IN THEIR DREAMS OF FIRE

A NOVEL

By

Maurice O'Callaghan

ᐱDESTINY

© Maurice O'Callaghan 2011

Paperback ISBN No 978-0-9549565-2-3
Hardback ISBN No 978-0-9549565-3-0

A Destiny Publication

Published in Ireland by Destiny Publications in 2011
18-20 Lower Kilmacud Road,
Stillorgan, County Dublin,
Ireland.
Tel: 00 353 1 2885281
Email: destinyfilpub@gmail.com

The right of Maurice O'Callaghan to be identified as the author of this work has been asserted by him in accordance with the copyright Designs and Patents Act 1988.

A CIP catalogue record for this book is available from the British Library

Portrait photograph: Philip O'Regan

Typesetting and Design by Artwerk Limited, Dublin.
Printed by CPI Mackays, Chatham ME5 8TD
Copying Services by Blueprint, Dublin.

CONTENTS

I sing of warfare and a man at war.

The Aeneid
Virgil

Men's memories are uncertain and the past that was differs little from the past that was not.

Blood Meridian
Cormac McCarthy

Some dream terrble dreams and in their dreams fire comes down from God to devour Gog and Magog and casts the devil into the lake of Gehenna, burning in fire and brimstone with this beast, this false prophet stalking the land..

In Their Dreams Of Fire

This book is dedicated to the memory of my parents,
Denny O'Callaghan and Yana Hurley, who lived
in troubled times.

ALSO BY MAURICE O'CALLAGHAN

Fiction
A Day For The Fire And Other Stories

A Man Who Was Somebody

Other Genres

Feature Film
Broken Harvest - Writer/Director

PRAISE FOR OTHER WORKS BY MAURICE O'CALLAGHAN

A DAY FOR THE FIRE AND OTHER STORIES
O'Callaghan has the true storyteller's gift of attracting the reader's interest and holding it to the last word.

Eugene McEldowney,
Irish Times

I was reminded of the great William Trevor. This is a vivid evocation of a West Cork childhood.

Alannah Hopkin, *Irish Examiner*

They are beautifully written and it is the quality of the writing that impresses.

Tom Widger, *Sunday Tribune*

This should be hailed a national masterpiece such is its descriptive power of language and its ravaged beauty.

Michael McMonagle, *Irish Times Books That Made Your Year*

A MAN WHO WAS SOMEBODY
Beautiful transcendant writing

Frank Hanover, *Sunday Tribune*

It has all the essential ingredients of the disintegrating Celtic tiger of today, bedevilled by tribunals, corruption and personal betrayal.

Joe Duffy, *RTE*

From 1919 to 1923 the Irish people fought a war to gain independence from British rule, when the Black and Tans were sent to crush the revolution by whatever brutal means necessary, followed by a bitter civil war, pitting brother against brother and friend against friend, ending with the devastation and partition of Ireland.

Out of these historical events, Maurice O'Callaghan has written a novel of extraordinary power and pathos, dramatic and precise in its depiction of landscape and dialogue, of life physical and emotional, and gargantuan in its conception of the wider cultural and political implications for Ireland and its long and troubled association with Great Britain. Here history's vanguard flows seamlessly, propelled by storytelling organic and profound.

He is born in winter at the turning of a new century. The youngest boy to a fragile mother who will produce fourteen children and expire in childbirth with the last. The father is of a bearing that suggests a long lost aristocracy but he now maintains an indolence anaesthetised by whiskey against the ruin of the world. The house has meagre furnishings, a stone-flagged kitchen floor, an open fire with hobs on either side, a clevvy, an iron crane for holding pot or kettle. There are barefoot wains about the mother's knees when she is strong enough to rise from the birthing bed and outside there is a farmyard, a cowbyre and stable for a horse or two. Some miserable greyhounds shiver in the cold and wait in vain for crumbs to fall from the rough-hewn table. But there is no falling save for stars that flame and burn out overhead in the night that is the solstice in the season of the Christ. The farm stands upon a plateau ten miles from the wild Atlantic, while in the valley there is a river called the Bandon and westward there are mountains. Along the riverbank are substantial farms occupied in large part by settlers of an Anglo-Saxon provenance with names such as Bateman, Jennings, Hosford and Eustace. Further from the river the holdings become smaller and the land poorer, wherein subsist families of McCarthys, Hurleys, O'Donovans, Hennessys and O'Mahonys, names of the Gaelic clansmen driven and burned out after Kinsale's rout in the year 1601: the year the great Gaelic nation died. O'Sullivan Beare, the last to fly, carrying the remnants of his clan north to Breffni in the dead of winter, over many rivers bridged with ice and many vales with snowdrifts dumb. Attacked on every side, the ghostly remnant of a great nation, gone north into the dark forever. The Elizabethan adventurers bring with them their work ethic, their dour puritan religion and their love of husbandry, order and beauty. Gradually the poetic Gaelic sounds will be replaced by the harsher, clipped English and there will be a new pecking order and class distinctions. On the lower rungs of the social ladder are the bag-carriers and the farriers of Mountjoy and Carew. These are called Shortens, Chinnerys, Pattersons, Welpleys, Deans, who, after the battle, will be parcelled out smallholdings of rougher ground as reward, whereon they will scrabble for the same allotments as the displaced Irish. The poorest of the poor will be the landless Catholic peasants, surviving in mudwall cottages of slate and thatch whose numbers will be devastated in the Great Famine of 1847, and millions will die on coffin ships bound for America, the promised land.

Unto this traduced and ravaged race this boy is born. He is bequeathed a long history of pain and death that can be traced, century on century, a palimpsest of failures and defeats. And what will lie before him? A great war between the nations of Europe, a crumbling of empires in Austria and in Britain, a rebellion of his own people in 1916 in Dublin against the forces of the Crown. In the year of his birth a young woman will return from fin-de-siecle Vienna, where she has been governess to the scions of Hapsburg, to inherit a well appointed farm from her parents who are minor gentry. She will give birth to a baby girl some years before Halley's comet illuminates the sky over the dark and brooding fields of this benighted country. And while this baby girl will not lack for the trappings of a comfortable life, this boy some years her senior, and born not far away, will see his mother dying, will witness the seizure of the farm by cold-eyed bailiffs sent by banks, and will experience the scattering of the family of fourteen children to the four corners of the world. He will recover from pneumonia at the age of nine to make his way into the world, with little to sustain him but an optimistic outlook and a determination to change things for the better for his family and his people. He will abandon a haphazard schooling at the age of fourteen, his head full of the fiery rhetoric of a schoolmaster who instils in him ideas of revolution and blood sacrifice. Around him young men are drilling in the night and he will join their ranks because he, like them, will no longer lie down before the marching armies of the Crown, as those who've gone before them have been forced to do. But what yet he does not know, is that a wind is sown that will grow and be reaped many years ahead in a whirlwind that will change this ancient land forever, because he does not have the gift of seeing the future, only seeing behind.

PART ONE

1

the bull riders

There was a lone man standing on a country road dressed in a tweed suit and cravat. He smoked a pipe and carried a slash-hook under his arm, which he used every now and again to snip a protruding briar. He was tall, heavy-shouldered, heavy-jowled. His eyes were set wide apart and they carried a rather cautious, wary look. His hair was longish at the back, as if to compensate for its almost complete disappearance above the high-domed forehead. He looked out upon the world with the ruddy assurance of a man with little to fear in his corner of the world. His name was Jasper Eustace and he owned six hundred acres of the ground beneath his feet. He turned and walked along by the edge of a deep wood called the Bull Riders. There was the sound of a stream flowing, the sound of hacking, a song of a lark in clear air. The stream flew faster as it narrowed, plunging downwards through a steep gorge, where broadleaved oaks grew. The trees were very old. Their branches spread outwards and up as if they would embrace and shelter all living things. In the wood there was birdsong, the pop of ladyfingers in the heat, dogs' distant barking across the river, a fringe of ghosts in Jasper's old walled estate and manor house. There was the shimmer of leaves and a fluttering downwards of white and pink-petalled flowers. Twigs crackled under the feet of squirrels and rabbits. Woodcock and pheasant came with curious eyes and throaty cries, pecking and bobbing in continuous motion. And sometimes there was a whoosh of wings as a sneaky weasel disturbed their nervous treading in the shadows.

As Jasper continued on the winding wood road, another man came walking around a bend towards him. This other man was dressed in a dark suit, waistcoat, white shirt and a bowler hat. He wore a fob watch in his waistcoat pocket and his boots were well polished. He had a handsome, humorous face, with laughter lines around his very dark eyes, giving the impression of a permanent smile. The eyebrows were thick and black, the hair equally so, beginning to fleck with streaks of grey. His forehead was high and noble and his mouth was strong. He was lean and quite tall and he walked with an elegant swing to his gait. His name was James Baldwin, aged in his mid forties and familiarly known as Doctor.

'Ah, Jasper, my dear fellow. Isn't it a most beautiful summer's day,' said Doctor Baldwin.

'Indeed it is, Doctor,' said Jasper, and stopped, but did not shake hands.

'I believe we're in for a fine spell,' said the Doctor.

'Good weather for haymaking,' said Jasper.

'Or horseracing,' smiled the Doctor.

'That too,' said Jasper. 'The Derby won't be long now.' He paused and then continued, 'Tell me, Doctor, how's Thomas Cody, and your sister, Madeleine?'

'As well as can be expected,' said Doctor Baldwin. 'Cody has the worries of the world on him as usual.'

'We live in dangerous times,' said Jasper.

'Too true,' said the Doctor. 'How's Mrs Eustace?'

'Like your brother-in-law, as well as can be expected,' said Jasper.

They both laughed, a little uneasily, and then ran out of things to say. Doctor Baldwin lifted his hat. 'Well, I'd better be on my way.'

'So long, James,' said Jasper, using the Doctor's first name.

The wood road climbed higher and soon Jasper emerged at a huge, grassy field that rose in gentle curves like waves upon a briny sea. He stopped and looked back the winding road where Doctor Baldwin had disappeared on his ramblings. 'A curious fellow,' thought Jasper. Then he looked in the other direction and saw a hooded crow floating over bulrushes and long bearded reeds like feathers, like brooms. It floated over snowy bog cotton, blue violets and yellow buttercups, until it came to where two men were building a stone wall bordering the far side of a bog in the distance.

One of the men was mature and beyond his prime, tall and angular with a straight nose and quite thick lips. His eyes were hooded, pale-blue and his forehead sloped backwards. His body was lank and loose emphasised all the more by his long, elegant arms and longer tapering fingers. He was dressed in black trousers, with an open-necked, white shirt. He wore a felt hat which he removed now and again to wipe his sweating brow.

'It's hot,' said the younger man.

'It is faith,' said the older man. He knelt and rolled a large boulder into position at the base of the wall. Although it was heavy, he manoeuvered it with ease and dexterity, as if the stone were lighter than it appeared. As if the stone were doing half the work for him. The way he touched it was almost a caress and in return the stone was happy to yield, as if alive and responsive to an artist's understanding. He carried on rising the wall, hour upon hour, stone upon stone, calmly and unhurried. From morning the wall had grown, stretching long and graceful through the day, a thing of beauty, as if moulded by wind, sand and water over a million years. The man's personality reflected that of the wall, solid and impregnable. The younger man, though eager and impatient at the start, had learnt by evening to temper his enthusiasm.

'You must let the stone do the work, Sonny boy,' said the older man.

The young man laughed ruefully, holding out his blistered hands.

'You're right, John James,' he agreed and did not need to say more.

The older man moved his head with a slow, repeated motion.

'The stones will best you in the long run. You must take your time to humour them. Life is long but a stone's life is longer than a man's. Tomorrow is another day.'

The younger man nodded. He'd learnt to listen. He was little more than a youth of eighteen. He had an open, slightly pale face, with a fair complexion and even features. He looked upon the world without rancour and also without fear. He had on a shirt, waistcoat and thick, frieze pants like an Aran Island fisherman. His movements were graceful and unhurried but his body, inside loose clothes, was wound like a spring. He was broad of shoulder and taller than he looked at about six feet. His eyes were smiling, summer-blue that could become cold, killer's eyes with winter in the iris. But they were not yet and had not been called to kill. The older man was John James O'Grady and the younger, Sonny Hennessy, a neighbouring farmer's son from up the road.

As Doctor Baldwin walked along he was wondering why Jasper's eyes carried the look of a man who had a constant fear gnawing at his insides.

'A curious fellow,' thought the Doctor. He followed the stream that had prefigured the looping road and when it emerged from the wood, it ran on through copses and under bridges until it reached flat, wide fields and another river flowing eastward to the sea. At the confusion of the two rivers a wider river formed, flowing on until it bisected the ancient, crumbling town of Bandon, which was also Doctor Baldwin's destination.

In a tavern in the town were soldiers getting restless from the heat and choleric from drinking whiskey. The more they drank the louder they became and they were looking for bait to draw their anger. Their leader was an English captain named Richardson, who had fought in the Great War in France. He had the blood of many people on his hands. He wore a uniform of black tunic and tan trousers, with a tasselled beret set at a rakish angle upon his head. His companions were dressed in similar fashion and were called the Black and Tans by the locals. He drained the last of his whiskey, stood up and growled, 'Let's go shoot some pork.'

Then, as an afterthought, he leant in over the bar with a swoop of his hand, clutching the neck of a whiskey bottle like the talons of a kestrel clutching prey. At the same time he kept his eyes cold and level on the bar owner, gauging his response. The owner quickly lowered his eyes and neither moved nor uttered a single protest. Richardson sneered at the man's timidity and waved the bottle to instruct his band of *desperados*.

They swaggered out, cigarettes dangling from the corners of their insolent mouths, muscling old men, women and children into the dusty street off the footpath. They crossed South Main and clambered noisily into a Crossley tender, with a flat-bed and high sides covered in mesh wire like a cage. In the enclosed, snub-nosed cab in front, Richardson took the wheel and another officer named Robertson sat beside him. They moved off down the narrow street, past shops with names carved over the doors. The names fell off the tongue with an Anglo-Saxon resonance. Lee, Good, Chinnery, Sweetnam. There were farmers driving horses and carts, other townsfolk on bicycles or on foot. Most of the people lowered their eyes and didn't salute the soldiers or acknowledge them in any way. To a disinterested onlooker they might have been moving in a parallel universe, such was the gulf of hostility that lay between them. The lorry turned left, past a Methodist church with long, elegant windows, then crossed a solid, granite bridge with seven buttressed arches. Up along the river the sun dazzled on a weir of white water where busy ducks harvested for minnows and other scraps. The ducks had their beaks in the river depths and their backsides turned tail-up into the blue afternoon, as if they alone had the temerity to insult these interlopers in as crude a manner as any the soldiers could contrive. At the bridge-end, the Masonic Hall stood imposing and implacable and directly opposite from it, the statue of the Maid of Erin was a cenotaph to a more innocent Gaelic past. The town straggled up North Main Street towards Kilbrogan Hill, where solicitors plied their arcane trade in a terrace of rather graceful, four-storey, Georgian houses, hidden from the suspicious eyes of the townspeople. Across the street was the entrance to the military barracks, a grim fortress from where the soldiers only ventured forth in the bright of day. They were aided and abetted by their counterpart police force, the Royal Irish Constabulary, in another barracks at the western end of South Main Street. As the hill went higher, the lorry traversed a wide open area dominated by a round, stone building called the Shambles, within whose cyclopean walls cheerful butchers had slaughtered cattle and pigs for consumption by the townspeople for many a hundred year. The town had formed on either side of a deep recess cut out by the surging river. On the near side, the tall-spired and Protestant, Christ Church, rose up against Kilbrogan Hill. On the opposite hill sat two further churches. St. Patrick's was Catholic with a plain, square tower that seemed too high for its flanking transepts, giving the impresssion of a large head and a stumpy body. St. Peter's, the second Church of Ireland, graced with beautiful stained-glass windows, bestrode an elevated site near Gallows Hill, a name suggesting a grim history.

Soon the Tans were going west along the banks of the river on the dusty, rutted road, the whiskey bottle passed from hand to hand like an unholy grail. They drank the liquor with greedy slurps, wiped their lips and swayed against each other as the lorry lurched over potholes. What gave them reassurance was the pressure of their fingers on rifle triggers, which they caressed like a child would a chestnut, or the smooth bannister of a stairs, because behind their crude bravado lurked fear, despite the Lee Enfields, Webleys and Sam Browne ammunition belts. They had learnt to be wary at all times, in all seasons, because this was a treacherous confrontation into which they'd been thrust as reluctant conscripts after the Great War. In the hellish trenches of France, they'd been taught to kill or be killed. Knowing no other way of life, they were redundant vagabonds back home in England. It seemed opportune to dispatch them to quell an incipient rebellion in Ireland that looked like it might get out of hand. Many grasped the opportunity, as the alternative was often the passage to a mouldering prison cell in Dartmoor or Pentonville, for felonies and misdemeanours, as if the devil always found work for idle hands. But now, emboldened by a mission that allowed them to exceed the restrictions imposed on the regular army, they were a dangerous and unbridled force.

As the lorry passed Doctor Baldwin on the road to Bandon, the drunken soldiers jeered at him, and one fired a pistol shot into the air. The Doctor jumped in fright and huddled in the ditch. The soldiers roared with laughter. When they had gone, he dusted himself down and walked on. 'The sooner these blackguards get their comeuppance, the better,' thought the Doctor

In the Hennessy household, Elizabeth, Sonny's eldest sister, was hurrying to finish baking a brown soda cake. She was conscious of the time, nearly 4 p.m. and the men liked their afternoon tea in the fields. Sonny always said food tasted better out of doors and John James kept to a strict schedule on the days he was helping out the Hennessy family. He had a small-holding himself of twenty acres and so he could only work part-time. He'd always start at eight in the morning and come back to the house at midday for the dinner. At four in the afternoon he liked a break for tea and was gone by six on the dot. Elizabeth kept snatching glances at the grandfather clock as it tick-tocked towards the hour. She was on her own today, like many days, now that the younger ones were gone. Because their mother died with the youngest in childbirth, Elizabeth bore a heavy burden as surrogate. How well she remembered the heartbreaking night her mother died. All the children big and small gathered round her in the eastern room, and her mother holding their hands and saying:

'Keep the little family together whatever you do.'

Then the long procession of sorrow to the graveyard, the words of consolation from neighbours gathered in their hundreds. Then her mother laid in her narrow grave and she and the bigger boys and little girls turning away, to face the great world alone.

She'd held things together for seven long years until she could no longer take the strain. Her father, Jeremiah, was getting on in years and, having sired fourteen children, he considered the world owed him a certain amount of leisure time, which he usually passed in the nearest public house. She'd reared the youngest ones in direst poverty. A kindly neighbour's wife with a baby of her own had come daily to suckle young Hannah. The kindness of strangers. But Elizabeth still ran the household, growing up before her time. The bank was pressing and evicted them. They had to leave the farm in the dead of winter and travel by horse and cart forty miles to lodge in a farmhouse with no roof. Sonny had caught pneumonia as a boy of nine. But eventually, using all her ingenuity and powers of persuasion, she managed to get the farm back. Then the little girls were swept out of her sight by a cousin priest, to the 'Black Country' coalfields of England and a new life. With their masses of golden hair, their freckles and trusting smiles, starting again with people of strange custom and language. To Elizabeth their departure was a great disaster but she felt relief because they were fed and clothed at least. To her mother it would have been an unforgettable wound; to her father it was washed over by the water of oblivion.

Elizabeth was a tall, dark-haired girl with a sculpted jawline and dark, dancing eyes which always carried the hint of a smile. She moved with an easy grace and was considered the best-looking girl in that part of the country. She was the eldest, at twenty-eight. Two of the brothers, William and John, were long gone to Boston and New South Wales. There were other brothers scattered about the place: Tull, volatile, talented, a good breaker of horses, gone riding across the neighbouring farms today, clearing ditches as he went. There was Richie, a cattle-dealer, tangling in ponies, sheep and pigs. Anything with four legs. There was Mike, the pragmatic one. And Sonny, smiling, warm and true.

She took the cake out of the bastible and placed it to cool on the solid, beechwood table. She hoped it wasn't too fresh for John James, but she knew he'd like the raisins. She cut a number of slices and smeared butter on them with a knife. She wrapped the bread in newspaper and put the package in a shopping bag made of string where she'd already placed a can of sweet, hot tea. Then she went out the back door into the farmyard. A slated stone building with stall and loft stood at right angles to the house and across the yard was a long, low outhouse that housed pigs, calves, and a stable for the horses. This was a former dwelling. Elizabeth had been born there and several of the older brothers. A previous generation of fourteen children had been raised there, taken wing and vanished. Before that, previous generations. She sometimes felt there were ghosts in every corner and behind every whispering tree. Her bicycle leant against the house gable and she slung the shopping bag over the handlebars. Because it was a downhill run all the way to the bog, she'd be there in ten minutes. Two barking collies raced her all the way.

Fr. Jerome Casey had completed his ministrations in the local church in the village of Ballycummin. He'd said Mass, possibly a little too quickly, for it was a weekday and his congregation was small: just the daily communicants. He had recited novenas for the dead and then cleaned and polished the golden chalice and silver thurible. He'd disrobed, neatly folding his long, white cassock, alb, silk rope with tassels, chasuble and stole: the ornate garments of his calling. He'd read his office from the breviary and finished his breakfast in the fine parish house he occupied with his housekeeper, Mrs. Lordan. It was twelve noon. When he looked out the window of his study he beheld a lovely day. He stretched and then sprang to his feet. He had one sick call to make to an elderly parishioner on the road to Enniskean, and after that he was minded to go on one of his occasional walks through the woods, which he liked to do when a fine day opened before him.

'I think I'll take the afternoon to myself, Brigid, while the day is fine.'

'Do Father,' replied Mrs.Lordan, like a satisfied hen. ''Tis a glorious day, thank God.'

'A day for the open road,' he said.

'Off you go and forget your responsibilities for a few hours.'

'I think I will,' he repeated.

'The very thing,' sniffed Mrs. Lordan, with a hint of smugness.

Fr. Casey walked down the tree-lined avenue from the presbytery with a spring in his step and a clear mind. Fulfilling your duties early in the day brought clarity of thought, ease, an uplifting of the spirit. Behind him the house hulked square and solid, with bay Edwardian windows and a roof adorned with red tiles: an imposing edifice, neither classical nor beautiful, but what of that? It was the house of a gentleman. He pulled the double, oak gates behind him, tying the hinged metal hasp and shooting bolt to keep wandering horses out of his green lawns. He struck westward. The road wound a little higher past a labourer's cottage and then swung sharply down. Although he walked this stretch of road most days, the view from this high eminence always took his breath away. The blue Caha mountains ranged the western horizon and, although Fr. Casey had never seen the Rockies, this is how he imagined them to look. In between was a vast, vaulting sky with white, bundled clouds moving slowly in the lazy summer breeze. He saluted two young men cutting around headlands with scythes in preparation for the mowing machine in a week or two.

Elizabeth was freewheeling down the shady lane towards the Bull Riders crossroads when the gun metal grey Crossley tender came around the turn at the big rock three hundred yards away. On it came, horn tooting, with the sound of raucous voices coming closer. She stopped in the middle of the four crossroads, putting one foot on the ground and the other on the pedal. She looked to her left and in the distance across the bog she saw her brother standing, while John James still worked on the wall. Whom she did not see, but who saw her, was Fr. Casey, hidden among a bunch of willows, where he had come to examine a phenomenon of nature in these parts: the imprint of a man's boot, a horse's hoof and the cut of a whip emblazoned on a flat rock about the size of a kitchen table. It was widely held by the locals to be a holy spot from where a priest in the days of the Penal Laws escaped from marauding yeomen. Was it an act of God or nature or of man? Whatever the explanation, it was there for all to see, and a point of pilgrimage for many miles around.

Fr. Casey saw the Black and Tans and pushed further into the willows out of sight. On the road, the quieter black and white collie stopped behind Elizabeth, perked up its ears and whined at the sound of the approaching lorry. The mottled-brown leading dog was already bounding across the bog towards the two men. It stopped suddenly, sniffed the breeze and cocked its ears. Then it turned about and returned at a gallop, barking furiously. Sonny looked up. He saw Elizabeth in the distance. Then he saw the Crossley tender. He was conscious of his mouth going dry and a knot forming in his stomach.

'John James,' he whispered. 'The Tans.'

John James dropped his trowel and stood up slowly, wiping the earth off his hands on the flanks of his trousers. He looked towards where Sonny pointed. He drew the back of his hand across his mouth, his face grew pale. They both stood, half crouching, in the lee of the stone wall. They saw the lorry stopping and Captain Richardson getting out of the cab. Elizabeth stayed in the same position with one foot on the pedal. As Richardson came towards her she stood off the bicycle and held it in front of her. But if she was afraid she didn't show it. She noticed his wide-set, cold eyes, prominent nose, heavy lips, high cheekbones. A rough, beefeating face with a scar slashed down the right cheek. He came on lugubriously, with two revolvers holstered on either thigh. The brown dog had reached them, still barking. Elizabeth shushed it and it stood, trembling and whining beside the other dog.

'Good afternoon,' said Richardson with a leer. Elizabeth said nothing.

'Where's a fine young filly like you off to then?'

Again no reply.

'No tongue, eh?' he sneered. 'So what's in the bag?' He looked roughly inside, 'Going for a picnic?'

Elizabeth was undecided whether to reveal the purpose of the mission, fearful of what might befall the two men. She remained silent.

'How's about a cup of tea for the rest of us?' He threw a sardonic arm towards his drunken rabble.

'Maybe she'll take us home with her, sir?' shouted a voice from the flatbed. Richardson smiled grimly and walked around Elizabeth, getting an eyeful of her sensuous figure outlined beneath her light, cotton dress. He leant in close to her swelling bosom and tumbling hair.

'How's about that then?' he drawled. There were lecherous guffaws from the lorry. Elizabeth could feel his whiskey breath, hot on the back of her neck. He put his hand on her shoulders, and thus caressing her, he pulled her around to face him. He put a hand on her breast. She slapped him as hard as she could across the face. Richardson staggered back in shock with his hand to his nose. Blood trickled through his fingers. He pulled his hand away from his nose, looking down at the blood, examining it in detail. There was a deathly silence until he whispered hoarsely, 'You'll pay for that.' The dogs started up barking again in clamorous unison.

'Shoot them,' roared Richardson. Two soldiers jumped down and trained their rifles on the furious dogs. Two shots rang out and the dogs toppled over with wailing yelps. The brown one, still alive, shivered and whined, struggling to rise. Another bullet finished it off. Inside the willow wood, Fr. Casey blessed himself and crouched lower, clutching the willow bark until the whites of his knuckles showed. He hated his cowardice, but his fear of bullets was stronger than his self-loathing. He prostrated himself on the holy slab.

A man who could shoot a dog like that was not a man to be trifled with. Elizabeth dropped the bicycle and the teapot clattered on the road. The tea spilled out and made a looping pool across the dust. She ran as fast as she could towards the men in the bog.

They were running towards her, oblivious to their own safety now. Despite his age, John James appeared the stronger and outran Sonny.

He held a spade in his right hand. Richardson lumbered down the road, shouting to his soldiers to follow. Like a hungry pack of beagles they grabbed Elizabeth, who kicked and screamed to no avail. Richardson had only one objective and he was going to get his way. Four soldiers held Elizabeth, one at each limb. They arched her back, and her summer dress was well above her spread knees, exposing the white softness of her inner thighs, the inviting darkness of her centre. Her wild struggles and screams only aroused them further. But the world was suddenly fractured as things happened in a whirlwind. Into the churning mass of arms and legs, John James crashed the blade of the spade against the poll of one of the holding soldiers. The soldier cried out and fell with blood pumping. Possessed of strength of stone, John James was swinging again, when a second soldier stabbed him in the gut with a bayonet, and the wind went out of him like the hiss of a stuck pig. Elizabeth was released, as a different lust possessed the soldiers. They fell on the prone John James in a frenzy of stabbing, and his ending was as swift as a fox destroyed by hounds.

Elizabeth ran to the unfortunate man, but he showed no sign of life. Sonny bent over them and then Elizabeth stood and Sonny held her close. They fully expected the fate of John James to overtake them too. Soldiers with bayonets pointed, surrounded them, waiting for the word. Time ticked busy in the stillness. But something had overcome Richardson. An evening tristesse fell over his face. He felt detached, no longer supercharged or out for vengeance. Sufficient blood today. The power was still his. He would conserve his energy for some future Armageddon. He felt these people had the power too. And how could he contain it? They were not afraid of him despite his overwhelming arms, this boy, this girl. He saw it in their faces. He was tired of blood today. The body of John James lay inert and ragged on the road. The soldiers, shocked from killing, were expectant, waiting for their captain to take command. They felt it in their sober hearts and knew perhaps that they had gone too far.

'Look to him,' said Richardson, pointing to his crack-skulled underling, who was wounded, but not dead. He spun on his heel and strode towards the lorry. The soldiers followed, holding their comrade between them. They reached the Crossley tender and Richardson said, 'Load up.'

The lorry went east along the road and climbed to the higher road where Jasper Eustace had been standing; was still standing; had seen all. Sonny and Elizabeth followed the trail of the departing lorry with their eyes. They saw it stop and saw words exchanged with their neighbour dressed in tweeds. Saw soldiers' respectful salutes and then pass on. And Jasper Eustace turned for home to his walled estate: his peacocks with spread tail-feathers, his pure-bred bulls, his hounds and horses. And washed his hands in a stream along the way, because all this did not concern him.

Fr. Casey crawled from his hiding place towards the bloody scene. Beads of sweat stood out on his brow. If Elizabeth and Sonny wondered where he came from they did not ask. He fumbled for his rosary beads and prayer book, and put the stole he always carried, around his neck. He whispered in the dead man's ear:

'Oh my God I am heartily sorry for having offended thee and I detest my sins above every other evil...'

2

the forests of the imagination

Anna Cody felt uneasy all that evening because the western sky was red. Southward the valley swooped low and red rays of the angry sun glinted off the river. Dragonflies and gnats whirled in the red rays in a dance of death and slowly the light changed as the red leeched out; became flat, then grey. She watched from the front door through tall trees as thunderheads built black, and, like soldiers stealing silently in to take up battle positions, stole in over the western mountains all that evening long.

Before dark she walked to the white gate down the avenue of trees in her ornate leather sandals strapped at the ankles, and met her older sister walking beside her bicycle. The tall trees creaked in a troubled wind rising, and the light was shadowy on her sister's face. Anna shivered a little in her light summer dress and pulled her cardigan around her. Her sister's face looked troubled.

'What is it, Margie?' asked Anna and searched her sister's face; a face that was ascerbic, proud and eagle-eyed, intelligent and fierce. Hair cropped short and unadorned made her look older than her seventeen years, giving the impression that her appearance was of little importance to her. An impression amplified the more by the plain, black coat she wore and the sensible, flat shoes. Anna's face, to Margie looking back, was soft, innocent, finely chiselled, eyes luminous and blue. And a sadness hovered always there behind her eyes. Her hair was rich and dark, tied back in a knot revealing her well-shaped head. Anna was aged sixteen.

'A man was killed,' said Margie and said no more. She pushed on with her bicycle up the driveway towards the twin-roofed house hidden among great beeches, elms and spreading oaks. A carpet of bluebells covered the grass, interspersed with daisies, violets and white-flowered stitchworth running riot. In the rustling wind they fluttered and danced like marionettes. Rhododendrons smelt stong and sweet, stronger in the twilight, their heavy flowers shivering and rippling as the wind passed through them rightly with a hiss.

'What man?' asked Anna in alarm.

'His name is O'Grady,' said Margie.

'From where?'

'From beyond Ballycummin.'

'How did he die?' asked Anna.

'Badly,' said Margie. 'Stabbed.'

'Stabbed?'

'Stabbed with bayonets.'

Anna, shocked, clutched her sister's arm. Margie walked on with quick, impatient steps and the weight of information, heavy but important, was a burden she relished in her way. They were breathless when they reached the hall door. Soft lamplight shone through the fanlight above the door. Through an open window a piano's tune trembled out into the welling darkness, a melancholy air, beautifully played. A delicate touch on a classical serenade. They hesitated, listening for some moments as the music streamed out into the thundery air. Margie left her bicycle leaning against the front, cut-stone wall of the house and they went in. Their mother Madeleine's face was rapt, serene and beautiful in the soft lamplight. Her eyes were half closed as her fingers strayed across the keyboard of the baby grand set down in the middle of the drawingroom, the finest in the ample farmhouse. She looked transported by the music; far away. Soundlessly they tiptoed in, not wishing to intrude upon the mood and stood, one on each side of their mother, and exchanged a secret smile. Their mother, sitting at the piano wore a light, white, cotton dress with a high collar tied at the throat with a brooch. Her dark, curled hair was tied back, coiffured and controlled, revealing a swan-white neck. Her face was delicate and pale with a finely-drawn, straight nose and aristocratic, bow-shaped lips. She had a face that hunted in the forests of the imagination to take refuge from the harshness of the world.

A high, mahogany bookcase behind the piano was crammed with books and two large paintings of a European city hung opposite each other on the walls, depicting views of Vienna and the Danube, the great cathedral of St. Stephen and the palace of the Hapsburgs.

Feeling their presence, Madeleine still played on and they waited for her, not wanting her to finish. Then Anna put her hands on her mother's shoulders, and gently pressed and kissed her curled hair as if she were another sister. 'You always play that tune,' she said.

'I do,' said her mother and sighed.

'The Blue Danube?' said Anna.

'Chopin actually,' sniffed Margie.

'No,' corrected her mother. 'It's Caprice, by Paganini.'

'It's beautiful anyway,' said Anna.

'It is,' said her mother a little wistfully. 'It makes me happy, but it also makes me sad.'

'Oh, mother,' said Margie with exaggerated, adult-like impatience, 'I think you spent too much time with the European aristocracy.'

'I suppose I did,' sighed Madeleine with a distant look in her eye. 'But you know, Margie, ten years among them was a long time.'

'But you're back a long time, nearly twenty years.'

'When you're young you make strong bonds. They stay with you. I became accustomed to the life.'

'I'd love to go to Vienna,' said Anna, 'and waltz to the music of Strauss.'

'And I'd introduce you to the great families,' said Madeleine. 'The Hohenzollerns, the Van Der Dorffs.'

'Oh, you two,' said Margie with a hint of scorn. 'What's wrong with dear old Ireland may I ask?'

'Nothing,' said Madeleine, still wistful. 'Ireland is beautiful, it's home, but Vienna was the centre of an empire.'

Margie put her hands on her hips and said defiantly, 'The days of empire are over. The socialists have risen up in Russia, Sinn Féin are on the rise here.'

Madeleine paused and looked, making as if to rebuke her but stopped. Anna cut in to scupper an impending argument. 'John James O'Grady was killed today.'

'What?' said Madeleine, alarmed. She looked from one to the other. They said nothing until she asked again, 'Who told you that?'

'Margie,' said Anna. Her mother faltered and put her hand to the brooch at her throat. 'Oh, my God,' she whispered.

'The work of the Black and Tans,' said Margie, grim-faced. She continued. 'I came upon them. I saw the bloodied man. He was like a pincushion, full of holes.'

'Oh Margie,' said her horrified mother, not wanting to hear more.

But Margie was intent on her description. 'I was in Enniskean and cycling home. The Hennessy family were there. I saw a girl, Elizabeth I think, and her brother. They had to bring a horse and cart to take the poor man back to his house. I watched them going. All the neighbours came running across the fields, shouting and confused.'

'The poor man,' said Madeleine, standing up from the piano and going to the window. 'What about his family?'

'They say he has a wife and four children. They were mad with grief.'

'Oh, the Lord save us,' said Madeleine. 'What's happening to the world?'

'There'll be hell to pay for this,' said Margie with the certainty of youth. Madeleine turned to her daughters and put an arm on each of their shoulders, as if she would protect them from the darkness of the world.

The mood of romance and longing was gone, and a long time gone when their father's imposing figure darkened the door. He strode in, powerful, broad-shouldered, choleric; handsome, strong-handed. He deposited his cap on the hook of a hall-stand and rubbed his thick, brown hair back with both hands. He blew out his cheeks and said, 'There's a storm coming, it could be a thunderfall.' He looked inquiringly at his subdued wife, wondering what was the matter.

'We just heard terrible news,' said Madeleine. 'A man was killed by the British soldiers.'

'I heard it already. I heard it in Bandon. He's not the first and by the sounds of it he won't be the last. Bad bastards.'

All eyes turned to him and all were quiet. Even Margie. Thomas Cody dominated without effort; a pragmatic, earthy man, dangerous with drink. He had drink taken, but was not drunk. He looked from one to the other and asked, changing the subject, 'Where's Seamus?'

'Inside with William and Doctor, finishing his supper.'

'Did he feed the pigs?'

'Doctor did,' said Anna.

'Worse again,' said Thomas, throwing his eyes to heaven. He headed for the kitchen saying, 'Anything to eat for a working man?' He was sour and in no mood for Doctor Baldwin's intellectual insights. The kitchen was large with high ceilings showing thick beech beams running across from high, Georgian windows. A huge oak table dominated, set down like a monument in the middle of the flagged floor. Eight sturdy chairs faced inwards with two coasters at either end.

Two youths sat amidships at the table. On the far coaster near the window and facing the door, sat Doctor Baldwin, also returned from Bandon. He moved in sprightly fashion and without hesitation when Thomas stood in the doorway. Like a lesser hound leaving the lair of a stronger adversary. The top chair belonged to Thomas Cody and if Doctor James Baldwin resented this, it was far too late to make a challenge now. The Doctor had been born here and Cody was no more than a *claon isteach,* as the older Irish called it: married in. Married Madeleine Baldwin, the Doctor's older sister. Cody was no more than a journeyman farmer, who never inherited his own father's farm. What did he bring with him? Nothing but the strength of his arms, the enterprise of his mind and the force of his explosive personality. Doctor Baldwin would call it crude. But Cody was a force of nature and the Doctor was effete and quite refined, if debonair. His only defence was a wicked sense of humour; he could only compete with Cody with his wit. He'd failed at his profession, although not because of lack of ability. He hated blood and the complications of human anatomy. So he never practised medicine although more than amply qualified.

The two younger men were Thomas Cody's sons. William, tall, distinguished, only twenty, but already with the bearing of a man of much older years. A student of medicine at University College in Dublin. An unlikely reach for the Codys, a costly investment. But there was background in the family and perhaps he hoped to improve upon his uncle's track record. There was pride and the relics of old decency, especially on the Baldwin's side. They'd been here a long time, came over with Elizabethan settlers from Devon or Somerset; were Protestant mostly, but this branch had turned Catholic a number of generations back.

The other son, Seamus, was the youngest at fifteen. A gentle soul, exhibiting his mother's sweet nature rather than his father's brooding demeanour. He was the farmer-to-be and showed the callused hands of the outdoor swain.

Thomas sat heavily into the supporting coaster and loosened the studded collar of his shirt. He also undid his shirt buttons at his wrists and rolled up his sleeves to the elbow. Madeleine poured his tea into the cup already placed for him.

Doctor Baldwin had moved to sit on a hob on one side of the huge fireplace, which had a large, iron stove burning coal or turf, on top of which the pots and kettle kept warm. The Doctor opened a hatch and poked at the embers inside, as Thomas ate his food. Doctor Baldwin looked askance at him betimes and whistled, as Seamus and William waited for their father to speak. Thomas flicked his eyes in the Doctor's direction and an irritated tremor of muscles bunched and unbunched in the middle of his forehead. Sometimes he fingered his moustache. 'Did you feed the pigs?' he asked of no one in particular.

'Doctor did, I was at the cows,' said Seamus.

'Did you leave them inside?' asked Thomas not looking at Baldwin.

'I let them out,' said the other blithely.

'You let them out?' inquired Thomas, and stopped chewing.

'Yes, I let them out. It isn't natural to keep pigs confined. They're forest animals. Foraging is their metier.'

'Metier my ass,' said Thomas. 'How are they going to fatten if they're out foraging?'

'My point entirely,' said the Doctor. 'The leaner the meat, the longer you'll eat. And the whiter the bread, the sooner you're dead.'

'For Christ's sake,' spat Thomas, and stood up, pushing back his chair. He strode out, grabbing his cap from the hallstand, and was gone out the back door into the cobbled farmyard. Seamus hurried after him.

'That bloody man will drive me daft one of these days,' Thomas shouted to Seamus. 'Why didn't you do the pigs yourself?'

'I...I was going to,' faltered Seamus, 'but he had it done already.'

'What next?' said the exasperated Thomas. 'What next?'

They made across the yard to a large, long, stone building with high, arched doorways and well-maintained timbers. Inside the solid, three-foot thick walls the building was subdivided into pens for the pigs, calves and stables for the horses. The calves mooed softly when they entered and the sound of horses chewing hay was familiar and soothing in the quiet. There were no noisy, restless pigs; just the eye-watering ammonia smell of their litter lingered in the air. Out under the great oaks is where they rooted for acorns, their contented snouts blackened from churning up furrows of earth and making chaos among Madeleine's flower beds. Thomas walked back into the yard and shook his head. There was faint light still in the sky, although it was after 10 p.m. There was a peculiar, clammy silence, an absence of birdcalls, a diminution of wind; like the silence that descends upon an audience before the prelude to a grand opera. Then out of the distance there was a low growl of thunder, a distant knell of mayhem about to be unleashed upon the world.

'Get help,' said Thomas to Seamus, 'before we're drowned.'

He felt the first splash of raindrops on his face. Seamus ran back inside as the first flash of lightning lit up the messuage, dwelling and curtilege. A score of red-eyed swine ran squealing in random paths as a rasping clap of thunder rolled, and then exploded overhead. Thomas gave chase, followed by Seamus with reinforcements already running from the house: William, Anna, Margie, and a reluctant Doctor Baldwin pulling at his braces. Up shady lanes went the cavorting pigs, over huge roots of elms, into escallonia bushes, grunting and squealing in gleeful flight. Huge raindrops began to fall, and then the deluge. The wet pigs became slippery as fish. Seamus collared one, but he slipped from his grasp. Another flash blinded the hunters, their eyes seeing stars of orange and pink and blue. And then they were plunged into a greater dark. Cries and curses echoed around as they tripped up on old ploughshares and abandoned harrows in the undergrowth. Bumps and welts rose on fragile shins. In the uneven contest, the two-legged were no match for the quadrupeds, who cunningly used the elements to their advantage, appearing and disappearing in the bright flashes and the enveloping darkness. Overhead, the thunder boiled as further peals cowed the pursuers and the acrid smell of brimstone filled the air. Amid the rushing and shouting, and the roaring thunder, Thomas fell to cursing the Doctor and all belonging to him who first set alien foot into these fertile valleys. He cursed all Elizabethan adventurers from Somerset and Devon; cursed Baldwins, Bernards and Beamishes, Kingstons, Perrots and Tanners. And every yeoman, sharecropper, interloper and landlord of whatever seisin or investiture, until all the pigs had disappeared and gone, bounding across the sodden fields to freedom. Eventually they gave up the chase and sloped home in defeat with bleeding hands and filthy garments. All except Doctor Baldwin, who had a peculiar look of elation in his eyes at the unexpected success of his enterprise. But not Thomas Cody. Because the thunder was the thunder of his heart and his railing was at his own plight and birthright and the circumstances of his life, which saw him cast as saviour and as slave to other more lithesome spirits, like Doctor Baldwin and his sister, who sought merely to live serenely in the world and did not try to bend life to their bidding in futile dissipation of their strength. He slept fitfully that night and was not the only restless sleeper in the territory. As the thunderstorm rolled westward, it shattered the belfry of the church in Ballycummin, clove a cottage in two a mile further on and a lightning bolt fried fourteen cattle sheltering under a solitary oak tree in a low meadow by the river. In the early dawn, all was calm, fresh and green with birdsong in the hedges, but those who travelled the roads noticed pillars at odd angles and windows in smithereens, where the storm had left its mark. And what the thunder spoke was a portent of something more fearful perhaps, of what was to come.

3

L iam Deasy and Charlie Hurley came over the high hill that rears above Kilbrittain in the early morning, and saw northward to blue hills and valleys wide and deep. They heard pigeons cooing, rooks cawing, swallows a-twitter. They smelt the pristine cleanliness after rain, the afterwash of brimstone and lightning. They saw a lorry load of English soldiers come around a bend and rattle menacingly towards them. They drew back behind a huge, briar-choked ditch and held their breaths. The chug-chug of the engine filled the air, approaching and then departing.

'Is it safe?' asked Liam.

'All clear,' answered Charlie.

'They're gone then,' said Liam, and stroked his stubbled chin.

'Gone for now, but they'll be back,' said Charlie. 'The murderers.'

'We'll be ready for them then,' said Liam.

'More than ready,' said Charlie.

They followed on the narrow road, tense as coiled springs, ready to leap from sight at the slightest alien sound. They knew every brake and burren, lag and hollow in the country through which they passed. They descended to Kilmacsimon Quay, a sheltered, hidden landing place amid the dense foliage of oak and beech trees on the Bandon river, six miles upstream from Kinsale. They stopped for sustenance at Liam's house and then continued westward along the banks of the river, past Inishannon and Dundaniel. They reached Bandon by mid-afternoon, coming in through lanes and by-roads only they would know.

Liam had a lean face, a long jaw, a long upper lip and a mouth with a stubborn set. He had a studious air about him, like a man with a mind for figures. He was strong, mid-sized, well set up. Charlie was six feet two in his stockinged feet, with deep-set, blue eyes, a generous mouth and straight nose, a smiling disposition and dark hair that fell along his forehead.

Onward they went, to Tinkers Cross and Mallowgaton, through Newcestown and Ballycummin crossroads, where a granite church bestrode the rolling fields. They saw O'Grady's house silhouetted against their tired eyes as the sun was setting. In the cobbled farmyard clusters of dark-dressed men stood about murmuring lowly. Solemn and sorrowful were their gestures.

The men made room for them with unobtrusive nods as they made their way inside, turning left into the parlour called, the "room," reverentially; used for Sunday dinners and greeting parish priests at townland stations and waking men like John James O'Grady, whose white, composed and handsome-headed corpse lay swathed in a brown shroud, facing the exposed ceiling beams, silent and unhoused. He lay upon no decorated catafalque, but on a flat, brass bed, bereft of furbelow or trimming, his unruly hair like a dark aureole displayed upon the pillow. Many women came and went, like silent auditors skilled in the time-honoured country ways of birth and death. Handmaidens of eschatology, who found their power and influence at laying out and afterbirth, keening and repose. O'Grady's emaciated young daughters looked like shy, forsaken wains towards the two strapping young men who came to pay respects. A plain-faced woman of slight and lowish stature accepted their condolences with the dazed expression of someone in a state of shock, and scarcely with the gifts to withstand the cruel blow dealt her by the hand of fate. Her skin was pale and tissue-like, transparent like the corpse upon the bed, as if she already were part revenant, soon set to follow on behind her mate.

Charlie and Liam finally rose from their knees beside the laid-out man and mingled with the neighbours in the kitchen. Elizabeth Hennessy, with her smiling disposition, came around with a pot of tea on a large, silver tray and a plate piled high with sandwiches. She went through the room passing the food around. Some people sat at the large kitchen table, while others used the steps of the stairs as a makeshift seat. Still others crowded onto the high-backed settle under the front window. Charlie and Liam stood beside the dresser crowded with colourful delftware and waited their turned to be served.

'Would you like some tea?' asked Elizabeth of the two young men, as she drew abreast of them finally, having skirted around them to other more familiar faces till they were the only people left. Charlie smiled, feeling an instant attraction. Elizabeth, in her turn, lingered beside him for a minute longer than was strictly necessary. They took the cups of tea and added milk and sugar and struggled to find words in the slightly awkward moment that can happen when subterranean emotions suddenly take hold and cause confusion.

They eventually edged outside to the yard where they were introduced to Sonny Hennessy, sitting beside his brothers, Tull and Mike on a concrete stand that held two churns. Someone produced cigarettes to pass around and as the night grew chilly around midnight, whiskey naggins were uncorked and swigged. Inside, the rosary was intoned and polished beads were fingered as Jeremiah Hennessy led the rosary in prayer

Doctor Baldwin, an inveterate attender of wakes, appeared outside under the quarter moon and said, 'It's cold, but not as dangerous as last night when the thunder fell. Nights can still be cold in May.'

'Don't cast a clout 'til May is out,' said a fellow called Maurice Mulcair, who was very thin and angular.

'That lightning did some wreck I tell you,' said a tall man named John Thomas Allen, who had a receding chin and protruding ears.

'Wreck isn't the word,' said Mulcair, with his sharp eyes and weak mouth. 'Tom Collins got his cottage cut in half. 'Twas a miracle no one was kilt.'

'The thunder is a force of nature. Even the house of the Lord didn't escape. Still, it's benign compared to these bad boys who did for our brave John James,' said Doctor Baldwin.

'A bad business,' said John Thomas Allen.

Mulcair spat and gave a kind of a shrug and hunched his shoulders, looking around him furtively. 'I wonder was he foolish, God forgimme?'

'How do you mean?' asked Doctor Baldwin, and wrinkled his brow.

'I mean to take on the Tans single-handed,' said Mulcair.

'Foolish maybe,' agreed Allen. 'But 'twas a mighty brave thing to do.'

'I don't think I'd have it in me,' said Mulcair.

'Which of us would, boy?' asked Allen. 'But then again, you wouldn't want to, Maurice.' He regarded Mulcair with a laconic smile.

'How so?' asked Mulcair quickly.

'Weren't you in the Great War?'

'I was,' said Mulcair. 'What's wrong with that? Weren't hundreds of

Irish? Wasn't that man's brother kilt in the Somme?' He pointed to Doctor Baldwin, who nodded and remembered.

'All I'm saying,' said Allen quickly, 'is that maybe ye'd have been better off at home and not doing the dirty work for the British.'

'Alas that's true, as regards my poor brother Henry anyway,' said Doctor Baldwin and sighed. They said no more as they noticed some other young men had joined the company. The yard suddenly seemed fuller and some of these were strangers. Charlie stood talking to a young man of erect bearing and a commanding aspect with dark hair swept backwards, who was greeted politely but who was regarded by some others with a slight suspicion, as if danger travelled with him as his permanent companion. Doctor Baldwin kept an ear on the murmured conversations of the younger men, collected in a huddle beneath a line of old ash trees, that were in a state of decay and erosion, with great holes at the bases of their trunks. He saw young Hennessy, whom he recognised from elsewhere; from Sunday Mass maybe, or sports days or fair days. He wondered what was up? He approached them with a curious intensity.

'Good evening, gentlemen.' He smiled and his dark eyes glittered merrily. 'And what, pray, brings you to these parts?'

Charlie stopped in his conversation and turned to the Doctor.

'We're here to support the family,' he said. 'In their hour of need.'

'Are you now?' smiled Doctor Baldwin. 'Well, support is what they surely need, by Dad.'

He kept nodding, looked at his feet, kicked a stone away and said, 'Would you be Crosby?' Like a sidewinder, he slipped up on them with questions.

'No,' said Charlie. 'My name is Hurley. Charlie Hurley,'

'And where might you be from?' continued Baldwin brightly.

'Southalong,' said Charlie. 'From Baurleigh, near Kilbrittain.'

'Baurleigh, by Jove,' said Doctor Baldwin. 'I know it well.'

'You do?' asked Charlie.

'I know a family not far from there named Hales. I know the father, Robert.'

'Well, there's one of them,' smiled Charlie, as he pointed to a sandy-haired young man with a high forehead, fair eyebrows, and a sullen chin, who said without smiling, 'I'm Tom Hales. You said you know my father?'

'That's a good one now. What a coincidence,' said Doctor Baldwin, 'Hales indeed. Could you beat that?'

This was a tough fellow, he noted. He pulled his long, black coat more tightly around him in the shadowy moonlight. Liam Deasy was introduced next.

'I think I heard about you,' nodded Doctor Baldwin. 'You're a bit of an adjutant I hear?'

'News travels fast,' said Liam, with the detached assurance some young men can muster, even in the company of older, more experienced men. Doctor Baldwin could only nod in admiration.

Charlie continued, 'This is Tom Barry.'

Doctor Baldwin took a step back as if all the better to get an overview of the man he had been particularly waiting to meet. 'Hello Mr. Barry,' he said, extending his hand. 'I'm James Baldwin.'

'You can call me Tom,' said the other, in his smart, white shirt, dark tie, and dark trenchcoat, belted and buckled. A fastidious dresser, with cold eyes, even features, thin lips, and a steady unblinking gaze.

'I'm delighted to make your acquaintance,' said Baldwin, eager to ease the tension.

'And this is Dick Barrett,' continued Charlie. Doctor Baldwin saw in Barrett a curly-headed young man in a rounded, white collar and tie, with heavy eyebrows, big, placid, brown eyes, a full mouth and a smooth complexion. He had a cherubic nose, which made him look younger and more vulnerable than the others.

'I think I know you, young man,' said the Doctor.

'I'm a teacher,' said Barrett, 'in Gurranes national school.'

Doctor Baldwin clicked his fingers. 'That's it,' he said. 'I've seen you before. I live not far from there, in Gatonville.'

'You're observant,' said the insouciant young man.

Doctor Baldwin gave a little gracious bow and said, 'My eyes are growing dim, but I can still spot a hawk from a hernsaw when the wind is southerly. I am but mad north, northwest, to bowdlerise Bill Shakespeare's phrase.'

Tom Barry lifted a detached, yet intense stare to Doctor Baldwin's characterful face, on hearing the quotation. He saw lines of laughter and of sorrow around the eyes. He saw hair luxurious, tousled, a straight nose, full mouth. A louche and graceful figure. Probably a man for whom each day brings dread and angst, yet still faces it. 'We don't hear much Shakespeare around here,' he said dryly.

'On the contrary,' said Baldwin. 'The language of the peasant is replete with Elizabethan phraseology. For instance, the sayings: *good morrow,* or *westalong* or *foreninst.* That's how they spoke in Shakespeare's day.'

'Peasants indeed,' said Barry, sardonically. 'You don't sound like one of them yourself.'

'Ah, but you'd be wrong. I come from a long line of Devon peasants. We came over as grooms for Mountjoy and Carew, over three hundred years ago. Bag-carriers and probably hod-carriers as well. The story runs that two of my ancestors were parcelled out land around Kilmichael, as a reward for putting King William back on his horse during the battle of the Boyne. After he was knocked off by a cannon ball.'

'And as a reward for cutting Irish throats,' laughed Barrett.

'In energetic numbers,' agreed Doctor Baldwin, fuelling the irony.

'It must have been nice for ye,' said Barry coldly.

'I know what you're thinking,' said Doctor Baldwin hurriedly. 'You're thinking, here's a black Protestant bastard, boasting about how well set up he is. How superior to the local rank and file. Looking down his Reformation nose at the rest of us. But you'd be a little bit off the mark there. You see, we're Catholics; apostates. The habit of apostasy seems to run deep in our lot. My great grandfather turned, apparently after he cursed some fellow and wished that he'd lose his limbs, wasn't his own son born without his right arm. My great grandfather became a Catholic after that to expiate his guilt.'

'Sounds like a likely story,' joked Dick Barrett and laughed.

'So you're some kind of professor then?' smiled Charlie, taken by his eccentric inquisitor.

'I'm a doctor,' said Baldwin, and his chest seemed to expand a fraction. 'A doctor of medicine. A most imperfect profession for the likes of me, who hates the sight of blood.'

'So how do you do your job then?' asked Barry.

'I don't,' said Baldwin. 'Alas, I haven't diagnosed so much as the common cold for thirty years. But I am a doctor for all that. I took the Hippocratic Oath at the Royal College of Surgeons in Edinburgh.' He turned to Barry again: 'You have the cut of a military man about your wise face.'

'Correct,' said Barry tersely.

'And what armies have you fought with?'

'The British, what else?' said Barry.

'I suppose you were in the Great War then?'

'I was.'

'Ypres, the Somme...Passchendaele?'

'I was with the Mesopotamian Expeditionary Force, fighting the Turks and the Germans. I served under Townsend at Kut el Amara.'

'Ah,' said Doctor Baldwin. 'The land between two rivers. The cradle of civilization; rich Baghdad with its turrets of Moorish mould; The Hanging Gardens of Babylon.'

'You're exactly right, sir,' replied Barry. 'But it was while there that I heard of less than civilized behaviour here at home.'

'You're referring to the executions of the 1916 leaders?'

'I am,' said Barry.

'And it shocked you?'

'You could say that.'

'Indeed it shocked us all. Young men like you went to fight for the right of small nations to exist. My own brother went. And yet, here we were, a small nation ourselves, being denied the very rights young men like you were urged to fight for overseas.'

'I knew nothing of small nations,' said Barry. 'I went to war for excitement, to fire a gun. For the thrill of it all.'

'So how did you end up here?'

'That's a long story, for another time and place. Let's just say I came back to where I was born and read my history for the first time.'

'And a tragic history it is,' said Doctor Baldwin. 'The Plantation of Munster, Kinsale and the flight of the Earls. And the United men of Mayo being hacked to death by swords in the battle of Ballinamuck. Driven into the bog to drown or be disembowelled. Unutterably sad. In every generation the English have cut us down. We rose up and they cut us down again.'

'Not this time,' said Barry.

He said the words with such considered vehemence that Doctor Baldwin was stopped in his flow. He looked Barry up and down, from his neatly combed hair to the shine on his shoes.

'You may be right,' he said. 'Do you have a plan?'

'I do,' said Barry. 'And there are a few more besides myself. Michael Collins and Eamon de Valera in Dublin, and the Brigadier over there.'

He pointed to Charlie, who gave a self-deprecating laugh.

The guarded conversation continued into the night. There was talk of the men of Tipperary: Dan Breen and Sean Treacy, who had tackled the RIC and were criticized for it. And Liam Lynch and Sean Moylan, swashbucklers from the hills of North Cork. And young men drilling and training with hurley sticks, because that was all they had. But how could they take on the might of the British Empire armed with hurley bats? As they parted in the small hours, the nagging question that lingered in Doctor Baldwin's agile mind was the same question that troubled Tom Barry, and it was this. Which side was the other man really on?

Charlie and his four companions retired for the night in a rough outhouse, where old mattresses were thrown down for them in a makeshift shakedown by the wall. Before settling into a deep sleep, he looked around for Elizabeth, but she had already slipped up the lane to home with her father and her brothers by her side.

A stray dog sniffed its way down the sloping street of Ballycummin. It sniffed at the wheels of traps and common cars, sometimes lifting its leg to make its mark and stake out its territory before moving on. Horses peeled their ears, if it came too close, but for the most part they stood patiently, still as statues, shackled and harnessed to the vehicles that were their quotidien burden, and waited for their masters to return.

Two black bicycles were parked inside the white wall of the graveyard, and two grave-diggers casually leant on their shovels, resting from their labours, and smoking. The bulk of their work was done and the freshly-dug grave yawned amidst crosses and headstones of various height and intricacy of design, depending on the wealth and standing of the interred. The fresh, chocolate-coloured earth lay neatly piled in a heap and the men continued to smoke down their cigarettes and waited for the priest to finish the funeral mass. And as they waited, they surveyed the cracked belfry high above them and wondered where would they get a ladder long enough to climb up to repair it.

Inside the church, the priest was in full flight in the middle of his homily, confident that he had his congregation's full attention, and flushed with the familiar feeling of power and influence his office bestowed:

'...and he was a good man,' the priest was saying. 'A decent, honest worker, a good father. No seeker after glory he, or hoarder of the jewels and baubles that some find comfort in, as if they could ward off or postpone the inevitable end that awaits us all. Many avert their eyes from the last encounter with the dust and who could blame them. But here the final quietus was so sudden, so stark and cataclysmic, that it cannot be easily put aside. The savage extermination of this good man has truly shocked and appalled us all. In recent times our country has been riven by unrest, and dark, ungovernable forces have been let loose upon the land. But in attempting to combat these adversaries, we are in danger of unleashing an even greater evil. Rather than take issue with these outside invaders, I say for God's sake, hold on. Let us pause and take a step backwards, or we'll have many more besides the good John James to bury. Christ said to turn the other cheek when struck by your enemy, and that is the course we should take. The day of reckoning will come eventually for the people who murdered our brother. Our own Royal Irish Constabulary are good, competent men, who will bring the perpetrators to justice. To you, young men, and indeed older men and women, who hold a certain point of view, and advocate a certain course of action, I say, stop now, before it's too late. Let the legitimate forces of law prevail, and do their job as they have always done...'

The priest paused and looked over the rims of his glasses from his lofty lectern. He heard muffled coughs, throat clearings up and down the aisle and his ears were attuned like antennae to see if he had correctly gauged the mood of his listeners. A delicate balance. A fine line. One had to tread carefully. He noticed a small ripple of movement that started somewhere in the middle of the left hand cluster of dark-suited men, and seemed to expand outward in a sudden wave, that disgorged into the centre aisle a tall, aristocratic-looking man of distracted air, well-dressed, if slightly raffish. At first he thought the man was sick or faint and maybe trying to seek fresh air, but to his surprise, Doctor James Baldwin advanced towards him with a steady, inexorable stride, like a man with something on his mind, intent on saying it.

'Hold on there, Father Casey,' said Doctor Baldwin. 'Hold your horses 'til I have my spake. Let an alternative voice be heard.'

'What?' asked the open-mouthed priest. Was the man raving? This was unheard of. 'Are you feeling alright, Doctor Baldwin?'

'Never better,' said the Doctor.

'Do you have something to say?'

'I most certainly do, Father,' said the Doctor, his voice rising to the stentorian levels of the priest himself. 'I wish to present a counter argument to the supine and craven nonsense which you have been spitting out.'

'But this is a church, sir, the house of God.'

'You're saying I have no *locus standi* in the house of God, and you may be right, in the normal run. But when you introduce a political point of view you are straying beyond the perimeters of your calling, and in such a circumstance, I as a citizen, reserve the right to respond.'

Doctor Baldwin had by now reached the step and the low-columned wall that divided the people from the priest in the holy-of-holies. He stood sideways on, and, as he spoke, he faced the priest and the rapt congregation, turn and turn about. A pin could be heard to drop.

'That was an excellent sermon you gave, Father, if I may say so,' said Doctor Baldwin, dropping his voice.

Father Casey regained his composure but said, a little puzzled, 'Excellent?..ah, yes, a tragedy, a great tragedy. I witnessed it myself you know.'

'Especially the bit about letting the forces of the law prevail,' said Doctor Baldwin, ignoring the response. His voice rose, 'But wasn't it the forces of the law that murdered the man?'

'What do you mean?' The priest was now quite confused.

'I mean, Father,' continued Doctor Baldwin, turning fully to face the people, 'that the law of the land has been broken by the very people who made the laws: English laws by Englishmen and English laws for Irishmen. But for hundreds of years they have killed us with the blind eyes of the law looking on. John James O'Grady knows all about justice and law doesn't he? He'd know who to accuse?'

Doctor Baldwin turned back to the priest, with a smile of rich irony playing on his lips, his eyebrows raised, eyes open wide.

The priest was now in a high state of agitation: 'Now look here, the police report says...'

'The police report?' said Doctor Baldwin scornfully, cutting him off. 'The police report? Jesus Christ almighty, don't we all know who the police are? Wasn't it they who brought the Tans through the country in the first place, pointing out targets to be shot at, houses to be burned down, people to be assaulted and terrorised?'

Doctor Baldwin flung a derisory arm towards Fr. Casey, his voice now at its highest pitch. The congregation was quite spellbound at the audacious challenge to the priest's authority. The priest's voice became a kind of whine.

'But...but...aren't the police Irishmen?' he stuttered. 'Don't they go to mass like the rest of ye? In fact they go more often than you yourself, if I may say so, Doctor Baldwin. Your presence here is rarer than a swallow in December.'

'A fair point,' said Doctor Baldwin. 'I won't dispute it, but rare as my visits are, I'm here today. Even some of our Protestant neighbours are here today in solidarity with this community. But I don't see the RIC. Now why is that?'

The priest opened his mouth as if to reply, but thought the better of it. He turned a page of his missal on the lectern, pretending to read, but not really seeing any words in his preoccupation. Doctor Baldwin allowed another few moments for his points to sink in and then turned on his heel and made his way down the centre aisle with his long, floating stride, as heads turned in disbelief to follow his progression. When he reached the door, a susurrus of voices started up. Someone said, 'Hear, hear!' and someone clapped. Then another clap, and then a burst of spontaneous applause gathered pace and volume; breaking around the church, echoing off the walls and high-beamed ceiling. As the clapping slowly subsided, some young men rose from their seats near the door and followed the Doctor outside to the cemetary.

The priest watched with a resigned expression and chose to make no further comment. He intoned abruptly in Latin: *'Ita missa est.'* He raised his right hand in benediction and made the sign of the cross over the congregation: *'Benedictio Dei, omni potenti, pater et filius et spiritu sancti, Amen.'*

And the congregation murmured, *'Amen.'*

He turned into the altar, gathered his covered chalice, descended the steps and, as the altar boys lined up, they genuflected in unison and turned. Preceded by the boys he walked with halting steps to the sacristy.

Doctor Baldwin's outburst was the talk of the graveyard as John James's coffin was lowered into the grave. As the earth thudded on the wooden box, in the absence of a tolling bell, some women huddling on the crowd's edge, looked in his direction with disapproving scowls. Still many others, having sympathised with the grieving widow and her family, approached the Doctor and warmly shook his hand. Doctor Baldwin accepted the approbation with the modest poise of a politician on the stump, quietly pleased to find himself the centre of attention. But his challenge to the priest in the open forum of the church may have been a heresy too far for all except the most audacious souls. Many expected and feared a retribution from the hierarchy, even more severe than that already visited upon them by the marauding forces of the Crown.

As the last decade of the rosary was finished, the priest hurried away, leaving small groups of people standing around. Some stopped near the widow at the grave, while others, further back, almost lurked in the country way, like awkward hobbledehoys around headstones. Reading the obscure dates and long forgotten names and commenting on the ages of the dead. Famine graves were pointed out; huge old mausoleums; sarcophagi overgrown with lichen and ivy, as if the dead were more real than the living. And in a land where death was so omnipresent, it was a national obsession. Death as a way of life.

At a discreet distance, Jasper Eustace stood with downcast eyes, hunched over, talking to Thomas Cody, another man of equal stature and respectability. Both men were dressed in dark suits, high collars and ties, both hatted. Cody moustachioed, confident, almost swaggering. Men of different faiths, but with a common interest in preserving the status quo, substantial landholders with money in the bank. Their other mutual passions were machinery and horseracing. Cody had recently taken possession of a steam engine and thresher, made by Ransome of Ipswich, the first such contraption ever to roll through the fertile valley of the Bandon, conferring on him a status beyond religion or politics. Eustace was among his principal customers, and in the golden days of September, the hum and grind of the threshing machine would resound across stubble and meadow, as it winnowed out the chaff from the rivers of ripe grain, reducing the giant stacks of corn in Jasper's wide haggard, and filling his lofts to bursting for another year. Enough to put a sheen on the coats of his three prized stallions, who stood at stud for substantial fees. They had many practical matters to discuss, apart from the obvious subject of the death of John James, which they studiously avoided. The ventilation of Doctor Baldwin's views in the church was a subject to which they gave an equally wide berth. And so it was to matters more congenial. The yield of last year's harvest, the likely outcome of this year's crop, the price of pigs and cattle, the state of the roads, the introduction of the new creameries and the likely winner of the Irish Derby up the Curragh.

Near them, Margie and Anna Cody stood, dutifully quiet in their long coats and peek-a-boo hats, styled after the new fashion. Beside them stood their mother, Madeleine. They talked low to each other and threw furtive glances towards Doctor Baldwin, who basked in the admiration of some younger men over by the churchyard gate. Among them were Sonny Hennessy, Charlie Hurley, Liam Deasy and Dick Barrett.

'I wonder who are those fellows talking to Doctor?' asked Anna, to no one in particular.

Margie turned her sharp, grey eyes in the direction of the group and said, 'I don't recognise them at all. They mustn't be from around here anyway.'

Madeleine overheard her daughters and, as she followed their gazes, she spotted Elizabeth Hennessy approaching her brother Sonny, who stepped away from the huddle.

Margie said, 'That's the Hennessy girl who was assaulted by the soldiers. I saw her the other day on the road.'

'That must be Elizabeth,' said Madeleine. 'Thank goodness she doesn't look the worse for wear.'

'That boy must be her brother then?' said Anna, admiring the good-looking Sonny, while pretending not to. 'He looks just like her.'

'He was with poor Mr. O'Grady,' said Margie, 'when they went to save the girl.'

'He must be a mighty brave young man,' said Anna and looked at her mother, who smiled.

'Oh, he must be commended for what he did,' she said. 'No doubt about that.'

Thomas Cody finished his conversation with Jasper Eustace and, putting an arm on Madeleine's shoulder, indicated it was time to leave. She smiled towards Eustace who doffed his hat and followed behind them. They passed close to the group at the gate and Doctor Baldwin spotted them approaching from the corner of his eye. He called the girls over. 'Margie, Anna, meet Sonny Hennessy; and this is Hurley. And this young man is Barrett from Gurranes.'

As they shook hands, Anna blurted breathlessly: 'We heard you stood up to the Tans. You were very brave.'

'Foolhardy more like,' said Sonny with a sheepish grin. 'But thanks for the compliment anyway.'

'You deserve it,' said Margie sensibly. 'Don't be so modest.'

Doctor Baldwin attempted to catch Thomas Cody's eye, but his brother-in-law deliberately averted his gaze. He beckoned to Madeleine with a slightly irritated wrinkle of his forehead, and she called, 'Come along girls. It was very pleasant to meet you, Sonny.'

She acknowledged the other young men, then followed her husband through the gates. Aware of the snub, Doctor Baldwin looked after Cody for a second and then beamed broadly as Jasper Eustace passed. 'Hello Jasper,' he said. 'Wasn't it good of you to come all the same.'

'Hello James,' said Jasper, with a faint smile. Doctor Baldwin thought he detected a sardonic glint in his stolid eye.

'Sure why wouldn't I have come?' said Jasper. 'Didn't I know the man well. A sorry business, a sorry business indeed.' He tipped his hat to Doctor Baldwin and crossed the road to where a man sat waiting for him in a hansom cab, the finest on the road.

As he watched Jasper climb into the cab, a voice with the sound of sunrise surprised his ear.

'An interesting foray, Doctor Baldwin!'

He knew the voice before he saw Eleanore Eustace. She'd come up behind him and was standing in a broad-brimmed hat and long, dark coat covering her svelte hips, a mocking smile playing on her voluptuous lips.

'My dear Eleanore, I didn't know you were here. You're not with Jasper?' he began.

She surveyed him coolly, her yellow, curled hair tied back in a bun underneath the hat. 'I'm still a Catholic you know. I've a mind of my own.'

'Meaning what?' he asked.

'Meaning I can go into the church even if my husband won't. I'm still devout, although my husband doesn't share my religion.'

'And you're still a sorceress,' said Doctor Baldwin, feeling a stirring in his loins, as he always did when he met Eleanore McCarthy, daughter of McCarthy of Castle Carthy, largest cattle dealer in Munster, and now wife to the Protestant, Jasper Eustace. Landed gentleman, with means to meet her means. She was pleased with the Doctor's remark, but didn't show it. She raised a languid arm and fiddled with the pin in her hair, adjusting her hat. Her well-shaped breasts were accentuated by the gesture. My God, was she tempting him? Even here on hallowed ground, and on this solemn day.

'Was that for show or did you really mean it?' she asked, and her white teeth dazzled in a mocking smile. He surveyed her up and down and felt the electricity in the air between them.

'What do you think?' he asked.

'I think you were showing off to the priest,' she said. 'Even though what you said made sense.'

'So you agree with me then?' he asked, pleased.

'I most certainly do not,' she said. 'Why should I agree with you? I said you made sense, but I don't subscribe to your republican rhetoric. You and your friends want to turn the country upside down.'

'You know what I said makes sense, Eleanore McCarthy, but you've joined forces with the powers-that-be. You can't afford to abandon the status quo.'

'Why should I?' she retorted. 'Would you have me be depending on the likes of you for sustenance?'

'Not for sustenance maybe,' he said moving close to her and staring intently into her eyes. He lowered his voice. 'But for something that you'll never have with that dull fellow, Jasper Eustace.'

She blushed in spite of herself and put a hand to her throat, fingering a gold necklace.

'Pedantic as usual, James,' she said. 'But it's just a lot of talk with you isn't it?' She looked towards the cab, where Jasper was waving to her impatiently. 'I'm sorry to meet on such a sad occasion, Doctor Baldwin,' she said loudly.

'I'm never sorry to meet you, Eleanore, no matter what the occasion,' he said. He watched her walk towards the cab with her long, elegant stride. She hitched up her coat as she climbed up beside her husband. He saw the fleeting flash of the back of her gleaming thigh. As the driver shook the reins, Jasper waved almost royally towards Doctor Baldwin, who followed his departure with a quizzical stare. Was that a man with something to hide? He always seemed to the Doctor to be a little on edge. He'd be feeling randy himself after his encounter with Eleanore for several days. Of that he was certain. A pleasurable prospect without doubt. But also one of torment.

4

S ome weeks after the funeral of John James O'Grady, Sonny went off with Charlie Hurley in a sidecar. He went with his brother Mike and some others, and they headed south to the coast. It was a fine evening close to the summer solstice. They went down the wood road and past the place they called the Bull Riders. Sonny liked the sound of the name but wondered where it came from. No one seemed to know. They turned left at the Doctor's Cross and in Murragh they turned right, crossing the Bandon river and the railway tracks at Desertserges. Down below they could see the signal men in peaked caps and navy uniforms waiting for a train. Soon they were on a road going east past the Lisselan estate where the Hon. R. Bence Jones, Lord Bandon's assistant, lived on the banks of the Arigideen river. This was beautiful country, rolling fields, rich and luscious with great stands of oak, ash and beech growing along the ditches and scattered across wide acres. Protestant estates.

'They have the best of it,' said Sean Hales.

'That's for sure,' said Charlie. 'And they don't like sharing it one little bit with the likes of us. Some of them anyway. But a lot of them are decent people too.'

'Sure it was ours in the first place,' said Mike Hennessy.

'Oh, they know that too. But what they have they hold,' said Dan Canty.

'A few of them would love to see the likes of us run out of our own country,' said Charlie 'And they're doing their best to help the British to do it.'

'Let them try,' said Sean.

'There's no turning back now,' said Charlie. The vehemence of his words, like those of Tom Barry a few weeks before, both thrilled and frightened Sonny. Soon they were on a winding, wooded road that snaked down to the sea. Then they would turn left well beyond Kilbrittain and head for a coastguard station that was built in the time of the Napoleonic Wars to guard against French invaders. And now this building housed soldiers with guns and ammunition. That was the prize they wanted.

A man waved them down as they came round a last bend to behold a narrow strand opening before them, and the dull, distant roar of the waves reached their ears. They could see the white surf on the beach, and flocks of shearwaters, divers, feathered waders and herons. The man beckoned them in under some trees.

Charlie said, 'Good on you, Jack,'

Jack responded back, 'Perfect timing, Charlie. This is Con Lehane.' He pointed to the other man. Both were young, athletic and determined looking.

They stepped down from the trap and Charlie introduced Jack Fitzgerald, the commander of the local battalion, who would guide them the rest of the way. Sean Hales held the horse as the others crept forward on light feet, almost on tiptoe. Charlie had a shotgun, Denis Manning had a sledge, Jack Fitzgerald had another shotgun. Con Lehane had a revolver, Dan Canty had a heavy blackthorn stick. That left Sonny and Mike with a hurley stick apiece. On a headland across the strand, the coastguard station stood isolated, tucked into the hill. It was a long, grey building with many windows and a tall chimney with smoke issuing from it. The windows were bright with lights. Back on the sloping ground behind the station, maybe four hundred yards away, stood a large Georgian farmhouse painted a daffodil-yellow, surrounded by a wood of oak trees bent inwards from the constant blowing of the wind. A walled yard and garden gave protection from the elements. A smaller house stood further down the hill before the station and, directly across the strand, another small fisherman's cottage stood almost on the very edge of the headland on the near side, dipping its toes in the water.

'Do we go across the strand?' whispered Sonny, not quite sure what was expected.

'No,' said Jack. 'We'd be spotted. Too exposed. We'll have to go round by the estuary, through the trees.'

They crept forward across marshy ground, sheltered by sally and willow trees and tall reeds. The reeds crackled as they inched through them, but the wind that always blew near the sea obscured the sounds. Pushing through briars and thorny furze they reached the farther side and slunk along a passageway until they were level with the building. They could see far out over the water and back to where Sean stood with the horse half hidden by a gorse bush.

Charlie held up his hand. 'Right,' he said. 'There's likely to be about six guards inside and some of them have wives as well. So there might be about ten people in there. They won't be expecting anything, so chances are they won't be holding their guns. Remember, our job is to get their guns and any extra rifles and ammunition lying around. No unnecessary violence, and try to avoid injuring anyone. Of course, if they resist we'll have to deal with them...right?'

The others nodded, pale-faced, tense, breath held. Charlie continued: 'Jack, Denis and I will go through the main door. Con, Sonny, and Dan, cover us going in, and follow fast behind us. Mike, you stand guard outside and watch for any sign of life from that farmhouse above. They're likely to be friendly with the guards and armed as well.'

They inched forward until they were under the lee of the hulking building. It appeared huge and ghostly with all its lights on. Their hearts were pounding. Every twig snapping seemed like a loud explosion. They stopped under the western gable and peered around to the back side of the building which contained the main door, facing away from the beach towards the rising field behind. All clear so far. They crept towards the door. Charlie climbed up the steps and tried the handle. Locked. He motioned to Denis Manning with the sledge. They sucked in their breaths as Denis raised the sledge and with a mighty swing smashed the heavy hammer against the door with all his strength. A gaping hole opened with a splintering crash. As Denis swung again the lock gave way and Charlie kicked in the door. They burst in over the fragmented boards. Four men were seated in the large living-room under the main window, playing cards. They were dressed in uniforms but appeared to be unarmed.

'Hands up!' roared Charlie as they crowded in. The four men at the table slowly raised their hands, looking from one to the other and back at these interlopers with looks of astonishment on their faces.

'Where do you keep the rifles and the ammunition?' asked Charlie fiercely.

'Who the devil are you?' demanded the boldest of the guards, and half rose from his seat.

'We're the Irish Republican Army,' replied Charlie.

'Under what mandate do you come here to demand arms?' asked the guard, getting bolder and playing for time.

'The mandate of the people of Ireland,' replied Charlie. 'Now shut up and give us the guns.'

At that moment a door burst open and a woman and a fair-haired girl who might have been eighteen ran into the room wringing their hands. The woman was sobbing: 'We came upon these intruders down the back,' she cried.

Behind her came Con Lehane and Dan Canty, training their weapons on them. In the distraction one of the cardplayers went for a hidden rifle under the table and swung it up. Jack Fitzgerald dived on him across the table and the rifle went off sending a shower of plaster and dust down from the ceiling, covering everybody in a fine white powder. Another soldier grappled for Charlie's shotgun, when Denis hit him on the side of the head with the sledge, and he slumped to the floor with a moan. Everybody was suddenly screaming and shouting simultaneously. Sonny shouted from another interconnecting room, 'Down here, the armoury's this way.'

'Cover them,' said Charlie to Dan and Con. He backed out of the room to where Sonny was hauling a large box of ammunition along the floor. Jack Fitzgerald raced in and they burst open a trunk that held a big bunch of rifles.

'What are they?' asked Jack, 'Lee Enfields?'

'They're Ross rifles,' said Charlie, hurriedly inspecting one. 'Grab them quick, come on Sonny.'

They gathered up a large bundle each and rushed back to the main room, where the guards still stood with their hands up, and the woman continued to wail. As they were heading for the main door, another guard hurried in pulling at his braces, awoken from sleep or from the privvy. He came from yet another room of the long building and he held a gun pointed at Charlie's head.

'Drop them, you Shinner bastard,' he said.

Sonny was quickest to react, attempting to wrestle the gun away from the guard. They stumbled around in a fierce embrace and another sharp crack sounded as the gun went off. The bullet ricochetted off a side wall back into the room, hitting the hapless teenage girl on the arm. She screamed and fell, clutching at her wound, which began to bleed.

'Oh, Jesus, I hit the girl,' said Sonny quite appalled. Everybody momentarily froze.

Then Charlie again seized control.

'Come on, get out,' he shouted, pushing Sonny backwards out the door away from the prone guard, who was too shocked at the girl's plight to react. 'Look to the girl, Jack,' said Charlie.

Fitzgerald went over to her. The mother, in hysterics, tried to push him away, scratching at his eyes. 'Will you let me look at it, woman,' he shouted, as Con Lehane pulled the wild woman away.

'It isn't serious,' said Jack, after a cursory examination. 'A flesh wound.'

'Do you people know a doctor?' asked Charlie. The soldiers nodded, slightly stupefied, the fight gone out of them. 'You can get him when we leave, but you can't telephone. We've cut the wires and we have your wireless equipment. She'll be alright. Tie up her wound. His as well.'

Charlie pointed to the first guard slumped on the floor with a gash on his head from Denis Manning's hammer blow. 'You must wait for half an hour 'til we're gone. If we see anybody following us we'll shoot to kill. Tie them up and let the woman get the doctor.'

Dan, Con and Jack raced around with hemp rope, lashing the cowed guards to chairs, table legs; whatever held them fast.

The wailing woman, reduced to whimpering, put her arm around her daughter and led her to a large armchair. 'You'll pay for this you cowardly so and so's,' she said, as they finally fled through the door. 'The brave rebels, shooting a young girl for sport. Mandate of the people how are ye?'

With the woman's scornful riposte ringing in their ears, they rushed down towards the strand from the building. Mike was waving a flashlamp to Sean who saw the signal and whipped the horse into a gallop across the hard sand. Herons flapped and squawked. Kittiwakes and oystercatchers rose in a flurry, and swarmed away. The sound of the sea was more thunderous. The night was all but in. Sweating and swearing, they managed to get the haul of rifles, the box of ammunition and the wireless apparatus into the trap. Shouts came from behind them further away. They came from the farmhouse in the oak trees. Bullets raked the sand and rattled off rocks. They could see flashes of shotgun fire coming from the oaktrees, like desultory lightning before a storm. They'd see the flash and then hear the echo. Down on one knee behind a rock, Charlie, Con and Dan Canty returned fire. Soon the flashes from the trees stopped. Sean turned the horse and galloped back across the way he came. The boys clutched at the back of the trap, racing after it as the sand was kicked back in their faces by the plunging hooves. They reached the road and never drew rein until they had put a good mile between them and their quarry. They stood panting in the silence, listening. Dogs barked in the distance, but no following voices were heard.

'I think we quietened them,' said Charlie looking around to his comrades.

'We quietened them right enough,' said Con. 'They're not too brave without the soldiers.'

'Sure I suppose they're only farmers like ourselves,' said Canty.

Charlie counted them. All were present. He then ordered them to disperse in groups, as they wouldn't all have room on the trap. Jack Fitzgerald had brought some bicycles, which lay hidden along the approach track to the beach, and in smaller twos and threes they made their escape into the night. Sonny sat on the trap with Charlie and Sean as they headed inland.

'You did well, lad,' said Charlie, looking at him finally with an admiring glance.

'But what about the girl?' asked Sonny, in terrible guilt and shame.

'It wasn't your fault,' said Charlie. 'But for you, someone might be dead, if that guard had fired.'

Sonny sat and noticed his shirt dripping with sweat, his hands all cut from briars and thorns, and his heart pumping as if it would burst. He thought of the bleeding girl and, try as he might, he could not let go of her mother's scornful cry. What kind of heroes they proved to be, to shoot an innocent girl? What was he getting into? Soon the countryside would be crawling with soldiers looking for them. In the midnight hour they reached a safe house, somewhere in the ancient parish of Kilbrittain. They slept in a hayshed and Sonny saw the terrified face of the stricken girl before his eyes. Until his dreams petered out and he lay dreamless.

Next morning they got a fresh horse and pushed northward early, before there was anyone going the roads and before word spread of the raid on the coastguard station. They parted from Charlie in Timoleague and promised to meet up with the others at the house of a man named John Lordan, which was hidden by a grove of pine trees on the road west of Newcestown. After that they would deposit their haul of rifles in a couple of different farms.

They pulled into Newcestown around six o'clock in the evening. They came up the winding road called *Bóther An Uisce,* the road of water, that lead from Farranthomas and Murragh. There was a big granite church in the middle of the crossroads, some low houses on the right and some others on the left in a twisting back lane with sheds and thatched cottages. There was a road leading east to Bandon, a road going north towards Crookstown and another going northwest to Castletownkinneigh. The schoolhouse was a couple of hundred yards out this road and the priest's fine house was up in a cluster of ash trees beyond the school. The sun was drifting westward, lower in the sky. They were thirsty and hungry. They tied the horse around in the backyard of O'Sullivan's pub, their precious cargo well covered with straw and half-sacks made of burlap, so as to give the impression of a farmer going to the fair. There was just the single pub in the village named after William Newce, who fought at the battle of Kinsale for the British in the year 1601. Newce was well rewarded by the Queen of England. She gave him several thousand acres of good land and he wanted to build a big town up here but later abandoned his plans because of the lack of water. And so Bandon eight miles away, built by his rival, Phane Beecher, became the favourite and grew the largest.

It was of no concern to Sonny who Newce was as he stood at the small, shadowy bar in the company of the swashbuckling Sean Hales, who lowered a pint of Beamish in one huge quaff and asked O'Sullivan to fill another. Sonny only had a lemonade.

O'Sullivan, a well-set up man with a smiling face, but a rather nervous disposition, refilled their glasses and said, 'Ye had a fruitful night, by all accounts.'

He was counting the change for Sean, because he was a careful man, and although a staunch supporter of the cause, he had to make a living. There was no tick with O'Sullivan. He was not given to handing out anything for nothing.

Sean Hales adjusted the narrow-brimmed trilby hat he was wearing and a humorous glint of warmth flickered into his cold eyes: 'Fruitful is right,' he said. 'News travels fast.'

'Twas here before ye,' said O'Sullivan, putting the empty glasses down in a sink under the counter, and wiping the oak top with a damp cloth. 'Even though ye must have had a good horse, the news was here before ye.'

'We changed horses in Timoleague, but I suppose our cycling men got here first.'

'Hours ago,' said O'Sullivan. He looked at Sonny the way an older man will look at a rising young competitor, sardonically, yet with reluctant admiration. 'I heard you gave a good account of yourself,' he said.

'He's a hardy boy,' said Sean Hales and bit into a sandwich which Mrs O'Sullivan, a demure woman with downcast eyes, had placed upon the counter.

'How old are you boy?' asked O'Sullivan.

'Eighteen at Christmas.'

'Sure you're still wet behind the ears.'

'Not after last night, he's not,' said Hales.

'Put that inside you,' said O'Sullivan, as his wife brought another plate for Sonny. He wolfed the food down.

'Nothing wrong with your appetite anyway.' O'Sullivan swatted at two flies buzzing through motes of dust caught in a shaft of sunlight arcing through the dirty window pane.

They had just finished their slim repast when a man on a bicycle rode into the dusty village square and leaped off, letting it clatter against a low wall between the pub and the small adjacent shop. It was Dan Canty. 'The Tans are coming lads,' he shouted. 'The scouts sent word they're coming up the Bandon road in two lorries. They're stopping at farmhouses and beating people up.'

'Come on Sonny,' said Hales and they bolted for the door.

'Lads...?' exclaimed O'Sullivan, raising his hand in alarm. They didn't look behind. He looked concerned for them, yet his mind carried the slightly distressing thought that they had left him no money for the food.

'Will you clear them plates away,' said his wife pushing past him brusquely. 'Do you want the soldiers to see the evidence?'

'Evidence of what?' asked O'Sullivan, still slightly diminished by the failure of his customers to fully settle the account.

'Oh, for God's sake, what kind of a poltroon are you?' she said. 'What's a few pence when they could be killed over-right us, and ourselves too maybe.'

As she looked out the window the horse and trap galloped out of the village on the Castletown road, with Sean and Sonny standing up like two charioteers urging it on. Dan Canty stood on the pedals of his bicycle, bringing up the rear behind them, eating dust.

And their fleet machine, that was stained with the soil of many parishes from Murragh to Howes Strand, had not long gone out of sight on the western road, when there was a low rumbling from the east and two Crossley tenders, covered high with meshed wire, growled slowly and menacingly into the village. They creaked to a halt in a far greater cloud of dust than that left dissipated by the fleeing sidecar. The flatbeds of the trucks were bristling with soldiers, loaded rifles at the ready, eager for a target. The only sound in the evening street was the furious barking of half a dozen dogs, dismayed by the invasion of their territory by strangers in strange garb. A few swift kicks sent the dogs howling back to their haysheds, as the soldiers jumped down from their flatbeds and stood around, waiting for command.

A tall, thin officer with a moustache covering his upper lip, a heavy lower lip, hooked nose, and a stubborn jaw, emerged from the cab of the leading truck. The initial impression was of an ugly man. He wore an officer's cap with a round rim, insignia of his rank on the front and the peak pulled low over his small eyes, as if to hide his unpleasant visage from the world. He was dressed in a tan tunic, belted at the waist, billowing jodhpurs that made him look pear-shaped around the hindquarters, and his boots were high-polished up to the knee. He walked with a slightly stooped, knock-kneed gait, but when he spoke any impression of weakness was immediately dispelled. He barked instructions with a clipped, upper-class accent that brooked no argument. Centuries of grooming and dominance seemed to echo in his words:

'Come on,' he bellowed as if starting a horse race. The soldiers milled about in a wild rabble, their heads covered in tasselled berets, many red-eyed with stubbled chins and rank-smelling from cigarettes and drinking whiskey. Two men from inside the bar attempted to slip out, but they were immediately whipped and manhandled back inside with kicks and blows of rifle butts.

O'Sullivan stood in rigid paralysis in the middle of the floor like a statue, and a few other straggling drinkers peered out of gloomy snugs, like sheep corralled in a pen.

'Percival of the Royal Essex Regiment,' said the officer, standing in front of the terrified owner. 'Major A.E. Percival.' He spat the words out a second time for emphasis.

O'Sullivan managed a faint nod and a gulp and Percival said, 'Are you the proprietor of this establishment?'

O'Sullivan nodded again. Percival started to walk around him as if inspecting a thoroughbred. 'Speak up man, have you lost your tongue?'

'I am,' stuttered O'Sullivan, and Percival asked his name.

'Sullivan...Richard Sullivan.'

'I thought you people like to put an O before your surnames?' sneered Percival.

'Richard O'Sullivan,' said the bar owner, beads of sweat breaking out on his forehead.

'I believe you've been harbouring Shinners,' said Percival raising one eyebrow under his peaked cap.

'What do you mean?' asked the dumbfounded O'Sullivan.

'What do you mean, what do I mean?... are you stupid? As if you didn't know what a fucking Shinner was?' The use of the expletive with the rounded vowels came as a further shock to the terrrified onlookers. Percival walked around through the crowd and pointed out individuals here and there. Names were proferred like Lynch, McSweeney, Lyons, Corcoran, O'Mahony, Hurley, O'Neill.

'Do you people all have the same bloody names?' asked an exasperated Percival. 'How many Dan Corcorans and Frank Hurleys are there in this Godforsaken place? All interbred no doubt. Lying, peasant scum.' He looked around and pointed to the barman, Jerry Lynch.

'Put that man up,' he said. Jerry Lynch was lifted roughly by two soldiers and Percival pulled a pistol from his holster. He held it against Lynch's temple and cocked the hammer.

'Well, Lynch you seemed in a terrible hurry somewhere,' he said. 'Where was your hurry taking you, eh?'

'No...nowhere,' said the terrified Lynch, his eyes rolling in his head. Percival pressed the barrel of the Colt .45 harder, creating an indentation in Lynch's temple.

'Do you know who attacked the Howes Strand coastguard station last night?'

'No..no sir.'

Percival noted the momentary hesitation. 'Our intelligence says some of the culprits were from around here?'

'I know nothing, sir, I'm just a barman,' gasped Lynch. Percival motioned to his second-in-command, Captain Richardson, who twisted Lynch's arm behind his back until he screamed in agony.

'Don't come the gormless innocent with me,' shouted Percival, his face very close up to Lynch. He was working himself up into a nasty state; the ugliness of his face expressed also in his personality. 'I'll ask you again. Who were you hoping to alert when we apprehended you going out the door?'

'No one,' said the fearful Lynch; but the more he snivelled, the more it enraged Percival. Suddenly he struck Lynch across the temple with the barrel of the pistol. Lynch collapsed, sagging in spite of the soldiers holding him up. He began to convulse uncontrollably.

Richardson peered around at him. 'The bastard's taken some kind of fit, Major.'

O'Sullivan found his voice at last. 'For God's sake leave the man be, sir. He's just a barman like he says; no more, no less. I can vouch for him. I can vouch for everyone here.'

Percival took a step back, controlling his rage just as quickly as he had engendered it. 'You can eh,' he said, breathing heavily. 'And who will vouch for you, may I ask?'

He started to pace around again. 'Listen here,' he spat. 'I don't believe a word from any of you. If you ask me, you're all dissembling Sinn Féin sympathisers. Every man jack of you. But I can tell you this. If we find any evidence of collusion we'll come back and burn you out. Any armed man will be shot dead on sight.'

He glowered at the trembling customers and wiped the spittle from his chin. He motioned to his men to leave the twitching Lynch on the floor and, as they left, they made a point of stepping on him rather than over him; delivering some surreptitious kicks to the poor man's groin for good measure. As he left, Richardson raked the beer glasses from the counter top, sending the smithereens down on the prone man on the floor. Some of the others hurled chairs and bottles through the window, sending shards of glass out into the darkened street. They grabbed several whiskey bottles and, with much whooping, began to consume the contents as they waited for the order to load up. As the liquor went to their heads, they let off sporadic bursts of gunfire, systematically shattering every window pane in O'Sullivan's house and several of the neighbouring cottages as well. The shocked and helpless customers watched as they embarked noisily.

The two lorries pulled slowly out of the village, with Percival and Richardson in front. They headed west on the Castletownkinneigh road. A huge yellow moon was rising over the eastern hills. The night was still. The setting sun had left a silver afterglow in the western sky. The lights of the trucks were on as they headed out. The only sound was the roar of the engines in the night.

Outside the priest's house, four hundred yards from the village square, Richardson's head snapped back as a bullet from a Lee Enfield .303 went through his right eye. A fountain of blood spurted from his head; the leading lorry spun wildly on the road and Percival attempted to grab the wheel. With Percival unable to shift the dead Richardson, the truck continued at a crazy angle to climb the ditch, until he managed to disengage the gear lever. But with Richardson's foot still pressed to the floor, the engine roared as if the pistons would explode out through the bonnet. Shouting and screaming the soldiers in the back fell, jumped and crawled out, as rifle fire raked across them from inside the ditch on the northern side of the road. Dan Canty, Sean Hales, Jim O'Mahony and Bill Desmond sprayed lead on the two trucks from their newly acquired weaponry, hastily unloaded from the trap at Lordan's farmhouse, half a mile west along the road.

Sonny and Sean had raced into the farmyard with the pursuing Canty, and roused John Lordan and thirty or forty resting Volunteers from billets in haysheds, barnlofts and outhouses. Flinging a rifle from the concealed stash to every available man who had the remotest capacity to use one, Lordan, a lion of a man with deep set eyes and a steely face, immediately took charge. He assembled an ambush party to hasten back towards the village before the soldiers had made their exit from O'Sullivan's pub. They lined up in random groups behind the ditches in the fields north and south of the road. The Black and Tans were suddenly getting a taste of the medicine they had lately dished out to the publican and his customers back in the village.

As the surprised soldiers, now shorn of their belligerence, ran for the sheltering ditch on the north side of the road, another volley of fire peppered the road behind them. Half their number were forced to face the rifles of John Lordan, Sonny and Mike Hennessy, Jack Fitzgerald and a dozen other ingénues.

Major Percival, unmanned by the loss of Richardson, rushed up and down the road like a headless chicken. As a cloud passed the face of the moon, the desolate road darkened and the targets became obscured. The soldiers stumbled around in confusion not knowing which way to turn. A cool-headed lieutenant named Robertson led a contingent back down the road and in over a ditch on the southern side in an attempt to outflank the Volunteers. They found themselves in a sloping field newly mown, with haycocks studded about. They ran from cock to cock returning fire from flashes that suddenly became very close up. It became impossible to distinguish friend from foe. Robertson ran around a haycock when he saw a shadowy figure, hoping to get a clean shot on John Lordan whose back was turned. As he sighted along his rifle a bullet hit him in the stomach and he fell with a muffled cry. There were soldiers and attackers running in all directions. There were shouts, sharp cracks of rifle and revolver fire. The soldiers fired blindly, but their more nimble attackers were like 'Jack O' Lanterns' in the half-light and easily evaded their blundering foes.

Sonny Hennessy, cool and composed for one so young, had got the hang of his rifle in a very short time. He remembered Charlie Hurley's words to him the first or second time they met: 'Know your weapon,' he'd said. 'It's the best friend you'll ever have.'

Out on the road, Percival lost all nerve and sense of purpose when Corporal Hoare of the Essex had his jaw blown off in front of him. As he tried to assist him, Private Ward of the same regiment had his arm shattered.

'Sound the retreat,' shouted Percival down the line. There were blasts of whistles, shouts of, 'Retreat' and, 'Fall back.'

A driver managed to start up the first lorry, driving it out onto the road. The soldiers tried to fight a rearguard action back to the second lorry, dragging their wounded comrades with them. With much effort they managed to load them onto the flatbeds.

Not quite sure what was happening in the dark, the Volunteers held their fire momentarily, and in that moment the soldiers made good their desperate escape west on the Castletown road. The Volunteers threw their caps in the air in the heady excitement of their blooding in the acts of war, embracing exultantly as they fell back on a surrounding wood, where they drew breath, sprawled beneath pine and beech trees. Some smoked, some drank water and someone brought a bucket of tea from a neighbouring farmhouse.

All was quiet half an hour later. The bright moon, now high in the sky, shone down upon the spangled field. A busy fox sniffed at a trail of blood, stopped, climbed the ditch and crossed the road, heading north. A dog barked from another distant farmhouse. A pleasant tenor voice from somewhere beyond the leafy wood sang, *Boolavogue*.

5

in search of the crab nebula

'*Perigee* did you say or *perigree*?' asked Lord Bandon.

'*Perigee*,' said Parsons, '*perigee* without the r.'

'I'm no damn good at these Latinisms,' said Bandon with a self-deprecating laugh. He was quite a neat man with a head of hair still black, slicked and centre-parted; red about the gills from too much whiskey, perhaps. He had keen, very blue eyes, which watered a little as he approached seventy, but he was fit as a fiddle. He liked to walk and tend his walled garden and he rode to hounds in winter with the Carberys. He was dressed in check shirt and cravat; tweed jacket and cavalry twill slacks. His brogues were light-brown, made by Barker of Savile Row. The full moon was rising over his estate and they were watching it. Parsons had thick lips, a full, moon-face and he looked well-fed, unlike Lord Bandon who looked rather malnourished. He was dressed in a smoking jacket extending over his fair, rounded belly and voluminous pants and he was a good twenty years younger than Bandon. He suppressed an impulse to correct his host. *Perigee* was Greek, not Latin, but what of that? Such distinctions would be lost on the older man who was more of a military type. A man of action. Parsons was soft and academic and descended from one of the most famous astronomers in the world, the 3rd Earl of Rosse, William Parsons of Birr Castle in King's County. So he had a firm understanding of science. Bandon was an enthusiastic amateur. Parsons went on to explain that when the moon was at perigee the declination of its orbit brought it closest to planet earth; a phenomenon occurring every twenty-one years or so. Usually associated with very high tides, higher than spring tides. 'And what do you call it when a planet is closest to the sun in its orbit?' asked the older man.

'That would be *perihelion*,' said Parsons.'

Lord Bandon took a breather. They'd been walking around his estate for some hours and it was time to go back for dinner and greet his other guests. But he enjoyed the company of Parsons more than the others. He'd met him at his club in London, because Parsons, like himself spent half the year in England where he had a Yorks connection. Bandon liked it better in Ireland, but his wife took a contrary view. And now his putative successor and cousin, Percy, whom the locals called Paddy, charmingly, was intent on a career in the Royal Air Force, hoping to become a squadron leader. Although still only sixteen, his head was full of romantic notions of fighting and flying, ideas fuelled no doubt by tales of derring-do by pilots in the Great War; further amplified by the poems of that Yeats fellow about Irish airmen foreseeing their deaths, lonely impulses of delight and tumults in the clouds. A lot of claptrap as far as Bandon was concerned. What did a bookworm like Yeats know of the horrors of war? And yet perhaps there was a grain of truth in it? Words had great power.

Bandon let the thought escape to concentrate on his duties for the evening ahead. He regarded them as a bloody damn nuisance, but a man in his position had obligations. He was British Deputy Lieutenant in Ireland and Representative Peer; ceremonial positions to a large degree, but involving, on a quite regular basis, the entertaining of important, but dull guests. He looked at the beautiful yellow orb rising over the distant town and wished he could stay outside with Parsons: 'My goodness that's a beautiful sight. And seems so huge as you say. Incredible what they're discovering nowadays about the firmament.'

Parsons nodded. 'This fellow Edwin Hubble has now established that there are as many galaxies again in the universe as all the stars that we can see with the naked eye. Each galaxy with billions of stars.'

'But I thought your grandfather discovered all that over sixty years ago?'

'Not quite,' said Parsons, aware that his host was perhaps flattering him a little. 'He discovered the Crab Nebula galaxy and he accurately gauged the temperature of the moon, but our store of knowledge has increased exponentially since then.'

'All the same,' continued Bandon, 'it's gratifying to think that here in Ireland we had the largest and most sophisticated telescope in the entire world for over seventy years. All thanks to your forebear, the 3rd Earl of Rosse.'

Parsons looked rueful and bent to pluck a tall, spiked piece of bog sage with clear, blue flowers, which he twiddled between thumb and forefinger. 'That's absolutely true, but alas the structure has fallen out of use in recent years. The mirror has become tarnished and the pulleys and apparatus for moving the tube and mountings have crumbled. It's very sad.'

'Is it a sign of the times I wonder?' asked Bandon. He gave a quick, uneasy glance at his guest's face as they continued to walk back towards the house over the enormous wildflower meadow and lawn that descended towards the river in the trees below.

Both men were Irish and immensely proud of it in their way, although their ancestral roots were English. Norman in Lord Bandon's case. James Francis Bernard, the 4th Earl could trace his ancestry back to William the Conqueror. Somewhere along the line, around the year 1600 the Bernards had acquired the lands of Castle Mahon, which had belonged to Cnogher O'Mahony, the fierce Gaelic chieftain and his ancestors, for a thousand years before. And the currency of the acquisition was blood, not gold or silver. But for all that, Lord Bandon would swear vehemently among his peers in London's parliament that he was Irish to the backbone. Although red in tooth and claw.

As they confronted the house, its pale limestone had turned to the most delicate honey colour in the kiss of the dying sun. It was a formidable pile. Built at the end of the eighteenth century, it was less graceful than intransigent. Set down as an enormous fortified castle in this lush and verdant valley, it was designed more for defence and intimidation than for beauty. There was nothing very inspirational about its crenellations. It bespoke belligerence not artistry. The county had many more beautiful great houses. The Whites of Bantry, sixty miles westward, owned possibly the most beautiful of all. Bantry House was exquisite. Its drawingrooms were hung with priceless tapestries from Versailles and its great windows opened to the Caha mountains of Beara across the bay on one of the most stunning vistas in the world. Its collonades and arcades were perfectly proportioned, its sculpted statues in magnificent terraced gardens flung out their arms as if to embrace the blue mountains far away: Glenlough, Knockowen, Hungry Hill. Castle Bernard had none of this. But it was a mighty fortress for all that and Bandon commanded an estate far bigger and wealthier than his western counterpart. And besides, although White called himself an Earl, he was really no more than a Viscount. As a last excuse before leaving the beauty of the evening, they walked through the walled garden, where Bandon enthusiastically pointed out the names of the many flowers he had personally cultivated: fragrant roses, cascading clematis, borders of overspilling campanelas and sweet smelling violas. He was particularly proud of a ribbon of deep red *gladiolus byzantius,* the daring colour of which drew the eye and complemented the tones of pink geraniums. Parsons threw an admiring glance at his host. He was a man of many parts.

Inside in the huge drawing-room, with its finely-wrought ceiling, a quartet was playing a Bach concerto that allowed the two men to integrate without too much effort into the spirit of the evening. There were various people standing around sipping glasses of his finest dry sherry and a butler in a black monkey suit went around replenishing the empty ones. The atmosphere was restrained.

Lord Bandon went first to shake the hand of Major-General Sir Peter Strickland, GOC of the Cork 6th Division. Strickland was a tall, gaunt man whose outstanding physical characteristic was a large, handlebar moustache, which flowed over his thin lips in quite an absurd fashion. He had sober, grey eyes and gave the impression of being steady rather than enterprising. Ponderous was a description that sprang to Bandon's mind. Bandon chuckled inwardly at the nickname, 'Hungry Face,' that had been given to him by his men in the War. He could imagine Strickland holding forth at some military briefing about a completely insubstantial matter, while puffing his pipe importantly, and using words like *ipso facto* a lot. Strickland was in charge of all military operations in County Cork and was probably a decent enough fellow in the old school way, although limited and cautious. They exchanged pleasantries and Bandon went to greet various other dignitaries and important members of the town community and its hinterland.

There were clergymen, general practitioners and solicitors. He greeted his agents, George and John Jones, Richard Wheeler Doherty and another fellow called Webb. Bandon had recently remortgaged his vast estates and it was amazing how accomodating these individuals were and no wonder. The prospect of substantial fees flowing from such transactions was sufficient to put a spring in the step of even the dourest soul. He noted two fellows in intense conversation over by the huge marble fireplace and he went to shake dutiful hands. Maguire was a Catholic solicitor who courted Bandon assiduously for business, and whereas Bandon was happy to throw him some crumbs, he was damned if he was going to give this jumped up corner-boy anything of substance. The other chap was that Jasper Eustace fellow, who had a stolid, ruddy-faced arrogance about him that Bandon couldn't relate to except when they talked about engines. Eustace was a man of the world right enough, but there was nothing cultured or sophisticated about him. In fact he was far more bucolic than many Catholics of Bandon's occasional acquaintance. He was put in mind in particular of the mercurial Doctor Baldwin who invariably cheered Bandon up any time they met. The one redeeming feature Eustace had was that he had married a damn fine filly. Eleanore Eustace would keep the lead in any officer's pencil. By Gad she would. He looked around to see if she was here this evening, but noted her absence. Pity. No sign of Doctor Baldwin either; Lady Bandon, no doubt deliberately, avoided sending him an invitation. Whereas Doctor Baldwin was scintillating company, he could, on occasion raise the hackles of the more sensitive guests and so his presence was best avoided at such a time as this. But he wondered at the absence of Eleanore Eustace nee McCarthy?

There were two dowager ladies, with ample bosoms and coiffured hair, sitting on a pair of early Victorian library chairs over by a high window, with views over the lawn and the river below. It struck Bandon that the chairs, each with an armorial panelled upholstered back and serpentine fronted seats of a deep crimson, were considerably more attractive than the posteriors they supported. The ladies gave him their most seductive smiles and he smiled back in as gracious a manner as he could muster. Despite his years, Bandon had an attractiveness about him that didn't go unnoticed by members of the opposite sex, no matter what the vintage. They eventually assembled and went into the diningroom for dinner, where grace was said by the rector of St. Peter's and they fell to without further ceremony, as the initial awkwardness in the atmosphere of the evening gradually gave way to a more relaxed complexion.

'I'd like to propose a toast,' Major-General Strickland said, 'to Lord and Lady Bandon and family for their splendid hospitality.'

All stood, clinked glasses and drank. They'd finished an excellent repast: tureens of potato and leek soup, starters of delicate lark's wings, entreés of stuffed pheasant and duck ardmagnac; traditional roast beef for some of the less adventurous of palate. They were well into Bandon's best reserves of Claret and the conversation had proceeded to such a relaxed point that it was acceptable to draw down the delicate subject of the political situation.

Someone asked Strickland about the news filtering in concerning the attack on the coastguard station of the previous night. 'A trifling matter,' he said. 'Nothing that our forces won't be able to sort out with the minimum of effort.'

'All the same General,' said Bandon with a look of concern on his face, 'These incidents seem to be on the increase, no?'

'I can assure you sir, things are well in hand,' smiled Strickland. 'Our Auxiliary forces are pervasive on the ground, the Essex regiment has been augmented and the RIC have been bolstered by additional forces from England. What are our present numbers, Brigade-Major?'

He turned to a slight, dapper young officer with a pencil-thin ronnie on his upper lip and a self-contained air about him. Bernard Montgomery had already made something of a name for himself in the Great War for his courage and organisational gifts.

'Approximately 14,000 as we speak, sir,' said Montgomery. 'Comprising front line infantry, Auxiliaries and Black and Tan support.'

'There you see, my lord,' said Strickland. 'My young friend is with the 17th Infantry and a most assiduous officer, if I may say so. Our forces are being completely effective and increasing in numbers on a regular basis as required.'

'I'm not doubting your word Major-General, and I must commend Brigade-Major Montgomery for his outstanding bravery in the War,' said Bandon.

There was a general nodding of heads and some of the ladies turned towards the dashing Montgomery with something more than admiring glances. Some whispered coyly behind their serviettes that he had about him a rather boyish air and a vulnerability that they found irresistibly attractive, not to put too fine a point on it.

After allowing a suitable interlude pass, Mr. Parsons again addressed a subject that was bothering him. He cleared his throat. 'Your forces are effective as you say, General, but their behaviour is scarcely conducive to bringing the people around to our way of thinking?'

'Meaning what exactly, Mr. Parsons?' enquired the Major-General evenly, brushing both ends of his moustache between thumb and fingers, fanning it out a little with the pinky.

'Well, for a start what about the way that unfortunate man was killed a few weeks back, what was his name...?'

'O'Grady,' said the Reverand Tarquin Prosser, Rector of St. Peter's.

'That's it, I heard the poor man came to a most hideous end,' said Parsons, his jowls jiggling as he nodded vigorously.

'But he attacked the Crown Forces,' said Strickland and raised a supercilious eyebrow.

'With a shovel?' enquired Parsons. Strickland looked nonplussed for a moment.

Maguire, the solicitor, always on the alert, came to his assistance. 'Oh, I believe there was more to it than that,' he said. 'The papers said the fellow ran amok.'

'Well they would, wouldn't they,' interjected Reverand Prosser, his mild manner belying a somewhat feisty interior. 'But why don't you ask Mr. Eustace?'

'Exactly,' said Lord Bandon. 'You saw the whole thing didn't you, Jasper?' There was little chance of his rustic neighbour letting the side down and Bandon wasn't at all keen to have his military guests embarrassed. The two-pronged attack from his friends, Parsons and Prosser came a little unexpectedly. Must be the Claret.

Eustace was taken aback to be thrust into the limelight. He fumbled around for room to respond. He cleared his throat. How could he describe it? 'Well on the one hand,' he began tentatively, 'I'd have to say the man, O'Grady struck first...and on the other hand it could be said the soldiers were a little hasty in their reaction.'

'Come, come, Jasper,' said the Rector. 'The girl was being assaulted and about to be raped by all accounts. This kind of thing gives the Crown Forces a bad name. I've heard these wretched Black and Tans drive around the countryside in a drunken state taking pot-shots for fun at farmers working in the fields.'

'Our behaviour should be beyond reproach,' said Montgomery. Strickland gave a sharp glance at him, but the young officer had a mind of his own.

Strickland demurred. 'I'm bound to say I haven't seen any newspaper reports of this kind of thing,' he said, 'and our own report from Captain Richardson, our officer in charge on that day, said exactly as Mr. Maguire has affirmed.'

Maguire nodded earnestly, delighted to have been acknowledged by his betters. The Major-General remembered his name.

'The newspapers are on the side of the Establishment,' said Parsons dismissively. 'You don't expect a balanced report from them do you?'

'And aren't you yourself a member of the Establishment?' asked Strickland, refusing to be ruffled.

'I come from the Liberal tradition,' said Parsons. 'The Whigs, if you will. I believe in prosecuting just wars, but not outside the bounds of what's acceptable.'

'Easy for you to say,' put in Lady Bandon. 'But if you're being ambushed from behind a hedge without warning, then surely the normal rules don't apply?'

'Exactly so, Ma'am,' said Maguire. 'Very well put. These fellows don't keep the rules. What's acceptable to them?'

'That's a moot point,' said Parsons. 'In the first instance it could be argued that we are not keeping the rules. I'm referring to the 1918 election. The Sinn Féin Party won an overwhelming majority of votes; nearly eighty percent in that election. Yet we have disregarded the will of the people as if they hadn't voted at all.'

'How so, Mr. Parsons?' asked Major-General Strickland, becoming more bemused by the minute.

Parsons was not to be stopped: 'We've sent in a military force without declaring Martial Law, to try to quell the spontaneous outbursts of resistance, without appearing to do so. Let's face it, things have changed fundamentally. I don't think our kind are welcome here anymore. We are no longer the representatives of the people, although we may still own most of the wealth and property.'

Montgomery again spoke up. 'There's our dilemma. On the one hand we are trying to maintain law and order, but to put down an incipient uprising like this you must be ruthless. And in 20th century, democratic Great Britain that is not allowed. I think Mr. Parsons is correct. The only solution is to give the Irish some form of self-government and let them squash the rebellion themselves.'

There was a long pause, and some eyebrows were raised. Was a decorated officer really making such a statement and seeming to agree with the excitable Parsons? Strickland looked at Montgomery out of the side of his eye and drew a long, deep breath.

'Look,' he said, 'this was a prosperous little country before this assassination started and it will be again, when this assassination is put down.' He spat out his words and took a long drink of his wine glass.

'It was prosperous for you, and people like my lord here, and Mr. Eustace,' said the Rector 'but the average family has lived in penury and a good deal of misery for years.'

'But come now, Rector,' said Lord Bandon. 'We've given them their Catholic Emancipation, and their Land League has caused the passing of the Wyndham Act, to enable them to buy their freeholds. Gladstone was about to grant them Home Rule until the Great War put everything on hold. What more can we do?'

'They want nothing short of a Republic I'm afraid,' said Parsons. 'Young Major Montgomery is right. Their leaders, Eamon de Valera and Michael Collins have said so in speech after speech.'

'What? And sever all our links with the United Kingdom?' asked

Lady Bandon in alarm. 'Why that's unthinkable, Mr. Parsons, simply unthinkable.'

'Unthinkable it may be m'lady,' said Parsons, 'but that's what's coming I'm afraid.'

Strickland gave a snort and stood up. 'What a load of tosh,' he expostulated. 'That will never be allowed to happen, not in a thousand years.'

There was a long, uneasy silence and Lord Bandon intervened. 'Gentlemen,' he smiled, 'I really don't think we're going to resolve this argument this evening, if I may say so. Can I suggest that we repair to the library for some brandy and cigars, while the ladies visit the powder room?'

There was a general sigh of pent-up relief from the assembled gathering. With much nodding and forced smiling, the dining room was slowly abandoned, like a tide going out, and they all moved through the hall. The subject had been well ventilated. Everybody had done their bit for the sake of civility. It was better to finish the evening on a congenial note.

At that moment there was a tremendous banging on the front door of the great hall. Bandon frowned in alarm and the butler hastened past him. 'Are you expecting someone, Joseph?' asked Bandon, puzzled.

'Not at this hour,' said the butler. He opened the door and a dishevelled Major Arthur Ernest Percival stumbled in, covered in blood. A woman screamed and nearly fainted. The men stood in open-mouthed astonishment, unable to quite comprehend what they were seeing. Behind Percival, two junior officers made their appearance in a similar condition. Strickland eventually found his voice and went to hold up the tottering Percival: 'What the devil happened, Major?'

Percival whispered hoarsely: 'An ambush, the Shinners, we were surrounded. Must have been a hundred of the blighters. Two...two officers dead...ten wounded at least. But we got ten of them I think, sir.'

Bandon rushed a glass of whiskey into Percival's trembling hands: 'Here, drink this Major. Joseph, get the nurse-maid down here immediately. We must tend to these injured men. And call a doctor at the double.'

Strickland looked reproachfully at Montgomery, who immediately took charge of the situation with maximum efficiency. 'Bring the General's car around now.'

He pointed to two NCO's who had accompanied them as security. They rushed for the door. Outside, one of the Crossley tenders was slewed across the front of the driveway where a dazed driver had managed to stop it. In the back, a number of soldiers lay as if shell-shocked. The armoured car was at the door in seconds with the engine running. Percival was helped back down the steps as Strickland had decided that all medical atttention should be administered back at the military barracks. The General saluted Lord Bandon smartly and jumped in his car. The vehicles took off from the front of the great house with a grinding of gears. The dumbfounded guests appeared at the door and various cars and carriages pulled up one by one to take them home. No further words were exchanged. Lord Bandon stood for a long time on the steps of his mansion and looked after the retreating lights. The steady clip clop of horse hooves faded out. His evening was in a shambles. Parsons, the only house guest, appeared at his side.

'So much for your liberal theories, Mr. Parsons. I trust you'll modify them now?'

Parsons could only nod rather shamefacedly and went inside without a word. Lord Bandon looked up towards the stars and tried to decipher what was in them. He picked out Alpha Centauri, Fomalhaut, Rigel. He saw Orion the Hunter. He looked in another direction and there were Arcturus and Izar in the constellation of Epsilon Bootes the Herdsman. By screwing up his eyes he could see the Seven Sisters. He thought he could see right through the Milky Way to the Crab Nebula swirling beyond. Or were his eyes deceiving him? He sighed and turned back inside, sidereal speculation abandoned for grim earthly reality.

6

loreto

The equinoxal sunset shone down upon them. Turning into twilight. Venus piercing the western sky, silver and beautiful. Soon more stars, the roads and railways darkening, no moon, and twilight disappearing. Autumn beckoning. They had come north from Gatonville by steam train through Bandon, Cork city and many far-flung towns. Past Mallow and the Golden Vale, past Cashel of the kings. All day from the deep southwest, onwards to the Curragh of Kildare; the blue mountains of Wicklow on the eastern horizon. Half-mumbled words of farewell to mother, father, brother Seamus and Doctor Baldwin in the early morning. And then the wave of a white handkerchief and tears in their mother's eyes, turning quickly away. The back-to-back trap getting smaller in the rising sun. All day travelling among tired children, choleric adults, soldiers with wary eyes at every station. The country in turmoil and suspicion on every face. Big-handed countrymen with broad accents and florid faces. Their furtive wives opening sandwiches wrapped in newspaper, slightly embarrassed to eat in public. A report in the Cork Examiner of a young medical student arrested in an ambush in Dublin: three British soldiers killed at a place called Monks Bakery. Shot collecting bread. The student, Kevin Barry, studying, like William, to be a doctor at University College Dublin. William and Margie in heated disagreement. Margie for the rebels, William against. Anna listening, caught in the middle. William saying: 'Total madness; you think things are going to change if we get a Republic?'

And Margie replying: 'Of course, we're following where France went before us, and America: *liberté, egalité, fraternité.*'

And William scoffing, 'The French Revolution created more problems than it solved. Thousands slaughtered, blood running red, nobody knowing who was next. Is that what you want for us?'

Margie accusing William of complacency, taking the side of the establishment, interested only in his own career. And so on the argument went until all eventually lapsed into weary, sullen silence as the lights of Dublin hurried past the windows of the train. Alighting in the confused bustle of Kingsbridge station; Anna embracing her older brother, holding him tight. Margie and he, rueful, but burying the hatchet for the moment. Promising to meet some Saturday in the months ahead around St. Stephen's Green when the exigencies of study allowed. Then, William, waving from the tram that would take him to his lodgings near the university at Earlfort Terrace, a lonely figure in the night despite his certainties; their brother dearly beloved, his sights set on taking on the world.

And now they were back in Loreto Abbey in the wide parklands of Rathfarnham, to begin the new school term. Grand mansion of red brick. Some would say magnificent. Georgian masterpiece built for William Palliser in 1725. Flanked by granite wings of grey; yellow-bricked architraves on windows and doors, St Joseph's, St. Anthony's, St Francis Xavier's: all added later by Reverend Mother Teresa Ball, the foundress of the Loreto Order. Spreading copper beech trees, holm oak, chestnut, cascading streams from Kilmashogue; mills on the Dodder, wheat harvested in the darkening fields of Taylor's Grange above at Marley House. The spirit of Patrick Pearse hovering over St Enda's and the winding pathways and follies of Hermitage Park. The tragic lovers, Robert Emmet and Sarah Curran. His body never found, but reputedly buried somewhere in the grounds of Priory House after his brutal hanging in Thomas Street in the uprising of 1803. And she far from the land where her young hero slept. One hundred and twenty long years ago.

Anna's heart always falterd a little when the great black gates adorned with gold filigree closed behind them. A kind of fortress where she felt trapped like a bird in a cage. The windows always rattling in the wind and a ghost walking the corridors of the novitiate. Perhaps it was the ghost of Thomas Moore who supposedly composed one of his enduring melodies in this stately home one night. Unable to sleep, the words of deathless beauty ran to him:

"Oft in the stilly night e'er slumber's chain hath bound me,
Fond memory brings the light of other days around me."'

Other days and other places. West Cork, father, mother now so far away. And the young men who followed their own stars, equally distant beyond the Pale from this sophisticated city. Those she'd seen at the funeral of John James O'Grady many months ago. They were not easily intimidated, and despite her brother William's reservations, she felt her heart was with them. She finally drifted into fitful sleep with the image of the smiling face of Sonny Hennessy rising in her dreams.

Sister Stanislaus was a florid-faced woman, with a plain face and an authoritative air. She ruled the Loreto convent with an iron fist and her mission was to make Loreto girls the best.

'Loreto girls are achievers in the world,' she said on a regular basis. 'Up there with the best the Jesuits of Belvedere and Clongowes Wood can produce.'

It was significant to be a Loreto girl. It carried more than a suggestion of elitism and what was wrong with that? Not a whole lot in Sister Stanislaus's eyes. Anna was a girl for whom snobbery had no great importance. She could talk to prince or pauper and felt equally at home with either. Margie on the other hand, whilst she subscribed to an egalitarian outlook, really was an intellectual snob, and also cock-a-hoop around the convent because Stanislaus was their aunt. This conferred an extra level of prestige. Margie always came top of the class, displaying an awesome mastery of every subject from the classics to science and mathematics. And even such arcane disciplines as economics and horseracing.

And so the term unfolded from September into the blue, crisp days of October. Up in Kilmashogue Woods and Marley Park the evening primrose had long since waned. Gone too was the purple loosestrife, the hogweed and hedge-parsley. Leaves were blown in tumultuous showers of russet, yellow and red from the oak, copper beech and mountain ash to make a carpet of crinkling colour under their feet when they went on their Sunday walks. There was a cooling from sweet summer; winds were stronger and broken weather heralded longer, frosty nights. Anna would look out her dormitory window to behold the wheeling stars and sometimes it was so quiet she thought she could hear the singing of the universe.

While Margie dominated every academic situation with a casual ease, Anna looked forward to reading the letters from home, which she received every Tuesday in response to the ones she wrote home every Friday. Madeleine would write with all the news from Cork: the harvesting of the corn, the eccentricities of Doctor Baldwin; her father's various enterprises with machinery around the farm. Anna always hoped to glean some fragment of information about the activities of the Volunteers, and in particular some word on a certain Sonny Hennessy, whose name she couldn't seem to get out of her mind. But her mother eschewed the mention of controversial topics. Her husband, Thomas, disapproved of the tactics of Sinn Féin and the Irish Republican Army. He was a Redmondite: Home Rule and self-government by all means, but achieved peacefully. Madeleine herself hoped these unpleasant troubles would disappear. In the absence of information from her mother, Anna hit upon another scheme. She would write a letter to Sonny herself with a view to arranging a meeting with him when she went home for the Chistmas holidays. She wasn't sure of his address but she felt fairly certain a general description would suffice for the missive to find its destination; the Hennessys were a prominent family in that locality.

In mid-October the newspapers were full of the impending trial of the young medical student, Kevin Barry, the boy from Belvedere, who joined the IRA. Anna was particularly interested in the outcome due to an unease that the same fate might befall the young man in West Cork whom she barely knew. In the refectory of the grand abbey, Margie read out at breakfast the news that General Sir Nevil Macready, Commander of the British Forces in Ireland, had ordered a court martial of nine officers under Brigadier-General Onslow, to try Kevin Barry.

'They won't find him guilty, be assured of that,' said Sister Stanislaus. 'That boy is well got, a Jesuit-trained student. No, it's impossible to contemplate.'

Margie quietly opined to her fellow students that she took a contrary view; the British were more than capable of barbarities to equal those of any other nation. Especially when it came to the Irish.

'I don't believe that at all,' said Jennifer Slevin with her accent of the Anglo-Irish aristocracy.

'You don't?' inquired Margie. 'Well, just listen to this.'

"When I refused to give them names they sent a sergeant out of the room for a bayonet. When he returned the officer ordered the sergeant to point the bayonet at my stomach. Then I was ordered to turn around and face the wall and the bayonet was pressed into my back sharply. The sergeant said he would run me through if I didn't tell. Then they put me face down on the floor, the sergeant knelt on my back and the other two placed one foot each on my back and left shoulder. One man

twisted my arm to breaking point, while pulling my head back by the hair. It was too agonising to bear and they kept it up for so long that I passed out. When I came to, they continued to question me. I refused to answer all questions."'

Margie stopped reading from the broadsheet and looked up. 'There's a lot more. Do you want me to continue or have you heard enough?'

Mary Higgins held her hand up as if to ward off the onslaught. 'No more for God's sake, you've made your point.'

'What's that from anyway?' inquired Jennifer, suspiciously.

'It's from a sworn affidavit by Kevin Barry, smuggled out by his lawyer, Sean O'Huadhaigh and printed in the *Irish Bulletin*, published by Dáil Eireann's Department of Publicity. Torturing a prisoner of war is against the Hague Convention. Of course they get around it by saying there's no war going on, only an insurrection by rebels, who have no military standing. All this despite the overwhelming vote by the people of Ireland in 1918 to set up our own government.'

'But surely they won't hang him?' said Anna more in hope than conviction.

'Wait and see,' said Margie.

On the 28th of October it was officially announced that the verdict was guilty and the sentence was to be death by hanging, fixed for the 1st of November 1920, All Souls' Day. The girls were plunged into a trough of despondency along with the whole country. A huge crowd of nearly one hundred thousand people paraded through the streets of Dublin in an attempt to stop the hanging. They cursed and prayed and wept. Margie read how it was argued that the bullet that killed Private Marshall Whitehead was a .45 calibre, while all witnesses said Kevin Barry was armed with a .38 Mauser Parabellum. But the court martial wasn't prepared to entertain any such fine distinctions. He was an accessory to the fact of murder, notwithstanding what gun he was carrying, or who fired the shot. Throughout All Souls' Night the people kept vigil. The young man was visited by Fr. Albert and Canon Waters who heard his confession and read the Mass in his cell in Mountjoy jail. He was calm but unrepentant. If he was to die, it was for a sacred cause, following the path already taken by Pearse and the 1916 martyrs four years earlier. He was hanged at 8 o'clock in the morning and his body was pronounced dead a short while later. Medical evidence was adduced that death was instantaneous. The city of Dublin ground to a halt in shocked disbelief.

Father Waters wrote to Barry's mother saying:

"You are the mother, my dear Mrs Barry, of one of the bravest and best boys I have ever known. His death was one of the most holy and your dear boy is waiting for you now, beyond the reach of sorrow or trial."

To Anna, these words were unbearably sad to read. Her sister Margie could argue over methods of execution and why they hadn't shot him by firing squad like a soldier instead of hanging him like a thief. But to Anna, death was final and one way of dying was no different than another. Nothing was going to bring him back. Dublin Corporation announced an adjournment of their meetings as a mark of respect and Sister Stanislaus at Loreto Abbey allowed the girls a half day in sympathy. They found it difficult to concentrate on their studies for that week and well into the next. In addition there was the tragic news that Terence MacSwiney, the Republican Lord Mayor of Cork, had died on hunger strike. Public opinion was aroused to a fever pitch of indignation that, despite the international attempts by American, British and Vatican officials, no reprieve had been given either to Kevin Barry or MacSwiney.

The following week the girls got a note from William saying he was anxious to meet them. It was suggested they would rendezvous at 9 o'clock on Sunday morning, the 21st of November, at the Royal Dublin Fusiliers Arch on St. Stephen's Green. It was a crisp morning, the sun was rising over Dublin Bay as they alighted from the train at the granite-grey Harcourt Street station. They walked down Harcourt, carefully avoiding the trams that squealed their way on tracks down the centre meridian, full of early morning churchgoers. The bells were ringing out from St. Patrick's, Christchurch, Adam and Eve's, and across the river from the Pro-Cathedral. There were sidecars parked along the western side of the Green and the smell of horse dung was pungent. You had to move gingerly to avoid stepping into it. They met William under the arch near the top of Grafton Street. He was reading out the names of various generals who fought in the Boer War: Kruger, Botha, Steyn, De Witt. There were other names inscribed in limestone of the many Irish who had fallen in the Great War.

Anna was reading aloud: 'Tugela Heights, Ladysmith, Hartshill, Spion Kop.' She repeated the name: 'Spion Kop, isn't that the name of a horse?'

Margie laughed. 'Quite right my dear, but the horse was named after a battle in the Boer War in South Africa. Spion Kop is a hill above the Tugela river. The English were beaten there by a rag-tag army of South African farmers on horseback who were crack shots with rifles.'

'Sounds a bit like our own crowd,' said William laconically. 'Or should I say your crowd.'

'My crowd, your crowd, what's the difference?' asked Margie.

'I was trying to be funny,' said William apologetically. 'It's just that you approve of their tactics and I don't.'

'And what about the young medical student who was just hanged?' asked Margie. 'You said you knew him?'

'I did, I met him several times. A hardworking and serious young man. He'd have made a fine doctor. It's a great tragedy. What more can I say?'

'So was he one of your crowd then?'

'Look Margie, I don't want to argue anymore,' said William. 'You know my views on the subject; they're the same as our father's. I believe in an independent Ireland, but I don't believe in getting it by violence that's all. I know you have a different view and that you and Anna are somewhat in thrall to these young rebels; Doctor Baldwin also. I'm not going to change your mind and you're not going to change mine. So can we agree to disagree?'

Margie shook her head with a rueful smile and then clapped him on the back. 'Oh, alright William, you're always so solid and sensible.' She paused and said, 'So what shall we do now?'

'We could go for breakfast in one of those cafés around Grafton Street; the Cairo or Davy Byrnes, or Bewleys.'

'And we could go to Croke Park afterwards,' said Anna with a bright idea.

'Croke Park,' frowned William. 'What's on there?'

'There's a football match between Dublin and Tipperary. It could be exciting.'

'Exciting? I'm afraid I don't find a bunch of fellows chasing a ball around a field exciting, but if you want to go I'll tag along.'

'Oh, William, you're such a fuddy duddy,' said Anna, and gave him a hug. They set off down Grafton Street, as the rising winter sun cast a long shaft of light between the buildings. They turned left into Bewleys Oriental Café and were shown a table under some beautiful stained-glass windows, where the smell of coffee beans coalesced with frying bacon. And the sound of animated laughter, mingling with the clink of cutlery on delph made a warm haven inside out of the chilly air. A flaming coal fire added a Christmas flavour, although the season of goodwill was still over four weeks away.

They were nearly finished their bacon and eggs when Margie leant over and whispered that they shouldn't look now, but two tables away there was a famous man sitting with a number of others whom she didn't recognise.

Anna looked furtively around. 'Who is it?' she whispered, always eager for a conspiracy like any schoolgirl. William eventually turned his head while pretending to look at something else. He spotted the men. 'I don't recognise anyone either.'

'Do you see the dark-haired fellow with the three piece suit? He's kind of swarthy,' said Margie.

'He's very attractive,' said Anna in admiration, 'but he looks a bit forbidding, dangerous even.'

Margie gave a kind of chortle, 'That's because he is.'

'Who is he then?' said Anna, getting frustrated.

'Michael Collins,' said Margie with a hint of triumph.

'Michael Collins?' said William, impressed despite his attempts to retain his insouciance. 'But I thought no one knows what he looks like. Doesn't he travel in disguise?'

'That's him alright,' said Margie, 'I'd be exacty one hundred per cent certain it's him.'

'Lucky for him you don't work for British Intelligence. Isn't he the most wanted man in Ireland?' said William.

'The most wanted by the British, the most beloved by the Irish,' said Margie. 'It depends which side you're on.'

Margie floated into a kind of suspended trance, which people sometimes do in the vicinity of the famous. She continued to talk to her siblings, but heard nothing of what they said. For her, the man so close she could almost touch him represented the acme of everything she found admirable. In so much as Margie ever allowed herself to fall under the influence of a member of the opposite sex, she did on this occasion. Her knees felt like jelly. Collins was a West Cork man, perhaps twelve years older than herself, but already he had assumed the legendary reputation that only the very great in any walk of life can attain. He was the man who epitomised the spirit of the Irish revolution; the embodiment of it. As a young teenager he'd spent ten years living and working in London before returning to Dublin to take part in the Easter Rising of 1916. He was imprisoned again in England and finally afer his release he was back in Dublin, organising the Volunteers and building up a network of spies and informers against the British State apparatus in Ireland. He and Eamon de Valera represented the twin leadership of the new Irish nation. They were already world-famous for their daring vision of a new Ireland and were determined that this time there would be no stories of abject failure. And here he was in the flesh, two tables away from her, his careful, hooded, blue eyes twinkling into sudden merriment whenever a smile crossed his face. He radiated everything not only women, but men also can find irresistible: power, courage and competence. Margie kept sneaking glances out of the corner of her eye. Such a dazzling smile, such white teeth, such saturnine good looks. On the one hand she thought she might faint but on the other she was determined to say something to him before they left. Collins had the reputation of being mercurial, and as William had said, he was the most wanted man in Ireland. But the British were unable to catch him. He was said to be a master of disguise, riding around the streets of Dublin in broad daylight undetected by the British Intelligence who strove so diligently to apprehend him. As Margie was girding her courage to go and make an introduction there was a sudden interruption as a number of men hurried past them heading for the door of the café. Some incoherent words were shouted and they all turned to look at the backs of the departing men. Heads turned to watch them run down the street outside the window. Then quiet returned. When Margie turned back to re-engage with her target he had disappeared. Gone like a scarlet pimpernel. Collins was quick on his feet. He had behaved true to form. It was as if he had been assumed, body and soul, out through the ceiling. He hadn't gone out the front door with the other men, of that she was certain. Had they created a decoy run so that he could make his escape out the back?

They had been no more than an hour in Bewleys. As they made their way slowly down Grafton Street to the corner of Nassau Street there was a blaring of klaxons and a convoy of British lorries and armoured cars roared past them heading in the direction of Merrion Square. Early morning worshippers and window-shoppers jumped out of the way in alarm. Something was afoot. Although disturbances of one kind or another had become the norm lately, this appeared to be something more serious. But then the military were gone and normality seemed to return to the streets. Margie, Anna and William made their way slowly over Sackville Street Bridge and headed past Nelson's Pillar and the General Post Office. Its walls were still pockmarked from hundreds of bullets after the bombardment of the Rising four years before. They headed up past the Gresham Hotel towards Parnell Street by Findlater's Church. Margie and Anna recalled how they had lodged here with a certain landlady during the Rising and were stranded there for six weeks. Margie was only thirteen, Anna twelve. Their mother had accompanied them to Dublin prior to their first introduction to Loreto and into the midst of their maiden voyage, the Easter Rising had reared its fateful head. For the first week all was chaos. Constant bombardment from a British naval ship on the Liffey pounded the rebel positions all along Sackville Street, Boland's Mills and Mount Street. Every night Margie would sneak out down past the burning buildings, unbeknownst to their mother, bringing back tales of extraordinary goings-on to Anna. These assumed dimensions of graphic horror and a kind of romanticism that neither of them had been able to forget. They became inured to violent and dramatic events from an early age, leading to a heady addiction for the excitement they created.

They had meandered for some hours around the seamier side of the city, known locally as Monto, because they had time to kill before the game in Croke Park started. Then word began to filter through that there had been a number of shootings in the city in the early morning. Some said it was an IRA ambush and others said it was something more sinister. Then a young man, who seemed to be in the know, standing outside a pub in Marino, down to where they had wandered, had it on good authority that the Cairo Gang had been wiped out by Michael Collins.

'Who are the Cairo Gang?' asked William in his innocence.

'The Cairo Gang are the most dangerous bunch of British spies in Ireland. They've been trying to destroy the Republican leadership for the last year.' said Margie.

'Really?' said William.

'And you said they were wiped out?' asked Anna, of the cocky young man.

'I'm only going on what I'm hearing through the grapevine,' said the young man conspiratorially. 'Can't really say anymore about it.' And he put his finger to his lips to indicate they were sealed. As they walked on towards the stadium, word was now widespread that as many as fifty spies had been assassinated. They had been out to get the Irish leaders, but Collins had got them first. The town was buzzing with rumour and counter rumour. Some said four British agents were killed on Lower

Mount Street, two more on Baggot Street, others on Fitzwilliam Square, Morehampton Road and Earlsfort Terrace. It was a massacre.

'Do you think we should still go to the game?' Anna had asked, somewhat alarmed when it was recounted that one of the dead spies had been shot in his bed, with his pregnant wife by his side.

'I think we should go. What harm is there in going to a game? It'll pass the time and take our minds off this unpleasantness,' said Margie.

'Life must go on I suppose,' said William, 'although we're all becoming a little war weary.'

The game was due to start at 2.45 in the afternoon. They went in through the turnstiles on the Clonliffe Road and sat on the terraces waiting for the teams to come out. There were thousands of people. William said he thought maybe four thousand, Margie said more like ten thousand. It seemed to take a long time for the game to start. When the teams finally emerged it was 3.15 p.m.

'Which team is which?' asked Anna

'Dublin are blue; Tipperary are blue and gold,' said Margie.

The ball was thrown in and the game started. They followed the play up and down the field. There were partisan shouts from the opposing spectators and excitement began to build. First, Dublin scored, and then Tipperary responded. After ten minutes the sides were still level. 'This is more exciting than I expected,' said William, blowing on his fingers. It was quite chilly. Suddenly there was a sound of gunshots over on the Canal End of the stadium. The teams on the field stopped playing. Then there was a further fusillade of rifle fire.

'Are those shots?' asked Anna.

'Sounds like it,' said William.

Then they heard screaming and below them they saw a group of soldiers running in through the turnstiles. People began to jump from seat to seat. The soldiers were firing rapidly. Bullets rattled off the sheet iron roof above their heads. Margie watched in disbelief as one Tipperary footballer, running towards the soldiers, was cut down. He crumpled onto the green grass, blood pumping from his chest. He appeared to be twitching and kicking, trying to get up. Anna screamed. Margie and William stood as if frozen to the spot, unable to believe their eyes. Another player was hit right in front of them and crawled on his hands and knees, gasping for breath.

'My God,' said Margie. 'What's happening?' Then everybody began rushing for the far side of the Park amid scenes of the wildest confusion. The shots kept coming from every direction, it seemed. People ran like flocks of sheep one way and then the other. An older man was hit by a bullet and fell a few feet away from them. William bent to try to help him, but was swept along by the panicking crowd. There were abandoned shoes, jackets, overcoats. A military voice was blaring over a loudspeaker, but the orders went unheeded: 'Keep calm, everybody keep calm. Make your way calmly to the exits.'

People began climbing over the Canal End wall, trying to escape. A young man had half his face blown off by a bullet. A running boy tripped over a seat and was trampled underfoot by the desperate crowd. There was blood on their clothes and on their hands. The three of them clung closely to each other and ran as fast as they could around by the side of the pitch. They could hear the sounds of machinegun fire. As they burst out onto St. James's Avenue, they saw an armoured car firing into the crowd. They kept running, down narrow side streets, past small artisan cottages, past moaning, bleeding people fallen in doorways. They ran on and on, their lungs bursting, but in their terror they appeared to have superhuman strength. To get away, anything to get away from the nightmare. They finally found themselves back near where they first met the young man near Fairview Park. The darkness of the November evening was drawing in. They were scratched, bruised and battered. William walked with a limp from smashing his knee against the concrete edge of a terraced seat. Anna's clothes were half in tatters. Margie had lost her handbag and her glasses. They were dishevelled, terrified, but alive. They somehow made their way back to the tram and spent the night in William's lodgings on Lower Leeson Street.

Back in Loreto Abbey a week later, Margie and Anna were still recovering from their ordeal. They relayed the dramatic details to an expectant assembly of students. Everything was described over and over. They had achieved the status of heroes and were treated with due consideration and deference for most of the week. By the weekend, the aura had worn off somewhat and Margie took to piecing together the details of what had happened from various newspaper reports. She intended to make a diary of the events to keep them for posterity. Margie was an inveterate keeper of diaries. The *Manchester Guardian* and the *Daily News* confirmed that the Black and Tans and RIC were commanded by a Major Mills. By the time he got them back under control, they had fired 114 rounds of rifle ammunition and an unknown amount of revolver ammunition; not counting the 50m rounds fired from the machinegun in the armoured car outside the Park. Seven people had been shot to death and five more had been fatally wounded. Another two people had been trampled to death by the crowd. The dead included Jeannie Boyle, who had gone to the game with her fiancé and was due to be married five days later. There were two dead boys, aged ten and eleven. Two football players, Michael Hogan and Jim Egan, had been shot. The military later issued a statement to say they had chased armed men into the ground and shots were fired to warn them, causing a stampede. *The Times* of London ridiculed this account. It reported that no arms were found and the Black and Tans had fired into the crowd with no provocation whatsoever. Margie noted that Eamon de Valera, in a speech, said the loss of the Cairo Gang had devastated British Intelligence in Ireland and the public relations disaster that came to be known as Bloody Sunday, severely damaged the cause of British Rule in Ireland.

As for the Cairo Gang, their fate had been ruthlessly sealed by Michael Collins and senior IRA men such as Dick McKee, Liam Tobin, Peadar Clancy, Frank Thornton, Oscar Traynor and Sean Lemass. Probably the men accompanying Collins that morning in Bewleys Café. If only she had known. The operation began when members of the Collins hit squad entered No. 28 Pembroke Street at precisely 9 a.m. About the time she orderered their breakfast in Bewleys. The first British agents to die were Major Dowling and Captain Price. Then three more members of the Gang were shot in the same house: Captain Keenlyside, Colonel Woodcock and Colonel Montgomery. Three more were shot on the roof of 119 Morehampton Road. At 92 Lower Baggot Street, Captain Newbury and his wife heard their front door come crashing in and blockaded themselves in their bedroom. Newbury rushed for his window to try to escape, but was shot while climbing out. His corpse hung out of the window for several hours as the Black and Tans waited to approach, fearing it might have been booby-trapped. Lieutenant Ames and Captain Bennett were shot and killed in a gun battle, after a maid led their attackers into No.38 Upper Mount Street.

The list went on. Margie took careful notes. One of the most lurid, she noted, was of a lucky escape by a Major Hardy and a Major King, who had spent the night in a local brothel. They were missing when their would-be assassin, Joe Dolan, burst into King's room to find nobody there but his mistress. Dolan said he took revenge by giving King's half naked mistress a right scourging with a sword scabbard and setting fire to the room.

Margie dryly noted Collins's subsequent comments:

"I have enough proof to assure myself of the atrocities which this gang of spies and informers have committed. By their destruction, the very air is made sweeter...for myself my conscience is clear. There is no crime in detecting in wartime the spy and the informer. They have destroyed without trial. I have paid them back in their own coin."

Margie sighed. He was something different, something dangerous, this man they called, the Laughing Boy, and others called, the Big Fellow. This man she was in thrall to.

7

Doctor Baldwin was restless. It was a long way from springtime, *teacht an earraigh,* but he felt it was time to hoist his sail and hit the road. And Thomas Cody was no help. The house was becoming too small for them. It was, Jim do this, Jim do that; let out the cows and feed the pigs. If you said black, then he'd say white. You couldn't please him. No point in trying to get Madeleine to put in a good word for him. She was in Cody's camp. Married to him. Blood wasn't thicker than marriage vows, but she did her best. That man could be unreasonable. Especially with a few drinks. Get wild and irrational, he could. The Doctor was the opposite. A few quiet ones and he got even quieter, but more amorous. Benign though. *In vino veritas.* Never was a truer word said. The real person inside came out. Street angel, house devil. That was Cody. Well be damned to him. James Baldwin wasn't going to lie down like a beaten cur in front of any man. He still had a few friends left around the country. He'd seek them out. Anyway, Cody wouldn't need him for awhile. Cheap labour, that's what the attraction was. Not for his scintillating personality, which other people appreciated. But not that curmudgeon. The harvest was saved long since and now it was the long nights after *Samhain.* No cheer till Christmas and that a month away. Cold winds blowing from the southwest. Sometimes wheeling around to north by northwest. That would redden a man's arse of a frosty morning, unless he had the long Johns on underneath. Shrivel up the pecker until it disappeared altogether nearly. Not much use to a man then. Ah, he was a quare one right enough. Not married, yet not without companions. Women were taken by him. He was a plausible rogue no doubt and yet a sensitive soul. They liked that in a man. Besides he'd always pay them compliments and bring them flowers. Maybe quote some verse to them. His head was full of verse, and his prowess in the bedroom was unmatched, or so said the rumours that filtered back to him. He loved a woman's body.

He'd go away back into West Cork and maybe Kerry. Stop in to see his ancestral home in Kilmichael maybe, then on to Baile Mhúirne and meet the girl from around the county bounds he left behind so long ago.They'd met in Cork city at the university. She went her way and he went his. But they kept in touch by letter. She still had a soft spot for him. Married and widowed was she? So it would be no more, "Stall up, stall up," with Thomas Cody, and his canteens and creameries at six o'clock in the morning. He'd go away back into Kerry, where they had fine turf fires, the houses would be hot. He'd sleep away 'til ten o'clock in the morning.

The political situation was gone to hell. Since the Bloody Sunday business, the Auxies and the Tans were rampaging through the countryside on a daily basis, looting, shooting and killing. Burning too. Families on the side of the road, sleeping in old sheds and *cabhlachs*. Like famine times again. And the IRA on the other side demanding contributions and a levy. If you couldn't pay they drove off your cattle. Sold them at the fair. People were caught on every side, but the vast majority supported the Volunteers. If they were the new Government of the people, then the people had to do what they decreed, which included paying their taxes. But it caused a lot of resentment in certain quarters.

'There was a man who nearly got shot except some lads intervened to stop it,' said Tim Hurley the blacksmith, as he bent to burn the imprint of a horseshoe into the hind hoof of an Irish draught. 'These fellows were looking for the levy and went into this farmer's yard. But their leader and the farmer couldn't stand the sight of each other. It went back years. The farmer refused to hand over anything to yer man and he kept insisting. The farmer pulled out a gun and they both squared off. Only for the other fellows being there, blood would have been spilt. I got the whole thing from a man who was there.'

'Did you indeed?' asked Doctor Baldwin as he blew the bellows for Hurley in his forge near Baxter's Bridge. A favourite port of call where news was obtained, stories swapped, gossip broadcast. Hurley was a big, friendly man who hummed away as he worked, while his acolyte and brother, James, did the hammering and heavy lifting. The forge was low and dark. It smelt of smoke, coal and a particular fleshy smell of burnt hoof. Like fried meat. Hurley would measure the shoe to fit the hoof and when it was accurately burnt in, the hot shoe was held hissing into a bath of cold water by a long tongs. If not accurate it was reheated until white hot, then battered and moulded into a more precise configuration on the anvil. Then Hurley tossed the fashioned shoe to James, who lifted up the horse's hind leg, holding it between his knees, protected by a leather apron, while he hammered in the long, thin nails, twisted off the protruding points with a *castóir*, like a pincers, and buffed off the back of the hoof with a rasp. There was a sense of a job well done when a horse was shod. Of course a man like Hurley was much more than a smith. He had to be a vet and horse doctor. He could shoe them, pinfire them, better than most; he could spot a curb, spavin or splint with one rub of his hand over pastern, fetlock or tendon. He could diagnose a horse with colic, deficiency of calcium, broken wind. He suggested minerals for cures: potassium, molassses, raw eggs. And he was philosopher and confessor to every man who came down the road.

'Things are bad enough,' continued Hurley, rubbing his leather apron carefully with huge, yet delicate hands. He always seemed to have time to spare, yet he got through a vast amount of work each day. In addition to horses, there were wrought iron gates to be made, ploughs and harrows to be fixed. The walls held a bewildering array of implements for mending: hoes, shovels, pickaxes, dibbles, clippers, rakes. Outside, parked at random angles, were buck rakes, wheel rakes, spring harrows, reapers and binders, whittle trees. All forged and battered on the ringing anvil. A trade as old as time.

Each to his own, thought Doctor Baldwin. Whither mine? Wasted in pursuit of half-cocked ideas, unfinished projects, a jack of all trades, unfocused, incoherent. He might be called a clever man by some, dealt a good hand by the Lord. Squandered talents. He felt himself a fraud compared to Hurley.

There came Jasper Eustace, big man in out of the rain. 'Good morrow men.'

'Morrow Jasper,' in unisoned response. No religion, no class distinction here amid the smoking ruins of iron. Jasper dismounted from his saddle horse. He pulled the reins over the horse's head, letting it dangle. The horse was trained to stay motionless while the reins trailed the ground. Unhurried, Jasper watched the work. In the time-honoured, country way he joined in the existing conversation rather than creating a new subject matter. The subject happened to be the price of pigs:

'They're down I hear,' said Jasper.

'They are,' agreed Hurley. 'But cattle are up. Ballineen fair was slack enough last week. Prices were high.'

'No wonder, with the way cattle are being taken from fellows to pay the levy,' said Jasper.

Each with his own point of view, advancing it gently, but leaving room for the other's. Jasper led his big-boned hunter into the floor of the forge, that was built up, sponge-like, by years of discarded hoof cuts. The horse had high withers and a shoulder sloping well back into his frame.

'He's a good sort,' said Hurley, looking the horse over.

'Fills the eye alright,' said Jasper. Things were understated when it came to horses. All assessments were slow, deliberate, considered. Doctor Baldwin looked mildly at Jasper, no hurry on him to speak. Their relationship was a kind of sparring duel. No quarter given, but nothing nasty either. Jasper was too dull for Baldwin. Baldwin was too harum-scarum for Jasper. Steady, thrifty Protestant, quicksilver Catholic with an elite pedigree. From the way they spoke no one could tell the difference. Doctor Baldwin had been in their church surreptitiously one day out of curiosity. Cody didn't approve, but what of that. Fine stained-glass windows, well upholstered seats, dedications to the King on plinths and catafalques. The 2nd Earl of Bandon laid out in splendid effigy. But little difference between the Catholic and Protestant faiths. They didn't believe the bread and wine became the body and blood of Christ. Neither did Doctor Baldwin. Symbolism is what they called it. He had to agree. Was this the nub of the matter? That and the Virgin birth. Again he had to agree. Immaculate Conception my eye. Or was there something more? Certainly they looked to the Empire, these Protestants with their Fusiliers, Foresters and Irish Regiments. And yet if you went back to 1798, the United Irishmen were organised and set up by Protestants: Wolfe Tone, Henry Joy McCracken, Lord Edward Fitzgerald. What had happened to their sense of Irishness since? Lost somewhere in the cauldrons of different rebellions. And now they were a wealthy minority in danger of losing their exalted position once and for all.

'How's Thomas Cody?' Jasper asked, perhaps to irk the Doctor a little.

'Minding his own business I suppose,' quipped the Doctor. Jasper gave him an ironic, humorous look and was about to respond. Noting the Doctor's slightly pursed lips, he decided not to continue that line of inquiry.

Slow, slow, the steady hammering, the flying sparks, the hissing steam. Rain drops steady on the sheet-iron roof. Schoolchildren peering in through the smoke in the dusky evening. Cackles of laughter, hoots and hollers. 'You'll die from the smoke, Tim.'

'There's no smoke here,' said Doctor Baldwin. 'Come up here and blow the bellows. There's no smoke here boys.'

And the amazed children gathered to take turns wrestling with the long arm, balanced like a see-saw, suspended from the bellows's end by a chain.

'Where does the smoke go?'

'Out the door, where else?'

All a calm, orderly procession of hours, days, years. The long years forged in the smithy of life. Ah, yes, James Baldwin, if time could be rewound. His father a hardworking, intelligent man. His mother ambitious for her children. Sending daughter Madeleine to Vienna to the heart of the Hapsburg Empire. Sending another sister to Australia to join the Loreto Order over there. Making financial sacrifices to send James to study medicine in Cork and Edinburgh. Losing older brother Henry on the Somme. Fifty-five thousand young Irishman dying in the British Army. Forgotten heroes now. And he a womanless man, beloved of women for many years. But who would have him? Too volatile, too opinionated, unwilling to commit. Afraid perhaps? Like he was afraid of blood. And so while the flesh occasionally tormented, the mind tormented more. The meaning of things, the warp and weft of life.

The rain continued to fall from Thursday into Friday. The sky was clearing as he found himself around mid-afternoon walking into Castletownkinneigh like a *spailpín*, a day labourer. And yet his step was lightsome. There was freedom on the open road that could not be found in hospital ward or doctor's surgery. Other contemporaries could do that, but not him. A square peg in a round hole. Was it parental snobbery that sent him on the wrong road, or was it his own sense of self-importance? A doctor occupied a prime position in society that was for sure. If he were truthful with himself, he would admit to craving that pre-eminence. But it didn't work out. Blinded by the position not the reality, it could only end in tears.

Castletown was a remote village on a road to nowhere. It had changed little for maybe two hundred years. Its street ran downhill into a hollow and ended with a slight rise like the last furlong to an uphill finish of a racetrack. To the west in a deep, leafy valley, about half a mile away was the ancient monastic settlement of Kinneigh, with a round tower dating back to the ninth century, a lovely old church and historic graveyard. Westward from there, the tops of the mountains, Sheha and Owen, peeked over the foothills. He passed Tade Crowley's forge on his left, abutting a large farm to its rear owned by Hosford. Further along on the right, Tim Callaghan, a carpenter, was planing a gleaming, honey-coloured shaft of a new cart and the curling wood shavings accumulated in a heap outside the door. There was a wholesome, resiny smell of timber. He stopped and conversed with Callaghan for a few minutes, running his hand as he did so along the smooth surface of the wood in unconscious motion. Then he moved on past Jack Lordan, the tailor. Lordan's door was open and he was inside, sitting on his kitchen table, legs crossed, sowing a suit-length of worsted tweed. Thimble on thumb, dextrous movement of fingers, neat, correct in action and in conversation. Across the street was O'Mahony's post office and even from here the droning voice of the proprietor, Master Jeremiah O'Mahony could be heard, carrying up the rising street from the schoolhouse further down. O'Mahony the demagogue. A man of certainties, a serious patriot.

There was a red bicycle leaning against the blue wall of Nyhan's public house and Doctor Baldwin made his way towards it, skeways from the school. Fehily, the postman was sitting on a windowsill smoking a cigarette. The rain had stopped and the low November sun shone in slanting, yellow brilliance into his eyes as he stepped onto the footpath and saluted the postman. In the adjacent grocery shop, Mrs Warren was talking to Mrs Duggan, and Moore's cows, from the farm in the centre of the village, slowly ambled down the middle of the street as if they owned it. They were driven by Stanley Moore, leading a white horse, and they all moved in a stately procession out of the village, over the brow of the low hill, until they dropped from view as if descending a stairs. Young Tull Hennessy, tall, lean and dark, was holding a horse tackled under a butt, with a crib containing a load of bonhams, that grunted and squealed trying to find a comfortable corner in the straw. The Doctor enquired after his well-being and the taciturn Tull replied that he was fine. He seemed a serious young man.

The Doctor walked into the pub through the narrow, hinged door that could be fully opened to accommodate a crowd. Inside it was smoky and dim. The sudden sun shone through a far window and a narrow shaft of light illuminated the stone-flagged floor. There was a turf fire burning in a grate on the left and the sweet, pungent smell of peat rose and mingled with the permanent smell of whiskey and the faint smell of urine from an outside lavatory. Good wholesome smells to the Doctor, who was inured to nature's putrefactions. There was a high, narrow-topped bar of smooth, stained oak and behind it one of the Nyhan girls washed glasses and busied herself, waiting for a call for further drinks from the few customers imbibing in the shadows. Jeremiah Hennessy sat on a low settle in the small snug on the right, talking to Daniel Hourihane, a powerfully tall man with huge hands and a gravelly voice. Jeremiah was dapper in a white shirt, with rounded collar and tie, a dark suit and a bowler hat. His nose was red from drinking too much liquor betimes. Further along the bar two men, Bill Sullivan and Richie Shorten were sitting on high stools and Tom Wilson stood between them. They were all lean-framed, weather-beaten men, who had raised large families and took a drink. Doctor Baldwin's spirits rose. All the customers were men after his own heart. Decent, spirited, civilized. Lovers of humour and good conversation.

He opened his arms in an expansive gesture of greeting. 'Ah, my venereal friends.'

Tom Wilson stood back with a glint in his eye and looked him up and down, from the top of his hat to the sheen of his shoes. 'By Christ, will you look what the dog dragged in.'

There was a general ritual of backslapping and handshaking. Wilson continued to inspect him.

'Come here to me,' he said eventually. 'Is it to a wedding you're going or to a funeral?'

'Neither I'd say,' said Richie Shorten, 'I'd say that man is going courting.'

The Doctor demurred. Fake modesty.

Bill Sullivan added. 'I'd say you hit the nail on the head there Richie.'

Tom Wilson reached up and took the hat off the Doctor's head. He tried it on.

'Take that hat off,' said Sullivan. 'You don't have enough qualifications to wear that hat.'

And he winked at Doctor Baldwin, who said: 'It's not about qualifications, it's a question of style. Some can wear a hat and some can't. Isn't that right Jeremiah?' He'd skilfully drawn Hennesssy into the conversation from the snug, where he stood up to see what the commotion was about.

Jeremiah nodded and cocked his head to the right in his bowler. 'Too bloody true, Doctor, too bloody true.' And he ordered a whiskey. 'You'll have a drop?'

'If you insist, Jeremiah,' said the Doctor. A half-one was put up on the counter for him by young Miss Nyhan. 'That's excellent service, young lady,' he said and gave a little bow.

'Begod then, but you can keep your eyes off that young lady,' said Tom Wilson digging him in the ribs. 'She's spoken for. Isn't that right, Jeremiah?'

'Who's the lucky man?' asked the Doctor.

'You've a good few bowls-of-odds on him anyway,' said Bill Sullivan, and they all laughed.

'Ask that man there,' said Richie Shorten, pointing to Jeremiah Hennessy.

'My dear Jeremiah, are your crowd joining forces with the Nyhan clan? Is that what I'm given to understand by this innuendo from these learned fellows?' asked the Doctor.

Jeremiah nodded modestly. 'You have to take these rumours with a pinch of salt,' he said.

'There's many a slip 'twixt the cup and the lip,' said Bill Sullivan.

'Not in this case I'm told,' said Tom Wilson knowingly. 'Mike Hennessy is a steady young lad. He'll deliver the goods alright.'

'If he can tear himself away from the Flying Column,' said Bill Sullivan almost truculently.

'What's wrong with the Flying Column?' asked Daniel Hourihane, getting in on the conversation.

'They should have listened to John Redmond,' said Bill Sullivan. 'He'd have got us Home Rule without a shot being fired.'

'He would in his town halls,' said Doctor Baldwin. 'With the greatest of respect, Bill, if we were here for another hundred years we wouldn't get Home Rule while those Ulster Unionists are opposing it.'

'You're bloody right,' said Wilson. 'The British never gave us anything without the persuader.'

'And they never will,' said Shorten

'Three times the Home Rule Bill has been introduced, first by

Gladstone, then by Asquith,' said Doctor Baldwin, 'and three times it's been vetoed by Carson and his cohorts in the Ulster Volunteer Force. They were the first to introduce the persuader. The first to use the gun.'

'What about Michael Davitt and the Land Acts?' asked Sullivan. 'And Parnell. Them boys got us a fair amount of concessions.'

'The British will give you concessions on the one hand and take them away with the other,' said Tom Wilson.

Richie Shorten said, 'When the results don't suit them, they change the rules.'

'Exactly,' said Doctor Baldwin.

Jeremiah Hennessy shook his head and drank. 'We could be talking about it all day and 'twouldn't make a blind bit of difference.'

'Lads like yours are making the difference, Jeremiah,' said Tom Wilson and raised his glass. 'Good health to them.'

They all drank and Tom Wilson changed the subject. 'You're a fair bit from home, Doctor?' he said by way of asking an indirect question.

'Home isn't what it used to be,' said the Doctor sadly.

'Cody working you too hard is he?' asked Sullivan with a wicked grin. 'A tough taskmaster I'd say, but sure he's the hardest worker of all himself. It isn't as if he's asking you to do something he wouldn't do himself.'

'He'll leave it all behind him too someday,' said the Doctor philosophically. 'What's it all for?'

'You can't take it with you right enough,' said Sullivan.

Tom Wilson went outside to the lavatory. It was in a whitewashed shed and the urinal was a once whitewashed wall now stained yellow, with a hole in the floor. The toilet seat was behind a half-ajar door in a small cubicle. Tom undid his flies, leant with one hand against his forehead, elbow propped to the wall watching his water flowing down. The last rays of the setting sun illuminated the narrow space. The sun was poised like a ball of fire on top of Sheha. He thought he heard a rumble of a lorry and he turned his head to the right. Over the brow of the road into the village, two lorries silhouetted like black harbingers of the coming darkness, roared into view. He caught his breath and tied his buttons. By the time he was back in the bar the lorries had screeched to a shuddering halt outside the window. The backs of each were crammed with soldiers in tasselled berets, holding rifles. There were Mills bombs attached to their belts, bandoliers around their shoulders, two revolvers holstered on each thigh. There was a sudden shout and a series of shots were fired into the air. The soldiers leapt down and began running around. Their Colonel, Francis Crake, barked orders. Tull Hennessy had a mighty struggle to stop the horse with the load of pigs from bolting. The horse pulled him across the street towards Moore's shop, almost crushing him against the wall, but he managed to contain it.

Crake's cold eyes saw his struggle. He laughed. 'Lucky you stopped that horse, son,' he said. 'It would have made a nice bit of target practice.'

Tull was panting but defiant. He soothed the horse, ignoring Crake who regarded him laconically. Crake was tall and thin with a finely-chiselled jaw line, a straight nose, dark eyebrows. His mouth was well formed and a cigarette dangled from it. His upper lip was shaded by a pencil-thin moustache. He wore a black Tam O'Shanter beret. He was neat, fastidious, self-confident. He looked out at the street like a man who wished he was elsewhere. He was about thirty-two years of age.

William Barnes and Cecil Bayley were already up at the top of the street, marching Tim Callaghan and Tade Crowley before them at gunpoint. Leonard Bradshaw and James Cleave were pulling Mrs Warren and Mrs Duggan roughly out of Nyhan's shop. From across the street, schoolchildren were screaming as they were herded out by William Pallester and Arthur Poole. The schoolmaster, Jeremiah O'Mahony was protesting loudly but was ignored. He got a sudden blow in the face from Frederick Hugo holding the stock of a Lee Enfield.

'This is monstrous,' protested the teacher. 'You've no right to come into this village and terrorize these children. Have you no families of your own? Have you no pity?' He put his hand to his head and looked at his bloody fingers.

'Shut your fucking mouth, Guv,' said Hugo, 'or you'll get worse.'

Jack Lordan, the tailor was dragged by his collar down the street, his legs trailing. He had tried to prevent the invasion of his property, but Horace Pearson and Ernest Lucas had smashed in his door with kicks and rifle butts. The tailor was bleeding quite badly from a gash on his head. Crake surveyed the work of his soldiers with satisfaction. An efficient bunch. 'Keep searching till you find them all,' he shouted.

Frank Taylor, Christopher Wainwright and Benjamin Webster went in search of people in other houses. Crake gestured to H.F. Forde and Cecil Guthrie to accompany him into the bar. There was silence inside as they loomed through the door. The drinkers were still as statues looking down. Crake came over. 'What have we got here then?' he asked almost mildly. 'Drinking in the afternoon. Not good. Have you people no homes to go to or farms to work? No wonder the little country is upside down. Of all the Godforsaken places I've ever been this is the worst. How can you people live here? I know I'd rather live in the Gobi desert.'

He walked around surveying Baldwin, Wilson, Shorten, Sullivan. Jeremiah Hennessy gazed steadily at them from inside the snug.

'Don't be hiding in there, Grandfather,' smiled Crake. 'Out here with you.'

He motioned to Forde and Guthrie, who manhandled Jeremiah and Hourihane out of the snug. 'Put up a bottle there, Miss,' ordered Crake. 'Your best whiskey. None of the firewater stuff you people seem to prefer. Three large glasses please.'

The frightened girl put the bottle of whiskey and the glasses on the bar.

'Fill them please,' said Crake. He watched the golden liquor rising in the glass. Heard its comforting gurgle. He knocked back a drink with one gulp. 'Another please.'

Forde and Guthrie swallowed theirs.

'Fill these men's glasses,' said Crake pointing to Doctor Baldwin and the others, who watched their glasses filling. They did not touch them.

'Drink up gentlemen,' said Crake. 'Never let it be said the forces of the King were mean-spirited. Drink up on me.'

Doctor Baldwin took a long look at him. He tried to gauge his personality. Crake was like a coiled spring. Putting on a show of amiability. The man had a neurotic look about him. The Doctor looked through the window. There was a line of people young and old lined up against the wall of Moore's farmhouse. He fingered the glass, hesitated.

'Come on, sir,' said Crake in exaggerated deference. 'Enjoy your drink.' It was more a threat than an entreaty. The Doctor swallowed. The others followed suit. Crake continued:

'Now then, that's all very civilized. Alright gentlemen, I need some names please.' He pulled out a notebook. They gave their names one after the other.

'Let me see, Hennessy...I have that name marked in red here. That means we have reason to believe you or your family are supporters of Sinn Féin? You have sons named Sonny, Mike, Tull and Richie. Is that right?'

'It is,' said Jeremiah.

'Where are they at the moment?'

'Tull is outside with the horse.' Jeremiah pointed through the window.

'The others are at home working the land.'

Crake took the whiskey bottle, filled all the glasses again and knocked back his own with one slug. He considered Hennessy's reply. He didn't like being lied to. It put him in a nasty mood. So did too much whiskey. His eyes narrowed as he looked away and then slowly back to Jeremiah and said, 'They are eh? You don't expect me to believe that do you? Out running guns more like and fomenting sedition against the Crown.'

'I can't make you believe, if you don't want to,' said Jeremiah with a shrug.

Crake raised an eyebrow and pursed his lips. 'True enough,' he said. He looked around. He picked on Doctor Baldwin: 'So who have we here then, Doc Holliday?'

'You have the first part right,' said the Doctor. 'The second part doesn't fit the bill.'

'So you're a doctor?' enquired Crake. His eyes carried a strange light, as if his mind was elsewhere.

'Yes,' said Doctor Baldwin evenly.

'And you can cure people?'

'I haven't cured anyone for quite a while, sadly,' said the Doctor.

'You haven't, eh?' Crake paused. His eyes glittered. 'Well maybe you can cure this.'

He moved suddenly and slashed Jeremiah Hennessy across the cheek with a knife, which appeared as if by magic in his hand. Jeremiah screamed out in agony; blood spurted, cut through to the cheekbone. Jeremiah fell back against the counter and began to slide down the barstool to the floor. His blood splashed over the clothes of the others and made a pool across the counter, dripping down off the backs of chairs. Miss Nyhan grabbed a dishcloth and ran around the counter. Doctor Baldwin held it to Jeremiah's face. He had fainted on the floor. When he had staunched the flow, the Doctor looked back up at Crake, who was standing nonchalantly with his arms folded, a strange smile on his face. The stunned Doctor tried to reconcile Crake's sudden mood change. A neurotic he'd thought initially; more likely a psychopath? Better say nothing. He eyed Wilson and Sullivan, indicating to keep quiet. This Crake was capable of worse. Mad perhaps.

'Everybody out,' roared Crake suddenly. 'And fill the glasses again, young lady.'

'But the man is seriously injured,' began Doctor Baldwin.

'To hell with him,' spat Crake. 'Either you take him outside or my men will drag him out. Out! Out I say!'

Sullivan and Wilson lifted the unfortunate Jeremiah to his feet and, with a shoulder under each arm, shuffled outside with him. Crake ordered his men to follow and then he started into the bottle of whiskey. He lit a cigarette and muttered incoherently to himself, sitting on the bloody barstool.

Outside, Crake's men had assembled all the village folk, young and old, male and female, against the wall of Moore's farmhouse and shop. They all had their hands in the air and the soldiers were going through their pockets, pulling roughly at their clothes. Women wept, children screamed in terror. Crake appeared behind them in the door of the pub and surveyed the procedure from across the street. He let it continue for some minutes, as he finished the bottle, drinking from the neck. When he had drained it, he smashed the bottle on the footpath. He came across the street. People eyed him expectantly. The soldiers waited for the word.

'Strip all the men,' ordered Crake. The soldiers had gleeful looks in their eyes.

'Strip them and give them a damn good thrashing.'

Soldiers tore and pulled at the men's garments. Coats, trousers, shirts, vests and underwear were discarded. The men stood shivering in the buff. Doctor Baldwin was more bemused than shocked. His eyes sought out those of Master O'Mahony. Their eyes carried worlds of contempt. Crake could see the scorn in their eyes. Or was it pity?

'This is for you traitorous Irish, who stabbed us in the back when we were in the trenches of the Somme and Ypres. This is for your 1916 rebellion.'

His soldiers were lined up in formation of two lines, eight in each line. They stood about three yards apart. The naked men were started along the line. Some soldiers had belts in their hands. As each man was pushed along, a soldier slashed at him. Some were battered with the ends of rifle butts, some were hacked at and cut with bayonets. The men ran, stumbled, crying out in pain as they were driven like cattle between the lines of soldiers who seemed to enjoy their work. Screams rose into the twilight, women wept and prayed, children huddled under their mother's skirts. When all the men were herded through, battered and bleeding, a soldier pulled up the crib of Tull Hennessy's cart and the squealing pigs began to jump out. As they jumped, Poole and

Pallester went down on bended knee and sighted along their rifles, blowing the unfortunate animals to bloody smithereens one by one. The soldiers howled and jeered like demented recusants. When they finished there were corpses of swine strewn over the length of the village street like burst balloons. Tull, unable to control this final insult to his livestock, suddenly jumped upon the two soldiers, clawing and tearing at their faces. Such was his strength that he overpowered them before he was felled by a blow of Taylor's rifle butt. Then Webster and Wainwright began to kick him into unconscious submission in the middle of the street. They stopped when Tull was a bloody, crumpled, naked mess of quivering flesh.

'You've gone and killed the lovely boy,' cried Mrs Warren. 'May God bring misfortune down upon you all.'

'We'll do our business, Grandmother,' said Crake indifferently. 'Let God do his. Our mission here is not to gain the Lord's forgiveness, but to bring you people under the Crown's control, where you have always been, and will remain.'

'You'll never control us,' said Mrs Duggan, fierce defiance in her eyes.

'You'll have to kill us all,' said Doctor Baldwin, as he knelt to soothe the unconscious Tull.

'We may have to, Doctor Holliday,' said Crake, surveying his handiwork. 'We may well have to.'

He stood nodding in satisfaction as moans and groans rose into the still evening air. Then he said, 'Load up.'

Some soldiers had emerged from the public house with bottles of whiskey under their arms, which they proceeded to imbibe greedily as they clambered onto the backs of the lorries. They pulled away down the street, heading west.

Coming back from his fields, Stanley Moore met Father Jerome Casey about a mile away from Castletown on the road to Kinneigh. 'Hello Father,' said Moore as he stood looking over a gate into a field, where his horse, just released, was bucking and kicking among the cows.

'Hello,' said Father Casey from atop his saddle horse. The priest's eyes followed Moore's white horse, which began to prance back towards the gate with high steps, and much snorting and whooshing.

'Whoa, me bucko,' said Moore as his horse slithered to a halt at the last minute before the gate.

'He's high-spirited,' said the priest.

'Tis a way he wants the company of your fellow,' said Moore.

'Horses are herd animals of course,' said the priest.

'They get lonesome right enough,' said Moore.

'I suppose they're like people,' smiled Father Casey.

'Oh then, the very same,' said Moore. He stood watching as his horse put his head over the gate and nuzzled the priest's horse, tails switching. With a sharp whinny, Moore's horse reared, his forelegs flailing.

'Will you look at that,' said Moore. 'Get back you devil.' He swung a rope at his horse's face and the horse took off across the field again, in high dudgeon.

'I'd better be going,' said the priest. 'Tis getting chilly.'

'Are you going far?' enquired Moore.

'To Ballycummin,' replied Father Casey.

'You've a nice bit to go yet.'

'If it stays dry we won't miss the time,' said the priest. He saluted Moore and asked. 'Are you Hosford?'

'Stanley Moore, you were close enough.'

'Good evening Stanley.'

'Good evening, Father.'

As the priest rode on, he was thinking what a pleasant fellow Moore was. Although of a different faith, he was mannerly and called him Father. Respectful and decent. Some of his own flock could take a leaf out of that book. The priest was not quite out of sight of Stanley Moore, when the two lorries full of Auxiliaries came round the bend from Castletown. The trucks bore down the centre of the road and the priest could hear raucous singing and shouting from the drunken passengers. The lorries slowed down, the horse began to jump and shy, agitated by the noise. The first lorry stopped in front of the priest, blocking his advance. The priest's face fell. He looked behind considering a hasty retreat, but thought the better of it. They'd probably shoot him in the back. Crake got out, and Pearson and Lucas jumped off the back and stood behind him. Crake approached the priest's horse, which looked wild-eyed at him. 'Steady on, now, there's a good boy,' said Crake, uttering soothing words to the horse.

'He's afraid of your men,' said the priest, trying to muster as much authority as he could.

'Don't worry, Padré,' said Crake. 'My men are conversant with horses.' He turned to Lucas. 'Tell them to be quiet.'

Lucas walked to the back of the lorries and ordered the soldiers into silence. The raucous voices trailed off. Crake smiled at Father Casey and held out his hands wide in a gesture of reconciliation.

'There now Padré,' he said. 'They'll do anything for a man of the cloth.' He smiled at the men, then back at the priest who sat rigid.

'Would you care to step down, Padré?'

'Why?' asked the priest sharply. 'I've a long road and it's getting dark. And it's Father, not Padré.'

'Ah, is it now, Father...?' enquired Crake, oleaginously.

'Casey, Father Jerome Casey. Now can I be on my way please?'

'Not until I say so,' said Crake. 'Can you get off the horse please?'

'But this is ridiculous,' said the priest, inwardly quaking. 'I really must protest.'

'We just want to ask you a few questions,' said Crake, as Father Casey climbed down.

'What about?' asked the priest.

'Nothing much,' smiled Crake. 'Just as to who you might have come across on your travels. You have been travelling have you not?'

'I've been visiting with my colleague, Father O'Connell, in Enniskean. Parish business. I've seen nobody.'

'Excellent,' said Crake. 'You're doing the Lord's work. We, as you can imagine, have to do the King's work.'

'That work has to be done too,' said the frightened priest.

'I'm glad you approve, Father Casey,' said Crake, with a strange glint in his eye. He looked up at the sky, then he gently rubbed the horse's velvet nose with his right hand. 'Will you look at him. I think he wants a lump of sugar.'

He continued in a vague, almost distracted fashion. 'Now, as I was saying, Father Casey, we've been doing the King's work in the local village, and that work is not quite finished. And there's nothing that bothers me more than to leave a job of work unfinished. Would you agree?'

He raised his eyebrows in a seemingly innocent question. The priest nodded. Beads of sweat began to break out on his forehead.

'Would you hold the priest's horse please,' ordered Crake. Horace Pearson stepped forward and took the reins. Crake put an arm around Father Casey's shoulder in a comforting gesture and drew him to one side. At that moment Stanley Moore was marched in front of the Colonel by William Barnes and Cecil Bayley, who had seen him skulking just out of sight.

'This fellow seems to be hiding something,' said Barnes. 'We caught him trying to climb over a gate.'

'My word, but there are lots of shady goings-on around these parts,' said Crake. 'You've interrupted my pleasant conversation with Father Jerome Casey here. So who are you then?'

'Stanley Moore.'

'Well, Stanley, what have you to say for yourself?'

'Nothing,' said Moore. 'I'm a farmer, I was fencing in my cows for the night.'

'And are you and Father Casey acquainted?'

'We met just now,' said Father Casey, 'Stanley is not of my faith but he's a decent man. I can vouch for him.'

'Splendid, splendid,' said Crake. 'So you're a member of the Protestant faith?'

'I am,' said Stanley.

'Well, you can be on your way then,' said Crake. 'And don't look back.'

'But...?'

'No buts,' said Crake, and pressed his index finger to his lips. 'Off with you now, as fast as your legs can carry you.'

Stanley Moore looked at the priest for a moment and a feeling of foreboding came over him. He looked at Crake and then hurried away, through the groups of leering soldiers, who made a reluctant space for him to pass. He looked around once as he was nearing a bend. He saw the two lorries and the soldiers still standing around the priest. He could barely see in the darkness descending. He thought he saw the priest kneeling in the road. He thought he saw a soldier behind him, holding a pistol to the back of his head. Then he heard a shot. He turned and ran. Panting desperately he flew towards the village lantern lights as fast as his legs could carry him. As fast as he ran, he could not outrun the priest's riderless horse who bore down on him with plunging hooves. It passed him with the saddle leathers swinging wildly and the loose stirrups whacking off its flanks. Its iron-shod hooves sent showers of sparks flying up off the road into the darksome sky.

8

' I'll toss you for it,' said John Lordan, his face intent. Dan Canty was sitting opposite on a sackful of oats in a barnloft, smoking a cigarette. He considered the bet.

'Toss you for my rifle?' asked Canty. 'Christ man I'd wager my wife first.'

There was laughter from others sitting around the huge old loft. It was late afternoon, late November. It was shadowy and the light outside would soon be fading. A lantern burned to illuminate the long space. Under the slates the roof narrowed to an apex of huge, high rafters. There were old bits of wire twisted around the rafters holding up thrown-away furniture and other tranglum. Horse tackling hung suspended: collars, hames, straddles, backbands, britchins, winkers. There was a winnowing machine in a corner, some bicycles resting near low windows. There were jute sacks full of oats piled high along one wall. These were used by the men as temporary seats and beds. There were about thirty men sitting in groups here and there. They were drinking hot tea in cups poured out of a large bucket and eating slices of buttered, brown soda bread. They were young men, ranging in age from eighteen to maybe thirty five. Lordan was probably the oldest. Sonny Hennessy sitting to his right was the youngest at nearly eighteen. They were dressed in long trenchcoats and caps, and they wore bandoliers full of ammunition around their shoulders. Some had revolvers, and all had a rifle except the one disputed between Canty and Lordan. A few played cards. Some were alert, but others dozed with waiting. They looked like a group expecting to go somewhere. There were murmurs of, 'Hit 'im with the 'tray,' as a cardplayer lashed a trump to win a game of twenty-five. In the background the debate over the rifle continued.

'But it's not your rifle, Dan,' said a young man with slightly bulging, fanatical-looking eyes, they called Flyer Nyhan.

Canty turned, a sceptical glance on his dark, handsome face. 'How d'you mean 'tisn't mine?'

'You didn't buy it,' said Flyer, with a grin.

'That's for sure,' said Canty. 'Neither did you buy yours, by Jesus.'

'Let's say he commandeered it,' said a round-faced, cheerful fellow called Spud Murphy.

'A nice word for stole it,' laughed John Lordan.

'Stole it off who?' asked Canty. 'Some bastard who stole our land a couple of hundred years ago? 'Tis a small recompense for him to give me a rifle.'

Sonny Hennessy was watching the faces of the older men. He knew it was a good-humoured disagreement, but there were only so many rifles to go around. Canty and Lordan happened to be in the last allocation, which was done by a kind of a lottery. Whoever drew the shortest straw was the odd man out. That was Lordan, but he was stubborn. He didn't like to take no for an answer.

'Possession is nine points of law,' said Canty dourly. 'I'm not budging.'

'Have it your own way then,' said Lordan phlegmatically.

At that moment some other men climbed the steps of the barnloft and came in. Tom Barry was to the fore, followed by Charlie Hurley and Liam Deasy. The men immediately sat up when they appeared. The disputed rifle was momentarily forgotten.

'At ease, men, at ease,' said Barry. He was smartly dressed in a military tunic, and he carried field glasses along with a revolver and two Mills bombs attached to his belt. He stood in the middle of the high-ceilinged loft with an easy authority. Although only twenty-two, his strong personality and extensive military experience meant his word was respected. His word was law. He also had an uncanny knack of remembering every man's name no matter how recently they'd become acquainted.

'Alright lads,' he said after a long pause to look into each man's face. 'The moment you've been waiting for has arrived. You've done your training for the last few weeks. It's not enough, but it's adequate. You've prepared well and you all appear to be brave and natural fighters. You're young and fit and healthy. You've learned to shoot straight and you've learned the concepts of enfilade and defilade. You've drilled and shown your committment to the cause we're fighting for. And now the hour has come to engage the enemy. I needn't spell out for you what kind of an enemy we're facing. As recently as yesterday, they terrorised the local village of Castletown, regrettably without our knowledge or we'd have attacked them. They killed the local priest in cold blood. They assaulted and humiliated men, women and children, without respect for the vulnerability of youth or the dignity of old age. They've burnt and killed without mercy for the past five or six months and not one shot has been fired at them by an Irish Republican. They think they're invincible and many of our own people think so too. If they're allowed to continue they will destroy our morale and will reduce the country to slavery once again, and set our struggle back another generation or maybe two. Maybe a hundred years. That is their objective and they are close to reaching it. So it's imperative to act now. There's not a moment to spare. Next week may be too late. You are the first recruits to the new Flying Column. We are calling it that because we will be continually on the run. Some of you will go back, after this engagement to your own companies, to be replaced by others from different areas. In due course you will return again, having spent time with your families and on your farms. We are a Volunteer army. We are fighting for our families, our friends, our communities. Our very lives. We will travel light and fast and hopefully live off the generosity of the people, who already have been so generous to us. The people are behind us and we cannot let them down. Above all we cannot allow a repeat of what happened yesterday in Castletown. This is going to be all or nothing. We have identified a location about six miles from here on the Kilmichael road where we are going to attack these Auxiliaries. Either we kill them or they kill us. Make no mistake, if we don't kill them, they will show us no mercy whatsovever. We've seen enough evidence of what they are capable of.'

He stopped speaking for some moments to survey his audience. Not a mouse stirred, not a breath was heard. Sonny, to the fore, had a rapt look on his youthful face. He was burning to avenge his brother and his father. The report of their treatment had shocked him to the core.

Barry continued: 'I am offering any man here a last chance to go with Commandant Charlie Hurley, who is going back east with Liam Deasy to organise other companies to engage the enemy.'

Charlie smiled at his comrades and they nodded to him.

'Any man who wants to go with Charlie and Liam can do so. Indeed any man is free to return home for good, because this is a voluntary force. Nobody is coerced into doing anything he doesn't want to do. Now, hands up all who are with me.'

Every hand in the dark, cavernous barn shot up as one. Barry nodded his head in satisfaction.

'Excellent,' he said. 'I'm very pleased. However I'm informed that one man here will have no choice but to go with Charlie because we're short a rifle.'

He looked around. Who was that man? Either Dan Canty or John Lordan. Lordan walked forward with a huge grin on his face. He'd snatched up the rifle from Canty while they were all engrossed in Barry's speech.

'Twill have to be Dan,' he smiled, 'I have the rifle now.'

All the men turned and laughed at Lordan's sleight of hand. Canty looked rueful, but did not argue with his friend. And did not want a fight.

'What do you say, Dan?' asked Tom Barry.

Canty threw back his dark-haired head in a kind of resigned way. 'What can I say, Commandant?' he smiled. 'There is only one rifle. My friend insists on keeping it. I want to go very badly with you, but I cannot go without a firearm. So I suppose I'll go with Charlie.'

The men applauded him spontaneously. He had been reasonable and fair-minded.

'You're a good man, Dan Canty,' said Tom Barry. 'Your chance will come again.'

Lines of marching men moved silently along a ridge above Kinneigh. The landscape was bleak, rocky, beautiful. They could see great distances but night was coming. Soon they would move in darkness, by instinct and guided by local scouts. There would be starlight perhaps, but no moon. They were moving north and would follow the stars if they were visible: the Plough and the North Star. If a man stood in a gap and watched the shadowy figures silhouetted against the western mountains, he would count three sections, twelve men marching in each section, formed into fours. At the head of the marchers, he would see a single leader in a military uniform and cap: Tom Barry leading his newly formed Flying Column on the road to Kilmichael. Behind him came his new recruits: Flyer Nyhan, Spud Murphy, Sonny Hennessy, Dan Hourihane, Ned Young, Dave Crowley, Michael McCarthy, John Lordan and nearly three dozen others. Soon it began to rain and the wind rose. It was cold. They marched through the night, silently. No dogs barked in distant farms. Nobody knew they were passing. They went by side roads and across fields and moors, and high brakes and foothills, mile on mile. They were drenched through to the skin, but their morale was high. Occasionally they stopped to take a short rest or smoke a cigarette in the shelter of a ditch.

Dawn rose over a bleak and rocky landscape. Furze brakes sloped away to knotty tufts of boggy grass and hollows draped with withered fern and vicious briars that would cut to the bone like the sharpest knife. Momentarily the clouds lifted and they could see the huge Sheha range of mountains that appeared so close they could touch them. Then the clouds descended again and they were in a country where it was impossible to discern east from west, north from south. The road from Macroom to Dunmanway snaked out before them. It ran for a quarter of a mile east to west in a deviation from its north to south trajectory.

'This is the spot,' said Barry. 'Unprepossessing it may look, but I believe it is the best position for an ambush on the entire Macroom road. Our information tells us the Auxies take this road without fail every day as far as Gleann Cross. Below that there is no guarantee where they will go. If we go further north we will be too close to Macroom and make ourselves vulnerable to reinforcements coming through.'

The men were wet to the bone, cold and hungry again. There was a cold wind blowing from the mountains. Water dripped from overhanging hazel branches, it flowed down gulleys, falling continually and grey in roaring streams from the sky. They considered their position with grim anticipation. No quarter given by the elements, nothing yielded by the terrain. Both bleak and unremitting.

'There is no provision here for a safe retreat,' said Barry. 'This fight will end either with the smashing of the Auxiliaries or with the destruction of this Flying Column. This will be a fight to the end.'

The Commander allocated out positions. Himself and three hand-picked fighters to the command post: Flyer Nyhan, Spud Murphy, Mick O'Herlihy. They lay behind a low, stone wall in a position at the farthest end of the ambush site down the winding glen. They would command a sweeping view of the approaching trucks, and should repel them one by one as they came on. Tom Barry himself would call the shots from there. He placed ten riflemen on the back slope of a heather-covered rock that rose up twelve feet from the road. He called this position number one.

Number two section of riflemen occupied another beetling rock one hundred and fifty yards up the road on the same side at the entrance to the ambuscade. Michael McCarthy, a young man from Dunmanway was in charge here. Across the winding road between positions one and two, Barry posted six fighters along a chain of rocks under the command of Stephen O'Neill, their purpose to prevent the British soldiers from gaining fighting positions on the south side of the road. He warned them to be careful with their aim, lest perhaps they fired on their own comrades across from them to cause disaster. At a distance of two hundred yards at either end of the glen, two unarmed scouts were posted. They would signal the arrival of their quarry.

The wait was long with nothing to do but lie in their positions and count the hours. Sometimes they stood to stretch their limbs and some smoked in the lee of further rocks. They nervously checked and rechecked their rifles and ammunition. Each man had thirty five bullets, a few had revolvers. When they fired their allotment of bullets, there would be no more. What might then befall? Sonny wondered. Would they resort to fighting with rifle butts hand to hand, or would they be run like lambs to slaughter into endless enemy rounds? And what of bayonets and the sting of cold steel? What would death by steel be like? Not quite as quick as gunpowder and shot. Intestines spilled out in bloody reams? Sonny banished the thoughts for fear of failure of nerve, and forgot the prospect of his own pain in substitution for the pain inflicted on his aged father and his naked brother in the days before; the bullet to the back of Father Casey's undefended head; the priest who favoured peaceful means, who trusted the forces of the Royal Irish Constabulary. Those were the thoughts he kept uppermost.

The clearing sky was streaked with coloured clouds as sunset came over the blue mountains, huge and grand. Flames of fire flew out from the sun to paint the clouds yellow and scarlet. An arcing rainbow rose brilliantly between receding rain and shining sun. Long shadows were cast of cattle in high fields and longer shadows of solitary men walking late across bare uplands in the distance. No stubble ground to scuffle, no horse and plough to follow, no wheat to harvest and to gather in. Just hibernating nature, trickling streams, whispering whin bushes. The smell of tobacco from a restless Volunteer's cigarette, the hissing of water on the rocks, as someone stood to piss. Men blowing on cold fingers that turned blue from clutching rifles in the chilly afternoon. Cattle calling westward, cows lowing as they were driven home for meagre milking, herded by a barking collie. Faraway voices saying,

'How, how' to the patient cows, oblivious to the absorbed and motionless men lurking near at hand, as if painted in relief at the end of destiny's rainbow.

At four o'clock in the afternoon the Auxiliaries came out of the west. They rode the glistening road like charioteers: swaggering avatars of destruction. Decorated with gimcrack paraphenalia accumulated from plunder: beads and bangles on their necks, rings on their fingers ripped from dead victims' fingers. As if to ward off evil greater than themselves they'd taken to daubing their faces red with the blood of those they'd casually killed. And it being late in the day they were infused with whiskey and with moonshine the Irish called *poitín,* which they'd sequestered in their trails of pillage. Some more outlandish than others wore feathers in their berets and hung gaudy little statues of the Virgin Mary, lipsticked red in blood. Such was their contempt for the natives, they'd taken to imitating their religious customs in mocking parallels of outrageous sacrilege. Colonel Francis Crake rode imperiously in the van, a slightly demented smile on his mystical face. Impervious and omnipotent was how he felt and passed this potion of delusion to his cohorts. Cecil Bayley beside him was the driver of the leading Crossley tender. As they swept around a looping bend, the sun was blood-red on their backs. Red was the road before them as a late sunburst shone in magnificent eclat to light up a distant figure etched like an effigy on the road, his arms outstretched.

Crake gestured to his driver. 'Slow down,' he said. 'He looks like one of ours.'

Bayley was unsure. 'Out here? You sure you want to, sir?'

'Yes,' said Crake. 'He's wearing a British officer's uniform.'

Bayley applied the brake with his right foot and the lorry slowed down, but did not stop completely. On it came as the officer on the road continued to wave. Ten feet away the wave became a recoil and the semaphoric arm drew back, then forward, in the snapping motion of Tom Barry's wrist. They saw the Mills bomb sailing through the air, but did not hear its loud explosion. Nor did they see their guts fly forth and vanish on the event horizon, mixed with shards of steel. Or see their spattered blood on dashboard, windshield, doorhandle. Crake the invincible was dead, with Bayley his accessory stone dead beside him when the cab fragmented in their faces. Then the silent evening became a bedlam of roaring gunfire, shouts and screams of pain. Centuries of pent-up frustration was released into the valenced air like an erupting volcano. Barry, at the command post, opened fire with revolver close at hand, aided and abetted by his elite cadré of Nyhan, O'Herlihy and Murphy, handpicked couriers of death. They poured murderous fire into the back of the drunken, keeled-over lorry and into the bodies of its passengers who jumped and crawled from the wreckage, firing as they went. But the element of surprise neutralised all previous combat experience, all toiling on the battlefields of Flanders. All skills of marksmanship went for naught. There were no bad shots from ten feet distant. Yelling and cursing, the Auxies tried to retaliate, but with cold fury the IRA kept their concentration and did not falter.

Fire and brimstone belched from Sonny's gun, becoming like a living thing in his hands. And it surprised him to see men falling when he pulled the trigger; appalled him too. But ricochetting bullets from the rocks around him, passing inches from his ears screwed his attention to his own survival. The battle once in motion acquired its own momentum and rationale, and could not stop. Things appeared to happen of their own volition and to Sonny they seemed remote and at a distance. The bayonets in the belly, the spurting blood from throats, the white terror in the eyes of men. He fought for life with an elemental power and reflexes were automatic. There was no logic on the battlefield. All was raw, visceral, and collosal beyond imagining. He saw Tom Barry bestriding the highway, cutting down random running soldiers. Lucas, Webster, Hugo were blasted to eternity by round after round. Arthur Poole, down, but not done for, tried to rise and fire with Barry in his sights. He fired and missed and Flyer Nyhan's bayonet cut him through the ribs below his heart and thrust upwards to sever his aorta, which burst in a shower of crimson in his face. Cleave and Bradshaw made for a narrow lane in a desperate run, but they were easy pickings for Sonny and his friends. From their high position they had commanding fields of fire as Barry had assured them that they would. Wainwright was the last of his group to fall. As he fired at Nyhan, the life was smashed out of him by the butt of O'Herlihy's rifle and his brains issued out like mustard on the grass. Within five minutes the terrible cacophony had ceased. With no targets left, Barry ordered all available men up the road towards the second lorry which was sloughed across the road one hundred and fifty yards away. The Auxiliary survivors were pinned down behind it by McCarthy's and John Lordan's men in position number two. With fire cutting across them from the Volunteers in the third position south of the road, they were caught in a cleft stick, and also unaware of the creeping figures on the road behind them, stalking them like hunters. Sonny saw a white cloth hoist on top of a bayonet tip, and heard hoarse shouts:

'We surrender! We surrender!'

There were six or seven in the group left alive. The firing stopped. There was a silence broken only by the groans of the dying. On the ridge above, Michael McCarthy stood up. Beside him young Patrick Deasy, the boatman from Kilmacsimon Quay who'd followed late, also stood, and a third named O'Sullivan. For a moment, trusting and uncertain, they waited for command. Then, as if possessed by some demons of perversity, the remaining Auxiliaries fired again. A bullet severed O'Sullivan's main artery under his jaw and he fell with a cry across the blood-soaked heather. Three slugs tore into Deasy's powerful chest and emerged to shatter his arms that once propelled the rowing crews to victory along the pleasant Bandon. Another bullet felled McCarthy, and he staggered backwards and collapsed across the bodies of his two companions.

'Fire at will,' ordered Tom Barry. 'Do not stop until I tell you.'

And with that the barrage opened up again more fiercely than before. The stalking hunters were now walking towards their quarry holding rifles belching lead. In a matter of minutes there was no Auxiliary soldier left alive on the Kilmichael road. Barry called ceasefire and there followed an eerie silence. Then he turned and ran up the heathered slope to his stricken recruits. McCarthy and O'Sullivan were dead. Deasy was dying.

'It's all over, Pat,' said Barry. 'They're all dead. How are you feeling?'

'I think I'm not too bad Commandant,' said the youth. 'Could I have a drink of water?'

'We'll take you to a farmhouse and we'll get you tea,' said Barry, knowing water would hasten his demise. He ordered some of the men to run to fetch a door to bear Deasy away and at that moment a sidecar with six Volunteers, who'd barely missed the arrival of the Auxiliaries drove back down the narrow lane from the farmhouse across the way. The dead Volunteers were loaded on the jarvey and Barry ordered his men around to collect rifles and ammunition from the dead soldiers. Many were shocked and shaken. Sonny felt weak and dizzy, but held himself upright. Some vomited in the ditches. Such are men's physiognomies that some revel in the blood and gore and some are rocked to their foundations. Some have a tougher carapace around their psyches, which makes them impervious to the suffering of others. In any battle maybe less than a quarter of the combatants actually kill. Barry mused on this and estimated that maybe no more than twelve or fourteen of his fighters had the chance to engage in combat. He could identify the killers from the sensitive ones. The Auxiliaries had a higher percentage of the former he surmised. That's why the British had chosen them in the first place. Unfortunately for them they came across an equal number of their own ilk on this fateful day. Their aura of power had been smashed.

Barry issued harsh commands, ordering his men to drill up and down the road amidst the dead. Then he ordered the lorries to be set alight. Within half an hour from the commencement of the battle they had marched away. The last rays of sunset had gone. Great plumes of smoke and flame towered into the disappearing sky. Curious crows came down to land amidst the scattered bodies. Soon there were no shadows on the winding road. Only fading embers.

Doctor James Baldwin had nearly reached his ancestral home in the parish of Kilmichael, where his forebears had been parcelled out a smallholding in the year 1690 by William of Orange after the defeat of King James at the Battle of the Boyne. His progress was interrupted by news of the Battle of Kilmichael. He stopped in the townland of Gortroe in the house of Buttimer, another planter gone native like himself many moons ago, where he attempted to save the life of Patrick Deasy in an outhouse. He tried desperately to apply every remedy he had learned in the Royal College of Surgeons, but it was all in vain. Such a tragedy to see so young and fine a man die in his arms. He cradled the young man's head and tried to soothe him with words of dubious wisdom. As the young man drew his last breath he had a peaceful look on his face. Doctor Baldwin wondered if the dying man sensed the imposter in the man whom last he looked upon? And yet he had not turned away, but riveted his eyes and his attention with all his might to ease the suffering of the stricken youth. For that he was grateful and perhaps he could someday hold his head up and finally say, 'I didn't run away.'

With the help of Buttimer and his family, Doctor Baldwin and some neighbours buried the bodies of the three young Volunteers around midnight. They took them to a great expanse of red bog beyond Gortroe and laid them in a shallow grave with pendulous sedge and moor grass for their rudimentary pillows. The small group worked with spades and shovels and Fr. Gould, the curate from the parish, gave them the last rites and said prayers for the repose of their souls. As the straight rain again descended on the thunderous Shehas and spread over Gortroe bog, there ascended into the sodden air the strains of a haunting tune, *Farewell To Ahilina,* played by a lone fiddler who had come down from Sliabh Luachra earlier in the day.

Doctor Baldwin slept little that night and early the next morning walked out of Buttimer's farmyard as the sun rose up into a cold, clear sky. Low shadows cast from the east made new shapes on the mountains. You could see new valleys and winding roads to the west where yesterday, when the sun was setting, all was an amorphous silhouette. He walked with halting steps towards the scene of battle, dreading the sight he would see. As he rounded the last bend in the narrow road he beheld before him the bodies of the British officers scattered in contorted shapes around the burnt-out husks of the lorries. He passed the prone and battered bodies of Barnes and Hooper-Jones; then he passed Graham. On the southern side, his feet wrapped in withered fronds of bracken, was Horace Pearson, while Albert Jones lay prostrate in the middle of the road. Up a lane was Taylor's body, with William Pallester and H.F. Forde a little further on. These were the men who'd lashed the ageing citizens of Castletown with their belts and gun butts to within an inch of their lives three days before. They themselves now lay so curiously tame and unintimidating. He felt no remorse, no anger; no shame, no *schadenfreude.* Just pity and a terrible sense of helplessness at the ineffable squanderings of humankind. These were the men who had killed without mercy and were now themselves but effigies under the rising sun and the vanished stars that had looked down with curious indifference on the diabolical enterprises of man. Those stricken here had followed orders, were assured of the righteousness of their cause, toiled for a warlike nation that had grown into an empire that bestrode the world; celebrating at all times its military achievements; erecting monuments to its generals, apologising to no country for its prowess. Eulogising the warrior; painting stained-glass windows in its cathedrals with images of St. Michael and St.George, with swords in hand.

Doctor Baldwin could only shake his head with sadness as further down he came upon a little cluster of the leading group of Hugo, Bayley, Lucas, Cleave and Bradshaw. Then down the little laneway, where he'd attempted to escape, was Wainwright, his arm flung out across his face as if attempting to ward off the inevitable projectiles from the massed Lee Enfields above him on the rocks. And there at last was Colonel Crake, beside the burnt out Crossley, his body laid out in a posture like an oblation to the God of war. The man who'd sneered at the civilised countrymen of the Doctor's acquaintance in Nyhan's pub three days ago. Who proclaimed his feeling of alienation amidst these heather hills, these rich and fertile valleys, this country with its huge and painted skies. Perhaps it was the loneliness in the evenings that disquieted him or the unnameable lure in the distance. And as the Doctor stood above his slain nemesis he felt a curious pang of pity for him and wondered was his deracination now complete? Or was he in some valhalla of peace at last?

He turned and walked slowly back up the road. He saw the detritus of battle. Empty shells, fragments of Mills bombs, discarded bits of cloth and leather. Torn papers, pictures of saints, a set of Rosary beads, a photograph of the Auxiliaries, smiling and at ease in full battle dress, taken the day they'd arrived into Cork city on their providential mission. He thought he heard a groan and looked down to his right. He saw a movement, a flutter in the eyes of one of the bodies. The man was still alive. The Doctor bent down and touched his hand. He felt the pulse. A faint fibrillation. Blood was oozing in quite a continuous flow from a perforation in the soldier's chest. Doctor Baldwin looked around for something to staunch the flow of blood. He'd have to pilfer some of the man's own clothing to make a bandage. Gritting his teeth, he opened the shirt of the dying man and tore a strip along the length. Then he wound this around the man's chest as tight as he could and watched the blood slowly coagulate and finally the bleeding stopped. Stifling his urge to throw up he forced his lips to the soldier's mouth and blew as hard as he could. At first there was no response, but as he continued the resuscitation, the chest began to rise and fall and the breathing suddenly increased. With a feeling of elation he knew he'd saved a life. At that moment he heard the sound of a vehicle and looking up he saw an armoured car making its way cautiously down the blood-stained road. It stopped beside them and the driver turned off the engine. There were about six soldiers fully armed in the car. The door on the passenger side opened and a tall, thin man in military uniform stepped out. For a moment the man stood looking at the Doctor as he knelt holding the soldier's head upright against his knee. The Doctor didn't look up until the officer spoke.

'Lieutenant Fleming,' he said. 'Division 13, C Company, Auxiliary of the Royal Irish Constabulary.'

The Doctor slowly looked up. He beheld a youngish man with a slightly callow look on his face. No trace of belligerence resided in it.

'Doctor James Baldwin,' he said laconically. 'FRCP.'

'Is he alive?' asked Fleming almost timidly.

The Doctor nodded and then said. 'I'm afraid he'll need more sophisticated attention than what I can offer. But, yes, he is alive, miraculously.'

'You've saved his life?' enquired the Lieutenant with a bewildered look on his face.

The Doctor turned a world-weary eye on him. 'Maybe he'd be better off I hadn't,' he said. 'He looks in very bad condition. You should get him to a hospital without delay.'

As the soldiers hurriedly brought a stretcher and lifted the injured man onto it, Doctor Baldwin stood up and rubbed his bloody hands along the flanks of his trousers. Lieutenant Fleming surveyed the scene with a look of shocked resignation in his eyes. 'Is he the only survivor?' he asked as if to himself.

The Doctor didn't look at him, kept looking away. 'He is,' he said.

'They've been decimated,' said the young Lieutenant, in disbelief. 'The finest fighting force the British Army had to offer.'

'Decimated?' enquired Doctor Baldwin, 'I'm afraid that is not the apposite word in this case.'

'What word would you use, Doctor?' asked the cowed Lieutenant.

The Doctor had a rueful smile on his face. 'It's purely semantics, but decimation comes from the Latin, *decem,* meaning ten. When there was a mutiny in ancient Rome, one in every ten soldiers was taken out and killed. A tenth of the mutineers were slain. In this case there is only one suvivor out of the seventeen that I counted. I think the word devastation is more accurate, for what it's worth.'

The officer looked keenly at the Doctor, noticing his dark suit, his waiscoat and his hat. 'Are you Irish at all, Doctor?' he asked.

The Doctor said dryly, 'Yes, Irish to the backbone. I was born here.'

The Lieutenant nodded. He looked down, then back to the Doctor, who stood examining his bloody hands. The Lieutenant sighed. 'Well I have an unpleasant job to do identifying these dead soldiers, I'd better get started.'

'Would you like some assistance?' asked the Doctor, with an ironic smile on his face. 'I know them all quite well by sight, but not their names of course?'

'You do?'

'I'm afraid I've already had the pleasure of their company,' he said.

The Lieutenant looked long and quietly at the Doctor. He understood. He extended his hand and said. 'Thank you, Doctor Baldwin We appreciate what you've done for Lieutenant Forde. It can't have been easy for you in the circumstances. Can we drive you anywhere? Home perhaps?'

'No thank you, Lieutenant,' replied Doctor Baldwin, 'I'm already at home.' He walked off up the road with a thoughtful, measured stride. Lieutenant Fleming stood looking after him for a few moments and then turned to his unenviable task.

As Doctor Baldwin walked along, the opening lines of Virgil's Aeneid kept asserting themselves in his mind: '*I sing of warfare and a man at war...*' Could the name Aeneas have metamorphosed into the Gaelic name Aengus after the fall of Troy? There were uncanny resemblances between the fort of Dun Aengus he'd seen on the island of Arainn and another more famous one at Mycenae he'd once beheld as a young man under the full moon of summer in the Peloponnese, on his visit to the theatre of Epidaurus and the shrine of Asclepius, the god of healing. The massive cyclopean walls, the jagged *cheveux-de-frise*. Were the Irish the descendants of the Greeks or the Trojans? A foolish notion or an interesting thought? A subject for debate with the Earl of Bandon perhaps, the next time their paths crossed.

9

royal crown derby imari

It was a crisp, cold, sunny day all through Ireland when the train dispatched Margie and Anna from Kingsbridge, going home for the Christmas holidays. Impending snow, the wind from the north, the sky blue and clear; early December. The term had finished early because the nuns had a foreboding the political situation might take a turn for the worst, and it would be safer for the students to be in the bosom of their families. As they travelled south through Ireland all that afternoon, the evidence of trouble and strife was everywhere: burnt-out farmhouses, broken bridges, groups of uniformed, fully armed soldiers at every station; hungry cattle in bare fields, beggars on bleak, grey village streets. By the time they reached Cork, the blue sky, like their good humour, became obscured. The cold sun had disappeared behind some opaque cloud as if an unexpected eclipse had descended without warning. At twilight as the lights came on, the tide along the river was high, wide and deep. Such a beautiful approach: ships from foreign countries plying up the huge harbour, one of the biggest in the world. Coming up from Roches Point, Haulbowline and Spike Island, where the British kept their prisons and moored their warships; past hissing estuaries alive with flocks of egrets, black-throated divers, curlews, great crested grebes; the flowing tide filling obscure coves and inlets, smelling of fish and seaweed. There were more soldiers than ever at the Glanmire station, more armoured cars and lorries. The girls had some time to kill before taking their connecting train to Bandon, so Margie suggested a walk into Patrick Street. Cork was a small, walkable city. A city of water. They'd be in the centre in ten minutes. High above them, the large Victorian mansions of Montenotte hung over the bustle of the running trains as remote as castles on the Amalfi coast. The merchant princes of Cork had made their money on trade and being loyal to the Empire. Their reward: the good life of gracious living in sumptuous dwellings, with overhanging gardens of sweet-scented azaleas and laburnum; their sailing-yachts down in Crosshaven at the Royal Cork Yacht Club, the world's oldest. A tight-knit bunch, unwelcoming to outsiders.

Margie and Anna walked on past small rows of cottages further down and heard the familiar sing-song lilt of Cork's unmistakeable accent. Today the faces of the poor seemed more pinched and bitter. Horses hung their heads under sidecars and seemed reluctant to cast off their torpor. They got as far as French's Quay and attempted to cross Patrick's Bridge, but it was blocked by stony-faced soldiers who told them to walk on up Camden Quay. On the high steps of St. Mary's Church they paused, and the Angelus bell pealed out at six in the evening from the North Cathedral high above, in counterpoint to Shandon's Steeple bell tolling the hour. Cork's hills ranged around like the seven hills of Rome, and through the flat, winding streets in the centre, the twin-branched river Lee flowed eastwards to the sea: Venice-like, the city on the marsh. There were flotillas of mute swans on the river by the North Gate Bridge, like white galleons on dark water, darker sky. Leaning over the parapet Anna threw the last crumbs of a white loaf of bread into the plashy depths. The swans gobbled eagerly, the stronger ones hissing to announce their prerogatives. The late-straggling street vendors on the Coal Quay were closing up for the day. Old 'shawlies': women with careworn faces in black shawls and Kinsale cloaks, were offering last-minute bargains: 'A penny for the last of the lovely red apples, love.'

Anna asked for two which the old lady grudgingly delivered. They bit into the sweet, rosy fruit as they walked towards Paul Street. A lone fiddler played The Snowy Breasted Pearl outside the graceful, limestone-clad wine vaults of Woodfourd Bourne's Emporium. They decided to walk over to the Victoria Hotel on Patrick Street for a cup of tea and a curranty bun.

Groups of marauding Black and Tans, Essex and Auxiliaries started to leave their various outposts around the county as night descended. They were in belligerent mood. Word had quickly filtered in of the annilihation of the Auxiliary force at Kilmichael the week before, and revenge was on their minds. In the town of Fermoy one of their lorries broke down and a heavily armed group decided to stay overnight in the town. They abandoned the lorry and dispersed to the bars around the town centre. They demanded liquor and did not pay for it as was their *modus operandi*. One group went into the Royal Hotel where they encountered an ex-British army officer, Captain Nicholas Prendergast, who had fought in France in the Great War. An argument broke out between him and an Auxiliary soldier. They accused him of being a supporter of Sinn Féin and dragged him from the hotel onto the town square outside. They beat him up and stabbed him to death with bayonets. They dragged his body to the bridge over the wide Blackwater and threw it into the fast-flowing river below. They returned to the hotel and insisted on holding a dance. The grovelling manager explained that the neighbours might object to the noise, so they left and tried to enter Mr. Dooley's shop next door. When he refused to open they smashed the door down, dragged him out, set fire to his premises and the adjoining houses as well. They beat Mr. Dooley up, took him down to the quay wall and threw him, still alive, into the river. Then, as he struggled to stay afloat they riddled the water around him with bullets. As he was going under he managed to grab some branches overhanging the water and eventually pulled himself to safety, bloodied, half-drowned, traumatised.

In Cork, several lorry loads of heavily-armed Auxiliaries left Victoria Barracks on the north side of the city. They stopped at a house where Fr. James O'Callaghan, a young priest from the pleasant ploughland of Laravoulta, way out west, had come to lodge and administer to the poor of the city. They knocked at his door.

'Yes,' said the priest. 'Can I help you?'

'No you can't, you Roman Catholic renegade,' said the officer in charge and, pulling his pistol from his holster, he fired three bullets into the priest's body. His liver punctured, his spleen ruptured, he fell at their feet and they left him to die a slow, agonising death.

Whooping and jeering the Auxiliaries slowly made their way in convoys of trucks down towards the city centre, stopping at every public house along the way, demanding whiskey and brandy to stoke their choleric tempers. Passersby, seeing the murderous disposition in their eyes, gave them a wide berth and hurried home.

As Margie and Anna were about to go into the Victoria Hotel, two lorry-loads pulled up on the street and the drunken soldiers jumped down. 'Ere, Missy,' said one. 'How's about you then?'

He put his hand on Margie's shoulder and attempted to kiss her. Margie drew back and gave him her most withering stare. 'Who do you think you're calling Missy?' she demanded, fearlessly.

The soldier, taken aback, stopped and took his hand away. He looked towards Anna.

'You take your beady eyes off my sister, and your filthy hands off me,' said Margie. Her flashing eyes and fierce demeanour caused him to pause. The tension was broken by the soldier's companions' laughter. They jeered at his timidity when confronted by the force of will that was Margie Cody.

'Bit off more than you can chew there, didn't you mate,' shouted one. 'Come on, before she scratches your eyes out.'

With Margie standing four-square, protecting her younger sister, the rebuked soldier turned sheepishly and rejoined his companions. They walked off down the street, pushing people off the footpath and firing their guns into the air every now and again. Margie and Anna hurried into the hotel and ordered tea.

By eight o'clock the shooting had become more indiscriminate and soon the Auxiliaries were joined by heavily-armed Black and Tans and regular military. The drinking became more copious and the soldiers' behaviour more unruly. The hotel porter informed Anna and Margie that the West Cork train was not running. Sensing that things were getting out of hand, they slipped out of the hotel and hurried away to the Western Road where they took lodgings for the night.

Soon after 10 p.m. further lorry loads of troops left the barracks with plentiful supplies of petrol in cans, and drove to join their comrades on the streets, where they embarked on an uncontrolled orgy of arson, looting and assaults. They set fire to all the large shops and businesses on Patrick Street, and the fires spread to the adjoining Winthrop Street, Oliver Plunket Street and Cook Street. The city fire brigades came out to try to quell the blazing fires but the British Forces fired on them and cut their hoses. Across the river the City Hall was singled out for destruction and so was the Carnegie Library with its thousands of books. Even the RIC joined in the mayhem, cutting off the water each time the fire brigades attached the hoses to the hydrants. By midnight the entire city centre was ablaze and huge palls of smoke, flames, ashes and sparks ascended into the night sky.

In the morning, Margie and Anna rose, and thanked their lucky stars to have escaped the destruction of the night before. They headed back into the city but their spirits did not soar as they crossed into Daunt

Square to behold the burnt out shells of the Queens Old Castle and the Victoria Hotel; the Grand Parade with no coherence to its streetscape, all reduced to smoke and ruin. People stood round in resentful, shocked huddles, pointing out one abomination greater than the next. The city of lights and water reduced to blackness and smoke. They walked in mute amazement down towards the South Mall and looked across a bend in the south fork of the river towards the devastated City Hall: 'My God,' cried Margie, 'My Palace of the Doges, destroyed.'

A shaft of sunlight eventually penetrated the soup-grey clouds to illuminate the granite pillars of Trinity Church in a golden noose of light.

'The only building left untouched,' said Anna in disbelief, as they walked on over bridges and past green and slippy, stone steps. Water everywhere, but the ancient, historic city reduced to rubble by the unbridled savagery of the Crown Forces. They finally faced the obliterated remains of the finest street in Cork: Patrick Street like a bombed out battlefield of the Great War. Gone was the beautiful Carnegie Library, and smouldering were, Roches Stores, Cash and Company, the Munster Arcade, the American Shoe Company, Forrests, Sunners Chemists, Saxone Shoes; and the Victoria Hotel where they had supped the night before. The heart torn out of the city.

They took the train to West Cork as quickly as their legs could carry them to the station. The countryside was green, but bare of leaves and bleak. They saw roads cut up and mined, bridges broken, evidence of a country in a state of disarray and chaos. They were glad to reach the great, sheltering beeches of Gatonville in the deep, secluded valley they called home. They went in at the white gate and their mother welcomed them with tears and kisses and a warm embrace. Their brother Seamus came in with blackened hands from repairing the thresher and they hugged him with relief. William had stayed in Dublin. Their father was out in the fields, Doctor Baldwin still on his wanderings, like Aengus.

'I don't know if I can let you go back to Dublin,' said their mother tearfully delighted they had made the long journey safely in the depth of dangerous winter.

General Sir Nevil Macready rose from behind his shiny, walnut desk and moved his large, soft body to a high Georgian window overlooking the main square of the Royal Barracks, in the Arbour Hill district of Dublin. As he stood looking out at the rain falling steadily on the cobblestones, he took small sips of sweetened Turkish coffee from a beautifully ornate cup of Royal Crown Derby Imari porcelain and considered how much he loathed this country of Ireland. And Dublin in particular. Good God what a place. Here he found himself, the cast of a fishing line from the northern bank of the river Liffey in the stale, wet heart of the city, attempting to carry out his commission as the GOC of his Majesty's military forces in Ireland. And what a dreary river it was, with a cold wind forever blowing down its featureless banks. He missed the sweet, gentle Thames with its broad reaches, its great loops and swirls; the grand houses and gardens out by Richmond, Twickenham and Hampton Court. This damned country was no place for a gentleman who'd reached the zenith of a fine career in the noble profession of arms. But such was Macready's vast discipline and sense of duty that he would invariably apply himself to his assignment no matter how unenthusiastic he felt about its implementation. God knows he'd seen enough of soldiering. From the Boer War to the Great War and now an increasingly nasty and ruthless conflict in this provincial backwater. He was beginning to think it better for a man to follow his passions at this hour of life, and, curiously Macready's lifelong passion was not the army as might outwardly appear to be the case, but the stage. Odd choice for a soldier, but there it was. Of course he'd been raised in the bohemian milieu, his father being the famous actor and friend of Dickens, William Charles Macready, and his mother Cecile, the granddaughter of the painter Sir William Beechey. Brought up around the urbane dinner tables of Cheltenham, he'd been exposed to theatrics from an early age.

'Don't even think of going on the stage,' his father always said. 'Bad enough for it to have ruined my life, besides ruining yours as well; always struggling to make ends meet while having to keep the bright side out. No, get a real job and do something useful.'

But though he'd taken the advice and followed a dutiful course as far from the theatre as one could get, the apple didn't fall far from the tree. Macready was never happier than performing in a Gilbert and Sullivan operetta or taking the lead in an amateur dramatics production. Not that he'd find much time for that kind of thing in this troublesome town.

He heaved a sigh, and, as he was contemplating how to outwit these fellows, de Valera and Collins, a sharp knock upon the door caused him to turn to see two uniformed officers entering smartly. Major-General Sir Henry Hugh Tudor, the minutiae-loving martinet, who headed the Royal Irish Constabulary, and Brigadier-General F.P. Crozier, a bluff, ruthless Unionist from Ulster, whom Macready didn't particularly care for. They both saluted and advanced towards the middle of the room. Tudor was recently commissioned to reorganise the RIC and Crozier was in charge of the Auxiliaries. Tudor waved a document on heavy deed paper in his direction. 'I think we've come up with a suitable wording, sir,' he declared with a rather triumphant smile on his roundish face.

'A wording for what?' asked Macready pretending ignorance, but really wishing to blunt the irritating eagerness of his provisional secretary. Hardly that. Perhaps amanuensis was a better description.

'Why, for the proclamation of Martial Law, as we discussed?' exclaimed Tudor, compressing his thin lips and staring intently at Macready.

'Oh that,' sighed Macready. 'Yes, yes of course. D'you think it'll make any difference?'

'But it was your idea in the first place,' remonstrated a perplexed Tudor. 'You asked me to find an appropriate format. I've spent the past two days with Colonel Winter and Brigadier-General Crozier coming up with this version.'

'Ah, of course, of course my dear Tudor, my apologies. My mind has been taken up with matters of extreme urgency lately. Carry on.' Macready moved behind his desk and almost flopped into his chair, as if he'd just run a marathon. The feel of smooth leather was cool on his nether regions.

'Quite, sir,' nodded Tudor, wondering what in the world was more urgent than getting to grips with the political situation, which was spinning further and further out of their control with each passing day. Macready motioned to them to sit down across the desk from him.

Tudor leant forward. 'Just to bring you up to date sir,' he began. 'One of our finest sections of the Auxiliary under an excellent officer named Colonel Crake, has been wiped out within the past week in a place called Kilmichael in County Cork. You are aware of that sir?'

Macready regarded Tudor with an even demeanour. Was he being sarcastic or did he take him for a fool? He continued to look at Tudor while addressing Crozier: 'I'm well aware of that Major-General Tudor. It has also come to my attention, Brigadier-General Crozier, that your Auxuliary and Black and Tan forces ran amok two nights ago and burned half of Cork city to the ground, aided and abetted by your constabulary, Major Tudor. In fact Major-General Strickland has sent me dispatches from Cork deploring the actions of both parties. It seems that when the local fire brigade attached their hoses to water sumps, the taps were continually turned off by the police. What's the world coming to when this kind of thing is perpetrated by the forces of a civilized country?'

Crozier's eyes glinted merrily underneath his peaked cap. 'I think Major-General Strickland may be mistaken, sir. The situation admittedly has become tense, and it is understandable that our forces would react to the loss of their comrades by a reflexive action, but I'm assured that the fire brigades were never interfered with as suggested.'

'Major-General Strickland is preparing a report,' said Macready. 'I'm given to understand it may not be the most favourable.'

Crozier threw his arms up in a gesture of frustrated acceptance: 'I'm afraid I have no control over the Major-General's perceptions, but given the provocation against my forces, I think their reaction is understandable.'

What he was really thinking was that these soft English generals, Macready and Strickland, had no stomach for slaughter. Given an unfettered hand he, Crozier, would give the Tans and Auxiliaries free rein to burn and lay waste at will. That would soon bring these recalcitrant southerners to heel. A bit of cold Unionist steel was required. The fist of God. He regarded Tudor out of the corner of his eye. There was a man he could do business with; him and that fellow Percival in West Cork, about whom he'd heard glowing reports. No shilly shallying there. As for the rest of this hierarchy, Lord French, Sir Hamar Greenwood: a lot of pompous English asses.

Macready looked steadily across his desk and beheld a slightly chubby soldier of fortune who wouldn't pay his gambling debts and a round-faced bureaucrat who only got the job because of his friendship with Churchill. All hush-hush of course. Crozier had been drummed out of the army in the early part of the century. Not cricket to dishonour your debts. Rehabilitated after a suitable interlude, because, when the going got rough, you needed a chap like Crozier by your side. Irish of course. Macready considered him a damned Ulster lunatic; but they had their uses. In particular they liked to slash as many Catholic throats as possible and hang the carcasses up on meathooks like butchers. They had a particular enthusiasm for that sort of thing. As for Tudor, a cold fish if ever he saw one. Would have to keep an eye on that chap, watch his back. So for the moment he'd play one off against the other in the time-honoured strategy of holding onto power. Let them huff and puff for awhile and think he was soft; call him General 'Make-Ready' behind his back, sniggeringly. As if he wasn't aware of their nasty little mockeries. The only thing that was soft about Macready was his posterior. He'd see them both off the premises in due course.

He puffed out his cheeks and reached without a word for the document from Tudor. He put on his reading glasses, and, holding the document at arms length, he started to read it disdainfully:

"NOTE WELL, that a state of armed insurrection exists. The Forces of the Crown are hereby declared on active service. Any unauthorised person found in possession of arms, ammunition and explosives will be liable on conviction by a Military Court to suffer Death. Anyone harbouring any person who has taken part is guilty of levying war against His Majesty the King, and is liable on conviction to suffer Death."

Macready looked over the rims of his glasses. 'You have a most annoying habit, Major Tudor, of prefixing ordinary nouns such as death and military with a capital letter.'

Tudor lifted one eyebrow and glanced quickly at Crozier. A faint suggestion of a smile played on his lips. 'You think so, sir?' he said.

'Here it is again,' said Macready:

"All meetings or assemblies in public places are forbidden and for the purposes of this Order six adults will be considered a meeting."

'Can you explain to me why the word, order, in the middle of a sentence, has to have a capital o?'

'Well, sir, for emphasis, I suppose...' began Tudor.

'A proper noun begins with a capital letter: Macready, Dublin, King George, for example. Common nouns are lower case. Did you not learn that at school? Where were you at school anyway Major?'

'The Royal Military College, Woolwich, sir,' said an unperturbed Tudor. 'And yourself sir?'

'As a matter of fact I was in Marlborough, then Sandhurst,' said Macready, safely superior. 'Don't remember seeing you in either.'

'Even if I had been at either, you would have already left by the time I started,' said Tudor smugly.

'But you weren't, so I didn't,' said an irritated Macready and returned to scanning the document:

"No person must stand or loiter in the streets except in pursuit of his lawful occupation. All occupants of houses must keep affixed to the inner side of the outer door a list of the occupants, setting forth their names, sex, age and occupation."

Tiresome claptrap. How was this going to be enforced? What manpower would it take? Certainly more than he had at his disposal.When he'd finished he said abruptly, 'This will have to do. But I'm bound to say there's a certain amount of tautology in there that we could do without.'

'Tautology, sir?' asked Crozier with a smile.

'Telling us what we already know,' said Macready and stood up. He handed the document back to Tudor. 'Very well Major, carry on. Post this up and circulate it to every military barracks, police station and post office in the country. Let's see if it has any effect, which I doubt.'

'Would the General care to suggest an alternative strategy then?' asked a peeved Tudor. He was also annoyed that Macready often called him Major rather than Major-General, obviously to get under his skin.

'As a matter of fact I would,' said Macready with a triumphant smile: 'Excommunication!'

'Excommunication?' frowned Crozier.

'Yes, excommunication. Dr. Coholan the Bishop of Cork has excommunicated all these blighters who are in the IRA. It seems it is working a treat in some quarters. You know how damned superstitious these fellows are. Most of them are Papists. They'll shoot you in the back from behind a ditch without a thought, but excommunication to them means their immortal souls are condemned to suffer in hell for all eternity. So rather than risk that, many of them are laying down their arms.'

Crozier laughed out loud. 'By God sir, I think you may have a point there. That may be the way forward without another shot being fired.' The look he exchanged with Tudor suggested that he thought Macready was barking mad.

The look didn't go unnoticed. Macready drew himself up to his full height, displaying his ample girth. He squared his shoulders. The set of his jaw below his rather jowly cheeks was ominous. He put his hand to his collar while swivelling his neck, as if to give himself more breathing room. Crozier waited expectantly.

'You're Irish, aren't you, Brigadier-General Crozier?' asked Macready as if they'd only just been introduced.

Crozier's eyelashes blinked quicker than usual. 'Why yes, yes, I'm Irish, Northern Irish, but I thought you already knew that, sir?'

'Northern Irish, Southern Irish. You all sound the same to me. What's the difference?' asked Macready.

Crozier's laughter lines crinkled a little more around his eyes. Was the General being facetious? 'Why not a lot I expect, but I don't understand your point, sir.'

'My point,' said Macready in his clipped accent of the Royal Military College, Sandhurst, 'is that you're not English.'

'Well... I'm British... I suppose,' faltered Crozier.

'But you're not English, like Major Tudor and myself. You're Irish. You were born in Ireland.'

'But no less loyal for all that,' responded Crozier, by now quite puzzled. 'I don't get your drift, General.'

'Because I've often wondered why you Unionists want to be British?'

Tudor was examining his finger nails, beginning to feel like an eavesdropper at a domestic row. He came to Crozier's assistance. 'They're British in the sense that they're part of the British Isles.'

Crozier shifted uneasily on his solid feet, noticing the sense of otherness in Tudor's use of the word, 'they' when referring to Unionists.

Macready addressed Tudor: '*We* don't consider them British though,' he said.

Crozier's Unionist insecurities began to bubble under. What was this wedge Macready was trying to drive? 'But we're the loyal subjects of his Majesty. We support the King,' he expostulated.

'But does the King support *you*? Except out of the burden of duty. And a heavy burden it is,' said Macready dourly.

'I'm bound to say I fail to see what you're driving at, sir,' said Tudor, noticing Crozier's thunderous demeanour. They'd have fireworks in a minute.

'As far as I can see, they're Irish when it suits them and British when they want something from us,' said Macready. 'Apart from some of them wanting to ape us, and of course I'm not including the Brigadier-General in this, most of them are just thick-brogued, boorish peasants, drinking too much and dancing steps of *cipín*.'

Crozier's face had reddened to a deep crimson. Now he was being insulted as well. What a bloody liberty. He felt his breath shortening, his heartbeat quickening, but still he held his counsel as Macready continued in full flight:

'What have the Irish ever accomplished except being good at brawling and fighting and drinking moonshine?'

'We've held this island for you for three hundred years,' said Crozier, finally finding his tongue.

'But the 1916 Rebellion and this present outbreak of violence is contained not by Irish soldiers, but by British. The Auxiliaries wiped out at Kilmichael were English officers to a man.'

Crozier's expression had hardened into a mask of contempt as Macready moved away from behind his desk and paced towards the window, gesticulating with his arms like a character doing a soliloquy in a play. 'Take us English,' he continued in full flow. 'We've sent armies and ships across the globe. We've brought civilisation to Africa, India, North America. We've invented almost every machine in the world today. We've brought our Common Law system to millions. We've produced the finest engineers, explorers and botanists since the Romans. We've produced Shakespeare, Milton, Tennyson. The sun never sets on our empire...'

'It will soon, if it keeps getting theatrical fellows like you to run its army,' cut in Crozier, with a sneer.

Macready wheeled away from the window and stopped suddenly. Perhaps realizing that he'd overstepped the mark. He cleared his throat, feeling ever so slightly ridiculous all of a sudden.

Tudor was gazing at him with a bemused expression. 'I think you've made your point, sir,' he said. 'If it's alright with you, Brigadier-General Crozier and I will carry on with this assignment.' He waved the deed paper in the air.

Macready looked sheepishly at the floor. He sighed and nodded. 'Yes, gentlemen, carry on,' he said finally. They both saluted and Macready returned the salute. They went through the door without a word, shutting it a little too sharply behind them. Macready watched them go and stood thoughtfully in the middle of the floor, halfway between the window and his desk. He pursed his lips and turned his head to one side. Had he been a bit too hasty? A bit over the top as they say? Not really. A chap had to say what was what from time to time. No, let them put it in their pipe and smoke it. He smoothed down his tunic on each side and straightened his tie. Then he poured himself another cup of coffee. He sipped it. It tasted cold, but he liked the feel and look of the porcelain as he held it delicately in his soft, wide hand, right pinky extended prettily. He examined the design. Such copious gilding, such sprigged vignettes. He particularly loved the cobalt-blue and iron-red colours of the ware and the globular coffee pot with its swan-necked spout.

He had a review of troops the next morning with Lord French, the

Lord-Lieutenant of Ireland. French was already there when he arrived into the main square of the huge building. Impatient as usual and perhaps no longer as cock-sure of himself since he'd been ambushed by the IRA up at Ashtown a year previously. Damned buggers attacked him in broad daylight as he was getting off the train coming from a private party at his country residence in Frenchpark. French had a walking cane and he stood wide-legged in his uniform and polished boots as Macready strolled towards him. They exchanged salutes and French's watery eyes were choleric above his full moustache. Macready smiled. He knew better than to upset his titular head. French had a reputation for being hot-tempered and defensive, perhaps as a result of his less than successful campaign as Commander-in-Chief of the British Expeditionary Force in the Great War. He'd made some serious blunders after the battles at Mons and Cateau and suffered the indignity of having his orders ignored by subordinates. And to cap it all, Lord Kitchener arrived for an emergency meeting at the battle of the Marne in his Field-Marshal's uniform, implying to French that he was his military superior and not simply a cabinet member. Macready was careful to ensure his epaulettes carried no superfluous insignia.

'Good morning, Lord-Lietenant,' said Macready urbanely and took his place in front of the line of troops.

'Can we get on with this, General,' said the red-faced French, 'I've come down from the Vice-Regal Lodge without my breakfast. You're three minutes late.' He really couldn't stand Macready.

'Sincerest apologies my Lord,' said Macready. 'I assure you this won't take a moment longer than is necessary.' He looked sideways out of the corner of his eye at the irascible older man. One had to walk on eggs around him in case one proferred an opinion which would shake the old man's world view and perhaps bring on a heart attack or a severe bout of the aigue. He was glad he didn't have the Lord-Lieutenant's company every day. He certainly couldn't vent his feelings around him as he did with Crozier or Tudor.

The troops went through their motions: order arms, present arms, slope arms, at ease, attention, by the left, quick march. All quickly accomplished and still only eight o'clock in the morning. After exchanging some information on the state of readiness of the army, Macready mentioned that he was going to the Theatre Royal that evening with Sir Hamar Greenwood, the Chief Secretary for Ireland. The Lord-Lieutenant got back in his car. He rolled down the window from the back seat and looked up at Macready. 'You can't be too careful in the times we live in, General. I'm told you like to take a walk unaccompanied through the city from time to time. You should discontinue that practice, especially at night.'

As the Lord-Lieutenant's car drove slowly down the huge square with its arcaded collonades, past the great neo-classical buildings, Macready's visage was as implacable as the granite that faced the mighty walls of the largest military barracks in Europe. One thing was for certain, he wouldn't be taking the Lord-Lieutenant's advice.

That evening General Macready and Sir Hamar Greenwood strolled down through a warren of narrow, cobbled streets in Temple Bar in the oldest quarter of the city. They had a dispatch of outriders on motor bikes at a discreet distance in front and behind them, but to the casual passerby they looked like two anonymous gentlemen going for a drink. Macready wore a cape, flung at a slightly capricious angle over his shoulders, while Sir Hamar was well muffled in scarf, Homburg and Kashmir overcoat, advertising the best of Savile Row haberdashery. They felt quite safe. There were armed soldiers standing at every corner and armoured cars with powerful cannon going up and down the streets. They'd left the Chief Secretary's offices in the grand environs of the Castle, where Greenwood had given him a quick guided tour. They passed through the Grand Ballroom with its painted ceilings by Vincenzo Valdre, depicting the coronation of King George 111, Saint Patrick introducing Christianity to Ireland, and King Henry 11 receiving the submission of the Irish Chieftains. They walked on through the Throne Room and the marching procession of vaults and arches on the Great Corridor. They went by the Picture Gallery, but skirted the luxurious apartments which were the personal accomodation of the Lord-Lieutenant; Macready quietly intimating that one encounter with the esteemed Field-Marshal John Denton Pinkstone French was quite enough for one day.

The Chief Secretary permitted himself a knowing laugh. His humorous eyes twinkled. A lawyer and politician, he was born in Canada and was free of the stiff upper lip mentality, which characterised the officer classes of the British Army. But he had his ruthless side. Macready was aware that he favoured the heavy-handed tactics of the Black and Tans, which Macready found rather appalling, though outside of his control. But this particular evening they were putting military matters aside for some well-earned *divertissement*.

'You know, General, this Castle has an air of grandeur superior to what is observable in any of the Courts of Saint James, the Royal Palace of London,' said Greenwood.

'You believe so?' said Macready, dubiously, as they strolled through the upper yard and passed down by the giant Record Tower and Chapel Royal, on their way to the lower pedestrian gate.

'Absolutely,' continued Greenwood, 'and that's not just my opinion. It was originally proferred by James Malton in his great, *View Of Dublin*, and I'm bound to say I couldn't agree more.'

'Perhaps I've been somewhat blinkered to its aesthetics,' said Macready, generously. Greenwood nodded vigorously. He liked Macready. The feeling was mutual.

By the time they'd passed by Sir William Temple's old house at Temple Bar, Macready was beginning to have a different appreciation of the ancient city, despite its putrid smells, its beggars crowding around the Roomkeepers Society for the Sick and Indigent, and its dangerous subversives who could shoot you in the back at any moment.

'As fine a city as any in the United Kingdom, outside of the Capital. Such beautiful Georgian Squares: Fitzwilliam, Merrion, Mountjoy. Such magnificent parks: St Stephen's Green, the Phoenix Park.' As Greenwood was expounding he was simultaneously chewing on a gravy-smothered *crubeen,* which he'd bought from a street hawker on Sycamore Street.

Macready smiled at the easy manners of the North American. He couldn't bring himself to munch in public with such unselfconscious ease. Too embarrassing. The English disease. 'Why is it called Temple Bar?' he asked to muffle Greenwood's slurping.

'A barr, spelt with two r's, is a reclaimed piece of land on an estuary,' said the Chief Secretary, wiping his hands on a rather greasy handkerchief. 'Sir William Temple, the first Provost of Trinity College built his house on such a piece of ground beside the Liffey back in the 16th century. Hence the name Temple Bar.'

'Interesting,' said Macready. 'They dropped the second r.'

'You got it in one,' said Greenwood, his Canadian accent slipping momentarily through his cultivated Whitehall tones. As they walked along, the bells of Strongbow's Christchurch rang out over the chilly, foggy waters of the Liffey. 'Oh for the life of a campanologist,' said Greenwood with lithesome step.

'A campanologist?' queried his caped companion.

'A bellringer,' said the Chief Secretary with aplomb.

Later that evening, they roared with laughter at the antics of the actor, Henry Lytton playing the Major-General in Gilbert and Sullivan's Pirates of Penzance up at the Theatre Royal. In tall-plumed hat, monocle and white gloves, he pranced around the stage as the well-known lyrics flowed from his lips beneath his bristling moustache. Macready knew all the words and sang along:

I am the very model of a modern Major-General,
I've information vegetable, animal and mineral,
I know the kings of England and I quote the fights historical,
From Marathon to Waterloo in order categorical:
I'm very well acquainted too with matters mathematical,
I understand equations both the simple and quadratical,
About binomial theorem I'm teeming with a lot o' news,
With many cheerful facts about the square of the hypotenuse...

The Irish audience clapped enthusiastically and rose to give a standing ovation to the actors at the end of a splendid evening. Macready turned to Sir Hamar and said rather laconically:

'Do you think Mr. Gilbert had our own Major Tudor in mind when penning those lyrics?'

The Chief Secretary slapped his thigh and almost hollered aloud. As they turned to leave, whom they did not see, but who saw them a few seats away, was a powerfully-built younger man in a three piece pinstriped suit, a dark, laughing face and twinkling eyes, who'd obviously been enjoying the evening just as much as themselves. Michael Collins turned discreetly to one of his entourage of bowler-hatted companions and discreetly pointed out the Chief Secretary for Ireland and the General Officer Commanding his Majesty's forces. They looked like fellows they could have enjoyed a drink with in another time and place.

10

horses in the snow

The horses came up through the snow. They came up over the hill from the northside where the wind was blowing. The sky was grey, falling down to the horizon, where land met sky and merged, so that it was difficult to distinguish one from the other on the horizon line. Sonny and Mike heard their muffled hooves thudding. There were four loose horses, their whooshing breaths bursting out in the cold air like bellows. Tull was roaring behind them. Driving them on as he rode bareback on a hunter. Sonny's eyes followed them as they hurtled along by the ditches of the eastern fields. In the background Greenhill passed from view, and then the high ground up behind Newcestown. He was aware of the background landscape, because he was high up on the highest point of the farm. But he was moving his eyes, following the horserace in the foreground. Clumps of snow and earth flew into the air behind the lead horses, spattering Tull and the grey hunter until they were turning black with mud. They descended to lower ground and wheeled westward towards the farmyard. They did not enter the yard, but kept going in a circle like wild horses from the Camargue. Tull was training them. He used the farm as a racetrack. The damn fellow was half crazy at times. But what a horseman.

'What's he doing?' asked Mike from inside the hole. He was in a concealed dump in a deep trench behind a ditch, where they were checking sequestered guns. He couldn't see Tull.

'He's racing,' said Sonny with a smirk.

'He's daft,' said Mike and continued to examine the guns.

'Look what he's doing now,' laughed an incredulous Sonny.

Mike started to climb up out of the trench. He was wiping his hands with an oily rag he'd been using to clean the guns. The rag had a string attached, which they called a pull-through. You put the rag into one side of the barrel and pulled it right through to the other side to clear any obstructions. Mike had a Colt .45 revolver in one hand with the chamber flipped out so he could see through the barrel. He squinted into the barrel, then switching his gaze to the galloping horses in the distance. Tull was nearly supine on the horse's back. His head was bobbing above the flying hooves.

'The bastard will break his neck,' said Mike.

They watched as Tull leant further back on the horse's rump and let go of the bridle reins. Then he slowly swung his right leg over the horse's withers and disappeared from view on the far side of the horse. When the horse flashed past him Tull was standing in the snow with his knees slightly bent.

Mike said: 'How the hell did he manage that?'

'He's like a cat,' said Sonny. They watched as the small herd thundered towards them up the long, wide, sloping field of snow. They heard Tull's sharp whistle and watched as the hunter slowed and went galloping back to him in a wide, turning arc. It slowed, then stopped, loose reins swinging forward on its neck.

'Will you look at that,' said a bemused Mike in grudging admiration, still hefting the cold revolver in his oil-smudged hand.

'He's good isn't he,' grinned Sonny, as the athletic Tull ran alongside the hunter, sprang with a bound onto its back and came cantering nonchalantly towards them. The loose horses had already swung by them in a blur of pounding hooves. Tull pulled the hunter to a slithering halt in front of them in a shower of kicked-back snow and clods of earth. Steam rose in clouds from horse and rider. There was a pungent smell of sweat and bridle leather. Tull patted and stroked the velvet-soft neck and dragged his fingers through the knotted mane like a rudimentary curry comb.

'Anyone would think you were training for the Grand National,' said a poker-faced Mike.

'You'd never know,' said a beaming Tull. Sonny grinned, looking from one to the other. Tull and Mike sparked off each other on a regular basis.

'Have you any saddle?' asked Mike. 'You can't ride the National without a saddle.'

'I'm practising without it,' said Tull. 'All the best riders in the world can ride without saddles: the Sioux Indians, the Cossacks in Russia.'

'You're a long way from Russia,' said Mike.

'I've been reading about them,' said Tull.

'So have I,' said Mike. 'About their Communist revolution, not their horsemen.'

'It takes all kinds,' said Tull. Mike nodded. It was hard to best Tull in an argument.

The horse's flanks were heaving. It pawed the slushy ground, impatient to be off again. The loose remuda wheeled around and came back towards them, slowed and eventually trotted to a stop on a square perch of ground half a furlong distant; panting, wide-eyed, curious.

'They're mad for galloping,' said Sonny.

'Horses love the cold,' said Tull. The beasts were well covered with their hairy winter coats. Their matted flanks glistened with sweat. There was white froth between their legs.

'Where are you taking them?' asked Sonny.

'I'm going to stable them,' said Tull. 'They need fodder. There's not a scrap of grass left.'

'Lucky for you we had a good crop of hay,' said Mike.

'Damn right,' said Tull. 'I saved most of it myself remember, while you fellows were off chasing guns. How's the cache anyway?'

'That's a secret,' said Mike, and winked at Sonny.

'Secret my backside,' said Tull, and jumped off the hunter, trailing the bridle reins over its head, where it dragged wet in the snow. The horse waited dutifully. Tull ran up the ditch to his brothers. His face and neck carried healing scars. He looked healthy again.

'Have a look,' said Sonny. Tull descended on the far side of the ditch. The branches of a blackthorn tree concealed the entrance to the trench. He pushed them aside and followed along a narrow path, where ferns and furze bushes grew in abundance on either side. Then he found himself under a man-made canopy covered in earth and grass, and then inside of a small chamber, where he could almost stand up to full height. There were rows of jute sacks lined along the floor, wrapped with binder twine. Sonny and Mike followed behind. Sonny bent and undid the twine on the first sack and pulled the mouth back. There were six gleaming Lee Enfield .303 rifles jutting out. Sonny pulled one out completely. He handed it to Tull, who held it in his hands like it was a fragile violin.

'No need to baby it,' said Sonny, taking the rifle back. 'These are tough boyos.' He pulled back the bolt with a sliding sound that echoed around the dugout. He sighted along the barrel.

'Where do the bullets go?' Tull asked.

Mike laughed. 'Jesus, Tull, you'll never make a soldier. You'd better stick to the horses and the pigs.'

'There's nothing I'd like better,' said Tull. 'I hope I don't have to fire one of these any time soon. Although I wouldn't mind putting a few bullets through them bastards who beat me up in Castletown.'

'No need for you to do that,' said Sonny grimly. 'We took care of them at Kilmichael.'

'But there's a lot more of them,' said Tull and looked worried.

Sonny slapped him on the back. 'We have them on the run,' he said.

'But you're on the run yourselves?' said Tull.

'We're home for Christmas,' laughed Sonny. 'Relax, be cheerful.' He put the rifle in the bag. 'Better cover these up. Charlie and the boys will be coming for these.'

The horses whinnied as the young men emerged into the grey light.

'It'll soon be Christmas,' said Sonny, 'although 'twill be a strange one.'

'The snow is nice,' said Tull. 'But it's not good for feeding the animals.'

'Not good for us either,' said Mike. 'If the Tans come they'll see our tracks in the snow.'

'Ah, we put the frighteners on them after Kilmichael,' said Sonny.

'I doubt it,' said Tull. 'I'd say 'tis worse they'll be.'

'They'll never find us up here,' said Sonny.

'Say your prayers they won't,' said Mike.

'Your prayers are no good now,' said Tull. 'The bishop has thrown you out.'

'How d'you mean?' asked Sonny, and stopped.

'Have you ever heard of excommunication?' asked Tull. 'It means you're no longer a member of the Catholic Church. You boys have been excommunicated after Kilmichael.'

Mike shrugged. 'It doesn't bother me,' he said.

'Me neither,' said Sonny, then paused. A serious flicker entered his eyes: 'But what if we're shot. Will our souls go to heaven?'

'That's what that bloody bishop wants you to think,' said Mike. 'He wants us to get so scared of going to hell that we'll stop attacking the Tans.'

'He won't stop me,' said Sonny and walked on with a grim expression.

'Nor the rest of us,' said Mike, and followed.

'The Bishop is doing the work for the British,' said Tull. 'But don't worry. A lot of people disagree with him, including Alfred O'Rahilly.'

'Who's he?' asked Sonny.

'He's the president of the University in Cork. A big intellectual.'

'Like yourself,' said Mike. They all laughed and walked on.

Until Tull said, 'So you don't like the Communists, Mike?'

'I don't know much about them, but I hear they don't believe in God.'

'But you don't either, if you defy the bishop.'

Mike frowned. 'You think you're too damned clever,' he said.

They got to the farmyard and Tull stabled the horses. Over in a piggery, Jeremiah was getting ready to kill a pig for the Christmas dinner. He was helped by Richie, the older brother, and Tom Wilson the neighbour. Wilson and Richie held the pig, one at his hind legs and the other at his front legs. The pig was spun upside down and Jeremiah skillfully drove the knife across its throat. The pig squealed high and lonesome, then gurgled, as the light of the world left its eyes. Sonny arrived for the denouement. He hated seeing a pig's end, but it was a necessary job. Jeremiah and Wilson were nonchalant about it. Richie had a huge pan and he collected the dripping blood, transferring it into a bucket. The blood would be used to make delicious black pudding, a delicacy mixed with onions and sauce. When the blood was all drained, Jeremiah sliced the pig down the middle and took out its intestines. Tom Wilson said, 'He's in great condition. There'll be a lot of eating in this fellow.'

'There will faith,' said Jeremiah, as he threw rolls of guts to a pack of hungry dogs. The dogs would wait, crouching, and gobble each piece before it hit the ground. Most of the pig would be saved for eating: the heart, the liver, even the feet they called *crubeens*. Pig's head was another delicacy. The pig's carcass would be salted and hung up in the dairy from the rafters for a week or so and then it would be sliced and boiled with fresh, green cabbage and eaten with floury potatoes and gravy.

'You can't whack the taste of fresh-cured bacon,' said Wilson, 'especially after a feed of drink.'

'My mouth is watering already at the thought of it,' said Richie.

Wilson was a man with a great turn of phrase. As Sonny and Mike loomed large in the doorway he said, 'By Jesus, if it isn't the return of the bold Fenian men.'

Jeremiah turned sharply around from where he was kneeling beside the stuck pig. He struggled stiffly to his feet. Tears filled his ageing eyes.

'Sonny, Mike,' he said. They came towards him, embraced him one after the other. Sonny held onto his hands at arms length and looked at the scar on his cheek. It was healing, but there were marks and scabs running down his face. Jeremiah looked self-conscious.

'How many stitches did you get, Dad?' Sonny asked.

'Twenty-four,' said his vulnerable father.

'We got the man who did that to you,' said Sonny, and that was all he could say. Jeremiah sighed: 'He was a bad article.' Tears fell from his eyes in sorrow and relief. 'You've been on the run a long time boys. We missed you here.'

'We missed you too,' said Sonny. 'We missed you all.' His face brightened: 'But you're managing well without us by the looks of it.'

'We have to,' Jeremiah said. 'We have no choice. But it's hard for us. Not knowing where you are or if you'll not come back at all some day.' He looked away and his chin trembled.

Sonny put an arm around his shoulder. 'Never fear about us. Me and Mike are hard to catch. We'll be around for Christmas and the new year with the help of God.'

'Yes,' said Mike, 'We'll be around to drink *poitín*. And we'll help you make some more.'

'That's the talk,' said Tom Wilson. 'A drop of the crathur is what's needed. Have you any sup left, Jeremiah?'

The old man cheered up: 'I'm running low,' he said 'We'll have to make another belt of it. But I might have a *taoscán* somewhere if you'll all have the patience.'

They finished cleaning the carcass and left the piggery. Richie hefted the dead pig on his shoulder. Elizabeth crossed the yard wearing rubber boots and carrying two buckets of water, which she'd drawn from the well across the field. She put down the buckets and rushed to embrace her two brothers. They tasted of earth, horse, salt, gunsmoke. 'Look at you,' she said, her eyes alight at seeing them. 'Have you eaten anything lately?'

'Not much,' grinned Sonny.

'You're as thin as greyhounds,' she said. She paused, searching their eyes. 'We heard about Kilmichael.' She looked anxious.

'We had to move fast afterwards,' said Sonny. 'We lay low for a few days and had a few close shaves where the army nearly caught us.'

'Are you home for long?' she asked, with hope in her eyes.

'As long as we can,' said Mike. 'Till early January anyway. Tom Barry wants us to re-form again after that. He has big plans.'

'Well, I think you should get your strength back for the moment,' said Elizabeth. 'Christmas is only a week away. We'll feed you up with plenty of salted bacon and a good fat goose. By the way, Sonny, there's a letter inside for you.'

'A letter for me?' said a surprised Sonny. 'Who'd be writing to me?'

'You could have a secret admirer,' said Tom Wilson, winking.

They went inside as the evening light was fading. The house was warm. A huge fire blazed on the open hearth. A kettle hung over the grate suspended on a black crane that swung in and out as required. In the corner was a fire machine that blew the fire to flame as a bellows underground. Sonny stood with his back to the fire and warmed his backside. Mike turned the familiar handle and the flames licked higher. Elizabeth scalded a teapot and heaped three spoons of tea into it and filled it to the brim with water from the bubbling kettle. Soon there was the smell of bacon, eggs, onions and black pudding pervading the cosy kitchen, wafting out into the yard, bringing all working stragglers to the table in a jiffy. 'By Jesus, this is good,' said Sonny. 'I haven't had a decent meal for a month. I could eat a Christian Brother's ass through a hedge.'

'You've been educated on your travels I see,' said Tom Wilson, laconically, as they all gathered in and sat on settle, stools and coasters. After Jeremiah prayed grace before meals they fell to like hungry hounds. An air of contented security descended on the homestead. Beasts and humans fed and watered. As the grandfather clocked ticked on, the night drew in. Tom Wilson and Jeremiah agreed that it was a long time since they'd had a visit together, or a *scoraíocht,* as the old people called it. They drank some *poitín* and told stories, but the most hair-raising tales that night were Sonny's and Mike's, of how they dared the Auxies and beat the Black and Tans. Tom Wilson sang a song and Tull pulled an old melodeon out from under the stairs. He played, *Sé Fáth Mo Bhuartha,* a sad, slow Gaelic air. Their eyes filled up with tears.

Sonny went upstairs and saw an envelope lying on the pillow of his newly-made bed. He picked it up, noticing the neat handwriting, and the letters S.A.G. across the top. St. Anthony's Guide. Someone was praying for him. He opened the envelope and took out the letter. He looked quickly at the bottom of the page for the signature - Anna Cody. His heart leapt up. He'd been expecting bad news of some sort, and the contrary was the case. He could barely read it with excitement. He missed whole sentences as his eyes flew down the page. He started again at the top.

Dear Sonny,

I hope this finds you well. I've been thinking about you ever since John James O'Grady's funeral, R.I.P. My sister, Margie and I are here in the Loreto Convent in Dublin. It's a beautiful place but the nuns are quite strict, and it gets lonesome at times. Things are very troubled here. First there was that awful hanging of Kevin Barry, and then Bloody Sunday. Would you believe I was at Croke Park that day with Margie and my brother William. It was very frightening, but we got out safely, thank God. There are ambushes and shootings every day. We saw Michael Collins one morning. I hope you're safe and well. I heard that you and some of your brothers are fighting the Black and Tans. Margie is mad Sinn Féin but my mother and father don't approve. Neither does William, but I think you boys are right. Good luck to you. I'll be home for Christmas and we'll be at Ballycummin Mass on Christmas morning.

Yours sincerely,
Anna Cody.

He felt slightly embarrassed as he re-read the letter, but entirely delighted. Such a smart girl, getting a good education up in Dublin. He'd never been there. He'd barely been to Cork, except for one trip on his way to Birmingham when he was thirteen, when his little sisters were taken to that convent by the priest, their cousin. Orphans God help us, what else were they? He wondered what did she see in him? He never went to school beyond the age of fourteen.

He put the letter back in the envelope and hid it carefully under the pillow. By the time he heard Mike's foot upon the creaking stairs, he was nearly asleep, with a warm feeling, as he thought about meeting Anna on Christmas morning. He'd blown out the candle so Mike wouldn't see the letter and when Mike came in he blundered around in the dark, swearing under his breath as he tried to find his end of the bed. It was pitch dark, and they slept, one at each end of the small, single bed.

'Where's the bloody candle?' swore Mike as he stubbed his toe against the leg of the bed. Sonny mumbled incoherently, feigning sleep. The last thing he remembered, as he fell through a sea of stars, was Mike's cold feet in his face, and Saint Anthony guiding him through a valley of soldiers with guns. Their faces were filled with blood. He couldn't look into their terrible eyes.

In the week before Christmas they cut the holly, and brought ivy from the ivy trees that grew around the flax pond. The berries were red on the holly when Sonny crossed over the river to cut the branches in the Bull Riders. Jasper's hounds howled and bayed from behind his walled estate, eager for the foxhunt on St. Stephen's Day. Berries fell here and there on the ground underneath the bare oaks, like drops of blood into snow; John James's blood. The wood was quiet now in winter sleeping, the moss growing over winter's bones. The hoar frost obliterating spawn and spoor. Covering John James up in Ballycummin graveyard, and Colonel Crake, and Richardson, wherever their bones were hurled.

Late that evening, two figures loomed out of the darkness, into the lantern light. Charlie Hurley and Liam Deasy. Pale-faced, stubble-chinned and gaunt, like wandering precursors to the coming Christ, seeking refuge in the winter solstice. Elizabeth pressed Liam to stay, but he was on his way to pay a poignant visit to his home at Kilmacsimon Quay, where his bereaved parents kept vigil for their late, beloved Patrick. So, after a pleasant interlude, and a hearty meal, he again went on his way on a borrowed saddle-horse that Tull lent him, to speed him homeward. Charlie was enfolded into the Hennessy household like a long-lost brother, and Elizabeth fussed about him, not wanting him to leave. Sonny and Mike vacated their cosy bed to make Charlie welcome, and they themselves slept on straw mattresses on the kitchen floor, made warm by cooking, and the dying fire embers that smouldered until dawn.

The bells were ringing out on Christmas Day, as they made their way to Mass in the common car. The wheels of iron rumbled on the hard road, the horse's hooves clip-clopped in syncopation. It was cold, but the sun was bright. They sat at various angles, their feet hanging out of each corner of the car. Tull drove. Elizabeth sat beside Charlie, and they were packed so close she could smell his manly scent, feel his breath against her cheek. It seemed right to have a strange man beside her. Although surrounded by brothers, she was a manless woman, heading for thirty. Could she dare to hope that this perfect man beside her would have eyes only for her? Was that too vain a hope?

She put that thought aside as the new priest welcomed and blessed his congregation. He spoke fleetingly of the troubled times and asked them to try to put the Bishop's decree into context. But he, Father O'Connell, neither endorsed nor agreed with it. Not after the atrocities of the Tans and Auxiliaries who'd terrorized the countryside and cruelly murdered two of his own contemporaries in cold blood: Father Casey and Canon Magner.

Sonny sought out Anna Cody after Mass and thanked her for her letter. She was even more beautiful than he remembered. Dark hair, dark eyes, a smiling, serious face.

'Are you home for long?' he asked her, as they mingled in the crowd of Massgoers outside in the churchyard. Neighbours wished each other the season's compliments.

'My mother is worried that the times are too troubled to go back to school,' said Anna. 'We may have to stay at home for the next few terms.'

'That will make it easier for us to talk,' said Sonny. 'Maybe we can meet again, when things get better?'

She looked anxious. 'Are you going back to the fight?' she asked.

'I'm afraid we've no choice,' said Sonny. 'We're all marked men now. If we stay at home, the Tans will find us one fine day. And show us no mercy.'

'We'll meet whenever we can,' said Anna. 'Don't worry. I'll be praying for you.'

As he watched her go in the company of her family, he felt a pang of regret not to have said more. But what was to be said? He was tongue-tied.

On St. Stephen's Day, the horns rang out across the country, as the red-coated riders rode in search of Reynard the fox. 'Tally Ho, hounds away,' shouted a sweating Jasper Eustace. Bucolic squire, pitchforked on top of a hunter, seventeen hands high and more. Arrogance in his demeanour, every inch the monarch of all he surveyed. But awkward, slouch-seated, no horseman. Behind him, in various modes of dress, came hard-riding country ladies and gentlemen, in green and red-coated raiments. In jodhpurs, high-booted, sure of their station and eager to let the peasants know they still held sway and hegemony in the land. 'On, on, on,' shouted the absurd-looking Maguire, the Bandon solicitor, in black bowler and cravat, taking his cue from Jasper or from Lord Bandon, who was noticeably absent today. Perhaps fearing for his safety in the times that were in it. As a fox was rousted deep in the Bull Riders Wood, the hounds' ululations filled the air. Off towards the Black Bog went the fox, beaten out by Tull Hennessy, poorly-dressed, but valued for his knowledge of the terrain and his superb horsemanship. They went off across a swathe of countryside called Killnacronnach, over large, wide, snow-covered fields owned by Shorten or Walsh or Hurley. The bugles sounded, ladies clung low over their mounts' withers, rounded backsides hoisted careless in the air, clearing ditches as they went. Some fell into drains, some were knocked off by overhanging branches. Woodcock and pheasant flew up and away in chattering alarm as the ruddy-faced pursuers, like charging cavalry, made havoc of stubble ground, of fallow field and pasture. Everyone loud and shouting and thrilling to the chase.

Tull was out ahead, unbridled, uncontained, hair flying back in the wind as his athletic hunter cleared fence after fence, some so tall neither horse nor rider were visible from the other side. Jasper Eustace and Maguire trundled along in his wake. Tull stoked the hounds into a frenzy as they got a clear scent of the fox and overhauled it, field by field. The fox darted this way and that, crossed small streams, went through dense bracken, crossed roads, lanes and byways, but Tull and the hounds clung tenaciously to its tracks. Eventually they were only specks in the distance as the main hunting party brought up the rear. In deference to the rules of hunting, Tull eventually gave way to the master of the hounds, and as the fox was cornered in a quarry over by Port Na Locha, the pleasure of its dismemberment fell to Jasper. With bulging eyes and tongue almost tumescent, he watched as the clever creature was cornered by twenty-five hungry beagles up against a rocky cliff. First, one grabbed its back and broke it, then a second tore out its throat, and then the savage pack ripped off legs, tail, intestines; ripped out its beating heart, its tongue, its haunted eyes. A harrier-handler on foot beat back the dogs eventually and salvaged the bushy tail, which he handed up to Jasper, to display as a totem on his saddle when they made their triumphant way home later in the day for stirrup cups, brandy and cigars.

Passing by the Hennessy laneway, Tull saluted Jasper, who rode along in weary satiation, but not so weary not to notice that Tull was joined on a bend in the lane by his brothers, Mike and Sonny, and another fellow whom he did not know, but was curious about. He thought no more about it as he was met further along by a motley bunch of colourfully dressed youths and men, with a dead wren bedecked in ribbons hoist on a furze bush. Some were camouflaged in straw coats and wore masks on their faces. They milled around the landlord and gave lusty vent to their atavistic rhymes:

The wran the wran the king of all birds,
St Stephen's Day he got caught in the furze

We hunted him up we hunted him down
We hunted him round all over the town.
Up with the kittle and down with the pot
All silver and no brass, a penny or two
To bury the wran.

Jasper was in ebullient mood. He tossed them some coins and so did Maguire. The wren boys danced jigs of gratitude, tooted on their tin whistles and beat their bodhrans. Jasper and Maguire guffawed at their antics and rode on. The wren boys cavorted along the line of riders, beseeching alms in exaggerated clamour. Flung coins jingled merrily into their tin buckets.

'Bloody pagans,' said Jasper. 'Very entertaining. But what did the poor wren do to deserve such a fate?'

'There are various theories,' said Maguire. 'Some say the wren betrayed St. Stephen to the Jews when he was hiding in some bushes in the early Christian era. Other legends derive from Scandinavian and Celtic mythology. Either way it was all about betrayal, and the poor wren was the culprit.'

'Interesting,' nodded Jasper. 'By Chrisht, Maguire, but you're a mine of information. What happened to St. Stephen by the way?' The accent was thick and broad, with plenty of purchase on the r's and s's, almost more exaggerated than those of the peasant. A different breed to the more effete Anglo-Irish like Lord Bandon.

'He was stoned to death,' said Maguire, with a wry smile. Jasper's eyes were shielded underneath the peak of his riding hat, but a flicker of unease crossed them for a moment, and then was gone. Maguire, for his part, allowed himself a congratulatory plaudit at the depth of his knowledge, as opposed to the ignorance of his more prosperous master of hounds. Even his own accent was more refined. They seemed to wear their lack of education as a badge of pride and distinction, as with their gutteral brogue, these landed Protestants. How could an outsider tell one religion from another? Except that they worshipped in different churches? Certainly not from their speech. There was a poor tradition of education among them, as if it was an impediment to their quotidian preoccupations: the accumulation of money and living the good life. Education was superfluous when you had lots of land. But education had given a fellow like Maguire a leg up, so to speak, propelling him close to the orbit of a celestial body like Jasper; had given him the polished sing-song lilt of the Cork merchant princes. But for how much longer would their stars continue to shine? In their vast complacency, were they aware of the runaway train that was hurtling towards them? Maguire suspected they were blind to it, or, like ostriches, kept their heads in the sand. Either way he would keep a weather-eye out himself, to test which way the wind was blowing. Best to be nimble-footed.

The wren boys followed Tull and his brothers up the winding lane towards the Hennessy farmyard. It being late in the day and a change coming in the sky, which looked like snow yet again to fall, they came on like a tiresome gaggle of relatives who had drunk too much at a party. In lieu of coinage, they'd imbibed whiskey or *poitín* at many doorsteps since early morning, and now, close to the fall of night, they were like a boisterous crew of *saltimbanques*, chiming their discordant instruments through the twilight. When the Hennessys and Charlie reached the farmyard, the wren boys were behind them, cloaked in a sinister anonymity. As if behind their masks they felt free of the shackles of good behaviour, and for a day believed they were allowed run rampant. They were initially a source of amusement, but eventually became an irritation as they overstayed their welcome, juggling about the yard, upsetting the cows. One in particular, more inebriated than the rest, eventually let his mask slip, and there stood the emaciated Maurice Mulcair from the adjacent townland, reeking, rheumy-eyed and demanding drink. Elizabeth came to the door and said, 'You've had enough to drink for the day, Maurice. You should be off home now with you before dark.'

'Ah, Elizabeth,' slurred Mulcair, as he reeled around. 'The finest girl in this part of the country. Have you a drop of mountain dew for a dacent man?'

Elizabeth was firm. 'Not a drop that ever was, Maurice. Sonny will walk you out the short cut now. It's nearly dark and the snow is coming.' And even as she spoke, the first flakelets curled about the bare tree branches, and began silently to fall on roofs and walls.

'Ah, then, to hell with you so,' said Mulcair, as Sonny took him by the arm. The remainder of his retinue dispersed, uttering cheerful maledictions, which, in the circumstances, were taken in good spirit and ignored.

Sonny took him across the yard and through a gate going up the fields, that would lead him in due course on a back lane to his cottage two miles away. As they were walking, Sonny realised he was retracing their footsteps from the arms dump, which were still etched in the frozen snow. Although the new snowflakes were now falling thick and fast, he steered Mulcair the long way westward for fear of drawing attention to the obvious signs of traffic. Although the man was drunk, there was no point in taking any chances and putting their precious hardware at risk.

'Can't we go by *páirc an tobair*?' complained Mulcair. Every field had a name that every neighbour knew.

'We'll go the *seana faiche*,' said Sonny. 'You might fall into a water hole and be drowned over-right me.' And so through the old meadow, not the wellfield. He bade farewell to Mulcair at the end of Sullivan's Lane and turned for home through the softly falling snow.

They went to bed that night as the candlelight cast shadows around the nooks and crannies of the kitchen, and the snowflakes gently fell throughout the night, forming a fresh shroud of white over roads and fields. Something caused Elizabeth to awaken deep in the night. She sat up in bed. The house was sleeping. Gentle snores came from bedrooms, parlour and hall, where heads were thrown down in shakedowns and makeshift mattresses. She got out of bed and it was cold. She took a candle, and holding the grease-streaked handle of the holder, made her way down the stairs. She saw the hands of the grandfather clock touching 5 a.m. The hour when wolves went roaming. The clock's sudden chime on the hour startled her. Some other light caused her to turn towards the window and, looking out, she saw moving headlights coming round the bend in the lane four hundred yards away, passing between the trees, blinking on and off like distant quasars. She knew it was the Black and Tans and her heart sank. She rushed around to the sleeping forms.

'Sonny! Charlie! Mike! Get up! Get up! The Tans are coming!' Sleepy eyes opened and they were up in a flash, inured to danger, trained to sleep like dogs or horses. Forty winks, then instantly awake. They'd slept with their boots and clothes on. They were gone out the door in the blink of an eye. Sonny and Charlie were armed with pistols. If they were caught with them they were dead men. So were the whole family. Where to hide them? In the milk churn that stood outside the door on a concrete plinth. The Tans would never think of looking there. Sonny lifted the tight lid and dropped the guns into the half-filled churn of creamy milk. They gurgled below the surface. If not left too long, the milk would not rust them as much as water. They were gone up the loft steps as fast as their legs could carry them, when the two lorries came round by the cabbage garden into the yard. The dogs ran from the straw rick and barked, as the the lorries slid to a halt. Crabby, angry soldiers piled out, led by Major Percival, the scourge of God. They burst through the door into the kitchen. Elizabeth had hidden behind the hall door, and made her appearance, dishevelled, as if just awoken. A bright torch was shone in her face. She could just make out Percival's figure. The light blinded her. She put her hand up to shade her eyes and was grabbed roughly by a soldier. Another torch picked out the vacated mattresses and discarded blankets. A soldier put his hand down:

'Still warm, sir.'

'Bring everyone downstairs at the double,' shouted Percival, his eyes never leaving Elizabeth's face. Soldiers rushed up the stairs. Tull, Jeremiah and Richie were roused from their beds.

'Where are the others?' roared a soldier. He motioned to two comrades who ran through the rooms, driving bayonets down through mattresses. If anyone was hiding, he was a dead man under a bed. They were all herded into the kitchen, half dressed. Percival had a piece of paper in his hand. 'What's your name?' he barked. 'Jeremiah Hennessy?'

'Yes,' said Jeremiah.

'Tull Hennessy? Richie Hennessy?' He got a grudging response.

'Mike Hennessy, Sonny Hennessy, Charlie Hurley?' No answer.

Percival's men had created pandemonium on the floor above. Wardrobes were knocked over, windows smashed out, glass splintered. Then the racket stopped and the soldiers came back down the stairs. 'We found nothing, sir. We've searched the house from top to bottom.'

Percival paused. The family huddled, traumatised and humiliated. 'Right, then,' said Percival. 'You're all aware that a state of Martial Law has been declared. That means anyone harbouring insurgents, or aiding and abetting them, is guilty of an offence punishable by death. General Macready's Declaration has been well publicised. There are no excuses. Now, we have reason to believe this family is heavily involved in the insurrection. Thus far we have no concrete proof, but we have *prima facie* evidence. We note three mattresses on the floor here which are still warm, suggesting to me that they have very recently been vacated. I mean within the last ten minutes. Now this is as serious a situation as can be imagined. I presume you all understand?' He paused and looked around at the family's alarmed faces. 'Do you understand the gravity of the situation?' he repeated. They nodded, the light trained on their faces.

'It's lucky for you,' he continued, 'that we've found no weapons, or you would all be immediately taken out and shot. We haven't found any weapons, so, in this instance, I'm giving you a reprieve.'

They shuddered, visibly relieved. Then Percival said, 'We're not going to shoot you, but we're going to burn you out.'

He clicked his fingers and three soldiers came through the door, with cans of petrol already filled. They ran around, scattering the liquid on armchairs, beds, and curtains.

'Everybody out,' ordered Percival. The family were herded like sheep out into the freezing yard, past the milk churn that had not divulged its deadly secret. Smoke issued from the kitchen door, and out through the broken windows. Flames licked up to illuminate clevvy, cupboards, dresser. Within three minutes the flames had engulfed the newel post, balusters and stringers of the staircase, and were eating through dry timber floors.

Half a mile away, Sonny, Mike and Charlie looked back to see clouds of dark smoke and flames issuing into the wintry morning half-light.

'We must go back,' said Sonny.

'But we're unarmed,' said Mike. 'We'll be sitting ducks.'

'The dump,' said Sonny. 'We'll get rifles there.'

'No,' said Charlie. 'Too dangerous. If they follow our footsteps they'll find it for sure.'

'We have to risk it,' said Sonny. 'We can't let them get away with this.'

He eventually persuaded them to get rifles from the dump. They dashed across two fields, and quickly armed themselves with a rifle apiece and thirty rounds of ammunition. They crept back towards the farmhouse and as they got closer, they could hear the crackle and roar of the flames, that by now had attacked soffit, bargeboard, fascia, rafters and joists. The roof was caving in. They crept in through a grove of trees behind the yard and, peering through dense branches, could see no sign of soldiers. Tull was leading his alarmed horses out of the stable and Richie was trying, hopelessly, to throw buckets of water on the blazing house. But it was a useless exercise. Percival had prevented them from going near the house until the flames had caught on, and he and his sidekicks stood around, their sinister shadows cast on whitewashed barnloft walls, like ghouls increate. They laughed as Tull and Richie desperately tried to enter the house to salvage some belongings, only to be beaten back, roasted, coughing and blackened by the flames. No further adjurations being necessary, and satisfied that he had well and truly done his monstrous work, Percival ordered his soldiers into the trucks. They were borne away, like vampires through the snow, as the first streaks of a cold dawn came forth in the eastern sky. Elizabeth and Jeremiah stood, crushed and helpless, as their home and their belongings were devoured before their eyes. When she saw her brothers coming back, Elizabeth wept openly, and Charlie put his arms around her. She leant against him in her distress and sought a moment's comfort from his strong embrace. There was little to be said, standing before the elemental thing that was a burning house in the dark of night. Tull came over when the horses had gone galloping off. They made a human chain with buckets and threw more water on the flames, but there was little impression to be made. Within an hour the house was a gutted ruin. They stood around, faces, hands and clothes blackened from smoke, their hearts faltering.

'Where are we going to go?' asked a bewildered Elizabeth. The men stood, trying to think, but it was as if all imagination had deserted them, until Tull said. 'We can stay with the Wilsons for a few nights, and then we can re-roof that outhouse. It used to be an old dwellinghouse.'

He pointed to the low-slung longhouse across the yard, that now provided shelter for the animals.

'With what?' asked Jeremiah, his eyes tired, his spirits fading. 'We have no slate, not even sheet iron.'

'We have straw in the rick and there's reeds in the river,' said Tull. 'We could thatch it.'

'God help us, who remembers the thatching trade?' said a resigned Jeremiah.

'I can learn,' said the enterprising Tull. 'I'll get a few neighbours to help me. Mick Shorten used to be able to do it.'

'Sure Mick Shorten has taken to drink,' said Richie.

'We'll give him plenty of that. We have the worm for making moonshine above in the loft, ready for road,' said Tull, in a half-hearted attempt at humour. They stood around in a circle, and then Elizabeth said, 'We'll go to Wilsons first. No point in standing here, shivering. We'll go to Wilsons and Tull can start on the thatching, like he says. It's better than being out beside the ditches.'

They took whatever they managed to salvage to Wilsons, who welcomed them with open arms. Sonny, Mike and Charlie bade them a troubled farewell and promised to return within a few weeks, when they would help Tull with the building. Before they left, Elizabeth said to Charlie, 'They knew you were here. Percival had your name on a piece of paper. He called it out.'

'My name?' asked Charlie, and his expression clouded. 'Are you sure he had my name?'

'He had your name alright,' said Richie. 'I heard him call it too.'

Charlie looked at Sonny and Mike. 'You know what this means? Someone must have told him. Someone who knows us well.'

They nodded, with heavy hearts, and turned to embrace the remnants and the ruins of family, as the crimson sun came up over Farranthomas Church of Ireland; graceful, clean and steepled, outlined in silhouette. They faced the hills again. No more to run like foxes, only now to run like wolves. And like wolves to hunt down spies who dwelt amongst them.

PART TWO

11

Somewhere around the lakes of Inchigeela, the images of dead men and pouring blood began to fade from Doctor Baldwin's mind. It took several days. He wandered in mute incoherence, a frenzied fire still raging in his head. Oh, for a glimmering girl to soothe the pain. How quickly all can change; life extinguished like a moth burnt by a flame. What fragile candles we all are, under the chilling stars. Lakes lovely, wide and deep, kissed by hazel branches leaning down, as if waving to him in pathetic fallacy. The lordly Lee flowing down from deep Valley Desmond, past Saint Finbarr's exquisite oratory at Gougane Barra, eastward under the shadow of Sheha, to the drowned oak forest of the Gearagh near Macroom. Then looping onward to the city Finbarr founded: *Corcaigh*, on the marsh. He wandered in the woods of oak and ash, of hornbeam and Scots pine: native trees of Ireland; growing since the ice-age, ten thousand years. Since the time of the Tuatha De Danaan, purveyors of magic; the Fir Bolg, small, dark, big-bellied; and the Celts of the yellow hair: *Fionnbarra*. Amidst these hilly, hollow lands, remnants of their mother tongue was still spoken; language of poetry and botany; an object described in twenty ways. An extravagant, generous, sensuous tongue.

Over the following weeks, he walked on narrow roads, through a country laid to waste. Burnt farmhouses, cottages, shebeens, desecrated villages; slaughtered cattle in fallow fields and barren meadows. At night, he saw for miles the flames of other torched dwellings lighting up the sky. In cottages and *cabhlachs* where he sought refuge, he heard of terrible things. A pregnant mother up in Galway, shot in the stomach, left to bleed to death on her own doorstep. Young men picked up at random, taken to military barracks and beaten to death, or castrated; or tortured until they went insane. The revenge of the Black and Tans; fearsome, complete and terrible. Random, burnt, human bones. A holocaust. As if the angel of death passed over, as he'd passed before in the Famine days of Black '47. Lucifer on a white horse. A dead child stretched on every cindered hearth in the parish of Kilmichael, the barony of Uibh Laoghaire, and southwest to Carbery of the Hundred Isles. And which was worse, death by starvation or death by fire and bayonet?

On the high road above Ballingeary, a farmer with a horse and butt stopped, near the townland of Reenaree. 'How far are you going?' he asked.

Doctor Baldwin jumped with alacrity on the buckboard and sat on the opposite side to the farmer. 'As far as you're going,' he replied.

'I'm going to Baile Mhúirne, to get yella male for the pigs.'

'That'll do,' said Doctor Baldwin. 'Yellow meal indeed.' His eyes twinkled. He observed a large-handed, florid-faced peasant, no longer young, hunched on his wagon like a perched crow. Thick-vowelled, curmudgeonly, suspicious. Plainly, but substantially dressed, in dark, tweed coat and pants. Underneath, the tops of his long Johns showing above the belt line. Upholstered with belt and braces, check shirt with stud, no collar, cloth cap, brown boots like a tangler. A well set up man, minding his business. 'Have you come far?' he asked, after allowing some minutes adjustment to pass.

'Kilmichael side,' said Doctor Baldwin, glad to give his weary feet a rest.

The other looked sharply down his hooked nose at him and tugged an earlobe with his right hand.

'You musht be mad,' he said, then shook the reins to get the horse to trot. The Doctor smiled at his directness and asked, 'Why do you say that?'

'Didn't you hear about the battle?'

'I did.'

'Twas an awful slaughter.'

'I know.'

'Twas a wonder you weren't kilt yerself.'

'It was.'

A wonder, a miracle even. Grotesque, cadaverous mouths agape, staring, unseeing eyes. Grey crows pecking at the corpses.

The farmer shot a glance at him again, looking him up and down. A full appraisal. 'What's a man like you doin' travellin' the roads on the wunter's day?'

Doctor Baldwin smiled, but did not feel the need to reply. If the farmer wanted to be truculent, so could he. They were on a high, winding road of dark bogs, brakes of furze and brown, withered bracken, silver birch and sally. They met nobody for a long time. The day was drawing in, the sky was grey. The snow was gone but a cold east wind was blowing. The killer wind of spring.

'That east wind is good for neither man nor bashte,' the farmer said, after travelling in silence, except for the scuffling horse hooves, the grating butt wheels on dirt and gravel, the harsh croak of ravens.

Doctor Baldwin nodded. 'That's a fact,' he said.

'It blows from the steppes of Russia, so they say.'

'You reckon?' asked Baldwin, dryly sardonic.

'I do faith.'

'From Novaya Zemlya or Vladivostock?' The Doctor rattled the names off with a grin.

'You said it,' said the old timer, looking askance, but impressed.

'Do you speak Russian?' asked Doctor Baldwin.

The older man looked at him as if he had two heads. He laughed sourly. 'Russian is it? Sure I can barely speak English. I was brought up with the Irish don't you know.'

'Do you know what Novaya Zemlya means?'

'Chrisht I don't then.'

'New Land.'

'Huh,' said the old timer and spat. ''Tis great to be a scholar all the same.'

They were descending to the valley of the Sullane river, past ancient, medieval oakwoods and the monastery of St. Gobnait. A holy place where people went on pilgrimage for cures and to have prayers answered. Ireland abounded with ruined monasteries: Clonmacnoise, Aghaboe, Cashel, Monasterboice. Island of Saints and Scholars, when the monks preserved European civilisation after the fall of the Roman Empire in the 5th century. A dark cloud of ignorance and barbarity descended on the continent. It was left to the Irish monks to translate the great Greek works of Homer and Aristotle; to keep the Sacred Scripture and create beautiful works of art: the Book of Kells, the Ardagh Chalice, the Cross of Cong. No trace of the golden age now, except for the walls of ruined churches, round towers, high crosses. As desolate as Delos, as lifeless as the Foro Romanum.

When the farmer and the Doctor came down the road to the holy site, there were crowds of pilgrims making a *turas* around the holy well, passing through a wrought-iron archway and under old trees that formed a dark, cave-like approach. A stile led from the holy well, where people did the rounds, encircling the well three times, always in a clockwise direction. Old women, young women, men, children; offering water in thanksgiving to the earth, then to their faces, then drinking the water. Among gravestones, a sculpture of the White Goddess, standing on an egg with a snake curled around her feet. Over one of the church windows, cast in stone, a Sheila-Na-Gig: protector from evil and inducer of fertility; one hand on her belly, the other on her vulva, guarding the sanctuary of procreation. St Gobnait, keeper of bees came here in the 6th Century from Clare, travelling south across Ireland. An angel told her that when she came upon nine white deer, that would be her place of refuge. And here is where she found them, beside the singing Sullane, with oakwoods full of birdsong in the hills above. A place of sunshine, peace and fertility. Here is where she made her stand and founded her community. Still surviving after fifteen hundred years.

The farmer had to stop his cart to let the crowds pass, so narrow was the road.

'It must be St. Gobnait's Day,' said Doctor Baldwin.

'Musht be,' said the farmer.

'Will we do the rounds?' asked the Doctor.

'Indeed and we won't,' said the farmer. 'A lot of oul pagan nonsense.'

'Oh,' said the Doctor a little taken aback. 'I thought you said you spoke Irish?'

'So I did,' said the farmer. 'That doesn't mean I subscribe to this oul cnamhshawling. A black man can speak Irish as well, you know.'

'A black man?' enquired the Doctor, surprised.

'A black Protestant.'

'So you're a Protestant. I'd never have guessed.'

'Hard to tell with a fella sometimes,' said the farmer, 'who he is, or what's on his mind for that matter.'

'I don't think what's happening here has much to do with what religion you are,' said Doctor Baldwin. 'You're quite right to call it a pagan ritual. It goes back through the mists of time, far beyond Christianity.'

'I don't care how old it is. I'll still have no truck with it.' said the old man stubbornly. He paused as he looked at the people mumbling, chanting and miming their rituals; and then he said, 'They tried to shoot my brother, you know.'

'Who did?' asked the Doctor.

'Your crowd.'

'My crowd?'

The old man looked suddenly bitter. 'The boys of the Column.'

'What makes you think they're my crowd?' asked the Doctor.

'I can feel it in me waters,' said the old man, pulling his coat tightly around him as if to ward off evil spirits like the pilgrims on their *turas*.

'It's dangerous to jump to conclusions,' said Doctor Baldwin.

'You can't fool me,' said the old man and curled his lip.

'What would you say if I told you I saved the life of an Auxiliary soldier at Kilmichael?'

The old man shrugged. 'I'd say you were a damn fool.'

Doctor Baldwin laughed. 'Damned if you do and damned if you don't, is that it?'

'You musht be a doctor, then?' said the old timer, unconvinced.

'Something like that,' said Baldwin. There was a further pause. Doctor Baldwin tried to get inside his skin, but he was a doughty old bird.

'What's this about your brother anyway?'

'He had to jump a nine-bar gate to get away from 'em,' said the farmer and continued. 'And he's not a young man. He's seventy, if he's a day.'

'And he escaped did he?'

'No, they let him go in the wind-up. Don't get me wrong. The brother is mad against the Volunteers, and why shouldn't he be? They tried to say he was a spy, but they didn't have the proof. They had suspicions, but their commander let him go because of the element of doubt. But they gave him twenty-four hours to quit the country.'

'And did he go?'

'Sure where could he go? He's an old man, a middling-small farmer. Where could any of us go?'

'Do you think they'll come after him again?'

'Let 'em come,' said the old man. 'We'll be ready for 'em the next time. With the shotguns.'

'You're a brave man,' said the Doctor. 'But do you think that's wise? You heard what they did at Kilmichael?'

'I did.'

'Well, I saw what they did. Not a very nice sight.'

The old man stopped feeling sorry for himself all of a sudden. 'You didn't really save one a' them lads, did you?'

'I did,' said the Doctor. 'His name was Lieutenant Forde. Your friends in Macroom Castle will verify that.'

The old man looked away, as Doctor Baldwin stepped down from the butt. 'They're no friends of mine. I'd sooner take a chance with the Column boys than trusht a British bastard.'

'You're a complex man,' smiled Doctor Baldwin. The old man looked at him with a steady gaze. Then his eyes drifted downwards, from his bowler hat, to his slightly frayed collar, down past his dandy waistcoat, gold watch and chain, to his scuffed, unpolished boots.

'You're no doctor,' he said eventually. 'I'd say you're a man of straw.'

Doctor Baldwin laughed long and loud at the old man's perspicacity. Laughed 'til the tears ran down his cheeks. He wiped his eyes and said, 'You're a perspicacious man. May I ask your name?'

'Jennings,' said the old man, bidding him farewell with an uneasy look, as if there was more to his passenger than quite met the eye. He spoke in Irish: '*Go neirí an bóthar leat,*' he said. May the road rise with you.

He drank too much in Scannel's tavern in Ballymakeera that night. He'd entered in the gloom where men were drinking at a long bar, garrulously, after saying their prayers up at the holy well. Earlier, some respectable women drank glasses of sherry in a livingroom off the bar, but they had hurried away soon after nightfall, in horses and traps, common cars and bicycles made for two. Driven by those husbands who were biddable. The residue who remained were rough men, corner boys and labourers, and a few brightly-clad younger women, whom pious older women might call whipsters or jades, or even *striopaigh*. These kept up an excited clamour over in a snug, where a fire burned in a grate. Doctor Baldwin threw the odd glance in their direction and noted one in particular, who returned his glances with a come hither look in her eyes. But his immediate focus was on a small group of drinkers who seemed to be in thrall to a strapping, rheumy-eyed fellow, straddling a strategic corner of the bar, saying, 'Up the Republic,' and looking around belligerently at anyone who didn't heartily condone his sentiments. From his position, he was able to command a view of both doors of the low-ceilinged tavern, and the comings and goings of customers, most of whom he greeted with a surly familiarity. Doctor

Baldwin saw him bristle as he ordered a whiskey from the put-upon barman, who was eager to accommodate new business, and at the same time keep his regulars reasonably constrained, without alienating them. A delicate balancing act.

'If Liam Lynch isn't the greatest bleddy man in North Cork, my name isn't Murphy Deirbh,' said the fellow. His hunched-over admirers kept saying, 'Hear, hear,' and winking to each other, as the big fellow broke into snatches of song, while being half-heartedly sushed up by the pusillanimous barman:

> *'On the twenty-eighth day of November,*
> *The Tans left the town of Macroom.*
> *They were seated in two Crossley tenders*
> *That led them right into their doom...'*

'That'll do now, John Joseph,' said the barman, and Murphy quietened momentarily, looking around for some other focus for his frustration.

Doctor Baldwin sank his first half-one and ordered another. How quickly the local bards got busy with their quills. A ballad already composed about the Kilmichael ambush. Boastful public house words. Empty sound and fury, that would rise louder as the night progressed, but by dawn would be lower than a cur's whimper. The more Murphy Deirbh drank, the more quarrelsome he became. Doctor Baldwin had fallen into conversation with a quiet, studious type of man of middle years, sitting down along the bar, who said he was a teacher named Tadgh Sweeney from Clondrohid.

Murphy Deirbh didn't like being ignored. He stood up off his high stool and advanced ominously towards the Doctor. 'I'll challenge anyone here to name a better man than Liam Lynch above in the Galtee mountains.'

Doctor Baldwin's new acquaintance replied, while still looking into his pint of stout, 'There's a lot of good men around.'

'Name one,' said Murphy Deirbh, moving closer. 'Name one, if your name is Tadhg Sweeney? Or maybe your new friend here has a tongue in his head?'

Doctor Baldwin turned slowly and looked him steadily in the eye. 'I know a few good men alright,' he said, 'but they don't go around spouting *ráiméis* in public houses late at night.'

Murphy Deirbh's big chin set into a pugilistic jut. 'By the Lord God I won't shtand here and be insulted by any man, no matter what the cut of his jib. I know a few fellows who'd put manners on the likes of you.'

'You might know them, but do they know you?' enquired the Doctor smoothly.

Murphy Deirbh was taken aback by the retort. His fists bunched and unbunched and his jaws clinched. There was a reek of whiskey and of sweat from him. 'By Jesus...' he began, and the teacher got up to intervene, 'Go on away now, John Joseph, and leave this decent man to have his drink.'

'Dacent man is it? He has the look of a Castle hack to me and so he does. Dacent my arse.'

'We have a name for the likes of you where I come from,' said Doctor Baldwin, by now a little inebriated himself, having downed three shots of booze in quick succession.

Murphy tried to get his eyes to focus. 'You do?'

'Yes,' said the Doctor, conceding no ground. 'We'd call you an armchair Republican. All talk and no action.'

'By Jasus, but you're a saucy boy,' said Murphy Deirbh, stumped for words.

The barman came down and said to the teacher, 'Tadhg, better take your friend over to the snug. I'll send ye over a few balls of malt on the house, and then ye'd better be on ye're way. Otherwise we'll have more trouble than we bargained for.' He turned to Doctor Baldwin. 'Sorry to have to interfere now, sir, but you see, I have regular customers who'll be here again tomorrow, while you may not.'

'No offence taken, my good man,' said Doctor Baldwin urbanely. 'I understand your position. Your customer, John Joseph Murphy Deirbh doesn't frighten me. I've come across many more intimidating characters in recent weeks than him.'

'I'm sure you have, I'm sure you have,' said the barman.

They were ushered over to the snug beside the gaily-dressed young women, who had by now become very quiet, as they listened to the drama unfolding. The one who had eyed Doctor Baldwin earlier, caught his eye again and said admiringly. 'Fair play to you, sir. There's not too many people round here who'd stand up to Murphy Deirbh.'

'Well, thank you young lady, you're very complimentary,' smiled the Doctor. 'But you see, with fellows like that, their bark is worse than their bite. If he was an IRA man, he wouldn't be inside here telling everyone. The IRA are serious men.'

'I like a man with gumption,' she said, and sat a little closer to him. The room grew noisier, and the talk resumed of war and weather, and the price of pigs. Murphy Deirbh sulked at the far end of the bar, which was now quite warm, from the pressing of bodies together in the cramped space, and the heat thrown from the dying fire. Doctor Baldwin basked in the glow which the attractive outsider will invariably get from members of the opposite sex in a remote outpost.

'I like the way you dress,' he heard the girl say. 'And the way you smell. Are you a gentleman or a scholar?' It sounded like the chirping of a sparrow, or a bee buzzing. Soothing, but inconsequential. Glasses tinkled, hands touched knees and shoulders; breasts.

He awoke in the late morning of the following day, in the dark confines of a caravan, down a boreen on the edge of the village. He'd spent the night with the colourfully-coiffured tinker girl, but he could remember little about the finish of the evening. Even less of his fumbling encounter amidst the shoddy furniture of the caravan. And then he felt a terrible guilt as he beheld the wraith-like creature, now without paint or powder, who'd comforted him in the small hours. He wanted to be gone and quickly too, but the girl seemed in no hurry for him to leave. Eager perhaps to make a return on her investment. He saw that she was maybe thirty; though the night before, in the seductive shadows, she'd appeared younger. He heard a baby crying in a small cot in a corner. Mother of God, what had he let himself in for? His immediate impulse was to gather his legs out of there as fast as he could, but the pleading hurt in the girl's face caused him to waver.

'Ah, sir, sure how is my lovely gentleman feeling today?'

'My head is pounding so badly I feel it's going to burst,' he moaned, as he stood up, stooping under the low roof. The baby became startled and began to shriek. He put his hands to his ears.

'Ah, he's just a bit scared of you, sir. Don't worry, he'll quieten down in a second.'

He looked around, appalled. 'I don't remember much about the end of the night. Did we spend it here?'

'Indeed and we did, sir,' she said, and gave a smile that was intended to make him feel ashamed.

'And did we? I mean, as it were, did anything...?'

'No,' she smiled. 'Sure you're like all men with drink taken. All talk and no action. A bit like that Murhpy Deirbh fellow in the public house.'

'Oh, Jesus, Mary and Joseph,' he said. He fished in his pockets and took out whatever remaining coins were left; the jetsam of his night of dabauchery. 'Here, this is for the baby. Is he hungry?'

'If he was, sure he couldn't eat money anyway,' she laughed. 'Here, come on sir, come over here, the bed is still warm. Maybe you'd like to stay a little bit longer?'

She lay on the unkempt bed and undid the top of her blouse. With that, there was a sound, a thumping noise outside, and a strapping young tinker stood in the door with a ferocious scowl on his face. His two ape-like arms hung loosely and his fingers twitched. The tinker girl sat up in the bed and pulled up her garments to cover her breasts.

'Is that your husband?' the Doctor half whispered to her out of the side of his mouth.

She laughed. 'Husband how are you. That's my man, Davy, back from the fair of Dunmanway.'

Doctor Baldwin took a pace forward, and squared himself. The tinker girl uttered a loud giggle of laughter, stretched out her arms and lay flat on the bed. Doctor Baldwin rushed for the door and the tinker stepped aside, striking him a terrible blow on the jaw as he passed him. The Doctor fell in a heap onto the muddy dyke of the road. The tinker jumped on him, swift as a cat, and began pummelling him. The Doctor was pinned down, but with a huge effort managed to flip the tinker over backward. Jumping to his feet, he turned and ran. The tinker stood panting from his effort, as the tinker girl came down the steps, waving and shouting. 'Goodbye, sir,' she said, 'Goodbye my lovely gentleman.'

When he was a good two hundred yards down to a bend in the road, he stopped and looked back. The young tinker had lifted the girl in his arms, and she was smiling and kissing him as he carried her into the caravan. The Doctor shook his head in disbelief. The country was gone mad. Things weren't half settled. It was time to head for home.

12

T he screams from the dungeons below invaded his ears all afternoon long. Maurice Mulcair sat in the big, cold, empty canteen in Bandon military barracks, and tried to shut his senses off against the infernal sounds. He shifted on his seat, he moved to another seat further away from the door, he pulled his cap down over his ears. But the chilling, sobbing cries seemed to come up through the cold, concrete floor like poisonous vapours from the earth's core. 'Oh God! Oh God! No more! Please, no more!'

He ordered another whiskey from the barman who came and went, silently, sullenly, like a ghost. He looked around the bleak, comfortless space: rough deal tables, bare walls, high ceilings. No pictures, no adornments. A stale smell of damp and urine. Seats as hard as granite against his bony backside, and cold as limestone to the touch of his shaky hand. The whiskey, sharp and burning, hit the back of his throat. Harsh as tar. He'd need a gallon of the stuff to quell awareness. To knock him cold. Sometimes, a squaddie or two came in, tossed back a couple of half-ones with cheerful bonhomie, and departed again. Some might look at him, some might nod, but none spoke to him. Mulcair was like an outcast, a leper, a pariah. Even the British soldiers hated an informer. Though he was a key facilitator to their abominable work, he was anathema, even to them. But did they not hear the screams as well? Or did they have hearts of stone?

Silence sometimes descended, quieter than thistledown falling on an August meadow. And he would momentarily forget his station. Then other sounds impinged upon his ears, coming in through the high, narrow windows, iron-barred and shuttered. A truck starting up outside on the square of the bleak building: a plain, grim, monolithic institution, from which no light or hope escaped. The house of the dead that always filled him with foreboding on his secret visits. He heard shouts of soldiers on parade, ravens croaking around the windy trees, jackdaws and magpies scavenging on roof and chimney. And then the dreadful screams breaking in once more. Oh, Jesus, make them stop.

He knew what they were doing very well, but the imagined horror was even more terrible than the actual. He'd been privy to their handiwork the day they brought Tom Hales and Patrick Harte in last July. Thanks to him. Betray your neighbour for five pounds a week. Judas Iscariot. How he hated his weakness for drink, for lucre. But he was caught in a cleft stick now. If he stopped, the British would turn him over to the IRA and death would be swift and unceremonious. No quarter given to traitors.

He'd watched through a secret vent as they got to work on Hales and Harte. Forced to watch. This was their game. Make him wait around for hours before they paid him. Make him suffer for his sins. Oh, how he wished he could fly. Mulcair had feet of clay. The images were seared into his brain. Both men brought in, shackled hand and foot. Already with evidence of mistreatment: welts, cuts, bruises, both staggering, bowed, half-broken. But they were tough, perhaps unbreakable in spirit, whatever of body. Hales was laid upon a table and three or four men got to work on him, like crude surgeons of the 17th century, intent upon their ghoulish experiments, salvaging living organs from a condemned man. Pinioned to the table with leather straps, his fingernails were pulled out slowly, one by one. Mulcair had to watch, as his neighbour and countryman was crucified before his eyes. All the while, his torturers kept up a tirade of haranguing shouts. Demanding details of colleagues, fellow travellers, armaments. With no information forthcoming from the bloodied man, his assailants set to work on his genitals. Mulcair had to close his eyes, the vista too unspeakable. His besieged senses could hear only moans of agony, see only blood and skin, smell only sweat and faeces. The romper room of hell.

Next, he saw Patrick Harte, with his hands tied in front of him, attached to a long rope, a blindfold around his eyes, being led like a blind horse to the top of a long, concrete stairs. At a given signal, two soldiers behind him at the top of the stairs gave a concerted shove, and another soldier at the bottom of the stairs pulled the rope. With no limbs to support him and no sight to his blinkered eyes, Harte was sent tumbling down, his unprotected head thudding on every step. When he rumbled to the bottom his head was battered to a bloody pulp. Half conscious, he was hustled and dragged again to the top of the stairs. Then the exercise was repeated.

That was six months ago. Harte went mad. His brain damaged beyond repair. The last Mulcair heard was that he was in a lunatic asylum. Locked in like a caged, peculiar beast, to be poked and prodded till he died. Hales was sent to Dartmoor or Pentonville, or was it Wormwood Scrubs? They couldn't break him, but they battered him bad. Mulcair sank another whiskey and sighed. At last the screams had stopped echoing up from the basement. The job was done for another day. The present pair that he'd pointed out for culling, O'Donovan and Hegarty, would be well rendered by now. Probably both shot through the head, but not before their testicles had been fed to the dogs. 'Twas one way of doing things, bejasus. Ah well. He was too drunk to care. No doubt they'd be found somewhere out along the road in the morning, or the morning after, or maybe a week later. Thrown out of a passing lorry like a pair of wet sacks, and left to moulder in the undergrowth until the rats and worms devoured them. Those British knew what they were doing right enough. Sow terror and fear by burning and degradation. Psychological stuff you'd call it. He'd gotten to know a few of them by name: Perrier, Hotblack, Halahan, and of course Major Percival. Although they were his paymasters, Mulcair knew they were bad eggs. They revelled in debasement.

He shrugged, rubbed his hands together and gave a chuckle; a kind of demented eructation. What a clever fellow he was? And it gave him a certain amount of power and influence, by Dad. If only those arrogant boys, Tom Barry and Charlie Hurley, and them wild Hennessy boys; if they only knew how many of their comrades he'd put paid to? That might take the steam off their piss, as the man said. Soften their coughs. Take them two fellows he set up just before Christmas, for instance, them two Essex soldiers from the barracks, who went to Tom Barry, saying they were deserters. That was his idea. The oldest trick in the book: sending out spies posing as deserters into enemy lines. Tom Barry thought he was too clever by half. Mulcair heard through the grapevine that Barry was thinking of making a huge assault with sixty Volunteers on the barracks in Bandon. If they could get past the main gate undetected, they'd have a free run inside, and with the element of surprise they'd go through the place like a dose of salts. They'd land a right prize if they succeeded. The bloody place could equip a small army with hardware. A battery of eight-pounder guns, a thousand rifles, four armoured cars, twenty-four lorries, two hundred and fifty thousand rounds of ammo, Mills bombs, shells, explosives. Christ man, if the IRA got their hands on all that, with three thousand men now fully armed, they'd go through Munster like Cromwell's army. Mulcair knew that. He'd been a soldier himself, fighting for the British in the Great War: most of the best fighting men were Irish.

Anyway, he'd planted the idea to have these two fellows from the barracks try to join the IRA as deserters, *mar dhea*. Barry was suspicious at first, but after a good bit of questioning, they convinced him they were genuine. The idea was that the brother of one of them, who was also a soldier, would leave the main entrance gate open on a specific evening, thereby allowing the IRA a free run at taking the barracks by surprise. The man was to be paid for his trouble. When they'd arranged on the agreed evening to get the spare key of the gate from the deserter's brother, an advance party of three Volunteers arrived at the appointed spot for the handover. Just at that moment, a large party of Essex soldiers who lay in in wait, jumped out from behind the ditch and arrested the three: Galvin, Begley and O'Donoughue. They were given short shrift. A shot each to the forehead and then dumped under some bushes in Lord Bandon's estate, minus their goolies of course. Mulcair had orchestrated the whole damn thing. They didn't show him any respect. Said he was a milquetoast, a fawning British lackey, for fighting in the Great War. He'd shown them not to trifle with Maurice Mulcair. Oh, yes.

He looked around the deserted canteen. The barman had turned on a dim light over in a corner. Outside, darkness had descended on the cold, winter's evening. He stood up and staggered drunkenly towards the door. Was there anyone in this damned place prepared to drive him home? He'd earned his crust for today, by Christ.

The night was still, clear and cold. A full moon shone down over wide fields, and glinted off the river in a long, silver streak. The river flowed slowly here and the land was rich, the soil deep. Some of the fields were ploughed, but fallow. Waiting for spring. The shadows of bare-branched beech and ash trees were flung far out across the cold land in the moonlight. No birds stirred or sang. Sometimes a hungry fox barked and a high, sharp cry pierced the silence; some small animal or bird meeting its end in the eternal battle between predator and prey. It was well after midnight. Four riders came slowly down along a narrow road that ran towards the river where it crossed another, larger main road. There was a sound of leather creaking, a jingle of bridle bits; but the clop of horse hooves was muffled because the riders kept to the grass verges. It was hard to see the riders' faces in the shadows. The road was wooded on either side and they kept their caps pulled low. Two of them rode ahead; the other two followed, a short distance behind, in single file. The wary eyes of the two in front swept the landscape, as if they were looking for something. Before they reached the crossroads, where the side road met the main road, they turned left through a gap into a field and rode along the inside of the ditch, that in high summer would burst out heavy with brambled blackberries, whortleberries, meadowsweet and ladysmock; but which now was beaten back and shorn of undergrowth. They rode along towards a corner of the field. The other two followed behind, still in single file. The two in front rode side by side. The horse hooves sank a little way into the softish ground and a hoar frost covered the bare grass, making the field look white and magical. The frost crackled under the horse hooves. The lead riders wore full soldiers' uniforms and peaked caps. The last rider wore a tasselled beret, and the one in the middle, a cloth cap. When they came to the corner, they turned left along the ditch that ran by the main road. Shadows of horses and shadows of riders travelled with them, like dark guardian angels. The two behind were silent and the two in front spoke scarcely at all, but appeared to be gauging the width of fields, the strength of ditches, the size of houses. Their communication with each other appeared to be monosyllabic, almost telepathic. They eventually went through another gap from the field onto the main road, and turned west, back towards the crossroads. They moved at the same methodical, slow speed for a couple of hundred yards. Suddenly the lead horse shied violently and reared backwards, nearly throwing its rider. With soothing words the lead rider controlled his horse and turned it back towards the source of its fright. The horse stepped high, snorted through its nostrils and blew out its breath. The other horses pranced and moved with sideways gaits, imitating the lead horse. Then the lead rider spotted the source of the alarm. A man lay in the side of the ditch, as if sleeping. The first two riders dismounted and came towards the sleeping figure. The lead rider shone a torch in his face. The man was asleep and the smell of whiskey suggested he was drunk as well. The lead rider kicked his boot and the man awoke with a start. He sat up, shading his eyes from the torchlight.

'What...' he asked. 'Who are you?'

'We're soldiers. What are you doing here?' said the leader. The man blinked, stood up slowly, shakily, and rubbed his hand across his mouth. Then he rubbed his eyes and scratched under his armpits. His clothes were crumpled, foul smelling, dishevelled. He looked keenly at the soldiers who had turned off the torchlight. He noticed the soldiers' uniforms. 'It's alright, sir,' he blurted. 'I'm one of ye're own. I just left the Bandon barracks.'

'What's your name?' asked the leader.

'Mulcair,' said the drunken man. 'Maurice Mulcair. I'm a friend. I know the Major well.'

'You do?' asked the leader.

The man gave a reassuring laugh. 'Indeed I do. I know Major Percival very well.'

'If you know Major Percival, what are you doing in a drunken stupor on the side of the road? I doubt the Major associates with many people like you?'

'The Major knows me well, I tell you,' said Mulcair, widening his bloodshot eyes. 'I work for him.'

The leader turned back to his second-in-command who had also dismounted: 'Have you ever seen this man in the barracks?'

The second soldier peered keenly at Mulcair and said, 'Never seen him before, sir.'

'Oh, here, hang on. I've never seen you either. But I go there all the time I tell you. I was driven here by a lorry load of Essex a couple of hours ago. I'd a few too many drinks so I fell asleep, that's all. That's why I'm out here in the middle of the night. I should be at home asleep in my bed long ago.' He gave a rueful laugh.

The leader turned to his second-in-command and spoke low to him. Mulcair couldn't hear what they said although he strained his ears to listen. He'd sobered up quite quickly. He suddenly felt anxious. He shivered.

'Listen, why don't you take me back in if you don't believe me? The Major will vouch for me.'

'Look here, Mr. Mulcair, you may or may not be who you say you are, but we can't take a chance with you in case you're a Shinner,' said the leader. 'Come along with us down the side road here. We'll be out of sight of any passersby and you can answer some more questions for us. If your story holds up we'll let you go.'

'There's divil a fear 'twon't hold up,' said Mulcair as they walked along. 'Who are the other two on the horses anyway?'

'One is a soldier, the other is a prisoner whom we suspect may be in the IRA'

'I'll soon tell you if he is or not,' said Mulcair. 'I might know him.'

'All in good time, Mr. Mulcair,' said the leader. 'First we must find out a bit more about yourself.'

'Fire away,' said Mulcair, feeling more confident.

'How long have you been working for us?' asked the leader.

'Since the beginning of last year, nearly twelve months now.'

'You say you've given us names of Shinners. Who exactly?'

Mulcair gave a little snort. 'So many, I can hardly remember them all. But let me see. There's two fellows called Hegarty and Donovan that are in there at the moment. I heard them getting a right going-over this afternoon. And them three boyos whom ye shot when they tried to get the keys of the barracks. I was responsible for delivering the goods on them.'

'And who do you know in the organisation that we may not know about?' asked the leader.

Mulcair laughed. 'Yerra *mo léir*, my dear man, I know them all. The Lordans, the Foleys, the Corcorans, the Callaghans. There's a nest of them up there around Castletown and Newcestown. Enniskean too. Hennessys, Crowleys, O'Mahonys. I could go on all night.'

'I see,' said the leader. 'And tell me, how much are you paid for all this?'

'Five pounds a week, and sometimes more, if I have good news.'

The leader paused and continued to regard Mulcair. The moon shone between the bare branches on the small group. Mulcair was feeling almost cocky. 'Anything else you want to know?' he asked.

'Do you work alone?' asked the leader.

'I do,' said Mulcair, 'But I know there's others who give good information.'

'Such as?'

'I know that Jasper Eustace, he's a big squire; I know he's involved with a group, an intelligence ring called The Anti-Sinn Féin Society. They're well organised. They know plenty.'

'So you believe they've also given us names of IRA men?'

'You can be sure they have,' said Mulcair. 'I'm good, but I can't do it all on my own. Them other fellows deserve some credit as well.' Mulcair gave a hearty, exaggerated laugh that belied his nervousness.

The leader gave a dry chuckle in response. He looked behind at his men and looked back to Mulcair. 'There is one final thing,' he said.

'The prisoner on horseback here. He won't tell us his name or anything about himself. I wonder could you identify him for us?'

'Bring him up, bring him up,' said Mulcair. 'I'm bound to know him.'

The two ridden horses were brought into the circle. The leader shone the torch up at the prisoner and Mulcair found himself looking into Sonny Hennessy's face. His jaw dropped. He grabbed the leader's arm and pulled him aside, whispering. 'I know him well. He's young Hennessy. Sonny Hennessy. He's a neighbour of mine.'

'We're taking him to Bandon for questioning,' replied the leader.

Mulcair looked alarmed. 'You can't do that,' he whispered in agitation. 'You can't bring *him* to Bandon. He knows me. He might get word out about me. I'd be finished. Shoot him. Shoot him here and now.'

'Shoot a man without an admission of guilt by him. We can't do that.' said the leader.

'You can,' said Mulcair, beginning to sweat. 'You'll have to. He knows me I tell you. Here, give me your gun. I'll do it myself.'

'You will?' asked the leader and stared at him. He produced a revolver from inside his coat.

Mulcair tried to grab it. 'I'll do it.' he said. 'Just give me the gun.'

'Would you really shoot me, Maurice?' asked Sonny from atop the horse.

Mulcair grew agitated. He walked towards Sonny. He walked back. He put his hands to his head, threw his arms out, spun on his heel, going back and forth.

'I'll have to. I'll have to.' He was mumbling to himself, quite unable to face Sonny.

'Would you shoot your neighbour, Maurice?' asked Sonny. 'I've known you since I was a boy. I thought you were on our side? We were always good to you.'

'Why should I be on ye're side?' asked Mulcair. 'Ye all sneered at me because I was in the British Army. But I had my reasons for going. To fight for the rights of small nations. And I needed money. At least the British Army paid my wages. I couldn't get work at home. We were poor. We were hungry.'

'What about this small nation, Maurice?' asked Sonny, smiling. 'Doesn't it have rights too?'

Mulcair suddenly smelt a rat. Why was he smiling so casually? He whirled around to face the leader. He found himself staring down the barrel of a Peter the Painter pistol. His eyes narrowed. 'What are you pointing that at me for?' he asked. Then it dawned on him. 'Who are you?' he asked. 'You're not a British officer are you?'

'No I'm not,' said the other. 'I'm Tom Barry. One of those fellows you'd like to betray.'

Mulcair's eyes flickered from Sonny on the horse to Barry, standing, and then to the other man beside him. 'And who are you?' he asked in panic.

The man took his cap off his dark-haired head. 'I'm Charlie Hurley,' he said. 'And that man on the other horse is Liam Deasy.'

Mulcair sat down on the side of the ditch. 'You're the leaders,' he whispered. 'You're the leaders of the IRA. But where did you get the British officers' uniforms? Of course, at Kilmichael. Oh, Jesus, you got them at Kilmichael.'

He began to shake his head from side to side. Then he began to sob. The cold moon still shone bright and brilliant in the midnight sky.

'Come along, Maurice,' said Tom Barry, putting his hand on his shoulder. They all walked up the narrow road, under the trees.

Moonbeams danced in through a tall bedroom window in a big, rambling country house and caressed Eleanore Eustace's strawberry blonde hair. She was sitting at a mahogany dressing table, with a large centre mirror and two slender wing mirrors, brushing her tumultuous, tangled tresses with a smooth-handled hairbrush. She could see Doctor James Baldwin reflected in the mirror, reclining nonchalantly on the large, four-poster bed behind her. She wore a black, satin nightslip, ornately hemmed, that reached to just above her knees, and her shoulders were exposed except for two thin straps that held up her slip. Her decolletage was deep and plunging, her soft, generous breasts thrown back in reflection towards Doctor Baldwin in the bed. The room was huge and airy with two panelled windows front and rear. There was a teak wardrobe, with its double doors ajar, revealing on one side, a selection of Eleanore's elegant dresses, and on the other side, Jasper's suits and shirts. She kept her blouses separately in an antique, carved portmanteau. A fire burned in a grate beneath a beautiful, marble fireplace. The room was warm, with a thick Persian carpet laid on the polished wood floor, and it smelt of sweet, Fragonard perfume.

Doctor Baldwin put his arms behind his head, stretched, and leant back against the headboard, supported by a pile of crumpled, downy pillows. The sheets and covers of the unmade bed were draped casually over the lower half of his semi-naked body. Everything felt soft, warm and silken to the touch. 'Did God ever make anything more perfect than a woman's bare shoulders in the moonlight?' he said eventually.

Eleanore's unruly hair had finally succumbed to the brushstrokes, and it flowed in cascades of curls down her back. She surveyed him in the mirror without smiling. Yet her brown eyes had a kind of an ironic twinkle. 'You'll be shot if Jasper comes home and finds you here,' she said.

He smiled and said, 'Pistols for two, coffee for one.'

'What ever do you mean?' she asked.

'It's a duelling term,' he explained. 'An honourable way to go. Shot at dawn, defending a lady's honour.'

'If you think Jasper would go to the trouble of allowing you to defend yourself in a duel, you're deluding yourself,' said Eleanore scornfully.'

'You don't think he would?' asked Baldwin, disappointed.

'A vagabond like you?' she laughed. 'He'd shoot you like a dog.'

'My dear Eleanore, you say the cruellest things,' he said. 'But it's that very cruelty that makes you irresistible to a man.'

'You're a great one for the idle words,' she said and turned to face him. Her face was soft, with enormous brown eyes, a wide, sensuous mouth, skin like alabaster and a magnificent mane of hair. Eleanore Eustace was made for love.

'You're a very pessimistic woman, despite the gifts of beauty nature gave you. Sure why don't you let me lie here in dreamful ease and drink in your beauty while the night is young?'

'It's four in the morning,' she said. 'Scarcely young. No more than yourself.'

'I thought you said he was gone for four days to the Cork Exhibition?' he said.

'Four days is up tomorrow, and I want no trace or tidings of you to be seen around here by then.'

'If you ask me, that man doesn't deserve to be married to a woman like you. Sure he gets more excitement out of a steam engine than he does from a woman's body.'

'Huh,' she shrugged, unconvinced, and began to move around the room, hurriedly putting everything back in its place.

Earlier, her cries of passion flew out through windows, over demesne walls and woods, so loudly that if her husband were a mile away he'd have heard them. Earlier still she'd met Doctor Baldwin on the road, just as she was turning her horse and trap in through the gates of the long, tree-lined avenue leading to the house on the hill. He'd looked forlorn and weary and on an impulse she stopped and told him to climb up. She'd welcomed him up to the house for tea. Since Jasper left three days before, she was alone except for the workmen in their cottages. But lonely long before that. Ever since the day her father made the match with the wealthy but unsympathetic Eustace, her life was comfortable but loveless. She herself was to blame as well, of course. She liked as smooth a run through life as possible, and she got that from Jasper: material support, but not spiritual or emotional sustenance. And the touch of his gauche hand on her body made her recoil.

On seeing the rakish, but darkly handsome Doctor, she was filled with a sudden and intense longing for the human touch. And a greater urge to give succour to the vulnerable wanderer, who seemed to her like a pilgrim in the wilderness. What strange creatures women were. Mysterious beyond all comprehension. He thought as he looked at her, now clothed again, how she, like all women, could justify two contradictory impulses without the least concern. In her nakedness she'd been unbridled, fiercely passionate, moaning unspeakable words to him. Scratching, tearing at his flesh, as if trying to wring some permanent, unnameable rapture from their interwoven limbs. She lead him on, teasing, touching, kissing; sounds and smells of ecstasy between them, ending with a long, shattering climax that buckled through the room and echoed out as if it would ignite with fire the cold, lifeless plateaux of the moon, and bring heaven down to earth. But now, reclothed, vulnerability, mystery and emotion were put aside, and a different person busied herself in putting house in order. Her clothes were like a shield to subdue and harness desire.

She looked at him and smiled in spite of herself. What was he? A child? What was it about some men that melted women's hearts? The dark, wounded eyes, the bruised mouth? Taken individually, Doctor Baldwin's features didn't fit a classical mould, but, taken as a whole, he looked as magnetic as a broken-down Italian count. Oh, how a woman could dream of taking such a man and changing him. But into what? Dutiful husband, hard-working breadwinner, dependable father, faithful lover? And change a prince into a frog?

What did James Baldwin represent to a woman? With his sympathetic ways, his gentle touch, his sparkling conversation and his knowledge of medicine, was he an alluring fantasy to be indulged and then forsaken? Little chance of taming his rebel heart. And so the perfect man wasn't really that. As if she ever thought otherwise. But he made her feel beautiful, admired and above all, desired. A woman could give herself to a man like that and let slip the chains of the begrudging world. If only for one night. But one night was sufficient. She finished her stowing away and gathering up. He regarded her from the bed with eyes that were uncritical and warm. God, how good he made her feel, though she did not let him see it, until tears suddenly flooded her eyes. She turned away from him, still not fully clothed, still uncertain.

He sensed her hesitation. 'Come over here, my dear, and dry your tears,' he said, extending his arms towards her. She came towards him slowly and he drew her down onto the bed. Her body shook with sobs.

'There,' he said, kissing her honey hair. 'Why do you cry?'

'I cry for hopelessness,' she sobbed. 'Why can't life be the way we want it to be?'

'But life is what you make it, my dear. You have comfort with Jasper, you have security and refuge. But refuge too has its price.'

'What price?'

'Loneliness perhaps; boredom, lack of control and independence.'

She sighed and laid her golden mane on his shoulder. He put his hand up to stroke her flowing curls.

When Doctor Baldwin finally left the Eustace house in the winter dawn, the sky was streaked with rose-red light that shone like backlights on a stage behind a curtain of purple cloud, standing halfway up the eastern sky. Above the jagged line of cloud the sky was crystal clear. The morning star still shone like a last ghost before the coming sun and hanging on the western horizon was the lost moon. Exhausted, but entirely content, he walked through the cobbled courtyard to the side of the house, past outhouses and stables, with red-painted windows and doors, out under an archway with a weathervane on top. Horses looking over stable doors, whinnied, and roosters were crowing. Some workmen, cleaning out the stables, saw the disappearing figure of the Doctor, moving down the winding driveway between the trees. They looked from one to the other with knowing smiles. 'Isn't that the bould Baldwin?' said a fellow called Joe Swanton, pausing to lean on his pitchfork.

'I'd say so,' said a small, squat fellow called Jer Leary. 'He looks mighty pleased with himself.' They exchanged lecherous looks and guffawed.

When the Doctor reached the main gates of the Eustace estate, he saw a body lying directly across the road on the grass verge. That was not sleeping, he sensed. Certainly not sleeping. Dead, he thought immediately, with the instinct of a medical man. He crossed the road with hesitant steps and approached with a sinking feeling. He saw the mouth agape, the staring eyes, the small, neat hole in the middle of the forehead. The skin was a pale pallor, with what looked like adipocere tissue already creeping over the fetid flesh from lying in the damp and frosty ditch. He stopped and leant over the body, and read the note pinned to the dead man's breast.

"Shot as an informer by the Irish Republican Army."

Doctor Baldwin straightened up in shocked disbelief. He looked up the road and then down the road. Then he looked back down at the stiffened corpse. Then he raised his head again and found himself staring down the barrels of three Lee Enfield rifles, pointing at him over the fence. Then he waited with his hands by his side as two men in full soldiers' uniforms climbed out over the ditch. Further back, he noticed four, then six, then up to twenty more men in caps and trenchcoats, with bandoliers slung over their shoulders and rifles in their hands. The two soldiers came towards him, unsmiling. He noted the revolvers in holsters, sitting on their hips. He regarded the two with a steady, unblinking gaze.

The leader spoke. 'So, Doctor Baldwin,' he said. 'We meet again.'

'Do we?' asked the Doctor with a raised eyebrow.

'Indeed we do.'

'I don't recall having the pleasure of your acquaintance,' said Doctor Baldwin, unphased.

'Do you recall the funeral of John James O'Grady?' asked the leader, doffing his cap.

Doctor Baldwin threw his arms up in recognition. He smiled broadly.

'Of course, you're Tom Barry, but you're cunningly disguised. I didn't recognise you in the British Army uniform.'

'You're not the only one,' said Barry grimly.

Doctor Baldwin continued to smile and nod his head. 'Very good, very good. And I believe I recognise your companion here now as well. Hurley, if I'm not mistaken. Charlie Hurley?'

'Nothing wrong with your memory, Doctor Baldwin,' said the unsmiling Charlie.

'Indeed, I could say the same about yours,' said the Doctor. He looked along the ditch at the line of armed men waiting expectantly.

Then he looked down at the corpse near his feet. 'So, what have we here then? An execution?'

'Yes,' said Barry, tersely.

'Not without good reason I presume?'

'Indeed not. You've read the note?'

'How do you know he was a spy?'

'He confessed.'

The Doctor nodded soberly. He sighed deeply. 'You don't look like a man who'd take such drastic action without very good reason,' he said.

'Correct,' said Barry. 'We only take such action as a last resort. He confessed to a litany of betrayals of us, our comrades and our families.'

'I daresay he did,' nodded the Doctor. 'I daresay he did.' He pursed his lips, looked down at the dead man, then looking up, he squinted into the rays of the rising sun which came up in a blood-red orb, bathing the road and the dark-dressed men with light. 'Which drives me to the question of what you want with me?'

'We want to ask you some questions,' said Tom Barry.

'Do you now? What about?' asked the Doctor. He adjusted his hat to keep from squinting into the bright sun.

'What are you doing out here for instance, so early in the morning?'

Doctor Baldwin said, 'I like to take an early morning constitutional.'

'We're told you like to sleep until noon,' said Charlie Hurley, with a deadpan expression.

'I've been known to,' said Baldwin. 'Depending on my mood and the company I'm keeping.'

'And what brings you out of Jasper Eustace's house?' asked Tom Barry.

'I was visiting.'

'With Jasper?'

'No, he's not there.'

'With whom then?'

'Why, with Eleanore, his wife. We're neighbours after all.'

'Look Doctor, you don't expect us to believe that do you?'

The Doctor laughed. 'Why not, my dear fellow?'

'You live about six miles away. That's hardly a neighbour.'

'I'm returning from my travels. I've been on the road.'

'So we've heard,' said Barry. 'We also heard you saved an Auxiliary after Kilmichael.'

'And why wouldn't I,' asked the Doctor. 'I took the Hippocratic Oath many years ago. An oath not to be taken lightly, despite my derelictions along the way.'

'And now we find you emerging from an informer's house,' said Charlie Hurley.

Doctor Baldwin turned sharply towards him. 'Who do you mean? Jasper Eustace?'

'Yes.'

'What grounds do you have for thinking Jasper is an informer?'

Tom Barry pointed to the body in the ditch. 'He told us,' he said.

'And who, pray, is he?'

'Maurice Mulcair.'

'Alas poor Maurice,' said Doctor Baldwin, slowly shaking his head.

'He gave us several names,' said Charlie.

'Including mine?' asked Doctor Baldwin, raising a disbelieving eyebrow.

'No,' said Tom Barry. 'But we have our suspicions about you too.'

'Really, Mr. Barry,' said the Doctor, unflappably. 'You're beginning to sound like Maximilien Robespierre in the French Revolution, seeing conspiracies in everything.'

Barry ignored the riposte. 'You must come with us,' he said, 'to the Eustace house.'

'There's nobody there except Mrs Eustace and some workmen,' said the Doctor. 'Don't you think they'll alert the RIC?'

'Not likely,' said Barry. 'They're our men.'

Doctor Baldwin smiled ruefully and said, 'You're clever boys.'

Barry waved his arm and the party of armed men emerged one by one from behind the ditch, and the entire troop moved swiftly up the winding tree-lined avenue to the Eustace house, with Doctor Baldwin marching in their midst.

The corpse of Maurice Mulcair lay on the road all morning long, and curious passersby would sometimes stop, read the note and then hurry away. No military patrol came out from Bandon to investigate. No Essex, no RIC, no Black and Tans, although the town was crawling with soldiers. Suspecting an ambush, no doubt, they kept their distance. Eventually Tom Barry ordered some of his men down to the road, with instructions to place the body inside the ditch, out of sight. Up at the house there was still no sign of Jasper. The main party of Volunteers waited in one of the huge sittingrooms with views through bay windows down the sweeping driveway. Scouts were posted at various corners of the yard, and the two workmen, Joe Swanton and Jer Leary, went about their daily chores unperturbed: milking cows, feeding pigs and grooming horses. Tom Barry, Charlie Hurley and Dick Barrett occupied Jasper's large study and questioned Doctor Baldwin and Eleanore Eustace for several hours. When they'd first arrived back with the Doctor, Eleanore had reacted in shocked amazement, but now, by mid-afternoon, she'd become reconciled to the reality of her position. Yet she was by no means cowed or intimidated. A fairly lengthy philosophical discussion had ensued after the initial element of shock and surprise had passed. Eleanore had even allowed them make tea for themselves, and the larder being well stocked, all the men had partaken with a certain amount of gusto. As regards the political situation, they'd agreed to disagree. Eleanore stuck to her view that she preferred the status quo to remain, and Barry said he respected her position. Doctor Baldwin, for his part, assured him that he was firmly in the Volunteers camp; that he agreed with their revolutionary methods and the sooner an independent Republic came about the better.

'Look, we're all in this together. The British have trodden us underfoot for centuries. It's time for them to go,' said the Doctor.

'What baffles me, Doctor Baldwin,' said Tom Barry, 'is how you can have that attitude on the one hand, and yet hob-nob with the landed gentry on the other.'

'Why ever not, my dear fellow? Are you saying there won't be any room in your new Republic for a bit of sophisticated interaction, whatever about sophisticated intercourse?'

And the Doctor laughed loudly, his infectious humour helping to thaw Barry's frosty demeanour to a considerable degree.

'On the contrary, Doctor, we have no problem with any of that. Our only concern is that we are not informed upon and betrayed to an occupying force.'

'I couldn't agree with you more,' said Doctor Baldwin. 'So why do you hold us here as prisoners?'

'Because you haven't yet explained to us, despite six hours of questioning, what you are doing in the house of an informer?'

'My husband may be an informer, but I certainly am not,' said Eleanore. 'Although I disagree with everything you stand for.'

'I respect your right to disagree,' said Tom Barry courteously, 'but I am still not convinced. Something still doesn't make sense here.'

There was a long pause. The only sound was the ticking of the clock. Charlie, Dick Barrett and Tom Barry had a whispered discussion.

Eleanore confided in Doctor Baldwin. He nodded, po-faced. Eleanore finally said, 'It's a delicate situation. I trust what I am about to tell you will go no further than this room.'

'Whatever you tell us in confidence will be respected and remain a secret,' said Barry. 'I give you this assurance and so do my fellow officers here.' The other two nodded soberly.

'Very well,' said Eleanore. She stood up and walked to the window and looked out for what seemed like several minutes, as if she were making sure there was no sign of her husband on the driveway. The others waited expectantly. Then she turned and walked back to the oak desk that Tom Barry sat behind, in Jasper's chair. 'My husband and I have had, how shall I put it, a less than satisfactory marriage. He is much older than I, nearly twenty years older. My father, who is a wealthy cattleman from north Cork, arranged the marriage. I was his only daughter, the apple of his eye. He wanted the best for me and I, of course, was happy to go along with it. There are many rewards being married to a wealthy man: jewellery, money, trips abroad, prestige in the community. But in our case there is no love. Jasper and I lead separate lives for the most part, although we still sleep under one roof, in separate beds. Our marriage is a sham to a large degree, but we keep up appearances.'

Her beautiful face looked disappointed.

Tom Barry shifted uncomfortably in his chair. He cleared his throat. 'Do we really need to know all this? It's hardly relevant to the scheme of things.'

'I agree,' said Eleanore. 'Except in one respect. It explains Doctor Baldwin's presence in my house in the middle of the night.'

Eleanore turned towards Doctor Baldwin with a beseeching look. 'Shall I tell them, James?'

The Doctor sat looking down at his boots. For the first time in a long time he felt ashamed. 'It's your prerogative, my dear. It's your decision.' He sighed and turned his hat round and round in his hands.

Eleanore's lips trembled. 'Doctor Baldwin and I are...are...we're lovers. There, I've said it. Are you happy now?' She sat down and burst into floods of tears. Doctor Baldwin immediately moved to her side and sat beside her, putting a comforting arm around her shoulders.

Tom Barry's eyes met those of Dick Barrett and Charlie Hurley. He stood up. 'I'm sorry to have had to put you through this ordeal, Ma'am;

and you too, Doctor Baldwin. I realise there are certain things better left unspoken.' He paused. 'But we had to make sure.'

'I trust you're sure now?' said the Doctor, with a slightly bitter look on his face.

'Perfectly,' said Barry. 'Please forgive us. We'll withdraw to the outside. We must ask you however, not to leave the house until our work is finished here.'

Jasper Eustace and Thomas Cody reached Bandon around midday on their way from the Cork Exhibition. They were travelling in Jasper's hansom cab and his fine harness horse had stepped out elegantly all morning on the long journey from the city. They were tired and hungry when they reached the town and they decided to stop at the Devonshire Arms Hotel on Kilbrogan Hill to feed and water their horse and fortify themselves for the remainder of the journey westward. They'd had a pleasant enough sojourn in the city, looking at new machinery and getting acquainted with all the latest gadgets issuing from the foundries of Birmingham and Sheffield. They left the horse with a livery man in front, with instructions to give it a bucket of water and a good feed of oats. Then they went into the restaurant and ordered up two sirloin steaks with all the trimmings, and a half bottle of Jameson double malt. The hotel had been taken over almost completely by a company of Black and Tans, but was open to whatever members of the public still cared to share its hospitality with such a notorious band of brigands. The townspeople gave it a wide berth for the most part, but the hotel was a traditional haunt for well-heeled gentlemen in from the country, and for such stout citizens as Eustace and Cody old habits died hard. They were prepared to put up with the proximity of their unsavoury fellow patrons, because frankly, there wasn't another establishment in the town with the capacity to equal the excellent bill of fare served up by the venerable Devonshire. Besides, on occasion one might bump into a contemporary of equal standing for a pleasant discussion, or even the occasional civilised British officer. They'd taken their time, enjoying a leisurely meal and lowering the contents of the whiskey bottle by degrees, until only a last spoonful was left at the bottom. Being men of even temper and disciplined appetite, and considering the waning hour, they resisted the temptation to order another half bottle of liquor. So they stood up and settled their account. They put their hats and coats on, and as they turned to leave, Major A.E. Percival of the Essex Regiment came through the door, accompanied by two other officers. Noticing the two, well-dressed gentlemen, Percival smiled and nodded. Just as he passed them he stopped and turned. 'Mr. Eustace,' he said, cheerily, 'I didn't spot you for a moment. It's good to see you.'

Jasper turned back and smiled. 'Ah, Major,' he said extending his hand. 'How do you do?'

'Very well, very well,' said Percival, his cold eyes lighting up a shade, as they flicked keenly from Jasper's face to his moustachioed companion's.

'Have you met Thomas Cody?' asked Jasper.

'Hello, Mr. Cody,' said Percival. 'No, I don't believe we've met.' He shook Thomas's hand and introduced his fellow officers, 'Meet Captain Hotblack and Major Halahan.'

After further handshakes all round, Percival continued, 'And what brings you gentleman to our humble quarters?'

'We've been travelling,' said Jasper, 'to the Cork Exhibition. We're heading home.'

'How interesting,' said Percival. 'You're brave men to venture such a long distance in the times we live in.'

'Well, the way I look at it,' said Jasper, 'you can't let fellows hiding behind ditches stop you from going about your business, or you might as well throw in the towel once and for all. And besides, with men like yourselves and your troops around, we don't see there's anything of great consequence to fear.'

'Very kind of you to say so, sir,' said Percival. He paused. 'Would you gentlemen care to join us for a ball of malt?'

Jasper looked at Cody who appeared to demur. He hesitated. 'We'd love to Major, but we're on the road now for nearly four days. If we don't put in an appearance on the home front we'll be in trouble.'

'In trouble with the war office you mean,' said Percival, and they all laughed knowingly. Then, tipping hats and caps all around, they went their separate ways.

About two miles out of Bandon town they came to a deep trench in the road. Jasper pulled the horse up. 'What the devil?' he asked.

'It's those boyos again,' said Thomas. 'They've cut the road so the military lorries can't pass.'

'Oh, for Jesus sake!' said Jasper. 'How the hell are we supposed to get through?'

'Look, there's a gap in the ditch. They've made it narrow enough for a horse and cart to pass through but not a lorry.'

Jasper turned the horse through the gap into a field. They proceeded along by the ditch until they came to another gap which allowed them exit onto the road again. Jasper shook his bewildered head. 'You know, it seems to me these fellows are doing more harm to the ordinary folk travelling the roads than they are to the British soldiers.'

'I couldn't agree more,' said Thomas. 'There's a certain lack of foresight at work here if you ask me. But they're clever, you have to allow them that. It's a good trick to stop a lorry, and not a horse and trap, which most of the people have.'

'And what about your fine steam engine and thrasher?' asked Jasper. 'That trench would stop you going about your business, wouldn't it?'

'Absolutely,' said Thomas. 'But they don't care about fellows like you and me. They think we have enough already. They have no sympathy for big farmers or businessmen.'

'They sound like those bloody Russian communists,' swore Jasper.

When they reached Gatonville, Thomas got down from the trap at the back entrance to the farmyard. 'Why don't you go in the front way?' asked Jasper. 'By the white gates?'

'You mean the entrance proper?' asked Thomas, with an ironic smile. 'That's reserved for gentlemen, don't you know, like Doctor Baldwin and his ilk.'

Jasper laughed heartily. 'Ah, indeed. So it's the entrance improper for yourself is it?'

'The very thing,' said an unsmiling Cody, and tightened his coat against the evening chill.

'And tell me,' said Jasper. 'How is the good Doctor these days?'

'I haven't seen him for over two months, thank God,' said Thomas. 'He's off tramping the roads somewhere, and solving the problems of the world.'

'I know what you mean,' said Jasper, with a dismissive smirk. 'Sure I suppose there's need of fellows like that in the world too.'

'Not around here, there's not,' said Cody. 'Good night.'

'So long,' said Jasper and whipped his horse into a trot. It would soon be nightfall and he had six miles still to travel.

When he drove his horse and trap up the tree-lined avenue to his mansion on the hill, the last streaks of the setting sun painted the sky behind his house to the west a beautiful shade of rosy pink. Over the low fields near the Bandon river to the east, the full moon was rising like a huge, golden ball. It was a magic-hour twilight, neither dark nor bright. He was dog-tired, and so was his horse. He longed for a hot bath and his bed. He jumped from the trap in the yard and called his workmen. 'Joe, Jer, will you untackle this bleddy horse?'

There was no response. He called again. Still no response. Irritated, he shouted louder. 'Swanton, Leary, where the devil are ye?' He looked towards the house. A dim candlelight burned in one window. There was no lantern light in the yard. That was odd. Then he noticed a movement from the corner of his eye. A soldier with a British Army uniform, wearing a Tam O'Shanter beret, hovered out of the shadows and approached him. He tensed up. 'Who are you?' he demanded.

As the fellow came on, Jasper noticed the uniform. 'Oh, the Army,' he said sourly, and relaxed. 'Ye fellows are showing up very late in the day. And I don't mean today. I sent for ye four days ago, before I went to Cork.'

The officer spoke with a Scottish accent. 'We're sorry to let you down, Mr. Eustace. But we have to tread warily these days. The countryside is crawling with rebels.'

'You don't have to tell me that,' said Jasper. ''Tis a wonder ye came at all. Does my wife know ye're here?' He looked towards where other soldiers hovered in the shadows.

'She knows we're waiting for you, but she has no idea why we're here,' said the officer.

'Thank goodness for that. Look, I won't invite you in if you don't mind. I'm tired and hungry. Let me get to the point.'

'Very good, sir.'

'You're Scottish, am I correct?'

'Correct, sir.'

'What's your name?'

'Monahan. Captain Monahan.'

'Right, Captain. I've been watching a group of local IRA for several months now. The Hennessys are the main family, Mike and Sonny in particular; and there's a fellow called Charlie Hurley who's been hanging around with them sometimes. I found where they keep a dump and I believe they have a stash of rifles there.'

'Have you seen them?' As he was talking the officer was writing in a notebook.

'What? The rifles? No, but I followed their footsteps in the snow. They went to a ditch and retrieved three Lee Enfields. I'm sure they have a lot of guns there. But at least the Tans burnt them out, thanks to me.'

'And who else do you know?' asked the officer.

'I know John Lordan is the leader. He's the big shot. He lives near Newcestown.'

'We heard a fellow called Tom Barry is the leader,' said Monahan.

'No, he's not I tell you, it's Lordan or Hurley. It could be Hurley,' said Jasper.

'Do you know these fellows by sight?'

'Sure I do. The Hennessys anyway. I might recognise Hurley too, if I saw him. But you must take action immediately. These fellows are getting stronger by the day. They're running everything in the countryside: cutting roads, arresting fellows. Do you know they even have their own courts? Most of the train drivers are working for them. If you don't wipe them out, they'll have control of the country in six months.'

'Oh, I think we'll have wiped them out in six months.'

'Not if ye don't take more serious action. How many soldiers inside in Bandon between all the barracks? Are there six or seven hundred... a thousand?'

'There could be, sir,' said Monahan.

'And what the hell do ye do all day? As far as I can see, all ye do is sit around and drink whiskey. And then go on the rampage through the town, frightening people who are no threat to ye at all.'

The officer smiled, a little condescendingly. 'That's not quite accurate, sir, if I may say so?'

'Don't come the lawdy-daw with me, young man,' said Jasper, suddenly conscious he was being talked down to. 'Only for fellows like me, ye wouldn't know ye're asses from ye're elbows around here. We're the people standing up to Sinn Féin. People like us and the RIC.'

'Of course you have the advantage that you're Irish yourselves,' said the officer. 'You know these people.'

'Damn right, we do,' said Jasper. 'And it's time manners were put on them. They think they can take over the country, set up their own government. Get rid of fellows like me. We're loyal to the King of England. He's a Protestant. If they take over they'll destroy our religion.'

'But they've taken action against wealthy Catholics as well. Catholics who don't want independence.'

'Huh,' said Jasper, unconvinced, and wiped his mouth. He'd worked himself up into quite a state. He looked around. 'Have you seen my workmen? They're supposed to be here.'

'I'm afraid I haven't, sir.'

'You know what they say. When the cat's away the mice are at play. I suppose the bastards are off drinking whiskey too, like the rest of ye,' said Jasper, exasperated.

The officer smiled, 'I'm afraid we can't help you there, sir. But I've taken note of what you said about the rebels.' He put his notebook inside his pocket. He turned to go, but paused and turned back. 'One last thing, sir.'

'Well, what is it?' said Jasper, beginning to remove the chains tying the shafts to the hames hooks on the horse's collar.

'Do you know Maurice Mulcair?'

Jasper stopped what he was doing and turned back to the officer. 'Of course I do. He's with us. He's a Catholic. He's given information to the Army as well. A good fellow.'

'Well, I have news for you. He's dead.'

'What? How do you know?'

'Because we shot him. His body is down on the road inside the ditch, opposite your gate.'

Jasper's brow furrowed. He saw figures emerging from the shadows. It dawned on him that it was a trap. Using the horse as a shield, he turned and ran. Before the Volunteers had a chance to lay a hand on him, Jasper had ducked down through a labyrinth of passages behind the stables. As he passed the scullery, he reached in, grabbing a double-barrelled shotgun and a bag of cartridges. Feverishly, he put two in the breech, and listened for running feet. They were trying to find him in the moonlight. He heard shouts. He turned and raced out behind the barns and across a field towards the woods they called the Bull Riders. He heard a shot and a bullet tore up the ground around his feet. He stopped and fired back, emptying both barrels. With shaking hands he refilled the breech. Panting and sweating, he struck for the shelter of the trees. His knock-kneed gait, trundling along, was not graceful, but Jasper was strong. The trees were thick and he knew the woods. He could outrun those fellows with a bit of a headstart. They wouldn't know the woods unless the Hennessys were with them. They'd know the woods. Jasper reached the sheltering trees and ran down the steep bank towards the swift-running stream. As the bank grew steeper he started to slither down, holding himself by dragging onto branches extending from the mighty oaks. The stream was ahead, he trundled into it. The water was running fairly swiftly but not too deep; halfway up to his knees. Gasping and drenched, he splashed up along the gravelled bottom. He stumbled on a boulder, fell headlong and dragged himself up again. He reached the opposite bank and, pulling at a branch, he hauled himself up. He stopped. He could hear no footsteps, or voices. Christ, he'd made it. Lungs bursting, he discarded his heavy, waterlogged overcoat. Lighter now. He was out of the woods and running up along a flat bog with a newly built stone wall on the left hand side. A nice wall it was. Made by a good tradesman, John James O'Grady. Random thoughts beset him.

He was nearly out of the bog when two figures loomed up in front of him in the moonlight, from the middle of a standing stone circle. They were armed with rifles. He couldn't make out their faces because they were silhouetted against the moon. Panting and sweating, he stopped. He raised his shotgun.

'Drop the gun, Jasper,' said a voice. Sonny Hennessy's voice. His heart sank. Jasper sighted along the barrel.

'Don't do it, Jasper,' said Sonny again.

Jasper hesitated a split second; then pulled the trigger. He did not hear the explosive crack of the Lee Enfield, but he saw the flash before the bullet hit its mark with unerring accuracy. A cry was wrenched from his throat as the force of the bullet that hit him just below the heart, lifted him, and knocked him backwards into a soggy boghole.

He did not see the two figures coming slowly from the middle of the circle of standing stones, nor did he hear Sonny leaning down and whisper in his ear. 'I'm sorry, Jasper, you should have dropped it. 'Twas either you or us.'

Sonny kneeling and Mike Hennessy standing, looked down upon the body of their dead neighbour. The moonbeams twinkled above. An owl hooted in the distant woods. The stream ran on.

13

Eleanore Eustace, all in black, with a lace mantilla covering her beautiful face, followed her husband's coffin down the centre aisle of St. Peter's Church in Bandon, leaning on her father, Walter's arm. Following the pallbearers, she passed the dignitaries in the choir and chancel, transept and nave. A cold light came through the exquisite stained-glass windows as she made her way out through the high, double doors to the graveyard.

'Like Niobe, all tears,' thought Doctor Baldwin, hovering a little uncomfortably behind the high, stone catafalque on which the carved marble effigy of the 2nd Earl of Bandon splendidly reposed. With downcast eyes, she moved at the head of the stately, solemn procession, headed by the current Lord and Lady Bandon, Major-General Sir Peter Strickland, Major Bernard Montgomery, Major A.E. Percival, and the great and good of the town. She scarcely noticed him at all. And if she did it suited her purpose to make nothing of it. All who came behind her were respectable, well-heeled Protestants for the most part, but there were upright Catholics too: Thomas Cody, Maguire, the solicitor of Bandon, and of course Eleanore herself and her father, the cattleman, one of the wealthiest of all. People came in from the countryside whom the Doctor did not know: big, red-faced, roastbeef-eating peasants from the Bandon valley who might be called Shortens, Kingstons, Jennings, Goods or Hosfords. But whereas he didn't know them, they had a stamp about them that was similar to Jasper. Stolid, materialistic men and women of the world. He saw a woman with a severe mouth and red hair whom he knew only by the nickname, Foxy Bess, which was name enough for him.

The coffin was laid down and lowered into the grave, and Reverend Prosser spoke some words of sorrow and of sympathy. Did Eleanore need such palliatives, never having received much in that way from Jasper? Still, the motions had to be gone through and the ritual enacted. As the earth thudded on the oak and the grave was quickly refilled, Doctor Baldwin noticed Maguire looking busy and important as he fumbled around for some notes he had written on a piece of paper. What was this fellow's function here, other than to thrust himself as usual into the limelight, seeking aggrandisement? He started out to pay some last words of respect to a fellow-huntsman, but not a client.

'No, Jasper would have favoured his own kind,' thought Baldwin, 'notwithstanding Maguire's eagerness.' He was forced to listen at the edge of the crowd as Maguire rambled on, tendentiously:

'Jasper Eustace was our neighbour, our friend, our brother. A man who minded his business and who bore no ill-will towards others. He helped his countrymen, attended church faithfully and was a staunch supporter of his own religion. He liked the sporting life, riding to hounds and enjoying a day at the races. He wasn't a flamboyant or loquacious man, but he was steadfast, loyal and true to King and country. His crime, in the eyes of some others, was that he disagreed with certain subversive forces who are out to change the *status quo* in this country against the wishes of men like Jasper and other people of this community. They wish to bring about an independent state, separate from the Commonwealth of the United Kingdom. They argue that Sinn Féin has been given that mandate in the 1918 plebiscite, and while it is true that this political organisation has grown strong and powerful in recent years, with undoubtedly a great many people voting for them – I can assure you I am not among them – nevertheless, they are entitled to their point of view; but their objectives must be brought about peacefully. Alas, this organisation has set its heart upon overthrowing his Majesty's Government by violent means and that is the rock it will perish on. Jasper did not want an Irish Republic. Neither do I. Neither do most of you people gathered here. But because Jasper allegedly gave information about the activities of these subversives to the Crown Forces he was ruthlessly gunned down, along with another unfortunate man, Maurice Mulcair, who was a Catholic like myself. So you see, these people have no care for creed or colour, if one is misfortunate enough to get on the wrong side of them. My friends, I say to you, we must not tolerate these bully-boy tactics a moment longer. We must be vigilant in seeking these murderers out and in destroying them without mercy. We must stand up and fight for what is right. Support the RIC and the military. Do not be afraid of sinister gunmen. Arm yourselves. Stand up. Go out and fight back. Give no quarter, show no mercy, burn them out...'

Maguire's voice began to quiver with barely-controlled hysteria. His lips trembled. He spat saliva towards his listeners in an increasingly seditious fashion. His audience nodded with clenched fists and murmurs of, 'Well said,' and, 'Hear hear.'

The ruddy-faced peasants from the Bandon valley were particularly exercised. Foxy Bess had a rapturous look on her plain face. Maguire finished up a little abruptly, perhaps realising that he'd overstated his sentiments in the company of his more esteemed listeners. Lord Bandon shuffled uncomfortably on his feet and looked around him as if to identify a more civilised face in the crowd. After all, he had little in common with these people, other than the commonality of shared religion. Was Jasper Eustace even Church of Ireland? Methodist more like, or Presbyterian. As the funeral-goers dispersed, Lord Bandon passed deliberately close to Doctor Baldwin and extended his hand in friendship. 'Ah, my dear Baldwin,' he said with a glimmer of humour in his angular face. 'It's been quite a while.'

'Indeed it has, my Lord,' said the Doctor, extending similar courtesy. 'But I had been thinking about you in recent times.'

'Had you, by Gad,' said Lord Bandon, pleased. 'In what context?'

'Some historical point or other, which now escapes me,' said the Doctor. 'Trivial in the present, sad context however.'

'History is never trivial,' said Bandon, gravely. 'History is a great teacher. I think we disregard it too readily these days. It has a nasty habit of repeating itself, often to our detriment.'

'That's very true,' said the Doctor. 'Especially where this little country of ours is concerned.'

'Correct, Doctor. The hand of history lays heavily on the shoulders of the Emerald Isle.'

They stood and continued to talk as the crowd dispersed. Bandon was in no hurry to leave the company of the unorthodox Doctor. When had they first met? Many years ago at a recital of Verdi's *Aida* at the Cork Opera House. Thomas Cody passed near them and didn't acknowledge the Doctor.

'Poor show,' thought Baldwin to himself. 'You could take the man from the bog, but not the bog from the man.'

Did Lord Bandon notice? If so, he didn't let on. Lord Bandon bade him good day and walked with his wife down the steep steps of the churchyard towards their carriage waiting below outside the gate. Strickland, Colonel Moffat, newly arrived from Kinsale, and Colonel Hudson of Skibbereen were in close attendance. In the time-honoured, stiff-upper lip tradition of the British officer class, things were, for the most part, left unsaid. Information was imparted and approved by innuendo and suggestion rather than directly and to the point.

'I say, who's the fire and brimstone man?' asked Colonel Hudson.

'Eh?' asked Strickland and said no more.

'The gentleman who delivered the oration, or should I say panegyric?' said Hudson.

Strickland frowned and then he chuckled, 'Oh, you're referring to Maguire.' His handlebar moustache shook for a moment like a rustling hedge that birds had just left. 'Where did we meet him before?' He fingered his moustache and then clicked his fingers. 'Of course, at your Lordship's soirée last summer.'

'An excitable fellow, evidently.' said Hudson.

They waited for Lord Bandon to speak. He made a sucking sound through his teeth and did not reply, his disdain for Maguire obvious from his studied silence.

Hudson continued after waiting for a suitable interlude for the Earl to reply. 'He's going to burn and lay waste I see. I thought that method was the specialty of the Black and Tans?'

There was a strong hint of disapproval in Hudson's voice. Strickland rubbed his cheekbone under his right eye with his left index finger. He inhaled deeply through his nostrils.

Colonel Moffat interjected, 'It's one way of achieving results. Major Percival would certainly approve.'

They looked back up the steps to where Maguire, Percival and Major Bernard Montgomery were deep in conversation outside the church door.

Lord Bandon said, 'It could be a double-edged sword.'

'Sir?' enquired Strickland, wondering what the Earl was getting at.

'Burning people out,' said Bandon with clipped intonation. 'That can be done by both sides. And there are many more of them than there are of us. I think you should tread warily in that area, Major-General.'

Strickland's eyes looked startled for a moment, like a stupid man realizing that others have noticed his inadequacies all of a sudden. 'Ahem,' he said to clear his throat.

Bandon looked sharply at him, as if he secretly took him for a fool.

'The Black and Tans burned Cork,' he said. 'To what end? It hasn't deterred the rebels one iota.'

'On the contrary,' said Hudson. 'It's made them more determined as far as I can see.'

'Really, Colonel,' asked Strickland. 'Is that what you're finding away down there in Skibbereen?'

The subtle put-down was ignored by Hudson. He continued, 'Yes, we're finding that, but even more surprisingly we're finding an honourable code of conduct among these fellows. Just a week ago they released some of my men whom they'd captured. They fed them and regaled them with ballads as they drove them back to the barracks.'

Lord Bandon laughed at Strickland's expense. 'What's your regiment Colonel?' he asked of Hudson.

'The King's Liverpool's, sir.'

'The IRA really let them go?'

'Yes sir. They let them go,' said Hudson, 'Because they understood none of my men in our regiment had been involved in burnings or in torturing their prisoners. So you see my point about burning being counterproductive?'

Strickland nodded his head, slightly nonplussed. At that moment Eleanore Eustace and her father drove away in their hansom cab. Lord Bandon tipped his hat to them. The officers looked after them for some moments.

'What will she do now, I wonder?' mused Strickland.

'The lady won't be short of suitors,' said Lord Bandon with a knowing smile, as his eyes followed another back-to-back trap leaving the street, driven by Thomas Cody. Sitting in front was his wife Madeleine, and in the back, with his feet dangling nonchalantly over the side, sat Doctor Baldwin, who raised his right arm in an ironic gesture of farewell to them. Lord Bandon did not smile, but his eyes twinkled in what could only be construed as merriment.

It was a cold February day as two brothers ploughed an upland with a pair of heavy horses. Overhead the sky was a steel-grey blanket from which no light escaped. A cold wind blew from the east, not strong, nor violent, but that chilled unto the bone. The ground they ploughed was stubbled from last year's harvest, and it unfurrowed, row on row; shiny, rich and dark, as the plough sock carved it through. A flock of seagulls followed the plough, screaming and squawking as they battled with jackdaws and rooks to gobble the fat worms that wriggled in the fertile earth. The horses were big-framed Clydesdales, with massive, deep chests, sloping shoulders, high withers, powerful, round hindquarters and clumps of hair flowing over fetlocks and hooves. Despite their enormous strength and power, they were gentle, good-tempered, and unshirking in their duty to their masters and the plough. The brothers reciprocated this goodwill, in an unarticulated bond between man and beast. They fed and maintained their horses better than they catered for themselves.

The brother leading the horses in a true direction along the furrows was called James Coffey. He was a youth of tender years, not yet twenty, with an intense, serious face, a steadfast chin, and deep, penetrating eyes. He was bareheaded despite the piercing wind, dressed in shirt, dark pants and waistcoat. Clumps of sticky earth clung to the soles of his boots, which he dislodged at each headland by kicking against the board of the plough. The other brother following the plough and guiding it with his powerful hands, was called Timothy. He might have been younger than James, but bigger, stronger, broad of shoulder, huge of forearm and of wrist. He wore a cloth cap on his curly-topped head and his face was open, unlined and sunny. He whistled while he worked and deferred to his older brother when decisions of importance were required. The field rose and fell in waves, and this was the pattern of the greater landscape for miles in any direction. It rose in ridges and fell to wide, green valleys.

Day in, day out, the brothers worked the land. Summer, winter this was their only calling. Their parents had passed on and left them well set up, with a good farm, as fine as any in the valley. They were simple and devout, but the political earthquakes of the moment passed them by. Their eyes were fixed on a longer view of history. They helped their neighbours of whatever persuasion, paid their taxes and baked their own bread. They liked to attend the horse fairs and would bid upon a likely brood mare to put in foal to some useful, up and coming stallion, which the likes of Jasper Eustace kept. They'd breed and feed the foals up to the age of three, and maybe sell them at the fairs of Ballabuidhe or Tallow or Cahirmee. Otherwise they'd stroll down to Enniskean after Mass on Sunday and follow the bowling lads along the winding roads, having the odd bet on the longest throw and then going quietly home to milk their cows at sundown.

A sudden blaze of blood-red sun shone forth upon the western sky, as if a lamp had lit in heaven's gloomy vault. James pulled the horses out onto the last headland and Timothy wrestled the plough around to make ready for the final furlong down. James did not lead the horses further. He stopped and said, 'That's a decent day's work done, Tim. We'll leave it for today.'

Timothy looked at the evening redness in the west. 'Whatever you think, James,' he said and did not need to say more.

James said, 'The weather will hold for a good while now. You'll get no rain. We'll be finished with this handy enough come tomorrow.'

'Sound as a bell,' said Timothy.

'You can untackle the horses,' said James. 'I'll drive in the cows and start the milking.'

James trudged home wearily towards the rook-filled trees around the farmyard.

By nine o'clock that night they had their milking done, their horses fed and their cats and dogs bedded in the hayrick for the night. In the kitchen after supper, they knelt and prayed the rosary solemnly; one leading with:

'Hail Mary full of grace the Lord is with thee, blessed art thou among women,' and the other answering, *'Holy Mary Mother of God, pray for us sinners, now and at the hour of our death...'*

Late into the night the dry wind rustled the withered leaves that still clung to the cut-down beech hedge around the haggard. There was but a hangnail, waning moon in the eastern sky. Wisps of cloud drifted across it, and across the bright Milky Way that was thrown like a ghost road above the constellations. There was a crackle of twigs underfoot as a furtive group of eight or ten people moved along by a high ditch towards a grove of trees behind the haggard. A disturbed night owl flew away with a fearful screech and a tremendous whirring and scratching of starlings wings started up within the evergreens. The group moved swiftly, led by two masked figures who beckoned them onward through gaps down by the beech hedge into the haggard. In the stall, the patient cows chewed peacefully on the cud, the two heavy horses looked over the stable half-doors and blinked but did not stir. As the group paused by the hayrick, two dogs leaped forth with sudden barking.

'Down, Shep, down Spot,' said the masked leader with soft familiarity, holding out two pieces of meat, which the dogs swallowed ravenously. At the same time their tails went down, their ears went back and they became docile and silent. As insurance, they were thrown further scraps. The masked leader raised a hand and the group halted, listening for any sounds of movement from the house. All they could hear was their collective inhalation and exhalation of breath, but if beating hearts had external sounds they would be loud as drums. The leader, noting with approval the shotguns, the .22 rifles and the Colt revolvers, as well as the cruder pikes and slash hooks in the disciples' hands, whispered, 'Follow me.'

They slunk towards the farmhouse and tried the door handle, which was locked. They went around by a back kitchen and, sure enough, a window lay open for the cats to come and go. The leader clambered swiftly through and opened the main door for the cohorts to swarm in. With lanterns lit they softly climbed the stairs that led directly up from the large, flagged kitchen floor to the bedrooms.

Stringers and balusters groan, floorboards creak, but James and Timothy Coffey sleep on beneath the rafters. In dreams they till the fallow fields of hope and reap the barley and gather in the harvests of the heart.

And then the door bursts open and a harsh voice calls, 'Arise you Coffey brothers and come with us!'

Timothy sits up, drowsed with sleep, and slowly James awakes. The lanterns wave like fallen comets in their faces and they imagine the room crowded with faceless people. Not sure if he wakes or sleeps, James asks, 'Who are you? How did you enter our house?'

'That's of no concern to you where you are going,' replies the masked leader.

Timothy looks at his brother then back towards the masked one, 'What do you mean?' He looks to his brother James again and his voice is shaking. 'What do they mean, James?'

'Up with you and come with us,' says the leader.

Guns are shoved close to their faces. They shrink back in dread.

'Get going,' shouts another man.

James throws his legs over the edge of the bed and stands vulnerable in his nightshirt and long, woollen underpants. Timothy goes to put on his trousers, but the man says, 'You won't need your britches.'

'What do they want with us, James?' asks the plaintive Timothy again.

The leader gesticulates and says, 'Get down the stairs with ye, the time for talking is past.'

They are pushed and harried down the stairs with gun barrels pressed against their backs. Their captors are excitable, cursing and swearing when they stumble. James goes to try to find his boots and is told no boots are needed. They are herded through the familiar kitchen that smells of dusty peat embers, fresh-baked bread, burnt bacon from the remains of last night's supper. They are pushed out in their bare feet to the farmyard. The cold, east wind carries the strong smell of animal manure to their nostrils from the dungheap. The dogs are bought again with scraps of bacon, and follow on behind their masters with troubled, guilty looks, aware that something sinister is afoot.

'Why are you doing this to us?' asks James. 'What have we ever done to you?'

The response is a push in the back which causes him to fall forward on his face. He is roughly dragged up by the hair of the head by two others.

'Shut your mouth and walk,' the masked one says. 'The hour of your judgement is at hand.'

They are well away from the house now, pushed out into the headland of the field they'd lately ploughed. Along by the sheltering ditch go the swinging lanterns, the whining dogs, the softly-sobbing Timothy.

'Stop your snivelling and face your maker like a man,' says the leader, from behind the mask. They stop beside the plough, and James says, 'I know you, Foxy Bess.'

'You know nothing,' says the masked one.

'I know you, mask or not,' says James. 'And I know these others too: ye might be Harbords or Hornibrooks, Howes or Chinnerys. Whoever ye are, ye're our neighbours that we helped out with the harvest; who walked to school 'longside us.'

He suddenly lunges and pulls the mask off the leader, and there stands Foxy Bess, exposed; her face a harder mask than that discarded.

'Your hour has come, James Coffey,' says Foxy Bess. 'May the Lord forgive you and your brother here. You must atone for sins against our people.'

'What sins?' asks James. 'We've committed no sins against you or your kind.'

'Wrongdoers have,' repeats Foxy Bess.

'If you mean the IRA, we have no dealings with them.'

'But you know them,' says the other masked one.

'No better than we know you, Henry Crawford,' says James. 'Your mask does not protect you or make you anonymous to me. I've bought horses from you and helped you with your calving cows. Why do you use us this way? You know us for what we are and that's as innocent men.'

'We know you for being Papists, intent on driving us from our land,' says Crawford. 'But you'll not succeed. Never, never will you do it. Heaven's wrath avenges us.' He turns towards the armed group lurking in the shadows. 'Get on with this,' he says.

Timothy lunges at him in sudden desperation, knocking the rifle from his grasp and pulling the mask from his face. They wrestle in the newly turned earth, scratching and clawing. Timothy is possessed of the strength of a drowning man. Two others try to pull him away from Crawford, but he drags them down as well. They tear at his hair and then a man with a two-pronged pike rushes in and sticks it in his back. Timothy screams out in agony as the tines perforate his kidneys. James jumps on the pikeman's back, but another hacks him with a slash hook, cutting his throat. Blood pumps from a severed artery like a gushing fountain. All is mayhem and confusion in the dark and in the dirt. The dogs begin to bark.

'Finish them,' screams Foxy Bess, as the stricken James is struck again by the man wielding the slash hook. His comely head is nearly severed from his shoulders. He falls into the furrow. His mouth and eyes are clogged with the new-ploughed earth.

'James, James,' says the badly wounded Timothy, and tries to crawl towards him on his hands and knees, his tattered nightshirt hanging loose around his body; his bare feet soaked in running blood. A man puts a rifle against his ribs and pulls the trigger. His intestines spatter forth across the half-ploughed field. As if to make assurance doubly sure, a revolver is pressed against his head, above his left ear, and the blast blows the side of his face away. The brothers lie twitching there until all breathing stops; and then they lie inert and lifeless in the furrows of the field they ploughed so well. Their assailants stand back, shocked and panicked at their own ferocity. A man goes on his knees and begins to scoop the earth over the bodies in a desperate bid to cover up the evidence of their evil work. Another shouts, 'Come on away. In the Lord's name, come on.'

Foxy Bess admonishes her motley crew and says sharply, 'That's enough. Get hold of ye're selves.' She goes round to each of them and looks them in the eye. She lowers her voice to a steely timbre, 'The deed is done. They won't be rising early.'

Crawford is buoyed up by her stern words and says, 'That will teach their brethern not to meddle with righteous folk.' He is panting, bloodied, begrimed, in disarray, but still with sufficient self-control to add, 'Write out the note, Bess, and pin it to their shirts.'

Foxy Bess scribbles hastily on a sheet of paper and attaches it with a safety pin to James's night shirt near the collar. "Executed to avenge the killing of our kinsmen – beware The Loyalist Action Group."

She calls it out and Crawford says, 'That'll do.'

The killers slope their rifles and put their pikes upon their shoulders, and walk off down the valley whence they came. The two dogs sit by the broken bodies of their beloved masters. Sometimes they move to lick their faces now growing cold, but mostly they sit on their haunches in their sorrow and confusion and whimper until dawn, when the sun will shine across the tragic acres on the feast of Valentine.

14

J ames Maguire, self-styled solicitor of Bandon, was working late on a document of title. He'd taken the deed home from his office on North Main Street and was sitting in the study of his big manor, overlooking the town. It was more than a week after the funeral of Jasper Eustace. He had pride of ownership in his house, which was once the home of a British Army colonel who'd fought in the Boer War, and who'd retired to West Cork, as large numbers of his fellow officers did, to enjoy the fishing, the hunting and the sailing down the river in Kinsale. Maguire had bought it when the colonel died, and it gave him a certain quiet satisfaction to occupy one of the finest houses in the town. Through dint of hard graft he'd risen from lowly cottier's son on the road between Letterkenny and Bundoran up in Donegal, to having probably the largest practice hereabouts, while also being influential as town councillor, alderman and registrar's committee member of the Incorporated Law Society of Ireland. Admittedly his clients weren't all of the blue chip variety; no Lord Bandon or Jasper Eustace among them, but he hoped to remedy that situation in due course with an assiduous, but discreet courting of the Earl and his friends. As it was, the raising of Probate to the estate of Jasper Eustace had eluded him and that was a disappointment. It would have been juicy. He'd hob-nobbed with Jasper as far as it was decently possible to do so, but the damn fellow had seen through him, while leading him along at the same time. No matter how many brandies he'd ply him with or house parties he'd invite him to, Jasper would retain his business with Dowdall, while cheerfully availing himself of Maguire's largesse. As for Eleanore, she was suspicious of him from the start and rarely gave him an opportunity to broach subjects of a legal nature. Never mind. He would continue to seek out opportunities, and in the meantime he was doing quite nicely, thank you very much. His daughter, God help her, was an eager student of the law and Maguire hoped to pass on the practice and keep things in the family for another generation. But his wife had been unable to deliver a son, much to his chagrin. There would be no solicitors with the name Maguire by and by.

Like a lot of solicitors, he liked the logic of the law, but even more so the inevitability of death. From death flowed the administration of people's estates, the conveying of their property onwards and the certainty of substantial fees accruing to himself. The sweetest logic of all. Even the occasional stray piece of land, unable to find a successor, would show up from time to time, which Maguire could then buy up on the cheap to add to his burgeoning portfolio. He allowed himself a quiet chuckle of satisfaction as he stood up from his desk and walked to the high, Georgian window, affording views over the town. He could see the dark river below, glinting dimly in the street lights, and out the other window the military barracks hulked on high in the distance. A sense of security and well-being gladdened his breast. There was a gentle breeze tonight, and the bare branches of the great oaks and beeches around the house swayed and creaked. Maybe rain was on the way. He sighed and turned back towards his desk. He'd better get on with drafting this deed of conveyance. He'd composed as far as the operative part: "Now This Indenture Witnesseth that in pursuance of the aforementioned agreement and in consideration of the sum of one hundred pounds (the receipt of which is hereby acknowledged) the Vendor as beneficial owner hereby grants and conveys unto the Purchaser All That And Those the property described in the First Schedule hereto To Hold the same unto and to the use of the Purchaser in Fee Simple..."

Conveyancing had such precise, interlocking parts, such accuracy of language, although archaic, even arcane; the chain of title passing from A to B as truly as a mathematical equation. A careful solicitor could trace the ownership and the history of a piece of land down through four or five hundred years. Back to when this entire barony of Kinalmeaky or Carbery was held by Gaelic chieftains. At what stage were their entitlements extinguished and their rights of ownership usurped? Maguire had a sneaking regard for those long dead clansmen, but of course it wasn't politic or even sensible for such a thought to be expressed by him in his present eminence. Sentimentality was all very well, but a man had to be aware on which side his bread was buttered. And not without good reason. The struggle to educate him had been exceptional. Most of his siblings were in service to big houses or worked as farm labourers. His parents had chosen him to lead the family to distinction and he had delivered on the promise. He'd been sent down to Cork to lodge with an uncle, his mother's brother, named Bill O'Donovan. Through careful cultivation of the right individuals, he'd been indentured with Dowdall's firm in Bandon and completed his examinations, incrementally, with the Incorporated Law Society. He'd stayed in with local magistrates such as Sealey King, J.P. and invited him and others like R. Bence Jones, Deputy Lieutenant to Lord Bandon, to dinner on a regular basis to ensure the bonds were maintained. He'd worked with Dowdall for a good seven years before setting up on his own, hanging his shingle out in gold lettering on a nameplate in rented rooms on North Main Street. He'd eked out his early living in a small, cramped office on the second floor of a damp, Georgian townhouse. Rickety stairs, sloping floors, toppling chimneys, these were his uninspiring surroundings; yet what did he require but a desk, a typewriter and some tomes of law reports and precedents? With painstaking steps he built up the practice; writing wills for small farmers and postmen in the town, securing dog licenses for old ladies, intoxicating liquor licenses for the odd shebeen, and defending quarrelling tinkers and petty criminals at the assizes. Year on year he grafted away, a slight, bespectacled figure with owl eyes, a mean mouth and a sense of his own self-importance. He did few favours for anybody, but liked to think he did no harm either. Lately however, these Sinn Féiners were invading his bailiwick, so to speak; setting up their own courts and administering justice separately from the British system. They ignored the established judges, magistrates and attorneys, dispensing sentences and dispatching land-grabbers, cattle-rustlers and corner-boys with a speed and efficiency Maguire could only envy. He was particularly bitter about that, and the fact they were taking the bite directly out of his own mouth. There was no greater bile on earth than that which came on the breath of an unpaid lawyer. Maguire suffered from a great hunger for money, for land, for power. Driven on from the hard-scrabble way he was raised, by residual fear of famine, deprivation, even death itself. In thinking along these lines he could work himself up into quite a state of righteous indignation. But there was someone for whom he reserved his deepest loathing of all: a fellow solicitor, and a Catholic to boot, named P.J.O'Driscoll, who'd also started up like himself from modest beginnings. By all accounts O'Driscoll was exceedingly popular with all and sundry in the town, had a reputation for efficiency and spoke fluent Irish. To cap it all, he had a bunch of strapping young sons to inherit his practice whereas Maguire had only the one daughter. There was no beating that combination.

His mousey wife came in through the double doors of the study with a silver tray upon which rattled a China tea set, barm brack and biscuits. Maguire momentarily forgot his misery and licked his thin lips, 'Ah, my dear Alice, thank you. Perfect timing, very welcome.'

His wife, a clone of himself, mean spirited, self-regarding and smug, laid down the tray and asked without much enthusiasm, 'Will you be working late?' The prospect of Maguire's parsimonious frame occupying the opposite side of the bed to herself didn't ignite any great fires of passion in her meagre bosom. They were birds of a feather right enough: a malcontent, treacherous pair.

Maguire bit on a biscuit and said, 'I have to finish this conveyance for Murphy of Myshells. He's coming in tomorrow and you know what he's like.'

'Indeed I do,' said Mrs Maguire, and shook her head with a kind of hopeless inevitability. Murphy was her husband's biggest client, his direct route to further riches. When he said jump, Maguire asked how high? She dusted off an eighteenth century Chippendale side table and straightened a Henry Mayer painting of *Hayfields,* on a wall. 'I'll be upstairs,' she said. 'You'll be late, by the looks of it.'

She went out into the large hall, where a fire burned in a grate, casting heat into the study and into the sitting room beyond, through which she disappeared. Maguire liked to throw all the double doors open in summertime to give himself and his guests a sense of the sheer spaciousness of the house, but such were the draughts that blew around his backside in winter that all doors were firmly shut. He gazed lovingly at his treasured antiques. He'd come a long way from the plain, deal table and typewriter on the North Main Street, and even further from the two-roomed cottage overlooking Bundoran Bay. He finished up his tea, sweeping the crumbs of the brack into the palm of his hand and depositing them in a rubbish bin underneath the desk. He heard a door creaking in the hall and thought that would be his wife locking up for the night. He returned to the perusal of the legal document. The study door opened softly but he did not look up; the wife was being particularly fussy tonight with her housekeeping. Then a shadow was cast over his parchment by someone standing between it and the lamp behind him. He turned round and nearly jumped out of his skin. A soldier in full military uniform stood at his elbow. He wore a long trenchcoat that was unbuckled, revealing two revolvers resting in two leather holsters on either thigh. He had an officer's peaked cap pulled low over his eyes.

'My God above,' swore Maguire. 'You startled me and so you did. I thought it was my wife. How did you get in?'

'Through the front door,' said the officer.

'Are you with the Essex Regiment?' asked the solicitor, looking the uniform up and down, absorbing every detail.

'No,' said the other, evenly. 'I'm with the IRA.' Then he walked casually from Maguire's side, around the desk and sat himself down in a swivel chair directly opposite. He took off his cap, undid the stud of his collar and loosened his tie.

Maguire's eyes watched his movements carefully and then he asked, 'Who are you?'

'The name is Barry. Tom Barry.'

The solicitor's jaw dropped. He licked his lips and his eyes blinked rapidly. 'To..To..Tom Barry?' he stuttered, and added, '*The* Tom Barry?'

'Is there another?' smiled the officer.

The solicitor did not reply immediately. He looked at the door which Barry had closed behind him, then he looked towards the window.

'Don't even think about it,' said Barry.

The solicitor frowned and pretended not to understand, 'I don't follow you, Mr. Barry.'

'The door, don't think of trying to alert anyone. You'll find your progress will be impeded.'

'Oh, really, Mr. Barry,' said the solicitor, with fake *sang froid*. 'Have you brought your dogs of war with you?'

'What do you think?' asked Barry and opened a packet of cigarettes.

'You don't look like the sort of man to take reckless chances.'

'You're a good judge of character, Mr. Maguire.' Barry extended the packet. 'Cigarette?'

The solicitor shook his head.

'You don't mind if I do?' asked Barry and tappped a cigarette on the back of the packet, before putting it between his lips.

'I don't think I'd be in a position to stop you, unless by appealing to your sense of good behaviour,' said Maguire.

Barry smiled again, struck a match to the cigarette, inhaled and blew the smoke in Maguire's direction. 'Good behaviour is a matter of taste. What you might consider good behaviour, I might not.'

'That's very true,' said Maguire. 'But where is all this leading? Is there something I can do for you?'

'If you mean of a legal nature, no thanks. We already have our own lawyers and do not subscribe to the redundant system which you still serve.'

'So I've heard,' said Maguire, and looked a little peeved. 'But from what I'm told there is somewhat less of good practice and fair procedure in your system, and a good deal more of the blunt instrument of persuasion.'

'We've learned from very good teachers, Mr. Maguire. The procedures of the Black and Tans could scarcely be called fair. In fact they've been condemned in most countries in the western world including by many in England, the United States and Australia.'

'What does all that have to do with me?'

'Mr. Maguire, don't come the innocent with me. At the recent funeral of the informer, Jasper Eustace, you inveighed against us in a vicious, sectarian speech that caused a bunch of thugs called the Loyalist Action Group, to butcher two innocent and upright young men, Tim and James Coffey, in cold blood. Your words, which were scarcely to be expected out of the mouth of a so-called upholder of the rule of law, were directly responsible for this crime.'

The solicitor shifted uncomfortably in his chair. 'I was merely stating a point of view. You forget, Mr. Barry that your IRA thugs assassinated my friend, Jasper Eustace, also in cold blood.'

'He was executed for betraying his neighbours and causing the deaths of countless young men by torture and mutilitation. You see, Mr. Maguire, the British have gone down into the mire and we have no choice now but to go down after them.'

'What does that mean?' asked Maguire, raising a supercilious eyebrow.

'Up to this point,' said Barry, 'we have only targeted British soldiers in the field, or those who have tortured and murdered our men. The only other people we target are those who have directly betrayed us. The British, through the agency of the Black and Tans, the Essex and the Auxiliaries have been riding rough-shod over this country for the past two years, burning, pillaging, murdering and raping. We have acted honourably. We've even released British soldiers who have not disgraced themselves or the flag of their own country by base acts. However, that will all come to an end as of tonight.'

Barry stood up. He took a pistol from his holster and placed in on the desk in front of the solicitor and he placed the other pistol on the desk in front of himself. Maguire looked alarmed. He shrank back in his seat.

'There's a pistol for you, Mr. Maguire, and here's one for me,' said Barry. Maguire's eyes flickered around like a cornered rat. Barry continued, 'You've been very vocal in your speeches, inciting your listeners to take armed action against us. You've urged them to kill, burn and destroy. Now here's a chance to make a start yourself.'

Maguire started to sweat. The two pistols, one a short Webley and the other a Colt automatic, pearl-handled and perfect, gleamed in the middle of his desk. He could make a lunge for one and become a hero, but that would only occur in his wildest imagination. The cold commander's eyes facing him were unlikely to blink. He mopped his brow with a handkerchief. 'I think I'll take that cigarette now,' he said.

Barry proffered one from the packet. Maguire's fingers trembled as he put it between his lips. Barry struck a match and put the flame to the cigarette end. The smell of sulphur from the match and the smell of smoke being exhaled by Maguire filled the room. Barry sat back down.

'So what do you intend to do?' asked Maguire. 'Shoot me? You know I won't fire that gun. I'm not a fighting man.'

Barry regarded him with a frank expression that lay somewhere between contempt and pity. 'You know why the British are so desperate to destroy us, Mr. Maguire? It's not because of our superior numbers, or our wealth, or even our ideas. It's because of these items here.'

He pointed to the two guns still reposing on the desk. 'You think you have power, but its parameters are severely limited. You have power as a lawyer to enforce the law, only because of an unspoken agreement by those who bear arms to enforce your decrees. If you were a judge you could sentence a man to death, but unless the hangman or the firing squad were willing to carry out your order, your power would be useless. All power is an illusion unless backed up by the threat of force. Bankers think they have power, so do politicians. But the real reason those very bankers and politicians are terrified of us is that we have real power. You could say power comes from a gun barrel, and a small minority prepared to wield those guns have power out of all proportion to their numbers. That is our secret. The British know that. We have demonstrated our intent. People like you will be swept away, along with all your vainglorious possessions.'

Maguire was now quite pale. 'So you are going to kill me,' he said, with a resigned look on his thin face.

Barry smiled at him. 'You shouldn't ever jump to conclusions as far as we are concerned, Mr. Maguire. We still operate by a series of rules and a code of honour, which may not look like such to you, but it will save your life. However it will not save your property.'

'My property?' spluttered Maguire in panic, and looked as if he were going to choke for lack of oxygen.

Barry stood up again: 'The British forces have been burning Irish families out of their homes in increasing numbers. Families have been left on the roadside, huddling under tarpaulins, sleeping in haysheds. But from now on we will burn two loyalist houses for every one of our houses burned by the British. Starting with your house and another on the eastern side of the town. This will continue until the British get the message and stop their crimes of arson against our people.'

'You can't possibly do this,' said Maguire. 'The soldiers are on curfew patrol through the town. They'll be alerted. You'll be trapped.'

'We've anticipated that eventuality. In fact your blazing house will not set a trap for us, but rather for them. We have companies of men coming into the town from three different directions. When the flames lure the soldiers from their barracks we'll be waiting for them.'

Barry replaced the two pistols in his holsters. A knock came to the door and Mrs Maguire was ushered in by two men armed with pistols: Sonny Hennessy and Mick Crowley. Maguire looked resigned, cowed and quite miserable. His wife had a look of hatred on her face. Not for the intruders in her home, but for her cowardly, lily-livered husband.

At precisely 8.15 p.m., Tom Barry left the Maguire household. Leaving Sonny and two others in charge, he instructed them to torch the house when they heard the first gunshots coming from the town. Then, accompanied by the lantern-jawed Mick Crowley, he made his way by a circuitous back route down to the corner of Cork Road and Watergate Street, not far from the river. There they met John Lordan and the main body of the Flying Column. The moon was bright but the wind blew scudding clouds across its face causing it to darken and brighten every few minutes. The men were hidden in doorways, and behind pillars and hedges.

'Are we ready, John?' asked Barry.

'All ready Commandant,' said Lordan.

'Has anyone seen ye?' asked Barry.

'We've confined all civilians indoors,' said Lordan. 'Nobody can come up or down Cork Road.'

'Very good,' said Barry. 'Charlie Hurley has men crossing the river from Castle Bernard Park. When Sonny Hennessy hears the first shots he'll set Maguire's house on fire. Hopefully that will bring the military in numbers out of the barracks and Charlie's men will be waiting for them. At the same time, Liam Deasy's men will come in from Shannon Street side. Some of them will stay there and the others will keep a shot on the RIC barracks at the western end of South Main Street. As for our party, its job is to destroy the curfew patrol when it crosses back over the river. Have you got that, John?'

Lordan nodded in his singular certainty. He was a man who feared little. A restless warrior, loyal to the core.

Then Barry said, 'I'll go across the river and see where the curfew patrol is.'

'Are you sure, Commandant?' asked Lordan. 'To risk it all alone?'

'Yes,' said Barry. 'I'll take Mick Crowley with me part of the way.'

They left the others and went towards the bridge. Mick Crowley waited at a granite-faced edifice called, The Allin Institute, and Barry continued on over. The moon came out again from behind the clouds and a cold wind blew colder across the bare expanse of the river from the west. When he got to the bridge end he stopped near the Post Office to talk to some people who knew him.

'God bless you, Tom Barry,' said an old man with a walking stick.

'Have you seen the curfew patrol?' asked Barry.

'They're gone up the South Main Street,' said the old man, and spat. 'Bad cess to them.'

'When d'you think they'll be back?' asked Barry.

'Give 'em ten minutes,' said the old timer.

Charlie Hurley ushered his men down a dark, tree-lined road, between the high walls of Lord Bandon's estate at Castle Bernard Park. At the bottom of a steep hill, they came to a double iron gate on the left and undid the latch and entered the wide fields that stretched out along the river's banks. There were huge, ancient stands of oak, hazel and birch. There were horses quietly grazing and a few started up and galloped away, snorting, in fright. There were many lights blazing back up in the big house but no guards or sentries impeded their way. The group approached the river where it flowed, sloe-black and silent. The smell of winter and of sweet decay was all around. Moss and lichen grew on barks of trees, and was soft to the touch of hand, as was the feel of mud, soft and mulchy underfoot. They disturbed a black cormorant, which flew upstream in the moonlight as they filed across the iron footbridge and made their way along the wooded banks on the northern side. Every now and then Charlie stopped if a twig crackled or a man coughed, so as to ensure they went undetected. He had ten men, all armed with rifles and revolvers, all battle-hardened and cool under pressure.

The curfew patrol stepped smartly up the South Main Street, oblivious to the encroaching danger. It marched in close formation and its forty-four rank and file soldiers carried full battle equipment, steel-helmeted, with their rifles at the slope. An officer marched in front. The townsfolk huddled in resentful, sullen silence, like penned sheep within the confines of their houses. Their hatred of the domineering patrol increased by the day, and the odd brave soul ventured forth at the risk of getting a bullet in the back any time a soldier caught him in the cross-hairs of his rifle. The curfew patrol related back to medieval times to apprehend robber bands who operated after darkness. Now resurrected to contain the IRA, it operated usually between the hours of 8 p.m. and 6 a.m. All citizens were ordered, under pain of being shot on sight, not to leave their homes during those hours. It brooked no excuses even for those fetching a priest or doctor for a loved one. No compensation was payable to a family whose breadwinner was shot down for breaching the rules. The powers of the army were completely unlimited and it was unanswerable to any British Courts since Martial Law was declared. No inquests or post mortems were allowed.

Liam Deasy, with ten Volunteers, occupied the raised bridge by Lee's Hotel and another few occupied houses at the corners of two lanes which branched south at Shannon Street from South Main. The men were well schooled as to their actions. They were to remain concealed until the enemy patrol hovered into view and at the blast of a whistle or a Mills bomb, fire was to be opened.

Constable Fred Perrier was in ebullient mood. He'd been commended by his commanding officer, Major Halahan, for his sterling work in extracting information from Sinn Féin prisoners. With his powerful, garrison-game build as rugby prop forward he was particularly well equipped to deliver thunderous kicks to the groins of his victims or to punch them senseless if they refused to divulge their secrets. He and his comrade, Constable P.J. Kerins, were adept at the black arts of persuasion and rendition and they'd been given a pretty broad brief to enforce them by their commanding officers, provided no proof of their methods leaked out to tiresome, bleeding-heart reporters from the *Manchester Guardian*, or that traitorous editor, Robert Lynd from the *Daily Mail*, who'd had the temerity to write in a leading article on the 4th of January, that England was ruling Ireland in the spirit of the torturer. Tonight, Perrier had a few hours off and along with Kerins and two other stout fellows, Corporal Stubbs and Private Knight, they were bound for Lee's Hotel to sink a right few whiskeys. The 'Paddy' brand had become their favourite tipple: a coarse Irish malt that burned the throat at the initial contact, but which quickly induced a sensation of well-being and euphoria. As a chaser, they liked to quaff a pint of the local porter made by Beamish and Crawford, a dark-as-midnight liquid, with a head that tasted like fresh cream. In anticipation of the beverage and with the prospect of stealing a few kisses or even something more from the loose-living doxies of the town, Perrier and his companions had a spring in their step as they marched down North Main Street.

Tom Barry thanked the locals and the topers he'd met at the Post Office and turned back along Bandon Bridge to rejoin his comrades on the other side. Armed with the precise information of the curfew patrol's movements, they'd be ready to ambush it on their own terms. He was about five yards from the corner of North Main Street when he heard voices, a sound of laughter and marching feet. He knew they were British forces, but had no idea how many. He thought of turning to run, but he'd be shot in the back halfway across. Here it was at last then. Perrier, Kerins, Stubbs and Knight swung around the corner four abreast. They saw Tom Barry straight in front of them. All went for their guns at the same time. Barry's first shot from the Colt automatic in his right hand hit Kerins just below the heart. He dropped like a stone. His second shot flattened Knight against the parapet of the bridge. Perrier dropped to the ground and blazed away, shouting and screaming as he did so, but in his haste his bullets went awry and missed their target. Stubbs, firing blindly, dashed across the bridge to the other parapet and Barry, throwing himself flat while firing with the Webley in his left hand, hit him with one deadly accurate shot in the side of the head. Stubbs fell, having emptied his revolver, all six chambers, into thin air. Perrier jumped up from his prone position, turned and ran. Barry leaped to his feet and gave chase. Perrier had a seven yard start as he turned the corner. His revolver was in his right hand as he pounded the pavement towards the barracks. Barry gained on him yard by yard. Perrier was surprisingly fast for a heavy man, but Barry was thin as a whippet and lithe on his feet. He kept the Colt in his right hand and slipped the Webley back in its holster as he ran. Had Perrier turned and dropped to one knee, he could have finished his pursuer off, but this never occurred to him in his blind panic. Neither could Barry have missed had he pulled the trigger. The race continued, pell-mell up the hill. An onlooker would have heard clattering feet, panicky cries and the panting of bursting lungs. Barry caught up with his quarry and grabbed him by the shoulder. Perrier had a look of terror in his eyes: the same look he'd so often relished when torturing his victims to death in the basement of the barracks. He suddenly darted in a doorway of a small shop. Barry's impetus took him past the door. He skidded to a stop and doubled back. He followed Perrier into the small, low-ceilinged *siopín i chúinne*. He vaulted the counter and found himself in the kitchen at the far end, facing Perrier. A man and a woman sat by the fire. The woman fainted as Barry pulled the trigger and hit Perrier in the face. He slumped to the floor and his revolver thudded on the floorboards. Barry fired again although Perrier was already dead.

Up at the barracks, the engines of lorries and armoured cars were revving loudly, as soldiers piled into them. Further along, flames were licking out through the windows and doors of James Maguire's prized mansion, bought and furnished with blood, sweat, tears and dubious legacies. The smoke rose into the windy sky, swirling and dipping around bare tree branches. Ashes and sparks traced the sky, cloud scuffed, moonbright. The soldiers emerged from the barracks in their vehicles and didn't know which way to turn in their haste. Some went towards Maguire's house and ran straight into a hail of bullets from Charlie Hurley's section, that had lain in wait having come over the river, and that was now bolstered by Sonny and his two companions who'd held Maguire and his wife hostage until the moment the shooting started. The solicitor and his wife, sobbing with rage and frustration, had no choice but to leave their entire hoard of antiques and gold ornaments unsalvaged, and take to the fields like common kern to escape the raging inferno, and head for Convent Hill, where they'd be lucky to find lodgings from the Sisters of Mercy for the night.

The curfew patrol, alerted by the unexpected encounter between Tom Barry and Perrier's men, had the opportunity to escape the worst of the fire from Liam Deasy's section near Shannon Street. Scattering to sidewalks, side streets and lanes, it doubled back up South Main Street, returning huge volumes of fire towards the flashes coming from Volunteers holed up in corner houses. As the patrol retreated, retaliatory gunfire also erupted from the RIC barracks in random salvoes that had no aim or target, but merely a knee-jerk reaction to the IRA gunfire directed at the patrol. Thousands of rounds of ammunition fell fallow on roof and river, street and footpath. Its only effect was to keep the citizens of the town awake and to generate an unexpected increase in heartbeats at the prospect of a counter-attack of such ferocity being directed at last against their hated enemies, who'd kept steel-tipped boots on their necks for far too long.

When Tom Barry emerged from the shop on North Main Street after his fatal encounter with Perrier, he found himself in an unexpected dilemma. Bullets raked the street from his own mens' rifles, after John Lordan and Mick Crowley had ordered them up the road to seek out the whereabouts of their commander, and to take the fight to the military barracks further up. Would he now be shot by his own men? Barry was waving and shouting frantically. The military vehicles were advancing down the hill towards him while his own men were simultaneously coming up the hill against him. He was caught in a cleft stick. By some miracle he was eventually spotted by Lordan, who immediately ordered his men to cease firing while their commander raced to rejoin them.

The bedlam continued for a further two hours around the town. Not knowing how many were attacking them and unnerved by the random but cunningly located sources of firepower, the British forces unleashed a barrage of rifle, machinegun and revolver fire out of all proportion to that directed against them. Well after midnight, with eight of their number dead, and several more injured, they reluctantly ceased firing. But most paced the perimeters of their outposts until dawn, with an alarming feeling in their hearts that the tide of war might be turning against them.

The Volunteers regrouped three miles away in ebullient mood. They'd suffered only one casualty and their morale was soaring. They'd taken on vastly greater numbers, with just seventy riflemen against hundreds of better armed enemy forces. They'd occupied the town for over four hours, and the close quarter attack on all three garrisons coupled with the burning out of two loyalist houses was a reassurance to them that they were a highly capable and confident force.

Major Percival was seriously perturbed at the effrontery of the IRA, attacking him in his fortress in the town of Bandon, the nerve centre of all British activity in Cork. He would have to seek urgent meetings with his commanding officers to put in place a strategy to counter the increasing audacity of the rebels.

15

'A cold oul devil of a day,' said Mick Shorten from atop the roof ridge as he pulled up a yealm of long reed and laid it on the brow course of thatch, which he and Tull were putting in place on the old outhouse. Tull was dressing the butts of reed on the spot board, combing them out nice and neat before handing them up to Mick.

'Tis cold,' said Tull, 'but we're nearly done. Another couple of days.'

'Ah Christ, this is no job for a harness maker,' said Mick, and blew on his icy-cold fingers.

'A man like you could turn his hand to anything,' said Tull. He was trying to jolly Mick along and he'd been successful for the past six weeks. Mick was a slight, lean man without an ounce of flesh on him. He was in his late twenties and no finer harness maker strode the roads of West Cork. Mick would move around from farm to farm with his brown leather satchel in which he kept the tools of his trade: awls, long needles, hemp, saddle cloth, pliers, pincers, leather laces. He was adept at repairing saddles, horse collars, straddles, backbands, bridles, britchins. A neat, fastidious tradesman, who worked all day long and drank a good bit of the night. He ate little, maybe a bowl of porridge and a rasher in the morning, but he had energy and skill in abundance. The big trick with Mick was to keep him from going on a batter. If that happened, you mightn't see him for a month and many the farmer would tear his hair out in frustration trying to contact him to fix a piece of essential tackling. If Mick was drinking, the job would have to wait. He liked Tull and agreed to forego his harness work for awhile until the outhouse was thatched. Besides, he had a good heart and felt obliged to help out his countrymen in their hour of need. There were a good few harness makers around, but very few men knew how to thatch a house. Mick could do both jobs very well, which made him a rare bird indeed.

Jeremiah kept the copper worm pipe going up in the loft making moonshine to whet Mick's appetite. 'He's a tasty tradesman right enough,' said Jeremiah, 'but 'tis a hoor to keep him at it.'

'You keep plying him with *poitín*,' said Tull. 'Not too much, just a little a day and with the help of God he'll see the job out.'

Tull had to use all his wit and powers of flattery and persuasion to keep Mick going, but talents such as his were rare, and the effort was worth the candle.

Since the Tans had burnt out the main farmhouse, Tull and Mick had been busy. Richie and Jeremiah helped a little but it was left to Tull to drive the project to completion. And without Mick Shorten, Tull could not succeed. Richie had helped with the rough work initially, cleaning out the calves houses and pitching the dung into the *súlach*. Then, when the outhouse was empty they removed the old rusted sheet iron from the roof and replaced and plastered the broken stone walls and the big open fireplace with its soaring chimney. They repaired the rafters and joists on the hipped roof and put wall plates in place. Then they laid battens and felt and contructed bargeboards, soffits and fascias. They didn't need to add gutters because none could be attached to the end of the reed. The rainwater would simply drop onto the ground. They went as far as Kilbrittain and Harbour View, where they cut large stelches of strong reed and built a high load on the cart, which a horse towed on the long road home. They made a half a dozen trips in all to the estuary, each taking a whole day. They'd bring back each load of reed, heel it out beside the renovated outhouse until they had a substantial rick, ready for thatching. They were lucky with the weather. No rain, just the wind that blew long and cold from the northeast.

When everything was ready they built a rudimentary scaffolding and set to work thatching the roof. Mick Shorten thatched in vertical stelches up the roof and used his legget to thump the end of the reed into place with steady strokes. They were soon up at the roof ridge, where Mick fixed a biddle into the thatch to enable him to work on the higher reaches. Getting nitches of reed into the ridge was slow and painstaking work.

'The most important part,' said Mick. 'The rain gets in here first and trickles down. A lot of people don't know that. If your ridge is sound, your thatched roof will last twice as long as it would if the job is botched. A dry ridge is a dry house.'

They placed hazel liggers on the outside of the ridge at the saddle and cut the ridge-yealm into a herring-bone shape along the apex of the roof. Then they bound it into the main stelch with spars split from gadds of hazelnut. By late February their work was done. The full spring moon shone down upon their handiwork. Elizabeth returned from the Wilsons and soon established a cosy kitchen, and fitted out the two bedrooms on the ground floor and the one upstairs in the steep-pitched attic.

'Sure this house is a better job than the one burnt out,' said Jeremiah, as they ate their first supper in their new home, having been bereft and homeless for two months. 'Thanks be to God, and here's a toast to a grand tradesman, Mick Shorten, whose likes you won't meet every day.'

'The boys should see us now,' said Richie. 'They'd never believe the style we're living in at all.'

Mick nodded. His eyes flickered. He looked troubled as he wiped his lips and said, 'They've raised the stakes I see.'

'You mean the barracks attacks?' asked Tull.

'Are they getting too daring?' asked Mick. 'One of these days that kind of thing could backfire on them.'

'It could,' said Richie. 'But the British are worried I'd say.'

'The retaliation is a good idea,' said Tull. 'Maybe the loyalists won't be so cocksure now, when they see their own houses on fire.'

'I hear Maguire took it very bad. He never expected his own place to go up in flames.'

'That'll teach him to be a little more compassionate. That fellow was too big for his boots anyway. Trying to play the squireen like Jasper Eustace.'

''Tis hitting my trade though,' said Mick. 'I used to do a lot of work for Jasper on his saddles and harness.'

'No matter,' said Jeremiah. 'A man like you will never run out of work. As long as there's horses in the country, you won't be idle.'

'Or thatched houses,' said Richie

'I suppose you're right,' said Mick. He slept on a downy mattress that night under the newly-thatched roof. All agreed that it was an outstanding success. It kept the heat in, in the winter, and kept things cool in the summer.

Before he left, Mick went up to the loft the following night to see some *poitín* being brewed. Jeremiah had been preparing for weeks. Initially he soaked a small heap of barley grain in a large barrel of water. Then he spread the grain on the floor near an old fireplace in the loft where he had a good fire going. It would take quite a while to dry and ripen and, when it first began to bud, it was dried and ground, and put into the wash barrel. Jeremiah then added a little yeast. After about two weeks the batch was ready for the still. The equipment consisted of three separate parts: the body, the head and the worm. The head was a cover for the body, with a connecting pipe to carry the steam to the condenser. Jeremiah would never connect the head until the contents of the still had almost reached boiling point, and then he sealed the loose joints with dough made from baking flour. The heady liquid was siphoned off and put into the pot. The fire was built up and the water was started running on the condenser coil, which they called the worm because of its twisting shape. The night he brought Mick up, Jeremiah was ready to dispense the first batch of moonshine. The first drops to come through the worm contained all the fusel oils, which were toxic, so the first naggin was dumped out the door. Then as the flow continued, Jeremiah filled up a bottle. Mick sampled a naggin.

'How is it?' asked Jeremiah.

'Powerful,' said Mick. 'A good smoky tang and a nice sweet after taste. Very subtle I'd say.'

They enjoyed a few glasses, which put them in ebullient mood. Mick had done a good job on the thatch and Jeremiah and Tull were exceedingly grateful. Apart from his pay, he was sent on his way the following day with four bottles of the illicit liquor hidden in his satchel. His step was lightsome and his mood was good. He sang a ditty as he strode along into the rising sun.

At 9.20 a.m. that morning, the west Cork train left Albert Quay station in Cork city. It carried an assorted collection of passengers: a man with two greyhound pups, a woman with two small children and a bicycle with a basket and carrier on which she'd arrived at the station; one child in the basket and one on the carrier. There were three priests with Roman collars, Homburg hats and long black overcoats to keep them from the cold. There were four farmers' wives, with their hair tied back severely off their faces, wearing headscarves, practical skirts and strong shoes. They carried baskets of eggs and pounds of salted, country butter well wrapped in old newspaper. A teacher, aged in his twenties, in a sensible suit and brogues, got on and sat in a carriage on his own, until fifteen British soldiers arrived as the whistle was sounding and gruffly ordered him to vacate the carriage, which they occupied exclusively. A solicitor with a pinstripe suit, white starched collar and bow tie, going down to Bandon to close a sale with Dowdalls, got on with his briefcase, his quills and quiddities, and proceeded to spread everything out on the seat beside him, catching up on his brief as it were, ticking requisitions on title off with a pencil. A young couple who appeared to be in love, arrived with a last minute rush and settled themselves in beside the solicitor, much to his irritation. They were panting and laughing, and making plans for all the sights they were going to see out around Ballydehob and Schull, and other far flung villages on the eternally grand and beautiful coast. There were other passengers of either sex who also got on board: young and old, rich and poor, each with his or her own particular itinerary, worries and troubles, and duties for the day. Many of the passengers caught the infectious mood of gaiety of the young couple, and as the whistle screeched again, the steam was released in great emissions of pent up energy, and the smoke towered upward into the morning air. It was cold, but the sky was cloudless, the sun was bright. The Great Southern & Western engine, painted black and green, with its number emblazoned in scarlet and yellow on the front, slouched slowly out of the station bound on a new day and a new adventure. The engineer, with cap and navy blue uniform, and the fireman with blackened face and sweating brow, nodded to the signalman on the platform who blew a final blast and waved a flag to signal the departure of the train, which ran, like the fabled Wells Fargo of America, come wind, hail, rain or snow, to take its passengers to their destinations.

Soon the train was rolling over the Chetwynd Viaduct, a fine feat of engineering, soaring nearly one hundred feet above a wide valley, designed by Charles Nixon a former pupil of the great English engineer, Brunel, and built between 1849 and 1851 by Fox, Henderson and Company, who had built the Crystal Palace in London. It consisted of four spans, each composed of four cast iron arched ribs, carried on huge masonry piers 20 feet thick and 30 feet wide. The overall span between the end abutments was 500 feet. The passengers looked down and gasped at the sheer height and length of the mighty bridge. No sooner had the train passed over the Viaduct but it was hurtling through another remarkable feat of construction, the Ballinhassig Tunnel, a half a mile in length, delving through rock and old red sandstone. When the train emerged from the tunnel it was well on its way towards the beckoning, romantic country to the west, where the sun shone down and mystery did unfold.

Charlie Hurley waited down the railway tracks from Upton station. He was agitated. He'd been wrestling with the idea of attacking a train for some time, given the increasing number of soldiers using that mode of transport, taking up valuable passenger space, paying nobody and treating decent people like thrash. A few rounds of lead might change their tune.

They'd received information that a small unit of soldiers would be on the train that morning, maybe ten or fifteen at most. Charlie brought his men down the tracks towards the station. There were fourteen including himself. They went towards the passenger platform on the north side of the line. They went into the station master's office and told him they were going to attack the train. The station master looked at the determined bunch of assembled Volunteers and quickly threw his hands up.

'I hope ye know what ye're doing,' he said. 'There's civilians on that train, women and children, not just the soldiers.'

'We know,' said Charlie. 'But they'll be in a separate compartment, like they always are. We'll make sure the civilians are nowhere near the shooting.'

'Lord help us,' said the station master. 'Sure how can you control things if ye start shooting.'

'Don't worry,' said Charlie. 'We have experienced men here, and we have two scouts who'll get on at Kinsale Junction to tell us which compartments the soldiers are in.'

'I still think 'tis a very bad idea,' said the station master.

Charlie put John Butler and Pat O'Sullivan in place beyond the waiting room. O'Sullivan had two Colt .45 revolvers and Butler a rifle. Sean Phelan and Flor Begley, with automatic pistols, he put in the waiting room, Paddy O'Leary at the wicket gate and Sean Hartnett at the signal cabin. Across the tracks at a goods store, Neilus Collins and Batt Falvey crouched, and behind a low wall were Dan O'Mahony and Denis Desmond. Back behind, at the goods yard entrance, Tom Kelleher and Denis Doolan were hidden behind another wall. All were armed with Lee Enfield rifles. Charlie himself ascended the iron footbridge over the railway line at the west end of the platform so as to afford himself a panoramic view of events unfolding on both sides of the track when the train came in. He was armed with a pistol, a Peter the Painter with a long barrel.

Three miles up the track at the Kinsale Junction station, the train stopped. One of the country women with the eggs and country butter got off and said so long to her companions. The woman with the bicycle and the two small children also got off. As the smoke swirled around and the signalman on the platform prepared to wave the train onwards, a large party of British soldiers, numbering at least fifty, began trooping onto the platform. Their leading officer, named Colonel Lattimer, curtly clicked his fingers at the signalman, ordering him to hold the train. 'Have you any spare compartments?' he asked.

The signalman looked at the assembling horde and raised an incredulous eyebrow. 'I have a few spare compartments but nothing like enough for that many soldiers.'

'Never mind,' said the Colonel. 'We'll use what you have, and the rest of my men will have to mingle with the civilian passengers. Can't be helped.' The soldiers began to file on, relaxed and laughing noisily.

Across the road from the station, there was a man scouting for the ambush party. His name was Bill Hartnett. His brother Sean was waiting back at Upton, at the gable-end of the signal room, oblivious to the new and unforeseen danger that was suddenly ahead. Bill was waiting for his fellow scout, John Beatty, to arrive, but he'd failed to show. The uneasy feeling struck him that his companion had drank too much the night before, as he was inclined to do, and had let him down. Bill was in a quandary. There were too many soldiers on the train now for him to get on board unnoticed. He'd have to try to make a dash for Upton on his bicycle. Before the train left he took off as fast as his legs could push the pedals. For a while the road was level and he was ahead of the train. He passed farmers in carts that he knew, others on foot. They saluted him and wondered why he didn't salute back. They stood looking after him, scratching their heads in puzzlement. He passed cows being driven out to fields after milking, and country swains leaning over gates, chatting in the morning sun. After two miles, the road wound around and bare trees bent down over the road in a canopy that would have been cool and pleasant in the summer, on a rising road where a man might stop and take a rest. But with pounding heart and bursting lungs, Bill Hartnett struggled up the rise. No time to stop today. He heard the train rumbling along behind him. Another couple of hundred yards and he crested the rise. With a horrified fascination he watched from a skew bridge as the train snaked out below him on the tracks. He could see well to the west. He could see the station in the distance and the smoke from the train blowing backwards like in a picture postcard. He flew down the hill on the western side, past the village crossroads of Killeady. Upton was half a mile ahead. He was three hundred yards from the station when he heard the gunfire erupting. He was too late.

The train pulled into the station and slowly ground to a stop. Charlie waited for thirty seconds for the scouts to jump off, as prearranged. No sign of them. Realising that something was wrong, he shouted, 'Fire!'

All guns blazed as one. Bullets ricochetted off iron railings and steel girders. They zinged as they hit the concrete platform, splintering the glass of several compartments. The man with the greyhound pups in the first carriage slumped over dead, shot through the neck by a stray bullet. The soldiers in their augmented numbers began pouring out of the train, returning fire. Passengers inside the train panicked and the young girl of the courting couple dashed out in the midst of the soldiers and began to run down the track. She was hit in the back and fell bleeding against the platform. Her stunned fiancé came running out after her, shouting desperately for her to stop. She died in his arms as soldiers milled all around them. The first of the attackers to be hit was Pat O'Sullivan. He fell, as two soldiers directed a salvo of shots at his stomach from point blank range. His companion, Sean Phelan, made a dash for the waiting room window, only to be mown down as he was halfway through. His body lay, half in, half out, as bullets fell all around him like showers of hail. Seeing what was happening from his high vantage point, Charlie shouted to his men to retreat and fall back to the west side of the station towards the level crossing and the gate house. His pistol had jammed after the first shot. He jumped from the bridge and as he jumped a bullet went through his right cheek and emerged at his left cheek just below his ear. At the same time he hit the ground, his ankle buckled awkwardly under him, in a severe sprain. As Flor Begley, Paddy O'Leary, John Butler, Sean Hartnett and Denis Desmond ran crouching under fire towards the level crossing, Tom Kelleher and Denis Doolan kept up a tremendous barrage of protective fire. Batt Falvey on the southern side dropped dead like a stone as a bullet hit him in the heart, and as Denis Doolan reached Dan O'Mahony, he realised he had also been wounded. He hoisted him on his back and carried him from the scene, eventually taking him for more than a mile to Cronin's house. All was pandemonium and mayhem on the platform. The soldiers had superior numbers, but panic set in and they began firing in random directions, often towards the train instead of away from it. One of the black coated priests was hit as he rose from his seat to get a glimpse of what was happening outside, and at the same time the young school teacher with the solid brogues burst out through a door and fell dead as a bullet hit him in the face. Tom Kelleher rushed towards Charlie and lifted him up. With a mighty effort he pulled him away from the platform. Charlie was seriously wounded and had no chance to make it on his own. Pat O'Sullian had a deep wound in his stomach. His entrails were hanging out. He found himself inside a deep trench beside the railway tracks and dragged himself along, until he also reached Tim Cronin's house in the townland of *Clais an Adhmaid,* a mile across the fields, where Doolan and O'Mahony also fetched up.

There were injured British soldiers strewn around the platform and six dead civilians. Five others were wounded. Colonel Lattimer shouted orders to his men when he realised the attack had been aborted. The station master came out and stood, slowly shaking his head at the scene of panic and bloodshed. His advice had not been heeded and he felt bitter about it. In his heart he was a supporter of the cause of freedom, but this was a high price to pay. The careful solicitor managed to make it to Bandon later in the day where he closed his sale and settled his nerves with several large brandies. One of the farmers' wives was not so lucky. She lay amid her running blood and her broken egg cartons as her life ebbed away, in the seat where she sat. Her sad companions in their head scarves and strong shoes, tried to help her, saying, 'God help us, Mary, wake up, girl.' But Mary would wake no more.

Tom Kelleher got his left arm under Charlie's right shoulder and, with his rifle in his right hand, they backed with halting steps away from the station. They kept looking at the smoke gushing from the train's funnel and the people running and shouting in disarray and confusion on the platform. Some soldiers pointed towards them and started to run after them. Kelleher coolly unleashed a volley of shots in their direction, holding the rifle one-handed. A few bullets whizzed over their heads, but the soldiers were half-hearted in their pursuit and appeared to have no appetite for further confrontation. They followed a straight road lined with trees and flat fields on either side. They reached a gate going into a field and went through it. They crossed the field and struggled through a gap at the far side. With Kelleher half lifting him, and Charlie hobbling along, they made it across another field and through another gap. They were getting further away. They came to an old Protestant church and they paused, gasping for breath. They were not being followed. Kelleher looked at Charlie's wound for the first time. There was a hole in each of his cheeks but by some extraordinary providence the bullet had passed though his face and the injury wasn't fatal. Blood was issuing forth, profusely at first, but then it slowed. He could put no weight on his ankle without excruciating pain. It could be broken. At this point they couldn't tell.

'What a disaster,' Charlie said.

'Never mind that now,' said Kelleher. 'We must keep going. They could follow us yet.'

He knew the country through which they passed very well. They crossed a main road, looking carefully to either side to ensure they were unobserved. They passed a public house in a sheltered hollow and climbed the hill beyond it. They took to lanes and obscure backroads rarely used by anyone. They kept going. Charlie, incoherent, groaning; Kelleher, stoic, determined, uncomplaining. Mile after mile they struggled along, begrimed, bloody, sweating, and thirsty. Having covered over five miles, Charlie gasped, 'I can't go on, Tom. You go on, on your own.'

'What are you saying, man?' said Kelleher. 'Here, sit down on this rock. Take a rest. You'll be alright.'

'I feel so weak, Tom. I've lost a good lot of blood. I'm fainting.' He slumped over on the rock and Kelleher had to move quickly to lay him down. Then he went to a stream flowing through the small wood where they'd stopped. He filled a tin mug he'd packed in his trenchcoat and brought it back to Charlie. He put it to his lips and Charlie drank the cold, clear water. It seemed to revive him.

'Where are we?' asked Charlie.

Kelleher looked around. Far to the east he could see the high, rounded hill of Knockavilla. 'We're a good way west,' he said 'Somewhere north of Bandon.'

They'd traversed a long ridge running westward, past many townlands with strange names. 'We might be in Queensfort,' said Kelleher. 'Or Roughgrove.'

The sun was sinking in the west, orange and cold. There were blue mountains far away. Charlie was cold. His punctured face was pale. He could barely speak. His will to continue was ebbing.

'We must go on,' said Kelleher. 'The military will be out in force looking for us. God knows what happened the rest of the boys. I think most of them got out alive, but poor Batt Falvey and Sean Whelan didn't make it. I think Pat Sullivan got hit too.'

'Where were the scouts?' asked Charlie.

'They must have let us down,' said Kelleher

'God almighty,' said Charlie again. 'What a disaster.' He shut his eyes and fell back down, 'You go on, Tom. I'm finished. Let me lay down here and sleep. You go on yourself.'

'I will not, Brigadier,' said Kelleher. 'Come on, I'll carry you. We'll head down the valley. There's some friendly houses in Carhue and Gatonville. We'll find shelter before night.'

Kelleher dragged the weakened Charlie up on his one good leg, and then heaved him across his powerful shoulders. He was broad of build and very tough. They emerged from the wood of ash and silver birch and headed down a long sloping byway to a green valley. The sun was blood-red in their eyes. Shadows of cattle and bare-branched trees were cast long over green fields. Rivers and streams glistened in the light that was now like purple haze. There was no wind. The evening was chilly and still. Dogs barked in distant farmhouses. There were trees in the valley. Black ravens croaked as they flew homewards to the woods. Smoke was rising from the chimneys of cottages on the sheltering roads. They staggered on, two figures silhouetted as one.

Margie, Anna and Doctor Baldwin were coming back from Bandon in the pony and trap. They'd been sent by their mother for some groceries and other messages and had received strict instructions from her to seek out their uncle from whatever den of iniquity they found him in, and to drag him home, by the hair of the head if necessary. He'd been slipping away into town a good bit lately, where he'd been spending too much time drinking with ne'er-do-wells, in various taverns and gin mills, often frequented by the lowest of the low, including Black and Tan jailbirds and criminals. Thomas Cody had been appalled when he heard of the affair between the Doctor and Eleanore Eustace and had given him a hard time ever since.

'The idea of it,' he'd exclaimed. 'Going behind a decent man's back like that, and consorting with his wife.'

'Sure that marriage was a farce,' the Doctor had responded. 'A sham in everything but name. The poor woman was shrivelling up with loneliness and neglect.'

'And a fine specimen she picked to help her get over it,' sneered Cody. 'The man with all his qualifications and who still couldn't earn a fiver. I'm stupefied by the idea of it. My God, when I think of what Jasper would have thought of me had he found out.'

'You're not your brother's keeper. Jasper knew that only too well,' said the Doctor.

'A fine day for the poor man he died when he did. Before he found out he was cuckolded by a man who'd had the temerity and the downright brazen gall to smile to his face and betray him behind his back. I'm shamed. You've shamed me in front of the whole community.'

'Too bad about you,' Doctor Baldwin replied. 'Concerned about yourself as usual, my dear Cody. And what community are you referring to? It's only the petty bourgeoisie that worry about what others think. You won't find people like Lord Bandon doing that. The aristocracy have always been sleeping with each other's wives. It's a matter of small consequence to them.'

'So now you're an aristocrat,' Cody replied in extreme irritation. Doctor Baldwin's superior education and breeding always rankled with him and occasionally drove him to violence. One word had borrowed another and Madeleine was forced to come between them. Cody had stormed off across the yard and up the fields, and the Doctor used the contretemps as an excuse to make himself scarce for a day or two, to head for town and drown his crocodile tears in whiskey and gin. Eleanore Eustace had departed in haste, back home to her father's estate in north Cork, and so there was no immediate opportunity for the Doctor to seek solace in that department. Eleanore wanted to let the dust settle, and to recover her composure, both from the aftershock of Jasper's untimely death, and the gossip mongering that attended the revelation of her illicit love affair with Doctor Baldwin.

The girls eventually found him in the late afternoon, stumbling out of a shebeen on the Cork Road. The Doctor brightened up when he saw his favourite nieces, and climbed up into the trap with alacrity.

'You've saved me from ruin again, my dears. Aren't I the lucky man. It's a fortunate thing for me that you two girls haven't gone back to school. Sure I'd be bereft of friendship and a kindly word but for your angelic selves.'

Anna laughed and slapped him on the shoulder. But Margie remained poker-faced. 'Don't think that we're going to provide a hackney service for you and be at your beck and call whenever it pleases you.'

'My dear Margie,' replied Doctor Baldwin. 'You have the disposition of an anchorite, but the heart of a saint.'

Margie was forced to smile in spite of herself. The Doctor had a way with words that could penetrate the stoutest defences.

When they were halfway home, they heard the rumble of engines behind them. Margie pulled the pony over to the side of the road, as six Crossley tenders passed them, one after the other. Grim faced soldiers stared at them impassively as they went by. The girls kept their eyes downcast and the Doctor avoided eye contact as well. They were aware that they were being carefully scrutinised because each lorry slowed as it passed them. Eventually they were all gone and Margie shook the reins to get the pony to trot on. 'They look like they mean business,' she said.

'Business is right,' said the Doctor. 'We know the kind of business those boyos get up to. There must be something up, or they'd have stopped to harass us just for the fun of it.'

A half a mile onwards the convoy of lorries passed through Tinker's Cross and came to a fork in the road. It slowed almost to a halt and the commanding officer in the leading lorry, deliberated, before pointing towards the right. The convoy started off again and was soon gone out of sight. The girls and the Doctor reached the junction a few minutes later and took the left fork. They travelled up the road for about a hundred yards around a bend and saw a man shuffling along in the twilight with another man on his back.

'What the devil?' said Doctor Baldwin, as they drew abreast. They observed the blood-soaked Charlie, semi-conscious, and the near exhausted Tom Kelleher, bent low under his heavy burden. They saw the rifle in his hand, the trenchcoat and bandolier. Kelleher half turned towards them but did not acknowledge them, unsure if they were friend or foe.

'Who are they?' asked Anna, concerned at the state of the two men.

Doctor Baldwin's brow furrowed in sudden recognition. 'My God, it's Charlie Hurley,' he exclaimed.

'Charlie Hurley?' asked Margie. 'The brigade commander?'

'That's him alright,' said the Doctor. 'Stop quick, those men need help.'

Kelleher surged, exhausted, against the side of the trap, relieved to hear friendly voices. The girls and Doctor Baldwin took hold of Charlie and lifted him into the trap. They had to help Kelleher up as well.

'Quick, Margie, home as fast as possible,' said the Doctor, suddenly sober and alert.

Margie whipped the pony into a gallop.

'What happened?' asked the Doctor, as they raced along.

Kelleher, barely audible, answered, 'We ambushed the train at Upton. It went badly wrong. We lost a few men.'

'Upton?' asked Margie. 'That's eight miles away. How did you get this far?'

'Walked,' said Kelleher.

'Did you carry him all the way in that state?'

'Most of it,' said Kelleher, and managed a weak smile. The Doctor started to examine the seriously wounded Charlie as the pony bore them swiftly back to Gatonville. Night was falling as they reached the great elms of home. Thomas Cody was inside in the piggery, looking over the pigs and feeding them buckets of yellow meal in a long, concrete trough. Seamus was up in a shed in the haggard, tinkering with the thresher; oiling wheels, tightening belts, adjusting nuts and bolts with a long wrench. He liked mechanics and was adept at fixing things. He had magic in his hands. In the house, Madeleine was preparing supper. She had a good fire going in the Wellstood range, her pots boiling up with potatoes and cabbage which would taste well with salty bacon. As the pony and trap clattered into the cobbled yard, Cody could already hear the girls shouting for help. He ran out of the long, stone barn to behold the pony in a lather of sweat pulling the tub trap with his daughters, Doctor Baldwin and two strange men.

'What's your hurry?' he shouted to Margie. 'Are you trying to kill the little pony?' He went to the pony's head and put his hand on its sweating neck. Then he walked to the back of the trap where he saw the Doctor holding a white handerchief to Charlie Hurley's wounded face.

'What in the name of God happened here? Who are these fellows?'

'They're injured,' said the Doctor. 'This man needs urgent medical attention.'

The girls looked expectantly at their father. They waited with bated breath for the explosion. Only the pony's panting disturbed the evening air.

'Who are they?' Cody asked again.

'This is Charlie Hurley,' said Margie, pointing to the wounded man. 'And this is Tom Kelleher.'

Cody's eyes narrowed. He pursed his lips. 'IRA men?' he said. 'You know what I think about IRA men. They have no business here.'

Anna climbed down and clutched him by the arm. 'Oh father,' she pleaded. 'They're desperate. We have to help them.'

'We do?' asked Cody. 'Why so? Aren't they the same fellows who shot Jasper Eustace, who was my neighbour and friend.'

'Nobody knows who shot him,' said Margie, and climbed down. 'For God's sake, father, we need your help.'

'And what if the military find them here? If we help them, you know what will happen to us.'

'Yes,' said Doctor Baldwin from the trap, where he cradled Charlie's head in his lap. 'We'll be shot. But we have to take that risk. We can't let this man bleed to death.'

'Says who?' asked Thomas scornfully. 'You? This is my place now. I'm the one who says what we can do.'

'Oh, for God's sake, father,' said Margie fiercely. 'Have you any heart?'

Cody looked from one of them to the other. The tension knots on his forehead bunched and unbunched. He held his gaze on Anna's pleading eyes. He pondered for what seemed like an eternity.

'Alright,' he said finally. 'But we could rue this day. Let him dress their wounds and then they have to move on. They can't stay here. They have enough safe houses besides using this house.'

Madeleine was already standing beside him with a look of alarm on her face. Seamus had come over from the haggard wiping his blackened hands with a cloth. Doctor Baldwin and Tom Kelleher helped the weakened Charlie down from the trap.

'Thanks,' he managed to mumble to Cody, who shook his head in irritation and walked to the pony's head as if to abjure responsibility.

Doctor Baldwin turned to his sister Madeleine. 'Do you think you could get a bandage and some hot, salted water?' Madeleine said nothing, but hurried away into the house. They helped Charlie towards the back door and into the kitchen and laid him down on a wooden settle. Madeleine brought a dish with hot water from the hissing kettle on the range. Anna ran in with a roll of bandages and the Doctor got to work with cloth and water. He firstly cleaned the wounds with the salted water which caused Charlie to wince in pain.

'The salt will sting for a bit but it will disinfect the wound,' said the Doctor. 'Better than getting gangrene.'

He then applied some ointment and wrapped the bandage in a rudimentary fashion around Charlie's face until only his eyes and mouth were visible. Madeleine brought him a glass of brandy which he drank gratefully. She also filled a generous amount for Kelleher. Their flagging spirits revived.

Seamus, who'd been helping, went out into the yard, where he saw his father untackling the pony near the car house. He did not interfere. He went around to the front of the house to the side lawn, and stood under the great, leafless elm trees. It was nearly dark. Through the line of trees he could see down the avenue to the white gate that guarded the front entrance to the farm. It was about one hundred yards from the house. His eyes were drawn towards a light coming up the road. He could see through the bare-branched trees. Then he saw another light, and then several more. At the same time he heard the sound of engines approaching. They were not loud. He knew it was the military. They were trying to take them unawares. He turned and ran around the house and into the kitchen.

'The Tans are here,' he said.

'Oh, the Lord save us,' said Madeleine. 'What can we do?'

'Get them out quick,' said Seamus. 'Come on, or we're all dead.'

'Where can we hide them?' asked Anna.

'Come on,' said Seamus. 'Fast.' They ushered the two men out into the yard. Kelleher held Charlie on one side, with Seamus on the other.

'The pigs' house,' said the Doctor.

'No,' said Seamus. 'They'll search there. They'll look everywhere. The thresher. We might be able to hide them in the drum.'

'The drum of the thresher?' asked the Doctor. 'They'll never fit in that.'

'The well, where the feeder stands. They might fit there. It's our only hope. They're too weak to run.'

Thomas Cody walked up and down the yard like a demented man. 'Now look what you've brought on us,' he said to Doctor Baldwin and Margie, through gritted teeth.

As the men struggled across the yard and up the loft steps to the haggard, Margie turned to her father. She looked steadily into his eyes and said, 'What will you say, father?' Her heart was racing. She felt powerless.

Cody said, 'I don't know.' He was agitated. He paced up and down, tearing at his hair. 'What happened to them?' he asked.

'They said they were in an ambush,' said Baldwin.

'They attacked the train at Upton,' said Margie.

'And you picked them up?' said Cody incredulously.

'If we hadn't, the Tans would have found them. It was a stroke of luck they took the left fork and not the right.'

'Good luck for them, but bad luck for us,' said Cody. He turned as he heard the lorries pulling into the yard. 'We're all for it now,' he said bitterly.

'What will you say, father?' repeated Margie.

Cody said nothing. The first lorry stopped and two others from the original convoy stopped behind it. The leading officer stepped down and his soldiers jumped down from the lorries. 'Spread out.' said the officer. He approached Cody, Baldwin and the two girls.

'We're looking for two fugitives,' he said. 'Have you people seen anyone?'

'Fugitives?' asked Doctor Baldwin. 'What kind of fugitives?'

'Rebels,' said the officer. 'They attacked the train. But the blighters got a taste of their own medicine.We put the run on them. They shot a number of civilians. We have reason to believe two of them came in this direction.'

'We wouldn't know anything about rebels.' said Doctor Baldwin.

The officer looked them up and down. 'Hmm,' he said. Then he turned to his men. 'Search everywhere,' he shouted.

The soldiers ran towards the barns and the haggard. Some of them went into the house. Anna and Margie followed them in.

'Would you like some tea?' asked Margie, brightly. The soldiers looked taken aback.

'Oh, no thank you,' said one. But he'd been disarmed. 'I'm afraid we have to look through the bedrooms, Ma'am,' he said to Madeleine.

'Of course,' said Madeleine in her most imperious voice, though inside she quaked.

The soldiers were quickly back down the stairs. 'We're sorry to have disturbed you,' said one.

'You're quite welcome,' said Madeleine. 'One can't be too careful nowadays.'

In the shed where the thresher was, Charlie and Tom Kelleher had climbed laboriously up the iron ladder to the top of the Ransome, and clambered into a well where a man would feed the sheaves of straw into the drum. They squeezed in and Seamus had pulled the hinged cover down over them. Then he climbed back down and made his way around the haggard so as to appear from a different direction when the soldiers arrived.

'Who are you?' asked the commanding officer, as Seamus approached.

Thomas Cody, who'd remained silent, finally spoke, 'That's my son, Seamus.'

At that, the officer looked keenly at him. 'Didn't we meet before?' he asked. 'I'm Major Percival of the Essex Regiment.'

'I believe we did,' said Thomas. 'But on a more auspicious occasion.'

'Remind me,' said Percival. His beady eyes on either side of his hooked nose were sharp, and still suspicious.

Thomas smiled. 'I believe we were introduced in the Devonshire some weeks ago.'

'Now I remember,' said Percival. 'Cody is it?'

'Your memory is good,' said Thomas.

'But I'm dashed if I can remember who was with you,' said Percival.

Thomas sighed and looked down at the ground. 'I was with a good friend of mine, but he's dead since.'

'And who was that?'

'A man named Jasper Eustace.'

'Of course,' said Percival. 'Now I remember quite clearly. And weren't you at his funeral later.'

'I was,' said Thomas. 'I was there with my wife, Madeleine, and my brother-in-law here, Doctor James Baldwin.'

Percival's look of suspicion and hostility changed abruptly. 'Look, I'm sorrry to have disturbed you, Mr. Cody. And you too, Doctor. But we have to follow a strict routine in these matters.'

He turned to a non-commissioned officer. 'Tell the men to come on,' he said. 'This is a loyal household.'

'Yes, sir,' said the NCO. 'I'll round them up, sir.'

'Let me show you where they're gone,' said Seamus. He hurried away with the officer towards the haggard. A number of soldiers were rummaging around in various outhouses. Some of them were in the shed, admiring the steam engine and the big thresher.

The NCO came in with Seamus. 'It's time to go, the Major's orders.'

'A nice machine,' said one of the soldiers. 'Ransome of Ipswich. That's my home town.'

'Really,' said Seamus.

'Oh, yes,' said the soldier. 'Would you believe I worked in their factory before I joined the armed forces. And that was the sorry day for me.'

'Come on,' said the NCO. 'These people are loyal subjects.'

'Mind if I have a look on top?' asked the soldier. 'Such a beautiful machine.' There was silence in the shed.

'Come on,' said the NCO. 'Major's orders.'

'Two minutes,' said the soldier, putting his foot on the rung of the ladder. Inside in the well underneath the cover, Tom Kelleher fingered the trigger of a Colt .45. He heard the steady climb on the ladder. Charlie, beside him, held his breath. The soldier was on the second last rung at the top when there was a sharp shout from the yard.

'What the devil's keeping you men,' barked Percival. His voice echoed around like a thunderclap in the still evening air.

The soldier on the ladder nearly fell off. 'Coming sir,' he shouted back.

He climbed back down in a hurry and they hastened back to the lorries. Percival glared at them as they came through the dusk. They jumped onto the lorries and the engines started up. The lights came on and the trucks turned in the yard. Madeleine had come out from the house. Percival gave a little bow and tipped his cap. 'My apologies for the inconvenience once again,' he said. He climbed into the lorry. 'Good evening,' he said.

They watched the lorries drive out of the yard and down the short back laneway to the road. They heard the sounds of the engines slowly fading and they watched the last lights disappearing. The assembled group in the yard heaved an enormous, collective sigh of relief. Anna came over to her father and hugged him tightly.

Margie came and stood beside him, slightly shy. 'Thanks father,' she said and was unable to say more. Tears filled her eyes. Doctor Baldwin gave Cody an admiring sideways glance and went into the house. Seamus and the girls ran towards the shed with the thresher. Thomas Cody and his wife Madeleine stood in the middle of the yard like people marooned on a desert island.

Late that night another horse and trap slipped furtively into the Cody farmyard driven by Sonny Hennessy accompanied by his brother Mike. Word had quickly spread through the grapevine, not only of the Upton disaster, but of the whereabouts of the wounded men who'd fled the scene. Pat O'Sullivan and Dan O'Mahony were tended at the Cronin household and had been conveyed to the hospital in Cork by diverse routes. The prognosis on either was not good. Falvey and Phelan lay dead and their bodies were recovered by relatives. The delinquent scout, John Beatty, who arrived belatedly at the Upton Station, was arrested by the military and taken into custody. The entire community was in shock at the severe reversal of fortune and deeply saddened by the deaths of Volunteers and civilians alike.

Charlie was quickly placed on board the horse and trap at the Cody household, and Anna, Margie and Doctor Baldwin came out to give a detailed account to the boys of the events as they had unfolded in the last few hours. The plan was to take Charlie to the Hennessy thatched house for a few days, where he'd be sequestered out of sight until he recovered sufficiently to move on again as necessity demanded. Anna waved them away down the lane with trepidation, yet with with hope in her heart at the pleasant surprise of meeting Sonny again. Tom Kelleher, the steadfast, had sufficiently recovered from his efforts to make his way across the country back to his own home around Crowhill and to report to his column commander the unhappy tidings of the day.

16

to take a long sleep

C harlie lay for two days without waking, under the thatch in the room at the top of the stairs. Elizabeth kept the huge, open fire stoked night and day, to keep the heat in, and the cold winds of February out. Never had she seen a man to sleep so soundly. Doctor Welply had come to examine him the day after he was brought over by Sonny. Elizabeth was taken by surprise, but she was happy to give her permission for him to stay, despite the danger and the serious consequences if the British discovered his whereabouts. The doctor had slipped in at the fall of night, transported by Tull in the back-to-back trap, pulled by his fastest horse. He gave Charlie a tetanus injection to avoid infection setting in, inserted stitches in the gaping holes in his cheeks, and wrapped a tight bandage around the swollen, painful ankle. After staying awake for the doctor's attendance, he'd then fallen back to sleep like an infant newly born.

During the following days Elizabeth was busy. She cycled the two and a half miles to the village of Enniskean to shop for the extra provisions which would now be required: loaves of white bread, flour, bread soda, oatmeal and salt. With the flour she'd bake brown bread that she'd leaven with the soda; with the salt she'd churn butter, and with the oatmeal she'd make porridge to augment Tull's drills of cabbage and turnips, his ridges of carrots and potatoes; and Jeremiah's salted bacon, cured in barrels. She greeted O'Donovan, the merchant, who had a fine array of groceries and hardware items, stocked under the low ceiling of his shop, which stood on the single, neat-facaded street with its grey, slate roofs sloping down, and stretching parallel with the river, a flat, wide field away. O'Donovan in his turn bade her good morrow, with sympathy in his eyes. If he was aware the brigade commander recuperated in the Hennessy household that information would never pass his lips. O'Donovan, small, dark, and fastidious, was a man to be trusted. He had his own ideas about the use of guns and violence, but was prepared to back his countrymen to the full against the appalling terror of the English invaders. He even allowed Elizabeth take some additional items, unasked for and voluntarily, on the tacit understanding that they would be badly needed, and that everyone had to pull together in times of trouble. If he could give a little more it would not go unrewarded because the Lord said each should give according to his means. O'Donovan was a careful businessman and a prosperous one. And with a heart as big as his bank balance. He produced his tot which he'd pencilled in pounds, shillings and pence:

	£	s	d
1lb tea, half stone sugar, cocoa		8	5
Soap, tobacco, candles		6	3
Brasso, 2lb rice, pepper		1	4
Polish, pig's head		4	1
Rinso, soap, tobacco	free of charge		
Currants, jelly, linseed	free of charge		

When Elizabeth pedalled on the long uphill climb to home she did so with a purpose that was missing from her life for quite a while, and with something akin to a spring in her step at the prospect of attending to her patient's needs, despite the other chores that were her daily burden. She still had to milk the cows, draw water in heavy buckets from the well two fields away, feed her hens, light fires, wash clothes. Tull fed his pigs and horses and helped her to keep the household together. Richie came and went, but spent a good deal of his time at fairs, buying cattle and horses; and looking the ladies over. Jeremiah kept tapping away, as he liked to say, doing small odd jobs, but he'd slip away some nights and walk to the public house in Enniskean or Castletown, for a glass of whiskey and a half pint chaser of Beamish stout. The return journey of five miles from either village was no bother to him despite his advancing years. Jeremiah was sprightly and carried no superfluous weight. On other nights, John Thomas Allen, Tom Wilson, or Richie Shorten would call for a *scoraíocht,* and they'd animatedly discuss the state of politics and the economic prospects in the present agitation, their voices rising louder and their laughter echoing merrily around the roaring fire, the more *poitin* they drank; oblivious to the important, secret, house guest whom nobody except Elizabeth and Tull ever saw. Which was not to say they were unaware of his presence. Few things went undetected in the countryside, but since spies were shot, the leaking of sensitive information was a rare occurrence indeed. When Mick Shorten came one afternoon to examine the spraggers and the ridge yealm of his recently finished contract, he remarked ironically, 'I hear you've already got a tenant for your new attic.'

Elizabeth looked reproachfully at him as Mick hastened to assure her that the identity of the occupant would not be revealed by him. 'Christ no, upon my soul not a word will ever pass my lips.'

The look he got from Elizabeth was like that of a tigress defending her lair.

Elizabeth was already beginning to treat the wounded Charlie like her own possession and already he'd begun to feel at home like he'd never felt since childhood. If only life could be always warm, safe and secure, and the cold world kept pemanently outside.

'I'd be lost without you,' he said to her one night, and held her hand. She smiled and let her hand rest in his. 'You've been through a lot,' she said. 'Your strength is not what it was. You'll need time to recover.'

He looked unhappy, his eyes were haunted. 'I really made a botch of things, didn't I.'

'That can't be helped now,' she said, with a practical tone.

'I led a lot of innocent people to their deaths.'

'Don't torture yourself,' she said.

'All the same,' he said, 'I should have planned things better. There's no excuse. I was careless.'

She hesitated before responding, seeing him wrestling with his conscience. She didn't want to rub salt into his wounded psyche.

He looked steadily at her and let go of her hand and said, 'You think we're wrong don't you.'

'In what way?'

'You think we should stop the shooting...the killing.' The words escaped his lips, painfully.

'There's killing on both sides,' she said, and continued, 'Of course I wish life were normal. But that's not the way it is.'

'But it could be,' he said. 'It would return to normal if we called it off.'

'But the Tans would take revenge.'

He shrugged. 'Oh, I think there's not a shadow of doubt about that. I've no doubt they'd round us all up, put us up against a wall and shoot us like the men of 1916.' His tired eyes were trained on her as if trying to read her mind. 'And then it would be over.'

'You don't really mean that,' she said, and stood up.

'My head means it, not my heart.' He struggled to find the words. 'You see, I think we've opened, what do they call it, Pandora's Box? All the badness in men's hearts comes out. Never mind that there's good intentions too. It seems like things are...turned upside down.'

She could see his struggle to find direction, to justify himself. He seemed to be looking to her for an answer, like a lost soul. She remained quiet for some moments and sat down again and took his hand.

'What are you thinking?' he asked.

She pushed the hair gently back off his hot, fevered forehead. She then held a cold, damp cloth against against his wounded face, where she'd removed the bandage as the doctor had instructed. It was slow to heal, looking red and raw. 'I can't answer your question for you, Charlie,' she said finally. 'But I myself will not give up. I'm behind you to the end.'

He squeezed her hand gently. He looked relieved. 'You think we're in the right then?'

'I think you're right...we're right, from our side. It's our country, our families and neighbours who are being murdered and burnt out every day by the English. Let them go to their country and leave us ours. We have a right to walk down the road and say, this is our land, these are our fields. You stole them from us. We want them back. I don't think that's too much to ask. They were taken from us by force, by terror, by planters and adventurers. They banished our people to hell or to Connaught. We lost this farm to the banks some years ago when all the children were young. But I fought to get it back. I say we continue to stand up and fight. No surrender when our cause is just, whatever it takes.'

The ferocity and the quiet passion of her words surprised him. 'Those are my sentiments too,' he said. 'But I wasn't sure if you shared them.'

She sighed, 'I know freedom comes at a great price. Look what happened to you. To many others. But we are not the invaders here. We are not the Empire devastating all before it for power and grandeur. The English have never helped us, except to have our young men slaughtered in their foreign battles and to use our land as their bread basket, leaving millions of our people to die in famines. No, when you have your own Government you control your own destiny. One final push and they will go.'

'You think so?' he asked, surprised. 'Even after this latest setback. Surely they'll be more confident now, thinking they have us on the run?'

'Now is the time to keep your resolve. To hold your nerve.' She stood up and pushed the blankets up around him. 'But you should sleep now. You need to regain your strength.'

She watched as he laid his head down on the pillow, watched his eyelids become heavy and close. She gazed a long time at his finely chiselled features, until his breathing became deep and measured. Then she slowly tip-toed down the stairs.

When she went out into the yard, an eager girl, aged about twenty, named Babe Lordan, cycled in on her bicycle, carrying some groceries in a string shopping bag which hung on the handlebars. She was John Lordan's sister and came over from the next townland some days to help Elizabeth. She produced some bread, fruit and cheese, and followed Elizabeth into the kitchen.

'You're very kind, Babe,' said Elizabeth, taking the groceries and putting them into the safe. 'And how are things in your household?'

'Just about the same as here,' said Babe. 'My brothers, John and James are on the run most of the time, like Sonny and Mike in this house. But we manage. Some of the neighbours take turns helping out when our men are away.'

'You're a great girl,' said Elizabeth to the younger girl. 'I wish some other people were as good as you. With some it's as if none of this is happening. They bury their heads in the sand and hope 'twill go away.'

She was only too aware that most people were like sheep, disposed to follow, not lead, but she also knew that the fight for freedom would not succeed except for the extraordinary support of these special womenfolk. They had their own organisation called, *Cumann Na mBan,* the Society of Women, set up specifically by Dáil Eireann, a Government which operated in parallel with the British Administration, both of which were locked in a terrible struggle for the hearts and minds of the people. But the heart and soul of the struggle resided within the bosoms of such youthful but formidable girls as Babe, Elsie Nyhan from the Castletown public house, and most of the sisters of the young men who fought in the local battalions, companies, and brigades throughout the country. With such passive but powerful background support it was becoming very difficult for the British to keep control, no matter how many troops they launched into the defence of their crumbling outpost of empire.

Soon, Babe had a big fire roaring in the kitchen, and two vases of fragrant flowers made the air sweet-scented. The house was warm and the smell of wholesome cooking wafted around to make a pleasant, homey atmosphere. Some days other girls came with Babe: Elsie Nyhan and a young lady named Kathleen de Courcey whom Tull had a fondness for. Tull liked the days the other girls came. It made the burden of his lot easier to bear and everything tasted better, sounded sweeter. And Kathleen De Courcey from a better off family was the apple of his eye, although her parents might not approve of the likes of Tull as a suitor for their daughter.

The days passed. They were long, quiet, deep-dark. Charlie lay awake under the rafters all afternoon long. The sounds he could hear were, birds twittering in the thatch, the moan of the wind, and sometimes the plop and scatter of rain against the eyebrow window pane. He'd hear the clink of cutlery and delph downstairs when Elizabeth came in from finishing her daily chores outside. Then he'd hear the hiss of steam escaping under the lid of the boiling kettle, hanging on the iron crane over the open fire, and the sound of the lid knocking up and down when the water bubbled. The men would come in for their midday meal and he'd hear the low murmur of voices, chairs being scraped against the flag floor, cups and knives knocking on the wooden table. When they left again the slow afternoon would wheel on; the grandfather clock ticking on into eternity, and the loud gong startling him when it announced the hour. From outside, he'd hear the low of a cow in a distant field as she searched for a newborn calf. He'd sometimes hear the rumble of galloping hooves and through the window he'd see Tull's horses thundering past, buckleaping, snorting through their nostrils, and blowing huge whooshes of air when they stopped, as if to warn off ancient predators.

He could see his home country in the far distance to the south, where the long ridge reared up from the valley of the Bandon river. Somewhere among those deep declivities and winding laneways was the plain and ample farmhouse of home where first he grew a man. On days when the rare sun shone brightly he'd see it sparkle on a square of blue ocean where the Atlantic peeped through a narrow, gouged out ravine. He thought of his parents, and his school days in Clogach, walking through sloping fields, wet with morning dew as the sun rose over the Old Head of Kinsale: a long, narrow peninsula running out into the sea where the tidal race was treacherous on even the calmest summer day, and which sent many an unsuspecting boatman to a watery grave. But he'd learnt the ways of the sea from an early age, messing about in small boats in Timoleague and Courtmacsherry. He could sail a boat with skill, could tack and gybe, run up a spinnaker and get in and out of small coves and harbours where he knew every hidden hazard. He'd forage for oysters, cockleshells, mussels and shrimp around the rocky islets where the seals lazed and the shags and cormorants lifted their wings to dry their feathers in the sun. He remembered bringing in the hay in the long, summer afternoons, from fields that towered above the foamy breakers, and thinning turnips in the springtime of the year with his siblings, kneeling on narrow drills with jute sacks tied around their knees, moving along towards a headland as if in some ascetic ritual of penance.

And he remembered saying goodbye to his family as a youth of fifteen, on a cold January morning, taking the train from Kinsale to Cork, and then the mailboat across the Irish Sea to Fishguard, a pretty Welsh town nestling on the western shores of a rich, pleasant valley. And there to take another train onward past the coal-dark towns of Wales, Swansea, Llanelli, Port Talbot and Cardiff; through the ordered, fertile fields of Gloucestershire, Herefordshire and into the great city of London, the centre of the world. Fetching up in the grim, industrial district of Harlesden, where a cheerful English foreman called him 'Paddy,' and put him to work in a bacon factory where he slaved around the clock from six in the morning, six days a week. A poor Irish lad, down in the trenches with the other wretches, never able to breach the social barriers erected by the English ruling classes, tolerated betimes but sometimes told no Irish need apply: untouchables in everything but name. Keeping the wheels of the industry of empire oiled and turning, recruited in their armies and sent forward to the front lines as cannon fodder, because the Irish were a fierce and warlike race, but considered, by some English as being not too bright, and so dispensable in the eyes of their officers. And when the wars were over, left on the slag heap of society, sometimes as crippled, eyeless, limbless outcasts. So when the Irish suddenly rose up in the midst of the Great War, it sent ripples of alarm throughout the empire and spawned what the Irish poet W.B. Yeats called, "a terrible beauty," and never again would the status quo between the English and the Irish be the same.

After the first ten days he felt strong enough to rise and go downstairs. He moved slowly around the house, leaning heavily on a crutch which the doctor gave him. He washed the dishes after meals, and brushed the floor for Elizabeth, and lit the fire with cippins, coaxing it aflame, adding a sod of turf and then another, until the smoke ascended like a prayer, its sweet, peat smell wafting from room to room and out through the chimney into the chilly air. Some nights when Jeremiah and Tull were gone to the pub or to a neighbour's house, he'd sit by the fire with Elizabeth and recount the happy story of his childhood, the drudgery and alienation of his time in England, and how only the strength and hope of youth had kept him going, and the dream of one day returning home to help create a new nation, with its own laws, its own Government; an independent Republic, forever beyond the reach of the British Empire. And having come home, and gone to work organising the Castletownbere Company of Volunteers in 1917, arrested and sent to prison, this time in an even more humiliating situation as a political prisoner in Maryborough Jail, Queen's County, where he languished for a further year. And here he was now, after all his wanderings, trials and tribulations, caught in the vortex of the great storm that was blowing across Ireland, and who knew when that storm would blow out, and what way the land would lie when it was spent.

Elizabeth told him of her mother dying in childbirth with the youngest baby, and how she'd found herself *in loco parentis*, in her mother's place, with the responsibility of rearing a brood of fourteen children at the tender age of seventeen. Not knowing what to do other than carry on from day to day, trying to put food on the table, washing and cleaning, struggling with debts, depression, poverty, some spirit of survival keeping her going, until her unmanageable burden was eased by Fr. Murphy, a cousin and a priest, finding a home for the little ones in the place she least wanted them to be: England. So, in that regard she had to admit, grudgingly, that England wasn't all bad, and that there were also people there with kind hearts and good intentions.

When they had each expended themselves in telling the stories of their lives, they would continue to sit there at the fire, night after night, often in silence for a long time. But it was as if the forced intimacy of their situation foreshortened the usual time necessary for strangers to get to know each other well. At the end of his three week stay, they felt an easy familiarity with each other that was hard to describe, other than a feeling of what could only be described as love.

Tom Barry, Liam Deasy and Sean Hales called around one evening in early March. Sonny accompanied them. Elizabeth made them welcome but with a foreboding in her heart that her happy interlude with Charlie might soon be over. She took them up the stairs to the open attic under the thatch, where Charlie relaxed, fully clothed, on the bed. She could tell immediately from the way his eyes lit up when he saw his comrades-in-arms that his heart would forever belong to them, and that she would always fill second place. They were jovial, smiling, delighted to see him.

'Tis no wonder he stayed so long,' joked Tom Barry. 'What man in his right mind would turn his back on this cosy place to be out running like a wolf in the hills like the rest of us?'

'Thanks for the compliment, Tom,' smiled Elizabeth, 'but all joking aside, he was lucky. Only for Doctor Baldwin he could have bled to death ever before he got here.'

'You mean the quack doctor? Sure maybe he's not such a fraud after all,' said Barry. 'One thing's for sure though, he's enthusiastic enough when it comes to the women, whatever about his fondness for medicine.'

'Whatever about Baldwin, I'd say only for yourself the man would be dead and buried by now,' said Liam Deasy to Elizabeth. 'I suppose we'll never be able to coax him back to work?'

'Oh, I've no doubt he's only champing at the bit to be off,' smiled Elizabeth like an indulgent mother of her son. 'I don't think he's a domestic animal by nature.'

They all laughed and turned to see Charlie's reaction. He was happy to let the good natured banter continue without interruption, until Elizabeth said she would leave them to their discussion and went downstairs.

Charlie looked around him at his friends, his brothers, his countrymen that he knew so well.

'Tis good to see ye boys,' he said simply. A secret tear welled in his blue eyes.

'How are you feeling?' asked Tom Barry, and stood at the edge of the bed. Elizabeth's warm, embracing presence was suddenly missed, a vacuum momentarily created. Charlie was leaning back against a pile of pillows. His raddled face had healed considerably, Elizabeth having removed the bandages, believing fresh air would heal the wounds quicker. 'I'm rearing to go,' he said. But his eyes looked more hopeful than convinced.

'You're looking well,' said Deasy.

Sonny nodded and smiled warmly towards the man he looked up to more than any other, and was taken aback to see the change in his appearance. The gaunt, pock-marked features once so seamless, the lank hair without lustre, the haggard, almost hollowed out body. He said nothing but felt sure the others were equally disappointed, despite the forced geniality.

Sean Hales had remained silent, not one to indulge in idle chatter. Sonny noticed the tall, blonde giant, stern of feature, with a stubborn chin, a high forehead, a dour almost Calvinistic demeanour.

'You'd want to wait another while,' Hales said eventually, standing as he was, looking out the window. Hales was an island.

Charlie looked towards his neighbour and long-time acquaintance and said, almost mockingly, 'Why don't you sit down, Sean?' He pointed towards a vacant chair.

Hales ignored the suggestion. 'I don't think you're fit to go back to the fight,' he said. 'But you'd better move to another house. It won't be long before the word spreads to the military that you're here. If it hasn't spread already.'

Charlie looked from one to the other: Deasy, precise, organised, driven. Barry, the cool and ruthless military strategist; the phlegmatic Hales; the fearless, generous nature of the youthful Sonny. He waited for them to speak.

Eventually Liam Deasy said, 'It's your own decision, Charlie, but Sean is right. You'd better move on.'

Two nights later Tull harnessed up the horse and trap and swaddled in blankets, Charlie bade goodbye to Elizabeth, kissed her once upon the cheek and quickly turned away. Jeremiah and the neighbours: Tom Wilson, Bill Sullivan, the loud voiced, laughing, John Thomas Allen; the Shortens, Richie and Mick, all materialised like mourners at a funeral to speed him sadly on his way. He went first to the house of Sullivan in Gurranereigh, and a week later, Bill Desmond took him to Forde's house in Ballymurphy twenty miles away.

Elizabeth went about her daily chores in her stoic fashion but with a feeling of great emptiness. She'd become accustomed to the upheavels of life: losses of loved ones to death and emigration. These were crosses she had to bear and her great faith in the Divine Redeemer brought her fortitude. But still, she felt diminished, with an aching in her heart and with hope less quick to spring again, once crushed. Nights would be long and colder now, with longer sleeping.

17

On a bright morning in early March in 1921, Majors Arthur Percival and Bernard Montgomery met at 7.30 a.m. at the Victoria Military Barracks in Cork. Percival had driven up from Kinsale, where his Essex Regiment was stationed and Montgomery greeted him in the enormous parade square as he stepped down from his armoured car. They saluted each other smartly and shook hands. They were both aged 33, separated at birth by only a month or so, Montgomery being the older of the two by a tiny margin. Both had distinguished themselves in the Great War. Montgomery received the Distinguished Service Order for gallant leadership, and Percival, in addition to that honour, had also been bestowed with a Military Cross for his power of command and knowledge of tactics. Both men were considered by their superiors in the military and political establishments, to be future leaders of His Majesty's Armed Forces.

Percival had taken the initiative to contact his fellow junior officer because he suspected an air of inertia and indeed complacency on the part of their superiors, General Macready and Major-General Strickland, that could lead, in short order, to the loss of the province of Ireland from the Empire if matters weren't taken in hand as a matter of extreme urgency.

Percival paused momentarily to take in his surroundings: the great panorama of the city spread out below them, the meandering river Lee and the broadening harbour that opened majestically down towards Haulbowline and Roches Point.

'Damn fine view you have up here, Major.'

'Wonderful,' agreed Montgomery. 'Does the heart good to be up here on a fine spring morning in the bracing air.'

He looked his fellow officer up and down with a slightly superior air. Although aware of Percival's fine war record and his reputation for enthusiastically seeking out and destroying IRA rebels, it struck him, nevertheless, that his contemporary hadn't an altogether impressive presence: a slight stoop, heavy jowled, uneven featured. The sort of chap that no matter how carefully he tried to present himself would still manage to look awkward and uncouth. But not everybody could be blessed with debonair good looks, overweening confidence and a sense of his own destiny, like himself. Neither could everybody be an alumnus of the Royal Military College in Sandhurst as he was, or be the son of an Anglo-Irish bishop. Percival, by all accounts was only the son of a land agent from the north of England, and had enlisted in the army as a private. Perhaps he was making up for his sense of inadequacy by taking matters to extremes when it came to the suppression of the Irish Revolution.

They observed soldiers passing on parade for a few minutes under the beady eye of an eager Sergeant-Major, who barked orders in staccato fashion as they went through their drill.

'You have them well tutored,' smiled Percival approvingly. 'That Sergeant-Major, a protegé of yours, is he?'

'Absolutely,' said Montgomery. 'That's vital. You pick the right men and give them the broad parameters to get on with the job, with the full confidence that you'll end up with a well-disciplined, well-prepared force, with clear objectives.'

Percival nodded, not quite able to disguise his admiration for his fellow officer. 'I agree with you one hundred percent, but as you and I well know, there is a certain amount of woolly-minded thinking at work when it comes to the Irish question.'

'You're referring to certain of our military superiors?'

'I am, and also to our political ones: Macready, Strickland, some of the members of the cabinet, apart from Lloyd George and Winston.'

'Mr Churchill is a beacon,' said Montgomery, 'and can always be relied on. People of his calibre only come along every few centuries.'

'Look,' said Percival. 'What do you expect from politicians when the King himself has come out as saying that some of the tactics of our Auxiliaries and Black and Tans are excessive?' He paused and looked keenly at Montgomery. 'What do you think, Major?'

'Of what?' asked Montgomery, knowing the question but evading it.

'Of our tactics, reprisals, burning out Shinners?'

'I have no great problem with it,' said Montgomery.

As they were talking they were walking down corridors, past gun rooms, store rooms, the officers' mess, the soldiers' canteen. Hanging at intervals on the corridor walls were pictures of generals and colonels, and paintings of battles from bygone days: Cornwallis at Ballinamuck, Nelson at Trafalgar, King William at the Boyne. The glory days of Empire. Montgomery paused for a moment to admire a bloody battle scene.

'We cannot say it too loudly, but don't you have the uneasy feeling that many of our present crop of leaders don't have the same stomach for conquest as these chaps?'

Percival's eyes took in the scene but his mind was elsewhere. He turned sharply to Montgomery.

'You may well say that, Major, but I am given to understand that you yourself have expressed the opinion that the Irish question cannot be resolved by force. In fact, and correct me if I'm wrong, but aren't you on record as saying that we should give them some sort of independence and let them settle matters among themselves?'

'You've done your research on me,' said Montgomery dryly.

'So I'm right then.'

'Except you omit the context in which I said it,' said Montgomery.

Percival was aware that he was dealing with a skilful soldier, with keen political instincts. He pursed his lips and turned from the painting to face him.

'The context?' he questioned.

'Yes,' laughed Montgomery. 'I was asked at a dinner party given by Lord Bandon, what I thought of the present unhappy situation obtaining in Ireland. There were various diverging opinions, some solid and sound, and some so outlandish they could have been uttered by one of those 'Bolshie' chaps from Russia.'

'And what did you say?'

'I said that in twentieth century democratic Britain it simply wasn't possible to suppress a rebellion with proper force because world opinion wouldn't stand for it. Not even British opinion. I'm afraid the days of pitch-capping and hanging, drawing and quartering are over, Major.'

'How do you justify the Tans then?' asked Percival.

'You don't. You pretend they're not operating as they are.'

'In effect you deny their existence?'

'If you can, but I'm afraid that bird has now escaped the nest as well.'

'So we're buggered then,' said Percival bluntly.

Montgomery put a companionable arm on Percival's shoulder, let it rest there for a moment and then he walked on, waving his arms expansively. 'The thing of it is, Major, and no one knows this better than you, that we could throw a vast force of men and arms into this country and wipe out these rebels within a month if the political will was there to do it. For God's sake man, we've just fought a World War, the sheer amount of firepower and manpower which we could have at our disposal would overwhelm these fellows in no time. But the Goverment is intent upon a policy of containment, not victory.'

'So that's what you would do then, if you had your way? Blitz them?'

Montgomery didn't rise to the bait. 'I'm only a junior officer. I must bide my time, like you. In the meantime we must work out a plan, which is the purpose of our meeting here today, to achieve the results we want in as diplomatic and pragmatic a way as possible. That is our brief. The Generals will be awaiting it with interest.'

'Indeed,' replied Percival and an irritated wrinkle furrowed his brow. Fellows like Montgomery would always be one step ahead of the likes of himself in the pecking order. For instance, he wondered, what was he doing, wining and dining at Lord Bandon's dinner party on the same evening that he himself and his Essex Regiment were slugging it out with the rebels in the village of Newcestown, when they were ambushed from behind a ditch and half his platoon was either killed or injured? Evidently he didn't like to get his hands dirty. That kind of thing was better left to Percival and his ilk.

They'd reached Montgomery's office and he stood back graciously to show his visitor into his quarters. A large map covered one wall, showing the entire of County Cork. Percival walked towards it, spending some moments picking out places of interest. Montgomery took off his cap and walked towards a cabinet.

'Whiskey?' he asked.

Montgomery, opened the cabinet and taking out a large bottle of Scotch, poured Percival a generous measure.

Percival continued looking at the map and sipped his whiskey. Montgomery sat back in his chair. He was feeling good. His star was inevitably on the rise, and sooner or later this vexed Irish question would be put to bed and he could get back to bestriding the world stage, where he liked being during the Great War and longed to be again. Chaps like Percival, while stubborn, could always be counted on to deliver the goods in the long run. Yes, thought Montgomery, a good NCO type, likes to huff and puff a lot and run around doing things that were often inconsequential. Trying too hard. But top officer material? He couldn't see it.

'You think we really can defeat these Shinners?' asked Percival, turning from the map to sit down opposite Montgomery.

'Yes I do,' said the other rather blithely.

'What makes you so sure? We've been pounding away at them now for the guts of a year and a half and they don't show any signs of weakening. As a matter of fact they seem to be getting more daring. Attacked us in Bandon recently and kept us busy for at least four hours. Must have been hundreds of the blighters. Maybe up to a thousand.'

'How many men do they have under arms, would you say?' asked Montgomery. 'In West Cork?'

'I've heard various numbers, hard to tell. No one on our side knows for sure.'

'Would you say a thousand?'

'Oh, ten times that,' said Percival. 'They're formidable. They have damn good officers. I hear their commander, a fellow called Tom Barry, is somewhat of a military genius. He calls himself a general, if you please.'

Percival gave a slightly disdainful sneer.

Montgomery raised an eyebrow and pursed his lips: 'Wasn't he one of ours?' he asked.

'He was with General Townsend in Mesopotamia.'

'We should have held onto him.'

'If I ever get him in my sights I'll make sure we hold onto him the next time,' said Percival a little bitterly.

'Quite,' said Montgomery, and paused to reflect before continuing. 'Why can't we be more certain of their numbers?'

'Because our eyes and ears have been destroyed.'

'You mean our spies and informers?'

'Yes, but our police officers in the Royal Irish Constabulary in particular. They know the countryside intimately. But those of them that haven't been killed or threatened have gone over to the rebels. We've now lost the RIC barracks in Kilbrittain, Schull, Castletownbere, Drimoleague, Ballydehob, and our post in Rosscarbery is in serious jeopardy. The IRA would love to destroy that. If they did, we'd be pushed completely out of West Cork, with only Bandon and Kinsale remaining.'

Montgomery nodded soberly. 'Rosscarbery? Isn't that where Collins is from?'

'It is,' said Percival, 'And Barry as well. Their two most capable leaders.'

'Must be something in the air down there,' said Montgomery and laughed.

'You may laugh, Major, but it's not one bit funny,' said Percival, like a scolding teacher.

'Of course, you're quite right old chap. Not funny at all.' Montgomery was thinking that perhaps deep down, his compatriot lacked a bit of bottle. He himself was really quite unperturbed. His eyes twinkled a little. 'What do you make of Collins?' he asked.

'The most bloody-minded of them all,' said Percival. 'He destroyed our Cairo Gang without mercy, shot men in their beds asleep, some in front of their pregnant wives. A fellow with a mean and vicious pathological streak, though the Irish call him a hero.'

Montgomery raised an eyebrow. He was thinking of his colleague, that it took one to know one. He didn't articulate his thoughts, but said, 'These fellows seem to know what they're about alright, but unless they are better armed and equipped they really have no chance against us in the long run.'

'They have brilliant propagandists, Desmond Fitzgerald and Erskine Childers. They know how to galvanise world opinion. On no account can we underestimate them,' said Percival.

Montgomery raised a supercilious eyebrow. 'The Irishman is like the Jew. Crafty and clever but lacking the polish to compete with our race of people.'

'I wouldn't have thought he was anything like the Jew,' said Percival. 'In the first instance the Jew won't fight like the Irishman. He's not as courageous.'

'The Irishman is a good fighter, probably the best in the world, except for the Ghurka,' said Montgomery. 'But the first thing he likes to do is fight amongst his own fellows. The tradition of faction fighting is long established in this country. There's nothing your average Paddy likes to do better than knock the stuffing out of his neighbour in the next parish. That's always been your Irishman's problem. No loyalty or discipline.'

'And the Jew won't drink, whereas the Paddy will drink all day long.' said Percival, looking agitated and appearing to level a veiled criticism at his fellow officer, who was part Irish though would prefer to deny it. Anglo-Irish he'd call himself no doubt. To Percival there was no difference. They were all from this infernal island. So utterly different from his own sceptred isle.

He held the whiskey glass up to his nose. The comforts of alcohol. He loved the smell of it, the colour of it, the taste of it, the way a shot of it hitting the back of the throat was like a bolt of lightning to the body. Everything seemed calmer, clearer, easier.

'You shouldn't fret so much, Ernest,' said Montgomery. 'We'll deal these chaps the cards in due course. Here, have another snifter.' He held the bottle up.

Percival held his hand up peremptorily, to refuse the offer. 'I really don't imbibe that much at all. It's just that I got a taste for it at a very young age and it has been my companion ever since.'

'Did your parents not supervise you properly?' asked Montogomery with a droll smile.

'They were pretty disciplined, but not unduly harsh. We did things the right way. Sunday school, local teachers in Bengeo. I then went to Rugby but I'm afraid I was not a good classic. My only academic qualification was a higher school certificate. I was more successful at cricket, tennis, cross country running, that sort of thing. But all in all, a solid upbringing. When I joined the army I found my true metier. Like yourself, no doubt.'

Montgomery hoisted his booted feet up on his desk and lounged back in his swivel chair.

'I hated my childhood, and my mother in particular.' he said.

'I beg your pardon,' said Percival, taken aback by the candid admission.

Montgomery was suddenly serious, almost petulant. He brooded for some moments with the absorption of an individual who would not brook interruption. Percival hated himself for not continuing, but it was as if the other man's natural authority and power made him helpless.

'My father was a Vicar who inherited the Montgomery ancestral estate at New Park, in Moville, County Donegal. But there was a large mortgage on the place and my father had to sell off several farms at Ballynally and there was still barely enough to pay for New Park and the summer holidays. We went there every summer. My father was then made bishop of Tasmania and he considered it his duty to spend six

- 238 -

months of the year there and leave the rearing of his children to my mother. His excuse was that we needed the money but I believe it was really to escape his domestic pressures. My mother was eighteen years younger than my father. While he was away she gave us constant beatings, and ignored us the rest of the time. She liked to present the public figure of the bishop's wife. A street angel, house devil, in effect. She took no interest in our education and had us taught by tutors. It was a loveless environment. I rebelled against it. I was a dreadful little boy and I don't imagine anybody would put up with my sort of behaviour these days.'

He paused and took his feet off the table. He leant forward, not looking at Percival - looking through the dark glass of the past. Percival was respectfully silent and quite taken aback at his compatriot's frankness.

'My sister Sibyl died prematurely in Tasmania. My other siblings, Harold, Donald and Una all emigrated. Eventually we returned home to London and my father became secretary of the Society for the Propagation of the Gospel. I was sent to St. Paul's School and then to the Royal Military Academy in Sandhurst. I was unruly, almost got expelled for setting fire to a fellow cadet during a fight with pokers. I joined the 1st Battalion of the Royal Warwickshire Regiment in 1908, and saw service in India until 1913.'

He stopped and looked directly at Percival, as if seeing him for the first time. He laughed disarmingly: 'And the rest, as they say, is history.'

Percival cleared his throat. 'That's quite a story,' he said. 'I'm afraid my background was much more prosaic. No great dramas. No highs or lows. All at a fairly steady, even keel.'

There was an awkward silence. Montgomery was thinking that such a nondescript background made his fellow officer limited in outlook. Percival, for his part, was slightly awed by the ferocity of his fellow officer's recollections. He would either conquer the world or die in the gutter. The situation was more volatile that he realized. He stood up.

'I'd better be getting along, Major,' he said.

Montgomery smiled, calm and collected as if nothing unusual had occurred. 'I'm sorry to have digressed from our agenda,' he said. 'Would you like some coffee?'

'No thank you, Major, duty calls. I'll keep you posted.'

They walked silently back down the long corridors and out into the bright morning air. Percival's entourage was waiting for him and he greeted them with a surly salute. He turned and saluted Montgomery, who returned the salute smartly.

'Carry on, Major,' he said and doubled back inside.

Percival was troubled on the return journey back to Kinsale. Their meeting had yielded little in the way of progress and instead had become a forum for Montgomery to unburden himself of the psychological traumas of his youth. No doubt the pressing urgency of addressing the serious military and political situation would be left to himself, as he suspected it might. Montgomery seemed to have his sights set a good deal higher in the firmament than on the difficult but marginal issue of the Irish question. And the way he had said, "Carry on, Major," to him, a fellow officer of equal rank, as if he were an underling. That was a particular irritant. The sheer arrogance of the man.

John Beatty was very cold. No matter how he tried to keep warm, the cold went through his bones. His cell was bare, with one hard bed, a chair, a rudimentary potty. His hands and feet were always cold, although he tried to exercise as best he could to get the blood flowing. His shirt and pants clung to his thin body like corroded extensions of his skin. He hadn't washed or shaved for several weeks. He could smell his own sour redolence, wafting against the bleak, red sandstone brick walls, and mingling with the foul-smelling waste from the potty, which was rarely emptied out by warden or maidservant. He survived on a meagre portion of thin, hot gruel in the morning made from stale oatmeal, a few crusts of unbuttered bread and a cup of cold tea. Otherwise he tasted only water, but in spite of the lack of variety in his diet, he wolfed it down like a starving cur every morning with eager anticipation. Hunger was good sauce. He was confined in a maximum security cell, deep in the bowels of Cork city gaol, a huge Gothic edifice built on a high, airy hill in the Sunday's Well district, designed in a H shape, with towers, turreted battlements and dripstones; considered a wonderful piece of Georgian architecture by its creators, William Robertson and Thomas Deane, but a living hell to its inmates, many of whom, once incarcerated, never ventured forth again to see the light of day. Most were so badly beaten that they died from their injuries ever before they saw a firing squad. Political prisoners like John Beatty were deemed especially dangerous and so very little leeway was afforded them. Beatty was allowed into a damp common room with one or two other prisoners on a Friday night where they played cards on a plain, deal table. He, dressed in his dirty, white shirt with no collar, belt and braces, and the others in similar rough-cut garb, with only a pot of tea by way of refreshment between them to while away the time.

Beatty was afraid. He'd been afraid most of his life. When he joined the Volunteers he soon realised he was in an organisation for which he was psychologically ill-suited, but he managed to keep a low profile, well away from the more dangerous enterprises of his compatriots, until time and fate caught up with him at the Upton ambush. Even there he'd attemped to wriggle free of his obligations and conveniently drank himself into a stupor the night before. In a half-hearted gesture, he showed up the following morning, knowing he would be conveniently late, but in an ironic twist of circumstances he was the one apprehended by the Crown Forces and taken to Cork gaol where he'd now been languishing for the past three weeks with little prospect of a favourable outcome to his predicament. He'd been awaiting the usual beating which people in his situation invariably received, but it never came. That was odd. Either they considered him an innocent, or his fate was already sealed. He'd been courtmartialled the previous week and was awaiting the deliberations of the Military Tribunal with a feeling of bleak foreboding. Three of his companions were dead and he knew the IRA leaders would be pointing the finger of blame directly at him. But that might only be a point of academic concern if the Tribunal found him guilty of aiding and abetting murder and treason against His Majesty's Forces. Beatty was smart enough to know that his chances of escaping censure were limited. He was clever. A small, slight fellow, with wary eyes and a thin face, he adopted a persona of bravado and arrogance when he had drink taken. He came from a reasonably well-to-do merchant family, an only child of a rather bullying father and an alcoholic mother. Neither parent had been of any great support to him in his youth and he was often left to fend for himself around the town of Kinsale, where he'd been reared. He was loquacious and sanctimonious in his cups, which was most of the time, and he liked to hold forth on the theories of Karl Marx and Lenin. He'd devoured the pamphlets of Voltaire and Rousseau and he'd studied the tactics of the Russian Nihilists. He was regarded by his fellow-townsmen as somewhat of an intellectual, but he was in no wise suited to the profession of arms. But what of that. Fellows like him were needed to devise and pronounce on policy, to bring about the long-term aims of the armed struggle. Some things troubled Beatty. Why for instance hadn't more bishops been shot? That's the first thing he would have done to Bishop Coholan after he excommunicated the Volunteers. The Church had far too much power and had an ambivalent relationship with the British Establishment. Revolution was all very well, provided the Church was not upscuttled. Beatty leant to the left. He was a follower of Larkin and Connolly. His Communist ideas were anathema to most of his comrades, but they didn't take him too seriously because he drank too much. When sober he hadn't a word to throw to a dog.

He was now sober, perforce, for quite a long time and a welling fretfulness beset him. The hours were long and crept in slowly until the morning when one of his gaolers roused him from a fitful sleep and he was marched down a series of long, interminable corridors by four heavily armed soldiers, and ushered into a room where three officers sat on a high dais, with looks of cold indifference on their faces. There was a prosecuting officer sitting at a table facing the Tribunal and a defending officer who gave a pitying glance in his direction and then turned to shuffle his papers. Beatty could tell by the dispirited slouch of his defending officer's shoulders that his prospects were not good. He motioned to Beatty to sit behind him. The Colonel chairing the Tribunal whispered some words of consultation to his companions and then cleared his throat.

'John Beatty,' he said, and his voice echoed around the high-ceilinged hearing room, as loud as the boom of a cannon. Beatty looked to his defending officer for direction, but all he did was to wave him to his feet in a kind of frantic gesture without looking around. Beatty stood up, alone, quaking, sick to his soul. The Colonel repeated: 'John Beatty, having carefully considered all the evidence at our disposal, and having taken into account the heinous offences with which you are charged, it is the unanimous verdict of this Tribunal, that you are found guilty as charged. The punishment for these offences is death, and you are to be taken from here, and you are to be executed by firing squad, at a date and time to be determined by this Tribunal in consultation with the Governor of this prison. You have no right of appeal. Nothing further occurs to this Tribunal.'

The words hung in the air and the antennae of Beatty's brain did not quite register their meaning. The room seemed to grow hot and stifling and the figures of officers and soldiers around him seemed to hover, wraithlike, in a kind of dream. Did he wake or sleep? He could barely remember his own name. Then, the three officers of the Tribunal stood and filed out of the room. Beatty couldn't breathe. His legs felt like jelly.

The room began to spin around him and he collapsed on the floor. He was hoist roughly to his feet and dragged, half sagging, between two soldiers back to his cell, where he woke up twenty minutes later, stretched out upon his horsehair mattress, his teeth chattering from the cold. He sat up and scratched himself. He felt his weeks of stubbled chin and remembered the words of the colonel falling on his head like an executioner's blade. No amount of scratching could keep the monstrous feeling of blind terrror out. His legs he threw over and sat on the edge of the bed. He vomited the wretched contents of his breakfast on the floor.

Two days later, Major Percival was finishing shaving in the washroom of his military quarters in the town of Bandon where he'd taken up duties. Through his window he could see outside to the square, where, on a patch of green lawn, pink flowers were sprouting prettilly on a Japaneses cherry tree. There was a luminosity in the air which heralded the arrival of spring, but that of course could be a false dawn as with many things in Ireland. The weather was as unpredictable as everything else. With phlegmatic thoroughness he finished his toiletries and strode the corridor to his office, to be greeted with the surprising news sent on a wire by the Governor of Cork gaol, that a political prisoner wished to enter into dialogue with the officers of the Crown Forces, with a view to having the sentence of death pronounced upon him, commuted. In exchange for such a gesture it appeared from what the Governor could gather, that the man was prepared to divulge information of a strategic nature concerning the 3rd West Cork Brigade. Percival re-read the dispatch to ensure he had understood correctly. After two frustrating years this might be the breakthrough for which he was waiting. He thanked his secretary and sat at his desk alone and took stock. The immediate thought which struck him, was to find out who else had this information. He lifted the telephone and spoke directly to the Governor. The prisoner was a man named John Beatty who'd been court-martialled and who'd broken down completely. No, he hadn't been put under duress. Yes, he had made the offer voluntarily. Percival instructed the Governor to keep the matter top secret and informed him he'd be at the gaol next morning at 10 a.m. sharp.

He put the phone down. So Montgomery didn't know. Neither did Strickland. Should he tell them? He stood up and strode in agitated circles around the office. He might be inclined to be more generous except for his recent meeting with Montgomery, which gave him an insight into the man that was less than favourable. The display of arrogance and sheer self-aborption had rather shocked him. Montgomery had a self-promoting, ruthless streak that had alienated Percival and that he felt sure would perturb his commanding officers too. Would Montgomery divulge this new information to Percival if the shoe were on the other foot? In a pig's eye he would. No, why throw an advantage to a possible future competitor, where there was no need to. Better let the hare sit.

The next morning he arrived in an armoured car at Sunday's Well, accompanied by his junior assistants, Captain Hotblack and Major Halahan, both battle-hardened soldiers and completely loyal to Percival. They were greeted by the Governor and shown into a well-appointed room with a large, shiny, mahogany table, comfortable armchairs, and a chart of West Cork covering one wall. The views over the city were impressive through the tall, Georgian windows. His two assistants seated themselves at one side of the long table and Percival stood, looking over the Lee fields, where the silver river flowed peacefully towards the city. Then the door was thrown open and the prisoner, John Beatty, was frog-marched in, handcuffed and cowed. Percival turned to behold, a thin, emaciated figure with hollowed-out eyes, a scraggy growth of beard, and an unkempt, musty-smelling suit. The three officers, to the prisoner looking back, seemed like beings from another, out-of-reach world; boots highly polished, tunics and jodhpurs immaculately pleated, shirts starched and ironed, smelling of expensive soap and aftershave lotion, belted and crisp, with holstered pistols on their hips. Beatty felt intimidated and unworthy. The looks on the faces of the junior officers didn't conceal their contempt. The prisoner stood with a warden on either side. Percival turned slowly from the window. What he beheld was a chicken ripe for plucking. He resolved on the benign approach.

'Won't you sit down, Mr. Beatty,' he said, pointing to a chair across the table from his captains. Beatty hesitated, as if he misunderstood. Was he hearing words of kindness or were his ears deceiving him? Percival, noticing his difficulty, moved to reassure him. He spoke to the wardens. 'You can remove the handcuffs.'

The prisoner had the look of a grateful cur receiving a piece of meat after getting a kicking from its master. Percival knew when to tread softly. Most of these Irish rebels were teak-tough and could endure endless amounts of hardship without caving in. To find one already ready for his programme was like finding a gold nugget in a mountain stream. He was pushing an open door. No need to break it down. He introduced his two companions and himself, and then sat down between them, directly opposite Beatty. He smiled more than usual. 'How are you feeling, Mr. Beatty?' he asked.

The other had a bewildered look on his face. 'I don't know,' he said. 'Not too good, I suppose.'

'How have you been treated, any rough stuff, any beatings at all?'

'No,' said Beatty, puzzled.

'Are they feeding you well?'

'Dry bread and water, porridge in the morning, thin and hot.'

'That's not good enough,' tut-tutted Percival. He turned to one of the wardens. 'Gentlemen, put on a pound of your best sirloin steak with plenty of onions and gravy. And bring in a decent bottle of Claret. This man is malnourished. Never let it be said that His Majesty's Forces acted in a mean-spirited manner towards a man intent on co-operating with the lawful authority of his country.'

Percival looked keenly to see if the deliberately provocative words would arouse any sign of resistance in his captive. He couldn't detect so much as the batting of an eyelid.

An hour later, John Beatty was sitting back in his chair, with his belly full and flushed about the gills, having lowered most of the contents of a bottle of Pomerol from one of the best vineyards in the Medoc. His tongue had also loosened in proportion to the number of glasses he'd drunk. Percival was listening keenly to his every word. Captain Hotblack was taking notes. Percival got up and, walking to the map, he lifted a pointing stick and let it rest at the townland of Ballymurphy.

'So you say this is their headquarters, almost right under our noses.'

'The very spot,' said Beatty, 'It has been Brigade Headquarters for most of the past two years.'

'What's the name of the family?'

'Fordes,' said Beatty, and continued: 'The Flying Column moves around as you may have guessed by now, but it usually returns from whence it started.'

'Does this so-called Flying Column really exist?' asked Percival. 'Sometimes it has seemed to us to be more phantom than real, such is its ability to evade capture.'

'Oh, it exists right enough,' said Beatty. 'The brainchild of General Tom Barry. I expect you've heard of him?'

'And how does he move so many men through the countryside undetected? How does he clothe and feed thousands of men? I know it's a huge job for us in the British Army, and we're the best equipped in the world.'

Beatty laughed. 'Thousands of men? Sure there's barely a hundred.'

Percival came towards the table and rested both hands on it, leaning down, staring into Beatty's face. He said nothing for some moments but his eyes didn't waver. 'Less than a hundred, did you say?'

'That's right,' said Beatty. 'You look surprised. There were only about thirty-five fighters at Kilmichael.'

'And what about the night they attacked us in Bandon?'

'Seventy at most,' said Beatty.

'Good God,' said Percival, 'they must be very efficient. They kept our three garrisons, plus the curfew patrol under constant fire for over four hours.'

'They're the best,' said Beatty, and his chest expanded with something approaching pride for the first time in many weeks.

'That is simply astounding,' said Percival, looking towards his captains who were equally agog. 'So our information has been all wrong. We were calculating in thousands.'

'There would be thousands,' said Beatty, 'if they could get their hands on enough weapons. But at any one time there's only enough for a hundred or so. But a hundred good men are better than a thousand uncommitted ones.'

'So you're saying our forces are uncommitted,' asked Percival.

'I'm afraid so,' said Beatty, and Percival thought he detected a smug glint in his eye.

'And does he use the same hundred men all the time?'

'No,' said Beatty. 'He rotates them. That's his secret. He keeps getting fresh men in while the others take a rest. That's why it's called the Flying Column. Very mobile, very fast and it never sleeps. Your conventional army is much too lugubrious and hidebound to compete with them. Especially in the mountainous terrain of West Cork.'

Percival sighed and nodded his head for several moments.

'Ingenious,' he kept muttering to himself. 'Damned ingenious. What do they plan on doing next would you know?'

'I'm afraid I can't help you there, Major Percival,' said Beatty. 'I've been out of circulation for several weeks.'

'But you're fairly certain we'll catch up with them at Ballymurphy.'

'If they're not there they won't be too far away.' said Beatty. He sighed and looked out the window. The haunted look returned to his eyes.

Percival snapped back to his usual, businesslike posture. He looked at Beatty. 'You've been extremely helpful to us, Mr. Beatty. Extremely helpful. I think we may well take a leaf out of the book of this fellow, Tom Barry, and catch him at his own game. In the meantime, I'll see to it that your sentence is immediately commuted. Unfortunately you will not be set free, but you will be transferred to an outlying barracks where you will be safe, not only from our side but especially from your own. Nobody will know of your whereabouts. In due course when we have destroyed this insurrection, as we are now very likely to do thanks to your goodself, and when peace returns to the land, you will be set free. Good day to you.'

Percival watched as Beatty was marched back out the door and then he turned towards his two junior officers. A smile of satisfaction played on his lips. He looked at his watch. It was high noon.

'Coffee?' he said. 'Or perhaps something a little stronger. A shot of Glenfiddich?'

18

A horse and trap, with two men on board, rolled over a hump-backed bridge. A second trap followed, one hundred yards behind, carrying three men. A dark river flowed underneath the bridge, black as coal in the deepest parts. The bridge had sharp cutwaters on the western side to prevent it being swept away in a flood. The road snaked away towards foothills and a towering, pyramid-shaped mountain. The river was the Bandon and the mountain was called Owen, from the Gaelic name *Abhainn,* where the river had its source. There were two swans in the river, where it meandered at this point, deep and wide through, flat, rich, fields, grudgingly yielded by the mountain, which surrounded itself for the most part with rough brakes and rocky breaknecks, down which the water furiously cascaded. The swans and their three cygnets trawled the bottom depths of the river for sprats, young trout, frog and salmon spawn. Spring was coming. Drooping snowdrops whitened the edges of the dirt road and thousands of purple crocuses spread across clearings in the hazel woods that grew along the riverbank. Amidst tall, green sedge, buttercups and marsh marigolds offered a splash of yellow. A kestrel swooped in a dizzy zig-zag through the morning light. The sun glinted off its wings as it harried chirping sparrows and bright-plumaged finches into groves of silver birch, in a rainbow of fluttering colours. It was quiet, empty country, with few inhabitants. The travellers in the traps heard only the whirring of rubber wheels and the clip-clop of horse hooves, the distant barking of dogs in the foothills, cattle calling to the west.

'Good country to hide in,' said Tom Barry, in the leading trap.

'But not to live in,' said Liam Deasy beside him. 'There's not grass enough to feed a snipe up here.'

'Those little fields are fertile,' said Barry.

'But few, and far between,' said Deasy.

'Have we far to go?' asked Barry, after a further silence.

'About three miles, to the northeast of Owen.'

'Do you have a map?' asked Barry.

'In my head,' said Deasy. 'I know every boreen in West Cork. I don't need a map.'

Barry smiled. His adjutant was diligent, and didn't make idle boasts. He looked at the blue sky, smelt the emerging flowers, saw the white buds peeping out on crab apple and blackthorn bushes. 'I think the weather is settling down.'

'Never trust the winter's day,' said Deasy. He was a pragmatic man.

In the trailing trap, Sonny Hennessy drove, and beside him sat the big-framed, soft-voiced, Bill Desmond, who smoked a pipe, and the red-haired Mike Hennessy. They were a little cramped because every square inch of space was taken up with bundles of rifles which they'd uncovered from their winter dumps on various farms. They were taking them to a gathering of the Flying Column, for a big engagement with the British being planned by Barry and Deasy. The Hennessys had supplied both sets of horses and traps. They'd all been lying low for the previous month and now looked forward eagerly to reuniting with their comrades. There was comfort and strength in numbers. There were stories to be told, news to be exchanged. There were new adventures to come which young men loved, oblivious to danger.

The small convoy passed the townlands of Malabracca and Coolkelure. Barry the postilion, Deasy the navigator; the three foot soldiers driving behind.

'One of our best men, Sam Maguire, was born in that farmhouse,' said Deasy, pointing to a snug, well-kept farmyard on their left. 'He's one of Collins's key men in London, and a Protestant to boot.'

'So is Gibbs Ross, in the Schull Company,' said Barry.

'And Robert Barton, and Childers. It's a shame some more of their brethern don't join the fight. If they did, we'd make a clean sweep of the British in jig time.'

'Maybe they'll come around to seeing things our way eventually.'

'I'd be saying that more with hope than with confidence.' said Deasy. 'Sure even our own boys don't all see things the same way. I hear that Collins and Brugha don't pull at all.'

'So I've heard,' said Barry, and said no more. The thought troubled him.

They drove on into a deeper fastness. Down deep, wooded valleys they went and ascended by corkscrew turns on the rough road. Clouds were fleecy, fluffy above the mountain tops, which folded into their own grandeur and felt as tall as the high Alps, which Barry had once beheld as he crossed France. They headed down a valley road to Behagh and Balteenbrack, where farmhouses were huddled and where their comrades would be waiting. A flurry of barking dogs greeted their arrival into the first farmyard. An old man in Wellington boots and a cloth cap turned back to front on his head, greeted them suspiciously. He looked the sweating horses up and down.

'Have ye come far?' he asked.

'Nearly thirty miles,' said Barry.

'Ye musht have started early,' said the old timer.

'We did,' said Deasy.

'Did ye come over Owen way?'

'We did.'

'Ye musht be half daft.'

'Why so?'

'That's a dangerous mountain. If the fog came down ye couldn't see ye're feet. Many's the clever man got lost up there. He did faith. Never found, until found dead.'

'Twas a fine spring day,' said Barry.

'Spring is it? said the old man scornfully. 'Sure you don't see spring up here 'til May. You could have hailstones in an hour.' He turned to look at brooding clouds moving over Sheha to the north.

'I suppose ye're hungry,' said the old man without smiling.

'We are,' smiled Barry.

'I'm Joe McCarthy. Come on, I'll make ye a sup a tay. There's hay in the stable for them horses. They look like they need some. And we've been feeding some of ye're companions for most of a week.'

No sooner had the old man shown them into his sparse, shadowy kitchen, than men in trenchoats began to materialise like spirits, from nooks and crannies where they'd been lying low. The same young men they'd been campaigning with had aged in sinew and psyche, from farm boys to soldiers in a mere six months. More confident in movement, more wary and watchful of eye, leaner and more powerful in physique. The company leaders came in first: the sandy-haired John Lordan, Christy O'Connell, huge of shoulder, wide-faced; Pete

Kearney of the large nose and twinkling eyes, square-jawed Mick Crowley, thick-lipped Denis Lordan; Sean Hales, the self-contained, blonde collossus. These were hard men, who'd endured long marches, rough living, who'd seen men killed and maimed in shocking situations. Who'd killed men themselves and whom nothing or no one could now surprise or intimidate. Yet they and their companions were no more than three score years alive, many in their early twenties; some like Sonny Hennessy, mere boys.

The old man fussed around, wetting tea and grumbling, accepting the easy ribbing from the young men he'd been sheltering, secretly pleased to help, to be important, his gruff visage hiding deeper feelings. After the humble meal, they assembled in the farmyard as evening cast long shadows of russet light through haggard and haybarn. More young men began to file into the rectangle of snug buildings: cowbyre and stable, stall and piggery. They came in twos and threes, tens and twenties, and from the cache of rifles they'd transported, each man was handed a Lee Enfield and a Sam Browne belt with forty rounds of ammunition. Some others already had their own revolvers: Colt six-shooters, Webleys, Mauser Parabellums, long-barrelled Peter the Painters. When they'd all been armed, Deasy asked them to fall in, and form fours. They'd come from the west in Beara, and from the Mizen peninsula: mountainy men with big hands and slow speech. Others came from the southern coast at Clonakilty and Kilbrittain, quick-witted, quick to laughter. From the east along the ridges above the Bandon came hardened warriors from fertile fields who'd left behind their horses and their ploughs, and forged their ploughshares into weapons. Liam Deasy counted carefully. One hundred and four men. Little was needed to be said once Barry had outlined their plans. Word had reached them from their spies in post offices and train stations, and in the heart of the Victoria Barracks in Cork, that a mighty force of British soldiers was being assembled to crush them once and for all. They were marching to meet this challenge and to upset the grand campaign of Percival and Strickland.

They waved goodbye to Joe McCarthy at the fall of night and marched eastwards. He pointed to the new crescent moon.

'That's a moon you could hang your hat on,' he said. 'A sure sign of nasty weather.'

It was a cold night, with a fresh wind blowing. They could see the stars and the bad moon on the rise. The roads were dry but rain was on the way tomorrow. They marched out of the deep valley and went east along the road they called the Bantry Line. Behind they left hidden valleys and uplands, with names that rolled like poetry off the tongue: Shanacrane, Shanlaragh, Coosane Gap. Off to their left was the killing ground of Kilmichael that they knew so well, but they kept their eyes on Coppeen, and turned right towards Castletown. They moved along winding stretches of dirt roads, with bogs and black water, and long fronds of greening fern and pale scutch grass, growing along the banks of small lakes, bending back in the cold night wind. Those who'd fought at Kilmichael did not welcome pale ghosts. They kept their faces towards the sliver of moon and kept a song of hope in their hearts

They reached Templemartin and Mountpleasant, where they finally found billets for the night in the ploughland of *Lios Na gCat*. The time was 4 a.m. The universe had wheeled above them. The Great Bear was overhead when first they started, but now burned in another part of heaven. Sirius was no longer brightest, fading lower. And still Orion the Hunter proclaimed its lustre, and near enough, the twins, Castor and Pollox, kept their equal distance. And all the stars moved to their own music, as did the young men marching, who kept rhythm with their footsteps all that night.

Charlie Hurley took Denny Forde's old mare, tackled under a trap, the following night and helped by the faithful Bill Desmond, he drove a back lane towards a townland across the valley from Forde's house. They were going to O'Mahonys of Belrose where Charlie had heard from Flor Begley that the leaders of the Column might be waiting. They were going down a hill around a narrow turn when they saw the red glow of cigarette butts in the dark. They stopped. Liam Deasy emerged from shadow and so did Tom Barry. Tadhg O'Sullivan stood with them, and Dick Barrett. Charlie pushed the hair back from his forehead. His face had healed but when he stepped down from the trap, he still walked with a limp. 'Goodnight boys,' he said quietly. The wind was light. There were more clouds over the stars tonight than last night. Wind sighed through the whin bushes. A startled night owl flew away across the Owenaboy river.

'We're going up to O'Mahonys,' said Barry.

'We'll see ye there,' said Charlie and climbed back into the trap. The horse hooves echoed up the lane to a big Georgian farmhouse on a prominent lookout over the valley. Below were the railroad tracks, the river, Kinsale Junction, with dim lights illuminating the station.

They talked late with the O'Mahonys and drank whiskey. Tom Barry said they were going to try to waylay the enemy the next day over by Shippool, eight miles distant.

'Where is the Column?' asked Charlie.

'In billets 'round about,' said Barry. 'In Tuough and Rearour.'

Charlie's eyes lit up. 'I'm coming too,' he said eagerly. 'For the crack of the rifles and the skirl of the bagpipes.' He was standing, holding himself straight. It was an effort for all to see. A show.

Tom Barry shook his head. 'You can't come, Charlie,' he said, 'I'm sorry. You're not well enough to fight. 'Twould be too much.'

Charlie sighed a little bitterly. 'So what am I?' he asked. 'Am I now a cripple? A permanent invalid?'

Deasy moved to reassure him. 'You're our inspiration. Our leader first and always. But you've taken a severe blow. You'll recover soon but not yet. Shippool is too far. When you're fit and strong you'll be back with us.'

Charlie sighed again. 'I wonder will I?' he said as if talking to himself. 'Or will I die alone. I always thought I would.'

'That's maudlin talk,' said O'Sullivan the quarter master. 'It doesn't become you.'

'You're right of course,' said Charlie and turned to Flor Begley. 'Will you play me a tune, Flor, if you have your bagpipes. A tune for glory.'

Begley produced his pipes and played, *The Cualann* and then, *The Croppy Boy*. Charlie had tears in his eyes. 'I'd better be getting back.' he said, 'Denny Forde will be waiting up for me over in Ballymurphy. He'll want to feed the mare.'

'I'll come with you,' said Bill Desmond.

'Don't,' said Charlie. 'The Column will need every able-bodied man.'

It was raining hard in the morning as the Column boys rose, from haysheds and from barns and back rooms, up around the high hill of Rearour. It was St. Patrick's Day. Their route was now towards the Bandon river, east of Inishannon where they halted at their chosen ambush site at a bend of the road to Kinsale, at Shippool. Across the river stood the historic castle of *Dún Na Long*. Not far from there, four hundred years before, the Gaelic cause was lost. The mighty chieftains, Hugh O'Neill and Red Hugh O'Donnell fought the British at a place called Ballinamona. They travelled three hundred miles, horse and foot from Ulster. But they planned poorly and drank too much and were betrayed. Mountjoy and Carew burst out from their encirclement and put the run on the superior Irish force. At the fort of ships they made a last stand. And Gaelic Ireland was forever lost.

The river was wide and grey and tidal here. The current was strong. The wind whipped waves up into white horses. Huge, ancient oakwoods grew along either bank. It rained with a vengeance. It was bitterly cold. Winter wasn't gone, just as the old man had predicted. They shivered all day by the sides of ditches but no lorry loads of Essex travelled the road. They were cold and hungry and drenched unto the bone when they retired that night to Skeough, to the families who gave them food and shelter, and who took great risks on their behalf. It was strange that the British hadn't come that day. They came most every day. Tom Barry felt uneasy. They must have been tipped off. If so, they were in mortal danger. They would have to confront soon before the opportunity slipped away. Before they were destroyed, like the men of Ulster, on the 3rd of December in the year 1601.

They slept late the following day and that night, through the inky darkness they ghosted back to Ballyhandle and Crossbarry.

There was a growl of lorries in the early morning. Furtive breakers of the curfew, skulking near a crossroads around the witching hours, saw headlights, smelt petrol from the sputtering engines as convoys of troops moved out of Bandon on the Kilpatrick road. There was no time to alert runners or dispatch riders. They were taken by surprise. The troops were crammed in, grim-faced, red-eyed and fractious from rising early, their Tam O'Shanters fixed at odd angles on their heads, their faces unshaved, their Black and Tan uniforms askew. Some were lonesome, some were anxious and fearful; all wished to be elsewhere. Away from this truculent country of lashing rain and cold winds, strange slanting light and hostile people they'd never been quite able to finally subjugate, until now, if Major Percival had his way.

In the last few weeks he'd been engaged in a feverish orchestration of men and arms, hidden in the bowels of the Victoria Barracks with Major-General Strickland and a select group of junior officers. They pored over maps, identified likely points of assault, memorised the names of obscure townlands. Strickland wished to enlist the assistance of Major Montgomery, but Percival demurred. This was his project and he was going to hold it in a vice-like grip. He secretly hungered for further honours and he would get the credit for his enterprise and diligence in extracting the crucial information from the prisoner, Beatty, in Cork Gaol. He'd marshalled forces from Kinsale, Cork, Ballincollig, Bandon and Macroom: The Hampshires, the Essex, the Auxiliaries, and the Tans. But Montgomery's 17th Infantry he'd deliberately omitted, using the flimsy rationale that they'd be required to bolster the rest of the county while he was engaged in an all out assault in West Cork. If he failed he'd have to take the blame of course, but that was inconceivable, now that he knew the minute size of the forces ranged against him. He could muster five hundred, a thousand, or even two thousand troops against a hundred IRA, the paltry number Beatty had divulged. Knowledge was power, and forewarned was forearmed.

Tom Kelleher was uneasy. He'd been parading the higher ground above Harold's farmyard in Crossbarry since midnight. In a circle thrown much wider, fourteen unarmed scouts from the local company were keeping vigil for any surprise attacks. Kelleher knew every hill and hollow in the territory. He was born up the road in Crowhill. He'd led the Column across the flat bogs from Skeough and Slievegullane that same night, and with Tom Barry and Liam Deasy they'd scouted the lay of the land, to see where best to set a trap for the invaders.

He heard the unmistakeable sound of lorries moving in the far distance. He moved a little higher up the hill and saw lights to the west moving slowly. He called to his companion, Mick Crowley.

'Come up here, Mick.'

Crowley hurried up.

'Do you see what I see?' asked Kelleher.

Crowley squinted his eyes: 'Moving lights.' he said.

'Shh,' said Kelleher. 'Can you hear anything?'

They held their breaths.

'Engines,' said Crowley.

'The military, for sure,' said Kelleher. 'Come on.'

They raced down the sloping fields and ten minutes later burst into O'Leary's house in Ballyhandle, where most of the Volunteers were sleeping for no more than two hours. They were quickly roused from their beds and marched to an agreed assembly point in the field behind Beasley's house. The ambush site ran for about six hundred yards along a straight stretch of the road from a lane going up by the side of Harold's farmhouse to a bend in the road before the village of Crossbarry. There was ample cover on the western side, where trees grew around Harold's farmyard, and Beasley's farm beside it. The further east the road went, the lower the ditch became and the less the cover, where the field rose sharply.

'The wester side is good,' said Barry. 'Not great further east if we have to retreat quickly. But it's the best we can do. We'll have the element of surprise.'

He marked the positions out from one to seven He put Sean Hales in charge of fourteen men in position section one, at the lane west of Harolds. Next he put John Lordan in front of Harold's yard, having advised the owners to stay under cover and keep their heads down. Harold looked truculent, Lordan noted. Not a likely supporter.

'Keep an eye on him,' he said to Dan Canty.

'I will,' said Canty. 'And Beasley too.'

Mick Crowley's section was in the third position and then Pete Kearney's section. At the last bend before the village, Denis Lordan and his fifth section took up their positions. They were all on the northern side of the road that ran east towards Cork except for a few men on the south to cater for any escapees. In position six, Tom Kelleher guarded the rear flank of the Column to the left facing up the hill behind the ambuscade about three hundred yards distant, and on the other flank, six hundred yards to the west, Christy O'Connell and his fourteen men guarded the western side and the line of retreat up the lane towards Skeenahaine Hill which rose above them, and Raheen Hill further back again, the highest ground around.

Around 5 a.m. they dug a trench in the road in front of Denis Lordan's position on the eastern side, at the last turn before the bridge. In the trench they laid a heavy 500 pound mine, packed with gun cotton. It was attached with wires to a plunger expertly configured by Peter Monahan, the mysterious Scotsman who'd joined the Column some time before. Tom Barry came to check the work.

'Will she blow, Peter?' he asked, laconically. 'We've had some duds in the past.'

'Not made by me, you haven't,' laughed the tall, angular man they called 'Scottie.'

'You're sure she'll blow then,' said Barry, more convinced by the smiling competence of the dark young man.

'She'll blow alright,' said Scottie in his rolling, Scottish brogue. 'She'll go up like a volcano.'

'I hope you don't go up with her,' laughed Barry. Monahan laughed too. Black humour eased the tension. Liam Deasy came over and then he and Barry walked back inside the ditch, checking each section of waiting men as they went. Words of reassurance and encouragement were offered. On the western side another trench was cut with another mine laid in it. The round-faced, cheery-eyed Dan Holland was in charge here. With two mines laid at either end, six hundred yards apart, they'd be ready for any eventuality. Whether the British came from Cork or Bandon.

They settled down to wait. Sonny was in Pete Kearney's section, in the middle. He felt cold and hungry, but not afraid. The months of constant danger made him hard. He didn't think about the men he'd fired on. The men he'd killed. When he killed, as he surely did, he thought, like every soldier about other things. The enemy became a symbol, a target. Barry had spoken quietly to them beforehand. Their scouts had told them the enemy was all around. Coming from every side. They'd have to fight their way out, in a calm, collected way. If caught in open country they'd be cut down and butchered. They were likely to be outnumbered ten to one, and possibly twenty to one. They were low on ammunition, but they were brave. The scouts said the lorries from the west would reach them first. If they landed the first blow they'd have the psychological advantage. Warfare was as much about psychology and strategy, as of might and men at arms. Barry was a very brilliant commander. He inspired confidence and projected a palpable calmness.

Sonny thought of his father, his dead mother, his brothers and his sisters. For too long all belong to him had been the victims. But now it was time to kill or be killed. That's what Barry said, and Charlie Hurley too. Sonny missed his great friend even more than his brothers. Charlie was like an older brother. He hoped he'd see him before long.

The night dragged on. The sounds of lorries still moving in the distance were borne on the gentle southwest wind coming slowly closer. Barry said to Deasy, 'They're taking a long time to get here. It must be a big roundup.'

'The scouts said they're stopping at every house,' said Deasy.

'Terrorising the people no doubt,' said Barry, 'and probably taking hostages.'

The sky changed colour and became streaked with grey. Thrushes and blackbirds started singing. Then chaffinches began chirping and pigeons cooing. As the sun rose, fractious rooks began to caw and scrabble for small sticks and papers to build their nests in the surrounding beech trees, completing their annual imperatives to reproduce.

Sonny looked down the long line of men huddled against the ditch. The sun made them warmer. Some were nervous and there was a steady line of them going towards the designated latrine, which was a quiet corner of the field surrounded by briars, where two ditches met. Men squatted to relieve themselves. The smell of shit mingled with the smell of sweat. The smell of fear.

There was a squawking of disturbed chickens in Fordes' farmhouse two miles from Crossbarry. A dog growled and got up and smelt the wind. The mare whinnied in the stable. The trap, yellow-wheeled, stood heeled, with its two shafts pointing at the sky like artillery guns. The family had retired late. Denis Forde and his wife, his son Humphrey, and his youngest daughter. Their special, honoured guest, Charlie Hurley, occupied the spare room at the top of the stairs He slept with his shirt and trousers on. He kept two pistols, locked and loaded under his pillow: a Webley, which you cracked open like a jacknife to load, and a Colt .45, which had a chamber that flipped out sideways when you slid the catch. The Colt he liked the best: lighter, smoother to handle. The Webley was a little heavier and more cumbersome, but he could handle each with ease in either hand. His face was nearly healed, but he still felt twinges in his troublesome ankle, though willpower had forced the healing faster. He was determined to join the Column tomorrow, come hell or high water. Enough of this malingering. Before he nodded off to sleep he thought of Elizabeth Hennessy. She'd be sleeping twenty miles to the west, in the secluded farmyard surrounded by elm trees, with flat wide fields to the north, the sloping wellfield and meadow to the south. Beyond that, the high brake, through which an ancient road ran. Elizabeth said it was the old road to Tara, seat of the Gaelic kings for a thousand years. He slept fitfully, waking every hour.

Major Halahan alighted from a lorry and adjusted his officer's peaked cap over his wide, Germanic face, his full mouth, his pugilistic nose. He drew himself up to his full height of six feet two inches, and tightened the wide belt around his tunic. Underneath, he adjusted his bulky vest. He held a pistol in one hand. He had another in a holster on his left thigh. He waved silently to soldiers following behind him. Some were on foot on either side of ten lorries, and others sat in the back. He had about three hundred soldiers under his command. Every few miles of the road the men would take turns riding and walking. They were now in Fordes' farmyard on the high hill of Ballymurphy.

Two dogs began an excited barking. Halahan ignored them. He looked around the deserted farmyard, towards stall and stable, hay rick and straw rick in the haggard. So this was where the storied IRA maintained their headquarters? He hoped Percival had his facts right. He'd left him back on the main road poring over a map having taken off his greatcoat. Halahan had noticed him taking a swig of whiskey from a bottle. Was he feeling pressure? There were about a dozen lorries in Percival's cavalcade, and maybe four hundred men. There were troops converging from all directions. Halahan hoped the Macroom contingent of Auxiliaries would turn up too. As yet there was no sign of them. The farmyard was unusually quiet. Halahan again adjusted his cap and nodded to two soldiers beside him. They made for the front door of the house.

Charlie awoke to the sound of barking dogs. The sun was blood-red, rising. It slanted in through the window, coming over the hills of Carrigdhoun to the east. He slipped out of bed and put the two revolvers inside his belt. He looked cautiously out the window. The yard was full of soldiers. Then there was a loud knocking on the front door, that became a pounding. He looked at a holy picture which he took from his pocket. He kissed the Blessed Virgin and blessed himself. The Fordes emerged from their rooms at the top of the landing, sleepy-eyed and frightened.

'What is it?' asked the girl.

'The military,' whispered Charlie. 'They're all around.'

The youngest Forde daughter gasped.

'Keep calm,' said Charlie. 'I'll go down. Everyone stay up here at all costs.'

They nodded, holding each other for comfort and security. Charlie inhaled deeply and exhaled slowly. He checked again the chambers of both revolvers. Downstairs the door came in with a crash, flattened back with a kick, in a shower of splintered wood and dust on the cement floor. Halahan and two soldiers crowded into the large kitchen. Charlie had a gun in either hand as he came down the stairs in his stockinged feet. He saw the guns of the soldiers pointing at him, but he was fast. He fired first. One, two, three shots. Each bullet hit its mark. The first hit one of the soldiers in the chest and he fell dead across the cold fireplace, amidst the soot and ash. The second soldier's hand was shattered by the second shot, and his pistol spun away. The third shot hit Halahan full in the chest. He toppled back, out the door into the yard. Charlie was now at the bottom of the stairs. He blazed away out the kitchen window. Soldiers outside ran for cover from the whistling bullets. Others returned fire, and the kitchen utensils on the dresser rattled and smashed, as bullets ricochetted everywhere. Charlie blew smoke from the pistol barrels, then released another round of shots which peppered the cobbled yard. His eyes shone with elemental fury. 'Come on you bastards,' he roared. Let them come on now and see what they were made of. The soldiers ducked and dived for cover in the yard. Halahan stood and dusted himself down from his temporary daze. A soldier ran to him and said. 'My God, sir, I thought you were done for.'

'Saved by the bullet proof vest,' Halahan whispered hoarsely.

'How many in there, sir?' asked the soldier.

'I only saw one. He has two revolvers. He's good. He hit the three of us.'

There was a lull in the firing. Charlie made for the back door and opened it slightly. Nobody there. He made a dash. A soldier was running past on his own. He fired from the hip more in hope than expectation. The bullet hit Charlie in the chest, but he charged on.

'Shoot you bastards, shoot away,' shouted Charlie, wounded, but still advancing. The soldiers from the yard raced around to the back, hearing their companion call. Charlie released a salvo of bullets, wounding four more soldiers. But then a bullet from a soldier's gun spun him around and he crawled on his hands and knees another twenty feet. Halahan ran around and took charge.

'Keep firing, keep firing.'

Rifles and pistols blazed again. Cold steel had its own will and soon made short shrift of human bones. Charlie's body bucked and convulsed, as he was struck by round after round. Eventually all movement stopped: muscles, pumping heart, sweet breath of life. Charlie lay dead on the grass in the garden behind the house. His blood seeped into the green, turning it red like the rising sun.

They heard the gunshots coming from the hill to the northeast. Tom Barry turned his head sharply to listen. He looked at Liam Deasy. They were standing with Denis Lordan's section, which they'd fixed on as their command position.

'That's coming from Fordes,' said Deasy.

'Only one man I know can shoot like that,' said Barry. 'It must be Charlie Hurley.'

Their eyes betrayed their unease, but dared not articulate their thoughts in words.

'He's alone, except for Humphrey Forde.'

'And Denis.'

'The old man can't fight.'

'Sean Buckly might be with him.'

'Maybe, but we'd better send help.'

Barry called Bill Desmond who was leaning against the ditch with the other Volunteers, rifle pointed towards the road.

'Go up to Fordes,' said Barry. 'Check up on Charlie. Bring him down with you. You won't need a rifle, in case you're apprehended.'

'I have this,' said Bill, and produced a short Webley from inside his trenchcoat pocket.

'That's the very man,' said Barry. Bill handed over his rifle and struck off up the fields. He went across a rough brake as the ground rose higher, and crossed the Kilumney road and forded the Owenaboy river which was quite shallow, running over smooth stones and gravel. Then he turned right and went uphill again along a lane that wound towards Fordes' farmyard, which stood on a height looking across the valley, towards Skeehahaine Hill to the west. He was going along by a high, bramble-choked ditch on the lane, when he was startled by a voice that shouted, 'Hands up.'

Bill stopped. A half dozen rifles were pointing at him from inside the ditch.

'Climb over,' said the Sergeant. Bill fumbled through the brambles which were long and treacherous, with arching stems armed with sharp thorns. He felt the Webley in his pocket. If found on him he was a dead man. His fingers found a small hole in the pocket and as he made an elaborate show of slowly climbing the prickly ditch, he pushed the pistol through the hole.

'Hurry up,' said the Sergeant.

'I'm coming,' said Bill, and pretended to slip back. 'Them briars are fierce.'

He deliberately drew the back of his hand along a jagged bunch of thorns and blood flowed. But the pistol had already fallen safely to the bottom of the ditch into a clogged drain. With a last heave he was up and over the ditch and down among the soldiers, blood dripping from his bleeding hand.

'What's your name?' demanded the Sergeant.

'Bill Desmond.'

'From where?'

'Ballintubber.'

'Where are you going?'

'To my sister's place up in Crowhill.'

'To do what?'

'To go ploughing.'

'Come with us,' said the Sergeant.

Bill was led across the field towards the Forde farmhouse.

'Who are ye?' he asked, faking innocence.

'Don't play the fool with us?' said the Sergeant. 'We're from the Hampshire Regiment, not that it will matter to you where you're going.'

Bill said no more. He looked at the soldiers. There were hundreds of them standing all around and down across the fields. Some had jute sacking tied around their boots, he noticed, probably to muffle the sound of marching. A thin, vicious-looking officer with a slight stoop, came up across the field from the farmhouse. The strawrick was aflame behind him, smoke rising into the bright morning sun. It would have been a pretty, pastoral picture on another, fairer day: blue smoke, yellow straw, green grass. The Sergeant said, 'You can answer some questions for Major Percival.'

'Percival of the Essex,' thought Bill. He didn't feel optimistic.

Percival huddled with the Sergeant, looking towards Bill, and looking back. Then looking again. After a few, whispered minutes, Percival came over. He looked Bill up and down. 'You're no ploughman,' he said. 'With your leggings and your breeches? You look more like a rebel commandant to me.'

'Yerra my dear man,' said Bill, feigning foolishness. 'A rebel is it? Sure I'm only dressed like this to ride a few horses over at the sister's place.'

Percival's eyes narrowed. 'I thought you were going ploughing? Do you use a ploughhorse to go riding out?'

'The Irish draught is an all purpose horse,' said Bill, mock seriously. 'He'll pull a plough, he'll pull a trap. And he's a mighty horse to jump a pole. You could win a trial stake with the Irish draught.'

Percival's demeanour softened. Either this fellow was genuine or else he was a plausible rogue. But he was not without a touch of blarney.

'That's enough of your horsey guff,' he said. 'Come this way.'

Bill, surrounded by soldiers, followed him down to the road. His hand had nearly stopped bleeding. He sucked the drying blood. It had a kind of sweet and salty taste. When they got to the road there was a back-to-back trap held up by two men. Bill recognised the Fordes, father and son. There was a body stretched, head to the rear of the trap, barefooted, dressed only in pants and shirt.

'Do you know this man?' asked Percival, pointing to the body. Bill stared. He recognised Charlie. He swallowed hard and wrinkled his brow. He shook his head and lied, 'I don't then.'

'Are you sure? Take a good look at him. Your life may depend upon it.'

'Is he dead?' asked Bill, playing the omadaun.

'If he's not dead he must be Rasputin,' said Percival. 'He certainly took as many bullets.'

Bill saw the riddled body, unseamed from the nave to the thrapple with bullet holes. The body of his old friend whom he'd lived with day and night. Nursing him back to health with the Hennessys, and then with O'Sullivans up in Gurranreigh, and then with Healys of Farran. He'd left him on his own with Fordes some weeks before. He thought his heart would break, but he could only say, 'I never laid eyes on him in my life before.'

'He was good, whoever he was,' said Percival with grudging admiration. 'I wish my own men could shoot like that. We got him, but not before he did us quite a bit of damage. Quite a bit.'

He nodded as if to himself, then he shot a quick glance at Bill, sizing him up. Looking for a chink in his armour. Bill was licking the blood from his hand again as if he hadn't a care in the world.

Suddenly, a soldier called urgently from across the field. 'More firing, sir, down in the valley.'

Percival kept his eyes on Bill. 'I'll be talking to you later, Mr. Desmond. I'm not finished with you yet. You can get underneath that trap now and bring that body down to the main road with these fellows.'

Bill went to the front of the trap and got between the shafts with Humphrey Forde. Old Denis Forde pushed from behind.

'Come on, Kinsale party,' shouted Percival to his troops. They ran down the side road towards Crossbarry at the double, rifles at the ready.

A long line of lorries came down the valley road, into the carefully laid trap. There were three vehicles to the fore, full of soldiers, about twelve men sitting in the back of each, with a driver and an officer in the cabs in front. There were further lorries stretching back along, with scores of soldiers marching in between, looking keenly to the left and to the right. They'd travelled laboriously in this fashion from Bandon, eight miles away, since 2 a.m. They'd searched every house along the way, ransacking, smashing furniture, burning haysheds, looting and terrorising women and children. They beat up some younger men and took some hostages, including young Ned White from Newcestown, whom they prominently displayed in the back of the first lorry. They caught him in Kilpatrick.

Christy O'Connell saw the convoy first. He put his finger to his lips and his men looked to him for a signal. The indication was to let the convoy pass them by. They kept their heads low inside the ditch and held their collective breaths. Their hearts pounded and their palms sweated on the stocks of their rifles. The lorries proceeded to pass Sean Hales's section next. Hales scanned his men's faces. They looked tense as coiled springs, but they knew the order was to let the convoy pass down to the end, as far as the mine laid on the road by the bridge before the crossroads. His men kept their heads down although they were well hidden by trees and thick fuschia hedges. Then the lorries came to Harold's yard. They were moving slowly, at marching pace. Inside in the kitchen, Harold, a long-faced farmer with a stoic demeanour, wearing a high hat like a Puritan, waited for his chance to warn the soldiers. There were Volunteers all around him and upstairs in his bedrooms. His wife and children were cowering in the back kitchen. Harold tried to grab the door handle. He succeeded in getting through it but was forced back in at bayonet point by Dan Canty. John Lordan, from his position at the front garden wall, directly opposite the farmhouse door, looked around. He raised a hand. His men waited for a signal. This troublesome Harold could upset the applecart. The lorries were twenty feet west of the postern gate. A young Volunteer upstairs poked his head out of a bedroom window to see what the commotion was about below. The first lorry was level with the gate. The driver looked to his left and saw the man at the upstairs window holding a rifle. He slammed his foot on the metal pedal of the brake. John Lordan saw the danger. 'Fire!' he roared.

Before the echo of his voice had bounced back from the farmhouse walls, fourteen rifles reported almost as one with a ripping, crackling blast. The first lorry was no more than ten feet away, stopped in the middle of the road. The fusillade marked and maimed every soldier in the back. The driver took his foot off the brake and pressed the accelerator. The lorry lurched sideways and the officer in the cab tried to open the door. He was crushed against the pillar of the wall before a hail of bullets blew his brains out. The hunt was on. First blood.

Red, viscous blood spouted from soldiers' chests, and from their bellies, eyes, aortas; burst by Lee Enfield shells. They fell and tumbled, keeled and crawled from side mesh and from tailboard, flattened like stalks or leaves blown before a hurricane. The men behind the hedges were possessed of one imperative, and that was to destroy, to annihilate, to extirpate. They set about their sombre work with gusto. The second and third lorries came on, but were now caught between the ferocious fire from John Lordan's men and Sean Hales' men behind them. In Beasley's farmyard fifty paces away, Mick Crowley's section had also launched its first obliterating volley. Lordan's fighters were like men exultant with the fury of blood and vengeance. The terrible cacophony broke out all down the tree-lined road as morning birds rose up in frantic consternation. Rooks and ravens, pigeons, blackbirds, wrens and robins went churring, squawking, cawing from branch to branch, forsaking their newly made nests, their primordial calls adding to the bedlam. Horses in nearby fields went racing in wild alarm, their canters collected, their tails in high display, their eyes rolling white with fear as they went round and round in ever-widening circles. The road was a river of blood, the dykes were fens of spilled intestines, gristle and bone. There were soldiers perforated with bullets and with bayonets if they stumbled too close to the attackers, and in their sulky ruminations back in Bandon, they had never dreamt up horrors of this dimension before their lives were smashed. And then, as if to mock their final agonies and intensify the darker images of their nightmare, a wailing sound hit the higher registers emanating forth on the bright air of that lovely dawning. The lone piper, Flor Begley, filled his lungs and played the bagpipes with a fierce merriment, striding up and down Harold's farmyard, impervious to bullet or bayonet, powder or shot. Notes climbed, shimmied, wailed, increasing in intensity between lulls in the firing. To hear such music, long the province of their English regiments going into battle, being flung back in their faces was a cruel irony, as Begley's fingers conjured up a manic energy and transferred it to his fighting comrades. At the same time a terrible aigue seemed to possess the British and render them impotent, transfixed by the dark enchantment of a demented pied piper.

To the west, the long line of soldiers and lorries who followed on behind the first three vehicles stopped and tried to take evasive action by turning up a side road to the left. As they moved up towards higher ground, O'Connell's section, cunningly deployed by Tom Barry, opened up on them before they could begin their attempted encirclement. Volley after volley sent them running, scampering, crawling, leaving many of their comrades dead in fields and gaps, some draped like rag dolls over ditches.

Ned White was the last man left alive in the leading lorry at Harold's gate. He leaped from the back into the face of furious firing from his own comrades' rifles, but some providential hand guided his footsteps and he ducked the bullets like a man evading raindrops on a rainy day. He stumbled into the arms of his surprised fellows as if he had dropped straight out of the sky.

When Tom Barry and Liam Deasy heard the bombardment starting up at Harold's yard, they left their command position, and with Pete Kearney, Whistler McCarthy, Tim Allen, and Denis Lordan they ran along the road towards the firing. Running towards them were scores of disorganised and panicked soldiers, who then scrambled and leaped over the ditch on the southern side of the road and headed for the railway embankment two hundred yards away. Barry and his officers followed them and cut them down until they were scattered all across that wide, green meadow in random, inert formations. No quarter given, no mercy in the heat and dust of battle. There was red blood dripping from rifle bayonets when the action joined in a fatal embrace, and there was a peculiar elation in the eyes of some who revelled in the gore. The field south of Beasley's farm was cleared. The pursuers turned back towards the road where the firing was still going on in sporadic bursts, that were less fierce and less frequent now. As Deasy was climbing over the briary ditch his cap appeared for a split second in the firing line and two rifles blazed as one. Denny O'Brien of Newcestown and John O'Donovan of Aultagh of the woods, were about to fire again when they recognised their adjutant rising towards them like some Lazarus from the dead. They ran towards him and helped him over. 'We are very sorry,' said O'Brien.

'I thought my goose was cooked,' said Deasy with a dry chuckle. He looked around. There were scattered bodies all over the road. The firing had stopped from Pete Kearney's section to that of Sean Hales. Tom Barry and Deasy huddled in conversation with their section commanders. The jovial John Lordan came down. 'I think we have them well in hand,' he said, casually, as if he'd merely mown a field of hay.

Barry laughed. 'It's not over yet, John, better not get too cocky.'

He turned to the others. 'Alright, men. Collect all the rifles and ammunition you can find, and then burn those lorries. There's a big Lewis gun on the leading truck. I don't think the gunner managed to fire a shot. Can we get a man to haul that with us?'

The young hostage, Ned White, put up his hand. 'I'll take it Commandant,' he said.

Barry regarded him laconically. 'How old are you boy?' he asked.
'Seventeen.'

'You've come through your ordeal well. You're the only survivor from the lorry.'

'I was praying hard,' said the young man.

'And your prayers were answered,' said Barry, soberly.

Bodies were ransacked for ammunition belts, rifles and revolvers. Sonny turned over one fair-haired youth and saw a man no older than himself. He sighed and felt a pang of remorse but had no time to linger. But when all this was over he would fight no more. Killing was a cruel road to follow. A road with no turning, only downward to the darkest pit. Maybe there was a better way, but in the weem and flux of a soldier's fortune there was no time to ponder on a better way. Some of these dead were also good men and had fought bravely. What more could they have done than what had been asked of them? No more than he himself. As he was going about his grim work his initial sense of omnipotence and elation had given way to a vague despondencey, when suddenly there came an echo of a large volume of rifle fire from far away up the hill towards Tom Kelleher's flank. Sonny lifted his head and listened. It wasn't over yet.

Barry and Deasy came over. They spoke to Pete Kearney.

'Can you spare a few good men, Pete?' asked Barry. 'Tom Kelleher will need some of your best.'

'These are my best,' said Kearney pointing to Sonny Hennessy, Nudge Callanan and Paddy O'Sullivan.'

Spud Murphy came over from Mick Crowley's section. He had his arm in a sling. He was unable to fire a rifle but he was one of the heroes of Kilmichael.

'Will you look after these lads, Spud?' asked Tom Barry. 'Make sure they hold their ground and shoot straight. The scouts report the enemy may be trying to engage in a pincer movement to the northeast. If they come across the hill they'll cut off our line of retreat.'

'No problem, Commandant,' replied the fearless Murphy. 'We'll give Kelleher a bit of a hand. I might take a few others as well.'

Barry ordered the rest of the sections from the western side to begin their retreat up the side lane by Harold's farmhouse to Skeenahaine Hill. Deasy took charge of the retreat. The only section left was back at their command position, where the cool Denis Lordan was holed up with his fighters, waiting for an assault to come from the east and south.

Sonny and his companions hurried uphill across the fields. The climb was sharp and quite steep. They were gasping from the effort. They crossed a lane and saw Kelleher and his fourteen men lining a long ditch facing the valley to the east through which the Owenaboy river ran, hard by the road to Begley's Forge and Kilumney. Over this fatal water, Bill Desmond had already crossed to Fordes of Ballymurphy, which was on the rising ground beyond it. There Charlie Hurley now lay dead. The forces of Halahan and Hotblack were advancing down from Ballymurphy. Somewhere further down, Major Percival was in charge of another four hundred troops.

'You're welcome boys,' said Tom Kelleher when he turned to see the reinforcements arriving. 'There's a big force advancing against us over there. We can't take them on in the open, there's too many for us.'

He looked at the smoke-blackened faces of Sonny and the others, he noticed the spatterings of blood on their hands and clothes. 'Are they finished down below?' he asked.

'Wiped out,' said Sonny and did not smile.

'Good work,' said Kelleher.

'Tough work,' said Sonny. He had scarcely opened his mouth when a bullet whizzed past his ear. He ducked for cover against the ditch. To the northeast they could see soldiers on either side of O'Driscoll's farmhouse. They had come up the old road from the Ballyhandle Quarry. The ground was higher up there. It fell away to a stream that flowed from left to right in a ravine that separated the soldiers from Kelleher's men. The stream flowed down into the Owenaboy to the east, itself little more than a stream. Skeenahaine Hill was whalebacked high above them, with wide fields of green growing grass being foraged by a scattering of cows. If the British troops reached the heights of Skeenahaine they could fire straight down on top of Kelleher and the newly arrived reinforcements. The advance guard had just passed north of O'Driscoll's farmyard and were moving cautiously westward, while the main party, of about one hundred and fifty, was heading straight for Kelleher. Cunning strategist that he was, Kelleher resolved to set a trap.

Sonny could see the advance and knew that in another few minutes their line of retreat could be cut off. 'We'd better get some men up there,' he said to Kelleher, who smiled calmly back at him.

'You're quite right, Sonny boy,' he said. He called two men, sent up by Denis Lordan. They were Con Lehane and Denis Mehigan, seasoned warriors. Kelleher pointed to the northwest. 'There's an old ruined castle up there. I want you two to make a run for it and hole up there. Hold your fire until the British are within twenty yards of you. Then let them have it, and make sure you get their commanding officer first.'

Lehane and Mehigan slipped off towards the intervening stream. They slithered down a steep, briary bank and then ran, splashing up along the shallow bottom. The high banks of the stream kept them out of sight from the enemy until they saw the castle ruins on a rocky crag above them. They scrambled up, pulling on drooping tree branches, into the crumbling, arched opening of the ruin. Through broken portcullises they poked their rifles, camouflaged by ivy hanging down the ancient walls.

Captain Hotblack was leading his platoon across a wide, undulating field, having passed to the north of O'Driscoll's farmhouse. They were heading for Skeenahaine Hill and would pass the ruined castle on their left in a few seconds. There were at least thirty men in Hotblack's group. They heard firing from their own men on their left flank, engaging Kelleher below them. Major Halahan was in charge. Hotblack was secure in his mission. Halahan would protect his flank. He forged ahead with his manoeuvre, waving his men on urgently towards the ruin. Once he got there he'd have cover, and then he and Halahan would squeeze the rebels in a pincer movement and snuff them out with overwhelming force. Hotblack was cocksure. He relished the din of battle, the smell of brimstone and smoke, the cries of agony as his enemy was butchered. Everything else was tame and inconsequential compared to the cut and thrust of battle. He was striding purposefully ahead, rifle at the ready, gesticulating to his men with a backward swing of his arm. He wanted them to lie up beside him. He was twenty paces from the ruin when Mehigan and Lehane opened up. The first bullet hit Hotblack in the throat and the second bullet hit him in the stomach. Blood spurted like a fountain from his larynx and his intestines issued forth like puddings from his burst belly. His rifle fell at his side. Mehigan and Lehane were firing rapidly. They cut down most of the thirty men behind Hotblack, before the survivors stopped, shocked, then turned and ran in panic, back towards O'Driscoll's long, low farmhouse.

Tom Kelleher, with quiet satisfaction, saw the fleeing soldiers and gave a little knowing smile to Sonny who said with understatement: 'It looks like they followed instructions.'

'I figured they would,' said Kelleher, dryly. 'Once they won the race to the castle, I knew they'd get the job done.' He pointed to the twenty-two men lining the ditch. 'Now we'll square away the rest of them.'

Halahan's large platoon had halted near the stream that Mehigan and Lehane crossed. They looked back in alarm towards their retreating comrades, and those slaughtered across the field around the castle ruin. Then they looked down on Kelleher's party, well covered behind the ditches that ran from north to south, and then, where the ditches intersected, from east to west. Before they could compose themselves or decide on a course of action, they clearly heard the shout from Kelleher as it echoed up the long valley, that rose up sharply first, then flattened out, then sloped up again in a series of graded steps to Skeenahaine on high. Bullets bit the turf all around them. Soldiers fell like skittles, some toppling headlong down the steep bank of the stream. There were howls of agony as grown men cried for their mothers, the look of fear fleeting through their surprised eyes, as the light of the world left them. When Kelleher's men fired again, Halahan's platoon turned and ran, like that of Hotblack before it. Losing all sense of formation, all shape or dignity, they scattered, terrified, across the green fields, among the ogling cattle who stampeded in between them as in the gadding summer season, with their tails in the air and their eyes crazed with fear. The sloping field was blood-spattered, gut-ridden, faeces-flecked, and there were broken bodies in khaki, and black and tan uniforms, thrown over ditches and into bramble bushes, like empty sacks. Soon every living soldier had fled. The blood of those who died trickled down the steep bank into Ballyhandle stream, turning it red as the Rubicon, as it flowed to join its sister Owenaboy, and from there two rivers fused into one, on the long journey to the sea.

As Kelleher, Sonny, Spud Murphy and the others continued to scan the high ground above them they saw a movement of men and arms. Kelleher put his field glasses to his eyes. He sighed in relief. 'It's Deasy and the boys,' he said. 'They made it up there first.'

'Thank God,' said Sonny with a huge sigh of relief 'For a minute there I thought it was more military.'

Kelleher was standing and waiting. 'That means most of our sections have retreated. But there's still firing down at Denis Lordan's and Pete Kearney's side.'

They saw heads coming up rapidly over the brow of the hill. Tom Barry led a group of rearguard fighters into view. They came up the steep slope from Harold's farm. Barry smiled grimly as he reached them. 'Ye've put the run on them,' he said. 'A good day's work all round.'

'Yes,' grinned Kelleher. 'They ran like scalded cats in the wind up.'

Barry looked around. 'Most of the Column have gone up with Liam.'

'We saw them throught the glasses,' said Kelleher.

'Come on,' said Barry. 'We must follow them up.'

'What about Lordan's men?' asked Kelleher.

'They'll have heard the whistle to retreat. They'll be coming.'

On top of Skeenahaine, Liam Deasy, Sean Hales, John Lordan and Christy O'Connell stood in a small circle. The views all around were panoramic. They could see the Atlantic away to the south where the last ridge before Kinsale and Timoleague reared up. There were several river valleys in between: the Arigideen, the Bandon and the Owenaboy which they beheld below them, They could also see, closer at hand, smoke rising from Denis Lordan's position near Crossbarry bridge as he came under heavy fire from British Forces approaching from three sides. The nearest was a detachment coming across from Killeen towards the Kilumney Road, intent on cutting Lordan off to the northern retreat. Deasy continued to watch through his field glasses. 'It's getting critical for Denis,' he said to Sean Hales.

'We'd better keep a shot on them,' said Hales.

'Alright men,' said Deasy. 'Line up along the ditch there and fire three rounds, rapid fire, at one thousand yards range towards that line of military coming across from Killeen.'

Sixty men lined the ditch and a volley rang out thunderously in the still, bright morning air. A second fusillade was followed by a third from the massed line of riflemen. The sounds rechoed from hill to hill. In the far distance, they saw random running soldiers racing back towards Hartnetts' farm in Killeen.

Denis Lordan was trying to hold his section together down at Crossbarry bridge. His men were fighting bravely but were under heavy fire from

Dunkeeran Road, as well as Killeen. It was too dangerous to attempt a retreat from their position up the unprotected field behind them. He had three men dead around him and then Dan Corcoran was hit. He was rescued by the brave Dick Spencer, who dashed out into the middle of the field under fierce fire, to rescue his badly wounded comrade. Lordan heard the firing from high on Skeehahaine and he noticed the attack from Killeen suddenly ceased. He turned his head and saw Pete Kearney waving to him from the west at Beasley's garden. Beasley was standing beside Kearney and appeared to be advising him. Lordan decided to risk a retreat. 'Alright boys, let's make a dash for it, but first let me check poor Peter and the others.'

He went to his three fallen fighters, Jeremiah O'Leary, Con Daly and Peter Monahan. He felt their pulses and listened for sounds of breath. There was neither. Nothing to be done but leave them there, faces turned up to the sky. He went to Monahan, the mine-layer, last. Peter had died in agony from a shot that felled him near the plunger of his mine, and as he writhed on the ground, the wires became entangled around his body. As Denis Lordan was unwinding the wires his hand slipped against the plunger. The mine exploded with an almighty reverberation, sending a huge cloud of dirt and smoke up into the air. The advancing military, under Percival, coming from Crossbarry, were thrown into momentary confusion by the blast and fell back towards the bridge. Under the huge, covering curtain of debris and dust, Lordan's men ran west towards Beasley who still stood on his garden fence. He beckoned to Lordan. 'This way.' he said.

Lordan stopped in front of his men for a moment. 'But I thought you weren't on our side?' he said, fearing a trap.

'I'm on neither side,' said Beasley. 'Only on the side of kindness and of pity. Follow me.'

He led them around the back of his own house, then across the back of Harold's large, rambling farmyard. 'There's the laneway,' he said. 'Your companions went up it some time ago. God speed.'

Lordan shook his hand and looked him in the eye. 'Thank you,' he said. 'That can't have been easy for you.'

'God's work is always easy,' said Beasley, as he watched them vanishing out of sight around the bend in the lane, that took them up to safety by the only route that was free for them to travel. Then he went back down to the road, to the scene of blood and carnage in front of Harold's gate. He began to lay the bodies of the soldiers side by side and whispered silent prayers into their unhearing and unhoused ears.

Major Percival walked up the road from Crossbarry bridge with the look of a man in a state of shock. He saw the broken bodies of soldiers lying all around him. The smell of burning lorries and charred flesh invaded his nostrils. He heard the moans of scores of injured men, some beyond all help, quietly expiring under the morning sun that had now risen bright and warm. He stopped and touched the chilling skin of a young private, whose blood was slowly seeping into the grass verge. He looked around for any sign of rebels, but they had vanished as if into thin air. All he could see were the three dead bodies they'd left behind, in torn trenchcoats, one blown up by his own mine. 'Hoist on his own petard,' thought Percival grimly, without a trace of irony. He had no stomach for wordplay. He himself was the biggest show of all. His carefully laid plans, his grand strategy was in ruins, like the remnants of his army. How could this have gone so badly wrong? Was it conceivable that the prisoner, Beatty had duped him? Given him false information? If the rebels were so few, how could they have killed so many of his soldiers? How had they planned so brilliantly, escaped so skilfully? What kind of men were they? What kind of man commanded them? He could see now why they called him General. As much as he hated to acknowledge it, this was one of the most astonishing military victories he had ever seen. Achieved at his expense, his humiliation, his shame. What would his rival Montgomery be thinking? He could imagine his condescending sneer. He reached a shaking hand inside his tunic and took out a naggin of Glenfiddich. It tasted bitter, like the gloomy thoughts that beset his addled mind.

He looked around him. His vaunted Essex Regiment had lost many men, the Black and Tans had been destroyed, the Hampshires had turned tail and fled across fields and valleys, leaving their dead companions strewn and dissipated on every acre. And now he was reduced to accepting the kindness and succour of the Harolds and the Beasleys, whose stoic women went about the invidious task of trying to apply soothing balm, and convey words of comfort to young soldiers with terrible injuries, many as bad as anything he had seen in the years he spent in France during the Great War.

As for the rebels, what a meagre reaping. Three raggedy cadavers and the barefoot man in the horse trap, which he could see pulled up on the road outside Harold's yard. He was still baffled by him, and curious as to his identity. A gunman of exceptional prowess, he must have been one of their elite, and obviously still recuperating from previous injuries at the time he finally succumbed to a hundred bullets. He'd noticed the scarred and pockmarked cheeks. Would he have died anyway? And there was the laconic fellow who'd pulled the trap down from Ballymurphy, still playing the fool and pretending he was as innocent as a new born babe. He'd get to the bottom of that chap's farrago of lies if it was the last thing he'd do. Ploughman indeed. Up to his eyes with the rebels almost certainly.

He walked outside and ordered Bill Desmond to load the dead bodies of his countrymen onto one of the lorries. He ordered his soldiers to give him a good kicking into the bargain and knock the lopsided smile off his brazen, rustic face. Soon there was a long line of lorries heading back on the road to Bandon, carrying the crippled and the dead. By late afternoon word had gone around the countryside and reporters from Cork and Dublin, and even London, were frantically trying to get in touch with military sources, to establish the alarming facts of the story. Major Percival brooded in his office in Bandon barracks and refused to speak to anyone, other than to his commanding officer, Major-General Strickland, to whom he tried to explain the details and get to grips with the obloquy which had fallen on his head. His immediate instinct was to strike back. Before the fall of night there were burning farmhouses all along the high ridges that ran in a line from Bandon to Cork city, chosen at random and without regard to the age, sex or state of health of their inhabitants. The rebels had disappeared but those who aided and abetted them would pay the price, and the earth would be scorched to such an extent that they'd think twice about supporting them again.

The Flying Column slipped away from Skeenahaine when Lordan's men joined them. There was a huge void in their hearts to leave their beloved dead, but there was nothing more the British could do to them now. They went up towards Raheen Hill, through Crosspound, and turned west along Raheen Lane towards Drews of Crowhill. That was the road they took and was rising ever higher, past smaller roads that criss-crossed at bewildering angles until they seemed lost to all time and place as they crested the long ridge. At the crest they stopped because they noticed a small detachment of soldiers below them, coming up from Aherla to the north. Barry sent three of his crack shots across Jagoe's field to engage them. They must have been Auxiliaries coming from Macroom who'd lost their way, or perhaps were reluctant conscripts in the first place, remembering their experience at Kilmichael. Mick Crowley, Pete Kearney and Jim Doyle lay against a high fence and fired a salvo which resounded across hill and dale. The officer in charge and his second-in-command were killed in the first volley. The rest fired a few half-hearted bullets which killed two goats grazing in a gorse-filled brake, and then they turned and fled, as the rest of the British Forces had done from early morning.

The Column moved on. There was a great urgency to get away to the lonesome west, where the hills would hide them and dark night cloak them. Gurranreigh was their destination, twenty miles away. To the west, the glowering red and purple sun was setting hugely between the far distant peaks of Sheha and Owen, and it cast long shafts of yellow and golden light east to illuminate the winding roads they walked on in the blinding silence of March. Tom Barry stood upon a high-banked ditch and watched his soldiers pass. And as he stood there, no wind moaned, but he heard a late blackbird singing, and a dim, deep-voiced choir of voices, humming low and throbbing, underneath the blackbird's song. There was a steady crunch of boots upon the gravelled road as they passed him with the sun bright on their faces that were cast and transfixed, some blackened, some drained pale of all emotion, serried lines of marching men, two by two and four by four, marching westward over the roads of grace. Their long trenchcoats were torn and frayed, and they looked a bedraggled yet amazing sight as they marched straight-backed into the setting sun. Some wore flat caps, some wore trilby hats and some were bare-headed. Over their shoulders there were Sam Browne belts, looped heavy with clips of bullets. They carried rifles slung over their shoulders, at the trail or sloped at arms. On they came, a raggle-taggle bunch with blood and dirt running down their faces, but in the extremity of their fatigue they were triumphant and sang softly that deep-vowelled chant, so sweet and dolorous and sublime. As they passed him in extraordinary brightness, some called to him, and some saluted, and others merely smiled. Some men looked like shadows or pale ghosts, some were gentle, smiling boys and others bore the stern badge of courage on their faces that was their legacy, their inheritance and the burden on their backs. On they went, brothers in arms, walking westward past fields of green, growing wheat, daffodils and snowdrops, into the ebbing sun's caress. As they crossed higher valleys into the gathering dark, they remembered the day an empire started falling, and they raised their arms skywards to the white evening star and the God of the great universe, to give thanks for their deliverance in that time and place.

19

requiescat in pace

Doctor Baldwin could no longer contain his curiosity. All day Saturday they were hearing snatches of information about the battle at Crossbarry. A workman told Thomas Cody that a hundred British soldiers had been killed. At Mass on Sunday morning at Farnivane the priest said it was the other way around and in fact the entire Flying Column had been wiped out. Cody refused to engage with the Doctor's speculations, but his daughters, Margie and Anna, avidly discussed every snatch of rumour and counter rumour that came their way. So obsessed with the details did they become that their mother, Madeleine, ordered them to shut up about it once and for all, banning all discussion on the subject from dinner or supper table.

Anna was especially keen to find out if Sonny was involved in the action and she was in a constant state of high anxiety until Monday morning, when she, Margie and Doctor Baldwin drove to Bandon in the pony and trap to buy the Cork Examiner. They made their way down the steep slopes of Convent Hill, past the nuns' sanctuary and the small, grey terraced cottages. When they went around the corner to Kilbrogan Hill, the houses became taller and more ornate, with classical Georgian facades, but they were suddenly confronted with a large blockade. The garrison town had become a veritable bastion, with sandbag defences erected in front of the Devonshire Hotel and barbed wire barricades outside the military barracks two hundred yards across the square, beyond the Shambles. There were Crossley tenders and Lancia lorries and armoured cars moving to and fro, unloading what appeared to be hundreds of extra reinforcement, being moved in, obviously, to stem the tide of misfortune befalling the forces of the Crown.

They were stopped and questioned several times by scowling soldiers before they reached their destination at Lee's Hotel, down on Shannon Street across Bandon Bridge. Other country folk, driving horses pulling common cars were similarly apprehended. There was an atmosphere of tension and fractiouness, as trigger-happy squaddies stood with rifles at the ready, looking for the slightest excuse to give vent to their sense of anger and frustration.

'Remember that the curfew comes into effect at 7 o'clock this evening,' said an officer to them, while menacingly levelling the muzzle of his Lee Enfield in their direction.

'Oh,' said the Doctor, urbanely, 'I thought it was at 8 o'clock.'

'It's been brought back an hour,' said the insolent officer. 'Anyone on the streets after 7 p.m. will be shot on sight. Is that clear?'

'Crystal,' said the Doctor, and shook the reins to continue.

As they moved on, Margie said, 'They're in no mood for joking. For a moment I thought you were going to say something to draw their wrath on us.'

'Not at all, my dear,' said the Doctor. 'I may be loquacious on occasion, but I did detect that this wasn't one time to be honing my witticisms.'

'Thank God,' said Anna, with a sigh of relief.

They bought the Cork Examiner in a topsy-turvy shop on the corner of South Main and Shannon Street. The proprietor was a heavy man named Hurley, with smudged spectacles and a distracted air, a strong supporter of the Republican cause. Margie began to read aloud the report of the ambush from the front page:

"The attackers arrived after midnight and took forcible possession of the Harolds and the Beasleys. They imprisoned the householders, made themselves comfortable, cooked meals and played the piano..."

'Played the piano?' asked Anna. 'Imagine playing the piano before going into battle.'

'It obviously helped them to relax,' said Baldwin.

'It did that right enough,' said Hurley with an ironic twinkle in his eye. A closer inspection would have detected a certain sense of satisfaction in his demeanour. He was sure of his ground with Doctor Baldwin, a long standing and stalwart acquaintance.

'Let me finish,' said Margie, impatiently,

'Who's stopping you?' asked the Doctor.

Margie gave an exasperated glare and continued: "'*By five o'clock all arrangements were completed for the ambush. Bedroom windows were barricaded and a cowshed loopholed, as were the ditch walls outside. At 8 a.m the fight began and the firing lasted in all over four hours. When the firing ceased the attackers made their escape in a northerly direction over the hills, and the occupants of the houses ventured out to find the road strewn with dead and wounded. Miss Beasley and Mr. Beasley were prominent in their helping of the wounded.*'"

Margie stopped reading. She looked puzzled. 'It doesn't say there were any Irish casualties in this report.'

'That's odd,' agreed the Doctor.

'I hope it's true,' said Anna, feeling relieved.

'Well, well,' said the Doctor. 'I wonder what the other papers are saying, or the military themselves?'

'Can't you guess what them sons of bitches will say?' said Hurley, looking around him furtively, as if someone might hear. 'God forgimme, but half enough of the bastards weren't killed. Naturally the military will put their own propaganda on the story. They'll make it sound as if they won the battle. They always do. They don't want their own people in England to question why so many of their soldiers are dying in a foreign country. For what? If the truth came out there'd be a clamour to bring their soldiers home. I've had all kinds of people coming into this shop for the last two days, including young British soldiers. They've said it was a massacre, whatever the official word is from the top brass.'

'And have you heard how many Irish were killed?' asked Anna.

'I heard there were three or four, that's all. I don't know who they were, Lord have mercy on them. I'm sure 'twill all come out before the end of the day.'

'We're going down to the hotel,' said the Doctor. 'We might pick up some further news there.'

'Doing things in style as usual, James,' smiled Hurley. 'Good for you. Don't tip the cap to any of those bloody foreigners.'

'Indeed we won't,' said Baldwin. 'I've never done so, and I don't intend starting now.'

They sipped their tea and ate their currant scones in Lee's Hotel, a block away. There were comfortable chairs, mahogany tables with white tablecloths and ornate, silver cutlery, teapots and delicate China cups. A waitress wheeled around a trolley, loaded with cakes and pastries, which the diners ordered while sitting in their seats. All very civilised. Doctor Baldwin noticed a thin, well-dressed man with a full head of groomed, grey hair getting up from a table at the far end of the restaurant. He carried a briefcase. Baldwin recognised a former fellow-student, now a prominent physician in the town, who unlike himself, actually practised medicine. Doctor Baldwin jumped up to waylay his old acquaintance. 'Good morning, William,' he said, extending his hand. The other stopped, surprised for an instant, then gave a terse laugh and shook the proffered hand. 'My dear James,' he said. 'It's been quite a while since I laid eyes on you.'

'Keeping a low profile,' said Baldwin 'Trying to stay out of trouble.'

'For a change,' smiled the physician.

'Meet my nieces,' said the Doctor, proudly. 'Margie and Anna Cody.' He liked to maintain an entourage, especially of attractive females. 'Girls, this is Dr. Welply.'

'I remember you as babies,' said Welply. 'My goodness how you've grown. What beautiful young ladies you've become.' He shook hands with the girls. 'The Welplys were always physicians to the Baldwins. How's your mother, Madeleine? And your father?'

'They're fine,' said Margie.

'Keeping a sharp eye on you two, I trust.'

'That wouldn't be hard for them,' said Margie. 'Sure we're at home all the time now.'

'And what became of your schooling?'

'We're at school in Dublin, but the troubles have become too dangerous for us to continue there.'

Dr. Welply frowned. 'All our lives are blighted by this business. I wish somebody would see sense and call a truce.'

'That's more likely now, after the latest incident,' said Baldwin. 'Maybe the British will tone down their high-handed rhetoric. It's their turn to see sense.'

'Rhetoric indeed,' said Welply. 'It's hard to get at the truth. Both sides say they are winning at this stage. Strickland has told Lloyd George that all this will be over by the end of May. Macready says the same.'

'Over in what sense?'

'That they'll have squashed the rebels.'

Doctor Baldwin gave a sardonic laugh. 'That's wishful thinking. But of course, there's none so blind as those who will not see. The evidence would suggest the contrary to be the case.'

'I know. *The Daily Mail* says there were nine rebels killed and six wounded at Crossbarry, and a large amount of arms captured. But that's not my experience.'

Anna gave an audible gasp.

'Are you feeling alright, my dear?' asked Welply.

'Did you say nine killed?' she asked.

'I didn't. *The Daily Mail* said it.'

Doctor Baldwin, inhaled deeply, and rubbed the back of his left hand with the fingers of his right. He straightened up and said, 'I know it's a delicate matter for yourself in your professional capacity as a medical man, but I daresay you are privy to the exact number of casualties, on both sides?'

Dr. Welply's eyes lost their professional detachment momentarily, and a flicker of a painful recollection was evident in them. His voice grew low, almost weak. 'I've never seen the likes of it. It was the most disturbing sight I've ever seen in all my years of practice. I counted over forty dead soldiers, and I saw as many again with horrific injuries. And I wasn't the only medical man at the scene. I heard from colleagues that there were many more dead and wounded scattered over a wide area, of maybe two square miles.'

'How many of our boys were killed?' blurted Anna, unable to contain herself any longer.

'Our boys?' enquired Welply, with a raised eyebrow.

'She means the IRA, Dr. Welply,' said Margie, with a steady stare. 'You may not consider them your boys, but we certainly do.'

'You do?' asked Welply. 'I wouldn't have thought Thomas Cody a revolutionary. Or Madeleine Baldwin either.'

'Indeed they are not, you are perfectly right there,' said Baldwin. 'But these young ladies are of a different generation, with a different mind set.'

'Come, uncle,' said Margie. 'You are a Sinn Féin supporter as well.'

Dr. Welply smiled, mindful of his old school chum's dilemma. 'Have you become a rebel in your old age, James?'

Doctor Baldwin sighed. 'I was always a rebel, or at least a maverick. You should know that. But the older I get the more I wonder what it's all about, and the less certain I am of everything. Youth, on the other hand is full of passionate intensity, to paraphrase our esteemed Mr. Yeats.'

He inclined his head towards the two young women, who gazed back, unflinchingly.

'Yes indeed, my dear Baldwin,' said Dr. Welply. 'I understand exactly what you mean. 'Tis a vext question, is it not?' He felt the clasp of his briefcase to see it was firmly shut and took a step backwards. 'I really have to be getting along.'

'You still haven't answered my question?' said Anna with surprising vehemence.

'What question was that, my dear?'

'How many of our boys were killed?'

Dr. Welply turned a friendly, compassionate gaze in her direction.

'There were four dead bodies of the IRA brought into the military barracks. They were brought in the back of one of the lorries. When I arrived they were thrown out on the ground rather unceremoniously, I regret to say. But in the circumstances, perhaps the reaction of the soldiers is understandable. Those were the only casualties I saw, and I have no reason to suppose there were any others. All the bodies from both sides were collected. None were left in the field.'

'What were their names?' asked Anna.

Margie shot a slightly apprehensive glance towards her sister, who was demonstrating quite a steely side to her usual pleasant personality.

'It was only with exteme difficulty that we were able to establish their identities, and even then we're not entirely sure of one of them. But from our investigations we believe the first three were called, Daly, Monahan and O'Leary.'

'And the fourth?' pressed Anna.

'The fourth man was so badly disfigured, that it was impossible to be certain who he was. I'm told he was killed in a gun battle early in the morning before the main hostilities commenced. He was riddled with bullet holes.'

'And you have no idea who he was?' asked Baldwin.

Dr. Welply stroked his chin with his right hand and adjusted his hat on his head, a little impatiently. 'This is purely conjecture on my part, and is not officially confirmed, but I did notice that the body carried the healed scars from an old wound to his cheek bones. Now, I attended a man with what appeared to be those exact injuries some three weeks ago in a farmhouse and it appears to be too much of a co-incidence for it not to be the same man.'

'Who was that man?' asked Margie.

'He was a fellow named Hurley.'

'Charlie Hurley?' asked Doctor Baldwin. 'He was the commander of the entire brigade?'

'So I'm given to understand,' said Welply dryly. He raised his hat to salute the two young women.

'Good morning to you, young ladies. Please convey my regards and best wishes to your parents.'

Then he turned to Baldwin. 'It was really good to see you, James, albeit in these unpleasant circumstances. I may have divulged more information than I should have, but I trust it will go no further than your own ears and those of your beautiful nieces.'

'You can depend on it, my dear fellow,' said Doctor Baldwin. 'We appreciate that the position you find yourself in is not an easy one. Caught between Scylla and Charybidis, as they say.'

'No more than your own,' said Welply, giving him an intense stare. 'You took the Hippocratic Oath as well. And tidings of your good deeds have not gone unnoticed among our esteemed profession.'

Doctor Baldwin scoffed. 'I doubt that's true. I'm a non-person as far as the medical profession goes.'

'You'd be surprised at how highly many of your former colleagues speak of you,' said Welply, and hurried away.

Doctor Baldwin resumed his seat beside the girls. There was silence for some minutes. Then he said. 'So there we have it girls. Now we know the truth. You can rest easy, my dear Anna, in the knowledge that your young man is safe.'

Anna blushed. 'What do you mean?'

'Come now, my dear,' said the Doctor with a broad smile. 'I may be an old fool but I still have eyes in my head and a nose for which way the wind is blowing.'

Anna sighed and smiled, and gave him a quick kiss on the cheek. 'You're not the worst of them, uncle James,' she said. 'I wish there were more men like you in the world.'

She looked happy as they rose and paid their bill.

Tull came back from Newcestown with a heavy heart. He'd met Mike after Mass and Mike told him that Charlie Hurley was dead. Sonny was safe, Mike said. He'd escaped with the rest of the Flying Column and they were now above in Joe Sullivan's farm in Gurranreigh, resting after their ordeal. Mike thought the bodies of the boys who died were in the Workhouse morgue in Bandon. He wasn't sure who'd claim them, but maybe the Cumann Na mBan would, with the priest. As ever, the harrowing, unpleasant work fell to the womenfolk; the harvesting and the gathering in, the comings and the goings. Mike said he couldn't come home because the house would be watched, and besides, he'd a job to do to scout the Column over the dangerous bridges on the Bandon to the south. They planned to bury Charlie at Clogach the following night, give him a hero's farewell. Then Mike went off with the Corcorans and Charlie Foley.

Tull rode the road in silence on his saddle horse. All silence but for horsebreath, hoofbeat, birdsong. He'd bought a few items for Elizabeth at O'Sullivan the publican's little grocery shop, and he had them in a satchel slung over his back. The saddle leathers creaked, there was a smell of oiled leather and horse sweat, and the horse's coat was well brushed and shiny. Smooth as satin to the touch of his hand. He was up high and felt good when he rode a horse. But what would he tell Elizabeth? She'd stayed home from Mass to tend Jeremiah who was feeling poorly with the bronchitis. She'd take the news badly.

He rode up the winding lane and saw the furze bushes coming into bloom. He'd burn them later, but they'd have to wait now till June, because you couldn't burn out the little nesting birds. Maybe he wouldn't burn anything this year. The Tans were doing enough burning for everyone. Maybe 'twould bring bad luck. He took the saddle off the hunter outside the stable door and laid it down on the footpath. He gave the horse water. He'd give it some oats later, but if you gave a horse oats first and then water it could get a gripe. He was a long time choring around and Elizabeth called him a couple of times from the back door to come in for his breakfast. He'd eaten nothing because he was fasting since midnight. You had to fast before receiving Holy Communion, the body and blood of Christ. He was starving now but still couldn't bring himself to go inside. Elizabeth called again as he continued to groom the horse with the dandy brush.

'You'd think you were getting him ready for the Gold Cup,' she said, laughing, when Tull at last came in. He took off his cap and placed it on the back of a chair and sat down. She was in a cheerful mood. He could see that. She put his boiled egg and brown soda bread on a plate in front of him on the table and poured his tea.

'How's the father?' he asked eventually, as he topped his egg with a teaspoon.

'He's a good bit better,' said Elizabeth. 'That heavy cold isn't helping his chest, but hopefully the better weather will improve it.'

'Maybe if he'd go easy on the liquor he'd improve faster,' said Tull, who had a rather jaundiced opinion of his easy-going father's drinking habits.

'I suppose you're right,' said the soft-hearted Elizabeth.

'Of course the weather might help too,' Tull hastened to add, making small talk. 'The forecast is good from the middle of the week. Before that 'twill be sunshine and showers.'

He continued to chew steadily. He was unusually quiet. Tull was a great talker. She wondered what was up?

'Who said Mass?' she asked.

'Father Cummins,' said Tull, and went silent again. He drank his tea with a slurping sound, and then emptied some into his saucer to cool it, and drank from the saucer.

'What is it?' Elizabeth asked eventually.

'What do you mean?' he asked in return, holding her gaze.

'You're very quiet.'

He put the saucer down and said. 'I met Mike at Mass. There was a big ambush at a place called Crossbarry.'

'Oh, my God,' said Elizabeth, putting her hand to her throat. 'Was Sonny in it?'

'He was,' said Tull, 'but he's safe. They all escaped except for four.'

'Four?'

'Four got killed, of our lads.'

'Jesus, Mary and Joseph,' she said and blessed herself.

'There were an awful lot of British soldiers killed.'

'Who were our four?'

'I only heard one name that I'm sure of,' said Tull. His eyes were anguished.

'Who?' she asked

'Charlie Hurley.'

Elizabeth put her hand to her throat again. She drew her breath in a sharp intake. She turned away from him and put the pot she was holding, down on the hob. The light of laughter left her eyes and she hurried out of the kitchen, into the room. She quietly closed the door. Tull would not disturb her. She'd be sorrowing, he knew.

They took the road to the south the following night, herself and Tull, with horse and trap. Jeremiah was up and about again, and John Thomas Allen came over to keep him company. They'd have a ball of malt. He'd be alright until they returned. She dressed in black widow's weeds, the cloth of sorrow, though no widow she. She spoke little for a long time, and Tull allowed her silence. They went down by the Bull

Riders and over the railway tracks at Desertserges. They went east by Kilcolman, along tree-lined roads with early leaves budding on chestnut and willow. The blackthorn was abloom with blossoms white as snow, which they could see in the bright light of the moon. The clouds would sometimes move across and the wind would rise. Then they'd clear again. It was chilly and it rained briefly once or twice. Equinoxal weather. Somewhere out there among those lawless roads, her brothers would be trekking like phantoms in the same direction, in the company of their fighting comrades. She and Tull had no such support, only each other and the dignity of grief. And she felt it all the more because so secret, introspective, unacknowledged. Tull knew, and her brothers had an inkling. Was she, like them, destined to live outside the law forever? No nuptial bells, no written contract to guarantee her house and home. *A mensa et thoro:* from hearth and table he was gone from her. It was hard on women as it had always been. When would her life of disappointments and defeats be over, and the grey clouds disappear? She wept silent, overwhelming tears.

The priest read out the words of comfort and benediction:

'Requiescat in pace.'

May he rest in peace.

'In vitam aeternum.'

Life for all eternity.

They filed out of the little chapel under the high hill of Clogach and a sad procession walked further on up the road. His fine Column boys with their rifles reversed, his six family mourners, and Elizabeth behind with Tull, holding her hand in kindness. Gentle, generous Tull. The moon came out and then hid behind the clouds, lanterns flickered, boots scuffled on the road. The cortége turned down a lane past a farmyard and stopped at an old, old cemetary above the Arigideen river on a green, grassy mound, with fields and low hills ranged around. And as they stepped along, the lone piper, Begley, played the Dead March, to lament the passing of a leader who was of the Gael and who thought in a Gaelic way, as Tom Barry said after they laid him down. Then Begley played the Last Post and three volleys rang out. There was silence for some moments and Sonny and Mike walked back to Elizabeth and Tull. They spoke some brief words, snatched with emotions too deep to articulate, before they were called back to march away again, because there was danger all around and they still had work to do, and promises to keep.

Elizabeth and Tull spoke some comforting words to Charlie's family. Tull accompanied them up to the road. Elizabeth said she'd follow in a moment.

She stood there in silence under the moon that shone and vanished and shone again. Now he was gone forever, and for his sweet love she gave God thanks. Oh, how she longed for the touch of his loving hand, his gentle kiss, but that would never come to pass again. He was gone on the river of time, and all she had left were sweet memories, blowing on the night breeze. She accepted her great loss with a stoic fortitude and faith. Some day they would meet again, of that she was certain, when they would all rise again and she would see him walking towards her when the sun would shine on a golden morning on the banks of the Arigideen, the little silver stream.

'Goodbye my darling,' she whispered, and turned away.

20

Hugh Martin, columnist with the *London Daily News*, fastidious, ascetic, dressed in black, neat and bowler-hatted, hurried down Harcourt Street in Dublin towards St. Stephen's Green. The blooms of May were bursting forth after dreary winter and rainy spring, and now presented a riot of colour to his eagle eye as he entered through the southwest gate of the park. He strode on under the high elms and beeches where thrushes and blackbirds caroled among the dense, green foliage. Workmen with rakes and wheelbarrows tended the well laid out flower beds of tulips, roses and dahlias. There was a sound of water from fountains and a splashing in the duck pond when bread was thrown to the tame water fowl by loitering secretaries, finishing their luncheon sandwiches. An echo of a violin floated from the direction of the Memorial Arch and children's voices floated happily from where the park widened, further over. Businessmen in three-piece pinstripes hurried across the shortcut, and more bohemian types lounged with their fancy ones on park benches, idling away the hours. There were horses and sidecars outside on the western and northern sides of the Green, and other more sinister presences: Black and Tans ceaselessly patrolling in gun-metal grey lorries and armoured cars. But in the park all was peaceful, dreamy and pastoral. The daily turmoil of the war for independence seemed far away.

Yet Hugh Martin was only too keenly aware of its proximity. He'd gravitated to Ireland like a lot of correspondents from the world's newspapers to cover the dramatic unfolding of this fascinating war, this gargantuan struggle between the David of Sinn Féin and the Goliath of the British Empire. The hotels and public houses of the city were hotbeds of gossip, intrigue and argument on a daily and nightly basis. There were reporters like himself, Robert Lynd from the *Daily Mail*, Francis Hackett from the *New Republic*, and Carl Ackerman from the *Philadephia Public Ledger.* There were others from the *Christian Science Monitor*, and Henry Wyckham Steed of *The Times,* all associating cheek by jowl, all eager for the latest titbit of information or to hear about the most recent shocking outrage, be it IRA ambush or Black and Tan reprisal. Thus, on any given night one could cross paths with Frenchmen, Americans, Germans, literary tourists like G.K. Chesterton and M.V. Pritchett or native artists of world renown like W.B. Yeats or George Russell. Some nights they'd congregate in the bar of the Shelbourne Hotel to mingle with the camp followers of the various factions, where sober, all would profess to the most complete detachment, but after numerous whiskeys and sodas or champagne, they would evolve into fanatical partisans of one side or another, and stagger out onto the pavements after midnight, hurling insults at one another to beat the band.

The situation seemed to be drifting from bad to worse. Last month there was the devastating ambush at Crossbarry in remote West Cork, and continuing shootings, burnings, hijackings and kidnappings on a daily basis, in Dublin and throughout Ireland. Martin had been around the country, travelling by train to Galway, Limerick and Cork, and from these hubs he'd travel out to small villages by bicycle or sidecar, to see for himself the burnt houses, the people living from hand to mouth under tarpaulins or in haysheds. He'd seen the dead bodies, the terrified children, the cowed old men. He'd sent his reports back to his newspaper on a daily basis and each week, Sir Hamar Greenwood, the Chief Secretary for Ireland would stand up in the House of Commons and flatly deny there were any British atrocities occurring in Ireland at all. But the more he denied the reality, the more people like Hugh Martin were believed. And behind the scenes, were two men, hand-picked by the master puppeteer, Michael Collins, to broadcast the Sinn Féin message through the weekly issue of the *Irish Bulletin.* These were, ironically, two Englishmen, who'd become apostates and avowed Irish Republicans: Robert Erskine Childers and Desmond Fitzgerald. Hugh Martin was now hurrying to meet them at the Shelbourne Hotel.

Martin was tenacious. Someone had described him as being like a moral accountant, keeping his British compatriots on their mettle, pushing them towards the high ground of moral probity in the maelstrom of the Irish conflict. He'd just taken tea with General Sir Nevil Macready up at the Royal Hospital in Kilmainham. Macready had been civilised enough though he was a man who lacked imagination in Martin's opinion, contrary to Macready's own rather exhalted view of himself.

He'd shown Martin through the beautiful Master's Quarters and the Great Hall of the most important 17th Century building in Ireland, with its grand forecourt, its splendid Gothic arches in the basement, magnificent baroque ceilings, outstanding woodcarving by Tabary, and he'd expressed the view that it was probably the most architecturally accomplished building in Dublin outside of the Custom House. On the merits of the building, Martin was in agreement with his host, though on most other matters they were at loggerheads. They'd passed veterans of the Crimean War, shuffling along corridors in their faded red and blue costumes, hanging about as broken-down reminders of the legacy of Britains's wars of empire, and the plundering of Irish manhood as cannon fodder in the front line trenches. Martin couldn't help but wonder at the sheer scope of the British Military presence in Dublin. There were enormous fortified barracks every few miles of the city. From Arbour Hill to Portobello, from Beggar's Bush to Kilmainham, from Marlborough and Wellington to the Royal Barracks, the list went on. Did it really require so many garrisoned redoubts to contain the wild Irish? Sequestered in their compounds inside the Pale, the original ditch constructed in a semi-circle around the city before the 17th century, were they really that terrified of the natives to warrant such defences? And now, these defences notwithstanding, the very edifice of empire was crumbling throughout the length and breadth of Ireland.

'You're really only giving one side of the story, old chap,' Macready had protested as they finally sat down to mid-morning tea in one of the palatial drawing rooms of the grand building.

'Are you suggesting, General, that I'm inventing my accounts?' Martin asked, quite offended at the implied impugning of his intergity. 'Are you suggesting that I'm lying when I report that of the six young men brutally murdered by the Tans at Kerry Pike in Cork, that one had his tongue cut off, another his nose, that another had his heart torn out and another had his head crushed in like a tin bucket? Are you suggesting I'm lying when I report that the two young brothers, found tied together in a bog in the West, had their legs roasted off them in a fire by crazed British torturers? Is it that you have no stomach for the truth? Is that it?'

Martin was spitting fire. Macready was nonplussed.

'No, no, of course not,' Macready blustered, half-heartedly. 'But there are atrocities on both sides.'

'Not to that degree,' said Martin. 'And surely it behoves us, as the leading power in western civilization to act with honour and restraint no matter what the provocation? Have we not subscribed to President Wilson's fourteen point plan, including the right of small nations to be free? Is every other small nation, Belgium, Holland, Serbia, entitled to choose its own destiny but not Ireland? What gives us the right to dictate here and to use the most brutally oppressive measures to prevent Irish independence? After all, hasn't Lloyd George, our Prime Minister, signed up to the principals of the Paris Peace Conference?'

He could see Macready was uneasy. No doubt a stiff letter of protest would follow to his editor at the *Daily News*, pointing out the bias of his correspondent against the Crown Forces. But Hugh Martin didn't care. There was no hiding from the truth, notwithstanding the vehement denials of Hamar Greenwood in the House.

'Are you saying Greenwood is right and I am wrong?' asked Martin, peevishly, as he put his cup down on his saucer with an almost petulant clatter.

Macready gave a sheepish laugh. 'I'm bound to say that the Chief Secretary's abundant energy has on occasion taken him beyond the boundaries of fact.'

'So you agree with me then?'

'Look, Sir Hamar is a capital fellow, and I have enjoyed his social company very much in the past. But I do agree with you that the louder and more outlandish his denials ring out in the Commons, the more we are playing into the hands of Sinn Féin's unscrupulous propagandists.'

'Unscrupulous is not a word I would use to describe them,' said Martin. 'Opportunists maybe, or nimble-footed fellows. But unscrupulous suggests they are inventing their stories, while it's the very accuracy and integrity, and lack of embellishment of their reporting that has endeared them to the world's press and has them winning the international propaganda battle, hands down. They have swung world opinion in their favour and against us.'

'You still consider yourself one of us?' asked Macready sarcastically as Martin rose to leave.

Martin straightened himself to his full height which was not tall, but which, along with his finely chiselled features and steely gaze, gave him a presence greater than his actual size.

'Democracy and the rule of law is what made the British Empire great, sir. Not the unbridled hooliganism of ruffians running around a small defenceless country, sowing terror and mayhem in their wake.'

Macready was taken aback by the ferocity of the retort. He stood back and then shook the proferred hand of his guest and watched, a little dumbfounded, as he strode away. A feisty fellow he thought. And not without a modicum of common sense in his opinions. Macready shrugged his shoulders, blew out his cheeks and called his batman to fetch him a brandy.

Hugh Martin did not disclose his destination to his host. His next port of call was to the Sinn Féin heartland in the city centre, and such an admission would have come no doubt with the accusation that he was supping with the devil, the personification of whom depended on which side of the argument you were on.

He stopped before he came out of the Green and headed towards a park bench. He sat down and took off his shoe. He had a blistered heel from tramping the streets of Dublin and he had a hole in his shoe. He took off his sock and massaged his foot and took stock of the situation. He was tempted to stretch out on the bench for a ten minute nap and looking around him furtively to see he was unobserved he lay back and pulled his bowler over his eyes. He drifted away.

Desmond Fitzgerald stepped through the revolving doors into the lobby of the Shelbourne Hotel with his dust-coat tails flying and a black Fedora set at a slightly nonchalant angle on his full head of tousled brown hair. He was smoking a Gauloise and underneath his overcoat a paperback novel protruded from the side pocket of his grey lounge suit. He affected an air of preoccupied intellectual superiority, and while his dress sense was correct for his environment, he had arranged his ensemble in such a way as to give the impression that cerebral matters were more important than mere outward image. That impression was false. Fitzgerald left nothing to chance and his vaguely haphazard appearance was a deliberate conceit. He was a man of careful thought and action while projecting the slightly raffish air of the bohemian.

Fitzgerald was the head of the Sinn Féin and Dáil Eireann Propaganda Department, which he ran with tremendous aplomb with his fellow Englishman, Erskine Childers. They were both connected to a wide international political and cultural network, that extended their reach far beyond the shores of Ireland, and enabled them, in the boxing vernacular, to punch far above their weight.

He went forward with mincing step and turned right into the elegant drawing room, which was a popular lounge for the taking of elevenses or afternoon tea. It was now past noon and Fitzgerald was late. His appointment with Hugh Martin was for 11.30 a.m. and 12.30 p.m. for Carl Ackerman of the *Philadelphia Public Ledger*. He now saw both men seated midway down, one on an armchair and the other on a *chaise longue*, obviously having introduced themselves to one another. They were engaged in wary conversation, as people will who have just become acquainted, when they beheld their host approaching with supercilious mien. If he was embarrassed about being late, Fitzgerald didn't show it. It came with the territory, this constant peripatetic movement, new faces, new names, even new offices on a regular basis. The *Bulletin* bureau had moved so many times under British pressure that Fitzgerald had to remind himself in his diary which address to go to every week.

'I'm sorry to keep you waiting, gentlemen,' he said, though he wasn't in the least bit sorry. After all, he held the key that would facilitate the introductions these chaps wanted in meeting the famous but secretive revolutionaries, who were the prized and exciting sources of news that was the *raison d'etre* of all correspondents. He nodded to Hugh Martin, whom he'd met previously, and observed the other urbane character in the dark, three-piece suit, white shirt and striped tie, who sat back with knees crossed, making no attempt to move. Fitzgerald noticed the long, thin face, the prominent nose, the dark, slicked back hair, and the pipe delicately balanced between the index and middle fingers of his left hand.

'You must be Mr. Ackerman,' he said, a little distractedly. Fitzgerald always gave the impression of having his brain focused on more than one thing at a time. Ackerman, who was in his early thirties, rubbed the palm of his left hand over his head, then stood and extended his right hand for Fitzgerald to shake. Martin stood at the same time and also proffered his hand.

'Sit down, sit down,' said Fitzgerald rather sharply, as if addressing two school children. 'Can I get you a drink, coffee, tea, anything...?'

His voice trailed off.

'Tea would be fine,' said Martin with monk-like brevity, and looked toward his fellow reporter.

'A pink gin for me, thank you,' said Ackerman, with the assurance of a man used to being received in the highest echelons of most Governments in the Western World and the Far East, not to mention Russia, where he'd recently published a volume on the Bolshevik Revolution.

Fitzgerald clicked his fingers and a waitress, familiar with his regular presence, hurried over to take the order, which included a French *espresso* coffee for himself.

'What are you reading?' asked Ackerman, with the keen eye and amiable diplomatic smoothness which enabled him to put most people instantly at their ease.

'Reading?' asked Fitzgerald, puzzled.

'The novel,' smiled Ackerman, as he sat back down. 'In your pocket.'

'Oh, that,' said Fitzgerald, fishing the book out and sitting on the other corner of the *chaise longue*. 'It's by a namesake of mine, an Irish-American author named Fitzgerald. A book of short stories called, *The Diamond As Big As The Ritz.*'

'Ah, Scott Fitzgerald,' nodded Ackerman.

'Are you familiar with him?'

'As a matter of fact I've interviewed him for the *New Yorker.* Very talented but drinks too much.'

'I'm afraid it's a bad habit of us Irish,' sighed Fitzgerald. 'An affliction which you Jews seem free from.'

'Oh, I wouldn't say we're that lucky,' laughed Ackerman, as his gin arrived on a silver tray. 'We just seem to hold it better.' He took his glass and said, 'Good health. It's a very great pleasure to make your acquaintance. Fascinating to have two men named Fitzgerald and neither speaking with an Irish accent.'

'We're products of the Irish *diaspora*. We were scattered far and wide in the Great Famine.'

'As indeed were our people,' said Ackerman.

'We have a lot in common,' said Fitzgerald. 'Both oppressed peoples, ambitious, insecure, driven.'

'Indeed,' said Ackerman. 'We demonstrate the characteristics of most minorities, unlike our British friend here who has the confidence to sit there quietly observing us prattling on, without the slightest compulsion to add his tuppence ha'penny to the conversation.'

Martin smiled gravely as he sipped his tea. If Ackerman was trying to be condescending it wasn't working. He responded to the point at issue, not the pseudo-flattery.

'I'm afraid there are as many oppressed Englishmen as there are Irish or Jews, if not more. We just happened to be dominated for hundreds of years by a ruling class which has spread the tentacles of empire to every corner of the globe, but the average working man in our country has no greater privileges than his counterpart in any other country.'

'Quite right,' said Fitzgerald, 'and we in this country are among the first to attempt to throw off the yoke of that empire, apart from the Americans of course, who have already done so many years ago.'

'The Bolsheviks have also done it in Russia,' said Ackerman, 'but there is a fine line between changing rulers and replacing one regime with an even more totalitarian one. I've seen it myself first hand. Revolutions have to be carefully planned and controlled.'

'That's exactly what we are doing here,' said Fitzgerald. 'I don't think our two leaders, de Valera and Collins have the Godless model of Russian Communism in mind for this country. We simply feel that we are entitled to rule ourselves, and most of your international newspapers agree with us at this stage.'

'Don't get me wrong, old sport,' said Ackerman. 'I agree with you. It's just that one would hope the eventual system that emerges doesn't throw the baby out with the bathwater.'

'We may be hot-headed with drink,' said Fitzgerald, 'but we're a pragmatic people. The hand of the Church is steady on the tiller, though I myself don't have any great enthusiasm for it.'

'You're more of a liberal intellectual?' enquired Ackerman.

'Well, I'm a great reader of poetry and I get my greatest pleasure from digesting the latest offering from our esteemed Mr. Yeats.'

'Not to mention, Mr. Joyce,' said Martin. 'It is amazing how such a small country can have a monopoly on the best writers in the world.'

'Joyce prefers to live abroad and pontificate upon us from a distance,' said Fitzgerald and paused before continuing. 'But it is an interesting place, I'll give you that. You see, I never set foot here myself until I was twenty-one, although I'm obviously of direct Irish descent. My father was a labourer from South Tipperary and my mother was Mary Anne Scollard, from Castleisland in Kerry. I myself am married to a Northern Irish Protestant, also a Nationalist, but I do have the detachment of the outsider which helps to keep my feet on the ground.'

'Well, I'd be fascinated to meet your colleagues,' said Ackerman. 'And perhaps your leaders, if that were possible?'

'We'll go to see Erskine shortly,' said Fitzgerald. 'But I'm afraid the arrangements to meet with our Sinn Féin Goverment will take a little longer.'

'I'm here for three weeks,' said Ackerman, 'I've been travelling the country like my friend, Mr. Martin, seeing things first hand.'

'I'll see what can be arranged,' said Fitzgerald as he finished his coffee. 'Shall we go to the offices of the *Bulletin* then?'

They rose and Fitzgerald paid the bill. Ackerman left a substantial tip for the waitress. As they were passing through the lobby, two striking-looking, well-dressed women came in the door. They were tall, statuesque ladies who might have been in their late forties, with beautiful clothes and refined, almost haughty looks in their eyes. Fitzgerald with his unerring eye, immediately spotted and recognised Maud Gonne McBride and Constance Countess Markievicz. He lost his easy *sang froid* and was suddenly all agog. The ladies recognised him as he bowed deeply and shook and kissed their hands.

'How pleasant to meet you, Desmond,' said the Countess. 'We've been reading your *Bulletin*. And very impressive it is too.'

Fitzgerald bubbled with delight and very nearly forgot his two companions. Ackerman introduced himself. 'Carl Ackerman,' he said, unaware of who he had.

'Please forgive me,' stuttered Fitzgerald, eager to bask in the reflected glory of the two famous women. 'Mr Ackerman of the *Public Ledger* and Mr. Martin of the *Daily News*. Gentlemen, may I present Maud Gonne McBride and Constance Countess Markievicz.'

Ackerman immediately stood back as if he didn't believe his ears. The two women were living legends, immortalised in poems by W.B. Yeats. Both were revolutionaries and had endured considerable hardship for the cause of Irish independence. Ackerman swallowed imperceptibly and bowed as if to atone for his earlier brusqueness. 'A very great pleasure indeed ladies, a very great pleasure.'

Hugh Martin was standing modestly aside. 'Mr. Martin,' said the Countess, 'your articles are outstanding and your courage in standing up to Mr. Greenwood is to be commended.'

The men stood around not quite knowing what to do with themselves. The Countess put them out of their difficulty. 'We are pleased to make your acquaintance, gentlemen,' she said. 'Unfortunately we have to meet with Mr. de Valera. Otherwise we'd stop for tea. Next time perhaps.'

The men bowed again as the two ladies moved like stately galleons through the foyer, all eyes following them left and right.

Robert Erskine Childers was going through his diary as he sat at a small desk in a large office on the second floor of number 11 Molesworth Street, around the corner from the Shelbourne. The diary read as a curious mixture of dates and meetings with foreign correspondents and politicians, intermingled with the mundane details of daily life in suburban Dublin. Thus, one page had notes of appointments with the editor of the *Christian Science Monitor*, Wedgewood Benn in the British House of Commons, and Henry Asquith, former Prime Minister, on the opening day of the British Parliament; the next page was a shopping list for wallpaper and linoleum with his American wife, Molly Alden Osgood, to decorate their apartment. He also had notes on his weekend at his mother's beautiful ancestral family estate in Annamoe in County Wicklow and observations of his dinner of pheasant and a good bottle of Chateau Margaux with his cousin, Robert Barton, a prominent member of the Sinn Féin movement.

Childers was rooting around, trying to make sense of the filing system. They'd been forced to beat a hasty retreat from an office up in Harcourt Street when their printing press was discovered and confiscated by the DMP, but they'd opened up again a few days after, and without any loss of publication of their weekly report, which in fact went out twice that week. The second was a fake, cobbled together by the incompetents at Dublin Castle from the data, names and addresses taken in the raid.

Some people were puzzled by the seeming *volte face* of the *Bulletin* in attributing the latest series of murders and burnings to the IRA, but it quickly became apparent that it was the handiwork of the Castle Administration, where, Hugh Martin satirically observed, "You would find chaos upstairs, downstairs and in my Lady's chamber, with Brute Force sitting in the drawingroom."

There certainly was an irony in the fact of having the Sinn Féin propaganda office now operating from the most snobbishly respectable Unionist street in Dublin. Next door was the Grand Lodge of the Free Masons. The Masonic Orphan's School, and Church Of Ireland Temperance Welfare Society were down the street. The halldoor flat was occupied by the Crown Solicitors, James and James, while the upstairs flat was jealously guarded by two elderly, rather snooty ladies who were engaged in some work for that bastion of Anglo-Irish ascendancy, Trinity College. The Sinn Féin people carefully prepared a gold plaque on the front door indicating that the first floor was occupied by a company that imported oil and nobody was any the wiser as to the true identity of the tenants. Only three days before, every house on the street was searched by the Black and Tans, and every floor in the building except the floor they occupied was thoroughly scrutinised. Their luck was holding for the moment. Childers got quite a kick out of it. There was nothing he liked better than to shock his fellow Protestants out of their sense of self-professed superiority. And he wasn't alone in this. His cousin Robert Barton took an equally gleeful and iconoclastic delight in exposing the hypocrisies of their mutual Church.

Childers was about 50, and he'd already had a chequered career in the British Army. A smallish man with a moustache, which had the desired effect of adding a sense of age and gravity to his rather round, callow face. He'd seen service in the Boer War and the Great War. He was a sailor, a lawyer, an author of the bestselling novel, *The Riddle of the Sands,* and he'd transformed himself from being a prominent and very well-connected member of the British Establishment: President of the Trinity College Debating Society at Cambridge, to a rabid republican and revolutionary in Ireland. His enemies would cavil and say he was disaffected, and that he'd never achieved prominent positions in the army or his other career choices, but he certainly possessed the zeal of the convert in his new role. He was a stickler for minutiae and his fiery personality would have him labelled as intemperate by some, and a downright uncompromising fanatic by others. But to his new-found fellow-revolutionaries in Sinn Féin he was a hardworking and ingenious promoter of their particular point of view. And amazingly, he still had entrées to the corridors of power in Whitehall which he visited on a regular basis, using his connections at every opportunity to put forward the cause of Irish independence. And like his colleague, Desmond Fitzgerald, he was brave. Both were literary men and soldiers. Fitzgerald had fought in the GPO in Dublin in the 1916 Rebellion, while apart from his wartime activities, Childers had used his yacht, the Asgard, to run guns to the Irish Volunteers from Hamburg in 1914. Fifteen hundred rifles and forty-nine thousand rounds of ammunition landed in Howth in the month of June of that year. He'd sailed the yacht himself, accompanied by Conor O'Brien, across dangerous seas patrolled by the powerful British navy.

There was a knock on the door in a pre-arranged sequence of taps and Desmond Fitzgerald hurried in with his two foreign visitors. Childers stood and gave a curt bow toward the two journalists as Fitzgerald introduced them.

'I've been reading your accounts in your newspapers,' said Childers.

'And what did you think of them?' asked Martin.

'Very fair and balanced I must say, unlike the British Chief Secretary for Ireland.'

'Anyone with any modicum of common sense who spends time here and takes the trouble to find out what's going on, will readily see a strong-arm attempt by a superior force to quell by whatever means necessary, an overwhelmingly popular revolution,' replied Martin.

'And such a tragedy for a charming and gentle people,' said Ackerman.

Childers maintained his deadpan expression. 'It's been going on for seven hundred years. The Irish are used to it. But they won't take it any longer. The IRA are a new, more confident breed who will see this thing out.'

'We were hoping to meet some of them, particularly de Valera and Collins.'

Childers looked sharply at Fitzgerald with questioning eyes. Fitzgerald quickly moved to reassure him. 'I think it will be alright, Erskine. Mr. Martin's and Mr. Ackerman's *bona fides* are assured.'

Childers sat down and pointed to two chairs opposite his desk, where the journalists seated themselves. Fitzgerald continued to stand, hovering like a fussing parent.

'To bring you up to date, gentlemen, de Valera is not long returned from an extensive, far reaching and successful sojourn in America for the past eighteen months. He has been raising finance and putting our case to Irish-American political organisations, and directly to the American Congress, which understands and is sympathetic to our situation.'

'Indeed,' said Ackerman, 'I can confirm that from my own conversations with various influential U.S senators. And I'm aware that other dignitaries such as Archbishop Clune of Australia are anxious to facilitate a rapprochement.'

'You move in high circles,' said Childers, dryly.

'It's an interesting profession,' said Ackerman smoothly. He wasn't going to let the spiky Childers deflect him.

'When you say rapprochement, do you mean surrender?' asked Childers bluntly.

'On the contrary, I would have thought the least Ireland could get was some kind of dominion status.'

'I don't think you will find de Valera or Collins amenable to that kind of solution,' said Childers. 'But can I ask you a further question?'

'Go ahead.'

'Do you have direct contacts with Whitehall?'

'I have my sources,' said Ackerman. 'At this point I'm not free to divulge their names. But I do have some influence.'

Childers nodded. He looked towards Fitzgerald, and looked back to the two men.

'Our leaders are in daily jeopardy. They are under constant threat of arrest and incarceration. We all are. Arthur Griffith is in jail as we speak, his only crime to have been elected as a member in a free election and to have helped form the Government and Parliament of our country. We can't be too careful.'

'We understand your concerns, Mr Childers,' said Martin. 'I myself have been harrassed and threatened here by British Forces on more than one occasion.'

'I'll see what I can do about arranging a meeting, with one of our leaders at least. It will take some weeks, you appreciate that.'

'We're the pack mules of patience,' laughed Ackerman. He reached into his side pocket. 'Do you object to my smoking?'

Childers shook his head. Ackerman had just produced his pipe when there was a sudden sound of running feet upon the stairs. A red-faced man burst into the office, panting from his exertions. It was Frank Gallagher, one of the *Bulletin* writers. 'Quick, quick, the military have thrown a cordon around Molesworth Street.'

'Not again,' moaned Fitzgerald.

'I'm afraid so. They're approaching the building. They must have been tipped off that we're here.'

Childers jumped up and called to his assistant, Kathleen McKenna. 'Come on, Kathleen.'

They all crowded through the door at the same time. Gallagher took a revolver out of his pocket.

'What'll I do with this?'

Childers grabbed it, looked around and then stuffed it into a pile of old newspapers that were ready for disposal. There was a honking of car horns and a roaring of lorry engines from the street. There were loud voices and shrieks from the ground floor. Soldiers were rushing up the stairs from floor to floor. Pandemonium reigned.

'Come on,' said Fitzgerald. 'We'll go down the main staircase. Don't flinch. Look the blighters in the eye.'

They stepped out onto the landing. There were soldiers milling all around. The two old ladies from upstairs were remonstrating with them and standing on their dignity. Hoighty-toighty to the end. When they reached the mezzanine, Childers, Gallagher and McKenna went down the outside stairs, while the others continued towards the front door. A pinstriped solicitor with a fob watch and waistcoat, and a pin in his necktie, was getting very exercised. Veins were popping on his forehead as he rebuked a junior officer.

'How many times do you people have to be told this is a loyal building? My God man, we're solicitors to his Majesty.'

'That may be so, sir,' said the officer. 'But we have to follow orders. Nobody is immune.'

Fitzgerald couldn't help giving a thin smile at the blustering lawyer's discomfort. They strode on confidently, heads held high, gazes steady. They were now out on the street amidst the jostling and confusion, approaching the barrier at the corner of Kildare Street, when another officer called to them.

'You there! Halt!'

The three men stopped.

'Names please.'

'I beg your pardon?' said Fitzerald, mustering as much authority as he could.

The officer hesitated, hearing the English accent. 'I'm sorry to have to ask you, sir, but we must establish your identities.'

'We're journalists,' said Fitzgerald. 'I'm Boyd of the *Manchester Guardian.*' He lied with a practised facility.

'And I'm Ackerman of the *Philadelphia Public Ledger.*'

The officer's eyes narrowed. 'Journalists, eh. We're sick and tired of you people writing lies about us and the so-called brutality of the army.'

'Oh, really?' said Fitzgerald, feigning surprise. 'Who are you referring to?'

'There's a fellow called Hugh Martin who's the bane of our lives. If we catch him we'll break his neck.'

'Well, he's not one of us,' said Fitzgerald smoothly.

The officer turned to Martin. 'I didn't get your name, sir?'

'I'm with the *Morning Post*. Carstairs is the name.'

The officer was unconvinced, but was interrupted by a soldier shouting to him. He hesitated, then turned to Ackerman. 'What did you say your name was again?'

'Carl Ackerman. Look, Mr Thomson can vouch for me.'

'Mr. Thomson?'

'Basil Thomson of Scotland Yard.'

The officer looked surprised. 'Basil Thomson can vouch for you?'

'Yes,' said Ackerman. 'He's a friend of mine.'

The officer raised his eyebrows, frustrated, but resigned. He looked away, and then looked back.

'Very well,' he said, indicating the two journalists. 'I'm prepared to let you two gentlemen go, but I'm going to have to question you further, sir.' He turned to Fitzgerald. 'If you are telling the truth you'll be released of course. If not there will be serious consequences.'

The cordon opened and Ackerman and Martin were allowed through. They looked helplessly back to Fitzgerald who was led away by the arm and ushered into an armoured car.

At 6.30 p.m. on the 19th of May, 1921, the evening train from Cork was approaching Dublin. It was a quiet day and there were few passengers on the train. In one carriage, deep in amiable conversation, sat two men. One was aged about 40, a military man in mufti, and the other was a civilian in his early 20's, dressed in a slightly ill-fitting suit. The older man sported a handlebar moustache which complemented his military bearing; he was a Major in the British Army, taking, as he put it, 'A few weeks well-earned leave from this damned country.'

The younger man in the oversized suit, with the shock of dark hair standing up on his head, was Tom Barry, pretending to be a medical student at University College. In reality he'd been summoned to Dublin by Eamon de Valera, to give an account of the latest military situation in the south. The preparations for his departure had been frantic, but thorough. He'd been briefed in medical terminology by his medical student colleagues, Pete Kearney and Nudge Callanan, and he'd assumed the identity of an actual medical student named Ted Ryder from Crookstown. He was armed with old posted envelopes, student bills, textbooks, forceps and other bits of paper, all addressed to Ryder, and the reason his suit didn't fit properly was because his sole previous one had been taken by the King's Liverpool's Regiment in Skibbereen, when they raided a house where Barry was staying two nights before. He'd been obliged to exit the house minus his clothes and his new apparel had been hastily stitched together overnight by a friendly tailor who'd guessed slightly optimistically at his measurements. It was delivered by pony and trap by Sonny Hennessy to O'Mahonys of Belrose, who then, along with the O'Mahony sisters, took Barry to the train station in Cork on the Glanmire Road. They pressed various pro-British periodicals and newspapers into his hands for good measure, along with his train ticket.

Tom had deliberately seated himself opposite the British officer in the carriage hoping to deflect any suspicions as to his true identity, by his association with such a gentleman. He soon struck up a conversation with the civilized Britisher, informing him of the necessity of his visit to a specialist in Dublin for suspected lung trouble, brought on through dint of constant studying for his examinations. The officer was sympathetic, and at every station when the military police inspectors came down the corridor, the officer assured them that the young medical student was travelling with him and that he was above reproach. Each time the subterfuge worked and it was with a warm feeling of gratitude and no little regret that Tom bade farewell to his travelling companion at Kingsbridge Station in Dublin, wishing him a pleasant vacation far from the troubles and confusion of the little isle.

'Welcome to the big smoke, you West Cork beggar,' roared Michael Collins as he bounded like a force of nature into the room where Barry had fetched up later that evening, in an elegant Georgian house with high triangular, capped windows, above Liam Devlin's Wine and Tea Merchants shop on Parnell Street. Barry rose from his seat and had his fingers nearly crushed by the strength of the handshake of the tall, powerfully built man in the dark, well-cut, three piece suit, white shirt, dark tie, highly polished brogues. He looked into the smiling blue eyes of the Minister of Finance. He beheld the wide face, the secretive mouth, the lips that curled into a mischievous smile. Several young men followed him, including his two intelligence operatives, Tom Cullen, with a flat boxers's nose and Liam Tobin, with a high forehead and slightly bulging eyes. There was also Gearóid O'Sullivan, the friendly-faced Adjutant-General, Sean O'Muirthille, and the thin lipped, thin-faced editor of *An tOglach,* Piaras Béaslai. But Collins dominated the room as if the others weren't there.

The two West Cork men stood eyeing each other like fighting cocks, each only too well aware of the legend of the other. Collins the organisational genius, Barry the military general *non pareille*. Although from the same rural parish they had rarely met. Collins was ten years older and had spent ten years working in the heart of London. Barry had fought in the British Army during the war. They had many bonds in common.

'How was your trip?' asked Collins.

'Uneventful,' said Barry. 'I was apprehensive, but I struck up a friendship with a British Major, who smoothed my path.'

'He wouldn't have been too friendly if he found out who you were,' laughed Collins, with quick repartee.

'Too true,' said the serious Barry.

'Have they given you anything to eat?' asked Collins. 'Your clothes are falling off you.'

'I'm afraid my tailor was flying blind,' said Barry, holding up his jacket cuffs, inside of which his hands had almost disappeared.

'Let me see that,' said Collins grabbing hold of the sleeve, and giving Barry a quick once over with his eyes. Then he said, 'You'll grow into it. Come on, we'll go over to Vaughan's Hotel to get you a sirloin steak.'

Having finished their meal in the row of three Georgian houses on the western side of Parnell Square that was Vaughan's Hotel, Liam Tobin hurried in and with an inclination of his head he indicated that it was time to go somewhere. Collins jumped up and said, 'Come on, Tom. Your belly is full now. We'll show you the town.'

Barry rose slowly, 'Where are we going?'

'A surprise,' grinned Collins, putting on his three-cornered trilby.

'What about the bill?'

'That's all taken care of,' said Collins expansively. 'I know you're a frugal man, Tom, but you're my guest for the next six days. You don't have to put your hand in your pocket.'

Outside, a jarvey car had pulled up to the kerb and Collins, Barry, Gearóid O'Sullivan and Sean O'Muirthille climbed on board.

'Where to?' asked the driver.

'The Phoenix Park,' said Collins, cheerfully.

The horse took off at a brisk trot down Parnell Street. Tobin and Cullen followed on bicycles.

They went along North King Street, and to their left they could see the Four Courts, the fortified centre of British legal administration in Ireland, dominated by a great domed central mass. There were soldiers everywhere. They sped on. Barry was uneasy. Collins was in ebullient mood, pointing out other landmark buildings as they passed them by. They went through Smithfield Market and up by Arbour Hill to the back gate of the Phoenix Park.

'Where are we?' asked Barry, noticing the enormous, red-bricked RIC barracks on their right and further on the shape of Marlborough Military barracks.

The sun was slowly setting in a red ball between the great beeches of the park, and large crowds of happy-looking people were proceeding in the one direction, some on foot and others in carriages. Then they beheld a green sward of track and an ornate grandstand.

'We're going to the races,' said Collins. 'The evening meeting in the Park has the best atmosphere in Dublin.'

'The races,' gasped Barry. 'Are ye mad?' He looked desperately around him as if searching for a means to escape. 'Is it safe to go to such a public place?'

'You're safer here than anywhere else,' said Collins to reassure him.

'I hope you're right,' said Barry uneasily. 'There's a price on my head you know. If I'm caught I'll be given short shrift at the end of a rope by one of their drumhead court martials.'

'There's a bigger price on his head,' smiled O'Sullivan, indicating Collins.

'You must relax, Tom,' said Collins. 'You're a long way now from Rosscarbery. You're in the big city, where everyone won't know you, anymore than you'll know them.'

Barry gave a half-hearted smile but the look in his eyes suggested he still considered them all mad.

They spent the evening until the sun went down and twilight made magic of the colours, the horses, the laughter, the chink of glasses, the far away war. They rubbed shoulders with the cream of the Anglo-Irish ascendancy in the reserved enclosure, where there was no detectable difference between the well-dressed revolutionaries in their waistcoats and hats, and the topped and tailed ladies and gentlemen of the gallery. There were shouts of, 'Get up you good thing,' and echoes of, 'Winner alright.'

Collins counted his winnings after the last race. 'Isn't it nice to see how the other half lives,' he said, nudging Barry.

'And get paid for it into the bargain,' said O'Muirthille with satisfaction. 'I got the winner of the last, at sixes.'

'You're too slow Sean,' laughed Collins. 'I got it at ten to one.'

Barry was neither a winner nor was he a happy man. He felt far from home and the green hills of Cork.

On their way to their lodgings with Mrs O'Donovan in Rathgar, they stopped for a drink at a pub on the Rathmines Road. They talked for several hours. Although well-travelled and fearless, Barry at first felt slightly ill at ease in the company of his sophisticated companions, with their easy references to familiar Dublin landmarks, their eloquence and their ability to discuss abstract political and philosphical concepts. After a while, however, he began to feel irritated by the condescending tone of the know-all Piaras Béaslaí, who kept on about the important work he was doing for the cause.

'What do you do, anyway?' asked Barry with a frown.

'Well I do a number of things. First of all I'm the editor of *An tOglach*, the weekly information broadsheet for the IRA, which keeps you fellows up to date about the goings-on around the rest of the country. You've read it no doubt.'

'Once or twice,' said Barry.

Béaslaí looked a little peeved and he continued. 'Secondly I'm a published poet, and thirdly I'm an elected member of the Dáil or a *Teachta Dála* as we say.'

'And what is your constituency?'

'Why, mid-Kerry of course.'

'And tell me,' said Barry, 'how many votes did you garner?'

'Ahem, well, I was elected unopposed.'

'He was the first man in Ireland to be elected three times without ever getting a vote,' said Collins, and then clapped his thigh and burst out laughing at his own wit. 'Tell me Tom, did you ever hear the bate of that?'

Barry smiled and shook his head not wishing to embarrass the other further. Béaslaí's expression was one of intense annoyance, but he was a mere acolyte moving in Collins's shadow and daren't interject. He depended on the Big Fellow for his exalted position.

Barry continued. 'This *Oglaigh* paper, I thought that was written by the little Englishman?'

'Which Englishman?' asked Béaslaí, haughtily.

'Childers,' said Barry.

'God, no,' spat Béaslaí. 'That's the *Bulletin*. He's doing it since Fitzgerald was arrested. But he doesn't understand Ireland at all. He has no real idea of what we are about. No real feel for what it means to be Irish.'

Collins looked at Béaslai with a long stare. Then his mischievous smile returned. 'Sure weren't you born in Liverpool yourself, Piaras,' he said.

'Yes, but I came over when I was young, only 21.'

'Is 21 young?' asked Collins. 'Sure Tom there is only 22 and he's already a general.'

Barry thought he'd better change the subject: 'My point about all this is that we don't have time to be reading papers. We're too busy grappling with the might of the Tans and the Auxies and the Essex. We're too busy worrying where we'll get the next .303 rifle or the next round of ammunition. Writing abstract accounts is all very well, but we have to deal with it on the ground, and I wish some of you fellows would come around to visit us more often.'

'You have a point there,' said Collins. 'Liam Lynch said the same thing and we have sent Ernie O'Malley around to give you fellows a gee up. But we're busy too. Come along with me for the next few days and you'll have a better idea of what it takes to run a revolution and a country.'

When Barry rose next morning and put on his suit he noticed that the cuffs were no longer too long and that the trousers fit him perfectly. He was perplexed. 'Will you look at that,' he said to Collins at the breakfast table where Mrs O'Donovan had prepared rashers and eggs.

'What?' asked Collins with an innocent expression.

'My suit fits?' said Barry.

'Another problem solved,' said Collins and winked at the landlady. Barry raised an eyebrow and looked from one to the other. The leader of the revolution had the presence of mind to tell the landlady to take in his trousers. There didn't appear to be any detail too trivial for the eagle eye of his compatriot.

They strode down Grafton Street. Barry wore a hat which Collins had lent him, saying: 'This place is crawling with spies and Castle hacks. You'll be less recognisable in a hat.'

The street was crowded with men in suits, waiscoats, cloth caps and slouch hats, and women in long dresses, bobbed hair and peek-a-boo hats. Many eyes were wary and suspicious. Friend or foe was hard to tell one from the other.

'Don't make eye contact,' said Collins out of the side of his mouth. 'Look straight ahead.'

The two confident young men got some admiring glances. Collins would sometimes tip his hat and smile to someone he knew. They passed sidecars, armoured cars, RIC men on horses, soldiers with rifles at the ready. They walked on, crossing into Exchequer Street and turned in the doorway of No. 10, a three storey, red-brick building with long, Romanesque windows in the baroque style. On the very top were two dormer windows on the slanting, slate roof. Collins leaped the stairs, two at a time and knocked at a door on the top floor. A voice called and they found themselves inside an office, which was a veritable hive of activity. There were young men in shirt sleeves and girls in blouses and tied back hair, all beavering away. There were typewriters clacking, people speaking on telephones, and others writing feverishly in longhand. There was a sudden respectful hush when the two men came in. Everyone saluted Collins and they all replied, 'Good morning,

Minister,' to his cheery greeting.

A dark-haired young man handed him a piece of paper that looked like a cheque.

'Do you see this, Tom,' said Collins, waving it in the air. 'This is one of our new Government Bond Certificates. We're raising thousands this way through the National Loan. You buy one of these and in due course you can cash it in and get your money back with interest. People are buying these wholesale.' Collins put the certificate inside his coat and put his hand on Barry's shoulder. 'Come on,' he said.

They were down on the street again in the twinkling of an eye and Collins powered ahead along Dame Street. 'That's one of our finance offices,' he shouted over his shoulder as they hurried along. Barry had to run to keep up. When they reached the junction of Palace Street, Collins suddenly dived in the main door of the ornate Munster & Leinster Bank. Barry followed behind him. Collins pointed to a seat inside the door. 'Hold on there a minute, Tom,' he said, as he went towards the counter. Barry sat on a comfortable chair that was located to the left. He observed the gorgeous marbled floor, the fine, corniced ceilings. He noticed a hatch being raised. Collins was inside the counter without breaking his stride. He was shown into a glass-panelled office where Barry could see him animatedly talking to the bank manager. He could see the manager looking over Collins's shoulder in his direction as if to get a better look at his guest. In a few minutes, Collins was back at his side, this time waving a cheque for 10,000 pounds under his nose.

'You see this,' he said. 'This is to purchase a consignment of Thompson guns for you fellows. You're always complaining that you don't have enough firepower. Well it doesn't come cheap. There are two American arms dealers over at the moment and we'll be getting a demonstration of these guns in a few days. Hopefully they'll do the job.'

Barry nodded. He looked impressed.

They went back down Dame Street towards Trinity College and turned sharply into the narrow, shadowy, cobbled Crowe Street, where bicycles leant against the walls. The houses were tall, grim and gaunt. Collins ushered Barry in the door of No. 3 and bounded up the stairs to the second floor. He went through a door with the name J.F. Fowler, Printers, emblazoned on the glass panel. Barry was panting from his exertions. Collins was breathing easily. A tall, thin man with bulging eyes stood up from a desk and Barry recognised someone he'd already met.

'Liam Tobin,' said Collins 'You met him last night.'

The young man extended his hand to Barry.

'I'm giving Tom a quick guided tour of our operations,' said Collins.

'You'd want to be fit to lie up with him,' grinned Tobin, noticing the puffing Barry.

'That's for sure,' said Barry leaning on the back of a chair. 'I feel like I've half a day's work done already and it's only 10 o'clock in the morning.'

'Liam is in charge of intelligence,' said Collins. 'He does a very important job.'

'I've no doubt he does,' said Barry. Collins exchanged a few hurried words with Tobin, and then beckoned Barry away.

'All the best, Tom,' smiled Tobin. 'Next time bring your running shoes.'

'I will bejasus,' said Barry and turned around. Collins was already halfway down the stairs. Barry wasn't used to playing second fiddle to any man, but such was the sheer force of personality and energy of his countryman that Barry didn't have time to feel like a spectator at someone else's party. He was simply swept along.

They ducked down a dark laneway with stone flags under their feet. Their footsteps echoed off the walls. There was a smell of dampness and of urine. They came to a red-bricked public house with an elaborate facade. The name 'Stag's Head' was written in bold lettering above the door. They slipped inside and went into the back where Collins pushed open the batwings doors of a cosy snug. There were five young men seated inside. They were drinking tea. One stood as the two came in. The others half rose. 'Sit down lads,' said Collins. Four of them sat back down. The first one stayed on his feet.

'Lads,' said Collins, 'I want you to meet a very famous county man of mine. This is Tom Barry.'

The five young men immediately lost their cold-eyed, nonchalant stares. Their faces became animated. 'Tom Barry,' exclaimed the young man who was standing. 'Your reputation precedes you.'

He extended his hand. Barry beheld a young man with a thin face, hooded eyes, fair hair, slicked back. He, like the other four, was wearing a white shirt with soft collar, a dark tie and a well-cut suit.

'I'm Vinny Byrne,' he said. He introduced the other four. 'Meet Michael McDonnell, Tim Keogh, Paddy Daly and Jim Slattery.'

Barry shook hands in turn with a wide-faced man with receding hair, a long, thin man with deep-set eyes, a cherubic-faced fellow with curly brown hair and a full-lipped, handsome young man with hair combed to o ne side and neatly parted. They looked quietly confident, as if they didn't feel the need to prove themselves to anyone.

'These boys are part of The Squad,' said Collins.

Tom Barry nodded. 'You got the Cairo Gang,' he said.

'By Christ they did,' said Collins.

Tom Barry took a step back. 'I'm in good company,' he said with a respectful smile.

Collins was on his toes. 'Lads,' he said. 'I have a few more appointments to meet. I think Tom here is getting a bit worn out following me around. Will you look after him for a few hours until I come back later in the evening?'

The young men nodded. Vinny Byrne said, 'We will, Mick. We'll take him up to the 'Dump' 'til you come back.'

'The 'Dump?' asked Barry.

'That's our headquarters,' smiled Byrne. 'Over in Middle Abbey Street. It's a cubby hole on the top floor. When you see it you'll realise it's well named.'

Collins hurried away.

'How does he remember all his appointments?' asked Barry. 'He has nothing written down.'

'He keeps it all in his head,' grinned Byrne. 'Your countryman is a bit of a genius. You should know that.'

'I'm beginning to think so,' said Barry.

'I see you are publishing my private correspondence before it arrives, Mr Ackerman.'

'Whatever can you mean, Mr. Collins?' asked Carl Ackerman evenly. He was sitting in a beautifully appointed drawingroom on the third floor of a splendid Georgian townhouse overlooking Fitzwilliam Square. Through the windows the sun was shining down on green grass and red roses in the small park, which was surrounded by wrought iron, arrowhead railings. Michael Collins had just come in and after a quick introduction by Erskine Childers, who sat on a sofa opposite Ackerman, Collins had moved to the window where he spent several minutes looking to the left and to the right, up and down both sides of the square. Collins turned eventually from the window and as he walked to an armchair set down between the two sofas he said. 'You can't be too careful you know.'

He sat on the armchair and produced a number of newspaper cuttings from his inside pocket and laid them on the low, mahogany coffee table. Ackerman saw they were a series of syndicated articles that he had written about Collins.

'I see you've been talking to the Special Branch about me,' smiled Collins, coldly. Ackerman was taken aback. He leafed through the articles to ensure they were his own. 'Well, I...' he began and cleared his throat.

'You see, Mr. Ackerman, I know more about you, than you know about me.' interrupted Collins.

'Such as?' asked Ackerman, trying to regain lost ground.

'Well, I know that you are somewhat of a devotee of Mr Basil Thomson, the head of Scotland Yard.'

'So?'

'So you feel that this connection gives you some kind of leverage with us.'

'I'm merely trying to help,' protested Ackerman.

'Look, Mr. Ackerman,' said Collins, a little impatiently, leaning down and taking a sip of tea from the China tea set that Childers had organised. 'We've had many people over here trying to help. People with a great deal more clout and influence than you might think you have.'

'Such as?'

'Such as Lord Derby, such as Sir James Craig, such as the Earl of Midleton. We've had Archbishop Clune bending our ears. We've had Smuts from South Africa.'

'I see,' said Ackerman, a little deflated but trying not to show it.

'These fellows have the ear of Lloyd George, and whereas your man, Thomson, is important, his job is to provide information to the British Government, not to set policy.'

'You've done your research,' said Ackerman. 'Very impressive. They told me you were formidable, now I can see why. And such a young man too.'

'Are you trying to flatter me?' asked Collins, and gave a look towards Childers.

'On the contrary,' said Ackerman, 'I'm merely trying to see what I can do to bring an end to this miserable war.'

'You can do that by returning to your patrons and telling them that the war will end when Ireland becomes a republic.'

Ackermen nodded. Some headway at last. 'And what exactly does that mean? In practical terms.'

'It means ceding to us total control over our army, our police, our courts and our finances.'

'But you could still get all that and not be a republic.'

'How?'

'You might still be required to swear an oath of allegiance to the Crown, and remain a member of the Commonwealth of Nations.'

Collins smiled again. He was aware the other man was fishing, trying to sound him out.

'I'm afraid that proposal would not be acceptable to our President, Mr. de Valera,' put in Childers quickly.

'But it might be to you, Mr. Collins, if I understand you correctly?' said Ackerman, looking for a chink of daylight.

'You're putting words in my mouth, Mr. Ackerman,' said Collins and levelled his gaze at the American.

'But politics is the art of the possible, surely?' asked Ackerman.

'We're not at the political stage yet, Mr. Ackerman,' said Collins. 'We're still very much at the military stage, and will be until the British Army leaves our shores.'

'And what if the army numbers are in fact increased?' asked Ackerman. 'What will you do then?'

'We'll still be able to wreak havoc on them. They may become more repressive but eventually they will lose so many men that the public will ask, is it worth the candle? Already the British public are asking that question in ever increasing numbers. There is a great deal of bluff and bluster going on, especially by the likes of Mr. Churchill. But we're calling his bluff.'

Ackerman nodded. He pursed his lips and sighed. 'Is Mr. de Valera in agreement with you on all this?'

'You'll have to ask Mr. de Valera that question,' said Collins, with an enigmatic smile.

'He won't talk to anyone below ministerial level,' said Ackerman, a little helplessly.

'That rules you out then,' said Collins, and stood up.

'I'm afraid it does,' said Ackerman, ruefully.

'Well, it was very nice to meet you, Mr. Ackerman,' said Collins, as Ackerman stood to shake hands. 'Erskine, will you see to it that Mr. Ackerman is given whatever other refreshment he desires.'

'Won't you stay for a quiet one?' asked Ackerman, hoping to continue to imbibe in the aura of the dashing revolutionary.

'I never drink on duty,' said Collins, and went through the door.

'What a fascinating young man,' said Ackerman, still standing, looking towards the door that Collins had firmly shut. The mood had changed, as if the bright sun had gone behind the clouds.

'You think so?' asked Childers, as he walked to a side cabinet and produced a whiskey bottle and two glasses. Ackerman turned and watched the golden liquid filling, heard it gurgling in the glass, sniffed its comforting bouquet.

It was nearing ten o'clock later that night. Collins was upstairs in a private room of Vaughan's Hotel where he was meeting IRA officers from all over Ireland. Tom Barry was there, observing. Collins had come back at 6.30 p.m. and drank a quick cup of tea in the bar. Barry was in the company of some members of The Squad, a dark, swarthy young man named Noel Lemass and a girl with short cut, bobbed hair named, Leslie Price, the chief organiser of Cumann Na mBan. There appeared to be an instant attraction between the dashing general from West Cork and the dedicated young woman, which didn't go unnoticed to the eagle eye of Collins.

'Cripes, Tom, you'll never go back to West Cork if you spend too much time with this lovely lass.'

'Maybe I'll take her back with me,' said Barry.

'By Christ you won't then,' said Collins. 'We can't afford to send a woman of her ability down to Cork.'

Collins stood back and looked around him at the other young men. He winked at Noel Lemass. He clapped him on the back. 'Has this Dublin hoor bought you a drink?'

Barry shook his head.

'He would if you were Dev's guest,' joked Collins. 'Sure this fellow and his brother only answer to the Long Fellow. They take no notice of me.'

'My brother is in jail in Ballykinlar unfortunately,' said Lemass.

Collins thumped him on the arm. 'I'm only joking. Don't be so sensitive.' He turned to Barry. 'This fellow and his brother Sean are tough fighters. They were out in 1916.'

Barry nodded admiringly. Collins continued: 'Maybe Noel here will make himself useful and take you out to Blackrock to meet the President in a few days?'

'Whatever you say, Minister,' said the laconic Lemass.

Afterwards, Collins had gone upstairs with Barry, where a parade of guerilla fighters had come and gone. All wanted Collins's time, energy and committment, which he gave unflinchingly. Liam Lynch, the serious, bespectacled leader of the North Cork Brigade, had discussed the setting up of a divisional brigade. Barry couldn't see the point of it.

Each brigade was an island, self sufficient unto itself. Guerilla warfare could not be centrally controlled. Only by stealth and secrecy could it prevail.

'That was Mulcahy's idea,' said Collins. 'You'll meet him tomorrow. You can decide on it then between yourselves.'

Collins was full of praise for some of the officers, and mildly critical of others. One arrogant Kerry commander who demanded more guns, got the sharp edge of his tongue. Collins stood back and faced him with a scowl on his face. He thrust his hands in his pockets and scuffed the floor impatiently with his right foot.

'Guns for you fellows is it? What the hell does a lot of lily-livered lousers like you want more guns for? You have more than enough rifles if only you'd use them. The Black and Tans are terrorising and shooting your neighbours and countrymen down there in Kerry and you fellows are afraid to take them on. Get out of my sight and don't come back here until you've done some fighting.'

The officer and his sidekicks were taken aback. They hastily left the room with their tails between their legs.

Tom Barry went to bed that night, his head reeling from the whirlwind of the day's events. He'd been on the go since early morning, and whilst he'd met many new people, it was, he knew, a trifle compared to what the Minister of Finance had accomplished in the same sixteen hours. How different the life of the city to the life of the country, with its sunrises and sunsets, its slow deliberate wheeling of nature's cycle. Even the gunmen had to accomodate the crowing of the cocks, the milking of the cows, the mowing of the hay. The ploughing and the reaping, the good seed scattered on the land. The tolling of the bells for Mass, for Angelus, for funeral. Here in the city all seemed a constant hum and grind of activity, without structure, without rest, without prayer. Here the soldiers of the brigades and the members of Sinn Féin had to go about their daily chores dressed in suits, harnessed by custom and necessity to regular jobs in offices and factories, and then obliged to assume different guises and personas after work hours, to continue the cause of the fight for freedom. How different for the brigades and columns of young men who, with Barry, roamed the mountains and the valleys and the wide fields of home, unfettered and untrammelled by the deadlines of factory clock, the timetables of omnibus or train.

Before he nodded off to sleep, the final scene of that eventful day which had set his nerves a-jangle, kept spinning in his head. As the quartet of Collins, Barry, O'Sullivan and O'Muirthille made their way back to Rathgar in their familiar horse and sidecar they were stopped on Portobello Bridge by a large party of soldiers. It was after midnight.

'Act drunk,' said Collins, instantly alert to the danger. When the officer approached and asked for their papers, Collins had put on such a show of fake drunkeness as would have done justice to the talents of the finest actor of the Abbey Theatre. With much gesticulating, laughing, joking cursing and swearing, he'd convinced the soldiers that they were a group of countrymen up in the city for a few days, enjoying their time away from the responsibilities of hearth and home, wives and children. With their well-dressed appearances and the slightly incoherent ramblings of Collins, the officer waved them on their way with a mystified shake of his head, reinforcing his already, firmly held conviction that the Irish were a completely incomprehensible species that the English would never understand.

Barry's final thoughts were of the extraordinary contradictions that comprised the personality of his countryman. A restless spirit, at one minute playing the joker and clown, the next, serious and choleric, he was a strange phenomenon. A man of tremendous confidence and natural authority, with a cunning and ever-active mind, he appeared to embody the heart and soul of the revolution. He appeared at times, too reckless for Barry's disciplined military instincts, and yet his far-seeing and natural organisational gifts made him the linch-pin around which every facet of the war revolved. He was a hard man to classify. Barry looked forward to meeting in the following days with the other twin pillar of the movement, the more shadowy *eminence grise* that was Eamon de Valera.

After four days in the big city he was beginning to get a clearer picture of the workings of the General Headquarters Staff. Apart from Collins and his immediate circle, he'd been to South Frederick Street to meet Richard Mulcahy, the IRA Chief of Staff, Kevin O'Higgins the Assistant Minister of Local Government, and Cathal Brugha the Minister of Defence. He'd also met W. T. Cosgrave the Minister of Local Government and Sean McMahon the Quarter Master General. What struck Tom were the titles they all rejoiced in. Ministers of this, that and the other. What did they all actually do on a day to day basis other than appear puffed up and important to impress their immediate underlings? And what contribution did they all make from their desks and offices to the likes of himself and his Cork brigades? Very little that he could see. Michael Collins on his own, appeared to do as much as all the others put together. He noticed a jealous guarding of positions and territory, and the adumbrations of emerging cliques. This dismayed him slightly. The slim, poker-faced Mulcahy and the austere Cathal Brugha didn't appear to have any great fondness for one another, while the tall, rather arrogant and patrician Kevin O'Higgins seemed more convinced of his own importance than was necessarily the case. The different factions of the secretive IRB, the Irish Volunteers, Dáil Eireann and the Cabinet, all appeared to promote their individual agendas with a disturbing enthusiasm. But he would reserve his judgement until he met the President himself, Eamon de Valera. Collins conveyed him in a horse and trap to meet the great man in the south Dublin suburb of Blackrock on the 23rd May.

'You're very welcome, Tom,' said the tall, dark-haired man with the long nose and round, thin-rimmed glasses, that gave him at once an owlish and slightly remote appearance. He put his hand on Barry's shoulder and showed him into a large room with views to the south, across a wide, tree-filled lawn to the Dublin mountains in the blue distance. It seemed a location, in this large, detached house, safely removed from the constant dangers of the city centre.

'How are you enjoying your visit?'

De Valera had a dry, precise way of speaking with a vague southern inflection, in contrast to the sing-song lilt of the more effusive Collins.

'I'm having a great time, Mr President. Michael here has taken me on a whirlwind tour of every department in the Government. I've barely had a wink of sleep at all.'

'Well you shouldn't try to compete with Michael. When God distributed energy he gave Michael a disproportionate amount compared to the rest of us.'

The two leaders chatted amiably for some minutes. To Barry they appeared to be on excellent terms, with none of the icy tension that was evident when Collins had earlier introduced him to Cathal Brugha, the monosyllabic Minister of Defence. Eventually Collins took his leave and de Valera requested tea from a warm and pleasant-faced lady who was introduced as his secretary, Kathleen O'Connell.

'I must congratulate you on the outstanding success of your Cork brigades,' said the President when they had finished their tea.

'Thank you, Mr. President,' said Barry.

'You can call me Eamon,' said the other but Barry continued to address him by his title. De Valera had the stamp and aura of a statesman, which created a distance between him and other men but which made him ideally suited to represent the new state that was struggling to be born. They talked for over two hours and Barry was impressed by his precise and comprehensive knowledge of all the major operations undertaken by the 3rd West Cork Brigade: Kilmichael, Crossbarry, Rosscarbery, Upton and the rest.

De Valera paused and stood up. He walked to the window and looked out, deep in thought. He turned round and stared intently at Barry and said: 'This war has now continued for the past two years. In that time a lot of people have been tragically killed, a lot of property has been destroyed, a lot of blood has been spilt. I have been criticised in some quarters for not defending the use of violence by our side, but I think I have justified our position of defending ourselves in more than one statement.'

Barry nodded and waited for the older man to continue.

'Neither side has been able to strike a decisive blow that would put an end to affairs once and for all. The British started out being overbearing and arrogant, but I think you and fellows like you, such as Sean MacEoin in Longford, Sean Treacey, Dan Breen, Dinny Lacy in Tipperary, others like Sean Moylan, Liam Lynch and Sean Hegarty in Cork have put manners on them. Now they are attempting a game of ducks and drakes with which to confound us. They are sending out emissaries on a monthly basis trying to sound us out, trying to gauge the depth of our military strength and our resolve. It's a game of bluff and counterbluff. It's the art of dirty politics, Tom, which, fortunately, you don't have to concern yourself with, but which I, as head of state, have to address. For instance, Winston Churchill has advocated putting an extra one hundred thousand men into the field against us. A massive blockade starting in Cork probably. He has proposed a tightening of security restrictions above and beyond anything we have seen to date with curfews. He has proposed a rummaging of every household in Ireland that is loyal to Sinn Féin.'

De Valera gave a dry chuckle. 'Rummaging is a nice word. Mr. Churchill is something of a literary scholar. He likes to use words with a quaint precision, and rummaging impeccably describes what the Black and Tans have been doing for the past two years. All the while seeking to talk peace, the British are also talking war. It is an attempt to unnerve us. They are of course assisted and abetted by the Protestant majority in Ulster who want no truck with our proposed Republic. Therefore they have introduced the Government of Ireland Act, to divide our country in two. They are playing a dissembling game and not for nothing are they called perfidious Albion.'

As de Valera was talking he was walking and gesticulating with his long arms. Tom Barry was quite mesmerised by his eloquence and logic. He spoke like a Jesuit or a Professor. An artist with the tools of language.

'There is an election in a few days. We expect to win a vast majority of the seats, but of course we won't be taking them up in the British Parliament. We're sworn to the path of the Republic. As head of state I am privy to certain communications that none of the other members of our Provisional Government are. The British feel that I am the man they must be talking to, and that is both my privilege but also the burden on my back. I cannot divulge all the information that I get for reasons of security and diplomacy. Neither can I disclose all the plans which are in the pipeline.'

De Valera stopped. Barry sensed that he was driving towards a question which came eventually. As the President sat back down behind his desk he said:

'The main purpose of my summoning you here today, apart from what you have already told me, is to ask you this. How long can we continue the fight against the British in your area and in Munster in general, assuming we can provide you with extra arms and ammunition?'

Barry considered the question. Then he said. 'With adequate arms and ammunition we could extend our reach, we could train a considerable number of extra Volunteers, we could strengthen brigades in other counties.'

'Assuming there is no British blockade,' said the President.

'Without a blockade, we could last five years,' said Barry.

The President leapt to his feet. 'Five years,' he exclaimed, his eyes shining. 'I was optimistic but not that optimistic. Thank you, Tom. You have answered my question and reinforced my resolve to hold out against them. For the next two months we will redouble our efforts. Let them do their worst. They might come to the negotiating table quick enough when we are finished with them.'

Tom Barry shook hands with Eamon de Valera and was driven back to the city by one of the Dublin Brigade. Two days later after testing one of the new prototype Thompson guns from America, he took the morning train back to Cork. The President had told him to keep an eye out for a spectacular incident which Barry's optimistic appraisal had convinced him to carry out, to give Mr. Churchill his answer in no uncertain terms.

By the time Barry reached Cork the Dublin Brigade of the IRA with 120 men had entered and destroyed the Customs House, the largest stronghold of British civil administration in Ireland. On the specific instructions of Mr. de Valera, Oscar Traynor, Tom Ennis, Jim Slattery and other key members of The Squad, had ordered the evacuation of all employees and then, sprinkling large amounts of paraffin throughout, they'd torched the building, sending up in smoke and flames, all the records of British taxation, commerce and property in the country. It was a devastating blow struck at the beating heart of the Empire. There were a number of civilians and IRA men killed, and a large number captured. The British press and the *Irish Times* called it a senseless and wanton destruction of a fine building, but Erskine Childers responded in the *Bulletin* that although it regretted the destruction of an historic building, the lives of four million people were more sacred than any architectural masterpiece. Barry could only smile grimly when he read the news. Dev and Collins were ratcheting up the pressure in defiance of British threats. He went back to his comrades with a mixture of hope and foreboding.

21

the men of the south

T hey came up the valley warily, like foxes or wolves, alert for sudden dangers. Prepared for fight or flight. There were distant dull booms of cannon coming from somewhere over the mountains. A scout said the British were shelling the slopes of Sheha, flushing out rebels. Word came over from the Kerry side that warships were landing troops in Kenmare and Bantry Bay. Thousands of troops. The start of Churchill's rummaging. They'd zig-zagged west over the last week, from Rosscarbery where they burned the barracks, north to Castledonovan, then south again across the main road to Cork, to hilly townlands near Ballydehob and Skeaghnore by the sea. But the reports followed them and made them anxious. Snippets of news from men on bicycles who slipped through the wide cordon of soldiers thrown in like a horseshoe around the southwest tip of Ireland. Led by Montgomery and Percival, Hudson and Lattimer, intent on pushing them into a corral from three sides with the ocean on the fourth. And on the ocean were frigates and destroyers with eighteen pounder guns from which there was no escape. Tom Barry had brought back word of the Custom House destruction led by Oscar Traynor. It was a big setback for the British administration, but an equal tragedy for the IRA. Many killed and over one hundred captured. They said it was de Valera's insistence which decided it. He wanted a large military confrontation. The tax records went up in smoke, but the Volunteers were badly weakened in Dublin. Lloyd George and Churchill were outraged, and now the British bull was turning to charge its tormentors, to stamp on them once and for all. Beginning here with its biggest adversary, the men of the south.

And so here they were at last, being encircled from every side. They went north from Kealkil and then they could see the sea spread out blue, huge and endless before them. They came out on the Bantry road that segued along a beautiful coast of bays, adorned with all the flowers of summer. Tom Barry led them with Jim Hurley and all the big men: Pete Kearney, Gibbs Ross, Spud Murphy, Christy O'Connell. And the young ones: Sonny Hennessy, Nudge Callanan and Dick Spencer, the men who fought at Crossbarry.

They headed into the deep, secluded valley of the Borlin to wait and wonder what to do. They stopped in the houses of Cronin, a big clan who inhabited the tree-filled valley, with towering mountain peaks ranged around. They were billeted out to houses and barns hidden in the trees. The long summer evenings were welcome, but made detection easier. Light lasted longer. They'd seen a spotter plane flying above them. They were thankful for the deep woods of birch and hazel. A slight zephyr blew up the valley. There were flies and midges that pinched the skin and made them itch. Swallows twittered. The cuckoo's call floated from over the way. They were tense and nervous, almost gloomy. But they were among trusted friends. Each man clutched his rifle more tightly and oiled his pistol more thoroughly, checking ammunition belts and preparing to make a last stand.

Before sundown they assembled and Tom Barry introduced them to a local man with a faraway look in his eye. They called him Sullivan The Mountain. He produced a long rope, which he'd coiled in a big loop and said phlegmatically. 'What did ye have in mind?'

Jim Hurley said: 'The British are on every side with large reinforcements. We could be trapped by the looks of it.'

'Could we get up the valley to the Kilgarvan side?' asked Tom Barry.

'Ye could I s'pose,' said Sullivan in his broad brogue. ''Tis high and narra, but there is an old boreen running up there.' He paused and then continued: 'But then again, if 'tis to Kerry ye're going, won't ye find them there too?'

'The British?'

'Aye.'

'You think so?'

'I heard they're sprad out north as far as Killarney and east to Ballyvourney and Macroom. If ye go Kilgarvan way won't ye be squez there too?'

'They'll squeeze us from the east and west if we stay here,' said the tall, intelligent Jim Hurley. 'And the sea is south.'

'They'll be here by tomorrow,' said Tom Barry feeling exasperated. Sonny sat and listened, looking from one face to the other. The leaders were poring over a map showing the surrounding mountain ranges. They appeared to be stumped. Sonny stole a look. 'Could we go up this way?' he asked, pointing to the Conigar peak.

'At night?' asked Sullivan, and gave a kind of mirthless, incredulous chuckle.

'Tonight is all we have,' said Sonny.

'You musht be mad,' said Sullivan.

Barry looked from Sullivan to Hurley and his eyes rested on Sonny. 'The boy is right. We have no alternative.' He turned back to Sullivan. 'If we attempted to go that way, where would it take us?'

'Into Gougane Barra,' said Sullivan. 'But you'd have to go up cliffs where even goats wouldn't go. And then when you get up, you have to cross a mountain with bog holes twenty feet deep. And then down the cliffs on t'other side. They're the worst.' He paused for emphasis, then continued: 'And do all that in the dark of night with a hundert men? Lord God almighty?'

'Is there a moon?' someone asked, half in jest.

'There's not then, only stars, and them covered mostly by clouds.'

'It's worth a try,' said Barry decisively. 'Otherwise we'll be shot like cornered rats by this time tomorrow.' He turned back to Sullivan. 'Will you chance it?'

'Sullivan shrugged: 'Whatever ye want.'

'And you know the way?' asked Hurley as if to make certain of his man. Sullivan had a droll smile in his eye. Cronin the householder spoke up at last. 'There's only one man would attempt it and that's that man there, Sullivan The Mountain. He's spent half his life up there herding sheep.'

'That's settled then,' said Tom Barry.

''Twill be dark in an hour,' said Sullivan. 'We'll strike out then. And eat plenty before ye go. This will take all night.'

Major Bernard Montgomery stood on a high ridge somewhere north of Kilmichael and surveyed the country around. It was an evening towards the first days of June and although the weather had been fine, the clouds to the west forecast a tempestuous morrow. They were piled in great bundles of grey with shafts of silver sunlight shining through, creating dreamy, hazy images, alluring and bewitching, as always with the Irish sky. Mirroring the landscape, instilling romantic hopes and false dawns, with treacherous waters below. You had to tread carefully in Ireland, as some of his compatriots had learned to their cost. As Montgomery looked north he could see the mountains of Mushera and Mullaghanish. To the west he could see the Paps in Kerry, and as his eyes ranged southwest, there was the round dome of Sheha and the pyramid point of Owen. Further south again, Corrin Hill stood sentinel over the vast Atlantic. He could see most of the main roads from where he stood: the Cork to Killarney road, the Bantry Line, the Bandon to Bantry road. He had convoys of troops on each of these roads, moving slowly and methodically towards a centre like a net closing on a shoal of fish. And when he finally pulled tight the strings of the net, he would have the shoal of the 3rd West Cork Brigade writhing inside. He smiled with satisfaction, not grimly, not triumphantly, just the smile of the professional soldier at the prospect of a job well done. Another mission accomplished.

He turned as he heard Major Percival coming across the rushes and the pendulous sedge towards him. He'd been forced to come cap-in-hand to Montgomery after Crossbarry. The man had the arrogance to presume he could prevail there on his own, but what a disaster that proved to be. The damn fellow was too impulsive, too angry. You had to be methodical, leave no stone unturned. Beat the bushes. Montgomery would show him how these things were done. Quietly, without show. No need for pedantry. Montgomery fingered his moustache and sniffed through his nose as Percival slouched towards him. He put down his field glasses and cheerfully saluted: 'Evening Major.' The inflection ended on a high, optimistic note.

'Good evening, Major Montgomery,' came the sour reply. The eyes had a rather hang-dog look about them. Montgomery was unperturbed. He was in charge now. Best to be charitable.

'How is it looking?' inquired Percival.

Montgomery was brisk. He pointed with his whip towards lines of lorries and armoured cars below them on the Bantry Line, supported by columns of infantry spread out across the fields and bogs on either side, all pushing west in a pincer movement designed to flush out and destroy every rebel in the territory.

'Lattimer is down there on the Bantry Line with five hundred men.'

He turned and pointed to the north on the Cork to Killarney road, where they could see a similar movement of troops and military vehicles, and said: 'On that side we have Major Halahan with another seven hundred men, and on the Bandon to Bantry road over this way we have Hudson with an equal number. From these tangents we have Blackthorn on the Clonakilty road closest to the sea, and on the far western side, McComber is pushing east from Kenmare with another thousand men. We have reinforcements from Cork sent out by Major-General Strickland's 6th Division and from the Curragh's 5th Division under Sir Hugh Jeudwine. All in all over seven thousand five hundred men.'

Montgomery pointed west by southwest towards the dreaming blue peaks. 'Somewhere in those lovely-looking mountain ranges the rebels are gathered. We've got them pinned in from every side. If they're on Sheha we'll flush them out with cannon which you can hear. Look at the smoke there.'

He pointed to puffs of smoke rising from the sheltered brakes of Sheha's rounded shoulders. He continued. 'If they try to go over the Cahas, we'll squash them from the west. Their only escape is by sea. Not a very inviting alternative under the noses of our destroyers.'

He smiled grimly.

Percival said: 'Overwhelming odds, Major. Congratulations. You've thought it out well.' There was a hint of grudging admiration in his voice.

'The job isn't done yet, Major,' said Montgomery, 'but in another two days we expect to let them have a taste of cold steel, gunpowder and shot that will put paid to their pesky adventures once and for all. This is the fourth day of our roundup. So far we've been persistent, deliberate, unwavering. We're covering twenty miles a day. We're closing in inexorably, to do what every British army has done to Irish rebels for centuries: put them in their place.'

Percival smiled dubiously. 'I admire your optimism, Major, but when it comes to Ireland, there's many a slip 'twixt the cup and the lip.'

Montgomery gave a scoff and clapped Percival on the shoulder.

'Don't be a pessimist, Major. Be positive. It carries one a long way.'

They moved off from their vantage point towards an armoured car waiting out on a laneway. They got in and the driver eased off down a narrow, winding road that would take them to the Bantry Line to rejoin their forces.

As the last light went off the black west, the Flying Column set out for higher ground. They went up through a grove of Scots pine and an invisible nightjar churred somewhere in the undergrowth. They could not see its brown-black plumage which resembled the wood bark in colour, but as it sat motionless it could discern these interlopers to its habitat well enough. It would take to wing soon and would have floated sooner to hunt for insects but for the presence of such multitudes. So for now it was content to sit and speculate with soft sounds which it could carry on all night for hours on end. No such timorous competitor was a long-eared owl which rose up out of the hawthorn hedges, streaked pale in flight, with staring orange eyes and rebuked the furtive line of climbers with clamorous screeches like the grating hinges of a rusty gate.

'A noisy hoor,' said Sullivan. He stood and paused for breath as they emerged from the last of the trees and pointed to a tumbling stream and a goat path that wound away up and out of sight towards the dramatic heights above. Being halfway up they had no conception of the mountain's size or scope, or the distance they had travelled, but hung suspended small as ants on a vast blackboard and trusted to the man in whom they had invested all their fates.

Barry and Jim Hurley led, hard upon Sullivan's heels, and strung out behind them the long line of men felt their way from rock to rock clutching the long rope Sullivan had paid out, with strict imperatives not to let go a hold on any acount. As he paused he pointed westward to a cone-shaped peak which stood up taller than any other on the Caha range. 'That's Knockowen,' he said. 'When you're up here you turn your back flat to Knockowen and head the opposite way and then you won't go wrong. If you stray from that angle at all you could be up here for days going 'round in circles. If the fog came down you'd scarcely see your hand.'

'The light is nearly gone,' said Barry. 'What happens then?'

'Then you trust your memory and say your prayers.' Sullivan was taciturn. The assignment gave him power.

Sonny climbed away and soon his guts began to rumble. He was obliged to slip behind a rock because the scours announced their imminent arrival. Other men followed soon after and a tug on the rope signalled an emergency halting while the gruel which they'd too greedily consumed before they left, was dispatched to manure the knot grass and the ragged robin, the bracken and the purple sage. When the emergencies had passed the rope was tugged again and they started up once more.

'No one better be short taken from now on,' said Sullivan sardonically. 'We're not stopping again for any man. He can lave it in his pants for that matter.'

They went up by high rocks, feeling and groping. Starlight emerged from behind a huge, black, cumulus cloud which heralded downpours before morning. You'd get that in these higher reaches when the valleys below would be dry. Jupiter shone huge and beautiful in the southern sky. Someone said it was nearly as bright as a new moon. But soon it disappeared. The wind lifted and blew the scent of moorland moss to their nostrils. Surprised sheep flared off into gulleys as the group invaded their nocturnal grazing grounds. Half-reared lambs bleated in a sudden panic. The rough trail levelled out and the ground became a soggy bog with tufts of Yorkshire fog and creeping soft grass. The men slipped and slid and a man in front of Sonny fell thrashing about into a hole as soft and treacherous as quicksand. He shouted and flailed under the weight of his knapsack, heavy gear and ammunition. Luckily he held the rope and with much grunting and cursing he was heaved out with a sucking eructation from the releasing mud and stood shivering and miserable in the dark. Someone produced a burlap half-sack and rubbed the clingy scales of mud off him and the party continued on its way with hardly a pause or word of sympathy to the unfortunate. Before the night was over it would be one of many such accidents, which could have proved fatal to the unwary, but luckily did not. They crossed an endless unseen expanse with their heads bowed, looking at the backside of the man immediately ahead and as the first streaks of dawn grew faintly in the greying sky the rain descended in cascades. It flowed down off their caps, inside their shirt collars and into their squelching boots until they stood in ragged, sodden misery above a cliff face that fell hundreds of feet below to a deep, wooded valley, and a lake hammered flat and glassy in the distance.

'There's Gougane Barra,' said Sullivan The Mountain with a nonchalant inclination of his head. 'There's not a whole lot more I can do for ye now, except maybe help ye down. That'll be the 'tarrawal.' He sucked rivulets of rainwater through bruised, bucolic lips.

They waited for the long straggling line of men to come up and they stood around, panting, sweating and uncomfortable in their wet clothes. But they'd shown fortitude to overcome the barren wastes. Barry counted them all and heaved a satisfied sigh: 'Men,' he said, 'we broke the back of it. But we have to go down there yet towards that lake and we have to do that before the spotter plane is up in the sky again. If that sees us our effort will have been in vain. But if we get down into that valley, we're home and dry.'

He turned to Sullivan. 'Where are the British, would you say?'

Sullivan screwed his eyes towards the eastern distance. 'They're probably gone down the pass of Céim An Fhia,' he said. 'There's no point them coming into Gougane. That's a dead end. Their spies would know that. So the odds of them finding you there are long.'

'How long?' asked Hurley, and stood in his wet trenchcoat, his statistician's brain working busily.

Sullivan pondered the question.

'Are you a gambling man?' asked Hurley.

'I am faith' said Sullivan.

'Would you say a hundred to one?'

'I would,' said Sullivan, 'and more.'

'How much more?'

'If they haven't been tipped off, I'd say more like a thousand to one.'

'Good odds for a horserace,' said Barry. 'Not quite so good when you have the life of every man in the Column in your hands.'

''Tis your call,' said Sullivan. 'But ye can't stay up here anyway.'

'Too bloody true,' said Barry. 'We'll go down.'

Sullivan went towards the cliff edge and just as if he looked like falling over he ducked to the right, past a giant bluff that hung out over the abyss. The men followed one by one. At first the escarpment was gradual and descended into a gulley, but then it graduated out to a ledge, below which the cliff plunged. Sullivan stood at a giant conifer that reared up tall against the sky with scarcely a branch until the top where a few uplifted arms gave the impression of penitential prayer in a thing inanimate.

'Reckon that'll hould a hundert weight or two,' he said, as he wound the rope around the gnarled trunk. When he'd made it fast he said, 'I'll go down first and then ye can follow one by one. Any slip and a man could end up three hundert feet below.'

They watched Sullivan abseiling down like a natural born climber of the Alps. Men who had faced Lee Enfields and Gatling guns paused before swinging out into space. A different kind of nerve was required for this enterprise. Hour after hour they swung out, trusting to the rope and to prayer, and as each man landed at the bottom, Sullivan clapped him on the back and shook the rope for the next man. Towards the end a younger man named Desmond got squeamish and let the rope burn through his palms until he let it go and landed with a crash at Sullivan's feet. He lay on his hands and knees gasping for breath, and his moans of agony suggested at least three cracked ribs and a twisted ankle into the bargain. The others had gone on ahead and Sullivan, Tom Barry and

Jim Hurley nursed the young man around until he sat up and regained his breath.

'I think I've broke my bleddy back,' he gasped.

'You haven't then,' said Sullivan. 'You've bruised your ribs bad and they'll feel like they're broke but probably not. If your back was broke you wouldn't be sitting up at all.'

After a while he came around sufficiently to be able to stand, and was helped the remaining way down a treacherous mixture of tussocks of grass and lichen-covered rock, that was sharp as a knife and slippery as ice. There were many falls, cuts and bruises before the entire party reached the sheltering oakwoods that grew up from the valley floor along the lower sides of the cliffs. Just as the last man gained the protective canopy of oak leaves the clouds lifted as suddenly as they had arrived in the pre-dawn hours and a magnificent sunburst illuminated the sheer granite wall down which they'd descended. At exactly that moment a Sopwith Camel aeroplane with an engine hammering its pistons like gunshots in the still morning flew across the mountain and over the woods where they crouched with breath held. They stood silently, faces upturned as the plane flew down the valley. They waited for it to turn and come back up and this they knew would spell mortal danger, if they'd been seen. But the engine cast its sputtering echoes further and further on against cliffs and mountain passes and did not return. They were safe.

The men gathered round Sullivan The Mountain and each man solemnly shook his hand one by one as if they were shaking the hand of a dignitary or a bishop. They were aware of the enormity of the risk and the effort he had taken on their behalf and for that they were grateful.

'Ye should hold on here for most of the day,' said Sullivan, 'to make assurance doubly sure. I'd say ye're well outside the cordon of soldiers and that they're gone on down the Bantry road, where they'll be mighty discommoded not to find ye. And unless that plane has seen us, ye have a free run of the country back east in the next day or two. I'll go down to Cronin's hotel on the banks of the lake and tell them to cook up some grub for ye and ye can slip down there in a couple of hours time. The Cronins are fine national people.'

'Is everyone called Cronin around here?' laughed Hurley in nervous relief.

'Except for Sullivan,' said the other, dryly.

Barry looked Sullivan in the eye and held his gaze. He grasped his hand with both his own. 'We're forever in your debt,' he said. 'And if there's anything we can do for you in return any time, just say the word.'

Sullivan's sardonic face creased into a rarely summoned grin. 'My needs are few,' he said. 'But if anyone has a good thing for the Galway races I'll be disappointed not to hear it first.'

'You can depend upon it,' said Barry and laughed heartily in return. Sullivan The Mountain went through the dappled shadows and the streams of sunlight that shone through the morning trees, and like a ghost he was gone.

When Bernard Montgomery stood in the great square of Bantry gazing out over one of the most spectacular vistas on the face of the earth, and realised that the IRA had slipped through his fingers, all colour drained from his rosy-coddled cheeks. As the midday sun beat down out of a cloudless sky, he watched his sections, battalions, brigades and the last of his divisions drive slowly through the huddled town, and as each commanding officer approached, he could see in the downcast look of the eyes that his great crusade had been in vain. A bitter taste filled his mouth as hope and confidence left his heart like water from a tub. He felt as if the shuddering beneath his feet caused by the trundling lorries were the omens of his ordered world begin to crumble. He went up to Bantry House where the sympathetic landlord, Shelswell-White, prepared tea for those officers with temperate tastes and whiskey for others more adventurous of palate. As they all stood around gazing despondently through great windows open to the west, clouds changed shape over distant Knockowen, casting light and shadows. Percival sidled up beside Montgomery, with a large double glass of Glenfiddich in his hand. There was no sign of disappointment in his pale-blue, watery eyes, which instead seemed to harbour a satisfied twinkle. Before Percival could utter a word of recrimination, Montgomery put up his hand as if in apology and said: 'Please don't say I told you so, Major.'

Percival laughed, threw back the whiskey in one gulp, smacked his lips and said with levity. 'Better luck next time, Major, if there'll be a next time.'

Montgomery shrugged and took off his cap and wearily rubbed his hand through his slicked back hair. 'This thing could go on for years. We could subdue these fellows on the one hand but this damned rebellion will keep breaking out like an ulcer on the other, until we're sucked into a quagmire that will drain our resources, our economy and our power.'

Colonel Hudson, standing nearby, nodded in agreement: 'Our resources are stretched to breaking point all over Europe and the Middle East. Ireland really is the straw that can break the camel's back.'

'What are you suggesting Colonel?' asked Percival almost with a sneer. 'That we sue for peace?'

'We've been sending out feelers for a truce for some time now,' said Hudson. 'I think our politicians should prevaricate no longer.'

'That may be your way of thinking,' said Percival coldly, 'but I agree with Mr Churchill. The sun never sets on the British Empire and while I draw breath it won't. Good day to you gentlemen.'

He saluted and strode across the room and out through the huge doors with the air of a man who'd been scorned and was now vindicated. There would be no more shilly-shallying as far as he was concerned.

One sunny Sunday morning in early June, before the roses graced the longest day, young Matt Donovan set out to hunt the brakes and burrens around Quarries Cross with his two harrier hounds, his horn, and his fiddle strapped in a leather satchel on his back. The sun was already high and hot and Matt had a song in his heart. He was dressed in a dark pants and waistcoat and a clean white shirt his mother had taken from the clothes line. He sported a cloth cap on his fair-haired head. The dogs ran on ahead and soon nosed their way into thickets of yellow-blossomed furze from where a fox was rousted. The chase began with yelpings, and the thrashing sounds of the heavy feet of dogs and the lighter scamper of the fox, racing off across fields and streams. Matt followed along a high, ridge road, from where he could hear the faltering wails of the dogs as they lost the scent of their more astute quarry and eventually sloped back towards him, mud-spattered, sad-eyed, their tails low down. He could see the undulating country all around and nearby, an industrious farmer working in his hayfield. It seemed another glorious summer stretching long and fine before him. His companions these days were few. Old school friends like Sonny Hennessy, the Hollands and the Foleys were long since on the run from the Black and Tans and so was his brother Maurice, who was rarely home. Matt helped his parents on the farm and sometimes his neighbours also, milking and ploughing and driving the cattle to the fair. The country was in turmoil and the burden of the daily chores fell to younger men like himself and other neighbours like Tull Hennessy, whom Matt met earlier that morning at Mass in Ballycummin. They agreed to rendezvous later in the evening at a pattern crossroads where they'd entertain the dancers; he on his fiddle and Tull on his melodeon. Sunday was rest day for most good country swains. By late afternoon the dogs had followed many trails and down at the creamery crossroads, as the sun was sinking in the west, Matt met Tull who'd arrived for the dancing session with his melodeon slung across his back, and a pair of pigskin shoes that would make him lighter and faster on his feet. They talked for an hour, leaning on a gate going into a meadow. They spoke of hunting and of hurling and of the likely crowd expected before sunset at the timber platform on the far side of the creamery building, set back a little from the road, under the shading trees. Far down the meadow the hardworking George Swanton, who stopped for neither priest nor minister nor tolling service bell, was working with a heavy horse and wheel rake, putting order on his swathes of new-mown hay. They saw the absorbed Swanton, sitting high on a metal seat, pulling the hay into long, clustered lines. He stepped on a pedal every now and then to activate a cog in the wheel of the rake and the tines reared up. Then he immediately pulled on a rope to again release the cog and drop the tines once more to resume the gathering. With this job finished, he'd come along the day after with a two-prong pike to arrange the hay into rounded cocks to be left to dry out under the sun for a further week before being drawn into the haggard for the winter. Sometimes Matt and Tull would give him a day's labour if the weather looked like breaking. Your neighbour in the country was your most important ally.

'George is a hard worker,' said Matt.

'He doesn't stop at all, keeps going day and night,' said Tull.

'He'll leave it all behind him in the end, like the rest of us,' said Matt, philosophical beyond his years.

'They're hard workers these Protestants,' said Tull. 'Sometimes I think we could take a leaf out of their book.'

'No chance George will shake a leg at the pattern,' smiled Matt.

'God help us, no,' said Tull. 'Nor lower a pint in Sullivan's pub neither.'

'No matter,' said the wise-headed Matt. 'We shouldn't judge him. His way is as good as ours'.

'That's a fact,' said Tull and turned to walk back towards the platform across the road. 'Come on,' he said, 'we'll set up a few chairs and you can tune that fiddle before the crowds arrive.'

By dusk they'd expect the country girls in their summer dresses and the young men in their polished boots to arrive in numbers and their laughter would linger far into the evening, as the music rose into the perfumed air and the stars came out and shone down the long, green valleys to the sound of skipping feet.

Matt had nearly finished turning the pegs of his fiddle when he heard a commotion at the far side of the creamery. 'The dancers are arriving early,' he said.

Tull was standing on the end of the platform holding his melodeon strapped to the front of his chest, his fingers straying hesitantly across the keys. 'No dancers,' he said and his hands dropped off the keyboard.

'Who then?' asked Matt as Tull kept standing, his back suddenly rigid. Matt got up from the chair on which he sat and walked across the platform to see what Tull could see. A grey military truck turned through the crossroads, followed slowly by another. Then a line of soldiers with rifles at the ready hove into view, and then a longer line of maybe forty men in shirts and waistcoats, with their hands holding up their trousers at the waist. Some were bare-headed, some wore caps or hats and some were in their stockinged feet. They looked a sorry sight, surrounded as they were on every side by further outriders on motorcycles and horseback.

'Company halt,' shouted a sergeant's voice. The soldiers and the bedraggled line of men stopped. They stood sweating, like a chain gang from a prison, as the evening flies buzzed about their eyes, and a cloud of steam rose off them into the rays of the evening sun. Major Percival, a sergeant and six soldiers with rifles presented, alighted from the first lorry and walked slowly down the hundred yards from the crossroads. They stopped in front of the two young men on the platform.

'Good evening, gentlemen,' said Percival disarmingly. 'Getting ready for a dance are we?'

'We are,' said Tull.

'Expecting a crowd?' continued Percival.

'The usual,' said Tull.

'And how many is that?'

'Maybe thirty or forty.'

'I see,' said Percival, climbing the two steps up to the platform. 'And tell me, is this a regular occurrence?'

'Most Sunday nights, in the summer anyway,' said Matt, nervously moving his thumb across the smooth butt of the fiddle.

Percival observed the instruments and the chairs. 'You are aware that it is illegal to congregate in numbers greater than six,' he said.

'Sure we're only having a little harmless fun.' said Tull. 'It's an old custom.'

'Harmless fun indeed,' said Percival. 'How many times have I heard that expression before? There's nothing harmless in this country as far as I'm concerned.'

He turned and pointed back towards the group of prisoners. 'Do you see that group of men holding their trousers up with their hands? We've arrested them in a sweep from Bantry to Macroom, and every able-bodied man whom we suspect of being a subversive will join their ranks. We're on a long march to Kinsale military barracks and in the course of that march there will be no escape. Why you may ask? Because a man can only reach full speed running with the use of both his arms free. We've taken their belts and braces so if they attempt to make off, their britches will fall down and they'll fall over. Quite an ingenious little trick don't you think?'

The two young men nodded, slightly bemused at Percival's eccentric need to boast about the most insignificant details. Percival continued: 'Major Montgomery has been hoodwinked by your brethren in the IRA, but unfortunately for them their scouts and supporters such as these fine fellows will no longer be around to aid and abet them. Not only have we arrested them, but we've burnt their houses down along with their crops and tossed their families out on the road. That will quickly knock the enthusiasm for revolution out of them. Don't you agree?'

The two young men nodded and said nothing.

'Who are you?' asked Percival of Tull.

'Tull Hennessy.'

'Look that name up,' said Percival to the sergeant who held a dog-eared notebook.

'And you?' His eyes rested on Matt.

'Matt Donovan.'

Percival and the sergeant had a whispered conversation as they bent over the notebook. Eventually Percival straightened up. 'Hennessy,' he said. 'You come from a long line of rebels. We've encountered you before. In fact, if I remember rightly, we burned you out last Christmas. As for you, Mr. Donovan, we have your brother noted down here as a notorious Shinner; one of our most wanted men in this area.'

He paused and walked around the two men, who stood straight and looked ahead. 'What do you say to that?'

'You must be mistaken,' said Matt. 'My brother is a farmer. He's never handled a gun in his life.'

'Very amusing, Mr. Donovan. Very amusing.'

Percival had a grin on his lips, but no laughter reached his eyes. 'Can you play those instruments? Or are they just for appearances to hide more sinister instruments, if you get my meaning?'

'We can,' said Tull.

'Play us a tune then.'

'What would you like to hear?' asked Tull, a great reluctance on him to oblige and doubting the sincerity of his audience to appreciate his compositions.

'You choose,' said Percival and went and sat on one of the chairs. The soldiers on the road below leant on the muzzles of their rifles with the stocks on the ground. Their faces carried amused, sarcastic looks.

Tull looked at Matt, who shrugged himself into a playing mode, putting the butt of his fiddle under his chin. Tull played a few notes of *The Boys of Blue Hill*. He stopped, faltering, and waited for Matt to commence. Matt took up the tune and gritted out some further notes with the bow. Then Tull followed on and soon they were running into a rhythm, which progressed into a chorus and then they were quickly into the hornpipe. Matt stomped out the beat on the timber decking with his right foot. The soldiers' cynical expressions turned to grins of amusement as the tune rose and dipped, careering along at a clinking spin. When they'd played the chorus again twice, Tull, with a nod of his head indicated a change to Matt, and they cruised seamlessly into *The Bucks Of Oranmore*. As the patterns became more complex and the beat surged and rippled, the sergeant standing beside Percival began to click his fingers and a few howls and cheers came from the soldiers below who started to relax, appreciating the virtuosity of the playing. Tull urged the squeeze box into different angles to his body and his fingers were blurs on the keys; his right hand tripping up and down the treble, his left hand regular on the bass. Matt's fiddle wailed and cried, its notes shimmying in the still evening air. When they finished there was a burst of spontaneous applause from the soldiery, who'd been prepared to scoff, but recognised good music when they heard it. Tull left the melodeon hanging from the leather belt around his neck and rubbed his sweating palms along the flanks of his trousers. He was puffing from the effort. Matt smiled with a kind of angelic innocence at the sight of the clapping soldiers.

Tull looked hesitantly at Percival, who said: 'Carry on, I'm enjoying this.'

Tull took up the first notes of *Lament for Limerick* and a strange hush descended on the soldiers, as if a cold fog had suddenly changed the complexion of the bright summer's day. As the notes climbed and drifted, Matt's fiddle embarked on the secondary motif, in counterpoint to Tull's elegaic lead and the solemn, sad melody stole up the valley over the lines of captured men, who shuffled on their weary feet and bowed their heads as if in involuntary prayer. The jeering soldiers assumed an almost reverential pose in the presence of such atavistic music that seemed to flow up from somewhere deep in the rocks of this ancient land, in which they'd never fully understood or felt at ease. The song spoke of an aching and a sorrow that no words could adequately describe. When Tull put the squeeze box down and Matt had wheedled the last dying notes out of the fiddle there was a silence. Then the gurgling of a nearby stream rose louder to the ear and rooks flying homeward broke the spell with their grating calls.

Percival finally stood and looked to the distance like a man recalling a memory. He straightened his peaked cap and patted the lapels of his tunic. Then he said matter of factly to the two men: 'Stand over against that creamery wall.'

As Tull climbed down from the platform he noticed a malevolent glint in the eye of one of the soldiers and a dreadful foreboding overtook him.

'Run Matt, run,' he shouted to his friend, dropping his melodeon on the road where it lay reverberating in a minor key, slowing the responses of the mesmerised soldiers. That moment was all the time that Tull required and he was gone over the nine-bar gate of Swanton's hayfield with an athletic leap, racing over the descending night dews as if there were wings attached to his lightly-shod feet. Though bullets ploughed and gouged the earth around him, Tull had got first run, and his zig-zagging gait among the haycocks made him a difficult target. In seconds he was gone out of sight into the sheltering trees of Swantons' farmyard. Matt's face still carried the innocent, beatific smile which first acknowledged the soldiers' applause, and as he stood alone against the creamery wall his heart leaped up in fleeting joy at the sight of his friend escaping in the gloaming. He seemed oblivious to the danger he was in. The sergeant, at a nod from Percival, beckoned to three of the six soldiers who were not firing after Tull, to come across the road, where they stood about thirty feet back from him and raised their rifles. Matt looked up the road to where the captured men stood with collective breath held, in anticipation of further horrors. He recognised

Charlie Browne, an old acquaintance from the harrier drag hunt and gave a little wave in his direction like a child might, under the admiring gaze of attentive adults. Matt still smiled out upon the world and the setting sun cast a golden beam of light which seemed to illuminate no face but his. Then there was a clicking of Lee Enfield bolts being pulled back as the three soldiers under Percival's command pressed the triggers. Matt's blood showered out in crimson red and flowed down the front of his newly pressed shirt, and spattered down the whitewashed creamery wall, as his body crumpled to the ground. His cap fell sideways to reveal his curled, yellow-haloed hair and his blood continued to slowly drip onto the frets of the fiddle that lay mute and tuneless at his side.

22

the seneschal

F rancis Bernard, the Earl of Bandon, shook hands with Doctor James Baldwin at the front door of his castellated pile and watched as his afternoon guest descended the steps a little uncertainly and pointed his face in a westerly direction. The Earl smiled as his occasional acquaintance, of whom his wife seriously disapproved, eventually gained momentum to his gait and was up to full speed by the time he reached the crested portal that guarded his demesne. His wife was away for the day and he'd taken the opportunity to spend a very pleasant afternoon with the Doctor, quaffing champagne and some wickedly expensive Bordeaux, as they listened to a number of .78 shellac recordings on his gramophone, including one by a very fine Irish tenor called John McCormack. It was midsummer's day, and the Earl and the Doctor had sat out on the front lawn under the great spreading beech trees. They discussed a wide range of topics, from history to astronomy, the opera, horseracing, and hurling which the Earl much admired. But very little politics. They both knew that particular subject could be combustible because of their conflicting views on the Irish question, so they avoided it. The Doctor was an ardent nationalist, while the Earl believed that *"patriotism was the last refuge of the scoundrel."* He had the luxury of such detachment of course, insulated as he was from the vagaries of misfortune and economic deprivation. In any event, why get oneself all hot and bothered in one direction when there were any number of themes on which they were *ad idem?* The Doctor had introduced him to the pleasure of listening to the lovely lyric tenor voice of McCormack, who could sing the great arias of La Boheme or La Traviata with facility, but whose especial gift in the Earl's opinion was his rendering of Moore's soft Irish melodies. The conversation had eventually turned to the subject of the welfare of the voluptuous Eleanore Eustace, and the Earl was particularly pleased to learn that her return to the southwest was imminent. There followed a little ribbing by the Earl about the Doctor's reputed courting of the lovely lady and the cuckolding of her deceased husband, but the Doctor assured him that this chapter of his life was closed and his contact with Eleanore was now purely platonic. The Earl was happy to hear of this though he wasn't quite sure if he could fully believe it. But in any event it would leave the way clear for himself to make an excursion to the Eustace estate in the near future, secure in the knowledge that he wouldn't be cutting the Doctor's grass in that department, so to speak. When the well-oiled Doctor had disappeared from view, he turned back inside with a spring in his septuagenarian step, humming the words of *Off To Philadelphia*, along with McCormack, as the song floated from the library, down the enormous long, high corridor, towards the exquisite stained glass window glittering at the end, designed by Sir Richard Morrison:

"With me bundle on me shoulder
Sure there's no one could be bolder,
I'm leaving now the spot where I was born in."

Nimbly the Earl turned right to go out through the huge, round vestibule that gave onto the garden where he could see Joseph O'Mahony, the man he called his 'seneschal': steward, butler, valet, rolled into one, gathering up the trays of glasses and the remains of his *al fresco* afternoons with the Doctor:

"For I've lately took a notion
For to cross the briney ocean
And I'm off to Philadelphia in the morning."

He was fairly skipping as he greeted the steward, who looked up, surprised, when he heard his master singing the words in his out-of-tune but debonair baritone.

'Ah, Joseph, my dear chap,' said the Earl. 'Thank you for clearing up. I would have done it myself you know.'

The Earl and his lady had an army of maids, cleaning men, gardeners and general dogs' bodies to cater for their every whim and so this admission came as somewhat of a surprise to the steward, who noted his unusually high spirits. 'I'm glad to see you in such good form, sir. I didn't know you favoured the melodies of our native land.'

'Oh, for goodness sake, Joseph,' said the Earl ebulliently, 'There's far too much made of all that foreign *cnamhshawling* by Verdi and those other French frogs, as my dear old mother used to say. Wasn't I born here? Why wouldn't I love the songs of dear old Ireland.'

'Born here, and Irish when it suited,' thought the phlegmatic steward. 'But not really one of us.'

Forever cut off from intercourse with the mainstream, in his ivory tower, with his impenetrable aristocratic accent, which he used as a defensive shield, but which he was quite capable of forsaking in favour of a lilting brogue as the occasion demanded. Joseph might have been more forgiving if the man wasn't so parsimonious. Despite his enormous wealth, it proved a marathon requiring persistence and stamina to prise even the most modest increase in wages out of him for his hardworking staff, who survived on subsistence rations for the most part. Yet he could spend six months a year travelling from London, to Switzerland and the Riviera, while people like Joseph kept his vast estate in working order. But that kind of thing rankled increasingly from year to year.

Joseph suspected that it was a different kind of intercourse altogether which now preoccupied the Earl and which accounted for his high spirits. As they went back inside, the Earl stood in front of a long mirror in the hall adorned with gold-leaved filigree and patted his stomach inside his waistcoat: 'Tell me Joseph,' he said, 'Do you think I look my age? I am seventy you know.'

'You don't look a day past fifty, my lord,' said the steward, adept, after years of practice, at flattering his master and gauging his moods.

'Oh, you divil you,' said the Earl, in exaggerated tones. 'Would you be after trying to butter me up now?'

Joseph gave an imperceptible snort as he pushed the trolley of dirty dishes down the corridor towards the kitchen in the west wing. No man was a hero to his butler. Then the Earl called after him, normal communication restored: 'Don't forget we're expecting his honour Sealy King, JP, for dinner tonight.'

'Very good, sir,' Joseph called back over his shoulder and kept going. For a moment Lord Bandon watched his retreating back and then his mind's eye turned to the altogether more pleasing image of Eleanore Eustace's haunches as they might be outlined in silhouette underneath a sensuous, satin gown, gliding seductively towards him.

He had to blink at the sudden rush of adrenaline coursing through his loins.

Sonny Hennessy left the Flying Column at its billets in the mountain fastness near the lake of Gougane Barra on the evening of the summer solstice. He rode a bicycle and he had a very important message to deliver to Sean Hales, the commander of the Bandon battalion, thirty miles away. Before he left, Tom Barry had called him over to a small table on the shores of the lake, where he sat, in deep conversation with Liam Deasy and some of the other section leaders.

'Sonny,' he said, 'I have an important assignment for you.'

'Yes Commandant,' replied Sonny.

'I want you to cycle to Skeaf and tell 'Buckshot' Hales to arrest Lord Bandon.'

'Lord Bandon?' Sonny paused for a moment.

'Yes, Lord Bandon. Tell 'Buckshot' to take him to a safe house near Kilbrittain and to also detain any other important figure in Bandon's company. He'll have to use his own judgement in that.'

'Very good, Commandant,' said Sonny and heaved a sigh. He knew the stakes they were now playing for were very high indeed.

'I want you to start right away and report back to me. It's thirty miles each way and you have four hours to do it.'

Sonny didn't hesitate. He leaped on his bicycle and pedalled eastward. 'Sixty miles of dirt road,' he thought, 'and four hours to travel it.' He'd have to make a superhuman effort and be lucky as well.

The evening sun cast long shadows on the roads that snaked out before him. He left the muscular mountain ranges where the cliffs were high and jagged, twisted into fantastic shapes aeons ago. Sheep clung to high strips of pasture between slashing rocks. Hooded crows and ravens flew homeward to deep woods and clusters of starlings swooped in ever-changing patterns against the sun's rays. Falcons hovered on draughts of rising air. The higher ridges began to level out the further on he travelled. Sometimes he'd glimpse vistas of the sea between indentations and devil's bits of land. Out there past Owenahincha and Inchydoney, was the bellowing wave of Cliona, rolling inwards to the Virgin Mary's Banks, where his youthful eyes first beheld the intense blue seas of childhood. Round, green hills like a bulwark on that southern horizon kept back that mythical wave, and then the land curved down in multicoloured patterns: deep green of grass and growing wheat, yellow of gorse and rapeseed, to the wide flood-plains of the Bandon river as it made its final majestic progress to Kinsale. As he crested a hill somewhere east of Dunmanway a full moon rose low in the eastern sky like a golden orange. He could hear the humming of the bicycle tyres on the road, his own steady breathing and the rhythm of his heart. He went down lanes and side roads few but he would know. Sometimes he'd pass a farmhouse and an alert sheepdog might chase him down the road, lunging for his ankles. If soothing words would not placate the dog, an expertly placed kick would suffice to put manners on the cur. He paused for neither friend nor stranger, his head bent low and his eyes upon the road. Exactly two hours after he left Gougane, he was freewheeling down the high hill of Skeaf towards a house in the valley where he knew Hales and his battalion would be waiting. He jumped off his bicycle and delivered his breathless message to the laconic 'Buckshot,' who immediately assembled his most trusted men, Denis Lordan, Jim O'Mahony and Sonny's brother Mike. Together with five others they set off northwards across the country towards the small village of Old Chapel, to come in on Lord Bandon from the blind side. Sonny swallowed a cup of tea and two slices of brown soda bread, and struck out west on his long and tortuous return journey. At the stroke of midnight, with ten minutes of his alloted time to spare, he was back at the little 5th century church and oratory on the small island in the middle of the lake, where the Flying Column boys were resting among headstones and urns, more than fifteen hundred years old. The golden orange moon of earlier had now become a silver apple overhead.

Sealy King, Justice of the Peace eased his long, thin frame into a well-upholstered coaster in the huge dining room of Castle Bernard. He adjusted the spotted bow tie at his throat, and grasping fork and cutting shears, he started into the plate of oysters, poached in their own juices in a delicate *beurre blanc* sauce, which had been delivered by a waiter to the table. On his right flank, Lady Bandon, a light-boned woman, was nibbling on some lark's wings, while at the head of the table, Lord Bandon who had plumped for the crab *au gratin*, was well into his mastications. Directly opposite the JP, his wife, a horse-faced lady of formidable build and a direct way of speaking, was savouring her dish of escalopes of monkfish with roasted peppers in a white wine sauce. The dishes came one after another and they demolished two bottles of Chateau de La Negly Coteaux du Languedoc, followed by a change to a Grenache from the Southern Rhone with overtones of fruit and white pepper. They were comfortable in each other's company. Ladies and gentlemen of standing, who, because of the intimacy of the occasion, felt uninhibited about venting their opinions on whatever subject came up. While it was mostly related to gossip and inquiries as to who might be seeing whom in the constricted, but elite social circles in which they moved both in Cork and in London, Sealy King, a good raconteur, had eventually turned to tales of derring-do and narrow escapes which he'd experienced in the course of his long career as a judge. He was finishing up a story about a particular incident in Skibbereen where the fates were surely on his side.

'...and there I was back in my hotel, the one where the railway tracks pass behind the Ilen river. It was a Friday in the winter as I recall and I'd put down a heavy day at the Assizes. I'd dispatched quite a few of those Sinn Féin buggers to Pentonville and Maryborough, so I suppose they weren't too pleased with me. So there I was back in my hotel room getting ready to throw my head down for the night. It was my third night in a row staying there. I was about to embark upon my usual routine of opening the window, when a maid came in and did the job for me.'

'How so?' asked Bandon.

'She opened the window for me, and found herself pointing straight into two ugly-looking pistols trained on her. She gave the most blood-curdling scream I've ever heard in my life and fainted on the floor. I turned in consternation and heard these two IRA men clattering across the railway tracks outside the window and jumping down onto the street. Now, by some act of divine providence I escaped that night, because if I'd opened the window myself as I normally did, I wouldn't be sitting here tonight.'

'Did you ever find out who tried to kill you?'

'I never did for sure, but I subsequently heard from a sergeant of the RIC that it was their two top men who'd come to get me: Tom Barry and Charlie Hurley.'

'Well at least our forces dispatched that fellow Hurley at Crossbarry,' said Lord Bandon, 'though I'm sorry to say Barry and his fellow travellers are still on the loose.'

There was a pause and a sudden change in the mood.

'I'm afraid he is,' said King.

Nobody spoke until Lady Bandon said: 'What's going to happen, do you think? I mean on the Irish question generally?'

Sealy King was grave. He sighed. 'It's balanced on a knife edge I'm told. Our forces have been making heavy weather of it in the field against them. Half the British cabinet, including Lloyd George, are in favour of a truce, while Churchill, Balfour, Greenwood, Wilson and the rest are dead against it. What do you think yourself, Francis?'

The Earl, who hated discussing politics, considered the question, pursed his lips and said finally: 'I'm afraid I'm on the side of my cousin, the Earl of Midleton. I think the writing is on the wall.'

Lady Bandon was taken aback. 'I never thought I'd hear you say those words, Francis,' she said.

'There it is,' said the Earl and looked around as Joseph O'Mahony came in with a fresh bottle of the Earl's best claret and refilled their glasses.

'Thank you, Joseph,' said the Earl. 'Now after you've locked up will you see to it that our honourable friends are made comfortable. They'll be staying the night in the west wing.'

'Very good, my lord,' said Joseph and went out. He went down the long corridor to the very end, where he went into the conservatory. He went to the outer door, but instead of sliding the bolt across to lock it, he left it on the latch. About half an hour later, after brandy and cigars, the Earl and the Justice of the Peace repaired to the library to discuss some matters of minor consequence relating to legal procedures, and had a night cap. The ladies had already retired to their bedrooms and the two gentlemen followed them up the winding stairs, swaying gently like old trees in the wind.

Moonlight shone bright as day. All was magical across the wooded landscape in Castle Bernard's huge demesne. Blood horses bent to drink the cool, bright waters of the slow, wide river and saw their own reflections and the high moon swimming in the languid pools below. A dog barked at a slinking fox off to the south, where the wide fields sloped down to the Old Chapel road. There was no wind. The scented smell of new-mown hay permeated the air well after midnight. It was a night for dreaming.

Nine men entered at a gate from the Old Chapel road in an opening of a ten foot high wall, constructed in the 17th century to keep native interlopers out and protect the new incumbents, who came from England with armies, seizing the land by pillage, fire and sword. The men did not go straight across the fields but went along by the shadowed wall. When the wall turned at a right angle, so did the men, and proceeded in such furtive but deliberate fashion. Their feet swished through the dewy grass and their boots were quite damp when they stopped on an eminence at the highest point of the long, wide fields, used for coursing hares and greyhounds in the sporting season. They could see below them the winding, silver river and the ghostly castle with its turrets and chimneys rising like some Camelot in the woods, heavy with summer leaves.

'There it is,' Hales said and stood breathing. His certain heart was beating calm and steady in the moon.

'Will there be sentries?' asked Mike Hennessy, and fingered his Colt .45, snug inside his trenchcoat.

'Not tonight,' said Hales. 'Joseph sent the word.'

'What about the hounds?' asked Jim O'Mahony.

'Fed to the gills with veal and venison. They wouldn't hunt a fox tonight if it came and lay down in their kennels, much less us.'

Their shadows followed them as they went swiftly through woods of oak, ash, beech and whitebeam. When they came to the walled, cobbled farmyard, there was no howl of dogs. They slipped across a clearing by the garden where the aroma of campanelas and violas was fragrant, contrasting with the pungent smell of horse manure from the stables, where Irish draught horses stood sleeping on their feet. They passed an older tower on the western side, built when the land was the clan O'Mahony's. Hales and four men went around to the front side of the newer edifice and climbed the steps up to the huge front door. Hales had a sledgehammer in case the communications of earlier hadn't been fully understood. Another man stood guard about the farmyard, while two more stood at either end of the enormous castle, guarding the approach avenues. Denis Lordan came in towards the large, round conservatory from the lawn and pushed the door left open by the 'seneschal,' Joseph O'Mahony. He tip-toed gingerly across the hardwood parquet conservatory floor and went through another door that led him into a vast, long hall with twenty foot ceilings, where wall lights dimly burned. He trod on carpets from Persia, Afghanistan, and Turkey: royal blue ground with stylized flowers on wide, brick borders. His grass-slicked boots smudged pictorial Herati rugs and ornately patterned Persian runners. He kept his head down, like a man almost afraid to behold splendours the like of which he'd never seen and did not imagine could exist. He reached the front door and slid the bolt to allow the others in. They stood as men transfixed for some minutes and tried to take in their surroundings. They wandered from room to enormous room, gazing at paintings and wall hangings, running their astounded fingers over smooth and beautiful bookcases, Regency mahogany chairs, side tables, hall seats, low boys and armchairs. Everywhere they looked they saw evidence of the amassing of a great fortune. Everything garlanded, adorned, gilded with more ornaments and *objets d'art* than a man would require for ten lifetimes never mind one. And for what purpose? None apparently, other than for him to sit and admire them as a reflection of his accomplishments, his status and his vanity. But deep in their hearts they knew they were, in spite of themselves, the butts of that specific display, which was intended to proclaim the ascendancy of the Anglo-Irish aristocracy and intimidate the natives.

Sean Hales called them into a circle after they had traversed the length and breadth of the mighty building without encountering a solitary human being, either master or servant. They waited for him to speak, which he eventually did in a low, but definite murmur. 'Well, boys, we haven't found Lord Bandon and since the bird has flown, we'll burn the nest.'

'Burn the nest?' asked an appalled Mike Hennessy.

'What problem do you have with that, Mike?' asked Hales with a grim smile.

Mike quickly composed himself and shrugged: 'Oh, nothing, except it's... well, it's so...beautiful.'

Hales looked around at his men. They were uneasy as if about to do something profane. He said, 'Beauty is a luxury Lord Bandon can afford, but we can't. Either we win this war or we allow the British to win. They have burned our people out of small-holdings and cottages, without a hint of mercy or remorse. Fear will beat the British, nothing else.'

They nodded in agreement and then started to pile the furniture in the middle of the floor.

In the old O'Mahony tower, Lord Bandon turned over in his bed and muttered in his sleep. His wife heard his incoherent moaning and thought she heard words of doom and sorrow.

She nudged him in his sleep and he sat up.

'What?' he asked in panic, momentarily caught for breath.

'You were talking in your sleep, my dear,' she said.

'What did I say?'

'You said the house is falling.'

'I was having a nightmare,' he said, and lay back down.

Then a servant burst into the room and shouted: 'Fire! The house is on fire!'

Lord Bandon blinked, then shot up in bed again and managed to throw his legs over onto the floor. He sat scratching, trying to collect his thoughts. His head was still groggy from liquor. Lady Bandon went to the door in her nightdress where she saw the servants rushing along the corridors. The smell of burning drifted up the stairs, followed by wisps of black smoke. The servants had already roused Sealy King and his wife. They looked lost and bewildered as they were ushered down the stairs, half dressed. Lady Bandon ran back inside the bedroom and helped her husband into his clothes. As he fumbled for his cravat she lost patience. 'The house is burning. Come on, you foolish man.'

Years of subordinate frustration were suddenly vented. The Earl looked startled. Befuddled, he stood and followed her like a man still dreaming. They reached the landing above the great staircase. They started down and as they did, four armed men leaped up the steps, two at a time, towards them.

'Are you Lord Bandon?' asked Sean Hales, as smoke swirled around them.

At the mention of his name, the Earl seemed to regain his dignity. He straightened himself and assumed a haughty posture. 'I am,' he said. 'Who the devil are you?'

'I'm the officer commanding the Bandon battalion of the Irish Republican Army.'

The Earl was truculent. 'I don't recognise any such military organisation.'

'Whether you do or not is immaterial,' said Hales, coldly. 'My orders are to arrest you and take you out of here, pending further instructions.'

The Earl was blustering, looking around him for support. There was none except from his frantic wife, whom he ignored. 'Joseph,' he shouted. 'Joseph come here at once and deal with these fellows.'

His voice rang through the cavernous reaches of the great building.

'I'm afraid you'll call in vain for Joseph,' said Hales grimly.

'Why?' asked the Earl. 'Have you shot him?'

His demeanour slowly changed from one of bravado and arrogance, to one of resignation. He was led meekly down through ash and smoke, and flames that were beginning to take hold in a grand conflagration. The dusty drapes and curtains were devoured in seconds. Then the flames attacked cornices and ceilings and oak floors. No sooner had the Earl come down, than the flames licked up around the stringers, risers and balusters of the sweeping mahogany staircase. Splinters cracked and flew like bursts of gunfire. The fire ripped through the interconnecting rooms: drawingroom, diningroom, ballroom and morning room. It jumped the corridor and Morrison's magnificent stained-glass masterpiece shattered in jagged shards all around the floor. On it raced through vestibule, library, kitchen and servants' quarters. It was sucked down to the vaulted basement, where the Earl's choicest Bordeaux vintages were lovingly laid down. It was vacuumed up to the third floor attics. There was the sour smell of burning carpets and the loud crackling of dry floorboards being consumed. Soon the flames were attacking rafters, crossbeams, bargeboards and soffits. They insinuated their way out through narrow portcullises and Romanesque windows, leaping up from the highest turrets. In a surprisingly short time the rafters started to collapse and the slated roof to crumble down through the floors.

The many servants ran around panic-stricken, without direction or purpose, waiting in vain for the steady voice of Joseph O'Mahony to tell them what to do. But Joseph, who'd laboured for Lord Bandon, man and boy for thirty years, had heard another call. In a final ironic gesture before joining the Brigade, he'd left the gramophone playing in the drawingroom, and as the inferno raged all around, the sweet lyric tenor voice of John McCormack rose in a bizarre reprise above all else like a grand, macabre opera:

> *"And some day I'll take a notion,*
> *To come back across the ocean*
> *When I start for Philadelphia in the morning."*

McCormack's velvet voice hit the last high note in a great sob and then dropped away in a dying, heartbreaking fall, before the shellac melted in the heat.

The full moon still hung in the western sky over Laravoulta, Ahilina, Shannawaddra. The flames of burning Castle Bernard reddened the pre-dawn skies until the rising sun of June eclipsed all other light, and all traces and accoutrements of a dynasty built up over four hundred years. And as the British soldiers arrived in convoys of Lancia armoured cars and Crossley tenders, all they were greeted by were the blazing eyes of the unbridled horses, escaping from the stables and thundering over the wide manicured lawns, sending clods of earth skywards from underneath their pounding hooves. Lady Bandon and the Honourable Mrs King stood like pale revenants on the verdant lawn, in their blackened nightgowns, as servants wandered in mute incoherence around them, wringing their hands in despair. The fire raged and roared and would continue to smoulder for the next several weeks, until only a shell remained, forlorn and hideous. But there would be no trace left of a lordly life and no vestige of a grand design that rose and held sway along the pleasant Bandon river from the time of the Battle of Kinsale.

Of Lord Bandon and the Honourable Sealy King there was no account. Hales and his men led them, like compliant sheep, out past the yew and hornbeam trees as the dawn chorus of blackbirds, thrushes, rooks and jackdaws swelled, chattering in the morning. By the time it had risen to a crescendo they were away southwards by the sea.

23

For most of June fires blazed across the countryside, in a game of tit for tat. The Black and Tans destroyed the safe houses of the O'Mahonys of Belrose and Kellehers of Crowhill. The Essex Regiment with the help of the vigilantes of the Protestant Action Group razed to the ground the homes of Sean Hales in Knocknacurra and Michael Collins in Sam's Cross. The IRA destroyed the loyalist houses of Colonel Peacock, Colonel Stephenson, Brigadier-General Caulfield, and Dennehys and Stennings near Inishannon. In the far west, Dunboy Castle went up in smoke, and so did the Skibbereen Courthouse. The Allin Institute and the Workhouse in Bandon were burned under the noses of the three British garrisons in the town, and no patrol ventured forth to stem the blaze or tackle the Volunteers. The coastguard stations at Howe's Strand, Galley Head and Rosscarbery were gutted and so were the Workhouses at Dunmanway, Schull and Skibbereen. Many important judges and notaries were taken hostage. If the British Army Maintenance Engineers required suitable acccomodation for their troop reinforcements, they would look in vain, and in pursuing the war they would pay dearly in terms of property, treasure and manpower.

But it was the arrest and burning out of Lord Bandon that caused the greatest shock waves to ripple throughout the United Kindom of Great Britain and Ireland. When the news broke there were frantic consultations between Major-General Strickland and his top officers in Cork. They'd detained a number of IRA suspects who were in prison awaiting a sentence of death and only the grim details of the time and place of execution were left to be confirmed. But the spine-chilling message they received from Lord Bandon was that he would get the first bullet if any further Irishmen were shot, and that if any more Irish households were burned by the Tans, there would be a multiple of loyalist properties destroyed in retaliation. Tom Barry had visited the Earl at the secret farmhouse destination to where he'd been taken near Clogach, a mere six miles from Castle Bernard. He made him aware in no uncertain terms that his fate was balanced on a knife edge.

There was much hand wringing and cries of indignation among the leaders of the British administration in Dublin, such as General Macready, Major-General Tudor and Colonel Winter, but they were obliged to defer to their political masters in London, where the dissembling of Lloyd George with de Valera came to an abrupt end. The endless prevarications were terminated. The game was over. It was clear that the IRA had called his bluff and it was difficult for the Prime Minister to envisage a graceful resolution to the conflict unless he took decisive and far-reaching action. Lloyd George summoned his brilliant assistant, Lionel Curtis, and dictated a letter to de Valera, inviting him to immediately discuss the terms of a truce which the British were prepared to enter into forthwith, the only condition being that the Earl of Bandon, Sealy King and any other agents of British power in Ireland be immediately released unharmed.

The offer took de Valera by surprise. Only a few days previously he'd been unceremoniously arrested by the British authorities and now, here he was, being courted by the most powerful politician on the face of the earth as if he commanded an army and resources of equal standing. The tail had truly wagged the dog.

The letter read:

From Mr. Lloyd George to Mr. de Valera
                                          "June 24th, 1921
"Sir,
"The British Government are deeply anxious that, as far as they can assure it, the King's appeal for reconciliation in Ireland shall not have been made in vain. Rather than allow another opportunity of settlement in Ireland to be cast aside, they felt it incumbent upon them to make a final appeal, in the spirit of the King's words, for a Conference between themselves and the representatives of Southern Ireland and Northern Ireland.

I write, therefore, to convey the following invitation to you, as the chosen leader of the great majority in Southern Ireland, and to Sir James Craig, the Premier of Northern Ireland:-

That you should attend a conference here in London, in company with Sir James Craig, to explore to the utmost the possibility of a settlement. That you should bring with you for the purpose any colleagues whom you select. The Government will, of course, give a safe conduct to all who may be chosen to participate in the conference.

We make this invitation with a fervent desire to end the ruinous conflict which has for centuries divided Ireland, and embittered the relations of the peoples of the two islands, who ought to live in neighbourly harmony with each other, and whose co-operation would mean so much, not only to the Empire, but to humanity. We wish that no endeavour should be lacking on our part to realise the King's prayer, and we ask you to meet us, as we will meet you, in the spirit of conciliation, for which his Majesty appealed."

> *I am, Sir,*
> *Your obedient servant,*
> *D.Lloyd George*

De Valera replied that he too earnestly desired to bring about a lasting peace but could see no avenue by which it could be realised if Britain continued to deny Ireland's essential unity. But therein lay the crux. The loyalists of the northern part of Ireland wanted no truck with republicans, and had persuaded the British to introduce the Government of Ireland Act, 1920, which was to divide the country into two parts. Nevertheless, a temporary truce and exploratory talks were worth a try. Without warning, the truce was officially announced on the 4th of July, 1921, to come into effect a week later on the 11th of July.

There was a mixture of joy, suspicion and frustration throughout Ireland. In Ballymakeera the bombastic Murphy Deirbh bought drinks on the house in Scannal's bar and proclaimed: 'We bate the British into the sea.'

In Bandon, when he read the terms in the Cork Examiner, Doctor James Baldwin, far from considering it a victory, surmised that the British were playing for time to carry on the war by other means.

In Dublin, Michael Collins's suspicions were equally aroused, when, a number of weeks later he discovered through his espionage system, that the British authorities were secretly carrying out a head count of all the able-bodied young men in every town in Ireland. To what purpose? To be in a position to make a quick roundup in the event of the truce talks breaking down? Probably.

'It's a start,' said Madeleine Cody. 'And at least all that dreadful killing will be at an end. The girls can go back to school.'

'Never trust John Bull,' said Doctor Baldwin, as he read out the terms over breakfast in the large family kitchen:

' "No incoming troops, RIC or Auxiliaries, no displays of armed forces, no pursuit of Irish officers or men, war material or military sources, etcetera, etcetera ..." '

'That sounds positive,' said Margie. 'And what do the Irish have to do?'

Doctor Baldwin looked back at the newspaper and summarised:

' "Attacks on Crown forces and civilians to cease, no interference with British Government or private property, and so on, and so on..." '

'That's a big step,' said Thomas Cody. 'Never before in the history of the Anglo-Irish conflict since the Treaty of Limerick and '98, have the British accepted anything in victory only unconditional surrender, followed by the massacre of the Irish leaders.'

'That's because the Irish haven't been defeated,' said Margie, proud in her youthful certainty.

Her mother looked away, and shook her head. 'Don't be talking about victories and defeats. It's a start and a hopeful one, after two and a half years of murder and mayhem. I hope that unfortunate Lord Bandon will be released, safe and sound now.'

'What's so unfortunate about him? He had it good for long enough,' said the Doctor.

'That's a bit rich coming from you,' said Cody. 'And you supping at his table and drinking his whiskey.'

'What does that prove?' asked the Doctor, indignantly. 'We always met at levels. We have a lot in common except in the matter of Irish independence, and on that score I never, ever conceded anything.'

'He's a reasonable enough fellow,' said Cody. 'Not the worst of them by a long shot.'

'I'm as sorry for his misfortune as the next man,' said Baldwin. 'But when you put yourself up as the King of England's chief representative for Cork and County, you have to take the rough with the smooth.'

Margie sniggered: 'I hear he's become a model prisoner.'

'What do you know about him?' asked Madeleine, sharply.

'I heard people talking. I heard he plays cards with his guards and tells them to shush when the British Forces are near, in case he's shot.'

'Who told you that?' asked Cody.

'Ask Anna,' said Margie. 'She heard it first from Sonny Hennessy.'

Anna gave her sister a dirty look.

Cody stood up and said: 'A fine way you're spending your time away from your books, running around with those fellows. Mark my words, they will come to a sticky end yet. You're better off away from them.'

'Didn't they just kick out the British,' said Anna defiantly.

'You have a lot to learn, my girl.' said Cody as he took his cap. 'Sure what do you know at seventeen?'

'I know a good man when I see one,' said Anna.

Cody scoffed, and walked out.

Doctor Baldwin looked towards Anna with sympathetic eyes. 'Never mind your father,' he said. 'He's only fearful for your future. Young Hennessy is a good lad. Very mature and responsible for his years. You won't go wrong with him.'

'Oh, for God's sake, James,' said Madeleine. 'Don't be putting ideas into her head. She'll be going back to school in Dublin in September and that will be that.'

Anna looked reproachfully at Margie for giving away her secret.

There was singing in the streets. Shots of celebration were fired in the air. Sonny and an IRA group met a lorry load of Black and Tans coming towards them on a road one day. They looked ominous as they approached, until it became obvious that their rifles were turned backwards. The soldiers saluted in mock deference and the IRA raised their fists in the air. But there was no resort to violence. Both sides claimed victory but in reality what they had was stalemate. They'd fought each other to a standstill.

Sonny and Mike went home to their family. Jeremiah opened a bottle of his best *poitin,* and they drank a toast. Elizabeth was relieved to have her brothers home safe and sound. Richie tended his cattle and his horses and Tull fed his pigs and played his melodeon, battered, but still in tune.

There were small kindnesses. One afternoon, a small, frail lady, the Honourable Albina Broderick, a cousin of Lord Bandon, and sister of the Earl of Midleton, knocked on the door of a young woman named Anna Hurley, in the townland of Tinker's Cross. Anna was a staunch member of Cumann Na mBan. Her visitor was tired and weak and she explained that she had walked the whole way from Bandon, looking to find Tom Barry and the Flying Column, to intercede for the safety of her cousin. A few months before, Anna Hurley's brother, Frank, had been shot in the back in cold blood by the Black and Tans and his body thrown in the undergrowth of Castle Bernard. She had no reason to give succour to a stranger who stood for everything she had fought against. But the good-hearted Anna invited the frail lady into her home and gave her a reviving cup of tea. Then she arranged for a horse and trap to convey her all the way to the fastnesses of West Cork near Glengariff, where Barry and the Flying Column were waiting for the next move in the great chess game to be played. Barry politely listened to her pleas and promised they would be fairly and carefully considered.

And there were farcical absurdities in the midst of war and peace. The Earl of Bandon was plied with the best of food, brandy and whiskey during the weeks of his incarceration. He conversed amiably with his captors and learned that the people of West Cork were humane and generous, and not without a sense of humour. One evening as the Essex Regiment encircled the farmhouse where he was being held, there was panic. The men guarding the Earl were obliged to make a run for safety, but the woman of the house was more resourceful. She quickly donned a nightdress and hastily urged the willing Earl into the double bed beside her, where they went through the faux ritual of lovemaking, as the soldiers crowded into the bedroom. On seeing the couple in virtual *flagrante delicto*, they hastily withdrew, uttering embarrassed apologies for disturbing the man of the house in the carrying out of his conjugal duties. The Earl was released shortly afterwards, a sadder yet wiser man. Deracinated, humiliated, but alive, unharmed, and with a greater understanding of his neighbours in West Cork than he had learned in seventy years living amongst them in his castle.

The summer passed and there was hope. In September the girls went back to the Loreto Convent and resumed acquaintances with their school companions. Their brother, William, was well advanced in his studies and had continued despite the years of war to follow his own star. Anna wrote more letters to Sonny, who had settled back at home in relative peace, but with responsibilities as a liaison officer reporting with Tom Barry. Their function was to attempt to enforce the terms of the Truce and to protect people and property from being molested by overenthusiastic "Trucileers," the name given to many men who'd never fired a shot in anger at the Black and Tans, but now, when the danger seemed past, were full of bravado. The British military stayed confined to barracks, but there were the inevitable skirmishes which thankfully were not considered serious enough to warrant a resumption of war. For the moment.

Margie was preoccupied with following the progress of de Valera's published exchange of letters with the British Prime Minister, Lloyd George, whom he'd already met briefly in July, with little success. It appeared the British were not prepared to enter full negotiations if the Irish held themselves out as representing a Republic. They would not concede such a crucial point. Eventually de Valera fudged the issue and agreed to send envoys to London to see what could be achieved, regardless. The envoys were to report back to Dáil Eireann before signing any final agreement. Arthur Griffith led the delegation. Michael Collins was also persuaded to go by de Valera, who, much to the surprise of many, did not go himself.

PART THREE

24

ship of fools

I t was a cold night in early December in the year 1921. A steamer was sailing out of the port of Dublin into heavy seas. On a metal deck seat, muffled against the cold, sat two men, well dressed in greatcoats and dark, three-piece suits with high wing collars and dark thin ties. They both wore trilby hats upon their heads and moustaches on their upper lips. The older man was ample of girth and might have been fifty years of age. His face had stress lines and he looked like a bank manager with worries on his mind. This was Arthur Griffith, the founder of Sinn Féin and the Minister of Foreign Affairs in the self-proclaimed Government of Dáil Eireann. The other man was Michael Collins, the Minister of Finance, twenty years younger, tall and powerfully built, and he, like his companion, carried the brooding dark of the troubled waves reflected in his eyes. Silently they watched the lights of the city receding, from Howth and Clontarf in the north, around the sweep of Dublin Bay, to Ringsend, Blackrock and Dun Laoghaire in the south. Ahead, somewhere in the blackness were the high, misty mountains of Wales. Dawn would see them bound on a train to London from the bleak little port of Holyhead.

Collins eventually stood and walked to the railing. He looked down for some minutes at the foamy wake of the steamer. He blew warmth upon cold fingers and eventually spoke low out of the side of his mouth so that his companion strained to hear.

'I can't understand why he didn't come himself.'

'What did you say, Michael?' asked Griffith, putting his hand to his ear against the wind.

'I said why the blazes didn't he come himself?'

'Dev?'

'Who else?' asked Collins. 'You might be a suitable debater, Arthur, but I'm not equipped for negotiating with a slippery customer like Lloyd George. What am I? I'm a man used to dealing in shadows, in smoky backrooms with a revolver in my pocket. Why didn't the Jesuitical so-and-so come himself?'

Griffith stood and moved a little shakily towards the railing, bracing himself against the swell. He kept one hand on his hat to keep it from blowing away.

'My sentiments entirely, dear boy,' he said and paused. 'Duty bade me come, but tell me, why did you agree?'

Collins looked away towards the fading lights and said: 'For the same reason as yourself, Arthur. For Ireland. If not we, then who?'

'For the much vaunted Republic,' said Griffith, wryly.

'Fat chance of that,' said Collins almost bitterly. 'Sure you yourself don't even believe in it.'

Griffith sighed and nodded in agreement. 'As I said to Dan Breen, "I'm a King, Lords and Commons man, Dan. And you are a Republican."'

'You're a poet as well,' said Collins, mirthlessly.

'What do you mean?' asked Griffith.

'That rhymes.'

'What rhymes?'

'The words you said to Dan Breen. They rhyme.'

Griffith gave a dry chuckle. 'They do don't they, come to think of it. But you know what I mean, Michael. Young men like yourself and Dan Breen will settle for nothing less than a Republic. My ideas wouldn't suit your age. And yet ironically here I am leading the delegation negotiating with the British to bring that same Republic about, while our great President and schemer-in-chief sits at home in Dublin and instructs us to sort it out.'

'And report back to him at every step although he gave us plenipotentiary powers. I'm sick to death of all this. There's no end to it.'

They'd been in London for most of the past two months, trying to reach agreement with the British on the terms of a Treaty to be signed between the two nations. But it had become a game of snakes and ladders. The British would suggest a proposal and the Irish would counter propose. They'd make progress on one point: defence perhaps, or finance, or the use of the Irish ports by the British, only to fall back in the other direction on the question of the Oath to the King or the status of the six counties. De Valera proposed external association within the Commonwealth of Nations; Lloyd George insisted on absolute loyalty to the Empire, while at the same time holding in reserve, like an ace up his sleeve, the threat of the resumption of war and the reconquest of Ireland. They were negotiating with a gun to their heads.

Just now they were on their return journey having spent the previous day in furious debate in Dublin with the other members of the cabinet: de Valera, Austin Stack and Cathal Brugha, with Childers like a hissing cobra on one side, having also persuaded his cousin Barton to his way of thinking. On the other side, Collins, Griffith and Eamonn Duggan, with the lukewarm lawyer, George Gavan Duffy, somewhere in the middle. They'd put the latest British document to their colleagues, who'd rejected it and put their own proposals. They were now more confused than ever and weren't even quite sure anymore what their instructions actually were. Some of the other junior ministers, W.T. Cosgrave and Kevin O'Higgins, had also put their heads around the door jamb, but they were essentially ineffectual yes men. Collins had to agree with de Valera's description of Cosgrave as, "That damned altar boy;" so insignificant as to be nearly invisible. And O'Higgins, all puffed up and preening, like a barnyard cockerel. He'd have to keep an eye on that fellow.

Childers and Barton were now on another steamer, in sulky rumination, keeping their distance from colleagues, with the entirely fraught situation compounded by Griffith's loathing of the apostate Englishman. The cracks in the hitherto united Sinn Féin party were beginning to show.

Collins turned and looked back towards the receding shoreline, distant in the dark. How different the two countries were; separated not only by the sea, but by a culture and a way of looking at the world. He thought he could detect the twinkling lights of the Grand Hotel in Greystones, where he and Kitty Kiernan had spent a last night of passion together before this mission began. Their interwined limbs, bound and harnessed to one another; kissing her lips, her eyes, her hair. He took out the small pocket watch she had given him as a memento before their engagement. He caressed his fingers across it. He touched it with his lips and he could still smell her perfume emanating from the smooth glass. When would the dark clouds disappear and this heavy burden of duty be gone? Duty, above and beyond the call, even to other

- 359 -

men, such as his visits to de Valera's family in that same town of Greystones, when the Long Fellow was away for a year and a half in America. Carrying small presents and tokens to Sinéad and the children on his bicycle. The long cycle out from Dublin each and every weekend. And to what end now?

A pessimism gripped his heart. What could he and Griffith do now that de Valera had failed to do last July, a week after the Truce came into operation? Lloyd George, the 'Welsh Wizard', scheming and dissembling. Churchill, bombastic, threatening, glowering. Birkenhead, at once charming and sarcastic, Austen Chamberlain, dull, dedicated, but unimaginative. And up in Ulster, James Craig, the most intransigent of all, unmoving and unmoved by the weekly pogroms against helpless Catholics being banished in their thousands by vengeful loyalist gangs. Waiting like a black widow spider for his adversaries in the South to make a false move. To seal their fates.

The black door of No. 10 Downing Street was not particularly impressive. It was narrow with a semi-circular fanlight above it and a single white step below it, surrounded by a modest brick front, with a black ironwork fence running up each side of the entrance. The number 10 was painted in white between the top and middle panels and below this was a knocker in the shape of a lion's head and a letterbox with the inscription "First Lord of the Treasury."

Unassuming was the word that first came to Collins's mind when he'd seen it eight weeks before, but on being shown into the most famous address in the United Kingdom he'd quickly changed his opinion. He would not forget that day as long as he lived. It was a Tuesday in October, the 11th as he recalled, at precisely eleven o'clock in the morning. He, Griffith and the other plenipotentiaries had arrived in taxis for a full session with all the members of their delegation and were greeted by a slim man with twinkling blue eyes, a huge walrus moustache and a high, domed forehead, with thinning, grey hair brushed back and side parted, foppishly. The Prime Minister, David Lloyd George, stepped back from the door into a black and white marbled entrance hall, with a Chippendale guard's chair sitting in one corner. He shook hands warmly with them one after the other and said, 'Come in gentlemen, come in. I trust you've had a pleasant journey and are not too tired. We've some hard work ahead of us.'

'We've had an easy passage,' said Griffith, 'but I fear the rough part is all ahead of us as you say.'

'Hard, but not rough,' laughed the Prime Minister. 'You can take it that the hatchet is buried and that you are among friends from now on.'

'Would that it were so,' said Griffith, to which the Prime Minister did not reply, but ushered them towards a triple stone staircase, with a wrought iron balustrade embellished with a scroll design and mahogany handrail. Engravings and photographs of past Prime Ministers, from Walpole to Pitt to Asquith, decorated the walls. They went through several interlinked rooms: the Pillared Room, the Terracotta Room and the White Drawing Room. They were vast in scope, some with Ionic pillars reaching from floor to ceiling and Persian carpets covering the floors. The huge State Dining Room had oak panelling and reeded mouldings with a vaulted ceiling that rose up to the floor above. Collins quickly realized that the house, unlike the front door, was enormous. The Prime Minister, who seemed anxious to impress them with a tour of the building, stopped before the Cabinet Room and Gavan Duffy said, 'It is much bigger inside than it looks from the outside.'

'Five hundred rooms,' said Lloyd George, nonchalantly.

'Five hundred,' mused Griffith.

'It is a vast, awkward house,' laughed the Prime Minister. 'William Pitt the Younger's words, not mine. It's built on a bog near the Thames and the foundations are constantly shifting. Originally three houses, it was built by a fellow called George Downing, whose portrait you may have observed inside the front door, and was completed in 1684. But he had to wait thirty years before building on it as some other obtuse fellow refused to relinquish a lease.'

'Nothing changes,' smiled Griffith, 'especially when it comes to land.'

'Prophetic words, Mr. Griffith,' said the Prime Minister. 'And for land you can substitute country, as in your own case.'

They nodded uneasily at the attempted humour.

'Who designed it?' asked Gavan Duffy, to breach the awkwardness.

'It was designed by Christopher Wren for so-called persons of honour and quality, and the first prime minister to occupy it was Sir Robert Walpole in the year 1735.'

'No place for the likes of us then,' laughed Collins with pointed irony. The half-in-jest remark broke the ice and the Prime Minister looked keenly at the man who had a price of 10,000 pounds sterling on his head three or four months before.

'On the contrary, Mr. Collins, there have been many colourful characters through here. In fact, if I'm not mistaken, Mr. Downing himself was a notorious spy for none other than Oliver Cromwell.'

'A name that to this day conjures up nightmares in every Irish heart,' said Collins.

'You mean Cromwell?'

'Indeed I do,' said Collins gravely.

'I am given to understand that Cromwell may not have been the most popular man in Ireland,' said the Prime Minister, 'but he is a hero to us British. He introduced democracy to our country and strengthened the role of the House of Commons immensely.'

'And he butchered men, women and children in Ireland without mercy until he reduced the population by nearly one third.'

There was a further pause for a moment, which now might be construed as a shocked silence, until Collins added dryly: 'What you see depends on where you're looking from.'

The Prime Minister shot him another keen look. This fellow had wit, he could see, and was not afraid to speak his mind. They had stopped in an anteroom where there was a huge map of the world on the wall, with the countries controlled by the British Empire outlined in red. Beside the map, Hendrick Danckert's painting of "The Palace of Whitehall" hung in another frame.

Lloyd George said: 'There we have it gentlemen, the British Empire in all her glory. Stretching from Ireland to India, from Africa to Canada.'

They stood in silence as the Prime Minister continued: 'We could use people of your undoubted talent to help us run this mighty enterprise. Why don't you come in with us and we'll run it together?'

Collins knew he was being flattered, but he had to admire the skill of the Welshman. He was a formidable opponent.

With adroitness the Prime Minister showed them to their places at the negotiating table which dominated the room, supported as it was on huge oak legs with carved mahogany chairs lined up for each member to take his place. Griffith as Chairman, in his jittery excitement, didn't notice that they weren't formally introduced to their British counterparts, who were already seated opposite them. One of the oldest tricks in the book: intimidate your rival by making him take the long walk to his place under the critical judgement of those already *in situ*. This also eliminated the embarrassment that might have been caused had they been obliged to shake hands with their counterparts when they came in. Hamar Greenwood in particular was a *béte noir* to the Irish and it had already been signalled by Collins that on no account would he be excused for his support of the Black and Tans. The Prime Minister formally introduced his team, who nodded superciliously as their names were called. Centuries of breeding and hauteur seemed to surround them like an aura. The names that rolled off the Prime Minister's tongue were like a roll call of every aristocratic family that had made the British Empire the mightiest in the world. He articulated the names with a singing declamation that rang up to the three brass chandeliers hanging from the high ceiling, and floated past the two pairs of Corinthian pillars, out through the enormous windows: 'Churchill, Chamberlain, Birkenhead, Worthington-Evans, Greenwood, Hewart....'

By the time Griffith got around to introducing his colleagues he already seemed to be apologising. And so the British had obtained a first, albeit minor, strike in their favour with barely a word exchanged. It was a signal lesson in the art of real political diplomacy that Collins and his colleagues had learned to their disquiet.

As Griffith embarked upon his laboured and tendentious opening statement, Collins became aware most eyes across the table invariably kept straying to himself. No doubt his reputation preceded him and to the considerably older British team he must have come across as something of a *rara avis.* Were they relieved not to find a grizzled monster with horn and cloven hoof, but an agreeable, smiling, well-disposed man who seemed rather youthful for the weight of expectation thrust upon him?

With his characteristic thoroughness, he had carried out his homework on them. Apart from the Prime Minister, he knew that Churchill and Birkenhead in particular were formidable imperialists and would defend the Empire with every fibre and instinct of their being. Both were already pushing fifty years of age, men of the world who were brought up with power and privilege and not easily intimidated. Churchill had seen action with the Admiralty, had established an Air Department and could fly his own plane. He'd commanded a battalion of the Royal Scots Fusiliers on the Western Front in the Great War, and was something of a scholar, artist and linguist.

Collins's intelligence network had established that Birkenhead was a powerful advocate, a *bon viveur* and, like Churchill, a heavy drinker. His family name was Smith, from Cheshire. He'd studied law at Oxford and was called to the Bar at Gray's Inn in 1899. He'd been Solicitor-General under Asquith and worked to secure the conviction and execution of the great-hearted Irish nationalist, Roger Casement. Collins knew that. He also knew that Smith was created Baron Birkenhead in 1919 and that he was often drunk in the street. Margot Asquith had said: "F.E. Smith is very clever, but sometimes his brains go to his head."

Having once beeen famously asked to give an opinion by a judge in a sodomy case as to what he ought to give a man who'd allowed himself to be buggered, he'd replied without hesitation: 'Oh, thirty shillings or two pounds, whatever you happen to have on you.'

Collins wasn't sure if the story was true or not, but it didn't deflect from the fact that if progress were to be made in these negotiations, Birkenhead was one of the principals to be won over. He might try to out-shine Collins with his wit and eloquence but Collins, with his forensic mind and prodigious memory might sway him in the long run. Several weeks later he was agreeably surprised to find that Birkenhead had conceived a particular liking and admiration for him, but that was not apparent on the first occasion they'd become acquainted.

As Collins surveyed the others while Griffith was speaking, he observed the clean-cut, handsome but somewhat plodding Austen Chamberlain, who'd a reputation for being a hard worker and an honest broker. As for Greenwood, Collins was already familiar with him from his days in Dublin. He considered him a clever bully and a braggart, but not somebody to be taken seriously. Of the other four, he knew that he and his "Envoys Plenipotentiary" would have their work cut out for them. Especially without the one man who could have matched any of them in brainpower and negotiating skills. The man with the great mathematician's brain who'd chosen to remain in Dublin: Eamon de Valera.

It had been a momentous two months. Most of the delegation were lodging in a tall, plain red-brick building at No. 22 Hans Place in Kensington, but Collins had chosen a different address at No. 15 Cadogan Gardens, a short distance away. This was another red-bricked Victorian house with bay windows and elaborate, white-painted brickwork at the arched entrance. He'd brought his own trusted men with him as bodyguards and assistants: Ned Broy, Tom Cullen, Liam Tobin and Emmet Dalton. He slept with a revolver under his pillow and one of his bodyguards in the room with him. Things were tense. At any moment the negotiations could break down and the safe passsage guaranteed them could be terminated. As a precaution he'd bought a Martinsyde Mk 111 aircraft, kept on standby at Croydon aerodrome, with two ex-RAF flying corps pilots, Jack McSweeney and Charlie Russell, designated to fly it in case a rapid escape was indicated. The constant breakdown of the Truce back at home didn't help and the British were particularly exercised over breaches. On one occasion he'd brought Tom Barry over to clarify points raised by the British regarding troop numbers and movements of ordnance. As Barry alighted from a taxi at the entrance to No.10 Downing Street, the wind blew back his trenchcoat to reveal two pistols underneath. At that same moment a photographer snapped his shutter and the armed guerrilla leader's picture adorned the front page of every newspaper in England the following morning. A furious Lloyd George took the matter up with Collins at their meeting and Collins laughed and threw his hands up:

'What of it?' he exclaimed. 'Aren't I armed myself.'

The Prime Minister paused, eyes like daggers for a moment. Then his face crinkled into a smile. He didn't insist on doing a search to verify Collins's boast. He wasn't sure if he could call his bluff. As for Collins, his one regret was that Barry wasn't a permanent member of the delegation. He wished he'd had a man like him at his side to face Lloyd George.

When they went into the meeting, Winston Churchill stood up and cleared his throat. With his great booming, solemn voice he read out a long list of the breaches of the Truce by the Irish. Collins was becoming irritated. He looked to his assistant, Emmet Dalton, and scribbled him a note while Churchill droned on. The note read:

'Have we any answer to these?'

'No we don't,' wrote Dalton, passing the note back. Collins listened for some further minutes and thought he'd better nip this speech in the bud. The Colonial Secretary was becoming dangerously animated. His jowly cheeks were turning red with indignation.

Collins suddenly banged the table with his fist and shouted: 'For Christ's sake come to the point!'

There was a stunned silence. The hairs stood on the back of the necks of the Irish delegation as they waited for the wrath of the Secretary to descend upon them. Before Churchill could gather his thoughts however, Collins burst out laughing. Then his adversary laughed too, in spite of himself. Collins had cut the ground from under his argument. Churchill sat down with a bemused look in his eye.

In between the hectic schedule of meetings and consultations there was little time for other matters. On a few occasions he went for dinner to the house of the painter, Sir John Lavery, at 5 Cromwell Place and the artist had painted his portrait. He went to Mass early every morning at Brompton Oratory, where he lit a candle for Kitty at the altar of the Sacred Heart. He also found time to visit old haunts from his days as a youth in London and to hold meetings with his brethren in the secret organisation of which he was head: the Irish Republican Brotherhood. As for Griffith, his main diversion and source of entertainment was to attend repeated showings of The Beggars Opera at the Lyric Theatre in Hammersmith. Every cripple had his own way of walking.

'They're split down the middle,' said Austen Chamberlain, his cold eye glittering behind his monocle. He seemed rather pleased with himself.

'To whom are you referring?' Lloyd George affected a puzzled air.

'Why, the Irish delegation of course,' said Chamberlain and walked towards the large fire in the Smoking Room in No. 10 Downing Street. He stood warming his long shanks and rattling the ice in his whiskey glass, taking the occasional sip through thin, aristocratic lips. The Prime Minister, sitting on a *chaise longue* across from him, looked sharply to his right, where Winston Churchill puffed on a long cigar. Lloyd George sat forward, narrowed his eyes and said: 'And tell me, Austen, how can you be so sure?'

'My spies tell me,' laughed Chamberlain and rocked back on his heels. He loosened the tie beneath his high collar and looked evenly at his superior in Government.

'Your spies?'

'Well, Basil Thomson's spies to be exact.'

'And who pray are they?'

'Any number of them. Disaffected Irishmen such as Tim Healy. International journalists like Carl Ackerman, to name but two.'

'And you think it's a good thing that they're divided?' asked the Prime Minister.

'Of course. It makes our job easier.'

'I'm not so sure of that,' said Lloyd George. 'If these fellows start squabbling we may not be able to reach agreement. And if we don't reach agreement our public will not forgive us.'

'You mean your public, Prime Minister.' said Chamberlain.

Lloyd George looked towards Churchill who was brooding, holding his own counsel.

'I mean our public,' said Lloyd George, gesturing towards his right. Churchill was in his own Liberal party, Chamberlain was with the Conservatives. They'd been in coalition since the middle of the Great War, but things were beginning to creak somewhat. Lloyd George had been all-powerful after the War, but that was over three years ago. There were rumblings from the unions because jobs were disappearing from the coalfields and steelworks that supplied the arms for fighting. He himself had been accused of accepting bribes for peerages. Scandals were rising around him. While he had Churchill he would be safe, but for how long could he depend upon him? If he could settle the Irish question it would be a major feather in his cap. He'd have to find a way. He stood up, walked to the drinks cabinet and poured himself a large measure. He walked back to the fire and stood beside Chamberlain projecting an air of forced camaraderie. But there was no love lost between them. It went back a long way to the Boer War, when, as a rising parliamentarian, he'd accused Chamberlain's family company, Kynochs Limited, of profiteering through favourable tenders accepted by the War Office. In recent years they'd learnt to work together to survive.

'We have to be united on this above all else, Austen.'

'But we are.'

'The Irish are not to be underestimated. They've fought us to a standstill. We will require all our ingenuity to get out of this with the Empire intact. If we let Ireland go, then India will be next, or Canada or Australia, or Egypt.'

'I think your fears are unfounded, Prime Minister,' said Churchill, from his armchair. 'In the last analysis we will always be able to go back to war.'

'But we've been at war with them for over two years.'

'Not serious war. You said we had murder by the throat, but you let it slip away.'

The Prime Minister turned sharply to face the Colonial Secretary.

'What are you recommending Winston? That we poison them with gas like you would the Iraqis? Sow, what did you call it, "A lively terror?"'

'What I'm saying, Prime Minister is that we've been fighting in Ireland with one hand tied behind our back.'

'With respect, Winston, you seriously misjudge the situation. The Americans would never stand for such strong-arm tactics. As it is, the Black and Tans besmirched our reputation quite badly.' Sometimes he could see a lunatic element in his Colonial Secretary.

'What you hold out is the threat,' said Churchill, 'if they will not see reason.'

'The threat?' asked Lloyd George and his face slowly changed as if a light had gone on in his head. He smiled broadly at Churchill. 'You may very well have a point there, Winston.'

At that moment the door opened and Birkenhead came in, removing his top hat, and blowing on cold fingers.

'Ah, Frederick, what news dear boy?'

Birkenhead came forward and Churchill pushed a glass of whiskey into his hand.

'The Irish are here.'

'Back from Ireland already?'

'Yes, but only three of them. There's no sign of Collins.'

'Really. That's odd. Are you sure?' asked the Prime Minister.

'Quite sure. I specifically asked Griffith. He said something about persuading the other two. It seems Collins may be persuaded already.'

Lloyd George straightened his waistcoat and pushed his tie up under his chin.

'Your charm must have worked on him, Frederick. Let's get to work on the others.'

'Surely Griffith is with us as well?' said Churchill.

'More or less,' said the Prime Minister. 'He wants the Ulster situation clarified.'

'But what about Craig?' asked Chamberlain.

'Craig can wait. 'Til hell freezes over if necessary,' said Lloyd George.

He waved to them to follow as he went down the corridor towards the Cabinet Room with something approaching a spring in his step.

'"I do solemnly swear true faith and allegiance to the Constitution of the Irish Free State to the Treaty of Association, and to recognise the King of Great Britain as Head of the Association."'

Arthur Griffith finished speaking and shuffled his papers. In the silence which followed his utterance, the sounds of the crinkling pages were like gunshots echoing off the high ceiling. Lloyd George's face looked like thunder.

'What's this?' he asked.

'Mr. de Valera's format for the free association of the Republic with the British Empire.'

'Mr. de Valera's format? What an exasperating man? First of all he doesn't come to talk directly to us himself and now his labyrinthine logic has concocted this. You're a reasonable man, Mr. Griffith, but dealing with your President is like trying to pick mercury up with a fork. The man is obsessed, with past grievances, the malignancy of Cromwell and the devil knows what else.'

'We're also under a strict imperative from the Dáil not to sign any final document until approved back in Dublin.'

The Prime Minister's optimistic mood of earlier disappeared instantly. Across from him sat Griffith, and beside him, the stubborn lawyer, Gavan Duffy, the independent-minded, landed aristocrat, Robert Barton, and his cousin, Erskine Childers. Two Catholics and two Protestants. The minority faith of Ireland was well represented at the highest levels. It didn't make dealing with them any easier. What a contradiction? Up in Ulster, Craig and his "Protestant Parliament for a Protestant People," while every second delegate from the South was a Protestant trying to secure a Republic? And the worst of all, the turncoat Englishman, Childers. What malaise was driving him?

'I thought we had an understanding,' said Lloyd George. He appeared wearily aggrieved. 'We've been talking for eight weeks. We've agreed on trade, on the ports, on defence, on your internal elections and taxation. You have independence on all those issues. Therefore the two remaining stumbling blocks are whether Ulster comes within a united Ireland and the Oath to the King. I cannot understand what is your difficulty in accepting the Oath, which Mr. de Valera's latest offering certainly is not?'

'Our difficulty,' said Duffy, 'is to come into the Empire looking at all that has happened in the past.'

'Good God,' sighed Lloyd George. He looked sideways towards his colleagues, who had very glum expressions on their faces. He turned back to Griffith. 'Does Mr. Collins concur with this?'

'You'll have to ask Mr. Collins that,' said Barton. The Prime Minister looked from one to the other, trying to find the weakness. There was none with Barton and Duffy. Griffith was unimaginative, but a stolid man of honour. He knew where he stood with him. But what of Collins? Were they playing a game of ducks and drakes with him? He'd have to find out. He stood up.

'You've gone back on everything we had agreed on. We're back to square one. You've broken on the Oath of Allegiance to the Crown. You realize this means war?'

'That is your call, sir,' said Griffith. He looked unhappy but resigned. Lloyd George stole a look towards Churchill. Their eyes met for a flicker of an instant and the Prime Minister hoped the Irish hadn't noted the imperceptible nod from the Colonial Secretary. He turned back to Griffith.

'I'll have to go to his Majesty, to tell him the talks have broken down.'

'We'll send a formal rejection tomorrow in that case,' said Griffith.

'Tomorrow is Tuesday, the 5th of December,' said the Prime Minister. 'Before your rejection is sent, make sure Mr. Collins is apprised of the situation.'

'Certainly,' said Griffith. He patted down his moustache and sniffed loudly through his nose. They rose and filed slowly out of the room. The British delegation remained seated. The Prime Minister turned to the others. 'What a sorry mess,' he said.

'On the contrary,' said Churchill. 'You played if perfectly. They'll be back.'

'You think so?'

'Undoubtedly, Griffith doesn't want war.'

'But Collins is the man,' said the Prime Minister. 'He's the one who controls them. I'll send Tom Jones around in the morning to try to persuade him. Meanwhile let them stew a bit overnight.'

There was a knocking on Michael Collins's bedroom door, at 15 Cadogan Gardens. Tom Cullen jumped up and looked at his watch. It was 5 a.m. He looked across at the sleeping form of Collins. He was surprised that the Big Fellow wasn't yet up. The constant travelling and talking must have worn him out. Cullen walked across the cold bedroom floor. He had a hand on the butt of his revolver as he opened the door. A porter stood outside with an apologetic look on his face.

'I'm terribly sorry to wake you, sir, but Mr. Jones, the Cabinet Secretary, wishes to see Mr. Collins urgently.'

Cullen went back and Collins sat up in bed. Cullen relayed the message. Collins swore and then jumped up. He hurriedly pulled on his clothes and grabbed his hat. He wouldn't have gone for many people, but he liked Jones, another Welshman. The man with "a thousand secrets." They took a cab to 10 Downing Street, through the damp, cold streets of London.

'We're in agreement on trade, on defence, but we're not in agreement on the North of Ireland or on the Oath to the King,' said Collins.

He was walking around the Cabinet Room with the assurance of a man who revelled in the machinations of the corridors of power. He turned to Lloyd George who sat at the long table, muffled against the early morning chill. Despite the constant stoking of the huge fire by a manservant, the ancient building refused to yield any warmth. Its curmudgeonly aspect seemed to reflect the parsimony of the Prime Minister, a man adept at squeezing the last shilling from his adversaries. Collins stopped and saw in him possibly a man who would go to any lengths to secure political advantage.

'What is Craig's answer on the North?' asked Collins.

'May I remind you, Mr. Collins,' replied the Prime Minister smoothly, 'that you yourself have agreed that the North will be forced economically to come in with the South.'

'Once the Boundary Commission has done its work,' said Collins. 'But are you guaranteeing us a Boundary Commission?'

'Most assuredly,' said the Prime Minister. 'It will be written into the Treaty. The Commission will go through Ulster, parish by parish, county by county. Those areas with a Catholic Nationalist majority will be allowed go with the South. Only those with a Protestant majority will cleave to the North.'

'By my reckoning that would only leave two, possibly three counties in the North. The rest all have Catholic majorities,' said Collins.

'Precisely,' said Lloyd George. 'How can two or three counties survive on their own?'

'Unless you gerrymander the boundaries of each county,' said Collins darkly.

'Why that's impossible, Mr Collins.'

Collins gave what could only be perceived as a snort of derision. Anything was possible with Mr. George.

'Alright,' said Collins eventually. 'I'll have to take your word on it.'

He walked back to the table, clapping himself around the chest with his arms to get warm.

'I don't understand your hurry?' he said. 'Couldn't we have waited 'til the sun came up? My brain doesn't work right when it's frozen over.'

'Sincere apologies, Mr. Collins. But I made a promise to Mr. Craig to deliver your answer by tonight. Besides I was given to understand that you yourself are always the first out of bed, and that your early morning wanderings are the bane of the lives of your compatriots, some of whom like to sleep late.'

'You've done your research on me,' said Collins, forced to laugh.

'As you have undoubtedly done on me,' replied the Prime Minister.

Collins stood looking down at his notes: 'Alright, what about the Oath?'

'What about it?'

'The form of the Oath concerns me greatly, as it does Mr. de Valera.'

'Oh really, Mr. de Valera, the master of casuistry.' Lloyd George was almost sneering.

'You're talking about giving us Dominion status, such as prevails in Canada?'

'I think that is very generous,' said Lloyd George.

The Prime Minister had his elbows on the table, touching his thumbs and fingers together. Collins noted the body language. This fellow was not being completely frank with him.

'The problem is,' said Collins, 'that the Dáil, or indeed the majority of the Irish people will never accept an Oath which proclaims such a Dominion.'

'But if the Oath does not proclaim it?' said Lloyd George.

'Then that is a different story,' conceded Collins.

'Although in practice a Dominion is what Ireland would be?' probed Lloyd George further.

'For the moment, yes,' said Collins, reluctantly.

The Prime Minister's eyes twinkled. His opponent took the long view of history. A pragmatic fellow like himself. He paused and cleared his throat. 'Well, Mr. Collins, I think we may have made some progress at last. We'll present to you at the next full session, a form of Oath, which I believe will be to your liking.'

'Any form of Oath to a King is not to my liking,' said Collins. 'I'm a Republican, first, last and always.'

'What I mean is a form of Oath that you can live with.'

'For the time being.'

'The time being is a matter of perception, Mr. Collins. For some the time being may be construed as, say, a week. For others it could be years.'

Collins smiled and nodded. Mr. George was a disciple of expediency, like himself. As they walked to the door the Prime Minister put his hand on the younger man's shoulder. 'Could I suggest the more civilised hour of 3 o'clock this afternoon for our final full session. Your brain will certainly have thawed out by then.'

Collins was more cheerful as he made his way back to meet his colleagues at Hans Place. As for the Prime Minister, he felt there was a decidedly more optimistic complexion to affairs. He had the door half open. One more push and he'd have them through it.

They met again at 3 p.m. Collins brought his entire team, including the secretaries, Childers, Chartres and Lynch. Across the table sat the familiar principals. There were also two British secretaries, Curtis and Jones. Hamar Greenwood came and went like an unwelcome guest at a party.

'Alright,' said Lloyd George, 'let's take the main three points, the Oath, the North and Defence. First the Oath. Frederick, can you read out the latest draft?'

Lord Birkenhead put on his glasses, cleared his throat and began in his most, solemn courtroom voice:

' " I do solemnly swear true faith and allegiance to the Constitution of the Irish Free State as by law established..." '

The Irish delegation strained to hear each line, and each man in turn pored over the individual copy provided in front of him.

Birkenhead continued: ' "And that I will be faithful to H.M.King George V, his heirs and successors by law, in virtue of the common citizenship of Ireland with Great Britain and her adherence to and membership of the group of nations forming the British Commonwealth of Nations." '

When Birkenhead stopped speaking there was a long silence. Lloyd George looked down the line of the Irish delegation looking for signs of unrest. Collins's face was not particularly happy, but neither was it turbulent. Griffith, he could see, was in a state of resignation, preoccupied perhaps with his own notion of being a jolly good fellow, a man of his word, a decent, upright citizen. A bank manager. He wouldn't last ten minutes in the British Cabinet.

But it was the spikey Childers whom the Prime Minister feared. He could see him in whispered, animated conversation with his cousin, Barton and with the truculent lawyer, Gavan Duffy. Childers then turned and whispered to Collins. His face was thunderous. He wasn't fooled by the British sleight of hand.

'There will be trouble with that fellow,' thought the Prime Minister, continuing to sit and wait, drumming his fingers on the table.

Griffith spoke up at last, though the fight had gone out of him. 'I'm afraid it's a far cry from de Valera's format which I read to you a few days ago.'

'Are you saying you are unhappy with it?' asked the Prime Minister.

'It's not myself but some of my colleagues who may be unhappy.'

'Which one? Surely not you, Mr. Collins? We have gone through this and met you fairly.'

'What about Craig?' asked Collins. 'I will answer only when Craig has replied.'

'I wish you had told me that earlier,' snapped Lloyd George, 'before the British Representatives had to face their die-hards.'

'I will accept inclusion in the Empire if Ulster comes in,' said Griffith, 'but I speak only for myself.'

'You have already accepted the alternative proposal if Ulster contracts out, sir.'

'Then in that case if you stand by the Boundary Commission, I stand by you,' said Griffith. He appeared to be confused. Did the man even know what he was saying?

Lloyd George noticed his dilemma. Keep pushing, he thought. A little more light through the door. Inch by inch. He stood up and produced two envelopes from his pocket. He held one in his left hand and one in his right. He declaimed dramatically: 'Is it a bargain between Sinn Féin and the British Government? I have to communicate with Sir James Craig tonight. Here are the alternative letters which I have prepared, one enclosing the Articles of Agreement reached by his Majesty's Government and yourselves, the other telling Sir James that the Sinn Féin representatives refuse to come within the Empire and that I have therefore, no proposals to make to him.'

The Prime Minister held up his right hand: 'If I send this second letter it is war - and war within three days, immediate and terrible. Which of the two letters am I to send? That is the question you have to decide.'

Winston Churchill stole an admiring glance at his Prime Minister. What a piece of theatre? The man was excelling himself. He looked at his watch. It was 7 p.m. Four hours had flown by like four minutes. He whispered to Lloyd George, who stood up again.

'I am reminded by Mr. Churchill that on this issue also depends the fate of this Government and you must also accept the obligation. Mr. Churchill and I are members of the Liberal Party. I need not remind you that if we fall, then you may be confronted by Mr. Bonar Law and the full spite of the Tories, who will be considerably less sympathetic to you and fully behind the Ulster Unionists. We shall adjourn now and we shall reconvene again before midnight, when I expect your answer in no uncertain terms.'

He walked to the door and shook hands with the Irish delegation, who filed out as if shell shocked.

Back in Hans Place, Erskine Childers had been haranguing the members of the Irish delegation for over an hour. He knew that Griffith and probably Collins had already made their minds up to sign. He hoped to sway some of the others. He continued, his voice rising urgently: 'You're tired, you're hurting and your country is broke. They know that. You're in awe of them and you're afraid to go back to war. They know that. But they're gambling. You can't see that, but I can. I'm one of them. I know how they think. After centuries of oppression you think they're better than you. You're mesmerised by them. But they are not better. The spirit that dared the Auxies and the Black and Tans, in Cork, in Dublin, in Longford, in Tipperary, that's the only thing they respect. The British are red in tooth and claw. Beneath the fatty tissue of their righteousness beats the hideous, imperial heart...'

He paused and Griffith cut in: 'We have Dominion status, like Canada, we have our own elections and taxation system. We have control of our own ports in peace time, the British Army will be gone...'

'Yes,' interrupted Childers, 'but what about the King? Will not all writs issued in Ireland still run in his name? Will you not pay to support him? Will you not still continue to pay land annuties to the British Government? And the army will be gone across the Irish Sea only. With the proximity of the two countries, they could be back within twenty four hours. No, you are back where you started. If you sign, all the past six years of struggle will have been in vain. Pearse and Connolly will have died in vain. All your great deeds, Mr. Collins, all your years of scheming, of organising? All in vain.'

Childers paused. He could see the pained expressions in their tired eyes. He would press on: 'And what about the North? Lloyd George says that he has to bring word to Craig tonight. Tonight? What nonsense. He would keep Craig waiting for years if it suited him. You have been out-manoeuvred with enormous skill and shrewdness by a man who knows that if you are not made to run, that you will jog along forever. But he is bluffing. As sure as I'm an Englishman, I can tell you he is bluffing.'

'I don't agree with you, Mr. Childers,' said Collins finally. 'We are guaranteed the Boundary Commission which will virtually ensure a United Ireland in no time. As for Mr. de Valera's external association and his document No. 2, pure semantics. It amounts to the same as what we're getting now, apart from a word or two here and there.'

He paused, sighed deeply and said: 'I'm going to sign.'

He stood up and reached for his hat. The other members of the delegation also stood and followed him like sheep to the slaughter.

Childers stood looking after them, his hands hanging helplessly by his side. 'You fools,' he shouted, as the door closed behind them. 'You hopeless fools.'

The Treaty was signed by all delegates at 2.10 a.m. on the 7th of December 1921. Lloyd George was surprised at how easy had been the Irish capitulation in the end. They forgot their instructions not to sign without consultation with Dublin, they even forgot the telephone, and they signed. They swore allegiance to King George V, they accepted the Partition of Ireland, they accepted Dominion status, they allowed the great strategic ports of Ireland to remain in British hands, fully manned with thousands of soldiers and sailors and naval warships. The list went on. They disregarded everything Childers had warned them against and they signed. It was as if their great battle for independence had been nothing but a charade of sound and fury. Afterwards, as they were offered a conciliatory drink, Birkenhead approached Collins in the anteroom beside the Cabinet Room and said: 'You did a very brave thing, Mr. Collins, and as for myself, I believe I may have signed my political death warrant.'

Collins took a long drink of whiskey and levelled a grave gaze at the man whom he'd come to like more than all the others. 'And you know, Lord Birkenhead, I may already have signed my actual death warrant.'

25

Margie Cody bought *The Irish Times* in a shop on Grafton Street in Dublin on the morning of the 7th of December. Underneath a headline that read "THE MEN WHO FRAMED THE SETTLEMENT," were seven headshots. Lloyd George, Churchill, Chamberlain and Birkenhead wore top hats and wing collars. Griffith, Collins and Barton wore trilbies and buttoned down shirts. The expressions on all faces were more wary and watchful than satisfied. More bemused than hopeful. Margie read every detail of every sub-paragraph, which carried captions such as: "FREE STATE OF IRELAND," "SURE AND CERTAIN HOPE," "WHAT NO PARTY COULD HAVE DONE," and "FEELING OF RELIEF IN DUBLIN."

Her youthful mind was confused. There would be an Oath to the King? A Governor-General appointed by the British Government? The Privy Council of the House of Lords would be the last court of appeal in the land? Britain retained the ports, Partition would be copperfastened except for some vague promise of a Boundary Commission to determine the final outline of the border. On the other hand, the twenty-six counties would have their own taxation system, their own members of parliament, their own courts, police and army. It seemed a mish-mash of conflicting directives. The more she read the more complex and ambiguous the wording became. All along the street people huddled in little excited groups and for most it came as a great and blessed relief. The fact that all the best information on the previous day led people to expect a decision the reverse of what had actually occurred, no doubt tended to increase the surprise. There would be peace at last. No more flames leaping at the window, no more jackboots on the stairs, no more mutilated bodies at the crossroads. Normal life could be resumed. For many people, probably the majority, that was sufficient. 'But then,' thought Margie, 'most people are sheep.'

Not everybody was so happy. Eamon de Valera, the President of the Dáil, was in the comfortable home of the O'Maras in Limerick when a telephone call came through. Richard Mulcahy, Chief of Staff of the IRA, took the call and relayed the information to the 'Chief.' De Valera refused to talk to the bearer of the news, Gearoid O'Sullivan from GHQ. Next morning when their entourage left on the train, the local papers were full of it. In a state of high indignation, the President returned to Dublin. The Treaty was signed without his consent and that was not a good thing. With Cathal Brugha, he sat in a carriage with Mrs Tom Clarke, the widow of the great patriot shot in 1916, and left Mulcahy and aide-de-campe, Michael Rynne, sitting on their own. The seeds of dissension had already been sown.

At 12 noon on the 8th of December, 1921, the Cabinet assembled in the Mansion House on Dawson Street. Griffith arrived in a horse-drawn hackney sidecar, Collins came in a Ford taxi-cab. They went up the steps into the old Georgian building under the elaborate wrought iron portico constructed to keep the rain off Queen Victoria for her visit to Dublin in 1900. The weather was no less inclement on this occasion. A cold sleet was falling. Overcoats, hats, and gloves were worn. In the long, narrow drawing room, de Valera, Stack and Brugha were already seated at a mahogany table, covered by a green table cloth, with files opened in front of them. One by one the other Members arrived.

Collins had a sudden sense of *deja vu,* recalling his first encounter with the British Cabinet two months previously. Beaten to the punch again?

'Good morning all,' he said with his usual cheerfulness, banging the small, black briefcase which he carried, on the table. If he was trying to break the icy glare on his President's face he did not succeed. There was barely a nod from the 'Chief,' who sat like a stern schoolmaster awaiting the arrival of his tardy class. W.T. Cosgrave tip-toed in behind Collins, followed by E.J Duggan, Robert Barton, Gavan Duffy and *The Bulletin* writers, Desmond Fitzgerald and Erskine Childers. Piaras Béaslai also showed up, along with Frank Gallagher and the gaunt, hungry-looking O'Higgins. De Valera's stony face softened for a moment as he motioned to Cosgrave to sit beside him. He was the man closest to him, who ran his errands, took him to lunch and arranged for his haircuts. He had a soft spot for the frail little man, who'd suffered a nervous breakdown after the Bloody Sunday massacre in Croke Park and who'd spent much of his time closeted with the Christian Brothers in Glencree, dressed in black soutane. He could rely on Cosgrave although he didn't have any great respect for his abilities.

Collins produced a copy of the Treaty from his briefcase. 'I presume you've read through this?' he said.

'Why should I have read it?' asked de Valera, his voice dry, deep and hollow as if dragged up from a sepulchre.

'Even the dogs on the street have read it at this stage,' said Collins. 'It's been published in every newspaper in Ireland and England.'

'Signed and published without my approval or consent,' said the President, 'or the approval or consent of Dáil Eireann.'

'Oh, well,' said Collins, 'that was the arrangement.'

'That's what Duggan said to me last night when he produced it from his inside pocket,' said the President peevishly. He breathed deeply through his long nose and in a tone of suppressed rage he continued. 'I was not consulted before this was signed. You know well, Michael, that was the agreement between us. I think this is an act of disloyalty to your President and to your colleagues in Cabinet without parallel in history. And you have made it a *fait accompli* by publishing it many hours before any of us have seen it.'

Collins levelled a steady gaze at the President. 'Don't you think that's a bit much. Unparalleled in history? In the first place, almost half the Cabinet was in the delegation. You yourself were urged umpteen times to lead it. You refused. Now you've already published a statement to the press that reads as if you're oppposed to the settlement.'

'And that's the way I intended it to be read,' said de Valera, coldly. 'I believe everything has been given away, without effort, without consultation and without permission.'

He placed his hands in an implacable gesture on the table and pursed his lips in a thin line.

Collins looked around at his colleagues. Griffith appeared too weary to argue. Robert Barton suddenly cleared his throat. He spoke in the carefully modulated tones of the Anglo-Irish aristocracy. 'Come, come, Mr. President,' he said, 'I have to reproach you. I believe you are going to extremes. In the first instance your own behaviour has given rise to this state of affairs, by your vacillation; by refusing to go to the talks. I'm not flattering you when I say that you were the best equipped of all of us to deal with the cunning stratagems of Mr. Lloyd George, and in not coming with us, you cast us adrift on the stormy waters of international intrigue.'

'A ship without its captain,' added Collins.

'A ship of fools,' interjected Childers, bitterly.

'But I had alternatives,' responded the President. 'I had a set of proposals to do with external association which would, I believe, have satisfied my more intransigent colleagues, such as Cathal and Austin here, but which would also have been acceptable to the British.'

Collins gave a contemptuous snort: 'Damned if I can see a ha'porth of difference between what we've got and your so-called document of external association, your document No. 2.'

Kevin O'Higgins leant his tall, bony frame into the proceedings. 'Gentlemen, gentlemen. I dislike this Treaty, as much as my President here. As much as Mr. Brugha and Mr. Stack, and as much as many of the IRA leaders, such as Tom Barry and Liam Lynch, who are already making subterranean moves to have it rejected with extremist support. I believe this Treaty should not have been signed, but the fact that it has been signed creates a situation in which unity among ourselves is imperative. Otherwise we will sow the seeds of dissent, which will be counterproductive and which will redound only to the benefit of the British and the Unionists in the North.'

De Valera stood and drew himself up to his full height. 'The terms of this agreement are in violent conflict with the wishes of the majority of this nation. I feel it my duty to inform you immediately that I cannot recommend the acceptance of it either to Dáil Eireann or to the country. In this attitude I am supported by the Minister of Home Affairs, Mr. Stack and the Minister of Defence, Mr. Brugha. He paused and looked over the rims of his glasses. 'So that there is no further confusion, I propose taking a vote on the acceptance of this Treaty right now amongst the members of the Cabinet, who apart from myself and my aforementioned colleagues, also include Mr. Collins, Mr. Griffith, Mr. Barton and Mr. Cosgrave. I might remind you, Mr. O'Higgins, that despite your enthusiasms, you are not a Cabinet member and therefore have no vote.'

O'Higgins shrugged. If the President wished to put him in his place he wasn't succeeding. 'What is your hurry?' he shouted. 'What is your haste? Why are you trying to split the greatest political movement, the solidest the world has ever seen?'

'Your knowledge of world history is limited,' said de Valera dryly, not even looking at O'Higgins. He smiled towards Cosgrave and said confidently: 'Now, can we have a show of hands please?'

'What are we voting on?' asked Griffith, mildly, as if no more than an observing spectator.

'We're voting to have this matter settled once and for all by the Cabinet.'

'Not by Dáil Eireann?' asked Collins incredulously. 'Wasn't it your own pronouncement that said only Dáil Eireann could ratify the Treaty?'

'And wasn't it you, Michael, who disobeyed that decree by signing the Treaty without the Dáil first seeing it?'

In the adjoining press room, Frank Gallagher and Desmond Fitzgerald could hear the voices rising louder. Gallagher smiled towards Carl Ackerman of the *Public Ledger* and said: 'A minor hiccup, I can assure you, Mr. Ackerman.'

Ackerman looked towards his fellow correspondent and sometime competitor, Hugh Martin, of the *Daily News* and raised a questioning eyebrow.

Back in the Cabinet Room all had voted except W.T. Cosgrave. The Cabinet was split fifty-fifty. Cosgrave had the casting vote. His face looked contorted. He looked from side to side, afraid to meet the penetrating eyes of his 'Chief,' who said, 'Well, William?'

Cosgrave apppeared to be struggling, mumbling like a man with a stutter. He finally looked beseechingly at the man he adored above all others. 'You put me in an impossible position, 'Chief.'

The stern schoolmaster voice cut across him: 'Well, Mr. Cosgrave?'

The frail man tweaked his moustache with trembling fingers, in nervous agitation. He exhaled: 'I...I can't do it Mr. President. I cannot vote with you. Let the Dáil be the final arbiter, not the seven of us here.'

De Valera's stern gaze changed from one of confidence, to scorn and then to one of acceptance.

'Is that your final word, William?'

'I'm afraid so,' said the other with a hoarse squeak. Beads of sweat stood out on his forehead.

The debate began in earnest on the 14th of December. They changed venues to the Council Chamber of University College Dublin at Earlsfort Terrace. The location was more impressive, a long, grey, stone building with Doric columns at the grand entrance. The Chair was taken by the Speaker, Dr. Eoin Mc Neill. Rev. Dr. Browne said the prayers and the Dáil Secretary, Diarmuid O'Hegarty, called the roll of Deputies, who numbered a hundred and twenty one in all. De Valera's saturnine presence dominated proceedings. He'd been leader of Sinn Féin for four years, the last great surviving leader of the 1916 Rebellion, the fountainhead of all recent Irish Nationalist aspirations. He was loved and respected by most. But what he was now proposing seemed destined to divide the Dáil and lead to great uncertainty. He leaped to his feet.

'The Dáil must consider this Treaty on its merits. The accidental division of the Cabinet, already known to you all, must not influence the further debate. Differences of opinion are inevitable, but my quarrel with the Plenipotentiaries is to have exceeded their instructions by signing without Dáil approval.'

His dry, precise voice carried to the furthest reaches of the chamber. Already there were hostile glares on the faces of some Deputies, nods of approval from others. There was genuine fear that all that had been fought for would be lost.

Griffith stood up and said: 'I deny that we exceeded our instructions.'

'You did not carry out your instructions,' responded de Valera.

'We simply signed on the understanding that each signatory would recommend the instrument to the Dáil,' said Collins. 'We did not commit the Dáil.'

The Speaker said: 'Can we press on gentlemen, we are re-hashing old arguments. Let us get to the nub of the matter.'

'The nub of the matter is that I have the perfect solution to all this,' said de Valera, waving a document in the air. 'I have here my alternative, which is the text of the Treaty already signed almost word for word, but without the Oath to the King, without the Governor-General and specifying that the legislative, executive and judicial authority of Ireland shall be derived solely from the people of Ireland, but that for purposes of common concern, Ireland shall be associated with the States of the British Commonwealth.'

'That is like offering a three-legged donkey instead of the four-legged specimen displayed at the fair,' laughed Griffith. There were grim smiles from the assembled Deputies. The majority did not vote for de Valera's new document. It seemed that Ireland would be half in and half out of the Empire. It did little to improve upon the document already signed.

De Valera withdrew his alternative and the debate resumed as to the merits of the Treaty itself. The arguments raged for thirteen days with a break for Christmas in between. Every Deputy spoke. The longer it lasted the more absurd and bitter the divisions became. All of the IRB were with Collins and Griffith; most of the IRA and all the women were with de Valera. The big farmers, the bankers, the businessmen and especially the Church were pro-Treaty. The small farmers, the men of no property and the men who had done most of the fighting against the British were vehemently opposed, and so were the women of Cumann Na mBan.

During the Christmas recess the arguments raged in public houses, at creamery crossroads, in churchyards and in households the length and breadth of Ireland. There were strong words from the pulpit from parish priests and bishops, urging the nation to promote the settlement. In the Cody household, the family, including Doctor Baldwin, had gathered from the four corners of Ireland. They sat at the solid, oak table and ate their Christmas dinner of turkey and ham.

'The women of the country are all against this Treaty,' Margie announced solemnly, as they finished their pudding before the evening light grew dim.

'Do we have to talk about it?' asked her irritated mother.

'If not us, then who?' demanded Margie in her certainties.

'What's that supposed to mean?' asked her mother.

'It's supposed to mean that we are educated people, with a serious interest in the outcome. For goodness sake, mother, do you always have to keep your head in the sand?'

Madeleine's eyes grew sad: 'It's easy for young girls to get carried away with passion and excitement, but when you get to my age you begin to wonder whether one is as good as another.'

'One what?'

'One form of Government, one system.'

'What nonsense,' said Margie, almost spilling her tea onto the lace-bordered tablecloth. She looked toward her father for a response. Thomas Cody was sitting back in cheerful mood, having partaken of a brandy or two after dinner. He surveyed the goings-on philosophically. William was sipping a glass of water and Doctor Baldwin was sitting on the hob near the stove, stoking the flames throught the hatch with a poker. He listened carefully, despite a cultivated expression of detachment on his face. Anna and Seamus were washing the dishes. Madeleine continued: 'You will find that most mothers of young soldiers will be in favour of this Treaty, whatever about the women you mention. Most ordinary women who have to raise a family want no further truck with disruption or violence.'

'And could you blame them?' said William, with studied maturity.

'What about Mrs Tom Clarke, Mrs Pearse, Mary McSwiney?' asked Margie. 'Those women suffered more than any, seeing their husbands and sons put to death. Yet they haven't yielded?'

'But there are others like Maud Gonne and Countess Markievicz, who make a virtue out of being firebrand revolutionaries, while remaining safe and unscathed in their upper class demesnes,' said William. 'The insurgency won't affect them.'

'It's not an insurgency,' said Margie indignantly. 'It's a revolution.'

William shrugged. 'Insurgency, revolution, whatever you want to call it. The results are the same.'

'Aping the British again, William,' said Margie. 'They'd like to call it an insurgency, like King George said to the Pope, implying a little restlessness among the subjects of his kingdom. De Valera quickly pointed out to the Pope that it was a great, popular revolution of the Irish people to establish their ancient nationhood once and for all, free forever from the shackles of the British Empire.'

Doctor Baldwin was finally moved to clear his throat. 'On the contrary, my dear William,' he said, 'my good friend Lord Bandon paid a heavy price. It certainly affected him. Margie is right. There is a great necessity to thrash this thing out. We need to know where we are going in this country, who's in and who's out.'

Doctor Baldwin's intervention was as much for Cody's benefit as for the others. He continued. 'The reality is that Britain, the invader, has for centuries imposed an Ascendancy of privileged people here, whose power has now been seriously diminished. The question is whether it is allowed to resurface under the guise of some superficial arrangement, or be smashed once and for all. I say the latter, and I am against the Treaty for that reason. It is a whitewash, not a liberation.'

'What do you propose to do about it?' asked Cody with a sardonic smile. 'Will you shoulder the pike and go back to war?'

'Only in self-defence,' said the Doctor.

'Sure who'd have you in their ranks?' asked Cody, his sarcasm increasing, but his temper even and mellow.

'It's not a question of me being in anybody's ranks,' said the Doctor, 'but I'm entitled to my opinion.'

'Whisht, will ye for goodness sake?' said Madeleine. 'We've had enough wild words.'

Anna listened, remaining stoic and aloof, but she knew she'd not be yielding either.

On Saturday the 7th January, 1922, Cathal Brugha arrived as usual at the University building at Earlsfort Terrace on a bicycle. He was hatted in a dark trilby, but only wore a longish, black body-coat rather than a great-coat, against the cold. His boots were highly polished. He was a neat, fastidious man, 47 years old, quite small and slim, with slicked-back, dark hair, thin lips, a pointed nose and blue eyes whose expression could alternate between humour and anger in fairly short order. He was the Minister of Defence in the Government of Dáil Eireann and this was not a position to be taken lightly. Previously he'd been Speaker of the Dáil and also Chief of Staff of the IRA. He intended to make his presence felt at today's debate. Things were coming to a head and he was going to be instrumental in the outcome.

Cathal Brugha was born Charles Burgess, in Dublin in 1874, to a Protestant father, Thomas Burgess, a cabinet maker, who was ostracised by his family for marrying a Catholic. Cathal was tenth of fourteen children and he attended the elite Jesuit, Belvedere College, near Parnell Square until he was aged sixteen, when his father lost his job. Thereafter young Charles was obliged to set up in business making candles for churches with the Lalor brothers, and he took to the road as a travelling salesman. He changed his name from the English to the Irish version when he joined the Gaelic League in 1899.

He was a brave man, of that there was no doubt. In the Easter Rebellion of 1916 he was blown up by a grenade and had also received multiple gunshot wounds. He was close to death, but clung tenaciously to life and made a miraculous recovery within a year, although scarred, and walking with a permament limp. He'd been a member of the secret Irish Republican Brotherhood, but disliked such underground organisations, and so formed the more transparent Irish Republican Army from an amalgamation of the Volunteers and the Irish Citizen Army. He was a serious man with a sense of duty and a high moral code. A man of honour, though some would say fanatical, with the unbending zeal of the evangeliser, like his party colleague, Erskine Childers. He was not for turning on the Treaty question and like his President, Eamon de Valera, and other senior cabinet colleague, Austin Stack, he was going to vote against it come hell or high water.

He hefted his high-handlebar bicycle up the steps of the University building and parked it against the wall. He undid his bicycle clips and when he straightened up he saluted a tall, elegant, athletic-looking man, with a handsome face and dark Celtic looks.

'Good morning, Austin.'

'Good morning, Cathal.'

Austin Stack spoke with the warm, rolling vowels of Kerry, but behind his smiling features lurked a will as stubborn as that of his Dublin compatriot. They were men of similar age, but Stack, unlike Brugha, had been blessed by the Gods, not only with the looks of a matinée idol but with the grace of a champion. He'd captained the great football players of Kerry to an All-Ireland victory in 1904 and his prowess was legendary in the southern county. He was imbued with the same selfless integrity and idealism as his colleague and both shared an antipathy to Michael Collins, whom they regarded perhaps with the wary eyes of middle-aged men towards a thrusting young rival. Was it a sense of jealousy that motivated them or was it something purer? Both were cut from the same cloth. Did they perceive in Collins, a man not only prepared to steal their thunder, but who had committed the unforgivable sin of compromising the sacred oath to the Republic by signing the Treaty with Britain? They walked inside the great hall of the building with a sense of bubbling anticipation that today was the day on which the Treaty would finally fall.

The fireworks started when Seamus Robinson, leader of the Soloheadbeg ambush in Tipperary, which had started the War of Independence, stood up. He was a fiery character. He directed his question towards Cathal Brugha.

'We've heard talk here from Mr. Griffith about Michael Collins being "the man who won the war." Can you tell us, Minister, what position Mr. Collins held in the IRA?'

'He was Director of Intelligence,' came the terse reply.

'Was he a brigade leader like Liam Lynch or Tom Barry, or Charlie Hurley?'

'He was not.'

'Was he ever an ordinary soldier in the IRA?'

'No.'

'Tell me, Minister, is there any evidence that Michael Collins ever fired a shot for Ireland, at an enemy of Ireland?'

'No, but he was very adept at getting others to do the firing for him.'

'And yet here we have this man leading the Plenipotentiaries in London, signing a Treaty without recourse to Dáil Eireann. Would you consider their actions to be treason?'

'I don't think treason is too strong a word,' said the dour-faced Brugha.

Robinson sat down, flushed and triumphant. Brugha got to his feet.

'We've heard the questions raised by Mr. Robinson, as brave a man as ever stood before the onslaught of the Black and Tans. We've heard him reiterate the words of Mr. Griffith, that Michael Collins was "the man who won the war?" Well I am affronted by that. It implies that others of our patriots have somehow done less than Mr. Collins. That he did it all himself. What nonsense. Mr. Collins was merely the head of a sub-section under the Chief of Staff, Mr. Mulcahy, who in turn was answerable to myself, as Minister of Defence. The headquarters staff worked conscientiously and patriotically for Ireland, without seeking any notoriety, with one exception, whether he is responsible or not for that notoriety I am not going to say. The press and the people put him into a position he never held; he was made a romantic figure, a mystical character such as this person certainly is not. The gentleman I refer to is Mr. Michael Collins.'

There was an outburst of sudden heckling from the pro-Treaty benches.

'Now we know the reason for the opposition to the Treaty,' shouted someone called Dan McCarthy. 'Personal spite!'

'Bravo, Cathal, bravo,' exclaimed Arthur Griffith, his voice dripping with irony. Another Deputy stood up and tried to stop Brugha from continuing, but Sean McGarry said: 'Too late. Let him carry on now.'

'The damage has been done now,' said Patrick Brennan, the bluff leader of one of the Clare brigades.

Michael Collins sat back with a smile on his face. 'No damage is done,' he said mildly.

Cathal Brugha continued. He spoke in colourful, awkward tones and with an honesty that could only be called unvarnished. He endeavoured to contrast the Treaty with de Valera's alternative, but under the onslaught of cross-examination from the opposition, could only throw his hands up and finally say: 'It's the difference between a draught of poison and a draught of water.'

He lifted a glass from the table in front of him and drank deeply and symbolically. He wiped his mouth and continued, his voice now lower and less strident than it had been. 'My final appeal is to Mr. Griffith and to the other Plenipotentiaries not to vote on this Treaty here today. To abstain, in effect. Mr. Griffith has earned great respect in Sinn Féin. He has been a great leader. He enhanced his selfless reputation when he stood down from that leadership in favour of Eamon de Valera, and if he agrees now to follow my advice and abstain from voting, his name will live forever in Ireland.'

Brugha finished with a flourish, his voice dropping to a lower octave eventually, until the final words were a sonorous whisper. All eyes then turned towards Griffith. There was silence in the chamber as he rose to his feet, rustled his papers and cleared his throat.

'I cannot accept the invitation of the Minister of Defence to dishonour my signature and become immortalised in Irish history. As I said at a Cabinet meeting two months ago, "If I go to London I can't get a Republic. I will try for a Republic but I can't bring it back."'

He paused and looked around at the assembly before continuing.

'We, as Plenipotentiaries, were sent to make some compromise, bargain or arrangement; we made an arrangement; the arrangement we made is not satisfactory to many people. Let them criticise on that point, but do not let them say we were sent to get one thing and that we got something else. Mr. de Valera in his own letter to Lloyd George wrote: "We have no conditions to impose, no claim to advance but one – that we are to be free from aggression."'

Griffith again paused and, like Brugha before him, took a drink of water. He put the glass down and continued: 'I now say to this House that the Treaty has met that claim. There are devout Republicans here who between them have taken seven separate oaths to the King of England, yet who now say the Treaty would stick in their gullets. This is damnable hypocrisy, which will involve the lives of brave young men. I have been told that this generation may go down, but the next generation might do something or other. Is there to be no living for Ireland? Is the Irish nation to be the dead past or the prophetic future?'

Over thunderous applause for Griffith, de Valera rose again and interjected: 'There is no Oath to the King in my document.'

Griffith replied: 'I do not care whether the King of England or the symbol of the Crown be in Ireland so long as the people of Ireland are free to shape their own destinies.'

'My document will rise in judgement,' said de Valera dramatically, 'against the men who say there's only a shadow of difference.'

Above the din, Michael Collins's voice cried out: 'Let the Irish nation judge us now and for future years.'

And then the vote was taken.

The speaker, Dr. McNeill rose slowly to his feet and solemnly proclaimed: 'The result of the poll is sixty-four for approval and fifty-seven against. This is a majority of seven in favour of approval of the Treaty.'

There was silence in the house for what seemed like an eternity. The sounds of the street seeped in and impinged upon the shadowy chamber: newspaper boys calling with shrill voices, the stuttering of car engines, a sudden wind rattling a skylight overhead. And then a shaft of bright sunlight shone through the skylight to illuminate the bench de Valera sat on. A light sheet of paper, part of his document No. 2, slid from the bench through motes of dust rising in the sunlight, and like a weightless object in space, floated gently to the floor.

And then the air was split with the cheers of those who had been victorious. Hats were thrown skywards and there was a melée, as over-enthusiastic Deputies rushed from the chamber to announce to the waiting crowds outside the glad tidings of the vote. The response outside mirrored that of the inside. Some howled with joy and triumph, but others spat and heckled the victors. There was mayhem on the steps of the building as it spilled down onto the street and along the footpaths. With no proper police force to restore order, chaos reigned for several hours around the area of Earlsfort Terrace, Leeson Street and St. Stephen's Green.

Attempting to gain access to his medical lectures, William Cody, who was essentially neutral, suffered the indignity of being abused by both sides for his unbiased opinions. 'A plague on both their houses,' was all he could think of saying.

And so a few days later, the levers of power passed from the hands of the man who had led the revolution and kept unity in Sinn Féin for four long years. A further vote was taken the following week on the retention of de Valera as President and when he lost this vote also to Arthur Griffith, he stood up and announced his resignation and took his colleagues with him. As the anti-Treatyites retreated from the chamber, a tirade of abuse and bile rained down upon them. Michael Collins stood, shaking his fist, his face purple with rage:

'Deserters all!' he roared. 'We will now call on the Irish people to rally to us. Deserters all!'

Not to be outdone, Countess Markievicz, by de Valera's side, retorted:

'Oath breakers and cowards!'

'Foreigners! Americans! English!' responded Collins, waxing more furious.

'Lloyd Georgites!' spat Markievicz.

When they got outside, a reporter from the *Freeman's Journal* confronted de Valera and asked him to defend his actions.

'We have a perfect right to resist by every means in our power,' he said.

'Even by war?' asked the reporter.

'By every means in our power to resist authority imposed on this country from outside.'

William Cody returned home to West Cork for a few weeks' rest and to wait for the hubbub caused by the Treaty debates to dissipate. He recounted his experiences to Doctor Baldwin and they engaged in a lively dialogue around the unfolding situation. Doctor Baldwin would read out sections of reportage from the Cork Examiner regarding the filling of the vacuum of power. He noted that, although shocked at first by the precipitate departure of the 'Chief,' Griffith and his colleagues quickly set about forming a new Cabinet. Griffith, with tears in his eyes swore that he had never met a man in his life whom he had more love and respect for than President de Valera and that he was thoroughly sorry to see him go. But, it seemed to Doctor Baldwin, that his love of power and that of the men around him was stronger than his sorrow for the 'Long Fellow.' Within a week, de Valera had faded from the scene like a disgruntled Agamemnon and Michael Collins had emerged like a triumphant Achilles.

To the Doctor's way of thinking, around Collins's burnished figure there clung not warriors but men of fear. The timid Cosgrave came out from the monastery to take on the mantle of Minister of Local Government, the ambitious O'Higgins became Minister of Economic Affairs. Griffith himself adopted the title, President of the Dáil and Collins assumed executive power as Chairman of the Provisional Government. There were other safe appointments: the balding, grey figure of E.J. Duggan with his waxed moustache, his striped pants and spats, became Minister of Home Affairs; the sad-eyed Gavan Duffy lent his hangdog appearance to the title of Minister of Foreign Affairs; the cautious and uninspiring Mulcahy took over the role of Minister of Defence from the fearless Cathal Brugha.

In regarding this constellation of mediocre men, Doctor Baldwin considered Collins, and wondered where were his Myrmidons to sail with him and smite the sounding furrows of the stormy seas ahead?

26

the drums of war

Back at school after the Christmas Holidays, Margie Cody followed the progress of events in Dublin with her usual thoroughness. Every few days as the nuns allowed, she would buy a copy of the *Irish Times* in a shop in Rathfarnham village, and with her classmates and her sister, Anna, she'd lead the debate on the pros and cons surrounding the establishment of the fledging Provisional Government of Ireland. Fellow students, Jennifer Slevin and Mary Higgins thought things were working out very well but Margie reminded them that the Government had no money, no army, no police force and no civil service. It didn't even have money to post a letter and instead used English stamps bearing the image of King George, with the legend, *Rialtas Sealadach Na hEireann* printed across the King's face. It had to rent temporary rooms in the Gresham Hotel on Sackville Street before decamping to further lodgings at the City Hall on Dame Street. The numbers of new recruits to the IRA had burgeoned enormously during the Truce, when it was safe to emerge into daylight and swagger about toting a gun, with no danger of a Black and Tan or an Auxiliary to be confronted. There were a lot of guns, some smuggled in to the country, some smuggled out from British Army barracks with many British officers carrying on a lucrative sideline in the clandestine sale of unlicensed weaponry. The British knew they were leaving anyway, no harm in indulging in some under-the-counter huckstering.

Mary Higgins pointed out that money was found to purchase uniforms and to pay the tiny regular army which installed itself at Beggar's Bush barracks on the 16th February.

'And where do you think the money comes from?' asked Margie with scorn in her voice.

'Well, from taxes I expect,' suggested Mary Higgins.

'Taxes?' asked Margie. 'Sure we don't even have our own Exchequer until the British set it up. No, Mary, the British have sanctioned an expenditure to the Provisional Government of the sum of half a million pounds sterling until the end of March, with the miserly proviso that it is to be "doled out cautiously, with great care to be taken to retain a substantial amount in hand." The new office of the Irish Exchequer won't open its doors until the 1st of April.'

'Well,' said Jennifer, 'it will collect all revenue in the country from then on.'

'If there's any money left in the country,' said Margie.

All of a sudden there were a lot of generals, smoking pipes and imitating the mannerisms of the departed elites of the Sandhurst officer class. Before that, on the 14th of January, Michael Collins stepped into the upper yard of Dublin Castle and took the keys of the premises from Lord Fitzalan, the British Lord-Lieutenant. While Collins was engaged within, taking over this enormous symbol of British power: citadel of the subjugation of Ireland for centuries, the new Cabinet Ministers sat pale and anxious in the Under-Secretary's room, as the former heads of all the British Civil Service Departments in Ireland sat glowering opposite them. There was a good deal of envy at the sudden elevation of Collins, the hitherto unfamiliar will o' the wisp and a longtime scourge of the British. Many officials, now losing their jobs, were bewildered that the Government should ever have come to such an agreement with rebels.

There was much jockeying for position amongst the Cabinet Members around Collins, eager and ambitious to bask in his reflected glory. On the day following the surrender of the Castle, Margie Cody again bought a copy of the *Irish Times*. There, on the first page, was a photograph of the triumphant Irish, emerging after the hand-over formalities. Margie was surprised to note that the man in front was Kevin O'Higgins, with his starched wing-collar, his hat pushed well back from his forehead, in the process of pulling on his gloves and dusting himself down as if having completed another very important job of work.

'You'd think that fellow was the "man who won the war,"' said Margie sarcastically, regarding the smug stuffed shirt on the front page. 'Sure Michael Collins is only trotting after him.'

And sure enough one had to screw one's eyes up to discern the shadowy figure of the new Chairman, sloping along behind, the hat brim down over his eyes. Perhaps it was that years of hiding in backrooms had made a habit of such behaviour, causing him to shun the limelight.

Yet Margie saw that he soon got the hang of it. Within a few weeks he was running, not only his own Department of Finance, but he was effectively the Prime Minister and the Minister of Foreign Affairs as well, meeting Churchill and Bonar Law in London and James Craig from Belfast. They made a pact, agreeing the South would no longer boycott Northern goods if the Ulster Unionists called off their death squads, which were rampaging throughout the Six Counties, murdering, maiming and burning Catholics out of their homes, in a reign of terror to equal anything perpetrated by the Black and Tans. Small wonder that the Catholics felt betrayed and cut off from the rest of the country, at the mercy of a majority intent on grinding them underfoot. Craig promised the earth, because the British gave him two million sterling to do so, but within a month or two things were as bad as ever. Collins soon found himself in the contradictory position of opposing his old IRA comrades in the South and simultaneously supporting those same comrades in the North.

He travelled the country conducting huge rallies in Cork, in Killarney, in Limerick, and in many other towns throughout Ireland, exhorting people to support the Treaty and to vote for its supporters in Government when an election was called in due course.

And Eamon de Valera went on a similar crusade, more or less in Collins's footsteps, but his message was the exact opposite. Under no circumstances should people vote for this nefarious document, and they should demonstrate their intent to the contrary by voting no when the plebiscite was held. But it kept being deferred. Neither Collins nor de Valera wished to put the matter to the test in case of losing face, so there was no legitimate Government of Ireland actually democratically elected by the people. The Provisional Government was an external British creation, coming about under the terms of the Treaty. There were, in effect, two Governments and two armies. Bloody conflict seemed inevitable, sooner or later. There would be "rivers of blood," as de Valera said.

There was great haste to get the British out of the country, because Collins and his Cabinet believed that their continued presence would provoke a major incident. Military barracks throughout Ireland were handed over to Irish soldiers. Sometimes the new incumbents were pro-Treaty soldiers, sometimes anti-Treaty. The British had no way of knowing and often the newcomers didn't know themselves. Men were known to change sides after a persuasive conversation in a public house, and change back again the following day. But increasingly there were a lot of guns in the control of wild and dangerous men and quickly the power slipped out of the hands of the politicians and into the hands of the gunmen.

Sinn Féin held a political Ard Fheis on the 21st of February and the IRA held a military Convention on the 26th of March. The Provisional Government banned the meeting and so the pro-Treaty members did not attend. A resolution was passsed declaring the Executive of the IRA to be the supreme authority and upholder of the Republic in Ireland, and the Irish Republican Army reaffirmed its allegiance. Two days later, the Executive, a body of sixteen men, including Rory O'Connor, Liam Lynch, Ernie O'Malley, Tom Barry, Dan Breen and others, anounced that the authority of the Minister of Defence and the Chief of Staff of the Provisional Government would no longer be accepted.

The drums of war beat louder. Ernie O'Malley, poet and warrior, led an attack on the RIC barracks at Clonmel and ransacked the place of grenades, guns and ammunition, loaded the lot onto a couple of Crossley tenders and drove away. The mid-Limerick Brigade under the command of Liam Forde occupied a number of key buildings in the city of Limerick for Republican Forces, and, not to be outdone, Michael Brennan from the 1st Western Division of Clare marched quietly down the railroad tracks into the city and took over six police barracks from the departing Black and Tans for the Provisional Government. The two factions remained growling and hurling insulting epithets such as, 'Irregulars' and 'Staters' at each other for most of a week, until Liam Lynch intervened and arranged a temporary truce to defuse an explosive situation.

General Sean McEoin, a belligerent pro-Treaty exponent, began to throw his weight around Connacht and North Leinster, moving through Sligo, Carrick-on-Shannon and on to Athlone, ejecting Republicans and installing pro-Treaty forces in many barracks. He was aided and abetted by a pompous fellow called General Eoin O'Duffy, who liked to give motivational speeches to his men before ordering them to blow the heads off their fellow-Irishmen if they disagreed with him. In Kilkenny an ex-American officer called Prout, ordered shots to be fired at several buildings occupied by Republicans, but nobody was killed. There was a constant flux with a lot of soldiers moving up and down the country. Men would exchange rounds of rifle fire with one another during the day and exchange rounds of stout in public houses with the same men at night, exemplifying the Irishman's uncanny ability to live with paradox.

In Cork, Tom Barry, Sean O'Hegarty and Michael Murphy led a group of Republicans to capture a huge consignment of rifles, revolvers and machineguns on board the 700 ton British vessel, *Upnor,* which had sailed from Haulbowline in the morning. A stolen ensign fooled the *Upnor's* skipper into heaving to and a boarding party from the tug, the *Warrrior,* ran her into Ballycotton Bay where the booty was loaded onto a convoy of some eighty vehicles and driven off.

The tension was ratcheted up several further notches when the Republicans seized the Four Courts of Dublin on April the 14th and threw out the peruke-wearing barristers and the whiskey-sodden judges, most of whom still clung like drowning rats to the old system of British practice and procedure. With gusto the new incumbents stomped on British writs and summonses, statements of claim and garnishee orders. Gleefully they lit their cigarettes with sheriff's execution orders, bank satisfaction pieces, judgements and bankruptcy orders. They were striking a blow for the common man and felt no guilt, no embarrassment and no remorse; only elation, which increased to euphoria when they discovered under the Law Library, a cellar full of the finest claret which the Benchers liked to imbibe at their monthly dinners up at the King's Inns, under the long-dead eyes of British kings, dukes, lords, viscounts and chancellors, whose rouged portraits lined the walls of the great dining hall.

From the redoubt of the Four Courts, the Republicans set out on regular forays around the city and country. They commandeered lorries and armoured cars, and conducted a huge raid on an ammunitions depot at the Curragh Camp. They robbed several branches of the Bank of Ireland, because the Provisional Government refused to pay them, like the new recruits in Beggar's Bush. But still Collins and his minions took no action against them. He was loath to drive a wedge between the two factions of the IRA because he knew that once the first real blow was struck all chance of a peaceful resolution would be gone.

In London, Winston Churchill and the new Tory Government kept a very sharp eye on affairs in Ireland. When they got wind of a potential voting pact between de Valera and Collins they grew extremely alarmed. The pact was to provide for all candidates to carry the Sinn Féin flag, with the number of Deputies from each of the pro-Treaty and anti-Treaty parties to represent their existing strength in the Dáil. The new Government, under this arrangement, would comprise an elected

President, a Minister of Defence to represent the Army, and nine other ministers, five from the majority party and four from the minority party. It seemed an Irish solution to an Irish problem and a compromise to avoid impending bloodshed.

But the British, in their blinkered righteousness, failed to see that an act of generosity and of justice towards the Irish would eliminate the cause of potential calamity. Was it that they secretly wished for a civil war to enable them to regain control over a country which seemed to be drifting far beyond the horizon they had envisioned when they signed the Treaty?

As it was, the new draft Constitution which the Irish had produced in a few short months, to give effect to the Treaty, had considerably watered down its provisions. In it, according to Churchill, the position of the Crown representative was reduced to that of a sort of Commissioner, the Judicial Committee of the Privy Council was excluded in favour of The Irish Supreme Court as the final Court of Appeal, the Irish claimed the right to make their own future Treaties with other countries, the Oath to the King was omitted altogether and the position of Ulster was not recognised. It appeared that Collins was leading his Provisional Government along the path of pragmatism far quicker than Lloyd George's understanding of the phrase, "for the time being," employed prior to the signing of the Treaty. Neither the pact nor the new Constitution could be allowed to stand.

Churchill stood up in the House of Commons and declared: 'The Ministers of the Provisional Government live far too much in the narrow circle of their own associates and late associates, and they think only of placating the obscure terrorists who spring up one after another all over Ireland.'

In his vast hubris, Churchill seemed incapable of appreciating that the man he dealt with now, Michael Collins, had been, until a handful of months before, the foremost terrorist of all in British eyes. Did the leopard so readily change his spots? It was as if the British, who were themselves the most nationalistic of nations, failed to see, like an over-protective parent, how a country, formerly living within their family of nations, would wish to strike out on its own path to freedom, like a fledging flying the nest.

Churchill continued: 'There is every reason to believe that the great mass of people in Ireland would gladly vote for the Treaty and the Free State, but on the other hand, the Irish Republican Army, whom we have not recognised, now appears to be largely unreliable and the

Provisional Government appears to be incapable of withstanding the extremists. In the event of a *coup d'etat,* the Commander-in-Chief of British Forces in Dublin will proclaim martial law at once, will attack the Republican Government and seize the dissidents, irrespective of the view of Mr. Collins and the Provisional Government. The existing garrisons who have not evacuated will be speedily reinforced and we have ordered two destroyers into the river at Dublin as an urgent precaution.'

Thus did the British convey to the Provisional Government that any attempt at circumventing the terms of the Treaty would be ruthlessly suppressed. Through influential pro-British Irishmen like Tim Healy, they let it be known that if the Provisional Government did not immediately take steps to kick the Republicans out of the Four Courts and put an end to lawlessness, the British would do it for them. As a further indication of their belligerent intent, and to add insult to injury, they appointed an arch-enemy of Collins and Irish Republicans, Sir Henry Hughes Wilson, to be special military advisor in the Six Counties to Sir James Craig and the Northern Unionists.

Back in the Loreto Convent, very little schoolwork was done. The daily developments were a constant distraction, but while dramatic events were unfolding, both sides were still talking, so there was hope of a rapprochement. Margie, in her animated excitement, liked to quote the line from Wordsworth's poem on the French Revolution:

"Bliss it was in that dawn to be alive,
While to be young was very heaven."

27

gunmen in the night

A retired magistrate named Thomas Hornibrook sat down to dinner with his son, Samuel, his daughter Matilda, and her husband, Captain Herbert Woods. They ate in silence. Their house was large and rambling, in a place called Ballygroman, near Ballincollig, not far from Cork city. A maid came with second helpings. The men ate roastbeef, bacon, fowl. Thomas Hornibrook drank brandy afterwards and his cheeks grew red. He took off his tweed coat and loosened his cravat. He poured a measure for the younger men. Woods held his hand up to stop the filling.

'That's enough,' he said. 'I have to work tomorrow.'

'Less work than before?' said Hornibrook. 'How many Britishers left in Ballincollig barracks?'

'Barely a handful,' said Woods. He was ex-British army with several decorations, DS, MM, MC.

'And they left with such unseemly haste, to leave chaos in their wake,' added Hornibrook. 'I'm surprised such stalwarts as Montgomery and Percival left without a whimper.'

'I'd imagine Montgomery was only itching to get back to bigger things,' said Woods, 'and Strickland is probably looking forward to retiring. As for Percival, I believe he'll achieve great things yet. The British Empire may have lost a small colony but it still bestrides the world.'

'All the same,' said Hornibrook, 'it must have really stuck in his craw to hand over his Essex barracks in Kinsale to a bunch of jumped up rebels. If 'twas me I know I'd resent it.'

'We must be vigilant,' said Woods, and drank, then put his glass down carefully on the coffee table to which they'd moved.

Hornibrook sat back in his armchair and grasped both its arms with a sense of entitlement befitting a superior man, although he was still indignant at the humiliation of Major Percival, an officer after his own heart.

'Collins is not to be trusted,' offered the more hesitant younger Hornibrook, Samuel, and continued: 'He's playing a duplicitous game.'

'Still, he's a very attractive man,' said Matilda, almost carelessly.

Woods scoffed: 'That's what all women say. Only thinking with their glands.'

'Don't be vulgar, Herbert,' said his wife, primly. 'With your army talk.'

'I'm surprised at such sentiments coming from the daughter of a staunch loyalist,' said her husband.

'I can admire him,' said Matilda, rather crossly. 'I didn't say I agreed with him.'

Thomas Hornibrook cleared his throat: 'We may be staunch, we may be loyal, we may be righteous, but either way, the Treaty is now done. And, as that fellow, de Valera said, "Twill be the mischief to get it undone." We must deal with new realities.'

Captain Woods demurred. 'The situation is fluid. Things could go either way yet.'

'You mean the British could return?' asked the wide-eyed Samuel, with his long face and fair eyebrows.

'If the Provisional Government of Griffith and Collins don't do the proper job, yes I believe it is possible.'

'That would be the 'tarrawal,' laughed Hornibrook senior, and sank his brandy.

There came a loud knocking on an outside door at the far end of the house down an untidy corridor cluttered with riding boots, saddles and sleeping dogs. They put down their glasses, breath held. When the knock came again, more loudly, the dogs in the pantry took to barking.

'What the devil?' said Hornibrook and looked at his fob watch in his waistcoat. 'Nearly midnight.'

Matilda exchanged a fleeting look of fear with her husband. 'Who could that be?'

The knocking came again, this time louder.

'Are you expecting anyone?' asked Woods of Hornibrook.

'I'm not. Most decent people are in their beds at this hour.'

Woods jumped up. 'I'll go,' he said. He pulled a pistol from inside his jacket.

Hornibrook struggled out of his armchair. He put a hand on the younger man's arm. 'Don't go to the door. Go upstairs to the bedroom window.'

Woods and Samuel Hornibrook hurried away up the stairs. Thomas Hornibrook shuffled after them.

Woods cautiously opened the casement bedroom window and called down. He could see shadowy figures around the backyard.

'Who's there?'

'We're looking for your car.' said a voice from below.

'Who are you?' asked Woods.

'Never mind,' came the voice. 'The car won't start. Where's the magneto?'

'I'll give you magneto,' shouted Woods. 'Clear off if you know what's good for you.' Woods tried to remain calm but his voice trembled.

'We don't want trouble, Mr. Hornibrook, but we want your car to use on an errand. We'll bring it back.'

Thomas Hornibrook, panting from the climb, had reached the window. 'Who are you?' he asked indignantly.

'The magneto, where is it?' the voice was calm, but insistent. Hornibrook and Woods were at the window, Samuel close behind. They exchanged fearful looks.

Woods pointed his pistol out the window. 'I'll give you ten seconds to clear off.'

'We don't want trouble, we want your car.'

Woods counted to ten. Then he fired a shot in the air. There was the sound of running feet, a rustling of bodies through trees and hedges. The dogs took to their frantic barking from below. The three men waited for some minutes and then the barking died down. There was silence. The moon was bright and cast long shadows. A disturbed owl flew.

'I think they're gone,' whispered Woods as they stood listening in the dark room. He was sweating. His hands were clammy.

As they moved across the room, Samuel asked: 'Do you think 'twas IRA?'

'Who else?' asked Woods. He walked back slowly towards the window and pulled it shut.

'What's to be done?' asked Samuel.

'Let the hare sit now,' said Hornibrook the elder. 'Come on. We'll go down.'

They slowly descended the stairs. They reached a turn and continued down to the ground floor. When their feet had cleared the last step there was a splintering of glass from down the corridor. The dogs started up again. The men rushed down. Matilda Woods came running from the drawing room with her hand to her throat. 'Lord protect us?' she whispered.

The men ran down the corridor. Confronting them in the moonlight, shining in through the downstairs windows, were three men. Shards of glass lay littered at their feet. Woods stood upright, Hornibrook and Samuel were on either side of him. Woods pointed the pistol.

'In the name of God, clear off,' he shouted. His voice was cracking.

The other voice was calm, cold, and more insistent: 'We want the magneto to start the car.'

'This is monstrous,' said the older Hornibrook. 'Breaking into a respectable house at midnight. What kind of ruffians are ye?'

'We're not ruffians. We're as respectable as yourself,' said the second man. 'We know you are a loyalist and an informer, but we're not here for that now. We want your car and we're going to take it. We need the magneto.'

The three intruders started towards the other three in the moonlit corridor. The dogs cowered and whined. Woods pointed the pistol. 'Stand back,' he said. 'Stand back or I'll shoot.'

The first man was Michael O'Neill. He came on towards them. Charlie O'Donoughue and another were a step behind. Woods fired. The shot was a loud, echoing blast in the high-ceilinged corridor. Blood spouted from O'Neill's throat. He fell back. Charlie O'Donoughue stopped, frozen in shock, as O'Neill slumped against him. 'My God, you shot him,' he said.

'Get out, or I'll shoot again,' shouted Woods, emboldened. The fear and panic that had gripped him was gone; transferred to his adversaries. The Hornibrooks, sensing Woods's confidence, opened their shoulders and stood firm. O'Donoughue held his hand up. 'We're going,' he said. 'We're going. Hold your fire.'

The two men dragged their wounded comrade towards the door. Woods followed, brandishing his pistol.

'Alright,' panted O'Donoughue again. 'We're going. This man needs a doctor.'

Blood poured down over O'Donoughue's coat and over the third man's shoes. It poured over the floor of the corridor, spattering the broken glass. The dogs sniffed and one began to lick the blood. The men struggled through the door. They lifted O'Neill, one on either side and staggered through the trees. Woods and the Hornibrooks followed into the garden behind the house. The dogs were at their heels. They listened and could hear the men grunting with the effort as they hefted the wounded man. They could hear the wounded man's groans. Soon they could hear no more, only the pounding of their own hearts, as Ballygroman's woods descended into silence.

Tull Hennessy lit a burning bush under the belly of a thoroughbred because the horse refused to budge. He'd been trying to break him all through March and April but the horse was stubborn.

'A pure mule,' he said to Sonny, who stood watching him. The watery April sun was going down in the west. A southerly breeze blew mildly. Tull sweated and swore.

'You can lead a horse to water, but you can't make him drink,' said Sonny, as he saw two men coming across the field near the farmhouse, where the spring grass was growing.

'That's what I always say,' said Tull.

'Say what?' asked Sonny.

'Say you can't make people do what they don't want to do. Like your crowd.'

Tull inclined his head towards the two men, now nearly upon them. Sonny shrugged and then smiled as Tom Barry and Tom Hales arrived and stood. Sonny shook hands. Tull ignored them and continued to goad the horse, which had planted its feet. Its eyes rolled white with fear. The bush blazed. There was a smell of singed flesh.

Tom Barry looked to Sonny, disquieted. Tom Hales, big, blonde and pale, had a query in his eye.

'He's tough, Tull?'

'He's a gadding bastard, Tom,' said Tull. He liked Hales. Back from two years in prison, from the dead.

Barry said nothing. He tightened his trenchcoat. Two pistols bulged in holsters underneath, two more under Hales's coat.

'Back from Dublin?' said Tull.

'Just got back,' said Barry. 'There's trouble brewing around here.'

'Is it any wonder?' said Tull. 'All the bad example ye're giving up there. What are ye trying to prove by taking over the Four Courts?'

'We've as much right to take over the Four Courts as the 'Staters' have to take over Dáil Eireann.'

'Huh,' said Tull, unconvinced.

'Are you coming, Sonny?' said Barry.

Sonny said to Tull: 'I have to go.'

'Go on,' said Tull. 'Go on, for all the good ye'll do.'

'Good luck, Tull,' said Hales.

'All the best, Tom,' said Tull. As they moved away he shouted after them. 'Ye're wasting ye're time with de Valera. That fella is only out for himself.'

Tom Barry stopped and shouted back: 'We're not taking orders from de Valera.'

'I forgot,' said Tull. 'The eternal revolution. That's ye're game, isn't it. The war is over, Tom.'

'It's only starting,' shouted Barry and turned on his heel again. As they got to the lane at the field's edge, the horse suddenly broke from Tull and raced away across the field with high buckleaps. The last they heard was Tull cursing in the twilight.

'There's a pair of them in it,' said Tom Barry. 'Horse and man.' He paused and looked back. 'He's gone with Collins, I see.'

Sonny rubbed his hair back ruefully. 'He is, but he's not alone.'

Barry nodded and stole a look at Hales who had a pained expression on his face. They all knew Sean Hales had done the same.

At dusk they reached the Bull Riders. The virgin leaves were glimmering on the great, primieval branches of the oak. The moon shone down. They could hear the running stream in the stilly night. A sudden sound of barking dogs came across the high walls of the Eustace estate.

'She must be having visitors,' said Tom Barry. He looked at Sonny.

'Your job is to stand guard for the next twenty-four hours. Denis Lordan will relieve you then. Things are getting dangerous. We've heard reports of attacks but we're not sure of the full extent of them. A family of Hornibrooks were kidnapped last night. Michael O'Neill got shot dead. We don't know the full facts yet, but we know these people are being threatened with revenge and we don't want that.'

'Would they threaten the widow woman?' asked Sonny.

'I'm afraid they would. Jasper was an informer. Fellows are still very bitter about that. But we don't want any more grudges. We have to live and let live. Tom here, Sean Buckley and others will be guarding various houses: Canon Wilson, Goods, Winters. But we can't guard them all. They're not so cocksure now. They're frightened, except for the odd few who'd like to bring the British back. But recriminations have to end. I hope we're not too late.'

He pointed to Tom Hales: 'Tom suffered the most from informers, first in Bandon barracks and then two years in Pentonville jail. But he's not bitter.'

'Let bygones be bygones,' said Hales, the greathearted.

Sonny nodded: 'Very good, Commandant. I'll go up the track through the woods around the back. I can sleep in the hayshed.'

'And you have your weapon?'

'A Luger and a Colt,' said Sonny, patting his thighs.

'Woe to the man that takes you on,' grinned Barry and slapped the young man on the back. They saluted and walked off through the woods. Twigs crackled underneath their feet. Sonny waited for them to fade through the dappled moonshadows. Then he went over the river.

There was a sound of digging around midnight in the hill country south of Kilumney: a shovel knocking against a stone, a pickaxe sparking on granite or socking through limestone. The land was rugged and high. In daylight, if a man stood on the highest point, he could see north to the Galtees in Tipperary, and east beyond Cork city towards Waterford. Down the valley to the south were Crossbarry and Upton. There were deep gulleys through which swift streams flowed, trees of hazel and sally grew dense in winding ravines. In a clearing in the moonlight there was a carpet of bluebells and a border of primroses and snowdrops. Two men stood in a half dug grave. One hefted a pickaxe and the other shovelled the red-brown earth up on the side. There was an older man, with his hands tied behind his back, standing a little way from the grave and a group of a dozen men with revolvers and rifles stood around him. The older man was well-dressed in tweeds, a waistcoat and a tie. His head was bare and his grey hair was thinning. He was red-faced, well-fed and prosperous-looking but his expression was one of ineffable bitterness. Some of the men around him sat on old fallen tree trunks while others stood leaning against silver birch trees. Some had kerchiefs covering their mouths and noses, others had makeshift masks with slits for their eyes to peer through. The older man sighed occasionally though he did not sweat, but the men in the grave sweated profusely from exertion and from fear. After a time the men stopped digging. The grave was shallow and wide. One sat on the edge and said: 'I'll dig no more.'

The leader of the gunmen shrugged. 'Have it your own way. 'Tis your bed to lie in.'

The leader motioned to his men to move closer. They huddled in a circle and drew straws. The three designated shootists lined up with their guns at the ready.

The leader said: 'Ye can stand where ye are or ye can stand out.'

One of the younger men who still stood in the grave said: 'You're not men at all, but savages.'

'That's rich coming from you, Herbert Woods,' said the leader, 'and you the man who shot Michael O'Neill in cold blood two nights ago. When you had the whip hand you didn't think twice about using it, anymore than ye showed mercy to James and Timothy Coffey this time last year. Hacked them to death ye did.'

Woods stared at the leader with a resigned look. Samuel Hornibrook, the man who sat on the edge of the grave said: 'What proof have ye that we did that?'

'We've a fair idea who did it,' said the leader. 'And if ye didn't, ye were hand in glove with those that did. The Loyalist Action Group sent many an unfortunate man to his death, either by direct action or by informing the Black and Tans.'

Thomas Hornibrook said: 'So it's revenge that's driving ye, just as I presumed.'

'Your Bible says an eye for an eye, a tooth for a tooth,' said the masked leader. 'If a man commits a murder, the law of the land says he must pay for it with his own life.'

'The law has procedures,' said Hornibrook. 'I should know. I was a magistrate. Extenuating circumstances are considered.'

'One law for the rich and one law for the poor, one for the English and one for the Irish, Mr Hornibrook. We have our own procedures, just as fair as yours.'

The leader motioned to the men again. They lined up their rifles. Thomas Hornibrook was taken over to the edge of the grave. A man took the bindings from his hands. The two younger men turned to face the rifles. Samuel Hornibrook wept and put his arms around his father. Herbert Woods looked straight ahead.

'Company, load arms,' said the leader. There was the sound of bolts sliding in mechanical motion.

'Present arms.'

Three rifles pointed at the three men astride the grave.

'Fire!'

The shots shattered the silence of the woods. The three men fell backwards into the grave and lay still. The leader climbed down among the bodies fallen akimbo. He felt for pulses. He turned and climbed out, wiping the blood and earth from his hands across his coat.

'That's it,' he said.

Disturbed jackdaws flew cawing up from the high tree branches. When the birds had flown the silence surged softly back and then other sounds impinged upon the glade: earth thudding on uncoffined bodies, boots kicking earth off shiny shovels, heavy breathing. The smell of gunpowder lingered on the air. The moon shone down in splendid streams of silver and a light wind rustled the green leaves of spring.

James Baldwin was taken aback by the change in Eleanore Eustace. For several weeks in the spring of 1922 he'd been receiving letters of entreaty from the lady. Would he meet her, perhaps for luncheon, to discuss matters of mutual interest? He wondered what that could mean? She'd been unconcerned about his welfare the last time they met, albeit a most pleasurable experience it proved to be. In the end, curiosity got the better of him and he agreed to a 12.30 afternoon appointment at Lee's Hotel in Bandon. It was well over twelve months since last he'd seen her, but it was clear that there was no diminution in her standing over that time in the eyes of the hotel management. The *maitre d'hotel* fussed like a peacock about them as they were ushered through the crowded dining room to the best table in the house, in a recessed corner, with a 'Yes, Mrs Eustace,' and, 'Of course, Doctor Baldwin.'

The best table for the best people. The Doctor noted the enthusiastic welcome, far greater than he might be accorded if dining on his own. As they commenced a hesitant reconnection from where they'd left off the previous year, he noticed a great lessening in her former bravura. Her cheeks were flushed as if a nervous uncertainty assailed her. As they sipped their aperitifs, an occasional glimpse of her former self-confidence asserted itself, in the way she arched her neck to smooth down her magnificent blonde tresses, now pulled back from her face. A sharp glance towards ear-wigging couples around them still held defiance and contempt, but somehow the regal haughtiness of yore was gone forever from her beautiful, brown eyes. Grey hairs were visible here and there and her alabaster complexion bore wrinkles around her eyes and worry lines along her forehead. Some spirit had died in her; the wild flame of youth was fading. The onset of age, not apparent when she was at Jasper's side was now visible to the Doctor's eagle eye. Even her humorous and sardonic voice had lost its music.

They both ordered roast beef from the menu but she barely touched it and soon suggested that she was becoming tired and that they should get her driver to bring her cab around to take them home. It seemed that this woman, who could charm and seduce the most indifferent heart, was at her wit's end. A sense of desperation seemed to permeate her heart. They drove the road home in sporadic conversation because she thought it best not to divulge too much to the driver, Jer Leary, her longtime workman, who in the last twelve months had lost his sense of deference and had on occasion become truculent. They passed the late evening becoming reacquainted and whilst a certain modicum of passion still burned in their lovemaking, neither the Doctor nor herself seemed to have any great desire to continue with that specific part of their relationship. Something had replaced the careless ardour. The sensual òdalisque had disappeared and there now lay beside Baldwin a needy woman, eager for support and continued companionship, but not of a sexual kind. And while the Doctor still prided himself on his vigour, and still felt strongly attached to the umbilical cord of his youth, here was a woman wavering on the cusp of youth and age. Where was the light of summer vanished from her eyes, replaced by winter's frost and gone like a setting sun? It saddened him, this change from merriment and laughter, to caution, fearfulness and the clutch of mortality's cold hand.

He moved to the window as the night drew on and as he was contemplating how a man such as he could possibly shoulder such a responsibility and such an expectation in her, he noticed a number of men moving across the front lawn, from tree to tree. He followed them with his eyes and saw them exchange greetings with the driver, Jer Leary, and he saw him pointing in the general direction of the upstairs bedroom, where a low light burned behind the Doctor, outlining him in silhouette. He quickly drew back from the window and turned to Eleanore.

'There are some men on the front lawn. Are you expecting anyone?'

'Only Jer Leary and the other workman, Joe Swanton, doing the chores.'

'There's more than two. It looks like there could be ten.'

'My God, what are they looking for?'

'I don't know, but I've been hearing rumours of assassinations.'

'Assassinations, of whom?'

'Of informers, of loyalists, of Protestants.'

'You think...? Oh, Jesus,' she whispered and buried her head in his shoulder. Her body shook with sobbing. 'I can't take anymore of this. Oh, Jesus, haven't we suffered enough?'

The sound of voices came from below. Doctor Baldwin tip-toed to the window and stole a look down. He saw a number of men in a semi-circle and they appeared to be confronted by a lone man brandishing two pistols. He held his breath and listened quite fearfully to the voices drifting upward.

Sonny Hennessy stood and did not waver, as a group of men tried to surround him. Some of the men were masked, but some were bare of face.

'Get out of my way now, Sonny boy,' said a swarthy man whom Doctor Baldwin recognised as the man Lord Bandon once called 'the Seneschal,' Joseph O'Mahony.

'I won't Joseph,' said Sonny. 'I can't.'

'Says who?' asked O'Mahony with a sneer.

'The Commandant's orders. I've sworn. We're still an army.'

'You mean Tom Barry?' asked Jer Leary, who'd joined in behind O'Mahony.

'Yes, and Tom Hales,' said Sonny. 'This woman is to be left in peace.'

'She's an informer's wife, looking down on us for long enough,' said Joe Swanton. 'Her and that fancy man of hers. They're up there in the bedroom this minute, fornicating.'

'You are her workman,' said Sonny. 'Have you no loyalty?'

'No more than she had to us,' said Jer Leary, 'or her husband either.'

'She was not an informer,' said Sonny.

'A likely story,' said O'Mahony. He paused before continuing, 'So you've joined the 'Staters' then?'

'I have not,' said Sonny, and stood cool and unafraid.

There was a jostling of men behind.

'We've had enough of this,' said one, and raised his pistol. Sonny eyed him steadily, and fingered his revolvers.

'Get out of our way now, boy,' said O'Mahony. 'The time for being nice to these people is over. Move aside or else.'

'Or else?' asked Sonny. His voice was quiet and cold.

'Or else we'll make you.'

There was a clicking of pistol hammers, glinting in the waning moon.

'I wouldn't do that.' said Sonny.

'Why?' asked a muffled voice. 'Would you shoot?'

'Maybe,' said Sonny.

'Like you shot Jasper?' sneered O'Mahony.

'If I have to, yes,' said Sonny.

The sudden information caused a ripple of uncertainty in the group.

'He's only bluffing,' said Jer Leary. 'He can't take on the six of us.'

'Maybe not,' said Sonny. 'But I have two revolvers here. That means I get a least two of you before you get me. You're easy targets from this distance.'

He brought the pistols up level with his eyes and said: 'Now clear off, and don't come back. If you do, you'll have more than me to deal with next time.'

'Like who?'

'Like Tom Barry, or Liam Deasy, or Denis Lordan.'

'All the big men,' said a voice. 'You think you're great, throwing your weight around.'

'We faced tougher men than you,' said Sonny quietly. 'We faced the Tans and the Auxies, most of you didn't.'

He cocked the pistols and drew back the hammers. His eyes were winter cold. There was the shuffling of feet and O'Mahony said: 'He means it. Come on.'

As they sloped away one by one, a voice shouted back. 'We'll get you yet, Sonny. We know a trick or two about you.'

When they were gone, Sonny walked to the hall door and knocked softly. Doctor Baldwin opened it. Eleanore was behind him, trembling and white as a ghost.

'You were very brave, Sonny,' said the Doctor. 'We heard it all. It looked like they meant business.'

'Don't be in any doubt about that.' said Sonny.

'How can we thank you?' asked Eleanore.

'No need to thank me,' said Sonny. 'When we fought, it was a cause worth fighting for. You have bad eggs in every group, who'd shoot a woman or steal her cattle. But most of us are honourable men. I hope you understand that?'

Eleanore nodded her head slowly. 'I do,' she said.

All through the night, Doctor Baldwin wondered at the irony of the woman saved by the man who'd shot her husband. But there was a difference of circumstances between then and now. A hair's breadth, but therein lay the depths of hell. Soon he heard, with increasing dismay, the filtering news the next day, of dreadful events. He and Eleanore had escaped the fury of the 'Trucileers,' but not so Chinnery of Port Na Locha, or Fitzpatrick of Dunmanway, or Howe or Grey, or Harbord of Desertserges. These, along with other prominent members of the Loyalist Action Group, were dispatched, unanointed, just as they themselves had dispatched others before them. And as Sonny listened with sadness to the grim details, he wondered whether the wave of blood that flowed along the pleasant Bandon was capable of being stemmed, or was it the flood-tide of a deeper gulf about to wash them down?

28

the flood-tide

A round 5 a.m on the 27th of June, 1922, Anna Cody was awakened from her slumbers by the sound of distant cannon. She was in a room in St. Anthony's wing of the Loreto Convent in Rathfarnham, and her sister, Margie slept opposite her in a single bed. Anna got up and opened the window and the dull booms grew louder. Margie also heard the guns and sat up, sleepily. She saw Anna by the window.

'What's that noise?' she asked.

'Gunfire,' said Anna. 'It seems to be coming from the city.'

Margie joined her at the window. The reports were loud and systematic, every five minutes.

'They sound like 18 pounders,' frowned Margie.

'18 pounders?' asked Anna.

'Heavy artillery. Only the British have those.'

'I thought the British were gone?' said Anna in alarm.

'Obviously not,' said Margie, grimly. 'We must find a way to sneak out to see what's happening.'

The summer holidays were nearly upon them. They lied and told Sister Stanislaus their brother William was to meet them at Kingsbridge to accompany them to Cork, but their journey was delayed. They stole away from the convent by mid-morning with alarming rumours of warfare being renewed. By then the sun was hot over the fields beside the Dodder. The cows were driven out from milking by the dairy farmers who sent milk to the city. There was a pall of smoke in the northern sky over Kilmainham, Stoneybatter and Smithfield Market. It drifted northeastwards on the gentle wind.

In the heart of the huge fortress that was the Four Courts building, Rory O'Connor exchanged a look of disbelief with Ernie O'Malley when the first shell shattered a window on the front facade near the river. O'Connor was a dapper man of about forty, with a long, saturnine face, a high, intelligent forehead with dark hair combed flat back. His eyes were sad and blue. He'd become the leader of the garrison by default, after Liam Lynch, the IRA Chief of Staff, had decided to return south to Tipperary earlier that night, having spent the previous six months making Herculean efforts to prevent a civil war. As he left the building in the small hours he had said, 'I am not thinking of war, I am thinking of peace.'

O'Connor now surrounded himself with men of high, unyielding principle, such as O'Malley, a brilliant writer and a firebrand, Liam Mellows, Sean McBride, Joe McKelvey and others such as Dick Barrett and Tom Barry, who had gone to Cork, but were making frantic efforts to return. O'Connor had been weapons engineer with Michael Collins at IRA GHQ before the Truce and had worked closely with Mulcahy, O'Duffy, and Kevin O'Higgins, for whom he'd acted as best man at the latter's wedding, the year before. The vote on the Treaty heralded a split in the ranks of the IRA, and now the thunder of the long range guns spelt the death knell of a thousand bonds of friendship and a breaking of the heart of the emerging Irish nation.

O'Connor had been warned. Michael Collins, at the urging of Churchill and the British Cabinet, had finally lost patience with the Executive Forces, and had delivered an ultimatum by motorcycle courier earlier that night, to have the Four Courts vacated and handed up to the Provisional Government by 4 a.m. O'Connor and his fellow officers had chosen to ignore the warning. At 4.25 a.m. the first salvo was launched. They never believed it would happen.

O'Connor rose from behind the fine walnut desk, where the former incumbent, the Lord Chief Justice of Ireland, Sir Thomas Moloney, usually sat, before being ejected abruptly back in April. This office was now the engine room of all operations directed by O'Connor, and others such as the barracks adjutant, Sean Lemass, who issued passes in and out to his men with the seal of the Chief Justice affixed to them: an act of effrontery, which would, no doubt, have caused the Chief Justice to choke on his whiskey and soda had he been aware of it.

O'Connor beckoned to O'Malley and they made their way down the long corridor on the southern side of the huge rectangular building. Outside on their left was the square, which you crossed to get to the

Law Library, Records' Office, the Solicitor and Bankruptcy Departments and other administration buildings at the rear. They passed soldiers, suddenly alert, clutching their rifles in the grey light of dawn as it began to illuminate the gloomy recesses of the cavernous building. They walked the length of the long, high-ceilinged corridor, past offices where judges used to work and where writs were formerly processed and stamped by civil servants and court clerks. At every door O'Connor stopped to clap a man on the back and reassure him, even as chunks of plaster came away from wall or ceiling, showering them in fine, white dust. They got to the eastern block, where Joe McKelvey of the Belfast Brigade was in charge of a small platoon sending retaliatory rifle fire out of sandbagged windows towards the guns from across the river at Wood Quay.

'How are we, Joe?' asked O'Connor

'We're well fortified,' said the Northern man. 'We have a few Lancias outside, blocking the road by the railings, and the armoured car is going up and down the yard. It's a pity Lynch left us though, and that Tom Barry and Dick Barrett are in Cork.'

'They'll be back,' said O'Malley. 'If there's fighting to be done it won't be done without Tom Barry.'

'I hope they can get in,' said McKelvey. 'There seems to be a huge crowd of 'Staters' gathering outside.'

As they looked out to the yard, they saw the armoured car, the *Mutineer,* wheeling up and down, releasing salvos of shells through the gate towards the 18 pounder on Bridgefoot Street, near the Brazen Head.

'The *Mutineer* is well stocked, and the gunner is good,' said McKelvey. 'We'll knock hell out of the British guns with her.'

'I hope we don't knock down the Brazen Head,' laughed O'Malley, 'the oldest pub in Dublin. It goes back to the fourteenth century.'

'We'd knock a lot of things before we'd knock a pub,' said McKelvey.

'If we'd spent more time drinking with those lads outside and less time arguing, maybe this wouldn't be happening,' said O'Malley. He shook his head wearily. They could hear the rattle of gunfire from the parapet on the roof as Sean Lemass came down a stairs and saluted smartly. He looked alert and in control, with his trim moustache and bright, intelligent eyes.

'I've put some of our best snipers up on top,' he said. 'They're trying to pick off the gunner on Wood Quay.'

'Good work, Sean,' said O'Connor. He and O'Malley hurried back along the corridor to the round hall, under the great dome, which was supported by twenty-four gigantic Corinthian pillars. They met Liam Mellows.

'How are the boys?' asked O'Connor.

'Morale is good,' said Mellows. He was a slim, youngish man of about twenty-seven, with a shock of fair hair that stood up on his high forehead. He had deep-set, intense eyes, a strong mouth and a determined chin.

'Will we call them together, to say a few words?' asked Mellows.

'We will,' said O'Connor, 'but you do the talking, Liam. You're better at speeches than me.'

'What about that fellow there?' asked Mellows with humour, pointing to O'Malley.

'Ah, he's too much of a poet,' laughed O'Connor. 'He'd have them all picking wildflowers and singing with the fairies.'

'You're being a bit over critical of him,' said Mellows. O'Malley, tall and handsome, only shrugged and said. 'Rory is right, Liam. You're the orator. Rouse the troops.'

Pale, sleepy-eyed young men emerged with their rifles at the ready from the courtrooms of King's Bench, Chancery, Exchequer and the Court of Common Pleas. They gathered in the great circular hall, and Mellows stood on a butterbox. As he started to speak, the boom of cannon and the rattle of rifle fire drowned out some of his words, but to his listeners, his fierce, fiery demeanour was all they needed to see.

'Oglaigh na hEireann,' he began. 'The hour we have all been dreading, and desperately trying to prevent, has come to pass. The Provisional Government has finally done the bidding of their masters, Churchill, Bonar Law and Birkenhead, and turned British guns on their own people. We've already received information that Emmet Dalton and Tony Lawlor went up to the Phoenix Park in the small hours of last night and finessed four 18 pounder cannon from the British, and that they've been given a further ten thousand rifles to try to destroy us. To destroy the Irish Republic...'

He stopped as a shell shattered a window high up near the dome, sending a shower of glass and shrapnel clattering down on the tiles like hailstones. Men ducked and dodged as Mellows continued:

'As I've said before, there would be no question of civil war were it not for the undermining of the Republic. The Republic has been deserted by those who have stated they still intend to work for a

Republic. Now we know we can have no faith in this chameleon Government. One moment when we look at it, it is the green, white and orange of the Republic, and at another moment, as now, it is the red white and blue of the British Empire. We, who have seized this building, have been termed mutineers, irregulars, and so forth, but are not mutineers. We have remained loyal to our trust. We are not mutineers except against the British Government in this country. We may be irregular in the sense that funds are not forthcoming to maintain us, like the other side are being maintained by subventions from the British. But we were always like that and it is no disgrace to be called irregular in that sense. We are not wild men. All you handful, who have assembled here to fight, are the lucky ones. We number a mere two hundred. There are probably thousands of new conscripts assembled outside this building now, including ex-British personnel, who have rejoined the Free State Forces with the specific instructions to shoot their way in. But we will not be moved. Let them come. We will meet them with everything in our grasp, with rifle and with pistol and with bayonet. In 1916 the British bombarded the GPO. Out of that great sacrifice the Republic was born. It still grows and will so remain. Remember the men of 1916. Take courage. Your cause is great. *An Phoblacht Abú*!'

A roar of approval echoed high off the bronze dome. The men hastened back to their posts with renewed vigour.

The fighting raged for the next eight hours, increasing in intensity hour by hour. The men inside the Four Courts resisted much more fiercely than their attackers expected. The artillery shells became more frequent and came at them from four different directions. Apart from Bridgefoot Street and Wood Quay, they now began to fire from Green Street to the northeast and the Bridewell to the northwest. Large chunks of masonry were knocked out of the 450 yard facade and innumerate bullet holes were gouged out of the six Corinthian pillars of the graceful portico. The waters of the Liffey at high tide reflected back the broken, disfigured building, plumes of smoke and dust, fires, running men and scurrying, children, admonished by their fearful parents for getting in harm's way.

Emmet Dalton, who had been promoted to the rank of General, stood across the river on the quay near the Clarence Hotel and casually lit a cigarette, as bullets from the sharpshooters, Tom O'Reilly and Bill Gannon on the dome of the Four Courts, peppered the cobblestones at his feet. He walked slowly along by the wall of the river, his only protection being the plane trees that grew at twenty foot intervals along the pavement, and gave no indication of any fright or even nervousness. Dalton had been appointed by Collins and the Provisional Government to take charge of the assault, and his assistant was Tony Lawlor. It was a task both men relished, having fought in the British Army in the Great War. Dalton was a young daredevil, who'd returned to Ireland, joined the IRA, and become one of Michael Collins's bodyguards. He had an uncanny nose for finding himself on the right side of whichever group was in the ascendancy, be it British or Irish, and whenever strong-arm tactics were required, he was the man to implement them, safe within the security of the power group. His ambition and easy familiarity with all things British made his present job of dislodging what he would call, the 'Irregulars,' a particularly satisfying one. He wouldn't lose any sleep if a couple of hundred of his former comrades were wiped out. Both his and Lawlor's experiences in the Great War meant they were well suited to confronting the new enemy within. They had no great allegiance to any flag. They were professional soldiers with a job to do, and high-minded ideals were matters for other people, like the men they now faced across the river. After standing out under the withering rifle fire for some minutes to demonstrate his fearlessness to the young recruits around him, he took a last drag of his cigarette through his thin lips and flicked the butt-end away. He walked back to Lawlor, who was directing the young gunners. He patted his moustache and his cold grey eyes carried a look of swaggering bravado.

'You're pushing it a bit Emmet,' said Lawlor.

'Not at all,' said Dalton, cocksure. 'It's good for the young lads to see there's nothing to be afraid of. Those fellows across the river will give up in a matter of hours. We'll roast 'em out of it.'

'I hope that's not wishful thinking,' said Lawlor. 'Some of the best IRA men are in there. They were our friends 'til six months ago.'

'Things change,' said Dalton, nonchalantly. 'That's life.'

Lawlor did not respond, but it struck him that his commanding officer, while ruthless and brave, was a pretty cold fish. There were a few others about too, he thought, such as General Daly, their overall commander in Wellington Barracks.

General Sir Nevil Macready recoiled in horror when a shell landed in the saddling paddock of the Royal Hospital in Kilmainham, directly outside his office window. He jumped up and grabbed his peaked cap.

'That's it,' he said to Colonel Winter, who had just come in to discuss logistical arrangements. 'That really is the limit.'

Macready made a dash towards the door and then turned as if in doubt and walked back. Then he made for the door again. Winter, noticing his commanding officer's confusion, enquired politely if there was anything he could do.

'Do, did you say?' asked Macready incredulously, as his jowls flushed crimson. 'By the Lord Harry, but there is something you can do, Colonel. You can send a message this instant down to the Four Courts and ask the officer in charge of these...these so called Provisional Government Forces to come here at once and explain to me why he is shelling the headquarters of His Majesty's Army in Ireland.'

As Colonel Winter departed in haste, Macready flopped his ample backside back down in his chair and took off his cap. He put the palms of his hands up to his face in a gesture of complete exasperation, and slowly drew them across his eyes, rubbing them all the while, like a man trying to see. He had had enough of humiliations. Ever since the Truce had come about twelve months ago, it had been all downhill as far as he was concerned. In the first instance, the Truce had been declared in the teeth of opposition from himself and his subordinate officers, Tudor and Crozier, who felt that with one more push the IRA would have been defeated in the field. But his political masters in the British Cabinet were fearful of world opinion and the bad press generated by the atrocities of the Black and Tans and the Essex Regiment. They had bowed to pressure from such pipsqueaks as Hugh Martin from the *Daily News*, who'd had the temerity to question his *bona fides* directly one morning as he gave him a tour of the Hospital. And then in the course of the supervision of the Truce, he'd suffered the extreme indignity of being called "a flat-footed bastard son of a policeman," by that notorious rebel, Tom Barry, who had come into his office one morning masquerading as a liaison officer. The absolute impertinence of the fellow. Macready had been so rattled that he spent the rest of the day shaking and taking nips of brandy from a hip flask to settle his nerves.

The list went on: the evacuation of the British Forces with unseemly haste, the handing over of all their best-equipped barracks to the Shinners, without regard to which side they were on. As far as Macready could see, both sides hated the British equally and couldn't wait to get rid of them, by hook or by crook. One of his closest associates, Field Marshall Henry Hughes Wilson, a staunch

Conservative and avid Unionist, had been assassinated outside his home at Eaton Place in London only five days previously by two self-confessed Republicans. Many, including Macready himself, suspected that it was done on the orders of Collins, in retaliation for the murders of Catholics in the North of Ireland, but in the murky political world in which they all now lived, it was impossible to prove for sure. But it shook him to his foundations.

Nobody consulted him anymore. Even as late as last night when he'd received word that the 18 pounder artillery pieces were to be handed over to the Provisional Government Forces to bombard the Four Courts, he'd objected strongly. But he was again overruled, this time by Sir Alfred Cope, the assistant under-secretary for Ireland. It was as if this makeshift Government of Collins, Cosgrave and O'Higgins, had somehow acquired greater influence with the British than he himself enjoyed. And now, the last straw: shells from his own artillery exploding on his front porch. How much more absurd could things become?

When he was summoned to explain himself by Macready, Dalton drove up from his forward command post in the Dolphin Hotel, behind the Clarence, with Liam Tobin and Pat McCrea. As he alighted from the armoured car, the first thing Macready noticed was the youth of the man and the second was his attitude. Before he got close, Macready saw him casually flicking a cigarette butt onto his green lawn. And then the jaunty swagger of his approach, the cap tilted askew on his head and the insolent smile on his brazen face. He gave a half-hearted salute, which Macready and his juniors, Tudor and Crozier, returned smartly, but with barely-concealed astonishment in their eyes.

'What's the meaning of this...General...Dalton?' demanded Macready, forcing himself to address the blackguard.

'What's what, sir?' asked Dalton, laconically, with the faint hint of a smile playing around his slack mouth.

Macready straightened himself upright in his shining brass buttons and inhaled. 'I mean these shells, General Dalton...you are a General, are you not?'

'Most certainly I am a General, General,' said the unperturbed Dalton, and continued: 'Shells, did you say, what shells?'

At that moment there was a whistling sound and another explosive from a distant 18 pounder flew over the roof of the Royal Hospital and landed with a splintering crash in a glass house in the walled garden at the rear.

'Shells...those shells...!' shouted Macready, ducking down and holding onto his cap. 'Are you deaf, man?'

'I wouldn't take much notice of those, sir,' laughed Dalton. 'It's just that one of our gunners thinks he's using a rifle instead of a cannon. He's behind in Green Street, a fellow named Ignatius O'Neill, he's from Clare.'

'I don't give a damn where he's from,' screamed Macready, losing all composure. 'Order him to stop this minute.'

'You see, he's canting the gun up like a rifle, trying to pick off one of the snipers on the parapet,' continued Dalton. 'Some of my men aren't used to artillery. When they aim too high, the shells sail completely over the Four Courts and land here in your back yard. Another fellow, Hackett from Kerry, well he did the opposite earlier. He aimed too low and blew a gaping hole in the quay wall and nearly killed us all with flying masonry.'

Macready looked fit to burst with rage as Dalton stood leaning casually against the car door with a grin on his face. He took a handkerchief from his pocket and wiped the dust from his brow. His face had small cuts and bruises from the hurtling stones.

'Can you return this instant, General Dalton,' said Major-General Tudor, coming to Macready's assistance, 'and order your men to take more careful aim. If they don't, sooner or later one of His Majesty's officers will be killed by your negligence.'

'What a shame that would be,' said the insolent Dalton, and saluted. 'I shall return immediately and ensure that we shoot straight from now on.'

He got back in the car and the driver, Pat McCrea, spun the wheels on the gravelled forecourt, as the car lurched off down the wide avenue with a screech of tyres. Macready was speechless. He followed the departing car, his eyes bulging from their sockets and it was all he could do to negotiate his way back inside, with Crozier and Tudor hovering behind him in case he stumbled.

Early in the morning of Friday, the 30th June, Michael Collins and Arthur Griffith climbed to the top of a building on Exchequer Street and stood on the flat roof. Collins was barely exerted, but Griffith was perspiring and out of breath. He stood bent double for some moments, holding onto a railing and panting laboriously. Collins waited for him to recover and then they both turned their eyes west along the Liffey, where they could make out the battered integrity of the Four Courts, lit up by the rising sun. The rain of the previous evening had passed, and it looked like the beginning of another glorious summer's day. As they stood, Collins produced a pair of binoculars and looked through them. He could see the damage more clearly, could see the smoke and flames and hear the shouts and cries of the wounded. Without a word he passed the glasses to Griffith, who perceived the same disturbing view. They stood for a long time, saying nothing. Eventually, Griffith stole a guilty look at Collins's face, and the expression he beheld was one of anguish and gloom. Griffith looked quickly away, unable to bear witness to the pain of his colleague any longer. Collins heaved a deep sigh and replaced the binoculars around his neck.

'What are we doing?' he asked in a voice that was barely more than a whisper. Was he speaking to himself? Griffith snatched another furtive look.

'What did you say, Michael?' he asked, cupping his ear with his right hand. His hearing, like his health, was deteriorating fast.

'I said what are we doing?' said Collins, 'turning our guns on our own race of people?'

Griffith cleared his throat. He didn't like to disagree with his Chairman, but he said: 'I would have done it a long time ago.'

Collins gave a bitter little laugh: 'You'd have unleashed the dragon before now, Arthur, but how could you contain him? How will we ever stop this now?'

'By restoring law and order,' said Griffith.

'With the greatest of respect to you, Arthur, restoring law and order will come at a terrible cost. The military men have taken control on both sides. We are more or less bystanders from now on.'

'Have you talked to de Valera? What does he say about this?'

'He's seeking a settlement, but he's as helpless as the rest of us now. Besides, he's not too pleased since we rejected his voting pact and lost him the election on June 16th.'

'The people voted in favour of the Treaty in that election,' said Griffith.

'A lot of good that is now,' said Collins. 'How can we govern with a civil war in full spate? And the elections were a show, to keep the British happy. I hope they're happy now.'

His eyes carried a look of bitter regret. Griffith looked lost for words. His big owl-like eyes blinked behind his prescription spectacles. His moustache drooped and he looked sad. 'Surely you can come up with some solution, Michael? You always have in the past.'

Collins smiled and put a spontaneous arm around the shoulders of the dejected older man. What a naive innocence resided in his portly bosom.

'Oh, Arthur,' he said, 'what dreams we had for Ireland? All going up in smoke.'

He blinked back tears of sorrow. 'We're fighting our own men. Some of our bravest and best are down there. I know them all: O'Connor, Mellows, Tom Barry, Dick Barret, Sean Lemass. They were the men who beat the Black and Tans, Arthur. Not you, me and de Valera, arguing behind our desks.'

Griffith looked like a broken man as they climbed down. When they got to the street, Collins turned and asked him: 'How are they treating you, Arthur, as President of Dáil Eireann?'

Griffith looked away. It was his turn to blink back sudden tears.

'What's the matter, Arthur?' asked Collins. Griffith heaved another sigh.

'They don't even give me a secretary anymore. They let me sit in my office with nothing to do. I'm a figurehead.'

He blew out his cheeks. Collins felt a tremendous pity for him.

'Never mind, Arthur,' he said, 'I know what you've accomplished in your life, but I'm afraid our new Cabinet has a different way of looking at things.'

'You do?'

'Yes, I'm beginning to think they've abandoned all idea of a stepping-stone to a Republic. Ever since the British rejected our new draft Constitution, my Cabinet colleagues seem bent upon a policy of appeasement and deference to the British at all costs.'

'But Michael, wasn't it we who ordered the bombardment of the Four Courts?' asked Griffith. 'Wasn't it you and I who agreed to the amendments to the new Constitution, after the drafting committee came up with a very republican document? Why do you blame the Cabinet when you and I were the leaders?'

'They did nothing to discourage us,' said Collins, glumly. He looked miserable.

Griffith looked away. His colleague was a complex man. Was he unable to decide for sure which side he was on?

They shook hands and Collins watched Griffith walk slowly down debris-strewn streets towards Government Buildings, lately opened in the stately mansion of the Dukes of Leinster on Kildare Street. For a moment he was lost for all words and ideas. Then a fresh clamour of firing broke out down towards Nassau Street. The trouble was spreading.

In the late, grey, rainy streets of Dublin the previous evening, Emmet Dalton had enough of treading softly. He ordered his gunners to take more deliberate aim at the facade of the Four Courts and make a bigger breach in the outer wall. Shell after shell slammed into the wall and soon it gave way completely on the western end. At the same time, he ordered 2000 new reinforcements up from the back streets and told them to present their rifles and fix their bayonets. Some were raw young recruits, eager for action and employment, while side by side with them were veterans of old wars, many of them British soldiers, just demobbed after the Truce. Dalton had personally re-hired many of them. With the rattle of Thompson machineguns, Lee Enfield .303 rifles and the blast of artillery shells ringing in their ears, they crossed the Liffey bridges in wave after wave, in the misty rain and wind, to batter their way into the fortified garrison.

There was a cacophony of ambulance sirens and motor cycle klaxons as the lonesome, broken streets came alive with the sound of running feet. The assault through the western breach was led by Joe Leonard, who received a bullet in the neck as he scrambled over rubble and masonry into the building. As Leonard fell, his men swarmed beyond him, but the men facing them inside did not back down. A terrible embrace of close quarter fighting began, with bombs, bayonets and bullets. Screams of gored young men rent the cavernous hall as the battle raged. Men who'd fought the Black and Tans side by side, now tried to cut each other to pieces. The Free State troops poured in but the gloom of the more cramped spaces gave the small garrison inside an advantage, until superior numbers overwhelmed them. They were forced to retreat over the bodies of fallen comrades as wild-eyed men with bayonets came lunging at them like they might have been ferocious Danes or Norsemen sacking Dublin a thousand years before. The small band of defenders retreated from pillar to pillar and from room to room, detonating Mills bombs in their wake to slow the onrushing momentum of the attackers. All was mayhem and confusion in the dark and in the dust. As the defenders retreated from the western wing and the round hall, they were replaced all along the three floors of the building by frightened young ingénues, who huddled for comfort in the dark chambers, wondering why they had ever volunteered to join this swaggering new army to fight their fellow Irishmen.

Outside the windows, the *Mutineer* roared up and down the yard between the main building and the rear, as its crew fired round after round in on top of the attackers. Rubble, broken glass, shattered masonry and spent bullets lay everywhere. By midnight the defenders had retreated towards the northeast wing after a heroic defence of their positions, and as the first streaks of dawn came over Dublin, the Free State soldiers occupied the round hall, the Law Library and most of the western wing. A temporary truce was arranged as a coal dray drawn by two horses, transported a large group of doctors across broken tram wires and mortar-strewn roads to take the wounded to Jervis Street hospital and the dead to the morgue.

Then the terrible din started up again, as the fighting resumed more fiercely than before. Soon the Solicitor and Bankruptcy Departments caught fire and men coughed and spat, as clouds of smoke filled lungs and burned eyes. Ernie O'Malley had a hurried conversation with Rory O'Connor and Paddy O'Brien.

'How are things now?' asked O'Malley.

'Getting critical,' said O'Brien. 'Our ammunition is nearly gone. So is our food.'

'But we still have lots of explosives,' said O'Malley.

'Enough to blow the place up?' asked O'Connor.

'And ourselves with it,' laughed O'Malley, grimly.

O'Connor nodded. He knew they had a lot of mines laid down throughout the fortress. He looked at his watch. 'It's nearly 11 a.m. Tell Lemass to gather the boys. We'll make a break out the far gate.'

Dick Barrett and Liam Mellows came over with Joe McKelvey. O'Connor saluted and said: 'It's not looking great. We're going to explode the small mines at the gate. When they go up, the 'Staters' will most likely fall back and we'll get through in the confusion.'

O'Malley looked sceptical, but he said: 'I'll go back and tell the bombardiers.'

He walked back down a long corridor, waving to bedraggled young defenders. He spoke to some bomb makers in a basement near the Records' Office. Quickly the order spread to evacuate the building, and there was a convergence of soldiers towards the eastern gate.

There was a lull in the sporadic shooting, and then a complete stop, as an eerie silence descended on the Four Courts. The morning sun shone in through broken glass, creating strange prisms of colour in the rising dust. The Free State troops looked up and waited. They wondered at the quietude.

Then there came a deep rumbling and a rising blast that rocked the city. Glass, masonry, bricks and mortar sailed skywards. Gigantic clouds of smoke and dust towered into the air and the sun was blocked out as if an eclipse had crossed the face of the earth. The men designated by O'Connor to rush the eastern gate were frozen to the spot, temporarily paralysed by the mind-numbing blast. Massed tomes were shifted from the walls of the Library. Like a huge, sinister snowfall, millions of fragments of paper floated through the air to settle far down the river on sidewalks and streets, parks and houses. Entire books were hurled for miles. All traffic in the city centre stopped and all eyes looked up along Batchelor's Walk to Arran Quay, where the mighty pall of smoke was slowly beginning to move away on the southwest wind. It floated slowly northeast over Drumcondra, Clontarf, Kibarrack and settled in due course like an angry wound in the sky over Howth Head. It took many hours for the blue sky to re-emerge.

The explosion had shattered the great dome of the Four Courts. In the round hall underneath it, over forty Free State troops were injured, some very badly. Long tongues of flame rose above the parapet and fires spread all along by the Records' Office and enveloped both sides of the western side of the building. Ambulances rushed from all over the city to carry the wounded away. Miraculously there were no dead.

The leaders of the Executive Forces huddled with their shell-shocked defenders in the northeast corner and wondered what had gone wrong. When his ears stopped ringing, O'Connor turned an enquiring eye on his smoke-blackened colleague, Ernie O'Malley. 'What in the name of God happened, Ernie?'

O'Malley removed the cotton wool earplugs from his ears and wiped the grime from his face. He removed his glasses, cleaned them on the tail of his shirt and put them back on. 'Our engineers must have put too much explosive in the mix,' he shrugged.

'But Ernie, we were only supposed to let off some small mines at the front gate, not bring down the building?'

'There were large amounts of explosives in the basement. Anything could have set them off, including Free State shells.'

O'Malley sighed. They'd probably never know, but it didn't matter. The battle was over. They were surrounded by a ring of Free State Forces. On the inside, more of those same Forces were within a wall or two of breaking into their last redoubt. O'Connor gave the word and Liam Mellows walked across the yard towards the gate with a white flag fluttering from his rifle bayonet. Behind him, groups of haggard, hungry young men emerged, with their rifles at the trail and their hands up. O'Connor stood at the gate. His officers and men lined up in a ragged line behind him. He asked Tony Lawlor and Emmet Dalton for terms.

'Unconditional surrender,' said Dalton tersely. 'Those are our only terms.'

'No better than the men of 1916 got from the British,' smiled O'Malley, a little bitterly.

'What did you expect?' asked Dalton coldly

'From you, not a lot,' said O'Malley. 'But what do your superiors have to say?'

'In this situation, they have no say. Only my military colleague, Major-General Daly has any input and my understanding is that he wishes to shoot you all.' Dalton gave a dry, cynical smirk.

At that, a bluff, red-faced man, who looked like he might suffer from high-blood pressure, came bustling over. It was Major-General Patrick Daly, who'd led the first Free State troops to take over Beggar's Bush from the British while still only a captain. But now that he'd been promoted to the rank of general, he felt quite triumphant and entitled to throw his weight around.

'What the devil are you doing?' he said to Lawlor. 'These fellows deserve only the firing squad. Why are you being nice to them?'

Lawlor was in the act of passing cigarettes around to devastated young defenders. He knew brave men when he saw them. The onslaught they'd withstood for three days was ferocious and their courage had been impressive.

'You've got to take their surrender before you shoot them, General,' said Lawlor with a shrug.

'Huh,' said Daly, not sure of the protocol. 'Which of these buggers is controlling them? Is it you, O'Malley?'

Ernie O'Malley turned a weary eye towards Daly. 'It doesn't matter much who it is at this point,' he said. 'My only regret is that we didn't blow you and your army to Kingdom Come in that explosion.'

'Big words, Ernie,' laughed Daly, 'but sure it's only sour grapes with you, isn't it.'

An orderly handed a sheet of paper to Daly with the surrender written on it.

'Sign this and give me your gun,' said Daly.

O'Malley signed the surrender without a word and then proffered his pistol to Daly, who reached for it greedily. At that moment,

O'Malley changed his mind and threw the pistol over Daly's head and it landed with a splash in the Liffey. Daly whirled about to see the pistol sinking in the water. Then he turned back to O'Malley with a look of thunder on his face. O'Malley looked elated. Daly said. 'We'll knock that grin off your face where we're taking you.'

'And where might that be?' asked O'Malley casually, his contempt for Daly clear in his voice.

'Mountjoy,' said Daly. 'Expect a long stay.'

William Cody had volunteered for the task of attending the wounded. With his fellow medical students he'd laboured day after day in the cauldron of destruction that had burned up Dublin. He'd seen many dead bodies. He'd never forget the face of one frightened, wounded young man whose hand he held, as his lifeblood ebbed away. What was it for and what purpose would this sacrifice serve? All for a form of words upon a page that some said were more significant than another form of words. To William there was little difference between one way of dying than another, whatever about one phrase and another.

When the Four Courts garrison surrendered, the fighting spread down along the Liffey. There were clashes in Westmoreland Street, Dame Street, Nassau Street, Gardiner Street, and in dozens of side streets and back alleys leading off them. After more than a week, the final focus was on the broad boulevard of Sackville Street, where the remnants of the Executive Forces held out all along the eastern side. For some reason the massed ranks of Republicans outside the city failed to materialise within it. There were few reinforcements coming to the assistance of the beleaguered Dublin men, but still the resistance was as fierce as ever.

Cathal Brugha, with the zeal of the fanatic, urged his fighters on from the roof of the Gresham Hotel. Oscar Traynor and de Valera managed to find their way into the middle of the defenders, but Brugha called the shots, literally. With a Mauser automatic grafted on to the stock of a rifle, he moved along the rooftops, from Morans Hotel to the Hammam, to the Gresham, praising, goading, comforting. His Forces had broken through from one building to another along Sackville Street, moving on planks stretched between walls. But the same 18 pounder cannon that had finally smashed the Four Courts had now been moved ominously into the mouth of Henry Street, the corner of Batchelors Walk, and south of the river on Burgh Quay. The Free State Forces controlled most of the western side of the street, but the

Executive Forces were also strategically entrenched in the Rotunda at the top of Sackville Street, near Parnell Square. Both sides set about demolishing the city with gusto.

Margie and Anna, with their schoolmates, Mary Higgins and Jennifer Slevin, finally managed to sneak out from the confines of the convent for a few nights and joined the hundreds of other spectators who roamed the centre of Dublin, to see the bullets and shells tracing the air like fireworks, smell the gunpowder and hear the roar of artillery. Soon, flames began to engulf the eastern side of the street and building after building began to blaze in a gigantic conflagration of smoke and sparks. By Wednesday the 5th of July, most of the defenders had surrendered except for a small group who held out with Cathal Brugha. The girls moved closer to the centre of the terrible, unfolding drama. They stood near the entrance to the Y.M.C.A. building on the western side of Sackville Street. The Republicans had held it, but now it had caught fire. There was a group of blind men inside trying to get out. They groped their way along by the walls of a corridor led by a young man, as smoke blackened the air all around them. Suddenly Anna recognised the young medical orderly.

'It's William,' she shouted. 'William, William.'

Her heart leaped up in fear and pride. William turned in astonishment when he heard the familiar voice. 'My God, Anna, what are you doing here?' he said. 'Are you mad?'

'Not at all,' said Anna, blithely. 'I'm here with Margie and some girls from Loreto.'

'Will you go back to the convent for goodness sake,' implored William. 'You'll be killed.'

They crouched down as a fusillade of shots ripped into the burning building. There was a tangle of wires overhead, glass littered the pavements. The street was in chaos. Margie appeared from a side street and ran over excitedly. William looked bemused: 'I suppose this is into your oil can,' he said, sarcastically.

The 'Staters' aren't getting it easy,' said Margie, with satisfaction. She pointed across Sackville Street: 'There are at least thirty women from Cumann Na mBan in there, fighting as fiercely as the men. I'm hoping to join them.'

'And be killed?' said William in despair.

Their voices were drowned out as an 18 pounder blasted the Granville Hotel across the street from point blank range. The block was burning furiously. The defenders fought bullets, shells and flames.

William and the girls watched in horrified fascination as another hotel, the Hammam, crumbled in a thunderous roar of falling bricks and mortar, sending forth dense clouds of dust and smoke.

'I don't know how anyone can survive that,' said William, as they saw the defenders move on to the next roof, continuing to fire their rifles and revolvers in the face of overwhelming odds. The watching crowds remained transfixed and curiously passive in the midst of the spectacle, impervious to the cries of the wounded and the suffering of the dying, as if deriving a ghoulish pleasure from it all.

'Is this what we have come to?' asked William, sadly. 'Fighting like rats in a hole?'

'It's the 'Staters' who are doing the attacking,' said Margie, 'just like their masters before them.'

'Masters? What masters?' asked William.

'Don't play the innocent with me, William,' said Margie. 'The real Irish will still prevail. The British will never beat us.'

William shook his weary head. His sisters were on a different wavelength, guided by another star. The convictions of the family mirrored those of the country, hardened into factions with no end in sight.

Suddenly there was a shout as the Granville Hotel caught fire. It was about 5 o'clock and the evening shadows were lengthening over the battered and bleeding city. Then, a group of defenders, men and women, emerged into a side alley with one holding a white flag aloft. There was a lull in the firing.

'Look there, look there,' said Anna. 'It's de Valera.'

'And Oscar Traynor,' said Margie.

'And Austin Stack, and Art O'Connor,' said someone else.

'There's Mary McSwiney,' shouted Margie, 'and Kevin Barry's sister.'

The group of women came forward defiantly into the middle of Sackville Street. Some men followed behind them, but in the milling confusion, some others slipped away, de Valera among them.

Margie looked ecstatic as the women advanced to the centre meridian. Suddenly she left her siblings and dashed across. They could see her standing in front of Mary McSwiney, shaking her hand.

'She's mad,' said William.

'She's not,' said Anna, fiercely. 'She's as brave as a lion.'

Their attention shifted to a lone figure on the roof of the Granville. Then there was a murmur of anticipation as the man ran across the roof, firing his pistol. A shout went up: 'It's Cathal Brugha. He's not going to surrender.'

'He'll be burnt to death,' said a second voice.

'That's what he wants,' said a third.

They could see the firemen battering down the door of the blazing building, and the Saint John's Ambulance officers rushing in. But after some moments the officers backed slowly out the door, repelled by the flames or perhaps by the defiant Brugha, waving his gun. The crowds of ogling people, the Free State soldiers across the street, the group of surrendered prisoners huddled in the middle, all waited, as the flames roared skywards and tall plumes of smoke, smelling of tar, towered into the evening sun. William looked around. In the strange hush, broken only by the crackling sound of flames, a small figure dashed out the front door of the Granville. He held his Mauser automatic with its rifle stock to his shoulder and fired blindly towards his attackers across the street. At the same moment, the Lewis gunner in Findlaters, directly opposite, opened up on the running man. Brugha was spun around as a bullet hit him in the shoulder. With eyes bright, like the devouring flames surrounding him, he still came forward, immune to pain. He tried to lift his gun arm but his strength was gone. The Lewis gun rattled. Bullets bounced all around Brugha's feet. Onwards he charged, until another bullet found its mark, and down he fell, with a gaping wound in his leg from which blood spurted like a fountain. His automatic fell from his grasp and he dragged himself along in the debris, his breath coming in broken gasps. William Cody started across the middle of the street towards him. He shouted at the Lewis gunner. 'In the name of God, stop firing. Can't you see the man is done for?'

'Be careful, William,' shouted Anna. The firing stopped as William reached the wounded man. By now he had been hit several more times and blood flowed from many perforations. William knelt beside him and tried to staunch the flow with bandages which he pulled from his pocket. Already he could see the glazed look in Brugha's eyes and hear the faltering breath. He put his hand on the stricken man's forehead to comfort him. Silence again descended over the ruined street, as when a door is closed or a curtain drawn. The Saint John's Ambulance men reached them and gently placed the heroic little man on a stretcher. As they bore him away, William stood up, letting his hands hang helplessly by his side, his face a mask of sorrow at the grand futility of it all. Margie and Anna stared at their brother and all of a sudden each felt an immense pride. He had proved to the world that he had a kind and generous heart and he'd shown them that he too was brave.

Slowly night drew in. The moon shone down on Sackville Street. Margie, Anna and William lingered with the aimless crowds, who now seemed to move like redundant ghosts on streets where brave men had died. There was no more excitement for today, no more violence to satisfy their blood-thirsty desires. The fires burned on and the sparks mingled with the moonbeams to create an eerie sense of otherworld. The stars looked down on Dublin and if they had feelings they would have cried.

Several hundred Republican soldiers were arrested and carted off to Mountjoy. Included in their ranks were Rory O'Connor, Liam Mellows, Joe McKelvey, Dick Barrett and Tom Barry, who was arrested as he had tried to inveigle his way back in dressed as a nurse. Others, such as Ernie O'Malley, Sean Moylan and Eamon de Valera, managed to escape, melting away over walls and through side alleys, past raw country recruits who held up the innocent bystanders while inadvertently allowing the schemers-in-chief to get away. Most of the Republicans had lived to fight another day. They would head for the south where the mountains were high and their numbers great, where they still had many friends and where the methods they used to beat the Black and Tans would be used again to challenge their new-found, bitter enemies of the Free State side.

29

the galtees were so beautiful

The Galtees were so beautiful, dreamy, blue and beckoning in the hot sun of July. Anna gazed at them in the distance all the long afternoon. She looked at Margie, lulled into sleep beside her. She'd miss the sun going down on Galteemore. They were travelling in a horse and trap driven by a young farmer, with a long nose and a thin face, who'd picked them up in a place called The Horse and Jockey, a funny name for a small crossroads with a public house and shop, on the wide plain of Tipperary. The driver was humming to himself to while away the tedious miles and Anna liked the words:

> "*And as we crossed Tipperary, we reeved the clan O'Leary,*
> *Oh, Sean O'Duibhir a'Ghleanna, we were worsted in the game.*"

The singing caused Margie to awaken. She looked about her. 'Where are we?' she asked.

'Near Cashel,' said the fellow.

'Cashel of the Kings,' said Margie, 'built by Dónal Mór O'Callaghan.'

'Twas the Ryans built that,' he said, with a twinkle in his eye.

'Are you Ryan?' asked Margie.

'Tommy Ryan,' he said and doffed his cap.

'The Ryans were but a minor clan,' said Margie, 'vassals to the O'Briens and O'Callaghans.'

He looked sideways at her. 'By God, you know your history.'

'Which repeats itself with unfailing regularity.'

'What does?'

'History.'

'By Christ you're wise, for a young wan.'

'Thank you,' said Margie, now fully awake.

They'd come by train from Dublin to Port Laoise, but the line was blown up there and the train stopped. They reached Abbeyleix and then Durrow by various means, motor car, on foot and on horseback. Margie thought how beautiful the countryside was in the shadowed light of sundown, rolling away from the Slieve Blooms to the Silvermines, yet how ugly the towns they must traverse. But the people were kind to them, farmers, jarveys, soldiers, no matter which side they were on. They got to Urlingford in a Free State lorry and the young soldiers were charmingly boastful. They swaggered in their uniforms and told them how they'd pushed the Republicans ever southwards until now they only held Munster. Margie looked askance at them. She recalled the fellow who'd ridden all the way from Dublin to Port Laoise, standing on the footplate of the steam engine. He must have been frozen with the cold and his face was black as soot from the smoke, but he liked to show how tough he was. McEoin they called him, a general now, though he started out as a blacksmith. Fellows got big ideas in wartime.

'How far are ye going anyway?' the young farmer asked.

'West Cork,' said Anna.

'West Cork,' exclaimed the incredulous driver. 'Ye'll never get that far, the way things are in the country.'

'Why not?' asked Margie.

'The 'Irregulars' are controlling everything from Limerick to Clonmel,' he said.

'Who are the 'Irregulars'?' asked Margie, sarcastically.

The driver looked sharply sideways at her. 'Ah, Christ, don't be codding me.'

'If you mean the Executive Forces, then I understand you,' she said.

The driver laughed. This one was feisty. 'Fair enough, the Executive Forces,' he said, 'or the Republicans, call 'em what you like. Liam Lynch's crowd, and de Valera's.'

'So you support the 'Free Staters' then?' asked Margie.

'Aye. The Ryans were always law and order men. We don't like blackguarding.'

'Where are you going anyway?' asked Anna after a pause.

'To Fethard,' he said, 'to buy a horse.'

'You're very kind to go out of your way,' said Anna.

'Why wouldn't I,' he said, 'war or no war, I wouldn't like young wans like yerselves to fall into the hands of the 'Irregulars.''

'We appreciate your kindness,' said Margie, 'but we're happy to meet with the 'Irregulars,' as you call them.'

'Christ, are ye?' He looked a bit taken aback, regarding them keener still.

When they got to Cashel there was confusion, with Republican soldiers moving through the town in lorries, cars and on horses. They learned that they'd been defeated in Limerick, despite being better armed. A Free State general called Brennan had transported a bunch of guns from Clare and sent them back and forth again and again, for the next round of troops. They only had two hundred guns in all, but they made the journey five times, giving the impression they had a thousand. Liam Lynch was fooled. He was also double-crossed after making a truce with an old, trusted comrade called Donnchadh O'Hannigan. General McManus came from Dublin and gave a countermanding order. Then the big artillery was brought in by sea. Up the Shannon it came. Limerick was pounded to bits, just like Dublin. The Republicans left blazing barracks everywhere behind them as they headed for the hills. Liam Lynch, once a moderate compared to Rory O'Connor, had moved on to Clonmel where he still felt confident of victory. Following the fall of Kilmallock, Liam Deasy was in charge in Buttevant, north Cork, which was a lawless crossroads like a frontier town in the American west. The beautiful river Suir was like the Rio Grande, all to the south were the rebels, the true Republicans, while northward were the compromisers with England, who'd sold the pass. At least that's what Margie and Anna thought. Some of their best fighters, like Tom Barry, were in jail in Mountjoy and their former political leader, Eamon de Valera, was reduced to the status of private, taking orders from the men who wielded the guns. The Provisional Government Forces were full of enthusiasm while the Executive Forces seemed to have no stomach for the fight, being loath to kill their former comrades-in-arms.

Michael Collins rose early from his bed in his new headquarters in Portobello barracks in south Dublin, and donned his new uniform: dark green tunic and pants, peaked cap and shiny boots. He tied a brown leather belt around his waist and slung his leather pouch containing his field glasses over his shoulder. He finally holstered a Colt .45 revolver on his right thigh and surveyed himself in a long mirror. He smiled wryly, kingpin at last, Commander-in-Chief of the Free State Army. Within the past week, at the urgings of Dick Mulcahy, he'd gone into uniform.

'You'll inspire the troops Mick,' Mulcahy had said. 'No one can do the job like you.'

'You really think so?' asked Collins, with a doubtful look on his face. Sitting with him in the red brick building that was now his headquarters, were military men, Mulcahy, Eoin O'Duffy, Emmet Dalton and Cabinet Members, Kevin O'Higgins and W.T. Cosgrave, who'd come along to rubber stamp the appointment. All seemed eager to flatter him, despite his reluctance.

'I was always a desk man, Dick, an organiser, sure I can't even shoot straight.'

Mulcahy moved to reassure him: 'We don't envision a forward position for you Mick, leave that to Emmet and Eoin here, both military men with proven experience. What the army needs is an inspirational figure, like yourself.'

'And what about you, Dick?' asked Collins. 'You weren't doing too badly.'

'I know my limitations,' said Mulcahy. 'I'm no Michael Collins.'

Collins frowned. 'But what about running the country? Who'll talk to the British, who'll organise the finances if I'm in the army?'

'You are a many-talented man, Mick, it's true,' said Mulcahy, 'but there are others amongst us who have abilities as well.'

He indicated Cosgrave: 'We're proposing that William here will take your position, temporarily of course, as Chairman of the Provisional Government. Kevin O'Higgins will take over Justice and I will continue in Defence and as Chief of Staff. Eoin O'Duffy will be Assistant Chief of Staff and GOC of Southwestern Command.'

Kevin O'Higgins, who'd remained silently watchful, sitting at one end of the long table where they'd held the Council of War, cleared his throat and smiled his smooth, oleaginous smile. 'We have the 'Irregulars' on the run, Michael. They're holding on in Munster, but we broke the back of them in the Four Courts. You showed your mettle there by ordering the bombardment. One more push and we'll smash them for good.'

Collins looked evenly at O'Higgins. His recollection was that he'd ordered the Four Courts garrision to be starved out, to force a surrender. He hadn't actually ordered the bombardment, which appeared to have been the initiative of some officers acting independently? But that was of no matter now. The deed was done. He turned his gaze on Mulcahy. He could feel the incipient rivalry between him and O'Higgins. He stood up and said: 'Alright, I'll agree to your proposals, provided Mr. Cosgrave is in overall control of the Cabinet, Prime Minister, in effect, and standing in my shoes, as it were.'

O'Higgins nodded vigorously: 'That's absolutely perfect, Michael,' he said, 'that's the way we want it as well.'

'What about Arthur?' asked Collins. 'Have you consulted him?'

There was an embarrassed silence until Cosgrave spoke up. 'Mr. Griffith is poorly these days. Not sleeping and drinking a lot we hear. I'm sorry to say he's not the man he was. The shock of civil war has upset him.'

'It's upset us all,' said Collins. He looked around from face to face. The glint he observed in O'Higgins's eye suggested less upset than satisfaction. Did the man enjoy the prospect of crushing his former comrades? He put the idea to the back of his mind and said briskly: 'That's settled then.'

The others stood and they all shook hands and filed out. Collins turned to the young general, Emmet Dalton, and said: 'I hear you've devised a plan to take Cork city.'

'I have,' said Dalton. 'From the sea. We've no chance of battering our way south overland. The 'Irregulars' have all the best men in South Tipperary and Cork County. Scarcely an IRA officer has defected to our side, except for Sean Hales and some others. Some are neutral of course, such as Florrie O'Donoghue. If we come up Cork Harbour by boat we'll catch them unawares. They'll never expect us.'

'It sounds like a clever plan,' smiled Collins.

'Do I have permission to commandeer two boats, the *Arvonia* and the *Lady Wicklow*, they're Irish Sea packets, suitable for ferrying troops?'

'Carry on, Emmet,' said Collins. Dalton saluted smartly, turned on his heel and left.

As the others stood in the courtyard of the barracks, Cosgrave said he was going to Mass in the church on Rathgar Road. Mulcahy had military business to attend to in Beggars Bush barracks on Haddington Road, so they went their separate ways. O'Higgins climbed into his car, driven by a junior officer named Vinny Byrne, part of Collins's former Squad. He sat in the back and told Byrne to take him to the city centre. As they drove along, he surveyed the ruined buildings, the burnt out husks of shops and warehouses. Everywhere he looked he saw chaos and destruction. An iron fist was needed and he was the man to provide it. 'Yes,' he thought to himself, 'a good day's work.'

He'd been surprised at how easily Collins had agreed to become head of the army. But he would no longer be in Government. He'd be answerable to Mulcahy, in a Civil Service post, in effect. Mulcahy would be his senior as Minister of Defence.

O'Higgins sniffed. That would give himself and Cosgrave a free hand to run the country as they saw fit. In fact, he would run it. Cosgrave would do as he was told, so would the others, McNeill, Blythe, McGrath, Duggan and Walsh. The one great figure standing in the way of his own progress had been subtly sidelined.

The Cody girls eventually got home to Gatonville. Anna stood in the green lawn under the magnificent elm and beech trees and thought how all had changed. Only two years ago she had stood in that self-same spot, the day Margie had told her of the death of John James O'Grady. It seemed as if a lifetime had passed since she'd seen the sun going down and its rays reflected off the ancient Georgian windows; since the balmy evening she heard her mother's beautiful playing of Paganini drifting through the soft summer air. In that time the British had mostly gone, but now their world was shaken by this terrible, fratricidal war. Who now was friend and who was foe? In fact friend had become foe in many cases and the dreadful, dark passions and acts of barbarism had shaken them all to their foundations.

News was even now filtering through of the fall of Cork. The 'Free Staters,' under Tom Ennis and Emmet Dalton, had crept up the foggy Lee in the *Arvonia* and the *Lady Wicklow* with over 800 troops. They'd put a gun to the head of the river pilot and forced him to sail past mine-laden wrecks into a narrow berth at Passage West. The Gods were on their side. It was the only unmined pier in all of Cork Harbour. Dalton had taken a chance, as was his wont. In the small hours they swarmed ashore in the village of Passage and fought a bloody, three day battle with 200 Republicans all along the Rochestown coast road, in Old Court Wood, in Maryborough and in Ravenscourt, until they finally reached Douglas. The fighting had been savage, in turnip fields and cornfields, where the golden wheat was stained red and many men on both sides died in a futile squandering of young life. Dalton was again triumphant and he marched on into the heart of Cork city, as a huge Republican convoy of cars, lorries and guns set out for the west country, leaving Union Quay barracks burning and the city to the Free State. To Margie and Anna it seemed another easy capitulation by the men who'd fought the Black and Tans so tenaciously for two long years. Some awful inertia had overtaken the best of men, who now appeared marooned and unable to rouse themselves, like lotus eaters, swooning and in thrall to woeful tidings come to pass, as if their spirits had forsaken them and melted away like blown roses on the grass.

30

'You'll get rain,' said John Lordan, and stood dressed in black in the cooling breeze of early morning.

'I doubt it,' said Tom Hales, 'while the wind is from the northwest.'

He adjusted his cloth cap down over his eyes to keep from squinting in the bright sun.

'You might get a smattering,' said the heavy-set Bill Desmond. 'The wind is turning, but 'twon't be much.'

A group of about ten men stood on high Greenhill. The views in all directions were sublime. They saw some late stragglers coming up. Sonny Hennessy was first, then Dan Corcoran and another they couldn't make out.

'Good man Sonny,' said the smiling John Lordan as the young man arrived, panting from the climb.

'Where's Mike?' asked Dan Holland.

'Coming,' said Sonny, as his brother followed Corcoran up by a long ditch.

'Sure when were the Hennessys early?' joked Bill Desmond, as Mike stopped at the crest.

'You'd be late yourself if you had to deal with that brother of ours,' said Mike.

'Which one?' asked Lordan. 'Not Richie? He's punctual.'

'Tull I s'pose,' laughed Tom Hales.

'Who else,' said Mike with a look of exasperation.

'What's bothering him now?' asked Dan Holland.

'With Tull there's always something,' said Mike. 'Horses or pigs, or politics, even women.'

'Women, by God,' said Lordan. 'Which one?'

Mike looked to Sonny who said: 'He was keen on Kathleen de Courcey, but her parents didn't approve and she went off without him.'

'She could have done a lot worse than Tull,' said Tom Hales.

'You know he's with the 'Staters,' said Mike, throwing an uneasy look to Hales.

'I do,' said Hales, 'like my own brother, Sean. 'Tis a disaster. They're the only two out of five companies from here to Bandon who've taken the other side.' He shook his head in weary resignation and said: 'No matter, it can't be helped.' There was a pause before he continued darkly: 'I hope he doesn't appear at the end of my own gun sights.'

There was a flicker of unease in the eyes of each man.

They looked down on the townlands of Lissarourke, Killinear and Laravoulta to the south. Westwards were Bengour, Monacreha and Coppeen. When they gazed to the north, they looked down on Pullerick and Gurranereigh and beyond the lowlands towered the Sheha mountains, the Paps and Mushera. The sky was big, the clouds were windblown and white horses rimed the southern sea.

'You can see half of Ireland from here,' said John Lordan.

'You can even see the Galtees in Tipperary,' said Bill Desmond.

'Liam Lynch country,' said Dan Corcoran.

'Lynch sent word that Dev is in Joe Sullivan's,' said Hales, 'but he said not to entertain him.'

'Who's with him?' asked Dan Holland.

'Tom Crofts and Liam Deasy,' said Hales.

Their eyes followed a hovering hawk floating in the updrafts above the valley floor. There was a glint of sunlight on glass. 'What's that?' asked John Lordan, pointing to a movement on the distant road to Mossgrove.

'It looks like a lorry,' said Sonny.

'More than one,' said Mike.

Tom Hales took a pair of field glasses out of their pouch and held them to his eyes. 'You're right,' he said, 'I see a lorry and an armoured car, and it looks like a touring car between 'em. 'Tis bright yellow. There's a motorbike in front.'

'It must be 'Staters,' said Lordan.

'If it is they have a damn nerve to be coming into our territory,' said Hales, grimly.

'They think they own the country now,' said Bill Desmond.

'Not yet by God,' said Hales. 'Come on, we'll go down to meet the others.'

They descended Greenhill in single file, rifles at the trail, pistols holstered, relaxed in their own ground, but wary nonetheless. Their grey trenchcoats and dark pants blended in with the yellow of the gorse and the many shades of green leaves and grass. Sonny followed behind and watched them. Brothers in arms, a small band left now. Hunted on every side, with the 'Free Staters' holding most of the towns and they back running in the hills like in the days of the Black and Tans. He recognised true hearts and comrades he grew up with. Here is where they hurled, bowled, rode horses, followed cattle. This was the land they fought for, would die for if they had to. Here was the land they cherished.

When they got down to Boxers Cross, they saw Liam Deasy and Tom Crofts coming against them from Horn Hill side. There was a tall, dark man walking between them. He stood out from the others because he carried himself with a kind of austere dignity. Everything about him was long and ascetic-looking, his nose, his jaw, his arms, his legs. Liam Deasy introduced Eamon de Valera. He still called him 'Chief,' although the man who'd taken America by storm and confounded Lloyd George and Churchill was now reduced to the status of foot soldier. They all lined up to shake his hand. He would never be a foot soldier in their eyes. They showed their respect for him and walked along like a bodyguard down the Bantry Line.

'The Bantry Line,' smiled de Valera, bemused at the grand name of the narrow road. 'It sounds like a big highway in New York.'

''Tis just as dangerous I tell you,' said John Lordan. 'We'd better take a side road in case of 'Staters.'

They turned right at Cronins and walked along a narrow boreen with high hawthorn hedges. A man with a roguish face called Tom Taylor waved them through his yard at Pullerick and invited them in for whiskey when he learned the name of their honoured guest.

'We'll go on, Tom,' said Liam Deasy. 'Thanks though. We have a meeting with IRA officers later and the 'Chief' has to go on to Ballyvourney and north Cork.'

'Does he want a lift?' asked Taylor, eyes twinkling. 'I've a good horse and a back-to-back with mighty springs. The most comfortable you'd ever see.'

De Valera smiled at the offer and said. 'Thanks very much, Tom, but

I believe Sean Hyde is looking after me. If he can't do it, I'll be back to you though.'

'Fair enough,' said Taylor, 'but come here to me.' He beckoned to Tom Hales and whispered low. 'I hear Collins is around.'

Tom Hales leant in close as if he hadn't heard properly. 'Collins?' he asked, in doubt.

''Pon me sowl,' said Taylor.

Hales stood back. 'Who told you?'

'Denny the Dane,' said Taylor. 'He spotted him in Béal Na Bláth, when the convoy went through less than an hour ago.' He pronounced it 'Balnablaw,' the local way.

They went on, past Norah Wall's farmhouse, then down a steep hill to where the river Bride flowed gently under a hump-backed bridge in the shadow of ash trees.

'Do you know which side every family is on?' asked de Valera.

'Every house and every man,' said John Lordan. 'Most of them are friendly and those that are against us are still friendly in these parts.'

'Like old Mr. Sullivan in Gurranereigh,' said de Valera.

'Old Joe is always against everything,' laughed Liam Deasy. 'When we were fighting the Tans, he said we weren't a patch on his old pals in the Fenians. Now he's mad Free State.'

'But he still gave me a bed to sleep in,' said de Valera.

'And no fear he'd turn you in either,' said Tom Hales.

When they came back out on the Bantry Line, Hales put his hand on Liam Deasy's shoulder and confided in a thought that was troubling him.

'We'd better be careful,' he said. 'Tom Taylor says Mick Collins came through in a convoy earlier.'

Deasy turned to de Valera. 'Did you know that Collins was coming south?'

'Collins?' frowned Dev. 'That's the first I heard of it.'

'It seems a local scout, Denny Long, saw him in a convoy.'

'The one we spotted from Greenhill?' said John Lordan.

'We'll know for sure when we get to the crossroads. 'Tis only half a mile,' said Tom Crofts.

When they reached the crossroads of Béal Na Bláth, they went into Jer Long's pub. In the dark interior there was the smell of stale beer and cigarette smoke and the forlorn air of an early morning tavern. There was a high counter on the left, with snugs off it, and a room to the back leading to the outdoor toilet. As their eyes got used to the gloom, they saw the shadowy outlines of men sitting here and there on hard settle seats, their stubbled faces and white shirts half lit by the sun filtering through the narrow side window. They were unusually quiet, as if anticipating something important.

Long's look of suspicion changed when he recognised John Lordan and then the others following behind. Some of the men sitting in the shadows stood up. Tom Kelleher was there and Pete Kearney, Con Lucey and Jim Hurley. From the room at the back, Mick Crowley emerged with Tadhg O'Sullivan, Sean Culhane and Denis O'Neill. Sonny and Mike Hennessy stood at the edge as they all crowded around to shake de Valera's hand. He still retained his ability to mesmerise even these most hardened of men.

Jer Long was suddenly relaxed and laughing in nervous relief. 'We thought 'twas the 'Staters' come back to interrogate us,' he said. 'But 'tis alright, they didn't spot anyone here.' He turned to de Valera. 'Will ye have a sup a' tay, or something stronger, for the 'Chief' anyway? You're welcome, sir, to our humble corner of the world.'

De Valera's long impassive face crinkled into a grin. 'Thank you, Mr. Long,' he said, 'but we got a hearty breakfast from Joe Sullivan.'

'No better man than the same Joe,' said Long dryly, his tone carrying a subtle hint that there were differences with his neighbour up the road. He fussed around and produced a few high stools: 'Sit up there won't you and have a ball of malt for the long road that's ahead of you to north Cork and south Tipperary.'

De Valera demurred, but Long insisted: 'Ah, Christ, if Joe Sullivan can give you the 'bruckisht,' you can have a drop of the crathur in this house. We mightn't ever again see you here.'

For the sake of harmony, de Valera agreed, and Long poured a measure. All the others declined and he filled one for himself. 'Bad cess to ye,' he said, 'we can't have the President of Ireland drinking on his own.'

As the hot *poitín* hit the back of his throat, de Valera brightened and said: 'It's nice of you to say so, Mr. Long, but there are others who carry that title now.'

'*Mar dhea*,' scoffed Long, 'but not around here. Those fellows will never be accepted in these parts. No, there's only one law around here and that's the writ of Dáil Eireann, and to hell with the begrudgers.' He drained his glass and smacked his lips. 'Yerra what,' he said and gave a shrug of satisfaction.

Tom Hales waited a suitably respectable interlude and then said: 'Tom Taylor tells us that Mick Collins is around.'

'He's around alright,' said the pub owner, 'I saw him with my own two eyes from the top room of the house. And they asked Denny the Dane for directions to Bandon.'

All eyes turned to a stocky young swain hovering in the corner.

'Will you come out here, Denny and tell the men what you saw,' said Long. Slowly the shy young man came forward. 'Like Jer says, they asked me the way to Bandon,' he said.

'How can you be so sure 'twas Collins?' asked Liam Deasy.

'Sure everyone knows Collins. Isn't he a West Cork man like ourselves?' said the Dane.

'He is, but he's been gone for twenty years. He's a West Cork man in name only at this point,' said John Lordan.

'Did you recognise anyone else?' asked Con Lucey.

'Only Tim Kelleher, Macroom, with the hackney car. He was scouting for 'em I'd say.'

'If they had a local scout why would they ask you the way to Bandon?' asked Liam Deasy.

'Ye can cross-hackle me all ye like, but there's no doubt 'twas him,' said the young man, suddenly indignant. 'Sure he was sitting up in the back of a Leyland, with another fellow looking important beside him.'

'Did you know him?'

'The other fellow? No, some Dublin jackeen I'd say. He didn't know where he was.'

'One last question,' said Tom Hales. 'What colour was the Leyland?'

'Ah, Christ, you must think I'm a complete omadaun. 'Twas yellow. Sure even Tom Barry wouldn't ask me as many questions.'

The Dane sat back down in the corner and sulked.

'Unfortunately, Tom Barry is in jail,' said Hales, looking at Deasy and John Lordan, as if the burden of a major decision now fell to him. He frowned and continued: 'Well, that puts a spanner in the works.'

'What do you mean, Tom?' asked de Valera, a trifle anxiously. He'd remained silent, sipping his drink.

'Well, we came here for a brigade council meeting, but it looks like we might have more urgent business to attend to now, '

All the men looked silently from one to the other and some looked at the stone-flagged floor. There was the shuffling of feet and an uneasy clearing of throats.

'You're not thinking...?' began de Valera.

'Why not?' asked Hales, cutting him off.

'It would be unfortunate if anything should happen to the Big Fellow,' added Dev.

'No fear of that,' said Deasy.

'I mean, he could be replaced by lesser men,' said the 'Chief.'

'Collins is a great man,' said Tom Kelleher. 'We all know that. But he's chosen one road and we another. And as John Lordan says, he's been gone from here for twenty years. He can't come down here and start telling us what to do.'

De Valera hastened to add: 'Nobody is telling you what to do, least of all myself. I'm only a humble foot soldier at this point. But Collins is the best of them by a long way.'

'Why isn't he with us then?' asked Pete Kearney, 'instead of them cutthroats.'

'That's a long story and an old one now,' said de Valera.

'Look,' said Liam Deasy, 'Collins has surrounded himself with bully boys and ruthless men like Dalton, McEoin and Conlon, who are after taking Cork city and Macroom under our noses. There's a mad fellow called Daly running riot in Kerry. These fellows don't care who they maim or kill. Most of the men here are retreating from bitter defeats at Limerick, Kilmallock and Cork, so we're entitled to fire a warning shot over Collins if he comes back this way. We will make a last stand here, where we started.'

'As long as it stops at a warning shot,' said de Valera, and stood up. He noticed an irritated wrinkle on Hales's brow and continued: 'Don't worry, I'll say no more. You wouldn't listen to me anyway.'

'You'll have to persuade Liam Lynch first in Tipperary,' said Hales. 'He's our military leader now.'

De Valera smiled an ironic smile as he shook hands with the men. He knew Lynch would never listen to him either. He lifted his hat as he went through the door. His car was waiting with the engine running. He climbed in behind the driver, Denny Crowley, who eased his foot off the clutch pedal and the car moved down the winding road towards Crookstown. It was about 11 o'clock on Tuesday morning, the 22nd August in the year 1922.

About six o'clock in the evening of the the same day, the Free State convoy carrying Michael Collins arrived back in Bandon. He was sitting in the back of the Leyland touring car and Emmet Dalton sat beside him. The hood was down because the day had been fine, but now it looked like rain, with a build-up of cumulus clouds in the western sky. Collins was tired. It had been a long day since they left the Imperial Hotel in Cork at ten past six that morning. They'd been to Macroom to deliver a machinegun and ammunition to Captain Conlon, the brash sidekick of Sean McEoin, and then on to Bandon, Clonakilty, Rosscarbery and Skibbereen. They were now on the way back to Cork city. They'd encountered broken bridges along the way, and trees felled to obstruct their passage. They'd met friendly crowds in Clonakilty and Skibbereen, but the touring party had an uneasy feeling that behind the smiles and the welcomes there lurked a hostile resentment in many quarters. In certain villages where Smith, the motor cyclist, would announce grandly that the Commander-in-Chief was coming, nobody came out to greet him. Although Collins was a native son, the position he'd adopted in the Civil War had made him an unpopular figure to many, who'd previously admired and supported him. Some of the criticism came from unexpected sources. At the Eldon Hotel in Skibbereen, where he stopped to meet with local military officers, he'd been taken to task by a crusty old amazon named Edith Somerville. She was a writer of popular fiction, living in a rambling and enormous estate beside the sea near the lovely village of Castletownsend, who couldn't understand why the sun no longer shone on the Anglo-Irish aristocracy. She bustled into the foyer of the hotel and demanded to see General Collins. Ignoring the officers who were talking to him, she stood in front of him in her billowing tartan skirt and sensible shoes and said: 'Mr. Collins, I am reliably informed that you are the person in charge of affairs in Ireland now.'

Collins slowly turned away from the circle of officers and regarded the interloper with a bemused smile.

'Who have I?' he asked.

'Who have you?' asked Somerville, taken slightly aback at not being recognised. 'You have Lady Edith Somerville of Castletownsend, sir, that's who you have.'

'I'm proud to meet you, ma'am,' said Collins, mustering his most charming smile and extending his hand which the rather surprised old dame shook weakly. 'And what can I do for you?' he continued.

'I demand that you keep murderers and ruffians away from my estate.'

Collins paused and considered the demand. 'There have been a lot of those in West Cork in the last number of years,' he said. 'Which particular group of ruffians did you have in mind?'

'Don't try to be smart with me, young man,' said the dame. 'I know people, you know.'

'Far be it from me to attempt anything of the sort, ma'am, but most of the murderers and ruffians in West Cork in recent years have been Englishmen, to wit the Black and Tans, the Auxiliaries and the Essex Regiment. You are familiar with them?'

'Come, come, Mr. Collins, the English have departed, unfortunately. No, I'm referring to the scum and the dregs of this wretched country who are now in power.'

'But we are the people in power now,' said Collins, mildly. 'Are you referring to us?'

The lady looked stumped for a moment, then recovered her equilibrium: 'So remind me, which side are you with then, the 'Irregulars' or the 'Staters,' as the say?' she asked archly.

'I'm the Commander-in-Chief of the army and I was the Chairman of the Provisional Government until the 12th of July when my colleague, Mr. Cosgrave assumed that position.'

'I thought the Chairman was that American fellow, de Valera?'

'He was,' said Collins, patiently, 'until the vote on the Treaty. He's now with the opposition.'

Edith Somerville looked confused, but even more annoyed. She sighed and pursed her lips.

'You're all the bloody same to me,' she said, then turned away, muttering, 'I don't know where my dear old Ireland has gone.'

Collins watched her retreating back and then turned to continue his conversation with his officers.

He was now weary from it all. He'd left Dublin two days ago with a heavy cold. He was feeling low. To add to his sombre mood, his sometime negotiating partner, Arthur Griffith, had died suddenly within the past week. He was greatly troubled at the turn events had taken, culminating in the bitter Civil War in which they were now embroiled. He'd searched vainly for a solution. He'd sent out emissaries to Liam Lynch and de Valera, requesting them to lay down their arms, but the men who'd faced down the Black and Tans had no intention of capitulating. Collins would have to crush them and the only way he could do so was with overwhelming arms, mostly supplied by the British. He wrestled with his conscience, hating himself for the task he had to undertake. But he felt he was left with no choice. The country was sliding into chaos and if this were to happen, then the British would most certainly return, triumphantly announcing that the Irish were incapable of governing themselves.

His last port of call was to Lee's Hotel in Bandon where he'd met up with the local commander, Sean Hales. As they rose from the dining table where they'd taken tea, the proprietor hastened over.

'A safe journey to you now, General,' he said, eager to please. 'Which way are you going back to Cork?'

'The same way we came,' said Collins.

'The Macroom road?' asked the proprietor.

'I believe so,' said Collins. 'You have the map there, Emmet?'

Dalton pulled a folded map from his inside pocket and opened it out on the front desk. He pointed and said: 'This is the way we came.'

'I think you should go the Inishannon road,' said Hales.

'But I hear the bridges are down,' said Collins.

'They've been repaired for you, Mick,' said Hales. 'I believe the Republicans have also guaranteed you a safe passage.'

'I suppose they'd hardly shoot me in my own county,' laughed Collins.

They went outside and Collins said: 'Do you think we can find a way to end it, Sean?'

Hales sighed: 'I'm doing all I can, believe me. But my brothers, Tom and Bob, are stubborn men. They all are: Deasy, Lynch, Lordan, Kelleher and the rest. They've been through a lot and won't give up easily.'

Collins clapped him on the back: 'Keep trying Sean. For old times' sake and for the future, keep trying. 'Twill be a great prize if we succeed in stopping this terrible business.'

Emmet Dalton stood and listened. His eyes showed scepticism, as if he believed his Commander-in-Chief was indulging in a bout of wishful thinking. 'Come on, General,' he said. 'It's starting to mist over and we've a long road ahead of us.'

'Are you sure you wouldn't rather go the Inishannon road?' asked Hales again.

'I am,' said Collins. 'You see, there's a few places I might call to on the Macroom side, if we have the time.'

'The 'Irregulars' are in control west of there,' said Hales. 'In Ballyvourney and Ballingeary: mountain country.'

'Exactly,' said Collins, enigmatically. He saluted Hales and got into the back of the touring car beside Dalton. The driver, Private Corry, started the motor and the convoy roared away over Bandon Bridge and up Kilbrogan Hill. Sean Hales stood and watched them go and wondered was his Commander on a mission of war or peace?

In the fading light, Collins could see the men in front of them in the Crossley tender standing up. Snatches of song echoed back to his ears. They were tired, they'd had a few drinks and were glad to be heading for bed. Collins was philosophical about it. They'd lost the armoured car, the Slievenamon, earlier in the day for an hour, when the occupants pulled in to a public house to wet their whistles. 'Sure the car needs a drink,' he'd said at the time, 'so why not the men.'

As they rolled through the green valleys of Carhue, Mallowgaton and Farnalough, the thrushes sang in the soft rain falling. The hedges were scented with sweet wild woodbine, birdsfoot trefoil and deadly nightshade: the small, bright flowers of summer. Collins's thoughts turned to the drumlins of Longford and his sweetheart, Kitty Kiernan. Would he see her ever more? He'd postponed their wedding following Arthur Griffith's death. One widow was enough to be in mourning.

The group of ten Volunteers who'd assembled in the early morning on Greenhill, started south along the Newcestown road. They'd been waiting in ambush positions all day on a bend in the road about half a mile from the crossroads of Béal Na Bláth. They were tired and hungry and with the coming of twilight, Liam Deasy and Tom Hales had decided to call off the engagement and go back to Jer Long's pub.

'They won't be coming back at this hour,' said Hales.They left Jim Hurley and Tom Kelleher behind with some others to dismantle the bomb and remove the four-wheeled dray and the crates of bottles they'd used to block the road. They'd chosen a spot to waylay the 'Free Staters' similar to that at Kilmichael and Crossbarry: a winding glen with ample cover on both sides of the road. Parallel with the main road was a higher boreen with two lanes leading off it, joining the main road, 400 yards apart, known as Foley's Lane, at the southern end and Walsh's Lane, at the northern end. Between the two roads was a small stream called the Noneen, that wound its gurgling way down to join the larger river Bride at Béal Na Bláth. There were saplings of hazel, silver birch and scrub oak screening the view and giving cover between the higher boreen to the main road.

Jim Hurley stood guard on the higher boreen with Tom Kelleher, watching John O'Callaghan, Dan Holland and some others dismantling the mine 50 yards directly below them on the main road. He saw John Lordan and Bill Powell walk off north towards Béal Na Bláth in the direction Deasy, Hales and Pete Kearney had already taken. He turned his head to look south to see if the party of ten had gone and saw Sonny

Hennessy, the last man of the group, standing on a ditch of a field the others had gone into, to take the shortcut through Foleys' farm in the townland of Maulnadruck. Hurley turned up the collar of his trenchcoat because the light drizzle was creeping down the back of his neck. He took out his pocket watch and ran his thumb over the smooth glass to clear the fogged up face. He saw that it was 7.30 in the evening. Suddenly he heard the sound of engines. As he took his eyes off the watch face, he saw an approaching convoy with a motor cycle in the lead, about half a mile away. He saw Sonny Hennessy jumping off the fence in the distance, between himself and the convoy.

Hurley was in a quandary. He wasn't expecting this. He shouted to Kelleher, twenty yards away. 'They're coming, Tom, they're coming. We must warn the others.'

Kelleher, stood on the ditch and looked. He could see the convoy now. He jumped back down and said: 'Right, Jim, you take the motor cycle and I'll take the Crossley.'

The convoy came on, each vehicle separated from the one in front by a distance of forty or fifty yards. Hurley and Kelleher loaded their Lee Enfields and took aim. The shots shattered the silence of the misty evening.

Sonny shouted to his other companions who were crossing the field towards Foleys. Led by Dan Corcoran, they turned and ran back. Sonny watched as the leaders of the convoy passed below him on the main road. He jumped back over the fence of the field onto the boreen and flattened himself against the opposite ditch. He slid a bullet into the breech of his rifle and waited. He heard the first two shots ring out. He saw they'd fired at the first two vehicles. He waited another few seconds and then pulled the trigger of his rifle, aiming above the head of the driver of the touring car which was third. The armoured car brought up the rear. Sonny was a crack shot. He shattered the windscreen of the touring car to smithereens. As his comrades rushed into positions all along the fence of the boreen beside him, they waited, as they had done so many times before in times like this. They were battle-hardened men, not prone to panic.

Three hundred yards away at the northern end of the ambuscade, shots were ringing out. The men dismantling the mine rushed back up Walsh's Lane and joined Kelleher and Hurley. They fired sporadically at the motorcyclist and the Crossley tender. Hurley watched, puzzled, as the motorcyclist came up Walsh's Lane beyond the dray on the main road. 'What's the bastard doing?' he asked Kelleher.

Halfway up the lane, a farm butt blocked the way. As the scout turned his bike, Kelleher said: 'Put the run on him.'

They fired as one, spattering the ground around the motorbike's wheels with lead. They grinned to one another as the motorcyclist weaved his way back to the main road, and finally fell off his bike into the dyke. Soldiers were shouting and running around the Crossley tender which had stopped fifty yards behind. They were firing randomly, like men in the grip of fear. The men on the boreen had to fire only occasional shots to contain them. 'Look at them,' said Denis O'Neill, beside Kelleher. 'Like headless chickens.'

The light was fading as the gunner in the armoured car opened up on Sonny and his companions on the higher boreen across the stream. Such was the ferocity of the assault that they had no option but to crouch in a line along the ditch and wait for the fusillade to go over. Sonny tried to count the shots which flew thick and fast like the clattering of a mowing machine cutting hay. Occasionally he'd peek over the ditch between lulls in the bursts of machinegun fire and take a pot shot back, but in the poor light all hope of accuracy was lost.

Down on the main road, Michael Collins had alighted from the touring car and had taken refuge behind the armoured car. Emmet Dalton was close by, with Joe Dolan and the two drivers of the touring car a few yards further away. Inside the armoured car, Jock McPeak was burning up the marshy banks of the stream with a scorching of shells towards the invisible enemy on the boreen above. After using up two hundred rounds of ammunition, he paused to reload a third belt. He glanced out to see his Commander-in-Chief with a strange, intense look in his eyes, blazing away at the attackers across the stream. McPeak frowned. The Commander was being somewhat reckless for a man with no training of fighting in the field. He clipped in the third belt and started firing again, but the weapon was now red hot and it jammed. He tried desperately to fix it, but his efforts were in vain. McPeak swore as he saw General Collins starting back the road the way they came, in the direction of Sonny Hennessy and his nine companions. He seemed oblivious to his own safety.

Sonny could clearly see the man on the road, but when Bill Desmond waved to him to retreat he followed his own party back along the lane towards Long's farmyard. It was nearly dark.

'There they are,' shouted Collins as he spotted the retreating figures. 'Come on. They're running away.'

Behind him, Dalton, Dolan and the two drivers, were joined by Commandant O'Connell, Lieutenant Smith, the motorcyclist, and some snipers who'd crept up with them, because the attack had ceased down at the blockade at Walsh's Lane. The attackers there seemed to have melted away.

John Lordan and Bill Powell, on their way back to Long's Pub had jumped over the right hand ditch of the winding main road when the shooting started behind them. They scrambled and grappled their way up the steep, tree-covered slope to try to gain an advantage on the high ground above them. When they reached the flat, wide fields on top of the hill they met Liam Deasy, Tom Hales, Tom Crofts, Pete Kearney and Mick Crowley, hurrying back by a circuitous route to the ambush site.

They all ran forward until they were directly above the spot where they'd waited all day. They saw sporadic bursts of gunfire coming from their retreating companions, and also retaliatory fire from the location of the armoured car. The firing at the brewer's dray, which had blocked the road, had stopped. They fired a few half hearted shots and then waited.

Michael Collins was leading his soldiers and exulting in the battle. He did not notice his isolation from his own party, preoccupied as he was with the fury of the fight. When there came no response from the retreating ambushers, he stopped and half turned to see where his own men were behind him. They were shadows in the gloom. The rain was falling. No birds sang. Suddenly, there was a moan, no more than that, and Collins slumped across his rifle near the low fence beside the stream.

Like men who were terribly afraid, his soldiers crowded close up beside him. They saw a jagged, gaping hole behind his left ear and a small, round hole on his forehead. They stared in horror for some moments. Then O'Connell, with the help of Private Corry, pulled the Commander across the road to the back of the armoured car. Dalton resumed a frenzy of shooting as if he could see phantoms.

Blood ran down Collins's greatcoat and onto the road, forming a large pool. He was gasping, and then his breathing stopped. His eyes were glazed over. Dalton stopped shooting and went across to the armoured car where he unloosed the stud from Collins's collar and threw it on the road beside the General's cap, which had also fallen off. Commandant O'Connell began to whisper prayers in the dead leader's ear. They lifted him and placed him on the back of the armoured car. All firing stopped. The men stood around in confusion and disarray.

'Load up,' said Dalton, eventually recovering his nerve. The word went down the winding glen to the scattered, frightened soldiers. Joe Dolan sat in the back of the Slievenamon and tried to administer to his old friend, but there seemed no hope or light left in the August evening.

The convoy moved out in the dark and stopped beyond Béal Na Bláth, where they transferred the General's body into the back of the touring car. His head lay slumped on Dalton's shoulder. They went blindly into the night, looking for a doctor and a priest.

Sonny and his companions walked back along the winding lane with high blackthorn hedges. They were tired and hungry. Some had scratches and cuts and one man had blood dripping down his legs, where a bullet had lodged in his backside. He felt no pain in the excitement of the battle. They passed Murphys and took a dog-leg turn to the left and then right again. They went shadowless in the dark and moonless night, until they reached Tom Taylor's house, where a hearty meal awaited them.

'Ye put the run on them by all accounts,' said Taylor, with a merry glint in his eye.

'We did,' said Bill Desmond. 'But 'twas only a bit of a skirmish.'

'Was there anyone kilt?' asked Taylor, stirring his tea. They looked from one to the other.

'No one,' said Sonny. 'Sure 'twas nearly too dark to see and the gunner would have blown our heads off if we tried to aim a shot.'

Taylor nodded. He tipped his tea into his saucer and drank. 'It sounds like a fairly good day's work,' he said.

'Oh my God, what now?' said Madeleine Cody, when she heard that Michael Collins was dead. It was early in the morning of the 23rd of August when Thomas Cody walked into the kitchen and told her the news. They both stood looking at one another for a long time, quite unable to say anything. Thomas finally sat down at the breakfast table with a heavy sigh and poured out his tea from a ware teapot, reposing under a tea cosy. Doctor Baldwin came in from the yard. He was in a cheerful mood.

'There now,' he said. 'I've fed the pigs, cleaned the stables and the calves houses, milked ten cows and it's still only nine o'clock in the morning.'

He removed his battered bowler hat and stood leaning against the dresser. 'Where are the academics? Not still in bed at this hour?'

Margie and Anna came sleepily into the warm kitchen. Doctor Baldwin raised an admonishing finger: 'Morns in bed and daylight slumber were not meant for man alive. Up lass, when the journey's over there'll be time enough for sleep.'

The girls ignored him and sat at the table. Their parents were unusually quiet. Doctor Baldwin was still standing, noticing Cody's downcast eyes.

'Nobody is interested in exercising their brains this morning, I see,' he said, a little miffed. As he was about to propound upon another subject, Madeleine whispered, 'Michael Collins is dead.'

The kitchen grew even more silent. The grandfather clock seemed to tick louder than Margie had ever noticed. The greyhound sitting near the doorway carried a wounded look in his eyes, as if he understood the enormity of the event. Margie wrinkled her brow and looked at her mother with her habitual, irritated impatience, whenever her mother spoke: 'What are you saying, mother?' she asked, disbelievingly.

'She said Collins is dead,' said Cody, and all doubts stopped together.

'Collins? Dead?' asked Margie, stunned. Her face grew pale.

'He was shot in an ambush yesterday evening,' said Cody.

'Where?' asked Doctor Baldwin.

'About four miles up the road at 'Balnablaw.'

'Oh, my God,' said Margie. 'Where is he now?'

'His body is on the way back to Dublin, I believe,' said Cody. 'By sea.'

'Where did you hear all this, Thomas?' asked Doctor Baldwin, discarding his usual edginess when talking to his brother-in-law.

'At the creamery. Everyone had it. It seems there was an ambush by some of the 3rd Brigade and some other officers who had convened for a meeting. When Collins was going back to Cork they attacked the convoy.'

'Who was in it?' asked Anna.

'In the ambush?' laughed Cody, grimly. 'I'd say 'twill be a long time before anyone admits to being in that.'

He looked somewhat reproachfully at Margie, and then stood up and put his hat on. 'Well, I have work to do. Someone has to keep the unfortunate country going. What's left of it.'

Their eyes followed his departing back as he went through the door.

They found the pool of caked blood on a bend of the road. They found a collar with a singe mark in the back of it and discarded shells all over the road. Many were from the machinegun that fired from the armoured car; some were from Lee Enfield rifles, some from Mauser pistols. They walked up to the high boreen and found the forms of the ambushers where they'd lain against the ditch, like the forms left by hares after sleeping. They had arrived as fast as the pony's legs could gallop. In their horrified fascination they'd pushed the animal faster than they should have. Seamus drove the trap, Margie and Anna beside him. They didn't tell their father or their mother. Doctor Baldwin declined to come with them. He'd seen enough bloodshed and like Thomas Cody, he feared more. Margie stood on the road where Collins died. Other neighbours started to gather. A young fellow twirled a soldier's cap with a hole in it, around his fingers.

'Is that Collins's cap?' asked Margie.

'I'd say so,' said the fellow. 'I'll take it back to Long's pub.'

'I disagreed with everything he was doing,' said Margie, as tears welled up in her eyes. 'I disagreed with the Treaty and with his policy of deferring to the British. But a great man has died and his likes will be hard to find again. I can't believe he's gone.'

They took the collar and the shells home and their mother put them in a drawer. For the next several days Ireland mourned a leader who promised much. His body lay in state at the City Hall in Dublin. Hundreds of thousands filed past the bier. He was buried in Glasnevin Cemetary, far from the coast near Rosscarbery where he was born, and from the winding road of flowers where he died. For a few days the war stopped.

31

red sky at morning

Tull Hennessy awoke from his lowly bed with a sinking feeling in his heart. He threw the rough blanket back and swung his legs onto the bedroom floor. He stayed sitting and the horsehairs of the mattress pricked against his backside like the thorns of a furze bush. For the third night in a row he'd slept in his clothes. He stood up and the room felt cold. It was September and the equinoxal weather had turned around from balmy summer. Leaves were blowing and grass was bending back in the sudden, cold, northwest wind. Spits of rain fell sleety and the shorter days were a reminder of the passing year, passing time for Tull. Through the eyebrow window of the thatched cottage, the sun was rising red in the southeast. 'Red sky at morning, the shepherd's warning,' he thought. He stood at the window, fingering a weekly growth of stubbled chin and smelling his own sour redolence. He tiptoed down the creaking stairs, not wishing to wake the sleeping Elizabeth and Jeremiah. In the shadowy kitchen, stocked with pots and pans, lanterns, horse tacking, bags of grain and tools of disparate kind, he was greeted by the sight of a sow and her sleeping farrow, stretched out in comfortable bliss on a litter of piled-up oaten straw. There lay the cause of his interrupted slumbers: up most of the night and the night before, as the squealing farrow was born: tiny pink 'bonhams' slipping out at intervals like scaly fish, until more than a dozen now crowded around the sow's abundant udder. There was the smell of swine mingling with the smell of last night's dying fire and the smell of dog from the langorous mongrels, stretched out cheek by jowl with the piglets in the enveloping straw. He leant down and counted the huddled babies, twitching and jerking in dreamful ease. Sows were protective mothers, but a tiny piglet was often smothered by the great maternal bulk, and so Tull was careful. He'd brought the sow into the kitchen because a long night in a freezing outhouse was a lonely vigil as well as a recipe for pneumonia for man and beast. He lifted the tiny pink bodies one by one and stroked them, soft as eiderdown to the touch and sweet-smelling of milk and curd, like all new-born things, be they calf or foal or human being. He stood there watching as the sow began to grunt and the piglets, with unerring precision, sought out the overflowing teats, gorging themselves on the patient mother's largesse. He clucked his tongue in rueful regret. Pigs had been both his salvation and his downfall in these times of sorrow.

He lifted the latch of the door and stepped out into the cool of early morning. He flapped his arms across his chest to propagate some heat through his lean, sinewy body. He was fit and strong, only twenty-seven, but sometimes felt like a much older man. Events of recent times had added to that ageing. He leant in over the large tank attached to the gable end of the house, splashing the icy-cold water on his face and behind his ears. Rivulets trickled down his neck inside his collar, but he felt more alert and awake. In the stable his four horses were muzzling together in a tactile display common to all herd animals. If only human beings showed such affection. As he stood there, having fed his horses, his thoughts turned to Kathleen de Courcey and the day she'd left without him on the train.

The de Courceys were well-to-do landowners with money in the bank; more than Tull could ever muster. When times of trouble started, Kathleen was an enthusiastic recruit to Cumann Na mBan. Tull met her often at election meetings and public gatherings and here at home when she helped to nurse Charlie Hurley. Emotions ran high in them days and it was "Up the Republic" and "Ireland for the Irish," morning, noon and night. Ah, but British dissembling and Unionist scheming soon put an end to that. Tull could see it all unravelling before most others saw it coming. And de Valera promising the earth, but knowing it couldn't be delivered. At least Collins was pragmatic. Some fellows were blinded by ideals, like Liam Lynch and Ernie O'Malley, but not Tull. He would settle for half a loaf. 'Twas better than no bread. But of course his brothers and sister and most of the local IRA men didn't see it that way. In spite of everything, Tull was faithful to his father, his sister and his brothers too. 'Twould take a lot to drive a wedge between them. But he'd seen it happening. By Christ he did, to the Hales brothers and many others.

The Republican connection didn't sit too well with the de Courceys. Kathleen's parents tried to persuade her to set her sights a good deal higher than Tull Hennessy. But Kathleen had a stubborn streak and she was impulsive too. She and Tull walked out together for most of a year when the Truce came. They talked about getting married, but that would not do at home. There would be war with her parents and to Tull there was war enough already and more on the way. Kathleen hit on the idea of eloping to America, but for that you needed money. Besides, Tull had his father and sister to look after, while his brothers were out fighting. When the Civil War started, a great urgency took hold of her. She was anxious to be gone from the fray, the violence in the towns, the lawless roads.The country was sliding further and further into ruin and Tull was on the horns of a dilemma. He had no money to go with Kathleen unless he sold his pigs, but the fairs were all cancelled and the price of pigs, cattle and horses fell to nothing. Tull blamed the die-hards who would not yield. Collins was the only true Republican among them. As far as he could see, Lynch and his crowd were pushing the Republic away. As for Cosgrave and O'Higgins, power was all they wanted for themselves and to hell with fellows like Tull who tried to work to keep the country going.

The killing of Collins was the last straw. Kathleen could see no point in staying. She would wait for Tull no longer. One evening she told him she was going to take the train for Queenstown next morning and then the liner for America. Tull thought she wasn't serious; only trying to test his commitment. It was a defenceless blow to him when he discovered she'd taken the train from Enniskean, as she promised she would, and went without him. People told him later that she waited all day in the street and when he didn't show up, she got the last train out. His heart was broken. How the two of them would have been happy on the farm and blessed by God with children. What a lovely life that would have been. But it was all in ruins now, like the sorry nation itself. He sighed as he turned away from the stable door, hearing voices coming up behind the cabbage garden.

Sonny and Mike came around the corner of the car house. Tull stood on the raised footpath outside the stable door and watched as they came towards him. They wore hats and trenchcoats, belted and buckled. On their feet were boots and they wore leggings up to the knee. There were no guns on view, but Tull knew they'd have concealed revolvers under their coats. They looked rank and weatherbeaten. Tull regarded them steadily and did not smile or show indulgence. As they approached, Sonny was smiling and Mike was stoical as he said: 'Well?'

They stopped a few feet from Tull, who displayed no emotion except a wry incredulity. He merely grunted, cleared his throat and looked away, as if spotting something in the middle distance. 'So, ye're back,' he said.

'Maybe for good,' said Mike, with a kind of apologetic grin on his face.

'Yeah?' said Tull and gave a snort of disbelief.

'It could be true this time,' said Sonny.

'Until the next time Tom Barry or Tom Hales clicks his fingers,' sneered Tull. 'Then ye'll be off again. There's other things to do in life besides fighting you know.'

'There's not a whole lot left to fight for,' said Mike with a shrug.

'And there's not a whole lot here either,' retorted Tull.

'What do you mean?' asked Mike.

'You heard what I said,' said Tull, a cold edge creeping into his voice.

'You don't sound too happy to see us,' said Sonny.

Tull looked at the ground and spat. 'I'm not,' he said.

Mike gave a short laugh. 'Ah, Tull,' he said, 'do you always have to have the bitter word.'

Tull straightened himself. 'Bitter is it? Why wouldn't I be bitter? Didn't ye shoot the best man the country ever saw.'

'We didn't shoot him,' said Sonny with a definite shake of his head. 'We only set out to frighten them a little. Let them know we were there. He was most likely shot by his own crowd.'

'You don't expect me to believe that,' sneered Tull.

'Why not?' said Mike. 'Most of our crowd don't want to kill our old comrades, even still. Most of the time we shoot over their heads. But the 'Staters' are serious. Power at any cost. That's their game.'

'But 'tis peace at any cost that most people want now,' said Tull. 'Ye should lay down ye're guns. Ye'll have to sooner or later.'

'Who'll make us?' asked Mike. There was a hint of steel in his voice.

Tull raised a sardonic eyebrow. 'I don't know what world you think you're living in. Sure the 'Staters' have captured more than three quarters of the country. The people are all against ye. It's not like the days of the Tans when we had support.'

'We still have some friends,' said Sonny, 'and while we have we'll keep going.'

'Not around here ye haven't,' said Tull. His eyes glinted dangerously.

Mike smiled, shook his head and looked at the ground. Then he raised his head and said. 'Look Tull, something else is eating you. We know that. You never talked like this before.'

'We're sorry about Kathleen,' said Sonny. 'We know you took it bad.'

Tull exploded as if a volcano was building inside him. 'By Jesus, you two have some damned nerve to stand there and tell me how sorry ye feel for me.' He walked in a circle, his face growing red as beetroot. 'Here I am keeping this place going for the last two years, working from morning 'til night, while ye're out fighting *mar dhea*. Avoiding hard work more like. And then because of all the roads ye've blocked and trains ye've blown up, the price of everything has fallen through the floor. Ye're destroying the country, nothing more. If ye have nothing better to say ye should clear off out of this yard this minute.'

'We won't clear off and you won't make us,' said Mike. He stood four square in front of Tull, who formed his lips in a thin line. He spun suddenly on his heel and dived into the stable. In a second he was back out, locking a loaded shotgun and pointing it at his brothers.

'I've heard enough of your oul blather for the last two years, Mike Hennessy,' he said. 'I'm not listening to anymore of it. Clear off out of this yard this minute or by Christ you'll be the sorry man.'

Mike had a look of amazement on his face. 'You can't be serious,' he said and laughed.

'I'm serious alright,' shouted Tull. 'Don't you test me.'

Mike slowly opened the belt of his trenchcoat. Beads of sweat stood out on Tull's forehead.

'What are you going to do?' goaded Mike. 'Shoot the two of us.'

'Get going,' shouted Tull. 'Other fellows might be afraid of ye, but I'm not. I don't care how many guns ye have concealed about your persons.'

'Are you sure you know how to use that?' sneered Mike.

Tull pulled back the hammer of the shotgun. 'Try me,' he said.

Sonny moved to Mike's side before he could bring his revolver out.

'Come on away, Mike,' he said, 'Tull is upset.'

At that moment, Elizabeth came running from the cottage in her nightdress. 'Tull,' she screamed. 'What in the name of God do you think you're doing?'

'I'm putting the run on these two,' said Tull. 'I should have done it long ago.'

Elizabeth ran in between the two brothers. 'Leave it be Mike, for God's sake leave it be. Isn't there enough bloodshed in the country besides our family starting it too.'

'He's gone a bit mad,' said Mike. 'Sure it's him you should be telling stop.'

Tull looked wild-eyed. Elizabeth could see he was near the end of his tether. 'Leave it be, Mike,' she said. 'In the name of our dead mother, leave it be.'

Sonny put his hand on Mike's shoulder. Mike relaxed and slowly buckled his belt. He kept looking Tull in the eye. 'I'll leave it for now,' he said. 'But you haven't heard the end of it, Tull.'

'Come on away, Mike,' said Sonny again. The two brothers turned and walked back out of the yard. Elizabeth put a comforting arm on Tull's shoulder. 'Put that down now, Tull,' she said. Tull looked at her, not really seeing her. He finally lowered the gun and the look of fear and pain slowly left his eyes. He then turned and walked the opposite way from his brothers, out into the vast fields, to embrace a change he could not come to terms with and that would last a very long and rainy season.

Tom Barry fled across the lush pastures of Meath as fast as his legs could carry him. He'd escaped from the Free State internment camp at Gormanstown near the east coast of Ireland, north of Dublin, and for four days and four nights he'd been on the run. For the previous three months, since the fall of the Four Courts, he'd been locked up, first in Mountjoy, then in Kilmainham and finally Gormanstown. He'd endured savage beatings, food deprivation, solitary confinement and the whips and scorns of men in uniform who were not fit to lace his shoes. It was as if a malicious intent had taken hold of those who represented the Free State and the more former giants of the War of Independence suffered, the better they liked it. To Barry's way of thinking, a terrible meanness had entered the hearts of men. Those who now held power seemed bereft of grace, generosity and nobility, and most perniciously, they did not keep the rules of warfare. Republican prisoners were starved in their thousands and kept in overcrowded, dank and freezing conditions. Many were tortured, some were beaten to death and it was now proposed to shoot anybody in possession of a firearm, without trial or court martial. Barry had begun to see a different side to the Irish psyche to that which he imagined it to be. In all his years of fighting with the British he had not seen such a degeneration into savagery as now prevailed in Ireland. Was this the land he'd fought for? Were these the people he'd sought to liberate? These were the thoughts that preoccupied him as he made his bid for freedom.

It was September and the nights were drawing in. He ran and rested and ran again. He followed the sun by day when the coast was clear and the stars guided him at night. He gave the city of Dublin a wide berth because the 'Staters' had a stranglehold there. Westward he'd have to go, following the bright, flaming stars, Sirius, Rigel and Vega. Sometimes he'd lie down from exhaustion in a ditch, sometimes in a field of golden wheat or barley and when he awoke a different constellation would have wheeled above him. He began to memorise the different positions as the earth rotated. He didn't know how many miles he'd travelled, maybe sixty, maybe eighty. The rich lands gave way to boggier terrain and he guessed he was skirting the Bog of Allen in North Kildare. It was flat, empty country. He'd see farms and cottages, long straight roads, cattle and horses in fields, but not many people. He stayed away from towns and villages, passing like a ghost in the witching hour. He ate over-ripe blackberries, plucked from thorny brambles and devoured apples hanging red from apple trees in pollen-dusted orchards. If a trumpery dog disturbed his stealthy treading, he'd quieten it with soothing words or dispatch it with a well-aimed kick if it proved quarrelsome. His clothes were threadbare and mud-encrusted: a pants, a shirt and a long jacket that reached to mid-thigh. His brogues were wearing thin and letting in water and he was careful not to lose his cap, which served as a shield against sun and rain and also a disguise, pulled low over his eyes. Not that anyone would know him on these endless roads of Westmeath, or Kildare. There were no mountain landmarks to guide him. He saw signs at crossroads for Trim and Enfield and Edenderry. He'd take a random road and trust his instincts, hoping to reach the broad, majestic Shannon from where he'd head southward into the warm arms of Munster. He'd missed all the fighting so far, but he'd heard reports of failures and defeats. He heard of the death of Collins and that saddened him. He saw a thousand Republican prisoners in Kilmainham, down on their knees praying for his repose the day after Collins died. Mick would not sanction this barbarity had he lived and Barry guessed that while he lived the fratricidal strife had grieved him to his soul.

He emerged from a copse of trees and found himself on the bank of a wide, deep-flowing river. He looked upstream and then downstream. The current was fast after heavy rains. He couldn't swim it and there was no bridge. He was desperate with hunger, cold and fatigue, his feet were sore from walking and his back ached from the constant beatings he'd received at the hands of his captors. But his heart was gleeful at finally giving them the slip. He chuckled at the memory. They were still assembling the huge camp at Gormanstown the day they brought their most dangerous prisoners up from Kilmainham, to incarcerate them there for years if necessary, maybe even for good, with a bullet to the back of the head. They thought they'd tamed their spirits, but men like Barry were ever viligant and restless. No sooner had he been brought into the compound than he noticed some workmen building a chainlink fence nearby. He immediately grabbed a plank of wood and pretended to be one of them and quietly sidled up beside an opening in the fence. In the blinking of an eye he was through the fence and away. It was several hours before he was reported missing.

As he stood here now at the fall of night, he suddenly spotted a small, red boat tied up with a rope to a spike hammered into the river bank. A landing place by all accounts. He looked across and a little way downstream saw a small, whitewashed cottage, near the river's edge.

'Poor people,' he thought. 'They can't be too bad.'

He untied the rope and clambered aboard, grabbing the oars. He was skilled enough at rowing from his childhood on the wide Rosscarbery estuary. He let the boat ride with the current, nudging it across by degrees. He lost his cap which floated off, but he was quickly alongside the little pier on the other side. He could see flat, stone flags leading upwards across a green sward of acreage, past a clothesline to the cottage door. He saw a woman spreading garments and she continued with her task, watching him from the corner of her eye. He edged the boat in, jumped out onto the pier and tied up on another iron ring provided for the purpose. He straightened himself up and hailed the woman. 'Good evening, ma'am,' he said.

'Good evening, sir,' she replied.

'Is that your boat?' he asked.

'It is but you're free to use it. That's what it's there for, so travellers like yourself can cross. There's no bridge for several miles.'

'That's very civilised of you, if I may say so,' he said.

'Thank you, sir,' she answered.

'What river is that?' he asked.

''Tis called the Brosnach,' she said.

'And what county are we in?'

'King's County, though some call it Offaly.'

Offaly, by Dad. He had travelled further than he thought. 'What town are we near?'

'The town of Birr,' said the woman.

'How far is the Shannon?' he asked.

'About twenty mile,' she said. She spoke with the flat accent of the midlands, dropping the T and S from the ends of words.

He walked slowly across the stone steps and stood before her.

'You look a fright,' she said.

'I've been travelling,' he said.

'Travelling rough by the look of you.' She was a woman with a lovely face. Her eyes were dark and her voice was musical. She might have been thirty. She wore a red dress with a green cardigan over it. Her feet were neatly shod with laced up, low-heeled shoes. Barry stood with his hands hanging by his side and felt unthreatened in her presence.

'I'd say you're hungry,' she said.

'I am,' he said.

She gave him a full appraisal from the top of his tousled head to the tattered boots on his feet. 'Come in,' she said. 'I'll make you a bit of supper.'

The woman gave him food and shelter. He slept for nearly twenty-four hours under the low attic roof of the cottage. He'd wake occasionally to hear the gurgling waters of the river, squabbling magpies on the window sill, or a singing boatman plying an ancient trade. He would gladly stay in that secluded spot with that welcoming woman, but duty of every kind called him. Deprivation and distance play strange tricks on the emotions. It was not that he loved his own wife, Leslie, any less, but they'd rarely seen each other in the two years of warfare, and strangers can be comforting in times of trouble. When he came down to the kitchen after two days resting, he looked a different man, washed and shaved. The handsome woman had cleaned and pressed his clothes, she'd a hearty breakfast heating on the stove and a man waited for him outside with a pony and trap to speed him on his way to a village where he'd meet friendly people to steer his homeward course. He ate his breakfast and was reluctant to bid farewell to his generous hostess. As he stepped up onto the trap, he hesitated and stepped back to kiss her. She looked embarrassed, but her dark eyes glowed. 'We don't take much notice of the fighting,' she said, 'but we think the Government are going too far.'

'How so?' asked Barry.

'Shooting unfortunate prisoners in cold blood,' she said. 'That's very wrong. I hope 'twill all be over soon.'

'So do I,' said Barry. He turned to look at the driver. 'Where will this man take me?'

'To Lorrha,' she said, ''tis near the Shannon. You'll find some of your own kind there.'

'How do you know who my kind are?' he smiled.

'You're an important man,' she said. ''Tis easy to see that. You'd not be hiding if you were a Government man.'

As they rode along the winding tree-lined lanes, he felt a surge of renewed hope, his faith in human nature reaffirmed. The driver said little and dropped him off in the village, four miles away. As they stopped in the middle of the narrow street, a man with a cap came out of a side alley and saluted them. Barry recognised Dinny Lacy, one of the leaders of the Tipperary brigades. The trap driver saluted Lacy and turned his horse around and drove away.

'Welcome to Tipp, Tom,' said Lacy.

'How did you know 'twas me?' asked a surprised Barry.

'The man with the trap told us.'

'He never told me his name,' said Barry as they stood watching the departing driver. A gentle veil of dust rose from beneath the wheels.

'He's the husband of the woman you stayed with,' said Lacy with a grin. Barry frowned, looked quickly at Lacy, then back to where the trap was just disappearing around a bend. He shook his puzzled head. 'Could you beat that,' he said half to himself. 'She never told me she had a husband.'

Lacy had a knowing smile on his face. 'Come down here, Tom,' he said. 'I have something for you that will make your journey a good bit more tolerable.' Lacy went under an arch between the houses to a ramshackle yard full of odds and ends and bits of iron, wire, horseshoes and other tranglum. He opened a creaking door and went inside a haybarn with a high sheet-iron roof. There was a large mound of piled-up hay in one corner. He groped it back and underneath lay a bulging jute sack bound with rope, which he untied. Revealed were several gleaming guns: Lee Enfield rifles and Thompson machineguns. Barry gave a whistle of amazement. 'That's more like it,' he said, bending to examine the weapons. 'They look spanking new.'

'They are,' said Lacy. 'Hardly ever used. We don't have enough lads around here to use them anymore. The fight has gone out of them.'

'Well,' said Barry, 'maybe we'll do something about that.'

'We badly need a man like you, Tom.'

'Can I have one of these?'

'Take your pick,' said Lacy.

'I'll take one of the Thompsons. I have to go on to Cork, but I'll be back.'

'You'll be a one-man army with that,' grinned Lacy.

Barry laughed: 'I've a long road before me, but I'll feel a lot safer with this.'

Lacy gave him a full belt of ammunition and a trenchcoat under which to hide the gun. He presented him with a dark grey Homburg hat and wished him God speed. Barry thanked him for his generosity and promised to be back before the winter.

He followed the mighty Shannon as it opened out into the great lake of Lough Derg. Green, brooding waters, long reeds crackling in the callows. Huge inland skies, wind rippling across from Clare. He passed through picturesque villages, looking out on the lake: Terryglass, Ballinderry, Coolbaum and Dromineer. He strode along and his heart was lighter. He asked for supportive names that Lacy gave him and he secured lodgings at night with no questions asked. The news was grim. A marauding band of 'Staters' was active in the territory. Among their number, it was reported, were former Black and Tans, who'd come back to settle old scores with the Republicans. People huddled by their fires at night and whispered the names of evil men. Many Claremen had gone with Brennan and the Free State. Limerick was held by O'Duffy and O'Hannigan. All enemies now.

Somewhere over the Silvermines mountains he came to a small village, little more than a crossroads with a bridge that followed the turn of a river, ringed with hills. Stands of hazel and mountain ash grew near small, rich fields on the river bank: a picturesque rural hideway. There were small cottages on either side of the winding street and a single public house with a balcony at the back that overlooked the pleasant waters, where the river was slow-moving and deep in a wide pool. The village nestled under a broken-backed mountain where silver had been mined for many years. But trade had fallen off, he was told, because of the fighting, causing people to be discommoded and unhappy. No soul stirred, no dogs barked, and furtive cats scurried away as he approached. He walked slowly down the street until he came to the pub: a low-slung edifice with the legend, "Ryan's Alehouse," emblazoned in white letters over the half door that swung idly in the gentle wind. The late afternoon sun was bright and sinking lower in the sky. It cast a single shaft of light through as he pushed in. He blinked to get his eyes accustomed to the gloom. A long counter ran down one side, with high stools on the outside and there were snugs with tables and chairs at right angles to the counter. There was the familiar smell of stale liquor, urine and something more musty suggesting decomposition. There was a smashed window at the back and glass strewn on the floor. Some chairs were knocked over. He looked around for any sign of life but saw none except a man lying on the floor with his arm flung across his face at an unnatural-looking angle to his shoulders. His eyes were open and seemed to carry the light of a smile, although unblinking. But that was not a smile. The throat was cratered with a rim of blood, where it had been unseamed by the slash of a knife. Further back lay two more bodies, lying askew a wooden settle by the side of a whitewashed wall, which was patterned in whorls and spatters of red that could only be blood. There were neat, round holes in the middle of both mens' foreheads.

'Shot at close range,' thought Barry, as he bent to feel for the fibrillation of a pulse, but there was nothing. He heard a scraping sound behind him and straightened, hand instinctively to the trigger of the Thompson inside his coat. A man with a half drunken leer sat on a high stool inside the counter, leaning back against rows of bottle-stocked shelves. He had a whiskey bottle uncorked on the counter in front of him and he held a glass canted at an angle from which he sipped the booze betimes. He was a man of about fifty, with receding hair and a face wherein lay the traces of anger and regret, but especially fear.

'Are you thirsty?' he asked, his voice a low croak in the shadows.

'I was,' said Barry, 'until I walked in here.'

'You'll have a drop anyway,' said the man, with a black, laconic inflexion in his voice. He stood and reached for the bottle on the counter and a whiskey glass, turned down on a tray.

'What happened here?' asked Barry as he watched the man's shaky hand filling the glass.

'Staters,' said the man. 'They came through here early this morning in a lorry. Must have been a dozen or fifteen of them. These lads tried to put up a bit of a fight against them. They were outgunned and then shot in cold blood after they surrendered.'

'And their bodies are left here since then?' asked Barry.

'The people ran away. They're hiding up in the mountains, frightened out of their wits. I'm the only one left. I saw it all.'

'Are you the proprietor?'

'I'm not faith, but I might as well be now. Help yourself to whatever you want.'

'Did you know these men?' asked Barry.

'Vaguely,' said the man. 'I believe they're North Tipperary men. They fought with Dan Breen by all accounts, against the Tans.'

'And what about yourself?' asked Barry.

'Oh, I was out too,' said the man, expanding his chest. 'I was a captain with Sean Hogan. But when this latest business started, I couldn't see the logic of it. Not that I take sides, mind you. Strictly neutral now. But I'll tell you this: them 'Free Staters' show no mercy. They're like the Tans, only worse.'

Barry asked: 'Is there no priest or doctor around here?'

The man shook his head. 'This is a remote spot. I'd say people are afraid to come back. The only people who'll come for them will be the 'Staters' because they run the Government now and all the local councils.'

'I think I'll take that drink now,' said Barry. He sat on a high stool, where the counter turned at a right angle to give him a full view of the door. He took the glass the man had filled from the counter. He drained the glass and the man filled it again. They lifted their heads as they heard the sound of an approaching lorry.

'Whisht,' said the man. 'A lorry. They're back.'

He walked to the low window at the end of the counter and peered out. The sun was setting and the street was bathed in blood-red light. There was the sound of orders being shouted and soldiers jumping off the back of the lorry, which stopped outside the door with its engine running.

'Tis them alright,' said the man. 'The same lads as this morning. I recognise a bunch of them. Lord God have mercy on us.'

'Keep cool,' said Barry. 'Take no notice and keep drinking.'

Heavy footsteps trod the dusty road. Orders were shouted. The door was kicked back with a crash and soldiers in full military regalia crowded in. Barry counted eight. There were two more out on the street at each end of the lorry. They were armed with a variety of pistols and rifles held menacingly in front of them. Barry stayed sitting at the counter but beneath the hat brim he squinted at the incoming figures, silhouetted against the sunset. He did not look the intruders in the eye after the first appraisal. The dead men were strewn on Barry's right. A soldier walked over to examine the bodies. 'Still here,' he shouted back to an officer behind him. 'Dead as 'banalanna.' He smirked and pushed one body over with his foot.

The other officer walked up to the bar. 'Fill a glass of whiskey,' he said to the man inside the counter. 'One for every man here.'

'I'm not the barman, you understand,' said the man. 'I'm not even the owner.'

'I don't give a tinker's curse who you are,' said the officer. 'Just fill them up.'

The man fumbled, looking for the glasses with trembling hands.

'For fuck's sake get out of the way,' said a soldier, vaulting the counter, grabbing the whiskey bottle and arranging a line of glasses on the counter top with alacrity.

'Christ, there was a great barman lost in you,' said the officer as the golden liquor sparkled in the row of glasses lit by the slanting sun. They knocked back the drinks and the soldier filled them again. The officer smacked his lips and patted his stomach. Then he sniffed the air. 'I'd say 'tis beginning to stink in here,' he said. The soldiers guffawed.

'Wouldn't you think these lazy hoors would bury them bodies,' said another. All eyes turned towards the man behind the counter, and Tom Barry at the end.

'You should have more respect for the dead,' said Barry, to no one in particular. There was sudden quiet as they directed their gazes fully on him.

'By Jesus, the man with the hat,' said the officer. 'What did you say?'

Barry tilted the brim of his hat upwards. His eyes were cold and steady. 'I said you people should show some respect for these dead soldiers.'

'Soldiers?' laughed the officer. 'They were only 'Irregular' scum.'

'Is that so?' asked Barry, his voice a low, menacing whisper. 'Well, I'm told they were soldiers of the Irish Republican Army.'

'If this man told you that, he's a lying son of a gun,' said the officer, turning to the cowering figure behind the bar. 'Did you tell the man with the hat that story?'

'I...I..,' stuttered the man.

'Stand over there against that wall,' said the officer with a click of his fingers. 'We can't have fellows bearing false witness against us now, can we? Sure isn't that one of the seven deadly sins?'

'Too right,' nodded the other officer, with cold intent.

'Can't you give a man a chance?' pleaded the barman, his eyes looked crestfallen.

'Stand over, I said,' said the officer, waving his pistol. He turned to Tom Barry. 'You too.'

Barry levelled a cold gaze at the officer. 'Were you talking to me by any chance?' he asked. He'd opened the belt of his trenchcoat.

'You're bloody right I was,' said the officer. 'Who the hell are you anyway? You're not from around here. Are you an 'Irregular' too?'

The soldiers were alert and fingering the triggers of their weapons. Barry turned his back slowly and walked to the wall where the barman stood, expecting the worst.

'Lord have mercy on ye're souls,' said the officer. The barman began to snivel. Barry winked at him as he walked towards him. Then, as he turned, he lifted the hat from his head and threw it like a discus towards the soldiers who followed its flight through the air. At the same moment, Barry opened his trenchcoat and the Thompson machinegun appeared like magic in his hands, spitting lead. The first round struck the officer in the heart and he staggered back dead against the counter. The machinegun rattled again and the soldiers fell like cornstalks before they'd taken their eyes off the spinning hat. Smoke and dust rose in the rays of dying sunlight. Men stumbled and ran, but were cut down before they could release a shot at the mysterious stranger. Glasses shattered across the counter top and bullets riddled the shelving. The sound was deafening in the confined space of the bar. In thirty seconds the machinegun had done its work. Bodies of dead and wounded 'Staters' lay beside those they'd lately killed in cold blood, as if an avenging angel had suddenly come among them to exact retribution.

'Come on,' shouted Barry to the barman. They burst out through the front door as the two sentries came rushing in against them. The machinegun spat again and the two sentries slumped forward on the footpath, blood spurting from their newly-pressed tunics. Barry jumped into the cab of the Crossley tender, its engine still running. 'Jump in,' he shouted to the shocked barman. He rammed the lever into gear as the barman scrambled into the passenger seat. The lorry trundled along the dusty street, gathering speed as it roared down the mountainside to the valleys below. In its wake, no voices keened or spake.

32

the wild west wind

D
octor Baldwin came out of a small public house at the Coppeen crossroads and looked left and right. Which road to go? To the left was the way he'd come, up from Béal Na Bláth on the Bantry Line, and to the right was the grand vista of the Caha mountains that always filled him with an intense longing, to wander on their blue ridges and descend to fuschia-crowded valleys of great loveliness. It was a mellow day of bright sunlight and the wind swirled yellow and red leaves in small tornadoes around his feet. 'Pestilence-stricken multitudes,' he thought, 'Shelley's wild west wind, the breath of Autumn's being.'

When he stood on the height of Coppeen his compass was always tilted westward, to the land of beauty, Kerry, the Kingdom. He'd go there.

He strode out and soon was passing the great expanse of Gortroe's red bog, where they'd buried the boys of Kilmichael two years before. Was their sacrifice gone for nought? These thoughts troubled him as he heard a clip-clop of horse hooves on the road behind. He turned and saw coming towards him, a horse and tub trap, with three men on board. As they drew near he stood back to hail them and was recognised by the driver, Sean Hyde, a soldier and pamphleteer.

'Good afternoon, gentlemen,' said the Doctor with his usual expansiveness, no matter what his dark mood.

'Well, James,' said Hyde, 'can we take you a mile of the road?'

'Do you have room in your mode of conveyance?' inquired the Doctor, peering at the crowded trap.

'We'll squeeze you in,' said Hyde. The Doctor gave a salute and stepped nimbly on board, beside a machine made of mahogany, with keys and silver-handled levers protruding from it.

'My word, what's that contraption?' asked the Doctor as he puffed into a tight corner beside a handsome young man with a full, smiling mouth.

'A printing press,' said the young man.

'Ah, men of letters,' said the Doctor, taking a look at the other austere-looking man of slight build across from him. He noted the greying, combed-back hair and the slightly protruding ears. The Doctor lifted his hat. 'Baldwin, by name,' he said, extending his hand, which the other shook rather weakly, but without changing his expression of hauteur.

'You've met Erskine Childers?' asked Hyde, as he flicked the reins.

'I'm bound to say I haven't,' said the Doctor, 'but your reputation precedes you, sir.'

The young man beside him put out his hand: 'I'm Frank O'Connor,' he said, shaking the Doctor's hand with vigorous warmth.

'I'm in exalted company,' said the Doctor with a gleam in his eye.

Childers's expression had varied little but his eyes softened somewhat.

'Are you going far?' asked O'Connor with interested eyes.

'I was thinking of Kerry,' said the Doctor, 'for a change of scenery. I've been promising myself a sojourn there for some time, but one thing and another held me up.'

'You might find yourself held up again,' said Childers, suddenly shedding his reserve.

'How so?' inquired the Doctor.

'Haven't you heard?' said Childers. 'There's fighting in the mountains.'

'Tom Barry is back,' said Sean Hyde. 'He's putting the cat among the Free State pigeons.'

'He's taken Dunmanway already,' said Childers, 'and McPeak has joined him with the Slievenamon.'

'The Slievenamon?' repeated the Doctor.

'The armoured car the 'Staters' had in Béal Na Bláth,' said O'Connor.

'Men are defecting wholesale,' said Childers. 'There will be a great rising up of the Irish once again.'

'You believe so?' asked the Doctor, with a trace of doubt in his voice.

'It's an inevitablility, sir,' said Childers, with the certainty of the polemicist.

'No second thoughts there,' mused the Doctor in his own mind. As they trotted along he stole a fuller glance at his companion sitting opposite. A strange fish he thought, but a man of some substantial intellect. He'd read Childers's book, *The Riddle of the Sands*, and he was also aware of his fierce championing of the Republic.

The Doctor turned his attention to O'Connor: 'And what brings you to these untrodden parts, young man?' he asked.

'I'm helping Mr. Childers with his publication,' said O'Connor.

'Are you a writer too?'

'A bit of a scribbler,' laughed O'Connor modestly.

'This young man is a very fine writer,' said Childers. 'You'll be hearing a lot about him in the future, when Ireland is finally a Republic.'

The Doctor peered admiringly at O'Connor. 'Well, I'll look forward to seeing you in print,' he said, 'in the light of such an encomium from Mr. Childers.'

They travelled in silence for awhile and soon were near Coole Mountain on the shoulder of Sheha. Eventually Doctor Baldwin addressed Childers again, because the latter showed no inclination to be civil.

'You're a long way from home,' said the Doctor.

'Home is where the heart is,' replied the stern man.

'So you like it here, in the deep southwest?'

'I like the mountains. They remind me of my native Wicklow. And the people are splendid.'

'It's my recollection,' said the Doctor, 'that Michael Collins held a similar view of the people, although he wasn't served very well by them.'

'Alas, yes,' said Childers. 'He was a stubborn man, although a fine one. But he should have taken my advice and not signed the Treaty.'

He looked across the hills and then looked back at the Doctor and continued: 'He should never have allied himself with the present crowd. He wasn't a natural conservative like O'Higgins and the rest. He was misguided as far as British intentions were concerned. They pulled the wool over his eyes and now they're using the puppets of the Provisional Government to do the dirty work they no longer have the stomach for.'

'Indeed?' said Baldwin.

'They've said so. If you read the statements of some of their brightest young officers such as Montgomery, that is patently obvious.'

The road became a switchback, winding higher through rocky breaknecks, ridge-backed and sculpted by glaciers twenty-thousand years before. They climbed higher towards Coosan Gap. On their right reared the round-shouldered Sheha and on their left, the sharp corrugations of Owen with its pyramid point: two noble mountains. Suddenly the sharp crack of rifle fire erupted across the cliffs above them. Little puffs of blue smoke rose in the air. The shots reverberated around from hill to hill. Frightened crows flew squawking away. They saw a man in uniform, running from rock to rock, followed by another man. They held their rifles one-handed, haphazardly. Then a further half dozen men dressed in similar uniforms rushed over the brow of the hill. As they came on, one went down on bended knee, fighting a rearguard action to protect his fleeing companions against the unseen enemy behind them.

Sean Hyde stopped the trap. 'Better take cover,' he said. 'This looks like a serious scrap.'

As they clambered down, bullets flicked around them off the twisting road. Hyde pulled the horse into the lee of a giant boulder and they crouched behind it. Childers jumped into the heather-covered escarpment and began to scurry upwards towards the shooting. He turned and shouted gleefully back: 'The 'Free Staters' are on the run!'

He ducked down as a bullet ricochetted off a rock beside him. The others craned their necks and watched his progress with a mixture of fascination and horror.

'Has the man lost his senses?' asked Doctor Baldwin.

Frank O'Connor gave a shrug. 'This is his usual *modus operandi*. Whatever you may say about Mr. Childers, he's not a coward.'

The shooting grew more intense, the shots came quicker and louder. Sean Hyde lifted his head to peer over the boulder. The pursuing group had now come over the top of Coosan Gap. They were about half a mile away, running hard after the 'Staters' and exchanging shots. The bulky outline of an armoured car appeared in the Gap, followed by a Crossley tender, with men leaning at all angles out of it, clutching rifles with an assured swagger.

Childers had worked his way up between the rocks until he was nearly between the two groups. He perched on a ledge and wrote furiously in his notebook. Bullets flew around his head like bees buzzing.

Tom Barry got off the running board of the Slievenamon and stood watching with satisfaction as his men routed the Free State troops down the mountainside. He saw Sonny and Mike Hennessy at the head of the chasing group. Tom Hales and Liam Deasy stood beside Barry. They saw Childers below on the rocks, scribbling away. 'Who in God's name is that?' asked Barry. Tom Hales looked through his field glasses and said: 'Some fellow writing.'

Deasy took the glasses and looked. 'I think 'tis Erskine Childers,' he said.

'Childers?' said Barry. 'Well, that explains a lot.'

'He must be half daft,' said Tom Hales.

'I've always thought that,' said Barry, 'but the man has a mind of his own.'

'What brings brings him down here anyway?' asked Hales.

'He's writing his newspaper, the usual anti-British stuff, but I don't know anyone who reads it,' said Barry.

'Still,' said Deasy, 'the man is a deep thinker.'

'But a bit of a liability to us at this point,' said Barry. 'Most of the men don't like him. It must be his English accent.'

'That's the irony of it,' said Deasy.

Below them, the Free State soldiers had surrendered. They were herded out onto the wide part of the road where the horse and trap had stopped. There were about twelve of them and they stood deflated, with their hands in the air and their rifles discarded on the ground. Sonny and Mike gathered the firearms. Doctor Baldwin looked on, slightly bemused, when he noticed one truculent individual complaining to his fellows. The Doctor stood out on the road and he recognised Murphy Deirbh, the man he'd argued with in Ballymakeera two years before. Murphy Deirbh regarded him with a scowl.

'I believe we've met before,' said the Doctor.

'Huh,' said Murphy.

'John Joseph Murphy Deirbh, if I'm not mistaken,' said Baldwin.

'How do you know my name?' asked Murphy.

'I recall you were a great supporter of Liam Lynch,' smiled the Doctor. 'Whatever became of your Republican sympathies? You don't remember?'

'Oh, I remember you alright,' said Murphy sourly. 'The quack doctor.'

'*Touché*, Mr. Murphy, from one fake to another. It's a great shame the country has been cursed with such fair-weather patriots as yourself.

If you and your ilk hadn't swelled the army numbers, taking the King's shilling, there would have been no Civil War.'

As Tom Barry approached with Hales and Deasy, the prisoners shifted uneasily on their feet. Barry walked past them and looked each in the eye. 'Well, gentlemen,' he said, 'I suspect you know who I am. I certainly recognise many of you, though there are a few imposters to your ranks, I hear.'

He stopped in front of Murphy Deirbh and looked back towards Doctor Baldwin with a twinkle in his eye. He continued: 'No doubt you thought the war was over and that you could do as you liked around here, thinking you'd seen the last of me and these brave men with me. Well, I've news for ye. We're back and we're going to go through West Cork like a dose of salts, and take back every town the Free State has captured. And then we're going to do the same in Tipperary and Limerick and Dublin itself. Ye don't look too brave now and no doubt ye're thinking the worst. Well, we're not going to shoot anyone, but if the shoe was on the other foot I wouldn't trust a 'Stater' to do the same. We've always fought honourably and still do. We're letting ye go now, and ye can go back to your superiors and tell them Tom Barry is back, and so is Liam Deasy, and Tom Hales and John Lordan and the Hennessys. Spread the word that we're coming for them like we came for the Black and Tans before them. Tell them to expect fireworks. Now, be off with ye.'

The soldiers turned and scuttled down the mountainside as fast as their legs could carry them. Barry and his men stood counting their newly-captured weapons with satisfaction. Childers came hurrying over, his notebook bulging. 'An excellent speech General Barry. What an inspiration to have you back. I'll be making sure this notable victory is broadcast far and wide in my newspaper.'

'I'd say the bush telegraph will spread the word a good bit faster than your pamphlet,' said Barry.

Childers looked disappointed. 'Alas, that's probably true, General. I keep finding unopened boxes of my publication in various farmhouses. Perhaps I'm becoming more of a burden than an asset at this stage.'

'Every man has a role to play,' said Barry. 'I'm not wishing to be harsh, but it's only action that will change things, not words.'

'Indeed, General, but words have great power. Do not underestimate them. When the Civil War is finally over we'll all have to resort to words in the long run. We can't shoot everyone who doesn't agree with our point of view.'

'I agree with you, Mr. Childers,' said Barry. 'I'm a pragmatic man myself. There are people on both sides who could do with a good dollop of reality.'

Barry turned and assembled his men. 'Company, fall in,' he ordered. 'Form fours.'

Baldwin, Childers and the others watched them march resolutely away. Then they got back in the trap.

'Where to now?' asked Baldwin.

'We'll go down to Joe McCarthy in Shanacrane,' said Hyde. 'He's one of the few safe houses we can depend on anymore.'

William Thomas Cosgrave stole a look at himself in a wall-length mirror as he strode through Leinster House. He was feeling good. The corridors of power made him feel secure and his sickliness of recent years had suddenly vanished. He still couldn't quite believe his luck. As he adjusted the black tie below his wing collar and straightened his top hat, he felt like pinching himself to be certain it was all real. Here he was at the age of 43, little Liam Cosgrave, the most powerful man in all of Ireland. Born into modest beginnings on St. James's Street in Dublin, schooled in Marino by the Christian Brothers, brought up surrounded by beer barrels in his father's public house, he was President of Dáil Eireann and Chairman of the Provisional Government. He'd neither sought high office nor coveted the success of others, but somehow fortune fell into his lap almost by default. He'd seen all the great men off, Collins, Griffith, Brugha, even the Long Fellow himself, Eamon de Valera, whose shoes he used to shine. The first three were dead and de Valera was hunted like a vagabond in the mountains, having taking the wrong side in the Civil War. By saying little, Cosgrave had manoeuvered himself into a position where his counsel was sought by the men of larger ego on the pro-Treaty side, such as O'Higgins and Mulcahy, who, rather than either of them agreeing to see the other as kingpin, had voted for the compromise candidate, William T. Cosgrave.

'Let them huff and puff,' he thought. 'Let them feel self-important. He had his hands on the levers of power and wouldn't let them go in a hurry.'

He had walked across the broad green lawn from Merrion Square to the Garden Front entrance and on the way he stopped to admire the magnificent three storey mansion with its facade of Portland stone. Once home of the Fitzgeralds, Dukes of Leinster, it was built in 1745 after a design of Richard Cassels, to reflect their eminent position in Irish Society. Things had come a long way for the modest Mr. Cosgrave, but he couldn't help taking a deep breath and expanding his chest and giving his moustache a quick twirl between thumb and forefinger. He'd utter a harrumph, if out of earshot of those surly tipstaffs, some of whom he couldn't help but feel resented his sudden elevation. No more of that now. He'd steer the country on a steady course. When he'd stood up in the Dáil Chamber some weeks ago he'd delivered an uncompromising speech, declaring that neither peace, order nor security could possibly be maintained if the Government did not take strong and definite action against the anti-Treaty Forces. 'There must not and there will not be an armed body in the community without the sanction of Parliament,' he propounded.

He'd surprised himself at the vehemence of his words. But other men of humble beginnings and retiring disposition had achieved greatness in the past. He recalled the Brothers in school mentioning some Roman fellow who went on to become Emperor, overcoming the handicap of a terrible stutter and other maledictions: Claudius or somebody. Not that he spent much time with his head stuck in books reading history. But, as they said, "Cometh the hour, cometh the man."

But now was not the time to become complacent. He was getting disturbing reports from General Mulcahy, the Minister of Defence and Commander-in-Chief of the Army since Collins died, that a new campaign had been started by Tom Barry down in Cork. It seemed Barry had rallied a great body of men and had taken back Macroom, Clonakilty, Bandon, and various villages such as Ballineen and Enniskean. He'd blocked off all the main roads leading into Cork city and was intent on squeezing the lifeblood from the Free State troops there. He had nearly 600 fully armed men in the field and if any man could upset the applecart it was Barry, the most brilliant commander of them all. Cosgrave would not take the threat lightly and agreed with Mulcahy that the army needed emergency powers in order to put down this new guerrilla threat.

Cosgrave slipped into the Dáil Chamber and took his seat on the front bench. He nodded to O'Higgins, Mulcahy and the newly appointed Minister of Foreign Affairs, Desmond Fitzgerald, whom Cosgrave noted had lost none of his flamboyance. The man had a red carnation adorning his buttonhole and wore a creamed-coloured suit that made him look like one of those British diplomats in India. Still, he was a fine propagandist, and his writings, once so effective against the atrocities of the Black and Tans, would now be urgently required to counteract the uncompromising anti-Provisional Government diatribes of his erstwhile colleague, Erskine Childers. Cosgrave looked around. They'd purchased part of Leinster House for the Dáil and the Chamber had turned out nicely. It was a former lecture theatre of the Royal Society and the floor had been raised and the seating capacity reduced. There were plush leather seats for the Government and the opposition, but the institution scarcely existed because the anti-Treaty Deputies had refused to take their seats.

'The Devil mend them,' thought Cosgrave. 'They could have maintained an attitude of opposition on constitutional lines to Government policy, but they'd chosen the path of continued violent resistance.'

He looked up at the lean, fiery figure of his new Minister of Home Affairs, Kevin O'Higgins, who was giving vent to their collective concerns about the military situation. O'Higgins had a way of shouting down others that irritated Cosgrave, but he was serving his purpose as an attack dog, nonetheless.

'The life of this nation is menaced,' said O'Higgins, spittle flying from between his thin lips. 'It is menaced politically, it is menaced economically, it is menaced morally. The country must collapse if the corrosion of Government power is not halted quickly.'

'Hear, hear,' murmured Cosgrave, with a sober glance sideways towards Mulcahy, whose motion for special powers for the Army they were now debating. Mulcahy wanted military courts to inflict severe penalties, including death, on anyone convicted of the possession of firearms, ammunition or explosives without proper authority. He was pushing an open door as far as the Government was concerned and the only opposition came from Thomas Johnson, the leader of the Labour Party, who presented only token counter-arguments in the absence of de Valera and all his missing colleagues.

O'Higgins was finishing up before Johnson took to his feet. 'I don't think any of us hold human life cheap, but when and if a situation arises in the country when you must balance the human life against the life of the nation, that presents a very different problem. The situation that now exists could see the country steering straight towards anarchy, futility and chaos.'

O'Higgins sat down with a final, emphatic flourish. Cosgrave stole another glance towards Mulcahy and noted an annoyed look on his face. There was no love lost between his two main Ministers. Mulcahy resented O'Higgins's meddling with the army, although they'd ostensibly put their differences aside for the good of the country. Cosgrave saw to that, but still he'd have to suffer the tendentious ramblings of Johnson to give the impression of democracy at work. He didn't have much time for that old democracy really.

Johnson had sprung to his feet: 'The situation that faces the country arises from a different interpretation of the promises, the undertakings, the pledges that men gave and of the temperaments of those men. Instead of trying to flatten opposition, it could be made clear that it is recognised that the country is accepting something very definitely short of its rightful demands...'

Johnson was quickly shouted down. It was asserted that he was rehashing old arguments that had already been exhausted in the Treaty debates. Things had moved on. Impatiently Michael Hayes, the newly-elected Speaker, asked him to finish up, because it was time to take the vote. By forty-eight votes to eighteen, the Dáil gave the Army the powers it sought. The new Special Emergency Powers Regulatons would apply from the 15th of October, 1922.

33

They moved from place to place among the rearing mountains, the deep, fertile valleys and the wild, high brakes of West Cork: Childers, Frank O'Connor, Doctor Baldwin and Sean Hyde. Another writer, Sean O'Faoileáin came by, so did Sean Hendrick and Robert Langford and Childers's cousin, David Robinson. To Doctor Baldwin, they were some of the happiest days of his life. Here at last he was in the company of individuals who understood his way of thinking, who could drink whiskey with him into the small hours and discourse on Shakespeare and the Romantic Poets, Homer and Virgil. Sometimes a man may wait many years for a soul mate to appear to keep him company on the winding roads of life. Sometimes it may only be a brief interlude, a short season, but it can be sufficient for him to draw resonance and fond memories until his days have run their inevitable course. They talked of Pearse's blood sacrifice, which had set young men upon the road of revolution, causing them to face up to and defy the mightiest empire the world had ever seen, and how within those same grand ideas were possibly contained the seeds of fanaticism, which had now bequeathed to them the legacy of civil war. They talked of turning the other cheek and they talked of an eye for an eye. In farmhouses where they were given bed and board with no questions asked, they saw the suspicion in the eyes of people who took a contrary view, but who welcomed them under their roofs because they shared a common heritage and humanity, stronger than any politics. A man may shoot his brother in the heart in an impulsive act of outraged passion and then weep his life away in the expiation of his guilt.

They left the good Joe McCarthy in the lee of Mount Owen and travelled to the hospitable home of the Woods family up a side road east of Coppeen. The Woods were Protestants, like Childers's and Doctor Baldwin's forebears, but that did not make them any less committed to the idea of an Irish Republic. Childers reminded them that Republicanism had been fostered by Protestants in America's Revolution and those same ideas had filtered down from Cromwellian self-expression and protest against the monolithic Catholicism of the Holy Roman Empire. Indeed it could be argued that Republicanism was a Protestant invention and there were many Irish of that persuasion such as himself who would cling to that idea no matter what the provocation of the apostate 'Free Staters,' who'd clearly lost their way and betrayed their oath to Sinn Féin, in the interest of their own aggrandisement.

October's bright blue weather ran its course and the gales of November came early. With increasing frustration they produced their publication, but Childers eventually lost heart when part of their printing press disappeared in a bog hole one dark, rainy evening at the foot of Mount Owen. It was near the lake where the Bandon river rose, and storied as the place where the handsome hero of the Fianna, Diarmuid O'Duibhne, slept with Gráinne, his light of love, on their flight from the angry, ageing Fionn MacCúmhail, in mythic times gone by.

'I've had enough,' Childers finally said.

'That's too bad,' said Doctor Baldwin. 'What do you intend to do?'

'I'll return to Wicklow, to my mother's ancestral home in Annamoe,' said Childers. 'I'll collect my extensive notes and perhaps I'll publish them as a memoir and as a historical record of the events of our recent wars. I will continue to speak out against this pernicious regime in Dublin and will continue to prosecute the cause of the Republic.'

They made their final bivouac for the campaign in the house of O'Sullivan at Ahilina, where the boys of Kilmichael first marched out on their fateful journey to defeat the Auxiliaries. In the morning Childers packed his few meagre belongings and showed Baldwin a small 'Destroyer' pistol which he kept attached with a safety pin to the inside of his waistcoat.

'Does that shoot real bullets?' asked the Doctor, peering at the small, ornate firearm.

'I'm given to understand that it does,' said Childers, 'though I don't have any bullets for it and don't know where to get them. It's a .32 calibre automatic, made in Spain. I got it as a present from our deceased leader, Michael Collins.'

'You considered him your leader?' asked Baldwin, surprised.

'Most assuredly,' said Childers. 'Head and shoulders above all but de Valera, who has great gifts too, but appears to be hiding them under a bushel at the present time.'

Doctor Baldwin waved farewell to Childers as he left the green, rocky heights of Ahilina, in a horse and trap driven by Sean Hendrick. They were going up to Longs of Shanacashel to meet Liam Deasy and Denny Crowley, to make arrangements for Childers's safe passage across Ireland to the Wicklow hills. He watched until they were out of sight and then he leant on a nine-bar gate looking through a gap to where the watery sun peeked through in a ray of silver, like sanctifying grace over the western mountains. He'd miss the contrary little man whom he'd come to admire for his tenacity of purpose and his egalitarian vision. He'd miss the arguments and the wit of the erudite young men, O'Connor and O'Faoileáin. They were fine types all. He'd deferred his trip to tarry with Childers and his friends. He now reset his compass for McGillicuddy's Reeks, but first he'd drink some *poitín* with the men of Ahilina in Forbes's pub in Kinneigh, by the old round tower.

A week later he took the old road west from Ballyvourney up through the Gaeltacht of Coolea. He slept in an abandoned tinker's caravan near the county bounds and in the morning strode down towards Kilgarvan. It was chilly and the wind blew up from distant estuaries. He could see the tops of high mountains, some flecked with snow. Kerry the magnificent, ringed with peaks of Himalayan grandeur. He stopped at a tavern in Kilgarvan where a man told him there was trouble with the Republicans.

'I heard the Free State Forces landed in great numbers from the sea,' said Doctor Baldwin, being diplomatic until he'd established the politics of his informant.

'They did, and a good thing they did. There's fierce blackguarding going on with the 'Irregulars,' said the other, a tall, wiry man, with an insouciant air about him.

'Blackguarding is it?' said the proprietor of the bar. 'Sure there's blackguarding on both sides. I hear some right hard men came down from Dublin, part of Collins's crowd. There's supposed to be a few bad articles among them.' He was a portly man with a red face, a bald head and a broad-vowelled accent that articulated every word.

'There is so?' said the wiry man, dubiously. 'Who told you that?'

'Everyone has it,' said the proprietor. 'There's supposed to be two fellows called Neligan and Daly, who're worse than the Tans ever were. All kinds of torture going on. They brought some poor lad in from Killorglin that they found with a rifle. He was only seventeen. For five days they used him as a shield against IRA ambushes and forced him to dismantle booby-trapped barricades. When word came in of an IRA ambush in Killarney they took the young lad and threw him down the stairs in the Great Southern Hotel before pouring bullets into him.'

'Who was that?' asked the wiry man.

'Young Bertie Murphy,' said the proprietor, warming to his subject. 'And what about Eugene Fitzgerald of Currahane Sands? A party of 'Staters' caught him at his aunt's house. They were blind drunk. On the journey to Tralee barracks, they broke his left leg and crushed it to a pulp, so they did. Then they shot the poor bastard in the side trying to get him to reveal the whereabouts of the local column. Yerra what, I could tell you dozens of stories like that, desperate barbarity. But you won't hear it from most people. There's a wall of silence I tell you. People are afraid to talk.'

'The barbarity isn't all on the Free State side,' said the wiry man. 'What about the Scarteen O'Connors down in Kenmare. Weren't they taken out of their beds one morning and shot through the forehead by the 'Irregulars' before they had a chance to defend themselves. And Tom O'Connor was a good man against the Tans. One of the best in South Kerry.'

'Most of the Kerry IRA who fought the Tans never joined the 'Staters,' said the proprietor with a hint of smugness.

'Well, Scarteen O'Connor did, and a terrible price he paid for it,' said the wiry man. He was becoming annoyed.

'Most of the fellows who joined the 'Staters' were herding goats up the mountains,' said the proprietor with a wink to Doctor Baldwin. 'They never lifted a finger against the English. But when they heard there was a few pound going, they took the Saxon shilling from Cosgrave.'

The proprietor was satisfied with his pithy rebuke of the wiry man, but Doctor Baldwin could see trouble brewing. 'Well, I think it's a tragedy the likes of which we haven't seen since the Greeks,' he said. 'Life has become cheap. We've become inured to cruelty and terrible violence.'

'Tell that to the Provisional Government,' retorted the proprietor. 'They have the power now. They need to show mercy and they won't 'til every Republican is crushed.'

The wiry man finished up his drink and saluted the Doctor. 'Good day to you, sir,' he said and tipped his cap. He did not acknowledge his host.

As he left, the proprietor continued to wipe the top of the counter with a cloth.

'Well,' said the Doctor, 'we know which side that man is on anyway.'

'Sullivan the Mountain is it?' laughed the proprietor. 'Sure he's not a bad fellow. But he listens to people spouting *ráiméis* about law and order and that kind of thing. Stuff O'Higgins and Mulcahy want us all to swallow.'

'Where's he from?' asked the Doctor.

'Who? You mean Sullivan the Mountain? Oh, he's from over on the Cork side in the Borlin Valley. A bit of a shepherd.'

He paused and gave the Doctor a look of appraisal as if establishing the value of a beast at the fair. 'And where are you from yourself?'

'Near Bandon, County Cork,' said the Doctor.

'Bandon, where even the pigs are Protestants, I always heard,' said the proprietor and chuckled.

'Too true,' said the Doctor. 'Well, I'd better be on my way.'

'Be careful how you go,' said the propietor

As he walked towards Kenmare, names of local places began to swim through his brain: the Gap of Dunloe, the Black Valley, Sceilig Rock. Treacherous beauties. He began to feel a strange alienation as if he didn't quite belong. These were an ancient people, *Na Ciarraíge*, first tribes of Kerry. They went back a long way into the dawn of history. Old scores to be settled. Black as midnight.

It was several days later that he found himself out near Sneem on the Kenmare Road, where the views were beautiful across the bay to the Beara Peninsula on the Cork coast. Truly a land fit for long-haired, bearded men, beating in from sea five thousand years before, to build Staigue Fort. He bought a copy of the Kerryman newspaper in a shop with a low ceiling in the square of Sneem and his astonished eyes read the headline that Erskine Childers had been arrested and was awaiting court martial in Beggars Bush barracks in Dublin. The charge was the unauthorised possession of a firearm, to wit a 'Destroyer' Spanish-made automatic pistol. The article confirmed that Childers had reached his ancestral home in Annamoe, County Wicklow and while resting with his cousins, the Bartons, he'd been apprehended.

Childers had made his way by tortuous routes to Wicklow. When he walked down the deep valley in the heart of the Wicklow mountains, where the Avonmore river flows out of the black lake of Lough Tay into the brown lake of Lough Dan, he'd felt a tremendous unburdening of his troubled spirit. Above him rose the rounded slopes of Djouce, further back Kippure, and ahead in the dim, blue distance, Lugnaquilla and Glenmalure. He liked to let the names roll off his tongue: Glendalough, Luggala, Avondale and Glenmacnass. He walked past the stone bridge built in 1828 and took the winding lane through the flat meadows to where the medieval forest began. How these great oaks filled him with peace and delight. Some of them may have been there nine hundred years, before the battle of Kinsale, before Shakespeare wrote Macbeth, some maybe saplings when Brian Boru fought the Danes at Clontarf, *Cluain Tarbh*, meadow of the bull. A home dog had welcomed him, barking and leaping up, then sniffing and urinating before him, as he made his way to the long, Georgian farmhouse that stood in the middle of the comfortable granite-faced buildings of the Barton estate. He'd grown up here, orphaned when his parents died. Ireland made him. He called it home. His cousins, the Bartons, welcomed him with open arms, though Robert, who'd signed the Treaty, was imprisoned by the 'Free Staters,' because he'd turned his back on them and espoused the Republican cause. His wife, Molly Osgood, was overjoyed to see him and he felt blessed at his good fortune in having such a companion, who'd not only stood by him through thick and thin, but who urged him fiercely on in his quest to influence the shaping of Ireland's destiny. He spent the first few days sleeping, then caught up with the latest happenings with renewed vigour. He noticed the Provisional Government had lost little time in implementing their new draconian measures of summary execution. Four young men, arrested near Oriel House in Westland Row, were its first victims. They were shot in Kilmainham, after a peremptory court-martial by the sinister military tribunal. Their fate was barely mentioned, mere footnotes in the self-righteous drive to destroy all resistance. Richard Mulcahy revealed his elitist condescension when he announced in passing: 'The men who were executed this morning were perhaps uneducated, illiterate men, and we provided all the spiritual assistance that we could to help them in their passage to eternity...'

O'Higgins had gone even further when he stood up in the Dáil and said with the lofty assurance of a man who now felt entitled to decree whether a man lived or died: 'The Nation's life is worth the life of many individuals. If we had chosen to execute first, some man who was outstandingly active and outstandingly wicked in his activities, the unfortunate dupes throughout the country might say that he was killed because he was a leader, because he was an Englishman, or because he combined with others to commit rape.'

'The breathtaking arrogance of the man,' thought Childers, 'pronouncing on the lives of others as if he'd earned the right to do so.'

How O'Higgins's words stuck in his craw. The brave men who'd so courageously fought the British to a standstill, must feel, as he did, impotent with rage. He noted in particular the epithet, "Englishman." Was O'Higgins referring to himself, Childers? He wasn't long in discovering that he was precisely the man in O'Higgins's gunsights. The hound dogs were soon on his trail and within days Childers was arrested as he took his afternoon tea on the lawn in the pleasant glades of Annamoe, where the peacocks strutted and fanned their bright feathers in the evening light.

He refused to recognise the military court that tried him. He argued that far from being an insurgency, the struggle now being pursued was one between two equal groups over a difference of ideology. To brand the soldiers of the Irish Republican Army, who derived their authority directly from the Sinn Féin victory in the election of 1918, as criminals, was a travesty and a grievous insult to all those who had fought and died for Irish freedom. He applied for a writ of *habeas corpus,* not for himself, but to assist the case of eight other young men who were awaiting trial by the same military court. The Master of the Rolls found that he was unable to deal with the application because a state of war existed, precisely the point the Provisional Government was trying to deny. Childers was a soldier fighting a war after all, as he had so eloquently argued. The Master of the Rolls delivered his decision late in the evening of the 23rd of November. Childers requested a stay of execution for an hour, until he could see the sun rise for one last time. In the morning he marched with his head held high and his gaze unflinching, across to the wall of the prison yard in Beggars Bush. The sun rose over Sandymount Strand and cast a bright shaft of light across the cobblestones. He could hear the dull boom of the sea at high tide, beating against the sea wall on Strand Road. The firing squad lined up and Childers shook each man's hand. Then he walked to the wall. He was offered a blindfold but refused to wear it. He noticed his executioners' hands were shaking. He smiled at them and beckoned them forward towards him to make a bigger target.

'Step closer lads,' he said. 'It will be easier that way.'

In Kerry, Doctor Baldwin followed the events of the last days of the strange, fanatical Englishman with sadness. His initial impression of the man was that he was aloof and austere, but then he'd come to admire his tenacity, his bravery and charity: the finest kind of Englishman. Would that the British Government Ministers, so niggardly and ungracious in their estimation of him, had his sterling qualities.

He followed the coast of south Kerry. West of Sneem the road twisted and turned, opening onto island-dotted bays: Derrynane, home of the Liberator, Daniel O'Connell. Then Waterville, Ballinskelligs and Caherciveen. He saw fishermen at dawn pushing black-beetled currachs into the pounding surf; he passed white-washed cottages where large families subsisted on a single acre, a donkey, a cow, a few mackerel for supper. This was a poor land. What would a Republic bring to these hard-scrabbled lives? The poet Yeats had written that "the riders had changed horses but the lash goes on." English landlords replaced by middle-class Irish merchants, bankers and big farmers, the elite of the Catholic Church. And so the present struggle lay between who would control the transfer of patronage from Dublin Castle to the Irish Parliament. But would Liam Lynch and Rory O'Connor guarantee more bread on the table for these poor of Kerry, anymore than Cosgrave or Mulcahy would? The Irish Revolution was not a real one in the Bolshevik sense. The Russians had deactivated the Churchmen; not so Collins, or Tom Barry for that matter. Connolly was the last real socialist, but the Labour party hadn't followed him. Dublin's working class were mesmerised by the nebulous idea of a utopian Republic, just as the West Cork small farmers were. The main opponents of the Free State: de Valera, Lynch and O'Connor seemed to have no alternative programme other than some vague notion of martyrdom; and martyrdom, to Doctor Baldwin's way of thinking, should be avoided. Ireland was destined to spill the blood of its finest young men and women in a display that was no more than a charade which would change nothing for the working man or woman, the people of no property.

He bought the *Kerryman* when he reached Caherciveen. In the distance out to sea rose the magnificent natural pyramid of the Sceilig

Rock, where Irish monks had preserved Western civilization, the works of Ovid, Homer, Sophocles and the Bible, when Europe entered the Dark Ages. Nothing left of it now but the beehive hut cloisters and the thousand steps ascending to Christ's Saddle; gannets, puffins and dolphins cresting the wild Atlantic waves. His eyes fastened on a headline: "Orders of Frightfulness issued by Liam Lynch."

What could that mean? He scanned the first paragraph. In response to the Free State Emergency Powers, the Republican Executive would retaliate by targeting for legitimate assassination all members of the Dáil, all judges and all newspaper editors who'd voted for or supported the new legislation.

He lingered on the road to Killorglin. The days grew crisp and cold but the sky was still blue. The mountains muscled northwards to his right and the broad Atlantic sparkled on his left. He heard stories of arson and robbery by anti-Treaty men, and floggings, murder, summary execution and torture by 'Free Staters.' The hopeless futility of it all. He was out near Castlemaine seven days later when he heard that Sean Hales was shot dead on Ormond Quay in Dublin as he climbed into a horse and trap on his way to the Dáil. Hales from Ballinadee, brave son of a brave clan. He knew them all, the father, Robert, an old Fenian; the sons, Sean whom they called 'Buckshot,' Tom, Bob, Bill; the sister Hannah and the others whose names he couldn't recall. Sean Hales, the only significant West Cork commander who'd gone Free State with Michael Collins. He'd paid the price for his apostasy.

34

silver and gold

D esmond Fitzgerald, Minister of External Affairs, sat and watched the glum faces of his Cabinet colleagues in Leinster House in Dublin. Richard Mulcahy, the Minister of Defence, had just made an astonishing proposal, which was to execute four political prisoners in Mountjoy as a reprisal and a solemn warning to the 'Irregulars' in retaliaton for the murder of Deputy Sean Hales. After the initial stunned silence there was an uneasy clearing of throats.

'Which four do you have in mind?' asked Kevin O'Higgins.

'One from each province of Ireland,' said Mulcahy. 'Four leaders this time, not four nonentities.'

'Which four?' O'Higgins asked again. His usual certainties appeared to Fitzgerald to be absent. But Mulcahy was fulminating: 'Barrett from Munster, Mellows from Connacht, McKelvey from Ulster and...'

He paused, as if confronting an obstacle in his mind.

'And who from Leinster?' asked Fitzgerald, appalled.

'Rory O'Connor,' said Mulcahy and went silent.

'Rory...?' asked O'Higgins, and blanched palely.

The room was overcome by something that went beyond silence. To the senses there was the touch of smooth mahogany and the smell of polished furniture. To please the eye there were marble statues and high-corniced ceilings. The men drank cold water from a jug and glasses provided, but still there was this silence from which there was no escaping. All heads were bowed, no gazes met. Cosgrave looked complacent in his regular inscrutable expression. Blythe's face was hard-masked, cold bulging eyes behind thick glasses. Eoin McNeill, the Minister of Education, was suddenly fiercely passionate: 'We're all in danger now. Anyone of us could be next. Hales is gone and Pádraic O'Maille, our Deputy Speaker, is badly injured. Do we wait until they come to our houses and shoot us in our beds? No, I say. I second the motion of the Minister of Defence.'

'Why so definite?' thought Fitzgerald. Perhaps they all were thinking what he thought. McNeill came from a house divided. One son on the Free State side, another shot in Sligo in cold blood, fighting for the 'Irregulars.' Shot through the head at close range, unarmed. Was McNeill so devastated, so blinded by guilt that his sentiments became distorted? Joe McGrath, a big, raw Dublin working man, elevated to the post of Minister of Industry and Commerce, nodded. He'd a carapace of steel around him. Cosgrave went with the flow, as was his wont. Fitzgerald looked towards Duggan who'd signed the Treaty: a natty dresser, a wearer of spats and striped pants. By his silence did he acquiesce? Patrick Hogan, the stolid Minister of Agriculture, with no discernible expression on his face to show his feelings. Fionán Lynch, Minister without portfolio, quiet as a mouse. Was there to be no dissenting voice, or were they all dissenting except Mulcahy and Cosgrave, but awaiting O'Higgins's say so? O'Higgins, the strongman of the Cabinet.

Fitzgerald ventured against the juggernaut of unanimity: 'It's retrospective, General, it cannot be sanctioned retrospectively. It would be illegal. These men have been incarcerated for over five months. How can they be guilty or complicit in a crime that did not exist on the Statute Books until the 10th October? What is the charge here? Where is the court? Where is the tribunal?'

Mulcahy stood up, a slight man with cold eyes, a hard, determined mouth, harder than his often featureless expression. He looked as if he was about to pound the table but did not: 'As I've said before, when this all started, to have a real revolution you must have bloody-minded, fierce men who do not care a scrap for death or bloodshed. A revolution is not a job for children, for saints or scholars. Neither is the suppression of an insurgency like we have now. Any man, woman or child who is not with you is against you...'

He paused and looked around the Cabinet table. His voice dropped a decibel, but the words were unmistakeably clear: 'I say shoot them and be damned to them!'

He sat down. The one man whose vote would carry most weight had said nothing after his first question. All eyes turned furtively towards O'Higgins, who appeared to be in a kind of preoccupied trance. He was thinking of gold and silver coins, transferred from his own hand to Rory's. The symbolic coins of security and fealty, exchanged with marriage vows. 'Til death do us part. Rory O'Connor, his best friend, best man at his wedding twelve months ago.

'What do you say, Mr. O'Higgins?' asked the formal, flat voice of Cosgrave. 'What is your answer?'

O'Higgins looked towards the high windows. Outside, the December sun was sinking low, illuminating the chamber with its shadowed winter light. It would soon be dark. He sighed and produced a white handkerchief from his top pocket with which he dabbed his eyes. 'It is a hard thing I'm being asked to do,' he said. 'I know all these men well, but Rory is my friend.' He paused and his lower lip trembled. 'I know all government is based on force and must meet its opposite with greater force if it is to survive. But that knowledge does not make what I am asked to do here today any easier. Indeed, I can see in all your faces that it is the hardest thing you've ever been asked to do. These men were our comrades in arms until very recently...'

He stopped unable to continue for some moments, then continued: 'Civil war is a terrible thing. Would that it were over.'

He blinked back the welling tears. The others looked surprised and a little shaken. O'Higgins was the last man they'd expect to cry. He sighed and looked as if he were struggling to say more, but then shrugged in a gesture of resignation. 'What's the use in talking. I will say no more. I very reluctantly cast my vote in favour of General Mulcahy's motion, as you all have done.'

He sat down and covered his face with his hands. Cosgrave raised an eyebrow towards Desmond Fitzgerald, who said: 'In the light of what Mr. O'Higgins has said, I have to concur as well.'

The silence surged back like an invisible cloud. They sat still as statues in the fading light.

'The motion is carried,' said Cosgrave. 'Our business is concluded here today.'

They all stood, and like shadows they slowly left the room.

In C wing of Mountjoy jail, Rory O'Connor was playing chess with young Sean McBride, the son of the beautiful Maud Gonne and Captain John McBride, the tragic hero of 1916. They were resting in cell number 32, which they shared, sleeping on a threadbare mattress, with three blankets and a bucket in the corner. Rory had carved the chess figures from a piece of wood. It occupied the long prison days and nights. He was winning the chess game as usual and was twirling a gold sovereign and a silver five shilling piece over his fingers like a magician.

'Checkmate,' Rory finally said, as he brought his queen into direct line with Sean's king, leaving him further blocked by a bishop and a knight. Rory stood up from his squatting position, patted the younger man's head and looked out the cell door, which hung at a crazy angle on its prised-off hinges. They'd used the bible, wedged in between the door and the frame, so the door couldn't close on its rebate. They valued their privacy but didn't want to be locked in. The Provisional Government had no money to repair the doors so the prisoners came and went with a certain amount of freedom.

Rory was looking towards the triangle hanging from the granite-flagged circle from where the warders could see to the furthest end of each of the four wings. Military simplicity at its best. He could see the squat, rotund figure of Paudeen O'Keeffe, the former secretary of Sinn Féin, now Deputy Prison Governor, sold body and soul to the 'Free Staters.' Paudeen was bustling about and issuing orders to subordinates in very colourful language. Rory smiled. Paudeen was a clown, but harmless enough.

Rory eventually turned back to McBride. He was in pensive mood. 'Did you hear the rumour?' he asked, 'about Sean Hales? Supposed to be shot this morning near the Ormond Hotel.'

'No one seems to know for sure,' said McBride. His accent was strongly French. He'd been born and raised in France until the age of 12.

'I'd believe it,' said Rory. 'But I wouldn't believe those who say our crowd did it. Hales was a very popular man.'

'So was Collins,' reminded Sean.

Rory nodded ruefully. 'That's true,' he said. 'No one is safe in war. Even less so in civil war. It will leave scars for life, I fear.'

'What will happen now?' asked Sean.

'Who knows,' said Rory. 'I wouldn't trust Mulcahy. He's a very cold fish.'

Dick Barrett stood leaning on the railing of a balcony with a distant look in his eye. He was thinking about a bend on the Bandon river near the creamery in Enniskean, where he fished for salmon as a boy. The river flowed through the flat, spacious fields of the valley and there the fish were big and fat. You needed a license from Conner of Manch, the local landlord, but Dick and his friends took great delight in poaching along the banks and gave no fig for riparian rights.

Peadar O'Donnell, on the landing below, was going into a cell with some others to discuss the subject of equal pay for equal work for women. He shouted up to Dick: 'Are you coming in to the debate?'

Dick smiled an angelic, boyish smile and shouted back: 'I'll leave the talking shop to you, Peadar.'

Barrett, despite his lovable, youthful demeanour, was a man of action, possessed of a keen intellect and a mind for conspiracy. A great friend of Michael Collins before the split, he'd learnt the dark arts from the master and had organised many the jailbreak, kidnap and military raid. One of the most dangerous adversaries the 'Free Staters' could have. He delighted in arguing political doctrine with Peadar O'Donnell, an avowed socialist.

Joe McKelvey was lying on a mattress in cell number 34, reading a book. He was a powerfully-built man of enormous strength. He'd led the Belfast Brigade with flair and dash and a certain recklessness, but no deep hatred resided in his bosom. He shared a cell with Liam Mellows. Dick Barrett was in cell number 36. The book was a popular novel called, *The Gadfly,* written by a lady named Boole from Cork, who'd married a Polish revolutionary. He read aloud to Mellows, a grim description of political prisoners, forced to watch the garrotting of helpless victims by sadistic executioners. 'God,' he said, 'I hope they don't mess up any of our lads this way.'

'Put that oul book away, Joe,' said Mellows, 'it'll only give you nightmares.'

'What if there's reprisals for Hales and O'Máille?' asked Joe.

'We're all clean here,' said Mellows. 'Haven't we been safe inside for the last five months. Whatever policy decisions Lynch and the others have made, they weren't made by us.'

Mellows, like O'Donnell, was a serious social thinker, working on the outline of a coherent social policy, which he hoped to put into operation when he got out of jail.

Dick Barrett called goodnight to them as he walked past the door to his own cell.

Paudeen O'Keeffe, short, fat and quick-witted, heaved his tired body into his bunk a little after midnight. He shared his room with the new governor of Mountjoy, Phil Cosgrave, the errant brother of W.T., the head of the Government. Paudeen could curse with the best of them and he reserved some of his choicest epithets for Cosgrave, especially at night when his superior kept him awake, snoring off drunken stupors. Tonight was no different to many other nights and he quietly swore foul imprecations under his breath. Bad enough to have to do most of the work, besides having to put up with his honking boss as well. Just as he'd finally managed to drift off several hours later, someone shone a flashlight into his eyes. 'Turn off that friggin' light,' he said as he recognised a Free State red cap named Burke, one of his security officers. He sat up, half dressed as he'd lain down.

'There's four names here for you,' said Burke. 'We've orders to bring them out and give them whiskey.'

'Whiskey?' said Paudeen. That could only mean one thing at this hour. The thought troubled him. There had been no executions in the 'Joy' on his watch.

Sean McBride heard the door of his cell opening in the dead of night. He heard someone come in, strike a match and lean over the sleeping form of Rory O'Connor. He recognised Burke, the red cap. He lay still and Burke went out again. Some hours later, McBride again heard people whispering and cursing inside the cell. Someone was trying to light the gas and only one man could curse like that: Paudeen O'Keeffe.

'This fucking gas,' he was saying. 'It never works when it's supposed to.'

Another guard came in with a lighted candle. Paudeen leant over the still sleeping form of Rory. 'Mr. O'Connor,' he said. 'Please get up and get dressed.'

'It must be something serious,' thought McBride, 'that he's being so polite to Rory.'

Paudeen looked miserable as Rory sat up, rubbing the sleep from his eyes. 'What is it, Paudeen?' he said. The Deputy Governor was generally a figure of fun and the butt of the prisoners' jokes. Why was he so solemn?

'I'm following instructions,' he said. 'Don't take it personal.'

He motioned to another guard. 'Bring out that bottle,' he said, 'and fill a glass of whiskey for Mr. O'Connor.'

He handed the glass to Rory. 'Have a belt of that,' he said.

Rory swallowed the drink without a word.

'You won't be needing one,' Paudeen said to McBride. 'You can go back to bed.'

When he was dressed, Rory took the gold and silver coins from his pocket. 'Take these,' he said to McBride. 'They've always brought me bad luck. They might work better for you.'

McBride faltered. He did not laugh, but Rory laughed.

'Goodbye Sean,' said Rory and firmly shook his young cellmate's hand.

Outside on the landing, Joe McKelvey had hefted a book bag on his shoulder. 'You look like Santy Claus,' joked Rory, as he came out.

A prison chaplain hovered behind Liam Mellows like a spurned solicitor. He'd been trying to persuade Liam to shrive his soul of sins without success. As they were led away, McBride also came out on the landing and watched them depart into the dark. Dick Barrett was first going down the steps. He was singing. He was singing, *The Top Of Cork Road,* loudly, defiantly.

They stepped smartly into the prison yard in the grey December dawn; the commanding officer mouthing, 'Left, left, left...'

The firing squad followed at the double. On either side of the four men were two soldiers, who led them to the wall. When they reached the wall the soldiers stopped, turned on their heels and faced the firing squad, which had stopped twenty paces away. The two soldiers produced blindfolds and tied them around the heads of the uncondemned men. Then the two soldiers stepped away. The four blindfolded men stood side by side a yard apart from each other. There was no sound except for the sound of their breathing. As the two soldiers stepped away their boots made a crunching sound on the gravel. There were twenty soldiers lined up in the firing squad and beside them stood the officer, the medical doctor and the chaplain. The seconds ticked away. Then the officer turned to the medical doctor by his side. The doctor nodded and the officer said, 'Load arms.'

His voice was a loud shout in the still morning. There was the click of rifle bolts pulled back as shells were slotted into the rifle breeches.

'Present arms,' said the officer, and the rifles were pointed horizontally, directionally.

'Fire!'

The volley rent the air. Three men fell and the fourth still half stood. Most of the firing squad had aimed at Rory O'Connor, although five men were designated to aim at each man. Rory's clothes were burning, so many bullets had hit him. His flesh began to burn. There was a smell like fried meat in the morning. The officer looked at the chaplain, who looked at the doctor. The chaplain vomited. There was a look of horror on the faces of the men who pulled the triggers. The officer half ran towards the other three mutilated men. Dick Barrett was still on his feet with the blindfold around his head, but he was sagging against the wall. The officer approached him. His hands were trembling as he lifted his pistol and aimed it at the side of Dick's head beside the temple. He pulled the trigger. Dick's skull caved in like a crushed egg and his blood splashed across the officer's face. He slid down the wall, leaving streaks of red across the brick. The doctor had run in panic towards the other two men on the ground. The officer turned towards Liam Mellows and shot him in the head as he lay on the ground. But Joe McKelvey was moaning in agony. The garrotte of *The Gadfly*? All messed up.

'For God's sake, kill me, Doc,' said Joe. He could see the doctor standing above him. The doctor tugged at the officer's Sam Browne belt. The officer was in a daze.

'Finish this man,' said the doctor, sworn by Asclepian Oath to defend life. The officer bent low over Joe McKelvey and he aimed his pistol at the piece of paper pinned as a target at his heart, where the firing squad had failed to hit him. Instead they'd hit him in the belly and the groin. His intestines were showing, visceral-red. The officer tried to aim at Joe's heart. He fired. Joe's body convulsed. He opened his eyes again and said, 'Another one.'

The commanding officer fired again. The bullet smashed through Joe's rib cage, severed his aorta, his blood spouted like a fountain. But it wasn't enough still.

'Another one,' whispered Joe. The officer had blood on his hands and on his face. The doctor had blood and pieces of flesh and gristle on his clothes. The officer fired again to make sure Joe was dead. Behind them the firing squad were men in shock. The chaplain turned and sloped away, unable to bear witness any longer.

A half an hour later the women prisoners who'd been lining up for Mass, were talking in hushed, excited whispers. Their section was near the front of the prison where the firing came from. After the first volley they'd counted nine individual shots. The male prisoners moved forward as the whistle went for Mass. It was the 8th of December, a Holy Day of Obligation, feast of the Immaculate Conception of the Blessed Virgin Mary. As the prisoners were filing across the circle they saw below them a squad of soldiers and beside them, some boiler-suited workmen. They did not look at the prisoners, but their boots were stained with blood and earth, and a white substance someone said was quicklime.

35

in their dreams of fire

They left the Sheha mountains the day after their four comrades died in Mountjoy: Sonny, Tom Barry, Liam Deasy and the best of their fighting men. They were going back to Tipperary where Tom Barry had promised to return. Dinny Lacy sent word. He said they'd built up a strong force of men around Carraig-on-Suir, a pleasant town, where the river turned south, confronted by the great bulk of Sliabh na mBan, and then east to skirt the northern flank of the Comeraghs, before joining its sister rivers, the Nore and the Barrow. The journey was long. Some walked in groups of five and six, north towards Mushera, then northeast to the Ballyhoura hills and the Kilworth mountains. They travelled at night because the roads were dangerous. The Gods and the people had deserted them, but they felt confident because Tom Barry was back to lead them. He'd fight more in a week than most men would in a lifetime. He was smart and careful, a great leader. A lorry travelled with them to take extra rifles and they took turns riding and walking. At every crossroads, Barry would order the men to climb down and scout ahead in case 'Free Staters' lay in wait. Somewhere around Glanworth they abandoned the lorry and headed over the Kilworth mountains in the dark. The mists came down and a man who'd led them lost his way, lost his nerve more likely. They roused another from his bed and he grumpily left them down beyond Clogheen, where the limestone clay of Tipperary was deep and fertile. They hugged the Knockmealdown foothills and went east through the valley of the Nire. After four days they saw the sun rise over the slender steeples and the grey backstreets of Carraig-on-Suir.

The river sparkled in the morning. They were welcomed by Lacy, Dan Breen, Bill Quirke, Con Moloney and Michael Sheehan: the last of Tipperary. They took the town with a hundred men. Tom Barry stood out on the road as he did at Kilmichael and fooled the Free State patrol. A Mills bomb dispatched vehicle and driver and the soldiers panicked. Word had quickly spread that Barry and the 3rd West Cork Brigade were on the rampage. They routed the Government Forces from the town and their haul of arms was large. They released all prisoners and the same day the Free State executed another seven Republican prisoners in Kildare.

They went over Windgap from South Tipperary into the broad plain of Kilkenny. They converged on Thomastown and famed Jerpoint Abbey on the Nore. Horsebreaths were white in the frosty air. In the trees above them they could see the beautiful Palladian mansion of Mount Juliet. Someone said they'd burn it, but Tom Barry refused. 'I don't agree with burning anymore,' he said, 'either of military barracks or big bouses. Neither should unarmed men be shot. If there's any shooting to be done, we'll get them in a fair fight where they can see the whites of our eyes.'

They let Major McCalmont in peace in Mount Juliet, but around the country others fared less well. Sir Horace Plunkett's house was blown up by a mine; Moore Hall in Mayo on the shores of Lough Cara was gutted and Sir Bryan Mahon's mansion in Ballymore Eustace, County Kildare was destroyed. Kevin O'Higgins's family home was burned and his aged father shot dead : all the work of anti-Treaty forces. To Barry it was an aberration and a throwback to tactics which worked against the Black and Tans, but which he now deplored as being counter productive.

The barracks in Thomastown gave in without a fight and they struck out for Callan, which itself quickly capitulated. Winter was bleak, with frost, rain and snow. Their clothing was thin. They slept in ditches and in haybarns. If it grew too cold they'd furtively enter a cowbyre to be warmed by the cows' breaths. They crossed dark bogs from Kilkenny back to Tipperary. They fought all day before taking Templemore. If men were wounded they were taken to safety on makeshift stretchers made of doors. They fought all through December and January, hungry, desperate for sleep, slogging through frost and rain. By late January they'd retaken parts of Limerick and captured 800 rifles from the Civic Guard in the Curragh of Kildare. But bright as their campaign blazed, it could not be sustained. The Free State executions of unarmed prisoners, and the killing of men who'd surrendered, continued: 55 in the month of January. The 'Free Staters' were ruthless and cold-hearted. Ernest Blythe, the Minister of Local Government, said they would go on executing anti-Treatyites until they had killed the last man.

They lost them one by one, imprisoned or dead. Ernie O'Malley had already been hit with over twenty bullets as he helped de Valera escape from a house in Ailesbury Road in Dublin. Dinny Lacy was killed in the Glen of Aherlow escaping from a house in Ballydavid. Liam Deasy was captured near Sliabh Felim and taken to the prison in Clonmel. He was given a choice of death by firing squad or signing a document calling on his comrades to surrender. He signed to save his life. Their forces numbered no more than perhaps 8000, mainly lying low. Their prisoners numbered 13,000. The Free State Army on the other hand, had nearly 60,000 men. Moves were afoot to call a ceasefire, but Liam Lynch, the IRA Chief of Staff, stubbornly held out. Eventually he agreed to hold a meeting of its Executive Council to be held in the Nire valley in Tipperary.

It was dawn in Bill Houlihan's farmhouse at the foot of the Knockmealdowns, a place of birch trees, dark cypress and cawing ravens. A place of rivers, the Tar and the Nire, rushing northwards, swollen in winter spate, to join the winding Suir going eastwards to the sea across the flat lands of Tipperary. A scout ran in to rouse Tom Barry to tell him Free State Forces were coming up from Goatenbridge in two files, silently, keeping to the grass verges on both sides of the winding road. Liam Lynch sat at the kitchen table drinking tea. He was a tall, austere-looking man. He wore round glasses with narrow, silver frames which accentuated the longitude of his face, his pale skin. A man of great convictions and in no hurry, no matter the worries of the scout. He was among friends here and guarded by his own people, the 3rd Brigade of Tipperary. They'd assembled Republican Army Council men from all over Ireland, and this for the second time. Only a couple of weeks previously, they'd met in Bliantas in Waterford, home of James Cullinane. De Valera had driven all the way from Dublin in a touring car dressed in trilby hat and fake beard, masquerading as an American tourist. Lynch had kept him waiting in a back kitchen while he and the Army Council debated a ceasefire.

Despite his putative position as leader of Sinn Féin, he'd not been allowed to vote and Lynch had carried the day, still believing in victory. They'd resolved on another meeting because of the imminent 'Free Staters' and they'd fetched up again further west near Goatenbridge. Sonny Hennessy, Tom Barry, Tom Crofts, Dan Breen and the others all assembled.

Tommy Ryan was in confident mood. He stood in a cold, bare officers' mess in Clonmel military barracks and with a pointing cane in hand he identified potential safe houses in the Knockmealdown mountains, where the Republicans could be hiding. General Prout, the overall commanding officer, was listening carefully. Tommy was resplendent in his new, darkgreen uniform. He adjusted the tight collar of the white, linen shirt around his thin neck and patted down his tunic over a hollow belly. On his nether regions he wore jodhpurs and his feet were booted up to the knee: Commandant Tommy Ryan, horse tangler turned officer, as imposing as any British Major Jeudwine or Montgomery, or Percival for that matter. He'd become well acquainted with Prout, who'd been inclined to keep his feet up on his desk in Kilkenny, while Tommy was busy in South Tipp. He knew all the safe houses. Didn't he stay in them all at one time or another in the fight against the Tans. Tommy's accent was broad and he used the uvular R of the region, a throwback perhaps to when the Normans first sailed up the river into Waterford city. He was a cheerful, bucolic fellow, but also cunning. He'd warned the Cody girls to beware of 'Irregulars' when he'd driven them into Cashel eight or nine months previously, but what he hadn't told them was his intention to become a big shot in the Free State Army. It hadn't taken him long. Prout nodded sagely, puffing on his pipe as Tommy elaborated on his plan to encircle Lynch and his Executive Army Council.

'Lynch is here,' he said pointing to an area on the large map, east of Sugarloaf Hill with Knocknafaillin towering above it. 'There's only two passes through the mountains that he can use to escape. We'll send a column out to cover the east and the western sides of his billet, which we believe is up near Croagh. I myself will lead two further columns up the Tar river from the north. We'll come up both sides in case he tries to slip back. Captain Taylor will go over the Vee gap tonight and come at them from the southern side as well. We've a thousand men under arms. I guarantee you we'll have their entire Executive GHQ back here by nightfall, locked up and the Civil War over.'

Tommy finished with a flourish of the cane, giving a lift of his shoulders and uttering a small 'humph' to indicate he was mighty pleased with his plan of campaign. Prout smiled. 'Carry on, Tommy,' he said. He'd learnt his military expressions equally as well as Tommy, from his superiors in the American Army.

When Commandant Tommy led his two columns up the Tar next morning, Captain Taylor was still in Goatenbridge, twirling his carefully-maintained handlebar moustache.

'You sir,' shouted Tommy. 'Bad cess to you, why are you still here?'

'Difficult terrain,' said Taylor with faux, clipped military speech. 'Slow progress.'

'Difficult terrain my arse,' roared Tommy. 'Sure I'd have walked a crowd of cripples to the top of Knocksheegowna by this stage.'

Tommy's men began to guffaw and for a while the situation looked to be about to collapse into a farce. A few of them started taking potshots at rabbits in the undergrowth. Then Tommy shouted to another officer in frustration. 'Captain Clancy, will you for God's sake take fifty men up there and seal the pass, although I doubt it'll do any good at this stage. Unless Lynch and his scouts are deaf he'll have cleared off by now. What will we look like then? Right eejits, that's what.'

Tommy scowled at Taylor who stood to the side with a wounded look on his face. Before Tommy could continue there was a shout that a party of men was seen going up the valley, 'Irregulars' most likely. Tommy's expression of thunder softened. He'd gottten lucky. Lynch must have been complacent.

Sonny and Tom Barry led the retreating party up the glen. They were going up a dry river bed when they saw a group of Free State soldiers off to their left coming over the rise. Barry immediately ordered them to fire their pistols, which were of little use against Lee Enfield rifles. But such were the reputations of Barry and Breen that the enemy was cautious. There were only a few half-hearted shots in reply. Barry cursed Lynch's tardiness and his own omission not to bring the lorry with the load of rifles. He looked back. All the members of the group were away safely from the farmhouse. They were moving along quickly. Lynch brought up the rear with Sean Hyde and Frank Aiken. They were safe in the river bed but once they crossed the ridge they'd be exposed. They kept on, scrambling higher over the tufted heather and the gorse bushes. They were several hundred yards ahead of the pursuing group of soldiers. When they came out of the river bed the rifle fire started up again. Bullets clipped at their heels but most of them were still out of range. If they could reach the passes above them they'd have a chance to get away. The higher they got the slippier the ground became, where winter snow still lay underfoot. They lined up behind rocks and ditches and fired volleys, rearguard fashion. They were heading into another gulch. Once there, they'd have shelter from stunted hazel trees and the 'Staters' would be unlikely to follow them in. There was no shooting for some minutes. The immediate sounds were of feet crunching over scree and gravel, heavy breathing in the cold air, grunts and curses as they stumbled and fell, and rose again. Suddenly a single shot rang out and echoed around the hills. Lynch, at the rear of the group, uttered a loud cry and fell across the heather. Hyde, Aiken and Quirke rushed to help him. The bullet had struck him in the back, just above the hip and had gone clean through his body. He was in great pain. It was a serious wound. They carried him onwards as the hail of bullets increased from down below. Tommy Ryan's men were gaining in confidence, sensing blood. Lynch eventually persuaded his carriers to leave him: 'I'm finished boys. Go on. God save Ireland.'

Tommy Ryan rushed up at the head of his column. For a moment he thought he'd landed the biggest fish of all: Eamon de Valera. He quickly recognised Lynch, an equally big prize. He orderd his men to keep chasing the others while the wounded leader was placed on an improvised stretcher made of rifles and coats. They faced back down the mountain with their heavy burden.

Sonny headed for Knocknafaillin, the highest peak above him, though he did not know the name. Dan Breen was close behind. He saw Tom Barry skirting off into a field where there were some cows. He saw Barry discard his trenchcoat and gesticulate at the startled cows. He saw a group of 'Staters' enter the field. They took no notice of Barry. Sonny turned his face to the summit once more. He climbed hard, running through bushes and scutch grass. Soon he was on the bare ridge and below him the 'Staters' had not followed. He could see north to Clonmel and south towards Cappoquin, blue fields, silver rivers, heartachingly rich and bountiful. Dan Breen came panting up. Austin Stack, Frank Barrett, Maurice Walshe and Andy Kennedy straggled along behind. They stood gasping in the cold morning light. Their clothes were bedraggled and muddy, their hands and faces scratched and bloodied.

'Lynch is dying,' said Breen. 'I'm not sure about Hyde and Aiken. They might have got away, but then again they might be captured.'

'What about Barry?' asked Stack.

'The last I saw he was herding cows across an upland,' said Sonny. 'The 'Staters' thought he was a cowhand I'd say.'

'Trust Barry,' grinned Breen.

'We can't stay long up here,' said Sonny. 'There's thousands of them. They'll be searching everywhere.'

'Aye,' said Breen, 'and that little bastard Tommy Ryan is in charge. He knows every nook and cranny up here.' He paused, surveyed the mountains ranged around and said: 'Mount Melleray is to the southeast. We'll strike in that direction. The monks might give us shelter.'

They moved all day through the mountains. Prout's men scoured the countryside. Whippet cars patrolled the roads. Boats were removed from rivers so no fugitive could cross. Spotter planes patrolled the skies above them.

They reached the Cistercian Monastery as the monks were at vespers. They walked down long, cloistered corridors on white Carrera marblestone flags. Drops of their blood fell on the white stone. A startled monk, standing at a holy water fountain looked up at the sight of these fierce men. He said nothing, but he dipped his fingers into the font and made the sign of the cross on forehead, breast and shoulders. They slipped silently into the chapel where the Abbot was standing at a lectern speaking in soft, comforting tones to cowled monks whose heads were bowed in prayer:

'...and we must continue to live in a school of love. In the Gospels Jesus calls unto us, "Come follow me. Pray always. Watch and pray." Our goal is the perfect love of God, expressed in the practice of obedience, silence, humility, service of others and in all things preferring nothing whatever to Christ...'

The fugitives knelt on pews of solid oak and tried to make sense of the Abbot's words.

'...if you meditate on the scriptures, if you practise your *Lectio Divina*, whatever fire of anger that burns in your hearts will dissipate, whatever torment, whatever pain. In the *Lectio Divina* you will encounter God. Christ gradually becomes your world; becomes the air you breathe...'

The monks gave them food and shelter for the night. They did not ask them questions or mention their excommunication which the bishops had proclaimed from altars throughout the land. The Abbot said that all were welcome, all sinners, provided they'd become men of goodwill.

They left at 4 a.m. with the monks at vigils. Their massed voices echoed out through stained-glass windows, chanting the *Magnificat:*

> *'My soul doth magnify the Lord*
> *And my spirit hath rejoiced in God my saviour.*
> *For he that is mighty hath done great things for me*
> *And holy is his name...'*

To be safer the group split again into smaller numbers. Breen, Kennedy and Walshe struck north towards Newcastle. Austin Stack said he'd try to reach Ballymacarbery to the northeast. Sonny said he'd soldier on alone. He headed eastwards where the Comeraghs reared their mighty summits on high. On his head he wore a cloth cap and he wore a warm, collarless shirt inside a single-breasted bodycoat, which the monks had given him. His pants were a worsted jodhpur, which billowed slightly on his thigh and narrowed below the knee to fit into the pair of sturdy, leather boots also donated by the Cistercians. They'd packed enough provender for him in a leather satchel: a loaf of brown soda bread, five hard-boiled eggs, a chunk of ham and a few apples to last him maybe three days if he was careful. He had twelve rounds of ammunition for his Colt .45 revolver, which he hid in his belt under the coat. Dan Breen had given him a Mills bomb and he stowed this in an outside pocket.

He kept to the southern shoulder of the Nire valley and ascended the right hand side of Lough Coumfea. He climbed all day and the wind blew from the northeast. He'd have to keep to higher ground because the 'Free Staters' would be in the valleys and on all passable roads. He went up over an arête from where the beautiful Coumalocha opened before him and a necklace of lakes reflected back the sheer sides of some unnamed cliffs as the sun set in an orb of blood. He nosed into a dense wood of Scots pine as dark descended. He ate some of the soda bread and ham with one of the eggs. Though ravenous, he rationed his provisions stingily and drank the pure cold water from cupped hands where a stream flowed off the rock in a small waterfall. He slept on a bed of pine needles in a hollow under a rock where the ground was dry. Strange sounds filtered through the night: an owl suddenly screeching when he disturbed its eyrie; stares within the evergreens flapping myriad wings, skittish for the slightest crack of a twig or the cough of an interloper. He heard the eerie moaning of the mountain winds, worrying across the heather and the sedge. Strange phantoms visited his dreams. He woke intermittently to remember where he was. He felt more lonesome than he'd ever felt before. How many of his comrades were even alive by now? The 'Staters' had been reaping at a grim and steady pace. What a gloomy ending to their three years of struggle for the cause, which now he felt must surely be all over; all familiar stanchions kicked from beneath his feet, no props were left for him to lean on.

He rose with the early spring sun streaming through the tall cathedral of pines. An apple was his breakfast and several gulps of water from the mountain stream. He struck up through the forest from Loch Mohra and ascended a spur to where the summit of Knockanafrinn rose. He climbed steadily all through that forenoon from dawn. As the sun grew warmer he felt better. Peregrine falcons floated like monarchs above the coums. Spring lambs bleated and gambolled. The first butterflies flew across the moors: red admirals and painted ladies.

On top of the ridge of Knockanafrinn there was snow. He could see across to the Blackstairs and Mount Leinster. He saw three figures coming across the plateau towards him, silhouetted by the lowering sun on their backs. As they came closer he saw they were boys of maybe twelve to fifteen, poorly dressed. Their hair was matted and they smiled gap-toothed at him when they stopped. 'Tinker boys,' he thought, 'or orphans maybe, of which there were many, augmented by the slaughter of fathers in the war that had overtaken them.'

'Howya, Mister,' said the most crabbit of them. His hair was red and his nose ran. He wiped it every now and then with the sleeve of his coat.

'Howya,' Sonny said back.

'Any smokes on ya, Mister?'

He shook his head.

'You wouldn't have a drop of the hard shtuff, then I s'pose,' said the oldest, being the tallest. ''Tis cold up here.'

He tried to speak like a man, exaggeratedly.

'Fraid not,' said Sonny.

'Where ya headin' Mister?' asked the redhead.

'Clonmel side.'

'You're a bit lost, by the look of ya,' said the tall one, 'or else you're on the run.'

'Are you on the run Mister?' asked the redhead. 'Me father knew Sean Treacy. He was a fierce man, but he's dead since.'

'I'm hiking,' said Sonny. 'I'm making maps for the Ordnance Survey.'

'Is that what's in the bag?' asked the redhead. 'Maps?'

'No, just a few apples and some stale bread.'

'I'd say he's got a gun in there,' said the tall one. He'd adopted a less friendly attitude: suspicious if not downright hostile.

'Will you hould,' said the redhead, rebuking his overweening companion. Then he said as if in second thought: 'Have you a gun in there, Mister?'

The third boy, the youngest, had not spoken. 'Gis a look,' he said.

Sonny opened the satchel and showed them the apples.

The redhead shrugged 'What'd I tell you, Petie. He's got no gun in there.'

Petie, the tall one said. 'We can show you where there's guns hidden.'

'Where?'

'In an old house down by Coumshingaun.'

'Where's Coumshingaun?'

''Tis a big lake halfway down the mountain. Come on, we'll show you. There's a shortcut down.'

Sonny hesitated. It would be dark in a few hours. Another night on this bleak plateau with nothing but an eternity of stars to keep him company? That was not a prospect he wished for. He'd take a chance on these vagabond boys.

He followed the boys along the ridge. They passed stands of rowan and holly here and there. They reached a sudden edge where a sheer cliff fell away to a black lake. There was a gulley sprinkled with heather and sundew, leading the way down. A waterfall sparkled in the sunlight, with rainbow colours dancing in the drops. The redhead pointed.

'That's the *Uisce Solais*,' he said.

'What does that mean?' asked Sonny.

'It means the water of the light.'

'You're good at the Irish.'

'I learnt it in Ring, in the Gaeltacht beyond Dungarvan. Me father was born there.'

They stopped to look at the long, pear-shaped lake. The water rippled in the wind. It changed in colour from steel blue to inky black. It looked a most mysterious place. A place of evil spirits? Sonny wondered as the older boy said: 'They say there's no bottom to that lake.'

They started down the gulley. On their right they could see sheer cliffs and a large, black moraine, deposited when the glaciers first carved out the valley and melted after the ice age. They slid along and were near the bottom surprisingly quickly. Before they reached the water, the oldest boy pointed towards a ruined house, with a sprinkling of ancient Scots pine and hawthorn growing around it and the remains of famine stone walls where people had created little patchwork fields through dint of toil and sweat.

'There's the place,' said the older boy.

The building was little more than four stone walls and half a roof.

'*Níl ann ach fothrach,*' said the redhaired boy. Only a ruin. Inside there was a rickety table standing in front of a window, beclawed with cobwebs. There was a huge old hearth with blackened hobs and an iron crane from which a kettle still hung. On the overhead clevvy stood tin jars of tea with designs showing Chinese scenes. There were some plates on a leaning dresser adorned with the willow pattern. It smelt of smoke and damp and desertion.

'Whatcha think?' asked the older boy, quite proud of himself.

'Nothing much,' said Sonny, his heart sinking the longer he stood there. Old houses had that disconcerting effect on him. No hope, no life. Ashes by the dead fire. Even in the best of times those who eked out life here must have had it hard. Was it for this they had fought, to change things for this kind? All gone up in smoke with only blackened hobs for evidence.

'Hould on,' said the tall one. 'Follow me.'

He pushed another door into a parlour with peeling wallpaper on the walls. He walked to one wall and pushed with his hands against it. Suddenly the wall gave way and a half door camouflaged by the wallpaper opened into what looked like an old scullery converted to a den. There were seats, a bed, a small black iron range for cooking and pots and pans.

'Someone lives here?' asked Sonny.

'They come and go,' said the boy. He lifted a cover on a long, low coal scuttle. He opened a bundle wrapped in cloth. Inside were three rifles and two revolvers, well-oiled and maintained.

'What'd I tell ya?' said the redhead triumphantly.

''Twas I tould 'im,' said Petie.

'You can sleep here too, if you like,' said the young one, his eyes wide with knowledge.

Sonny pondered the situation. He looked from one boy to the other.

'Who else knows about this?' he asked.

'No one else,' said the tall one. 'God's truth.'

'Well,' said Sonny. 'It looks like a place to spend a night.'

'Are you going to?' asked the redhead.

'I'll see,' said Sonny.

They went back outside. The boys said they were going back along the lakeshore to where they had a camp, a caravan with a round roof and a few horses.

'So long, Mister,' said the redhead. 'Sleep tight.'

'May the flays bite,' said the youngster.

'Are you brothers?' Sonny asked.

'Me and the young fella,' said the redhead. 'Not him.'

'Who'd want youse for brothers?' said the one they called Petie.

Sonny watched them going down the rough, boulder-strewn trail towards their distant camp, joshing and jibing one another.

After they'd gone he walked around by the far side of the lake, to accustomise himself as to the lie of the land. At twilight the cliffs looked huge and menacing, dwarfing all human and animal dimensions. He saw some feral goats treading across a ledge and ravens came to the edge of the black water and croaked hoarsely, out to where their cries echoed in the gathering dark against the moraine. As he walked back to the ruin he saw the smoke from the tinkers' campfires across the lake and he could hear the voices of adults and the voices of children as if they were close at hand, though they might have been half a mile distant. He stood in that silent place and the stars came slowly into view, burning brighter as the night descended and the flames from the campfire increased in luminosity. A feeling of disassociation took hold of him and he felt as some anchorite in the desert, atoning for the sins of the world, or like the cloistered monks at Mount Melleray consecrating their lives to God in solitude, silence and prayer. Perhaps that would be a life to contemplate and now looked a fairer, sweeter road than the one he'd lately travelled and which led him to such trouble and such strife. And he took to wondering if this was a life he'd chosen or had the life chosen him, as if his providence was prefigured and his destiny already ordained. And was it really written in the stars, now blazing acknowledged but indifferent overhead, that he should become a vagrant and defenceless man, stripped of all dignity and importance, without a shilling to his name, with barely food to eat and hunted like a common criminal? And he took to wondering was this a fate that could overtake any man, no matter how rich or powerful. Was security "mortal's chiefest enemy," as his father, Jeremiah, always said, and were the ways of man, his laws, his political systems, his religions and ceremonies but a membrane through which all could slip at any time as if through a thin sheet of ice, to be swallowed by the dark and depthless waters of the cold lake of death.

He went back inside the old house and felt for the wainscotting on the wall as the youth had done. The secret door opened and he went inside. He got the old stove going with some dried wood and matches left lying underneath by the previous occupiers, whom he guessed were Republicans like himself, on the run and now probably dead or captured. He boiled water in the kettle which he filled from the lake and made tea from the loose leaves in the caddy and he drank it down quickly and ate the last of the brown bread and the remains of the ham. He felt better after eating and the morose thoughts seemed to swim away, so that when he went searching to find them in his mind he could not quite remember what they were or what they meant. His last act before throwing himself to sleep on the bed was to take out one of the revolvers in the coal scuttle, flip open the chamber and put six bullets in the breech. That way he'd have two loaded guns rather than one in case a situation came about in the days to come when he'd need to use them. He put his jacket over the bed to use as a supplemental blanket and removed his boots, but kept his trousers and shirt on.

Something awoke him in the early hours. He'd been restless since the first small birds began twittering outside the porous walls, but some louder sound broke in and he realized there were voices in the parlour and men moving around. He was instantly awake and up, slipping on boots and coat and pulling the cap low over his eyes. He picked up both revolvers and felt to make sure the Mills bomb was in his pocket. There came a scuffling at the false door and then it was kicked open and a voice shouted. 'Whoever is in there, come out with your hands up.'

He slipped a pistol into either side of his belt beneath the coat and waited. The voice came again: 'Come out I said, or we'll shoot.'

He was a dead man either way, because if caught in possession of weapons as he surely was, the inevitable punishment was death by firing squad. That it should come to this then? He took a deep breath and said: 'I'm coming, don't shoot.'

He climbed slowly through the false door with his hands up. There were two soldiers with revolvers trained on him in the parlour and beyond in the kitchen, through the open door, he could see at least four more. He guessed they'd have another sentry or two outside. To exit he'd have to push the table out of the way and he made a sudden lunge and toppled it over against one of the soldiers, pulling one pistol with his right hand and the Mills bomb with the other from his coat. He fired with the pistol, two shots, deadly accurate from years of practice. Both soldiers went down, moaning, wounded if not dead. There were too many in the kitchen to take on with a revolver. He stuck it back in his belt and in one lightning movement he pulled the pin from the Mills bomb and flung it through the door into the kitchen, where it exploded with a deafening sound. He burst out over a tangle of broken bodies, through dust and smoke, a revolver in either hand. The two sentries stood no chance against him as they turned their rifles in his direction. As he came out the door, he fired with both guns, four, five, six rounds. The sentries were dead before they hit the ground. He leaped over them and as he raced away with one last look behind he noticed that one of the bodies killed by the bomb, lying at a forlorn angle half out the door of the old ruin, was the tinker boy of the day before: the taller of the three. The one they called Petie.

He raced along the lakeshore as fast as his legs could carry him. There were shouts from behind and he guessed some other soldiers who'd not entered the house were now upon the scene. He was at the tinkers' camp in minutes. He'd run faster than he'd ever run before. He saw the redhaired boy leading a bay cob up from the lake. He had a rudimentary bridle and bit but no saddle.

'I need your horse,' he said to the redhead. 'I'll leave it back sometime when I can.'

'Sure you can keep him, Mister,' said the redhead. 'I tould Petie not to tell the 'Staters.' I tould him I figured you were a Republican hero like Sean Treacy, but he wouldn't listen. I'd never have betrayed ya. I'm sorry he did, Mister.'

'Don't be sorry,' said Sonny. 'Thanks for the horse.'

He sprang up on the horse's back and kicked it into a furious gallop away down the shore of the lake. The redhaired boy watched him, willing him on as two soldiers reached the camp. They took aim after the flying horse and rider but man and horse were well out of range. The shots fell harmlessy into the flat, calm water, making little splashes as if fish were jumping for flies in the morning sun.

Doctor Baldwin sat in a small alehouse by the shores of the ebbing tide and watched the sun declining beneath the blue sea. Somewhere behind him over Mount Brandon, the pale moon was rising. He'd wandered Kerry from the south unto the west. He'd tramped from Castlemaine to where the Slieve Mis mountains rose like the high back of some unimaginably gigantic dinosaur, petrified in time and sleeping until the day of cosmic judgment came to pass and the God of all creation called sinners to give an accounting of their stewardship and hand in their ledgers for scrutiny to the magistrate of heaven. His footsteps were printed in the sands of Inch, the magnificent wide beach that curved along its outline for miles, where the white dunes glistened in the spring light and where at night in the cold clear air, he slept in stands of whin bushes, wondering what the stars were and what the moon? From long acquaintance with the night sky he recognized Aldeberan in the constellation of Taurus, Betelgeuse in Orion, and Polaris the northstar in Ursa Minor. He tried to dredge up memories of past charts and jotters, where he'd studied physics, Latin and Greek names, astronomical patterns, infinite permutations of constellations and galaxy clusters to which there was no end of counting and for a man to attempt to comprehend it would lead him to a black hole of confusion and maybe even a descent into madness. So he'd given the conundrum short shrift and turned his thoughts to earthly matters, which in these poignant declensions of his days were equally terrible and unfathomable. The war of brother against brother was dwindling down, but in Kerry the most beautiful old grudges died hard. Daily there were reports of soldiers blown up by mines laid by their adversaries, reprisals, killings of unarmed, defenceless prisoners, as if an appalling bloodlust had taken collective hold of the people and raged like the hectic in their veins. And the grim tribunals going about their relentless business, like some latter day Committee of Public Safety in the French Revolution. But who was left to kill? Maybe only a handful of die-hards on the unyielding coast of Kerry.

So he sat in this shebeen away out beyond Dingle, where the people spoke the lovely, poetic Gaeilge, in which he was, regrettably, unschooled, except for a smattering of words in common usage. His thoughts turned to home and his own people. No word of Thomas Cody or sister Madeleine for many months, nor of his feisty nieces and his hardworking nephews. Whither Lord Bandon and the sad, retiring Eleanore? It was time for him to cease his wanderings. His way of life was *"fallen into the sere, the yellow leaf."* He composed a letter to his sister and paid the *bean a' tí* his last few shillings and took a lift from a farmer who was going to the fair at Dingle. He stopped in a doss house for down-and-outs and the next day reached Tralee in a lorry driven by 'Free Staters' who stopped to ask him to produce his papers, and from whom he'd then brazenly cadged a lift back over the peninsula.

He sat on the flatbed in the back with nine or ten soldiers. Hard chaws with cold, suspicious eyes, caps tipped back over their foreheads or tilted sideways at rakish angles. Cigarettes clamped between teeth, smoke drifting upwards in rings blown by the most artful, a skill learnt in idleness: a badge of distinction like their carelessly buttoned uniforms, their rifles held at wanton ease. Enforcers they were, with casual power of life and death over people.

There was silence for a long time. They were in no hurry to make him welcome. He began to regret now his over-hasty request for a ride to Tralee.

'You men must be worn out from soldiering,' he said at length, to make small talk.

'Worked to the bone,' said the sergeant, turning small inquisitive eyes on him, looking him up and down.

'Irregulars' still giving trouble?' asked the Doctor, to indicate his *bona fides*.

'The fuckers blew five of our men up in a roadmine in Knocknagoshel the other day,' said the sergeant. 'But by Christ, that's the last time they'll do it.'

There was a further grim silence until a soldier addressed the Doctor.

'You don't sound like a Kerryman?'

'Cork,' said the Doctor trying to lighten the tension. 'Neighbours, don't you know.'

'What brings you down here?'

'A change of scene, and a bit of business thrown in.'

'What business?'

'Professional business.'

'Which profession?'

'The medical line.'

'You're not a doctor are you?'

'In a manner of speaking.'

'You mustn't have too many patients if you're bumming lifts off the National Army.'

'Very grandiose,' thought the Doctor. 'National Army indeed.'

But he resisted the temptation to pour scorn on the presumptions. 'A sign of the times,' he laughed. 'We all have to tighten our belts these days.'

'Huh,' grunted the sergeant, unconvinced. The men were silent until they stopped at Ballymullen barracks on the outskirts of the town. As they climbed down he said to the captain in the front: 'Many thanks for the lift.'

Nobody acknowledged him as he walked away. He might well have been invisible. But he noticed the sergeant huddled with the captain. They appeared to be talking about him, throwing furtive looks in his direction. He was nearly through the gates of the compound when the captain called him. 'Hey, you there. Come back here a minute.'

He walked back.

'The sergeant tells me you're a doctor?'

'Well...'

'Are you or aren't you?'

'I am a qualified physician,' said Baldwin, 'but I've never really practised.'

'Better again,' smiled the captain. 'You'll do. Come with me.'

He was led into a bleak room with high ceilings, bare walls and a few chairs lined up. There was a deal table standing in the middle of the timber floor. Their boots made a hollow, echoing sound as they walked through.

'Wait here,' said the captain.

He sat on one of the chairs. There was a dim bulb tepid in the corner. It was cold. There were no curtains on the high, iron-barred windows and the rising moon shone through in cold glimmers of light, broken by the shadows of branches swaying in the night breeze. Soldiers came and went and did not make any indication of recognition. He detected an air of menace. There was a glass panel on one wall separating the room he was in from the guardroom and he could see through it as the soldiers led a number of men in. He counted nine in all. From where he sat they appeared to be poorly dressed in civilian clothes, unkempt and bloodied. Their eyes looked pained and fearful. They looked like the remnants of the halt and the lame. He stood up and walked over toward the glass. He could see men with broken arms, suspended in makeshift slings. Some had black eyes and bruised faces. One man was bent like a corkscrew as if his spine were damaged.

'Tortured,' thought Doctor Baldwin. 'Unmistakeable evidence even to an untrained eye.'

The captain noticed the Doctor at the window and went to open the door.

'Come in here, Doctor,' he said. 'I want you to have a look at these men. Just a cursory glance will do. We want them to go out the road with us to remove a mine, which we believe is laid by their comrades, the 'Irregulars.' They look in good enough condition to do that job of work, don't you agree?'

The Doctor stood in front of the men. It was one thing to form an opinon from a detached distance, but to be asked to make a professional diagnosis was all of a sudden almost beyond him when he knew it was a lie. 'Well...' he began.

'Good, Doctor, that's all we wanted to hear,' interrupted the captain. 'Now gentlemen, I want you to hand over any packets of cigarettes you may have in your pockets. You can retain one apiece, you won't be needing more.'

The men looked crestfallen as they fished in their pockets and handed up their squashed boxes of cigarettes.

The moon is bright as they are marched into the barracks yard. There are two lorries. The soldiers keep their rifles trained on the men as they climb in, but there appears to be no resistance left in them. They go along docile as sheep.

'You come with me, Doctor,' says the captain. He is ushered into an armoured car with the captain and a driver, as the convoy moves out. They travel for a few miles on a long, straight road. By the light of the full moon the Doctor can see the fields on either side. They are flat and fertile. 'North Kerry,' he surmises, 'where the terrain differs from the dramatic highlands of the south.'

No words are spoken as they proceed along the road. The two lorries stop ahead and the armoured car stops. The men are ordered out and marched along for a couple of hundred yards to where there is a side road leading to the right towards a wood. It is bitterly cold and the full moon shines down, reflecting off a small river that flows through the wood. In the distance among the trees the moonbeams glance off the slated roof of a castle standing still and sentinel in shadow and light. The Doctor is marched close behind the men until they stop at a large log, which looks like a barricade roughly erected to block the road.

'There it is,' says the captain.

'Is there a mine at the log?' asks the Doctor.

'Underneath,' says the captain, but does not explain further.

Doctor Baldwin watches with keen anticipation, but sees no shovels or equipment handed to the men. Instead the soldiers begin to tie the prisoners' hands behind their backs as they stand near the log where the earth is disturbed and loose stones lie about. They bind each man's legs with a shackle at the ankles and knees so that each man is individually bound and also bound to the next man, hand and foot. The soldiers work methodically as if trussing beasts in stall or manger.

'Why are they not digging for the mine?' asks the Doctor in alarm. 'You said they were coming to remove a mine?'

The captain has a look in his eye that to the Doctor is not a look of fear and neither is it one of concern. It is more the look of pleasurable anticipation.

'Can we have a minute to pray?' asks a bound man's plaintive voice. A soldier turns and strikes him across the head with a knotted rope. 'I'll give you prayer, you Irish bastard,' says a voice that is, to the Doctor's ear, unmistakeably English. An eye for an eye then. So that's why they brought him here, as witness to a sacrifice of blood. He feels sick. His hands shake and sweat. His head reels. The men are bound so tightly they cannot move from their fixed positions in a circle around the log.

'That'll do,' says the captain. 'Move back, men.'

Some of the soldiers move back through the gate into a field that rises behind, looking down upon the road. The Doctor is ushered back toward the lorries. He turns as he sees the sergeant who accompanied him from Dingle, walking along to each man and removing each man's cap. 'Ye can be praying away now,' he says.

His work complete, the sergeant turns to follow the others to the lorries.

The men at the log stand and shiver in the moon. Some weep quietly and some cannot control their bowels and there is a smell that wafts rank and noisome, but the men only try to feel for the warmth of each and they utter words of love the last they'll hear. The Doctor hears their distant voices: 'Goodbye boys, goodbye, goodbye.'

He cannot take his eyes away and he thinks he sees them try to hold each other through their bonds and then the night is riven by the exploding mine, laid, primed and detonated by a plunger in the hands of a Free State soldier.

After the blast there comes a silence, surging back as the explosion surged out, like the comings and the goings of the sea. But the natural order of the night has been disturbed. Rooks asleep in Ballyseedy Wood fly forth into the air as if confusing night with morning, moon with sun. Dogs begin a tumultuous barking from farm to farm across a lengthy distance, but no human soul ventures out to seek the cause of the disturbance, though Gabriel's last reveillé would not be louder. To sleepers in their beds, it was not the call they were seeking, resembling more the tumbling of the mountains and the crumbling of the earth at Armageddon. So they listen and they pray and some dream terrible dreams and in their dreams fire comes down from God to devour Gog and Magog and casts the Devil into the lake of Gehenna, burning in fire and brimstone with this beast, this false prophet stalking the land.

The minutes tick by after midnight. Then there are looming shadows of soldiers converging from highway and from field to survey their terrible handiwork. The captain lays a hand on Doctor Baldwin's shoulder and escorts him down the road. As they draw near they find themselves stepping amidst headless corpses, tibiae and fibulae of severed legs, forearms, entrails and heads: a grotesque choreography that contains the faint voices of smitten men, some still alive and crawling, blinded and maimed, across the earth, their bonds sundered by the force of the explosion. The sergeant, on hearing some dying moans, orders his grenadiers to pull the pins of their Mills bombs and hurl them into the unspeakable stew of quivering flesh and brussed-up bone, until nothing remains but fragments where once were men, to be scraped from off the ground and shovelled into coffins, numbering nine, which they'd prudently brought with them for the purpose.

When they got back to the barracks there was a very faint ring of brightness in the night sky, precursor to the coming dawn. The chorus of birds heralding a new day had not yet begun and there still was work to do in the shadow of night that the light of day could not countenance. The coffins with the unrecognisable human remains were hefted in and stored in a freezing basement that acted as a temporary morgue. Doctor Baldwin was asked to wait in the guardroom and two armed soldiers kept him company. The captain went into an office where he spent maybe twenty minutes working on a statement with the sergeant, and then he reappeared and handed the statement to the Doctor for his perusal. The Doctor got as far as the words: *..nine prisoners died while working to remove a booby-trap mine laid by their own comrades in the* IRA...

'Would you be good enough to sign this, Doctor?' asked the captain. 'You were the medical officer present at this unfortunate incident. You will of course be entitled to the usual fee for such an undertaking.'

Doctor Baldwin reread the document and the captain waited in anticipation.

'Have you any problems with that?' he asked.

Doctor Baldwin looked at the captain, then back to the document and said: 'I can't sign this.'

'But you assured us you were a medical man,' said the captain, eager for a satisfactory outcome to his night's work.

'It's not that,' said the Doctor. 'I am a medical man, duly qualified. That is not the reason I can't sign.'

'What then?' asked the captain.

'Because it's not the truth,' said the Doctor. He looked at the men on either side of him. They appeared uneasy, on tenterhooks.

'Come now, Doctor, you look like a man who could do with some emolument. Just your signature is all we require. We need an independent arbiter to confirm what happened, and what you read here is essentially the substance of the matter in a nutshell. Why quibble over the meaning of a word here or there? The nub of the thing is as set out.'

'On the contrary,' said the Doctor, 'it is a bowdlerisation of the truth and an affront to the dignity of those unfortunate men whom you murdered in cold blood, premeditated and preconceived to look like an accident. What I saw was not an accident. The mine was laid by yourselves and detonated by yourselves. There is no excuse for such ineffable barbarity. It is beyond the bounds of all the codes of warfare that I've ever read or heard of.'

'But...' said the captain.

'There are no buts,' said Doctor Baldwin. 'I will not sign and furthermore, I intend to make known to the world-at-large what transpired here tonight, notwithstanding your cynical attempt to put a plausible face on it.'

The captain's demeanour lost its accomodating regard. His eyes narrowed and flickered to the two soldiers sitting beside the Doctor.

'I don't think it would advance anybody's cause for you to discuss this incident beyond the walls of this compound, Doctor Baldwin.'

'I intend to,' said the Doctor, 'and neither you, nor God, nor man will stop me. Now, I think I've said all I want to say. Am I free to go?'

'My dear Doctor, you've always been free to go.' said the captain. 'It's just that it occurred to me, from what I observe of your personal situation, that a modest remuneration for services rendered would not have gone amiss. But it's your decision. Have it your own way.' He turned away and said: 'Sergeant, will you escort the Doctor to the gate?'

Doctor Baldwin stood and the captain shook his hand. 'It's been a pleasure meeting you, sir,' he said, but his eyes did not smile.

The Doctor did not reply. He turned on his heel and the soldiers led him to the door. They went down a long corridor and the sergeant opened a heavier steel door at the end. He held it open and the Doctor stepped out into the yard. It was raw and cold outside. A bitter, black wind blew in from the sea. The yard was shadowy and there were some lorries lined up down near the gate by the high wall. The two soldiers walked with him, one in front and one behind. The sergeant walked ahead. As they were passing the lorries, where shadows were thrown by the moon that was now low in the western sky, the soldier behind pulled his pistol and shot the Doctor in the back of the head. As he toppled forward against the gate, the soldier fired again, this time hitting the Doctor in the small of the back. As Doctor Baldwin lay face down on the ground, the *coup de grace* was delivered by a third shot that went through his heart, entering higher up on his back between the fifth and sixth vertebrae.

36

the savage loves his native shore

When Madeleine Cody received Doctor Baldwin's letter she did not know her brother was already a fortnight dead. Seamus brought the crumpled envelope which the postman had given him into the kitchen and as he handed it to his mother he said: 'A letter for you, Mam, it looks like Doctor's writing.'

Madeleine felt the roughened edges of the tattered envelope and said: 'That's James's writing alright, but it must have been posted some time ago. What does the postmark say?'

Seamus scrutinised the stamp. 'Posted in Dingle, County Kerry, it looks like sometime in March. It might be the 5th or 6th. I can't make out the date.'

'Thank God,' said Madeleine. 'At least we know where he's been. He's gone so long I was beginning to worry about him.'

Seamus laughed as Madeleine opened a cutlery drawer. He said: 'Doctor is one person who will always make his way. He's very resourceful, for a man with no job.'

Madeleine shook her head with a kind of weary resignation, 'He's had a queer old life.'

'But he's happy,' said Seamus. 'At least I always thought he was.'

'Appearances can be deceptive,' said Madeleine, as she used a knife to slice open the cover. Her eyes lit up as she began to read:

My dearest Madeleine,
I feel compelled to put pen to paper being as I'm away so long. I sincerely hope all is well, and that the girls and the boys are healthy. Give my regards to himself, although I doubt he'll reciprocate. For my

own part, I am wandering on a distant coast, though at this point languishing might be a more apt word. I see the Blaskets sitting out on the western ocean. What is it about going west? Following the sun I suppose. When it shines this place is close to paradise, and more mysterious than our fertile valleys in Cork. The news becomes more depressing day by day. This dreadful war must stop. Both sides have to pull back or we will all be destroyed. We all have to compromise. Is life not a series of compromises? I wouldn't have said so once but I do now. I feel the pull of home, in spite of my wanderlust. The savage loves his native shore. Lately I've been thinking of when we were young and swinging on the great elms going down to the white gate. Wouldn't it be nice to stay forever young? What am I saying? I'm becoming a sentimental old fool. But life is a solitary business is it not? There are moments of warmth and camaraderie interspersed with long days of great loneliness. Is this the lot of man, and woman too? I will finish now and God willing I will see you all in a couple of weeks.

Farewell my dear and fondest regards.

James.

When she finished reading she was overcome by an overwhelming sadness. Seamus noticed her silence but did not intrude. He was aware of his mother's sensitive nature betimes. She left the kitchen after some minutes and went out to the piano room where her paintings hung on the wall: scenes of old Vienna, *fin-de-siecle*. Her life lay behind her. Time had driven onward fast. Time was the great enemy. She took down a box of old photographs and through sudden tears and smiles she regarded her younger self, brother James, and brother Henry dead on the Somme. There they were in their little summer clothes, frolicking among the bluebells on the wide green lawn, under the spreading elms. She uncovered further sepia-coloured images of her own dear girls and boys. Margie aged 7, already so certain and self-contained, William so earnest, Seamus so gentle, Anna trusting and innocent. The innocent and the beautiful. She herself sitting in, perhaps, a pose, her long summer dress buttoned up to the collar. Standing behind her, Thomas Cody, the man she married, the father of her children, authoritative, strong, impatient. Already the girls and boys were grown. Already she and Thomas were in middle years.

There was a light sound at the door and Anna came in. 'What are you doing?' she asked brightly of her mother.

'Oh, nothing,' said Madeleine and put away the photographs.

'What's that?' asked Anna, tuned in automatically to her mother's subdued mood.

'Just going through some old photos,' said Madeleine, putting her hand up to brush away a drying tear. Anna came over and stood beside her mother. Madeleine put her arms around her waist from her sitting position and drew her close.

'Things change so fast,' said Madeleine. 'Life is so fragile.'

'What brought this on, Mother?' asked Anna, gently patting her mother's hair.

'James sent a letter,' said Madeleine, and sniffed a little from her tears. 'It just prompted me to look through these old pictures. I suppose it made me sad.'

'Why? Is he alright?'

'He says he is, but he's lonesome to come home.'

'Where is he?'

'Somewhere in Kerry.'

'Kerry?' said Anna. 'Terrible things are happening in Kerry.'

'No worse than what's happening here at home, like the trigger mine in Newcestown last month.'

'I wonder did Doctor hear about that?' asked Anna.

'He mustn't have or he'd have surely mentioned it,' said Madeleine. 'But I'll tell him in my reply.'

'He'll probably be home before he gets it,' said Anna.

'Maybe, maybe not,' said Madeleine.

Anna sat down beside her mother. 'Can I have a look at these photos?'

Madeleine handed her the box and watched as her daughter scanned through them, blithely, untouched by sorrow. She said nothing for a while and then said: 'I hope you'll always be happy. All of you.'

Anna looked sharply at her mother and laughed: 'Of course we will, Mother. Don't worry about us.' Then she frowned and asked: 'Are you happy, Mother?'

Madeleine stiffened. Anna continued: 'I mean with us, with father?'

'I'm accepting,' said Madeleine, 'or should I say resigned. Life catches up on you and you start running out of time. But yes, I'm happy to have children, to be married to a good man, your father. People learn to live together and it's only when they part or someone dies that we realise that the comings and the goings of the day, of the week, are the things that hold life together.'

She stood and looked down at Anna and said: 'Look at you.

Eighteen already and all grown up. It seems like only yesterday you were the little girl in that photograph. Now you're finished boarding school.'

Anna was suddenly serious, as if to confirm her mother's observation. 'I'll go to Cork,' she said. 'I'll get a job.'

'You will? Where?'

'I'll work as a secretary, or maybe become a nurse. I want to be married too and have children of my own.'

'Oh God bless you, my darling,' smiled Madeleine. 'Only eighteen and already intent on marrying. Have you anyone in view?'

'Maybe,' said Anna, and said no more.

Madeleine waited and finally said: 'Have you heard from young Hennessy?'

'No,' said Anna abruptly. 'He's on the run. Hunted by 'Free Staters.' But I will. He'll be back someday.'

'You're so certain of things,' said Madeleine and touched her daughter's shining black hair. She was self-willed, made of stern stuff. More stern than Madeleine herself. She could see that.

In Bandon, Thomas Cody met Margie off the Cork train the same day Madeleine received Doctor Baldwin's letter. It was nearly two weeks after St. Patrick's Day and Margie was returning home for the Easter holidays from her studies at the University in Cork city. Loreto lay behind her and she was now embarked upon a Batchelor's degree in politics, history and economics. She was nearing the end of her first year and she could see new horizons stretching before her. It was her intention to graduate, *cum laude* if at all possible and then obtain the Higher Diploma in Education. After that the world was her oyster. She might go to Trinity College for advanced studies or even to Oxford to complete a Phd. Margie was ambitious, although her father fretted that her reach might exceed her grasp.

As she got off the train, carrying two bags, the steam from the engine gushed into the evening air. The days were lengthening. There was an echo of spring in the song of a thrush from a sycamore tree above the platform. Thomas hefted the heavy book bag and said, 'My word, that's a heavy bag. What's in there?'

'Books of course,' said Margie, herself carrying the suitcase with clothes. 'They're heavier than clothes.'

'Imagine that,' said Thomas. 'I wouldn't have thought so but now that you mention it, it's obviously true.'

They crossed towards Shannon Street where Thomas had tied his horse and trap in the tanner's yard. 'How's the study going?' he asked.

'Very well,' said Margie, 'and I'm meeting a lot of interesting people.'

'Really?' said Thomas. 'What kind of people: sons of wealthy businessmen?' There was a hint of irony in his voice. He spoke more with hope than expectation.

'No, the opposite, as a matter of fact,' said Margie. 'Intellectuals, thinkers, writers, people interested in politics.' Her expression, to combat Cody's, was slightly scornful.

'Don't you think we've had enough of politics?' asked her father.

'We've had enough of the Civil War,' said Margie. 'But you can't have enough politics. Somebody must govern the country one way or t'other.'

'Well, the Civil War is all but over,' said Thomas.

'Bar the shouting,' said Margie. 'But that's only beginning.'

'What do you mean?'

'I mean that if the people in the Provisional Government think they have *carte blanche* to do as they like, they have another think coming. Already people at the University are forming alternative political parties. The vanquished have as much right to be heard as the victors.'

'I've no doubt you're right. That fellow de Valera won't be quietened easily I'm afraid.'

'And why should he be?' asked Margie. 'Doesn't he represent the opinion of at least half the population.'

'If you ask me,' said Thomas, 'most people don't give a damn as long as they have a quiet life and enough to eat and drink.'

'As I've said before, most people are sheep,' said Margie.

'Well, even that most incorrigible of men, Tom Barry, is now advocating the ending of the fight. If he can do so, surely you can.'

'It's obvious that the Republicans have been defeated in the Civil War,' said Margie. 'But that doesn't mean that we are all going to kow-tow and be puppets dangled by the British as they see fit.'

'That's a bit harsh,' said Thomas.

'I don't think it is,' said Margie. 'Ever since Collins died the Provisional Government has been rubber-stamping British policy. Collins was the last great leader this country had. You know that yourself. Are you seriously telling me that W.T. Cosgrave is a leader? I'd do a better job myself.'

Thomas chuckled. 'Well, I'm bound to say you have a point there.'

'You know I'm right,' said Margie, triumphantly.

Thomas put a fatherly arm on her shoulder and said: 'How I wish I had the certainty of youth.' His eyes twinkled. 'Are you hungry? Would you like a snack in Lee's Hotel?'

Margie softened. 'Oh, alright then.'

'Sure we can't be serious all the time,' smiled her father.

As they entered the lobby of the hotel, Eleanore Eustace was walking out accompanied by James Maguire, the solicitor.

Eleanore looked a little embarrassed to encounter them. Thomas said: 'Ah, Eleanore, how are you keeping these days? I haven't seen you for quite a while. Are you going out and about at all?'

'As little as possible,' she said. 'Only on business.' She inclined her head towards Maguire, coming up quickly behind her in case she escaped his clutches if he lost sight of her. The look wasn't lost on Thomas. Maguire was no doubt ferreting around the Eustace estate, hoping to gain some advantage. Once a scrooge always a scrooge. Thomas was aware that Maguire viewed everybody in terms of pounds, shillings and pence. Everything was reduced to a benefit or preference that might accrue to him. Thomas really didn't like the abominable little man.

'Ah, Thomas,' said Maguire, feigning friendliness. 'How are you? How are the family?'

'Growing up,' said Thomas, indicating Margie.

'My goodness, I wouldn't have recognised this young woman. Margie is it?' asked Maguire.

'It is,' said Margie coldly.

'And what are you doing with yourself these days?' asked Maguire.

'I'm at the University in Cork.'

'Studying anything useful? Medicine, the law?'

'Politics,' said Margie.

'Steer clear of politics,' said Maguire. 'Nothing but trouble in that department. My own daughter is pursuing the law. She's going to be a solicitor, like myself.'

'There are too many lawyers,' said Margie, 'and not enough people to lead the country out of the abyss we're in. We need scientists, engineers, serious people.'

'Are you saying lawyers are not serious people?' asked Maguire.

'They're serious about making money for themselves and little else,' said Margie.

'Come, come my dear, that's a very biased point of view,' laughed Maguire, clearly ill at ease.

'How's Mrs Maguire?' asked Thomas, to break the ice.

There was a noticeable hesitation on Maguire's part. He looked furtively toward Eleanore. 'Oh, she's busy...ah...busy putting the finishing touches to our newly restored house, since those blackguards burnt it out some years ago. Well, at least they've got their comeuppance, as I predicted they would.'

'You mean the Irish Republican Army?' inquired Margie haughtily.

'I mean those damned 'Irregulars,' spat Maguire. He turned to Thomas. 'I see you've raised somebody with different views to yourself, Thomas.'

'What you learn, is that your children, as they grow older, can have different opinions. You don't own them,' shrugged Thomas.

There was an uneasy silence until Eleanore said: 'We'd better be going. Good evening to you, Thomas, Margie. Give my regards to Madeleine.'

'We will Eleanore,' said Thomas and lifted his hat. 'I'm glad to see you looking well again.'

'Good evening, Thomas,' said Maguire curtly. He did not salute Margie. He took a few steps and then turned back in an afterthought. 'By the way, Lord Bandon is poorly by all accounts and may not last out the season.'

'I'm sorry to hear it,' said Thomas.

As they watched them go, Margie said: 'I notice she didn't ask about Uncle James. I wonder why?'

Thomas gave her a rueful look. 'Now Margie, no need to drag up the past.'

'Well, it looks to me as if she's establishing a relationship that will be mutually beneficial to herself and that little weasel.'

'You shouldn't judge people so severely,' said Thomas, though he was equally as intrigued as Margie at the apparent signs of something more than cordiality manifest in the behaviour of their departing acquaintances.

Before Margie and Thomas returned from Bandon, Madeleine composed her letter of reply to Doctor Baldwin.

Dear James,
It was with great relief that I received your letter. We've been reading about dreadful things happening in Kerry: Ballyseedy, Countess Bridge and so forth. It seems people have sunk to new depths of depravity. I

hope you were nowhere near these awful events. Sadly, we have not been unscathed back here in our own parish of Newcestown. I'd imagine you didn't hear about it, otherwise you'd have mentioned it in your letter. It's about six weeks ago now, in early February, two young men lost their lives when they were forced at gunpoint to remove a trigger mine laid under a ditch across the road between our place here and the village. It seems the Republicans were trying to prevent a roundup of their numbers by the Free State Forces and they laid this mine to stop them rushing the church when all were at Mass. The 'Staters' came up to the church and forced about fifteeen young men at gunpoint to come down and remove the mine. They had nearly finished when they saw smoke coming from under a flat stone, and in a second there was an explosion that killed two and wounded seven others. It was a great tragedy. People in the countryside are very distressed about it. There is a lot of blame on both sides, but alas that won't bring the dead back to life.

Some very bizarre things are happening. Canon O'Connell's horse was shot dead by the Republicans because the canon has taken the Free State side. Imagine shooting a horse over the views of its owner. Canon O'Connell has said of the perpetrators that "the crops in their fields will grow downwards and they will never comb their hair grey." He also had an amusing encounter with Dan Holland of Timoleague one Sunday morning in Castletown church. Holland got into an argument with him (a la yourself) over the meaning of Bishop Coholan's excommunication decree, and as Dan was expounding from the body of the church, the canon suddenly roared: "Holland from the sea, what would you know about Canon Law?"

I thought you might enjoy that story. Anyway it was great to hear from you and hopefully we'll see you before long.

Much love,
Madeleine.

After signing the letter and putting it in an envelope, she called Seamus and asked him to post the letter for her on his way to the creamery next morning.

'Where's this going to?' asked Seamus.

'To your uncle James.'

'But there's no address on the envelope.'

'What?' asked Madeleine, a little mystified, seemingly.

'There's no address,' repeated Seamus.

Madeleine took the envelope back from him and looked at it.

'So there isn't,' she said. 'There was no address on the letter he sent me.'

'But you can't send a letter to nowhere,' said Seamus.

Madeleine was suddenly overcome with emotion. Her body shook with sobs. Seamus put his arms around his mother.

'What is it mother?' he asked. 'Why are you so upset?'

'James is living nowhere now,' she said. 'I can feel it in my bones. He's living nowhere now.'

'But why did you write the letter then?' he asked gently.

'We live in hope,' she whispered. 'We live in hope even when we know all hope is gone. It's all we can do.'

Seamus held his mother as tears of sorrow swept over her like a mighty wave.

After Sunday Mass in Ballycummin the following week, Madeleine and Anna met Elizabeth and Tull Hennessy emerging from the church. There was a subdued atmosphere, visible in the downcast eyes of the worshippers, the heavy trudge of feet, the slope of shoulders. The shock of the trigger mine lingered raw and bleeding in the collective consciousness. The trauma of a society torn apart, the reality of civil war at their own front door. A greater evil than even that of the Black and Tans. No glorious monuments to victory, only headstones to the dead.

People stopped to talk in the usual way outside country churches: the gathering at the Mass a way of connecting with your neighbour or fellow parishioner. A place to put differences aside and concentrate on the great mystery of life.

Madeleine smiled as Elizabeth, the younger by maybe twenty years, drew near. 'Ah, hello,' she said. Madeleine was from an upbringing where formality, above all, existed in public. No unnecessary displays of emotion or effusiveness. The Hennessys were a slightly more relaxed breed, easy smiles, immediate warmth.

'Hello, Mrs Cody,' said Elizabeth. 'And this is Anna is it not? You're all grown up.'

'Grown up in appearance,' said Madeleine, 'whatever about otherwise.'

Anna gave a kind of shrug indicating her disagreement.

Elizabeth included Tull, as he came into the circle. 'You know my brother Tull?' she said.

Madeleine smiled and nodded at Tull. 'Only slightly,' she said.

'We've met your other boys more often. Particularly Sonny.' Madeleine raised an eyebrow slightly, a faint suggestion of disapproval lingering in her expression. She looked quickly toward Anna whose face was as close to a scowl as she had ever seen. Things were left unsaid and then Elizabeth glanced toward Tull briefly, then turned back to Madeleine and sighed. 'We haven't heard from him.'

'Do you mean Sonny?' blurted Anna, unable to contain herself.

'He's been gone for over five months. We're very concerned. Mike has given up and come home, but not our Sonny. I'm afraid he's a die-hard to the end.'

'He's right,' said Anna darkly. 'Sonny doesn't quit.'

Madeleine put her hand to her throat and caught her breath. She looked pale, shook a little.

'Are you feeling alright, Mrs Cody?' asked Elizabeth, noticing Madeleine's sudden distress. Madeleine struggled visibly to compose herself. She put her hand to her forehead. Sudden tears glazed her eyes. Tears had been her constant companion of late. She put her hand out and held Elizabeth's arm. Elizabeth looked surprised at the uncharacteristic show of intimacy.

'I'm afraid our two families have been drawn together by circumstances beyond our control...by war. The folly of war. When we're all gone, the coming generations will look back and ask, what was it all for?' She paused and a veil of pain passed over her lovely face. 'My brother James has been gone too. For as long a time. He sent a letter from Kerry...' Her lower lip quivered. 'I'm sorry my dear, I shouldn't get so upset. But, you see, I have a premonition that...that he won't ...be coming back.'

She put her hand to her trembling lips and motioned to Anna to go. Anna turned to Elizabeth. 'We'd better be going, Elizabeth. My mother has been crying a lot lately. She's easily upset at the moment. I keep telling her uncle James will be back but she's disconsolate.'

'I sincerely hope she's wrong,' said Elizabeth. 'Our two families are affected like everyone else. I'm worried sick about Sonny you know.'

'Don't be,' said Anna and looked steadily at her. 'Sonny is a survivor. Sonny will return someday.'

'I hope you're right my dear,' said Elizabeth and kissed Anna on the cheek in a sisterly fashion. 'You're a lovely girl,' she said. 'Sonny would be lucky to have a girl like you.'

'Thank you,' said Anna. She hesitated, and then said 'Goodbye, Elizabeth. Goodbye Tull.'

'We'll keep praying,' said Elizabeth. 'For your uncle James and for Sonny, and for all the living and the dead.' Elizabeth watched Anna and Madeleine depart toward their horse and trap, where Thomas Cody and Seamus were waiting for them. She called after Anna: 'I've kept all your letters to Sonny. They're lying unopened for him, if...I mean when, he comes back.'

Anna responded: 'Thank you so much Elizabeth. You are a very kind person.'

Elizabeth turned to Tull and said: 'We'll go home, Tull.'

Her heart was heavy, and truth to tell, the burden on her worried mind was equally as heavy as that on Madeleine Cody's.

EPILOGUE

Sonny made it down from the Monavullagh mountains. He went unrecognised though observed over foothills and uplands, riding down to Kilrossanty and Leamybrien, where he was sheltered by folk with broad accents and florid faces, bighearted people who asked him no questions, but understood his plight. He left the cob with a powerfully-built man named Lonergan, who let him sleep beneath his rafters for two weeks solid, fed him and cheered his spirit. As payment he left the cob there on that farm of pleasant orchards beneath the Comeraghs and Lonergan said he'd return the horse to the tinkers if he could find them or if they came looking for it. When Sonny thought he'd overstayed his tenure, Lonergan advised him to proceed towards another man named Andrews who'd make him welcome near wide Clonea strand, where the Atlantic waves rolled in and the seabirds cried in the spring evenings that were lengthening into summer. He left one gun with Lonergan but kept the other as insurance against attack until the end of May, when de Valera called on the soldiers of the legion of the rearguard to dump their weapons and cease firing at their enemies. He then left the second gun with Andrews, who helped him to get to Abbeyside on the outskirts of Dungarvan. There he changed clothes to look like a farm labourer rather than a gunman, and although he encountered many in taverns and meeting places, he was greeted not as some base kern, but as a man to be reckoned with, because of his bearing and the look of experience and danger in his eye. In a small public house on the narrow streets of Abbeyside he learned, after many months, the full truth of the

Ballyseedy massacre from a Free State officer, who had left the army in shame at what he'd been party to. What he'd heard and witnessed was that not nine had perished therein but only eight. The ninth man had been sheltered from the brunt of the blast by his unfortunate companions and was blown clear across the road into a stream running at the edge of Ballyseedy Wood. The force of the explosion had stripped him of garments but had also unfettered the ropes that bound him to his fellows, so that he fetched up in the stream unencumbered save for the arm of the dead man beside him, still attached to the manacle locked around his wrist. Now this man, whose name the Free State officer said was Fuller, heard and saw the vile deeds of that night from his occluded cover under the freezing waters of the stream, until he could no longer stand the cold and took his chance to crawl away from that terrible place of shattered skull and bone, reaching a farm that he knew a good mile distant, where he was taken in and given succour by decent people and kept hidden for a long time until the war was over. And thus it came to pass that out of that darkness the truth came to the light and gradually the word spread through lanes and byways, from farm to farm and from town to town, not only of the fate of the men of Ballyseedy, whose flesh was eaten by dogs, and by scavenging crows off tree branches for weeks afterwards, but of similar enormities in Countess Bridge and Caherciveen in the days that followed, bringing ignominy to the noble name of Kerry.

He left Waterford in due time and travelled north all over Munster, remaining vigilant and cleaving to obscurity, because a great round-up of the vanquished Republicans continued for that year of '23 and well towards the end of '24. He briefly met some former fighters that he knew and one night on a podium in Ennis, County Clare, he saw de Valera shot in the leg and captured as he addressed a crowd of supporters, antecedent to a plebiscite held in the summer of that year, in which Republicans garnered one third of all the votes, but could not take their places in Leinster House, being locked away in jails like Arbour Hill, Kilmainham, Mountjoy and Sunday's Well.

He dare not go home nor did he hear of home, but all his waking thoughts were of grazing cattle chewing the cud into the sun-drenched evenings and the sight and smell of sweet contentment attendant thereto. He missed the feel of turning the handles of a plough into a furrow and the sound of seeds spitting from a turnip machine in the sowing spring season, and the grip of a reins between his fingers as he rode a horse. He often thought of Anna Cody, but unlike her, he was not the writing kind, and besides she'd probably forgotten about him long since. She was a star beyond his orbit, but he missed her more, not less as the time passed and wondered would they ever meet again.

But he did not miss war and he resolved to fight no more, although he knew some of his old comrades-in-arms were still intent on rekindling a hopeless situation and resuming where they'd left off. There were hunger strikes against the appalling prison conditions and the detention without trial by vengeful victors, of men who had no resources left or patent to obtain any. Many thousands of the best were forced to leave the land and quit the country, in their mouths a great bitterness and in their hearts a deep regret.

He made a brief return home in 1925 for the wedding of his brother, Mike, and he learned from Elizabeth that some of their younger sisters had returned from England and had again departed, finding nothing to keep them there and no apparent hope for any future. He reached a rapprochement of a kind with Tull but left him to his own devices, which he managed in his haphazard way. His father endured, but hinted that his time was running out and that he wasn't long now for the meanness of this world. He saw a sadness in Elizabeth's eyes and a resignation that was not there before, but he knew that women have a way of coping better with adversity and she found her comfort more frequently in the contemplation of the spirit of the Lord and the prospect of the religious life.

Tom Barry, in his wily fashion, avoided capture and, like Sonny, went from town to town disguised as a tramp or strolling player but never in that two years of wandering exile did their path cross that of the other. Former comrades like Tom Hales, Dan Breen, Sean Moylan, John Lordan and Frank Aiken took the political road and by 1926 there was a further rift within Sinn Féin and the IRA, and soon after, de Valera formed his political party, Fianna Fáil, which in Gaelic parlance meant, 'The Soldiers of Destiny.' On the 10th of July the following year, Kevin O'Higgins, the Minister of Justice in the Government and Vice-President of the Executive Council, was shot dead as he walked to Mass along Cross Avenue in south County Dublin. Richard Mulcahy had long since resigned his seat as Minister of Defence, because a storm blew up within the army which was known as the Curragh Mutiny, led by men who were disillusioned with the progress towards a Republic and the abandonment of the objective of gaining a united Ireland. In 1927 de Valera walked into the Chamber of the Dáil with his new party, brushed the bible aside and declared the oath of fealty to the

King to be an empty formula and took his seat across the aisle from his nemesis, William Cosgrave, and from that day forth continued to heckle and harangue, until the edifice of the Government of Cumann na nGaedhael finally gave way and Fianna Fáil took power.

It was 1932 and Sonny was in his 30th year. He'd survived doing menial jobs for many years and found himelf at that time in a factory in Cork, working for subsistence wages and living in a tiny, cramped boarding house on Sullivan's Quay, on the south fork of the river Lee. One evening as he walked across the bridge down by French's Quay he saw coming towards him, as the sun was setting, a young woman whom he thought he knew but had not laid eyes on for many years. He slowed down as he neared her and his heart skipped a beat. The young woman slowed as well. Sonny stopped and stared, and his look was so intense it was as if she felt it without looking up. She stopped and the shadows of the years raced across her face like clouds across a landscape from darkness into light. It was Anna Cody and she'd grown into a young woman of rare grace and independent means.

'Anna,' Sonny said, 'Anna Cody?'

'Oh my God,' she whispered. 'Sonny, you're alive!'

They continued to stand there transfixed in the silence and they both could hear the pounding of their individual hearts above the waters of the river cascading down a weir. And then Anna could no longer contain the pent up emotion of her long years of waiting. A single tear appeared in her eye that quickly became a flood she could not staunch and Sonny embraced her in his arms for the first time though it was a gesture as natural as if no time had passed at all. He held her in his arms until the great storm inside her subsided.

'Where have you been, my darling,' she began.

'Shh,' he whispered, 'I've been gone a long time but now I'm back. Are you glad to see me, Anna?'

'Never so glad in all my life. I waited for a long time, Sonny, but you were so slow arriving. I thought I could wait no longer.'

Oblivious to the looks of strangers they stood there holding hands, entranced, until the sun went down and exchanged the story of their lives during the ten years since they had met.

He inquired of her parents, Thomas and Madeleine Cody, and she divulged that they were hale and hearty, the family long since grown, all fledglings flown. Her sister Margie had finished university and despite her former antipathies, had gone to England for further studies, from where she reported that the plain English people were a good and decent race, who had taken in many of the refugees from Ireland after the Civil War, allowing them make their way in the world without hindrance for the most part. But she remained wary of the ultimate intentions of their ruling class. Her brother William had qualified as a doctor and her brother Seamus was working on the farm at home. Of Doctor Baldwin they'd neither trace nor tiding, and it was with a great sadness that they finally gave up the search to find him. He was listed as missing, presumed dead, somewhere on the lawless roads of West Cork, where he loved to wander, or perhaps lost somewhere in the deeper fastnesses of Kerry, where he'd last reported he was travelling during the dark times put behind them. His former lover, Eleanore Eustace had taken up with the solicitor of Bandon, James Maguire who'd found himself bereft when his wife left him for another man, a situation and arrangement that would have surely brought a smile to the lips of the good Doctor and at which he'd have chuckled at the telling in fair or market.

Sonny and Anna began walking out together soon after that fortuitous encounter and they set their eyes upon the future with a renewed hope. Some months later Sonny's father, Jeremiah, died, and in his will bequeathed the farm to Sonny. After a period he returned home. Elizabeth felt obliged to leave, though Sonny entreated her to stay. Approaching forty, as she was, she joined an order of nuns and sailed for France with no education, no money in her pocket and sorrow in her heart. Tull remained disgruntled, his condition not helped by a blow to the head received one day in a brawl with the 'Blue Shirts' at the local train station, during the upheavels which again flared up around the country when de Valera took power.

But Sonny and Anna were now embarked upon another voyage, of lost moments to recover and old dreams to reconsider. And in the surety of their embrace they felt strong and proud, untrammelled by all life's petty undertakings, failures and defeats. Still beautiful, unbroken.

They were married one autumn day in 1935, and as he gazed upon his steadfast bride, Sonny's face was once again innocent, eager and reborn, as when he and all his blood brothers first strode down through valleys ripe with corn. All things from the past were laid aside and as the future years unspooled before them, they looked towards a better, brighter day; to raise a family that would grow up free of the wounds of yesterday and where somewhere down the road the scars might heal and the ideals for which they fought would come to pass. That they'd become companions on life's journey was a thing chance or fate decided. It mattered not, so long as they both remained together 'til the journey's end.

The End

Principal Fictional Characters

Sonny Hennessy, young republican fighter, 3rd West Cork Brigade.

Elizabeth Hennessy, keeper of the household, sister to Sonny.

Mike Hennessy, republican fighter, brother to Sonny.

Tull Hennessy, keeper of the farm, brother to Sonny.

Jeremiah Hennessy, father to Sonny.

Anna Cody, student, sweetheart to Sonny.

Margie Cody, student and older sister to Anna.

William Cody, medical student, brother to Anna.

Seamus Cody, brother to Anna.

Thomas Cody, strong farmer and father to Anna.

Madeleine Cody, wife to Thomas and mother to Anna.

Doctor James Baldwin, brother to Madeleine, uncle to Anna.

Jasper Eustace, strong farmer, friend to Thomas Cody.

Eleanore Eustace, estranged wife to Jasper, lover of Doctor Baldwin.

Father James Casey, parish priest of Ballycummin, Co Cork.

John James O'Grady, farm labourer with the Hennessy family.

Maurice Mulcair, wren boy and ex-British soldier in the Great War.

James Maguire, solicitor of Bandon, Co Cork.

John Beatty, republican scout, at Upton ambush, Co Cork.

Principal Historical Characters

Carl Ackerman, reporter with Philadelphia Inquirer Newspaper.

Lord Bandon, Anglo-Irish landlord, British Deputy Lieutenant in Ireland.

Dick Barrett, republican fighter, 3rd West Cork Brigade.

Tom Barry, republican commander 3rd West Cork Brigade.

Lord Birkenhead, Member of British Cabinet.

Dan Breen, republican fighter, Tipperary Brigade.

Cathal Brugha, Sinn Féin Minister of Defence.

Dan Canty, republican fighter, 3rd West Cork Brigade.

Austen Chamberlain, Member of British Cabinet.

Erskine Childers, writer of Sinn Féin Bulletin and secretary at Treaty Negotiations.

Sir Winston Churchill, Member of British Cabinet.

Michael Collins, Head of IRA Intelligence and Head of Provisional Government.

William Cosgrave, Chairman of Provisional Government.

Col. Francis Crake, Commander of Auxiliaries at Kilmichael Ambush.

Mick Crowley, Republican Fighter, 3rd West Cork Brigade.

Brig-Gen F.P. Crozier, commander of Auxiliaries in Ireland.
Emmet Dalton, commander of Free State Forces.
Liam Deasy, republican adjutant, 3rd West Cork Brigade.
Bill Desmond, republican fighter, 3rd West Cork Brigade.
Eamon de Valera, President of Sinn Féin.
Desmond Fitzgerald, Head of Propaganda for Sinn Féin.
Maud Gonne, republican activist and mother of Sean McBride.
Arthur Griffith, Founder of Sinn Féin, leader of Treaty Negotiations.
Sir Hamar Greenwood, British Chief Secretary for Ireland.
Sean Hales, republican officer, 3rd West Cork Brigade.
Tom Hales, republican officer, 3rd West Cork Brigade.
Charlie Hurley, republican commander 3rd West Cork Brigade.
Jim Hurley, republican fighter, 3rd West Cork Brigade.
Pete Kearney, republican fighter, 3rd West Cork Brigade.
Tom Kelleher, republican fighter, 3rd West Cork Brigade.
Sir David Lloyd George, Prime Minister of Great Britain.
Denis Lordan, republican fighter, 3rd West Cork Brigade.
John Lordan, republican officer, 3rd West Cork Brigade.
Liam Lynch, republican commander and Chief of Staff Executive
    Forces IRA.
Sean McEoin, republican commander and Free State General.
Joe McKelvey, commander Belfast Brigade of IRA.
General Sir Nevil Macready, commander of British Forces in Ireland.
Hugh Martin, reporter with London Daily News Newspaper.
Liam Mellows, Member of IRA GHQ.
Maj. Bernard Montgomery, officer with 17th Infantry of British Army
    in Cork.
Richard Mulcahy, IRA Chief of Staff and Minister of Defence.
Flyer Nyhan, republican fighter, 3rd West Cork Brigade.
Christy O'Connell, republican fighter, 3rd West Cork Brigade.
Rory O'Connor, Member of IRA GHQ.
Kevin O'Higgins, Minister of Justice Provisional Govermnent.
Ernie O'Malley, republican commander and writer.
Maj. A.E. Percival, officer with Essex Regiment, British Forces,
    Bandon, Co Cork
Maj-Gen. Sir Peter Strickland, GOC British Forces, Cork 6th Division.
Maj-Gen Sir Henry Tudor, commander of RIC in Ireland.